To S

f

Susan

Susan Durst grew up in a Tyneside colliery village before leaving Newcastle to take a degree in French at Reading University. She subsequently settled in Paris, where she held various senior management positions in the international travel and tourism sectors. Married with two sons, Susan and her French husband currently live in the Dordogne area of southwestern France.

This book is for my sons, William and Alexandre.

Susan Durst

THE TIME MOSAIC

AUSTIN MACAULEY PUBLISHERS™

LONDON • CAMBRIDGE • NEW YORK • SHARJAH

A CIP catalogue record for this title is available from the British Library.

ISBN 9781528928519 (Paperback)
ISBN 9781528965514 (ePub e-book)

www.austinmacauley.com

First Published (2019)
Austin Macauley Publishers Ltd
25 Canada Square
Canary Wharf
London
E14 5LQ

Disclaimer

This novel's story and characters are fictitious. Certain historical events and Northumbrian place-names are real, but the characters involved are wholly imaginary.

Table of Contents

Principal Characters in the Robertson Family Tree

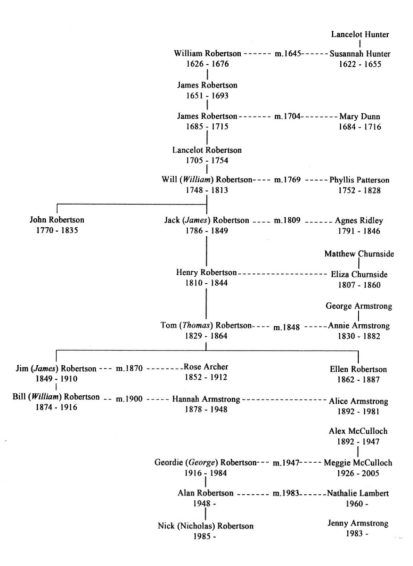

Lancelot Hunter
|
William Robertson ------ m.1645------ Susannah Hunter
1626 - 1676   1622 - 1655
|
James Robertson
1651 - 1693
|
James Robertson ------- m.1704-------- Mary Dunn
1685 - 1715   1684 - 1716
|
Lancelot Robertson
1705 - 1754
|
Will (*William*) Robertson---- m.1769 ----- Phyllis Patterson
1748 - 1813   1752 - 1828

John Robertson   Jack (*James*) Robertson ---- m.1809 ------ Agnes Ridley
1770 - 1835   1786 - 1849   1791 - 1846

                                                         Matthew Churnside
                                                         |
                        Henry Robertson----------------- Eliza Churnside
                        1810 - 1844   1807 - 1860

                                                         George Armstrong
                                                         |
                        Tom (*Thomas*) Robertson---- m.1848 -----Annie Armstrong
                        1829 - 1864   1830 - 1882

Jim (*James*) Robertson --- m.1870 -------Rose Archer   Ellen Robertson
1849 - 1910   1852 - 1912   1862 - 1887

Bill (*William*) Robertson -- m.1900 ----- Hannah Armstrong------------------ Alice Armstrong
1874 - 1916   1878 - 1948   1892 - 1981

                                                         Alex McCulloch
                                                         1892 - 1947
                                                         |
                        Geordie (*George*) Robertson--- m.1947----- Meggie McCulloch
                        1916 - 1984   1926 - 2005
                        |
                        Alan Robertson ------- m.1983------Nathalie Lambert
                        1948 -   1960 -
                        |
                        Nick (Nicholas) Robertson   Jenny Armstrong
                        1985 -   1983 -

Nick Robertson, January 2016

Despite his best efforts, Nick could not repress a faint smile of satisfaction as he gazed unseeingly at the icy rain streaming down the dark windows of his London office – if the glass cubicle he occupied could be called an office. He leaned back on the swivel chair, stretched out his long legs and put his feet on the desk; triumphantly, he raised his arms high above his head and then lowered them, clasping his hands at the nape of the neck. Out of the corner of his eye, he could see members of the overworked staff at One Better Productions glancing in at him as they bustled past his office; he suspected his posture of smug contentment might not meet with their approval. But for once, Nick felt that a few moments of self-congratulation were in order.

He had just emerged from an impromptu meeting with his boss. Mark Goodwin was one of the three directors who fifteen years earlier had started the television production company where Nick was currently employed.

"Good news, Nick," Mark had announced laconically. "The Beeb has confirmed they'd like you to present a second series of *In Those Days*. The audience ratings for the first series were significantly higher than forecast, and it seems you're building up quite a following among the viewers. The female variety, in particular." He smirked knowingly. "Must be nice to have a pretty face."

This last remark came as no surprise to Nick. Having received a constant flow of fan mail for the past several months, he was well aware that the series – the first he had presented on national television – had been hugely popular. Nevertheless, he had not dared hope that he would land a second series.

"There's still a lot of mileage in the concept of *In Those Days*," he pointed out, keen to avoid further discussion about his face, pretty or otherwise. "And as you know, we've already done a fair bit of research on potential topics and locations for a new series."

"Sounds good," said Mark, reverting to his usual deadpan expression. "The Beeb wants it on the air by September. Twenty weekly slots, forty-five minutes each. I'll need a detailed budget and schedule by the end of the month, okay?"

Nick nodded enthusiastically and started to outline his initial ideas for the new series. Mark, his eyes already riveted once more on the computer screen in front of him, raised a warning hand to cut him short.

"Sorry Nick, but I can't spare you any more time right now. But we do need to get together again at some point to review your contract with One Better Productions. You're turning into quite a valuable asset for the company, and that needs to be reflected in your package."

Those last words were still buzzing in Nick's head now, filling him with exhilaration. At the age of thirty, his career in television production was finally taking off. He was on the verge of becoming an established, well-paid presenter.

His first instinct was to call his father and give him the news, but he held back. Why, he wondered, did he always feel the need to impress Dad? Alan Robertson had never taken his work at One Better Productions seriously. Nor had he approved of Nick's decision to take a degree in media studies in the first place; there was no intellectual substance in media studies, in his view. And when Nick had graduated, Alan could not understand why he had chosen to go into television production, working long hours as a menial researcher.

"Where the hell is this hard slog leading?" Alan would protest. "You're doing all the leg work and reaping none of the benefits. Surely you can do better than a dead-end job like that?"

But Nick had persevered. It was he who had developed the original concept for *In Those Days* – a documentary series showcasing life as it used to be lived in Britain. The programmes aimed to demonstrate how different occupations, both industrial and agricultural, had forged strong regional communities and cultures. The project was initially greeted with scepticism by the management of One Better Productions, but Nick had finally been given the go-ahead – albeit on a shoestring budget – to produce a pilot programme on the Lancashire cotton mills. In the end, he not only managed to sell the series to the BBC but even persuaded Mark Goodwin to let him present it. When it went on the air, *In Those Days* unexpectedly took off, attracting bigger audiences week after week. Millions of viewers enjoyed the nostalgic appeal of the documentaries, reminding them of a bygone Britain that was fast fading from memory. And they also grew to appreciate the show's telegenic and articulate presenter; they liked the way Nick brought the past alive, his sensitivity and enthusiasm. *In Those Days* became the surprise hit of the season, making Nick Robertson a new name to be reckoned with in the world of television. Today, with a second series confirmed, he felt that his determination and hard work had finally paid off.

His reverie ended as Evie sidled into his office, startling him as ever with her bizarre appearance. Evie, who was in her early twenties and worked for Nick as a junior researcher and general gofer, always looked as if she was in a time warp. Today was no exception. Short and seriously overweight, she was dressed from head to toe in a punk style she herself was too young to remember. Her spiky yellow hair was streaked with green and her face was heavily made up, stark white with thick black eyeliner. Nick looked her up and down in amusement, taking in the black t-shirt with its 'Destroy' message in gory lettering, the ripped jeans and Doc Martens boots; as always, a large razor blade attached to a heavy silver chain swung back and forth on her ample bosom. But by now, Nick had learned to look beyond Evie's outward weirdness to the good-natured, hardworking girl concealed within.

"I saw you coming out of Boss Man's office," she said pointedly. "You look pretty pleased with yourself, I must say."

What had just transpired with Mark Goodwin was clearly none of Evie's business, but Nick was in an expansive mood. When he told her about the forthcoming series of *In Those Days,* a smile broke through Evie's ghoulish make-up.

"Cool." It was her favourite word, and one which never failed to irritate Nick.

"I know you've been working on possible topics for a second series. Get the team together for a meeting tomorrow morning, would you? We need to kick off with something hard-hitting."

"Cool," said Evie again. "I've already got a lot of stuff together on Newcastle coal miners. Why don't we start with that? Everyday life a hundred years ago in colliery villages, that kind of thing. We could work in a political slant too – you know, oppressed miners on starvation wages battling for survival."

Evie should be working in Hollywood, thought Nick wryly. "Mmm..." he responded pensively, his mind already playing with the possibilities. "Actually, this may come as a surprise but my family's originally from Tyneside. My Dad's a proper Geordie, born and bred in a colliery village. Just a thought, but it might be nice to weave a personal note into the first show of the new series?"

Evie gawped at him in disbelief. "Your family comes from Tyneside?" she repeated incredulously, as if Nick had announced that his father was born on Mars.

"That's right, although sadly I have to say we seem to have severed family ties over the years. Look, Evie, why don't you research some contacts for me in the area? People to interview, local historians who could point out places of interest... I might even go up north myself before we start production and get a feel for the old place again. Breathe in that bracing Newcastle air!"

Evie nodded, too astounded to say 'cool'.

The smartphone on Nick's desk buzzed, and he consulted the text message flashing onto the screen: "Home for dinner tonight? Dad." He glanced briefly at his watch, realising it was already after seven.

"Speak of the devil," he remarked to Evie with a grin. "I need to get out of here right now." He got to his feet and shrugged on his overcoat and the scarlet cashmere scarf he had been given for Christmas. "Bye, Evie. Don't forget to set up that meeting tomorrow, will you?"

Evie stood to one side as he squeezed past her and made for the door. "Cool," she said, fingering the razor blade dangling from her neck.

* * *

Not having bothered to take an umbrella to work, Nick was soaked through and shivering with cold in the short time it took him to walk from the tube station to the family home in South Kensington. His parents had opted to buy a large ground floor flat there shortly after their wedding, mainly because at the time, Nick's French mother felt at home among the Parisian-style bookshops and cafés in the area. She was also already planning to have her as yet unborn children educated at the nearby Lycée Français. Over the years, the couple had managed to buy two other flats in the same building, gradually transforming their home into a spacious, stylishly decorated town house. Nick had never lived anywhere else and at thirty years old was still in no hurry to move out; given the price of real estate in London, he doubted in any case whether he could afford to buy more than a garden shed.

He climbed the steps from street level to the imposing portico entrance, let himself in and hung his coat and scarf up in the hall. Pushing open the door to the elegantly furnished lounge, he found his father sitting contentedly by a cosy log burner and engrossed as usual in a book. In Nick's eyes, Alan Robertson never seemed to change.

The sandy-fair hair and beard had turned grey over the years, but the horn-rimmed spectacles, baggy corduroy trousers and slightly unkempt appearance were permanent fixtures. In fact, thought Nick in quiet amusement, his father looked exactly like the retired university professor he was.

Alan looked up with a smile and laid his book to one side. "Ah, there you are! I'd almost given up on you. Thought you might have to stay on at work again and burn the midnight oil."

"Not tonight, Dad," said Nick exultantly, flopping down next to his father on the Italian-design sofa. "Tonight I feel like celebrating! I've just had some really good news."

"Oh?" Alan glanced at him with interest. "Well, your mother always likes to keep a bottle of champers in the fridge for just such occasions. Why don't I grab it now and then you can tell me what's going on?"

"Any excuse, eh?" laughed Nick but did not protest when his father got to his feet and disappeared into the kitchen. He stretched out his legs and leaned back comfortably against the silk cushions until Alan returned bearing a tray; on it were two crystal flutes and a bottle of champagne in an antique silver ice bucket.

Ceremoniously, his father poured two glasses and handed one to Nick. "Well?" he asked expectantly.

Nick needed no further prompting, and every detail of his earlier meeting with Mark Goodwin was recounted with relish. Knowing that his father thought he was undervalued at One Better Productions, he added that his remuneration as a television presenter was about to improve significantly.

"Very well done, I'm impressed," commented Alan as they clinked glasses.

"Well, I know you don't think very highly of my show, Dad, so don't feel you have to fall over backwards or anything." Nick smiled self-deprecatingly.

"I do find the format rather trite and predictable at times," conceded Alan cautiously. "But my opinion is immaterial. You appear to be on your way to fame and fortune, which I suppose is your ultimate goal. And even I can see that your talent as a presenter is undeniable. You know how to draw people in and captivate them. Your mother is always ranting on about your natural charm and charisma on screen, although I suspect she may be somewhat biased." His blue eyes twinkled as he took another sip of the champagne.

"Where is Maman, by the way?" queried Nick, eager to share his good news with her.

"Oh, she should be back any minute," Alan said airily. "Actually, she was expecting some good news herself today so we may have to open another bottle!"

At that moment, the two men heard the click of a key in the front door, and then Nathalie Robertson joined them in the lounge. Her eyes lit up at the sight of Nick.

"Nee-co-la!" she exclaimed, pronouncing her son's name in the French way and holding out her arms in a theatrical gesture. "*Mon chéri!* I feel as though I haven't seen you properly for ages... I hope you're staying in for dinner with us tonight?"

"*Bonsoir, Maman.*" Nick got to his feet, glass of champagne in hand, and kissed his mother warmly on both cheeks. As always, he was struck by the way she seemed to fill the room with her presence and fluid grace. Now in her mid-fifties, Nathalie looked at least a decade younger thanks to her tall, slender frame and strong, patrician features. Tonight as usual, she was the epitome of the *chic Parisienne* in a figure-skimming grey jersey dress – plain but expertly cut – and her trademark Hermès scarf at the neckline; expensive gold jewellery adorned her wrists and hands. Her dark hair was casually arranged in a loose chignon and her flawless skin appeared to be devoid of make-up, although Nick was well aware that this effortless elegance was the result of long hours spent daily in the bathroom. Not for the first time, he wondered what bound his parents, outwardly so dissimilar in style and taste, together. And yet after more than thirty years of married life, their relationship was as vibrant and harmonious as ever.

Alan handed his wife a glass of champagne, and they all ensconced themselves happily around the fire, chatting animatedly. Nathalie was thrilled to hear about the latest developments in Nick's career.

"How exciting," she enthused. "*Mon bébé est une vedette! (1)* I always knew you had star quality, Nick, I was sure of it."

"Hang on, Maman! I'm a long, long way from being a star," protested Nick with a laugh. "Still, I've got a foot on the ladder now and I'm going to do my best not to fall off it." He suddenly remembered his father's cryptic comment earlier.

"Dad mentioned you might have some good news yourself, Maman. Does it have anything to do with InnerBeauty?"

Nathalie heaved a sigh, although whether from relief or regret was still unclear. "It does. And good news or not, I'm absolutely exhausted! So many meetings, so much pressure… *je suis sur les rotules. (2)* And now that there's no turning back, I feel rather sad to be losing my baby. Of course, the paperwork will take quite some time to complete – I'm leaving all that to my army of legal eagles. But the bottom line is that the final offer for the takeover bid was agreed today. InnerBeauty is about to be part of the leading multinational cosmetics group in the world."

"But that's wonderful, darling!" interjected Alan. "Think how hard you've worked all these years to take the company to where it is today. Isn't it time to cash in now, sit back and enjoy life for a change?"

Nick nodded agreement. He couldn't remember a time when his mother had not been totally committed to the business she jokingly referred to as her baby. Back in the 1980s, Nathalie had been a pioneer, one of the first to understand the growing interest in health and wellbeing and the trend away from conventional skincare products. With her flair for marketing and innate sense of style, she had spotted a niche at the high end of the market for a skincare range – cleansers, moisturisers, masks and scrubs – using only botanical ingredients. He remembered how in the early days, when he and his sister Charlotte were children, his mother had run InnerBeauty out of the family kitchen, working around the clock, throwing herself body and soul into her new venture. And year after year, with a combination of sheer drive and ruthless charm, Nathalie had transformed InnerBeauty from a cottage industry, known only to a small circle of neighbours and friends, into a quality skincare brand sold in every major European market.

"Dad's right," he told his mother. "It's time to let your baby go and start thinking about yourself. You'll be rolling in money when the takeover goes through! So why not take it easy, do all the things you've been too busy to do until now?"

"But what things?" wailed Nathalie. "My business is my life; it's the only thing I'm really good at. And anyway, can you imagine me as an idle housewife, bored out of my mind, shopping and lunching and pretending to have fun? *Mon Dieu,* just like my mother! Not to mention I'd get in your father's hair all day and drive him mad." She leaned forward and tweaked Alan's beard affectionately.

"Very true," remarked Alan drily. "But I'm extremely proud of my brilliant, successful wife all the same."

Nathalie stood up, finished her glass of champagne and smoothed down her dress. "Well, right now your brilliant, successful wife is absolutely starving. I think I'll pop into the kitchen and see what I can rustle up for dinner."

"Need any help, darling?" offered Alan, although he made no move to join her.

"No, I can manage – it won't be anything complicated. I'll give you a shout when it's ready." She blew them a kiss and promptly disappeared.

Nathalie was an excellent cook but usually too busy running her business to spend much time in the kitchen. Nevertheless, everything she produced, however simple, was invariably prepared and presented with care, and tonight was no exception. When the two men were called into the dining room a few minutes later, they were met with candles glowing softly on a table set with heavy linen, silver cutlery and crystal wine glasses. Steaming on a large platter was a fluffy omelette stuffed with Nathalie's favourite *cèpe* mushrooms, together with a bowl of crisp green salad, an array of French cheeses and slices of crusty *baguette* purchased from their local *boulangerie*. A bottle of Saint Emilion was already opened and waiting to be served.

It was only after dinner, as the three of them lingered at the table finishing the last of the wine, that the conversation turned once more to *In Those Days*.

"Any thoughts on subject matter for the new series, Nick?" asked Alan.

"Actually, I'm planning to start with a programme on Tyneside coal miners. We'll be going back to the old colliery villages around Newcastle, just like the one you grew up in." He noted the sharp interest in his father's eyes and pressed on. "I thought you might be able to share some of your childhood memories with me? Even give me one or two contacts in Burnside?" Nick's expression was eager, although he knew that Alan had grown apart from his old home.

For a moment, Alan looked wistful. "I'm happy to share what I remember about Burnside with you, Nick, although it was all such a long time ago. I left that part of my life behind me when I went to university, and since then, I've always lived down south. My life took a very different direction from theirs, and I was always so caught up with my academic work. Does that sound very snobbish? I don't mean it to. It must be ten years now since I set foot in Burnside, when we all went up for your Grandma's funeral. Mea culpa, I'm afraid…"

Nathalie rolled her eyes dramatically and shuddered. "Why would anybody want to go to Burnside if they didn't have to? Such a grim, depressing place… *quelle horreur!"*

Nick understood his mother's aversion to Burnside but did not share it. As children, he and Charlotte had often made the journey north with their father, although seldom accompanied by Nathalie; he had very fond memories of the warm welcome they always received. Sadly, Nick had never known his grandfather, Geordie Robertson, who had died the year before he was born. But he had adored his plump, affectionate grandmother, who spoiled them all endlessly with her delicious, home-cooked meals and who always gave him her undivided attention, unlike his mother. And he had also liked the tough, forthright people of Burnside with their no-nonsense talk and gritty sense of humour. It was a different world from the sheltered, privileged life he led in South Kensington, surrounded by well-bred, cultivated people with modulated voices and understated views. His childhood visits to Burnside had always been like a breath of fresh air to Nick.

"I'm thinking of going up to Newcastle in the next few days," he added. "I rather fancy doing the preliminary research for the programme myself."

Nathalie raised her eyebrows. "In the middle of January?" she said incredulously, as if Nick were planning an expedition to the North Pole. "Is this some kind of northern nostalgia trip?"

"Of course not," said Nick defensively.

"Don't listen to your Mam, man." A faint Geordie accent had suddenly crept into Alan's voice, as it always did when there was talk of Burnside. "I think it's a grand idea."

(1) *My baby's a star!*
(2) *I'm on my knees.*

Jenny Armstrong, January 2016

Jenny had just finished her second – rather large – glass of dry white wine and was beginning to feel distinctly annoyed. Lightheaded too, as she had skipped lunch and eaten nothing since breakfast. She glanced at her watch for the umpteenth time and saw that it was 8:45, a full three-quarters of an hour after the appointed time for her meeting with Nick Robertson.

She felt conspicuous on her own in the bar of this smart four-star hotel in Newcastle's city centre, although in fact no one was paying much attention to her. She wondered resentfully if she was in the process of being stood up by the famous Mr Robertson and resolved to walk out of the bar with her head held high if he failed to turn up in the next five minutes.

When Jenny had received a call the previous week from Nick's assistant, a pleasant-sounding girl by the name of Evie, she had felt flattered to be asked for her input and advice. It was exciting to hear that *In Those Days* was scheduling a programme on Newcastle later that year, and even more exciting to be told that her recently published book, *The Rise and Fall of the Tyneside Pit Village,* was considered to be a valuable source of information. Nick Robertson, Evie announced in a slightly mystified tone of voice, was flying up north for the weekend and was eager to discuss the project in more depth with her.

Jenny could not resist telling Heather, her oldest and best friend, about her forthcoming meeting with a television presenter.

"Oh my God!" Heather squealed. "A date with Nick Robertson! I'm green with envy, I just love him! Make sure you look drop dead gorgeous on Friday night, won't you?"

"Don't get carried away, it's definitely not a date. He just wants my input for the programme, that's all." Jenny put on her most blasé expression. "Anyway, I bet he's conceited and arrogant – these TV personalities always are. And as for looking drop dead gorgeous, he'll have to take me as I am. Why should I get dolled up for him?"

And Jenny had been as good as her word. She had deliberately not gone home after work to change, deliberately not applied fresh make-up. She had also refrained from searching on internet to find out more about Nick Robertson. Why the hell should she? In his eyes, she would be nothing more than a frumpy provincial schoolteacher, just a name on a long list of useful contacts. And in any case, she was off men for good, she reminded herself sternly. Once bitten twice shy had been her motto for the past two years, and there was no reason to change tack just because Nick Robertson was in town. She was not about to fall at his feet like a gormless teenager.

Looking at her watch again, Jenny noted that five more minutes had elapsed. She reached for her coat, feeling both irritated and disappointed. It was at that precise moment that a rather harassed-looking young man with an overnight bag strode into the bar, dressed in a tailored navy blue overcoat and crimson scarf. *Wow,* thought Jenny in spite of herself, *this guy is seriously good-looking.* In her – albeit limited – experience famous people were often less attractive in the flesh than on screen, but Nick Robertson certainly lived up to his television persona. Tall and slim with thick, wavy dark hair and deep blue eyes, it was no wonder millions of female viewers up and down the country tuned in every week to *In Those Days.*

Jenny waved discreetly to catch the young man's eye. Looking relieved, he hurried over to her table.

"Jenny Armstrong?" He smiled apologetically and shook her hand. "I'm Nick Robertson. I can't tell you how sorry I am to have kept you waiting. The plane took off from London on time but then circled for ages over Newcastle airport before coming in to land. I grabbed a taxi and came straight here, but you must be thoroughly fed up by now. I hope you'll forgive me and let me at least buy you another drink."

"That's okay," said Jenny coolly, determined not to be taken in by the suave manners and effortless charm. "I've had quite enough to drink, thanks, and anyway I can't stay long."

Nick ignored this last remark and signalled to the waiter for a beer and another glass of white wine. Jenny watched with amusement as he downed half his beer in one gulp, before leaning back in his chair with a sigh of satisfaction. "I needed that!" he told her with a boyish grin.

"Let me brief you on our initial plans for the colliery village show," he went on more earnestly. Jenny listened intently as he launched into his ideas for possible angles and locations; she was captivated in spite of herself by this glimpse into the world of television production. "I must say, your book is proving to be a veritable mine of information," he added.

"A coal mine of information, you mean," Jenny shot back, and they both laughed. "Have you actually read my book?" she continued, pleased at Nick's compliment.

"Well, not quite," he conceded with disarming frankness. "Bit short of time, I'm afraid. But Evie, my assistant, has read it cover to cover. She thinks it's absolutely brilliant."

"Well, that's something at least," said Jenny ruefully. She was warming slightly to Nick Robertson. It would have been easy for him to pretend he had read the book, but he had opted for honesty.

"What about *In Those Days?*" Nick asked curiously. "Have you been following the series?"

"Of course."

"What did you think of it? I'd be interested to hear your views as a renowned local historian." He leaned towards her with a humorous glint in his blue eyes.

"Renowned is stretching it a bit, and I'm really just an amateur," Jenny pointed out. "Local history is my hobby, nothing more. My real job is teaching maths at a secondary school not far from here, in Jesmond."

Nick gave an airy wave of his hand. "You're not getting out of it that easily, Miss Armstrong," he quipped ironically. "Come on now, spill the beans!"

Jenny sipped her wine as contradictory thoughts whirred through her mind. Nick Robertson, she assumed, would expect her to enthuse about the programme;

as a successful presenter, he must be inundated with compliments from hordes of admiring fans. Well, she didn't intend to be one of them.

"It's good entertainment," she replied brusquely. "But everything's so smooth and superficial. The shows all follow the same format; they lack subtlety and depth…" She paused, realising how harsh she must sound.

As she had expected, Nick's ego was stung. "Well, *In Those Days* aims to appeal to a wide audience, not a handful of academics and intellectuals," he snapped. He folded his arms defensively, and an awkward silence fell.

"Look, my point is that you never really get to the heart of the subject," she blurted out. "There's no sense of authenticity in the interviews. They all sound rather bland, as if people are only allowed to say what you've briefed them to say."

"It seems you're quite an expert on television production," retorted Nick scathingly. He looked sulky and resentful, the boyish charm suddenly gone.

Thoroughly annoyed now, Jenny pushed her chair back and stood up abruptly. Her head was spinning; three large glasses of wine on an empty stomach had not been a good idea. She pulled her coat on roughly, grabbed her bag and glared down at Nick.

"You're quite right," she said tersely. "Who am I to judge a big star like you, eh? Well, there'll be no more words of wisdom from me. I've wasted quite enough of your precious time already, and mine." She delved into her bag and threw a twenty-pound note onto the table. "That should cover the wine."

Nick leaped to his feet and began to protest, but she pushed past him and ran out of the bar into the street, her stomach churning and oblivious to the bitter cold outside. *Serves the arrogant git right*, she thought fiercely and congratulated herself for giving the great Nick Robertson a piece of her mind.

* * *

The phone rang as Jenny was washing up after lunch the next day, Saturday, in her small terraced house in Jesmond. Drying her hands on the kitchen towel, she picked up the phone and at the same time peered into the living room to check on her five-year-old niece, Emma. Jenny had agreed to babysit Emma for the weekend, so that her sister Kim and Kim's husband, Ian, could escape to the Lake District as a wedding anniversary treat. The little girl had been dropped off by her parents that morning.

"Thanks a million, Jenny, you're a star," Kim had called out through the window as the car drew away.

"No problem," Jenny had responded cheerfully. "It's not as if I've got anything else planned for the weekend. Have a great time and see you tomorrow night!"

Noting with relief that Emma was engrossed for now in a children's cartoon on television, Jenny turned back to the phone. As she had expected, the caller was her friend Heather.

"So how did it go last night with the gorgeous Nick Robertson?" demanded Heather. "I want a blow-by-blow account of the entire evening."

"Actually, it was a bit of a disaster," sighed Jenny. Knowing that Heather would not be satisfied until she heard every detail of what had transpired, she proceeded to relate her stormy exchange with Nick.

Heather's voice rose to a near-hysterical pitch. "You mean you actually said all that to him? And then just walked out? For God's sake, Jenny! Why do you always have to get so aggressive every time you meet a new man?"

"He's just an obnoxious big-head who can't take a bit of constructive criticism," declared Jenny stoutly.

"It doesn't sound very constructive to me. What were you thinking of, Jenny? Local history is your passion – nobody knows that better than me. You spent three years researching and writing that book about pit villages, the very topic Nick Robertson came all the way from London to discuss with you." Heather paused to catch her breath before resuming her diatribe. "And then when you get the chance of a lifetime, what do you do? Get on your high horse and give him stick." By now, she was practically screaming into the phone.

Jenny held the phone away from her ear. Ever since last night, she had thought of nothing else but her clash with Nick. She was beginning to regret her impulsive behaviour, knowing that she had missed a rare opportunity to talk about her favourite subject on national television. Nevertheless, she had no intention of admitting as much to Heather.

"Well, it's too late now," she said stubbornly. She suddenly felt a small hand tugging at her sweater and looked down to see Emma's chubby face and beseeching brown eyes.

"I want to go to the MetroCentre, Auntie Jenny. You said we could..." Emma's expression was at its most appealing.

"We're going right now," she said soothingly and turned back to the phone. "Look Heather, I'll have to love you and leave you. I've got little Emma here for the weekend and we're just leaving."

Heather's voice was resigned. "All right, then. But if you ask me, you should call Nick Robertson and try to patch things up."

* * *

Well, at least one of us is having a good time, thought Jenny, watching fondly as Emma frenetically jumped and bounced her way around the ball pit. As promised, she had taken the little girl to the enclosed soft play area at the MetroCentre, the huge indoor shopping centre in Gateshead. The play facilities were packed with boisterous children, their parents only too glad to find a place to keep them entertained on this bitterly cold Saturday afternoon. And Jenny, nursing a carton of weak coffee in the seating area for adults, was relieved to see her niece so happily occupied, at least for now.

Idly she rummaged in her bag for her mobile phone and checked for new messages. Nothing from Nick Robertson, she noted and instantly chided herself; why on earth *should* there be anything from Nick Robertson? But it was no good... she couldn't get the television presenter – and her disastrous encounter with him – out of her mind. Impulsively, Jenny typed his name into the internet search engine. It made no sense, she knew, but if she was never going to see him again, she might as well know what she had missed. A long list of links instantly appeared on the screen, most of them about *In Those Days* and Nick's apparently meteoric rise in the world of television production. Jenny scrolled on until she found his personal profile.

21

Nicolas George Robertson was born in London in 1985. Not a good start, thought Jenny grimly, that made him two years younger than her. *He and his younger sister Charlotte,* she read, *were both educated at the French Lycée in South Kensington. Nick later went on to graduate in Media Studies at City University, London.*

Jenny was intrigued in spite of herself. Why should Nick have attended a French school? He had seemed so utterly English last night. She read on. *He is the son of Alan Robertson, author and former professor at the London School of Economics, who is widely recognised as one of the UK's leading specialists in European Union affairs.* Hmm, pretty impressive, thought Jenny, although she was unsurprised; Nick exuded the kind of inbred confidence that came with a privileged background.

Nick's mother, she read, *is Nathalie Lambert, founder and CEO of the upmarket skincare company InnerBeauty.* Oh my God, breathed Jenny, instantly thinking of the horrendously expensive jar of InnerBeauty moisturising cream in her bathroom at home. She clicked on the link to Nathalie Lambert and was confronted with dozens of photos of an impossibly stylish French woman; she recognised her as the beauty icon who had appeared in countless glossy magazines. Jenny's heart sank as she wondered what Nick had thought of her unmade-up face and shapeless sweater last night; with a glamourous mother like Nathalie Lambert, he must have a trained eye when it came to women. And of course the reason he had been educated at the French Lycée was now clear… Nick Robertson must speak perfect French, she guessed, as well as being incredibly handsome, intelligent and successful.

Jenny heaved a sigh. There was clearly no point in developing a crush on the smooth and sophisticated Nick Robertson. She thought ironically of her own uneventful life and mentally wrote up her profile alongside Nick's. *Jennifer Hannah Armstrong, thirty-two years old and overweight, was born on a council estate in Burnside, the daughter of a bus driver and a switchboard operator. Following a disastrous and short-lived marriage, Jenny currently works as an underpaid maths teacher and is struggling to pay off a huge mortgage on her tiny terraced house in Jesmond.* A pretty accurate summary of her existence to date, she concluded. Nothing there to attract a man like Nick Robertson, even if she wanted to attract him – which, as she reminded herself yet again, she didn't.

She scrolled down to the end of the profile. *Nick Robertson is unmarried, although his name has been romantically linked to several women, including most recently the Swedish model Klara Nilsson.* Jenny laughed out loud, surprising some of the mothers sitting nearby. If Nick's taste in women ran to gorgeous leggy blondes, she would never even get past the starting block.

Jenny stood up and waved energetically at Emma, who had made friends with another little girl and was now racing up and down a giant slide. Emma was pretending not to see her, clearly reluctant to leave the soft play area and go home. Jenny sat down again, wondering whether Emma – a fussy eater – would like the lasagne she had planned for tonight's dinner.

When her phone rang ten minutes later, Jenny groaned inwardly. She felt sure it would be Heather, primed to berate her again. But the voice on the line was not Heather's, but Nick Robertson's. Jenny's whole body tensed with an unfamiliar mixture of sheer terror and wild excitement.

"Hello? Is that Jenny Armstrong?" she heard Nick repeat anxiously and realised she had not yet uttered a single word.

"Yes, it's me," she blurted out, feeling like an awkward schoolgirl.

"Oh, good," said Nick, sounding relieved. "Look, I hope you don't mind me calling you, but I think we got off to an unfortunate start last night. It was the end of a very long day – as it probably was for you too – and I over-reacted to your… errr… remarks about the show. In fact, I behaved like an absolute prat." He paused, waiting for Jenny to speak.

"Oh well," she stammered, trying to sound calmer than she felt. "I did go over the top slightly. When I have strong views, I tend to be a bit… up-front."

"I like up-front," said Nick, the humorous note back in his voice. "Listen, Jenny, I really would appreciate your input for *In Those Days.* I've spent most of today going through my contact list for the show and to be honest, I'm not making much headway. I wonder if you'd let me take you to dinner tonight? That is, if you're free of course? I want to apologise in person, and I'd really, really…" he repeated the word emphatically, "like to hear your ideas for the show."

Jenny wondered if Nick could hear her heart hammering over the phone. She tried to keep her voice professional and neutral. "That would have been nice, but I'm afraid I'm tied up this evening."

"Oh, I see." Nick sounded genuinely disappointed. "Well, I should have guessed you'd be out on the town on a Saturday night."

"No, no…" said Jenny impulsively. "The thing is, I have my little niece staying with me. She's only five, and her Mam and Dad have gone away for the weekend." She cursed herself as she said the words, realising she had stopped sounding professional and neutral.

"Well, of course in that case…" Nick's voice trailed off, unsure where Jenny's explanation was leading.

Jenny took a deep breath and made a spur of the moment decision. "In that case, why don't you come around to my place and we can talk there? Make it after eight, though – Emma should be asleep by then. And it's only lasagne for dinner, but you're welcome to have some if you like."

The pleasure in Nick's voice was unconcealed. "That's so kind of you, I can't think of anything I'd like better. If you'd just give me your exact address…"

* * *

For once, Emma had been as good as gold. She had eaten most of her supper, obediently brushed her teeth and consented with hardly a protest to be tucked into bed and kissed goodnight. *Worn out with pleasure,* thought Jenny fondly as she tiptoed into the room a few minutes later to find her little niece already sound asleep. She went into her own bedroom and scrutinised herself in the mirror. She calculated she had just enough time to spruce herself up before Nick arrived at eight, although she was still unsure why she felt the need to do so. Nick was a journalist working his way through a contact list for his television series, nothing more. Even if she were a toothless old hag, she reasoned, he would still want to meet her.

Nevertheless, when the doorbell rang half an hour later, Jenny had managed to shower, wash and style her hair and smother herself from top to toe with body cream. Rifling through her wardrobe, she opted for the designer jeans she had just bought in the January sales, which Heather had assured her 'took pounds off her backside'. She teamed the jeans with a long cream cashmere tunic – casual but classy, she hoped – and a gleaming rope of gold and amber beads. The outfit, she knew, offset her tawny hair and pale skin.

She opened the door to find Nick, the collar of his navy blue overcoat turned up against the cold and bearing a bottle of red Côtes-du-Rhône in one hand. With the other, he held a small but exquisitely wrapped bouquet of white peonies and winter roses. "Peace offering," he proclaimed as he handed them over, with the diffident half-smile that female viewers of *In Those Days* found so irresistible.

"Oh, there was no need for that," Jenny demurred, trying to sound less delighted than she felt. "But thank you, they're beautiful," she added as she hung Nick's coat up in the hall and ushered him into the house. He stood stock still in the middle of the living room, surveying his surroundings with keen interest. Jenny had decorated her home with an eclectic mixture of Ikea and vintage furniture gleaned from junk shops and auction rooms. Bookshelves lined one wall, while another displayed a series of antique etchings, perfectly framed, of Northumbrian landscapes.

"This is really nice," said Nick admiringly. "Quirky but cosy."

"That's one way of putting it," laughed Jenny, thinking back to the personal profile she had read that afternoon. She had a feeling Nick's family home in South Kensington would be neither quirky nor cosy.

But the ice was broken, and Jenny felt the tension drain out of her body. As Nick opened the bottle of wine in the kitchen and helped her set the table for their simple supper, the atmosphere was easy and relaxed. It was as if their disastrous first encounter had never occurred.

They exchanged more easy banter as they tucked into Jenny's lasagne, which Nick assured her was the best he had ever tasted. "Delicious," he declared with relish, scraping the last morsel from his plate. "But now, I'd like to get down to more serious business, if you don't mind."

"Of course – that's why you're here tonight, after all. I've been thinking about different angles for the programme, and I've come up with one or two ideas you might be interested in. All constructive advice this time, I promise!" She flashed him a rueful smile.

"Any advice gratefully received." Nick leaned towards her, his expression suddenly earnest. "The thing is, Jenny, I really want to get this particular show right. What you said about the series last night – that it was trite and superficial – irritated me because… well, it was almost word for word what my father keeps telling me. So if only for his sake, I want to get the Tyneside collieries show right – handle it more sensitively, make it more personal. You see, Dad's a Geordie himself, born and bred in a pit village."

This unexpected revelation hit Jenny like a bombshell; she could not have been more astounded. It certainly didn't tally with what she knew or had assumed about Nick Robertson so far. "Really? Your Dad was born here?" she repeated stupidly. "Whereabouts exactly?"

"Oh, a little place you might have heard of, a few miles north of Newcastle – Burnside."

"Burnside!" she shrieked, unable to control her excitement. "But that's where I'm from! And your Dad's a Robertson? Of course… why didn't I see the connection before?" She jumped to her feet, her face flushed with pleasure and stared down at a stunned-looking Nick.

"What an amazing coincidence," he stammered. "I wonder if our paths ever crossed at some point. Dad moved down south many years ago, but when my sister and I were kids, he used to take us to Burnside quite regularly to visit Grandma. Maybe you've heard of Dad… his name is Alan Robertson, and his father was—"

"Geordie Robertson," interrupted Jenny. "I know! He was great friends with my Granddad – they worked at the pit together. And I knew your Grandma very well – she lived in the same street as my family. I remember she was so proud of her brilliant son, always talking about how well he'd done for himself in London. It's just that I never for one moment imagined that her son and your father were one and the same person… Robertson is quite a common name, after all."

"Jenny Armstrong," breathed Nick. "Your name didn't ring any bells either. But now I come to think of it, there are quite a few Armstrongs in Burnside, aren't there?"

"There are," smiled Jenny. "And plenty of Robertsons too. In fact, the Armstrong and Robertson families are among the oldest in Burnside, they go back for generations. Oh Nick, this is incredible! It must sound weird, but I know everything about your family – everything!" By now, she was frantically pacing up and down the kitchen, her mind aflame with a million possibilities.

Nick poured them both a glass of wine and held hers outstretched, patting the empty chair next to his. "I want to hear all about it, but I'd rather you were sitting where I can see you!"

Jenny promptly sat down and took a rather unladylike swig of wine. "You must think I'm acting like a lunatic!" she exclaimed. "But for me, this is all so exciting."

"What did you mean when you said you knew everything about my family?" Nick's expression was both amused and curious.

"Well, maybe not everything," corrected Jenny. "But back as far as the early nineteenth century, it's fair to say I know most of what there is to know. You see, I'm an amateur genealogist – the Sherlock Holmes of Tyneside family history, so they say! I don't charge a fee or anything, but over the years, I've helped a lot of families in the area to trace their ancestry. I love doing it, that's all."

"But why did you research the Robertson family?" Nick was clearly intrigued.

"Partly because there are certain links with my own family," explained Jenny. "And partly because the Robertson name crops up over and over again in Burnside. It's fair to say nearly everyone in the village has a Robertson at some point on their family tree!"

Nick laughed. "I've never thought about trying to dig up my Tyneside ancestry – and neither has Dad, I'm sure of it. I suppose I assumed there'd be nothing much to uncover, apart from a long line of ordinary people living uneventful lives."

"But that's where you're wrong!" Jenny felt her voice vibrate with passion, but this was her favourite subject and she wanted to have her say. "Most people are only interested in history with a capital H – that is, if they're interested in history at all these days. They only look at the grand sweep of history – the kings and queens and nobles, the wars and revolutions, the great statesmen and inventors and writers… But history is so much more, Nick. I see it as a gigantic mosaic spread out before us. The mosaic stretches back through the centuries and is made up of billions of colourful fragments. Of course, certain fragments in the pattern immediately catch our eye because they're larger and brighter – that's history with a capital H. But the pattern would be incomplete and the whole mosaic would fall apart if it weren't for the myriads of other fragments, almost invisible to the naked eye. They're the people you mentioned – ordinary people living uneventful lives. Yet every one of them is an essential part of the bigger picture. They hold the gigantic mosaic together, tiny pieces in the grand sweep of history." She paused for breath and gulped down the rest of her wine. Nick, she saw, was scrutinising her intensely.

"Wow, I'm really impressed," he said finally. "I thought you were a maths teacher, Jenny Armstrong, but the way you talk about genealogy is sheer poetry."

"You're taking the mick out of me now," said Jenny archly.

"I'm not," Nick assured her. "But isn't it hard to find out anything at all about these ordinary people, the tiny pieces in the mosaic? There must be so little to go on, so few records of their existence apart from when they were born and when they died."

"Ah, you mean the BMDs," replied Jenny. "Births, Marriages and Deaths… those are the bare bones of genealogical research. But you can discover so much more if you put your mind to it, you can flesh out the skeletons of individual lives. For me, the exciting part is reading between the lines. I don't mean making things up to suit my fancy – there's no cheating with genealogy if it's done properly. But still, with a bit of logical deduction and a grasp of historical events of the time, you can build up quite a clear picture of their lives. You see, at first the tiny pieces of the mosaic look faded and dull, but if you keep polishing them the true colour starts to come through."

"To some extent, I suppose," said Nick musingly. "But even if you manage to put flesh on the skeletons, you can never get into their minds. Never really understand how those people felt, how their minds worked when they were alive."

"No," admitted Jenny. "That's the frustrating part. You know, sometimes when I'm researching an individual who particularly interests me, I long to somehow break through the mists of time and experience their daily life back then, their reality. That's the genealogist's fantasy – to press a button and step back into a person's life, just for a short while."

They sat in silence over the remains of the evening's supper, both of them lost in thought.

"Jenny," began Nick tentatively, his eyes intensely blue as they met hers across the kitchen table. "You've opened the door to a whole new world tonight. Talking to you has convinced me you're just the person I need to work with me on the Tyneside colliery programme. I even think there might be a way to weave Burnside into the show. But it's much more than that. I'd love you to help me put together the Robertson family history… help me break through the mists of time, as you put it, and find out who my ancestors really were. Would you do that for me, Jenny? You'd be doing me a huge favour."

"I thought you'd never ask." It was a deliberately flippant response, although she was secretly thrilled. "Seriously, Nick, it's no favour – I'd be glad to do some research on your family. First of all, I need to double-check the data I already have, and then – that's the exciting bit – see how much more I can find out."

26

Impulsively, Nick pushed his glass of wine to one side and gently took her hand in his; to her surprise, she felt every bone in her body respond to its warmth. "This has been quite an evening. I can't thank you enough, Jenny," he said. They lowered their eyes, looking at their hands still clasped together on the kitchen table. Neither of them wanted the moment to end.

A loud wail reached them from upstairs. "Auntie Jenny, Auntie Jenny!" sobbed Emma from her bed. "There's a monster in here, I can see him!"

Reluctantly, Jenny withdrew her hand from Nick's and jumped to her feet. "Duty calls," she said with a mock sigh of resignation. As she made her way upstairs to comfort Emma, the tips of her fingers were still tingling from Nick Robertson's touch.

Nick and Jenny (1)

Nick had been sitting in front of his laptop for over two hours but found himself unable to focus. On the computer screen were the detailed budget figures the production team had prepared for the next series of *In Those Days.* He had decided to work from home this evening, in what he usually referred to as his den. The den was in fact a comfortably appointed studio flat on the top floor of the family home in South Kensington; it consisted of a large bedroom with en-suite bathroom and an adjoining study-cum-sitting-room.

Tired of staring at the screen, he rubbed his eyes and stood up to stretch his legs. It was Friday night, exactly two weeks since he had first met Jenny Armstrong, and he wondered what she was doing this evening. As far as he knew she was single, but did she have a man in her life? Was she making love with him at that precise moment in her cosy little house in Jesmond? The thought was not a pleasant one.

Nick wished he could stop thinking so much about Jenny. She was not the kind of girl he usually found attractive. He had always been wary of opinionated women, and he suspected that Jenny – whose attitude towards him was so guarded – had some kind of chip on her shoulder. Objectively, she was no great beauty either, and yet he found himself inexplicably drawn to her like a magnet. She had what he thought of as a womanly body, too full and rounded to be fashionable. His mother would say she needed to lose a few kilos, but Nick had found himself fantasising more than once about those generous curves. She had a striking face too, framed by a luxuriant mass of tawny hair – the colour of autumn leaves, he thought whimsically. The face was expressive, with somewhat irregular features and a faint dusting of freckles. But what made the face unforgettable were her eyes – large and green, like twin pools of emerald water. He remembered how those eyes had flashed with anger when she stormed out of the hotel bar. He remembered how they had lit up with passion when she talked about walking back through time. And he also remembered how they had shone softly when he had taken her hand and their eyes met over the kitchen table. He was sure he had not imagined the connection between them at that moment.

It was a pity the end of the evening had been such an anti-climax. Jenny was upstairs with Emma for over half an hour, comforting her and assuring her the monster was no longer around. Nick, left to his own devices in the kitchen and not wanting to outstay his welcome, had simply called out a casual goodbye and let himself out of the house.

Since then, Jenny had e-mailed him a long and very well documented draft of her ideas for the programme, some of them with an unusual twist no one on the production team had previously thought of. There had also been a few text messages about the Robertson family search she had promised to undertake, although there was nothing in these messages that could be construed as personal, much less romantic. All in all, it was a frustrating situation, and one which occupied Nick's thoughts more than he liked to admit.

The smartphone next to his laptop buzzed, instantly identifying the caller as 'Klara'. Nick let the phone ring, certain that Klara would leave yet another message and feeling guilty that he had not replied to any of them. He had never been good at ending relationships, always preferring the cowardly option of letting himself be dumped rather than do the dumping. He knew, however, that it was high time he ended this particular relationship.

He had met Klara in a London nightclub almost three months ago and had instantly fallen – like every other man in the place – for her stunning good looks. Klara was a twenty-two-year-old Swedish model, tall and willowy with short, platinum blonde hair, a generous, rather sulky mouth and perfect legs. She was also, as Nick was soon to discover, fanatical about ashtanga yoga, her strict vegan regime and – above all – maintaining her own gorgeous physique. These turned out to be Klara's only topics of conversation, and her sense of humour – limited at best – vanished completely if Nick made fun of them. On the other hand, she had a totally uninhibited approach to sex, which was the main reason why Nick had allowed the relationship to go on for so long. But even in bed, Nick was now tired of Klara's athletic expertise; she made him feel like a competitor – and not a very good one at that – in an Olympic sporting event. The crux of the matter was quite simply that he was bored; Klara was shallow, narcissistic and – out of the bedroom – as dull as ditch water. Inevitably, his thoughts drifted back to Jenny, and he wondered how old she was – probably his own age or even slightly older, he guessed. The realisation only made her more desirable to him. Jenny was a real woman, a woman with brains and a mind of her own.

He padded downstairs in his stockinged feet and got a can of lager out of the kitchen fridge. He was surprised at that moment to hear the front door slam noisily; Alan and Nathalie were out to dinner with friends and it was too early – only just after ten – for them to be back. Still holding the can of lager, he went to investigate and was surprised to see his younger sister Charlotte, windswept and dishevelled, dragging a battered suitcase through the hall.

"Charlotte!" he exclaimed, greeting her with an affectionate hug. "We didn't expect you home this weekend."

"Change of plan, too complicated to explain," said Charlotte tersely. "I've just got in on the Eurostar. But I'm only here till Sunday, then I'm off to Burkina Faso."

She pushed her uncombed hair out of her eyes and took off her old brown parka with the fur-lined hood. In some ways, Nick thought, she looked very much like their mother, with her dark hair and eyes and patrician features. But Charlotte was a distorted, less attractive version of Nathalie – shorter and heavier and plainer, with none of her mother's innate grace and style. Luckily, this unflattering comparison had never affected Charlotte. A brilliant student with a razor-sharp brain, she had opted to study medicine in order – as she put it in her overly earnest way – to allay some of the misery in the world. Now twenty-eight and a qualified doctor, she was working for Médecins du Monde, a French-based humanitarian NGO. Nick was very fond of his altruistic sister and admired her unswerving dedication to helping the poor and needy. He just wished she were not quite so relentlessly virtuous. Charlotte was scathing about anyone who did not share the same moral high ground as herself.

"At least we've got you for a couple of days, then," he said. "Have you eaten? Shall I make you a sandwich or something while you unpack?"

"*C'est pas la peine, Nico, je suis lessivée,*" (1) she moaned, unexpectedly reverting to French. "I'm so exhausted I could sleep for a hundred years. Sorry but I'm going straight to bed – we can talk in the morning." She turned away and started hauling her suitcase upstairs.

Nick watched her disappear along the landing and finished his can of lager. He drifted aimlessly into the kitchen again and helped himself to another, trying to work up enough enthusiasm to finish reviewing the budget figures. He plodded back upstairs and into his den, idly picking up his smartphone to check for any messages. His heart missed a beat as he spotted a new text message from Jenny: *Have come to the end of your family line. His name is William Robertson.*

What did she mean? Without thinking, he punched back a reply: *Sounds exciting. Are you busy? Can I call now?* It was a long shot at this late hour, he knew, but for some reason he longed to hear her voice, if only to talk about his ancestors.

To his delight, it was Jenny who rang only a few seconds later. "Hi, it's me," she said, sounding cool and distant.

"Jenny! How lovely to hear from you," he responded warmly. "I'm very grateful to you for wading through the murky past of the Robertson family. But what do you mean by the end of the line?"

"Well, as I told you, I already had quite a lot of data on your family, at least as far back as the early 19ᵗʰ century. But now, I can trace the Robertsons right through to the mid-17ᵗʰ century. I found the parish record for the marriage of your earliest ancestor, William Robertson, in 1645 – and also a record of his death in 1676. So if we assume he married young, as most men did in those times, that would fix his date of birth somewhere between 1620, let's say, and 1627." Nick could hear the rustle of paper as she consulted her documentation.

"Fascinating!" he exclaimed. "But surely if you have a record of his marriage and death, you must have a record of his birth?"

"That's what I mean by the end of the line," explained Jenny, sounding frustrated. "There's no record of his birth, either in that parish or any other. So this is where we have to start reading between the lines."

As he listened to her voice, with its Geordie lilt so like his father's, Nick felt a rush of exhilaration, as if he were embarking on an adventure. He made a snap decision and prayed silently that Jenny would not rebuff him.

"I'd really like you to talk me through all this, Jenny. I don't think we can do it on the phone, though. I'm tied up all day tomorrow, worse luck, but I think I can escape on Sunday and take an early flight to Newcastle. That would give us all afternoon to go through my family history, or at least make a start. I know this is really short notice, but…" He waited with trepidation for her response.

"Oh, don't come all the way up here just for me," she said crisply, her voice instantly guarded.

Why was she keeping him at arm's length again? "But I want to come all the way up there," Nick insisted. "And also take you out to dinner afterwards."

There was a long silence over the phone. "All right, then," she agreed finally. "I mean, if you're genuinely interested in your family history and not just humouring me…"

"Jenny, I'm genuinely interested," he said slowly, deliberately making his reply ambiguous. He hoped she could hear the more personal implication, the unspoken words 'in you' hanging in the air between them.

(1) Don't bother, Nico, I'm worn out.

***

They were back in Jenny's kitchen once more, armed with ham sandwiches and mugs of coffee. Most of the kitchen table was taken up with the large roll of paper Jenny had spread out, displaying the Robertson family tree. The tree showed every generation of Nick's direct ancestors, along with their brothers and sisters, their wives and children.

Jenny watched covertly as Nick poured over the dozens of names and dates she had inscribed in her small, neat handwriting. She noticed how his dark hair curled at the nape of the neck, the way he bit his lip and narrowed his eyes in concentration. She studied his hands, which were well shaped with long fingers. Stop it, she checked herself; there was no way she would let herself fall for Nick Robertson.

She had been a bundle of nerves all morning, her heart fluttering like a silly schoolgirl at the prospect of seeing Nick again. When the airport taxi dropped him off at her house, she was struck afresh by his dark good looks and the easy, fluid way he moved. Yet now that he was actually here in the flesh, she felt surprisingly calm and relaxed; it was as if they had never been apart.

"I'm blown away," Nick announced finally. He drew back from the table and looked at her admiringly. "They're all here – every single Robertson ancestor for the last four hundred years. You've done a fantastic job, Jenny."

"Oh, it was nothing," she said modestly, although in fact she had spent every waking moment – when she wasn't at work – completing the research. She had found the Robertson family tree fascinating in many ways, but that was not why she had lavished so much time and attention on it. Secretly, she hoped that Nick, in discovering his Northumbrian roots, would truly connect with his ancestors, let them touch his heart and soul. And she wanted more than anything to be the person walking by his side on his journey through the past.

"I'm still waiting for a few transcripts to come through," she added. "But every name on that family tree is documented." She patted the huge pile of folders at her side, one folder for every generation of the Robertson family.

Nick stared at the folders in awe. "Did you uncover any blue blood in the Robertson veins?" he quipped lightly. "Or come across any shock-and-horror family scandals?"

"Watch this space and all will be revealed," she smiled. "Why don't we start at the very beginning, with William Robertson? He's the first tiny piece of the Robertson mosaic. As I told you on the phone, I can find no trace of his birth, although I'd guess it was between 1620 and 1627. What we do know is that he was married in 1645 in Northumberland, in the parish of Embleton."

31

"Embleton?" mused Nick. "I've never been there, but the name rings a bell. Isn't it near Alnwick?"

"Yes, Embleton's a pretty village – and a very old one too – a few miles north of Alnwick. On the coast near Embleton is Dunstanburgh Castle, the largest castle in Northumberland, although sadly there's nothing left of it but ruins. Ever go there?"

Nick shook his head. "So this is where the Robertson family originated, is it?"

"Well, we know that your earliest known ancestor, William Robertson, lived and worked at a large country estate near Embleton – a place called Dunstan Manor. At that time, the estate was owned by the Thorburns, a wealthy local family with considerable political influence." Jenny unfolded a map of Northumberland and pointed to the area in question.

"So the Robertsons are true Northumbrians, then?" said Nick eagerly. "Do you think William was born at Dunstan Manor?"

"Possibly," said Jenny cautiously. "Parish records in the early 17th century are often sketchy, so it's entirely feasible that the record of William's birth has been lost or destroyed. But there's another, more likely, hypothesis."

"The suspense is killing me," laughed Nick. "What is it?"

"Well, my hunch is that William wasn't a native Northumbrian. Robertson is a Scottish name after all, one of the oldest clans in Scotland."

Nick looked taken back. "I suppose so, now I come to think of it. I've never really thought of myself as anything other than English."

"I'm pretty sure that William – or possibly his father – originally migrated to Northumberland from Scotland. He certainly wouldn't be the first. At that time, many thousands of Scots crossed the border to England, looking for work. You might think that life was harsh in the wilds of Northumberland back then, but it was still an improvement on the poverty and lawlessness in most parts of Scotland." Jenny downed the last of her coffee and put the kettle on to replenish their mugs.

"So you're saying William was some kind of economic migrant?" Nick was captivated, trying to picture this distant ancestor desperate enough to leave his homeland forever and seek a new life in England.

"He may have been," she conceded. She had been spooning instant coffee into their mugs but now turned to face him directly. "But in your case, I don't think so. You see, I have a great deal of documented evidence proving that the Robertson family was Roman Catholic."

Nick was speechless. "But that's impossible!" he protested. "Our family has always been Church of England, as far back as anyone can remember."

"As far back as the mid-19th century, certainly," corrected Jenny. "But before then, every single Robertson in your family tree was staunchly Catholic. So it all makes sense now, doesn't it?"

"It doesn't make any sense at all to me," said Nick, trying to get his head around so many unexpected revelations.

"But can't you see, man?" Jenny's green eyes lit up with excitement. "At the time of William's marriage in 1645, there was civil war on both sides of the border. England and Scotland were torn apart by religious and political strife. Roman Catholics like William were outlawed and persecuted in both countries. Many Catholics took up arms to support the Stuart king, Charles I. There were fierce

32

battles all over Britain, in England against Cromwell's Puritan Roundheads and in Scotland against the Presbyterian Covenanters."

"Well, I know that much from history lessons at school," interjected Nick, still puzzled. "But that still doesn't explain why William Robertson suddenly headed south to Northumberland."

"Many Scots fled across the border at that time," said Jenny patiently. "You see, the Earls of Northumberland – the powerful Percy family – were known to be sympathetic to the Catholic cause. Unfortunately by 1645, the Percys had converted to Protestantism and refused to support the Royalists. Even so, in Alnwick and the surrounding area many of the nobles and gentry were still fervently Catholic." She leaned forward eagerly and clutched Nick's arm. "Including the Thorburn family of Dunstan Manor."

"Crikey," breathed Nick.

"At the time of William's marriage in 1645, there were hundreds of poor Catholics in that part of Northumberland. They weren't allowed to practise their faith openly and lived in constant fear of arrest, but the Catholic nobles and gentry in the area took them under their wing and protected them to a certain extent. Dunstan Manor would have been a relatively safe haven for William in those troubled times." Jenny took the top folder, marked 'William Robertson', from the pile and started leafing through the various documents.

"Now I understand," said Nick, pondering over his mysterious ancestor. "But we still don't know exactly how William came to settle in Embleton."

"We'll never know for sure," said Jenny with a sigh of resignation. "This is one of those genealogical conundrums I told you about. William's story will be shrouded forever in a mist of uncertainty. But Nick, wouldn't it be wonderful to break through time and see William Robertson as he was then? Find out what really happened?"

I

William Robertson, September 1645

The last thing William saw before he stumbled and lost consciousness was the massive ruins of a castle, jutting out of the headland at the far side of the wide sandy bay. Below him, huge waves crashed onto the windswept beach. Staggering over the grassy moorland, clenching his teeth from the pain in his shoulder, he wondered if the fortifications signalled the mighty Northumbrian town of Alnwick. Was he nearing Alnwick at last? Despite the hunger, terror and grief gnawing at his very soul, William's heart lifted at the thought.

He could not recall how many days had passed since he and James had fled south over the border from the battlefield at Philiphaugh. Scotland was in the grip of a fierce civil war. The zealous puritanical Presbyterians who held sway over the country were sworn enemies of the Stuarts. They were determined that King Charles, with his French wife and extravagant ways, must not be allowed to re-instate Catholicism in Scotland. So the Covenanters, as they called themselves, had raised an army and set about burning, pillaging and slaughtering all those suspected of loyalty to the King. But after long years of persecution, the Catholic chieftains had risen up to fight the hated Covenanters in armed combat. Alexander Robertson of Dunkeld was one such chieftain. He had called on his clan kinsmen to take up arms for the Royalists, and every able-bodied man in Dunkeld had rallied to defend the Cause. This was their chance for revenge at long last. A triumphant victory would be theirs, King Charles would restore the Old Faith to Scotland and they would all live in peace as free men.

This was what William truly believed as he and his elder brother, James, had set off from Dunkeld on that summer's day in 1645. There was no mistaking they were brothers, for they were close in age and had the same wiry frame, sandy hair and blue eyes. Bursting with pride and elation, they marched south with their Robertson kinsmen to the Border country. As they approached Selkirk, they were excited to find hundreds of fellow Royalists camped at Philiphaugh under the command of the great Marquess of Montrose. But their high spirits were short-lived, for even before the battle commenced apprehension and foreboding had spread through the Royalist ranks. William and the other foot soldiers, underfed and poorly armed, rapidly discovered they were heavily outnumbered by the well-trained disciplined Covenanters. As for the Marquess of Montrose, it was rumoured in the Royalist camp that he had once been a Covenanter himself; like all-powerful men, he might turn coat again if it meant saving his own skin.

William knew he could never erase from his memory that bloodbath of a battle at Philiphaugh. Through the smoke, the noise and the stench he had fought on, hundreds of his kinsmen lying dead or wounded at his feet. Musket fire caught him in the shoulder but he barely noticed, as if his senses had been deadened by the savagery all around him. As the hours passed, the Royalists, battle-weary and their numbers depleted, fought with increasing desperation but it was clear the day would end in defeat for the Cause.

It was then that William was roughly grabbed by his elder brother and hauled off out of range of Covenanter musket-fire. James was wounded too, for William noticed blood was flowing freely down his leg, but his voice was fierce as he shouted to make himself heard above the deafening noise of the battlefield.

"Come, William, we must flee! We will surely die if we stay here and fight on."

William, bewildered and anguished, stared at his brother in disbelief. "But how can we flee, James? The battle is not over yet and it would be dishonourable to go home to Dunkeld without our laird and kinsmen."

James spoke more urgently now, holding William's face close to his own to make every word clear. "Listen to me, laddie, we're not going back to Dunkeld, at least not before this war is at an end. We are fortunate, for we have no wives or bairns waiting for us there. And you heard the news the messenger brought the laird only days ago. His castle has been burnt to the ground by the Presbyterians and all his lands laid waste. Do you think we can just go home and start tending sheep again? The Covenanters will not rest until every Robertson is in his grave, and make no mistake, William – you will be one of them if you set foot again in Dunkeld." He was panting for breath now and gripping his wounded leg.

Speechless, William could only listen as James pressed on. "We will flee south to Northumberland until peace returns to Scotland. The Covenanter Army is fighting the Royalists in England too, but I have heard there are many Catholics in Northumberland. Why should Scots like us not fight alongside them? King Charles is their monarch as he is ours. We should go to Alnwick, seek protection from the English Royalists and take up arms with them against the Covenanters."

And so, they had escaped from the hell of Philiphaugh as night fell over the battlefield. The pain in William's shoulder was excruciating, but he staunched the wound as best he could and followed his elder brother across the moors and marshland of southern Scotland. James's plan was to follow the course of the River Tweed east towards its estuary in Berwick, on the English side of the border, and then head south. They had no idea whether this was the safest or quickest way to reach Alnwick, but it was the only plan they had. So like hunted animals, they fled towards the coast, avoiding farms and villages and taking cover in woodland as far as possible. Two days later at dusk, they managed to cross the Tweed near Norham and collapsed in exhaustion on the opposite bank.

Only then did William fully realise that James's wound was far more critical than his own. His heart contracted with fear as he looked more closely at his brother stretched out alongside him on the riverbank, his head and shoulders propped against a tree trunk and moaning with pain. Inspecting the wound, William tried to conceal his horror as he examined James's leg, swollen and discoloured from infection. They had had nothing to eat since the battle two days ago, and James no longer had the strength to move or even drink the river water William carried to him in the palms of his hands.

As darkness enveloped them, William could barely see the outline of James's body, but his brother's groans of agony kept him awake all night. James had wrapped his tartan plaid tightly around him like a blanket, although the late September weather was still quite mild and thankfully, there was no rain. William prayed through the long dark hours and tried to comfort his brother until he finally passed away just before dawn. James spoke only once, his voice hoarse as he grasped William's arm.

"Take heart, laddie, we are in Northumberland now and you must continue south until you reach Alnwick. May God go with you, William."

Wordlessly, William made the sign of the cross as James let out one long last moan and closed his eyes forever. Then he broke down sobbing over the inert body, grief and despair mingling with fear and a feeling of intense solitude. He had always relied on his hardheaded elder brother for guidance, and it had never occurred to him that they would not reach Alnwick together, that James would not be with him to decide on the best course of action. And now here he was, completely lost in a strange land, miles away from his kinsmen who would doubtless already be retreating north to Dunkeld.

After what seemed a long while, William raised his head. The sun was already high, its rays shining through the trees and glinting on the river as it flowed east to the sea. He was surprised by the rush of energy that coursed through his body, an iron resolve not to let James down. He suddenly wanted to prove to his brother that he was man enough to survive, to brave the unknown and continue fighting for the Cause.

But first, he must prepare himself as best he could for what lay ahead. Gingerly, he took off his blood-soaked linen shirt, although he had to grit his teeth to stop himself crying out from the pain. Then, shaking with trepidation, he un- wrapped the plaid around James's dead body and removed his brother's shirt. Would it be a sin to leave him lying on the riverbank, without even a shirt on his back? But what else could he do? Racked with remorse, he donned James's shirt and discarded his own. Finally, he ripped off a length of his brother's plaid and concocted a makeshift sling to support his shoulder. With a heavy heart, he took the dagger attached to James's belt and hung it alongside his own; a dagger was a valuable item and he had no intention of leaving it here on the riverbank.

There was one last thing – the hardest of all – William still had to do. Tears running freely down his face, he opened the rough leather pouch also attached to James's belt. Gently, he took out the wooden crucifix he knew he would find there and examined it in the palm of his hand. James had made the crucifix himself, the image of Christ overlaid on a beautifully worked Celtic cross. William had watched admiringly during long evenings by the fire in Dunkeld as his brother carved and polished the wood. The finished article was truly exquisite, William thought. Carefully, he placed it in his own sporran, convinced that in some mysterious way the cross would shield and protect him, just as his brother had always done.

And so, William left James's corpse on the banks of the Tweed and set off alone in what he hoped was a southward direction, steering clear of any human habitation and avoiding open tracts of land where he would be easily spotted. His shoulder wound was a source of constant pain, but even worse was the hunger gnawing at his belly and sapping his strength. He gulped down water whenever he came across a stream, but the Northumbrian woodland offered little in the way of food.

Then one morning, totally unexpectedly, he glimpsed a vast expanse of grey water on the horizon and realised it must be the sea. William was familiar with the peaceful lochs back home in Dunkeld but had never before seen such a huge mass of water, although he had heard tell of it from his kinsmen. He stumbled towards it and stood spellbound on the cliff top, hypnotised by the ceaseless ebb and flow of the waves and the rhythmic sound they made as they lapped and crashed onto the shore. There was not a soul to be seen in any direction. It was about midday, William guessed, as he turned towards the sun with the coastline directly to his left. Surely, if he stayed on this course, keeping within sight of the sea, he would be moving south and would therefore reach Alnwick sooner or later? It seemed as good a plan as any, he thought.

Shortly afterwards, William came across a lone cottage, nestled in the shelter of a copse and seemingly deserted. Hiding behind a tree, he observed the cottage for a long time but saw no one emerge. Dagger in hand, he quietly entered the tiny habitation; in the gloomy interior was a female form, her back bent over a huge pot on an open fire.

Years later, William still felt ashamed when he thought back to his behaviour that day. Grabbing the woman from behind and thrusting the dagger to her throat, he had yelled at her incoherently and forced her to give up every last morsel of food in the cottage. But he had been half-crazed with hunger, and his need to survive was stronger than any consideration of right or wrong. Like a wild animal – or so the terrified woman must have thought – and still brandishing his dagger, he had stuffed as much food as he could into his mouth and secreted the rest away in the folds of his plaid before he lurched off again on his journey south.

That had been the day before. And now here he was, watching the grey clouds scud over the mighty castle in the distance. Alnwick, surely this must be Alnwick at last? His eyes fixed on the huge fortifications ahead, he tried to break into a run but almost instantly twisted his foot on a rocky outcrop. As if in slow motion, he watched himself fall forward and his head hit the grey stone underfoot.

* * *

When William opened his eyes again, it was to see the round pale face of a girl; she was bending over him and wiping the sweat from his brow with a damp cloth. He was lying on a straw mattress, covered with an old rank-smelling blanket, in a gloomy interior. Instantly on the alert, he reached wildly for his dagger, only to realise his plaid and belt had been removed.

"Rest easy," said the girl calmly. "You have nothing to fear. Nobody will harm you here."

"Where am I?" William croaked weakly. "Is this Alnwick?"

The girl looked at him in astonishment. "No, Alnwick is a good way from here. This land belongs to Sir Charles Thorburn of Dunstan Manor. My father is his shepherd, and he found you senseless on the moor. We managed to carry you back here, but you've had the fever these past two days."

William tried to take in this information but felt too weak to think clearly. Turning his head wearily to one side, he saw that he was in a tiny one-room hut with stonewalls and a fire glowing in the hearth. The girl was alone, and he did not appear to be in any immediate danger. She gazed at him dispassionately with strange colourless eyes.

"Now I will tend to your shoulder," she went on, indicating a small earthenware bowl in her hand. It was filled with a sticky-looking unguent smelling faintly of honey, which the girl proceeded to apply to his wound. "This will bring the poison out and help with the healing."

Too feeble to respond, William lay back on the straw mattress and gave himself up without protest to her ministrations. He found his shoulder was less painful than before his fall and wondered if the girl had been treating his wound with the unguent during his fever. He hoped he had not been so delirious that he had betrayed his identity or plans. The girl clearly meant him no harm but he must be careful what he revealed about himself in Northumberland, for as yet he did not know whether its inhabitants were friends or foes.

The girl was busying herself now at a huge black pot over the fire. She returned a moment later with a large bowl of what looked like rabbit stew and helped William to sit up with his back against the wall so that he could eat it. Feeling suddenly ravenous after so many days without proper sustenance, he devoured the contents of the bowl in a matter of seconds. A faint smile appeared on the girl's moon-like face, although her eyes remained expressionless.

"You must sleep now," she commanded in her flat calm voice. "When you're feeling better, my father will speak to you. He'll tell you what is to be done." At these words, William closed his eyes almost dutifully and drifted off into a deep refreshing sleep.

It was several days before William felt strong enough to stand and move about the tiny room. The girl spoke very little but when asked, told him her name was Susannah. With quiet efficiency, she fed him, brought him warm ewe's milk to drink, applied the honey unguent to his shoulder and made him as comfortable as possible on the straw mattress. Occasionally, William glimpsed what appeared to be an old man in the hut, small of stature and stooped, but he was always gone by daybreak and did not attempt to question William or engage him in conversation.

But today was to be different. In the morning, William had left the confines of the stone hut for the first time, determined to find his bearings in this potentially hostile environment. His shoulder still ached, but he felt his strength returning and youthful energy coursing through his veins. There was no other dwelling to be seen near the hut, nothing as far as the eye could see but sheep dotting the grassy moors. The land sloped down to the high cliffs overlooking the bay. The castle he had spotted on the far side of the bay before his fall was much closer now, but as he approached to inspect it more closely, William was stunned to discover it was entirely uninhabited. The massive fortifications were in decay, the twin-towered gatehouse in ruins. There was a bite now in the early autumn air and the wind blowing off the sea was bracing, whipping colour back into his cheeks. William was struck again by the wild beauty of the place. With renewed vigour, he made his way along the cliff-top, seagulls screeching above him and the wide sandy bay spread out below.

It was then that he saw the figure of the bent old man emerging from behind the high stone towers of the castle, still a good distance away but walking – shepherd's crook in hand – in his direction. The moment of truth had arrived at last, William thought as he hastened towards him. He planned to glean as much information as possible from the shepherd, while disclosing as little as possible about his own identity. But the old man had stopped walking and was raising his crook, beckoning William to meet him in the sheltered ruins of the castle. When William joined him shortly afterwards, panting slightly from the unaccustomed exertion, he found the old man sitting with his back to one of the massive crumbling walls, gazing intently out to sea.

"I must thank you, sir," began William as he sat down next to the shepherd, "for your kindness in taking me in and your daughter's in attending to me through my sickness. I hardly know what would have become of me if you had not rescued me."

But the old man barely acknowledged his words, apparently eager to discuss more important topics. Without further ado, he looked William straight in the eyes and spoke to him in a slow, deliberate voice. "It looks like you're a stranger to these parts, lad, so I'll tell you where you stand. My name is Lancelot Hunter, and Susannah is my daughter. This land belongs to Dunstan Manor, the estate of Sir Charles Thorburn, and I am his shepherd."

"I'm a shepherd too," interjected William eagerly and was heartened to see a sympathetic gleam in the old man's eyes. Impulsively, he told Lancelot his name, that he was nineteen years old and had travelled many miles from his home in Dunkeld. "In Perthshire," he added as an afterthought, for he doubted that the old man would have heard of Dunkeld.

"Aye, I can see you're a Scot, lad," retorted Lancelot drily, casting a baleful eye over William's belted plaid. "And I know you're a Roman Catholic as well."

William was aghast. England was a Protestant country, he knew, and most likely no less dangerous a place for Catholics than Scotland. But how could Lancelot possibly have unearthed his secret? He glanced at the shepherd in alarm and was relieved to see no animosity in the Northumbrian's gnarled old face.

"We're Catholics too, lad, so you can rest easy. When you had the fever, Susannah dried your clothes over the fire and found a crucifix in your pouch."

Tears pricked unwanted in William's eyes as he remembered the precious Celtic cross he had taken from his brother's dead body. Instinctively, his hand flew to the sporran attached to his belt, but Lancelot grasped his arm reassuringly. "You'll have it back when you're ready, lad, but in the meantime it's safely hidden... and the two daggers as well."

It was time to come clean, thought William, making the sign of the cross and thanking God for his mercy in leading him to this particular Northumbrian. Almost eagerly now, he told Lancelot about his clan's support for King Charles and the Royalist cause, their hopes of defeating the Presbyterian army and restoring the true faith to Scotland. Sorrowfully, he related the debacle of the battle at Philiphaugh and his flight to Northumberland with his brother James.

"James died of his wounds just after we crossed the border," he ended in a low voice, "and the crucifix is all I have to remember him by. But even though he's gone, the cause lives on. That is why I must go to Alnwick without delay and join the Royalist army there. Tell me, please, how far are we from Alnwick?"

"You're in the parish of Embleton, no more than a few miles to the north of Alnwick. A man could walk there in little more than two hours."

Seeing William's eyes light up, the old shepherd raised his hand for silence. "Listen to me, lad, and listen hard. You must not think of showing your face in

Alnwick for many a month, or anywhere else in these parts for that matter. Have you not heard, man? The whole of Northumberland, all the way south to Newcastle, has fallen to the Scottish Covenanters. They invaded our lands these five years past and defeated the King's army. The bastards laid waste to every village and town they marched through, sacking Newcastle and plundering Alnwick. They are hated by every man in the county, for they have brought nothing but misery and starvation in their wake. May they be damned for all eternity! They have raped our women, burnt our villages to the ground, stolen our livestock and even the very pots and pans from our homes."

William's heart sank on hearing this tirade. Not content with ruling over all Scotland, the Covenanters had felt strong enough to cross the border and overcome the King's forces in Northumberland.

"But King Charles reigns over all England," he protested desperately. "Surely, he can raise an army mighty enough to defeat the Covenanters and drive them back to Scotland?"

"The whole of England is at war, lad," Lancelot responded bitterly. "Englishmen are fighting Englishmen. The Parliament in London has disputed the King's God-given right to reign over this country. The Puritan zealots have raised an army to defeat the Royalists, and we hear tell there are bloody battles the length and breadth of all England. Their evil commander Cromwell shows no mercy and thinks nothing of killing the King's soldiers in cold blood, even after they've surrendered. The Scottish Covenanters have formed an alliance with the Parliamentarians. They'll not relinquish their grip on Northumberland until Cromwell pays them handsomely to march their troops back to Scotland."

William silently berated himself for his ignorance and naivety. He had stupidly believed he could simply walk into Alnwick and be welcomed into the ranks of his Royalist comrades-in-arms. But it was now clear that the situation in Northumberland was infinitely worse than he could possibly have imagined. The whole county was occupied by the same hated Presbyterians who had persecuted his kinsmen in Dunkeld for so many years.

More thoughtfully now, he questioned Lancelot further. "Yet my brother told me there are many Catholic believers in Northumberland?"

"Aye, lad, there are – not only among the common people but also the nobles and gentry. Sir Charles Thorburn himself keeps the faith, as do many of his friends in these parts. But rich or poor, we must all keep our beliefs close to our chests, for it is unlawful in England to be Catholic. A man can be convicted and hanged for hearing mass, and even powerful men like Sir Charles would have their lands seized if they practised their faith openly."

"Then I am no more a free man in England than I was in Scotland," replied William disconsolately. "The Presbyterians will not be satisfied until they have tortured and killed the last Catholic in the land."

Lancelot crossed himself at these sombre words. "We must pray the Scottish Covenanters will not stay long in Northumberland and leave us to settle our own affairs, as we have always done. True, England is a Protestant country and as Catholics, we must conceal our faith in public. But you must understand that the people in these parts, Protestant and Catholic alike, have no love of the English Parliament. Those who make the laws in London are hundreds of miles away and understand nothing about our ways here in Northumberland. We have no need of their laws or their damned interference! Take it from me, lad, there was no persecution of Catholics in these parts before the Covenanters came. We kept ourselves to ourselves, and the Protestants let us be. Hereabouts even a poor shepherd like me could live in safety, as long as he served a Catholic master like Sir Charles and didn't stray from his land. The Hunters have been under the protection of the Thorburns for as long as my family can remember, and we've never come to any harm."

William was impressed by the old shepherd's gritty common sense and his insight into Northumbrian ways. He got to his feet and walked a few steps away from Lancelot, staring out to sea and trying to assemble his thoughts. The wind ruffled his unkempt sandy hair and the salty air filled his nostrils. He turned back to Lancelot with renewed determination.

"Then if Sir Charles is sympathetic to our cause, he must be acquainted with many Royalists in high places. Perhaps your master could help me enlist in one of the King's regiments?"

Lancelot sighed wearily. "Have you not been listening to me, man? These are dangerous times and the King's army is defeated. Northumberland is in the hands of the Scots, and the Royalists are lying low for the present. Sir Charles will not lift a finger for the cause now, for fear the Covenanters confiscate his lands. In the old days, the Earl of Northumberland would have protected us all. The name of Percy was respected by every man in these parts, rich and poor alike. But the present Earl is a coward and has sided with the Scots." The old shepherd spat on the ground to show his contempt.

"And another thing," he went on with a twisted smile. "You'll not survive long around here dressed in that Scottish blanket of yours. The men of Embleton will kill you as soon as look at you. The Scots have used savagery and violence these past years to oppress our people, and the Northumbrians are out for revenge. You'll be a dead man before you even draw breath to tell them whose side you're on."

William looked down at his belted plaid in despair. It had not occurred to him that his Scottish dress would be like waving a red flag to a bull on this side of the border. Lancelot, however, had clearly given some thought to the young man's predicament.

"Have no fear, I'll find you some breeches and a jacket to wear. But you must promise me not to leave these parts for many months, at least not before spring of next year. You tell me you're a shepherd? Then why not stay on with me and Susannah and help tend Sir Charles's flock? I feel God has brought you to me in my old age and sickness, lad. This is where you were meant to be, next to me and my lass."

Lancelot's tone was almost pleading now. Was the old shepherd trying to strike some kind of bargain? William felt frustrated and trapped but at the same time could see the sense in Lancelot's plan. What was the point in recklessly putting his life at risk, exposing himself to a hostile population and almost certain death? He sat down again beside his would-be protector and saw that Lancelot did indeed look ill, his weary demeanour betraying more than just old age. Suddenly curious, he tried another tack.

"Have you no wife, Lancelot? Is Susannah your only child?"

It was as if he had given the shepherd the cue he had been waiting for to confide in William. "My wife's name was Margery. God blessed us with nine

41

children, although six were sickly and taken from us in infancy. We thought Margery's time for childbirth was past, for we were both in middle years. But Margery gave me one last child, Susannah, although she died having her. God took my beloved wife from me but left me a dear daughter in her place."

Lancelot almost choked on the last words, his grief still raw even after so many years. Yet he continued with his story, as if eager to unburden himself at last. "My sons live nearby and also serve Sir Charles, but they have children and now even grandchildren of their own. As for me, I'm an ailing old man but I have no fear of death, for God will unite me again with my dear wife. So you see lad, I live only for Susannah and will not rest easy until I see her married to a good man."

Lancelot was staring out to sea again. He was reluctant to meet William's eyes, but it was impossible to misunderstand his meaning. So Susannah was part of the bargain the old shepherd wanted to strike? Lancelot was offering him an arrangement that he hoped would be beneficial to them both. William would have a safe haven in Northumberland, a wife and a quiet life as a shepherd at Dunstan Manor; Lancelot would have a man to help him tend the sheep and take care of Susannah after his death.

The young Scot turned impulsively to the older man and noticed then that Lancelot's face was lined not only with age but with suffering. There were no outward signs of infirmity but some deeper ailment seemed to be consuming him, racking his thin frame with pain. He reminded himself that he owed the shepherd and his daughter some gratitude for their kindness and generosity. Yet he was only nineteen years old... surely life had more in store for him than just tending sheep in this wild corner of Northumberland?

"I know you mean well," he began tentatively, "but you see..."

But Lancelot would not allow any objections that might stand in the way of his plan. "Susannah is a good lass," he said firmly. "She'll serve her husband well. It's true that God has afflicted her sorely, for she's nearly blind in one eye and sees only partially in the other..."

His voice trailed away as he waited for William's reaction, but the young man was dumbstruck. The poor girl was almost blind! So that was the reason for those colourless eyes, that strange look in her round placid face.

"I know what must be going through your mind, lad," Lancelot pressed on earnestly. "But think carefully before you cast us aside. Susannah is used to her affliction and tends to her duties in the home as well as any other lass. She has the same strong body as her mother and with God's blessing will bear her husband as many sons as he has a mind to give her."

Lost for words, William watched as Lancelot rose laboriously to his feet, leaning heavily on his crook and visibly trying to hide the pain searing through his body. His ragged, stooped frame looked even more pitiful silhouetted against the hard grey stone of the castle walls. Mumbling that he had work to do and that they could talk further during supper, the old shepherd simply raised his hand in farewell and turned away from William with the faintest of smiles on his face. Picking his way carefully through the ruins of the castle, he disappeared from William's view.

William had no idea how long he stayed there, his back to the castle wall and his thoughts churning like the turbulent grey sea before him. He found he had no desire to leave the safe haven of the castle, feeling protected within the confines of its stark ruins. Eventually, however, his body stiff and chilled, he stood up reluctantly and set off in the direction of the shepherd's hut. Lancelot had made him painfully aware that his clothing branded him instantly as a Scot, so he was relieved to see no one on the way back; he had no wish to be set upon by a horde of Northumbrians out for revenge. He prayed that Lancelot would keep his promise to bring him something more nondescript to wear.

As he drew near the humble stone dwelling, he spotted Susannah outside, kneeling to pick vegetables from the rough patch she tended. Although he was still a good way off, she seemed to sense his approach and got to her feet, wiping her hands clean on her bulky skirts. She neither moved towards him nor turned back into the hut, simply waiting motionless for him to join her. His mind still reeling from Lancelot's proposal, he observed her more attentively as he came closer. She was short and squat, the coarse material of her jacket and skirt making the outline of her body thick and shapeless. Her face was round and plain, with dull mousy hair tucked into a grey linen cap. His thoughts strayed to one or two of the bonny lasses back home in Dunkeld, but Susannah could not be termed bonny by any stretch of the imagination.

As he walked up to her with what he hoped was a friendly smile, Susannah's hand flew to her mouth as if a thought had just occurred to her. She turned away and ran back to the stone hut, standing on tiptoe to remove something small from under the eaves of the roof. Then she walked purposefully back to William, handing him the object without a word. Looking down, William recognised James's Celtic cross. It lay in his hand, the smooth wood gleaming dully in the autumn sunshine, reminding him of his faith and his kinsmen in faraway Scotland. He tucked it safely away in his leather pouch, overjoyed to have it back in his keeping.

As he raised his eyes to thank Susannah, she reached up and kissed him on the mouth. It was not a chaste kiss by any means, and Susannah's lips were pleasingly soft and warm. Startled at first by this unexpected intimacy, William found himself responding to the girl almost in spite of himself. He pulled her closer and felt her heavy breasts and broad hips pressing against his body. The lingering kiss continued until both of them felt the need to take breath. Keeping his arms firmly around her waist, William stared down at Susannah. The girl's strange colourless eyes were closed, but the expression on her face was one of intense yearning. This time, it was William who kissed her, gathering her tightly into his arms and closing his eyes as she had closed hers.

When the kiss ended, he relinquished his hold slightly and gazed over Susannah's shoulder at the sombre ruins of the castle at the far end of the bay. "What's the name of that castle?" he asked, his voice filled with newfound tenderness.

A look of surprise came over Susannah's face but she answered readily enough. "Why man, that's Dunstanburgh Castle. They say it's the biggest and grandest fortress in the whole of England. No heathen invaders will land on our shores while Dunstanburgh guards and protects us."

"But it's in ruins!" protested William with a laugh.

"Aye, it's in ruins now," responded Susannah earnestly. "But before the castle was built, our shores were invaded again and again, for hundreds of years, by

43

marauders from across the seas. The castle was built to defend Northumberland and keep our land safe from foreign devils. Dunstanburgh may be in ruins now, but that's only because no marauders have dared to invade this coastline for many a long year."

William refrained from pointing out that even as they spoke Northumberland was controlled by the Scottish army and therefore far from being a safe haven. Dunstanburgh Castle, in ruins or not, had failed to keep the Scottish Covenanters at bay. But the girl had spoken with such fierce conviction that William was in no mood to argue; perhaps everyone hereabouts felt as she did. They both turned to gaze in wonder at the massive outline of the castle, suddenly illuminated by a ray of autumn sunshine emerging from behind scudding clouds. For some reason, William had the odd sensation that his fate was sealed. He took Susannah's hand firmly in his own and led the girl back to the hut.

Nick and Jenny (2)

Although it was only four o'clock on that Sunday afternoon, the January light had already faded outside; a cold rain pattered steadily against the windows of Jenny's house. They were still sitting at the kitchen table, mulling over the mystery surrounding William's life.

"What we do know for sure," concluded Jenny, "is that in 1645, William married Susannah Hunter. She was the youngest daughter of a local family, and her parents' names were Lancelot and Margery."

"Lancelot!" exclaimed Nick. "How romantic! What do we know about the Hunter family?"

"My research shows that Lancelot was employed on the estate at Dunstan Manor. There are clear indications that the Hunters were also Roman Catholic."

"I don't see what real proof you have of their religion," argued Nick.

"Oh, I have proof," said Jenny firmly. "You see, in the old days when parish clerks used to register christenings for Catholic families, they would often annotate the inscription with the words *'privately baptised'*. That meant that the baby had already received a Catholic baptism at a prior date – it was the clerk's cryptic way of identifying the family as Catholic without actually betraying them. I've found several such annotations for your Robertson ancestors, and for the Hunters too."

"Whew…" Nick let out a long breath. "Was it really so dangerous to be Catholic back then?"

"It was indeed, and for a long time to come. We tend to forget how religious faith defined a person's identity in those days – their place in society and the people they would or wouldn't mix with. Don't forget that Catholicism was illegal for hundreds of years – Catholics were barred from voting or owning land or serving in the army." Jenny suspected that Nick had not fully grasped the implications of his ancestors' religious convictions.

"Yes, but the Robertsons wouldn't have been affected by all that surely? It looks like they were all as poor as church mice, so it was immaterial to them whether they could own land or not."

"That's true of course, but Catholics like the Robertsons who clung to their faith were usually banished to the outer fringes of mainstream society. William Robertson and his kind weren't just poor, they were outcasts in the parish. At Dunstan Manor, for instance, most of the workers would have been either farm labourers or servants, but the men in Catholic families were often shepherds – cut off and isolated from their Protestant neighbours on the estate." Jenny saw Nick's eyes widen as the reality of life in 17th century Northumberland sunk in.

"In that case," he said, "why did they bother having their children registered at the parish church at all?"

"They were fined if they didn't," explained Jenny. "It was compulsory to register marriages and deaths too. There was no civil register at the time, so this was the only way the authorities could keep track of the local population."

"Poor old William," said Nick. He turned back thoughtfully to the family tree, his fingers moving down to the next generation. "I see he and Susannah had four children?"

"Yes, although only one of them, James, seems to have survived beyond infancy. I wonder why he was named James, rather than William or even Lancelot? Perhaps James was the name of William's father or brother... At any rate, those two names – William and James – appear somewhere in every Robertson generation right up to the present day."

"That's amazing," said Nick, feeling strangely moved. "So what do we know about James Robertson?"

"Not much." Jenny shrugged her shoulders. "Life went on at Dunstan Manor as it had always done. James married and had six children. One of his children – also called James and your direct ancestor – is very interesting, though." She removed the relevant folder from the pile and opened it for Nick.

"Here he is, see?" she continued. "William's grandson – James Robertson – was born in 1685 at Dunstan Manor. In 1704, when he was only nineteen, he married a Mary Dunn. They had three children – Lancelot, Susannah and Jane..."

"All pretty much business as usual so far," remarked Nick wryly.

"Not quite," corrected Jenny. She took the transcript of an ancient document from the back of the file and pushed it across the table towards Nick. "This is the record of James's death in 1715, aged thirty."

Nick scrutinised the transcript closely and gasped. "Bloody hell," he muttered, staring in horror at Jenny.

"Quite," said Jenny grimly.

II

Mary Robertson, October 1715

Mary had been standing for the last two hours on Market Place in Alnwick, her three children huddled close to her skirts and the driving rain soaking them all to the bone. Her husband James was to be hanged at noon as a Catholic conspirator. Along with eight other Embleton men, he had been found guilty of fomenting a rebellion to overthrow the Hanoverian King George. It was a ridiculous charge, for the men were far too humble in station to play a political role in the Jacobite movement sweeping Northumberland. But they had confessed to being Catholics, and in these dangerous times, that in itself was a crime punishable by death.

Northumberland was torn apart by political and religious conflict. After years of plotting and planning, a Jacobite Rising – supported by many nobles and gentry in the county – was now underway to restore James Stuart, the Old Pretender, to the throne of England and Scotland.

Tears ran unchecked down the cheeks of Mary's two daughters, Jane and Susannah; they were only five and seven years old, too young to understand the charges laid against their father but old enough to realise he was about to die. Lancelot, Mary's ten-year-old son, refused to cringe and weep like his sisters; he stood straight and steadfast, his face chalk white and expressionless.

"Father always said a man must be prepared to die for his faith," he had reminded them sternly. "We can be proud of him today, for he'll die a martyr."

It was the first time ever that any of them had stepped outside of the relatively safe confines of Dunstan Manor. That morning before sunrise, they had left the tiny stone hut they called home and walked seven miles to Alnwick, for word had reached Mary that the hanging would take place today. Approaching the town from the north, they crossed the old bridge over the River Aln, staring in amazement at the busy corn mills along its banks. They were even more overawed at the sight of Alnwick Castle, the huge sprawling seat of the mighty Percy family, looming in the distance; its size and grandeur took their breath away. The town itself was bewildering and intimidating; never before had they seen so many buildings or mingled with so many people.

The crowd on the market square was not as large as Mary had feared, and the few dozen people assembled to view the hanging were strangely subdued; in fact, the tension in the air was palpable. The local population was largely sympathetic to the Jacobite cause and disapproved of Catholics being hunted down and persecuted. Mary did not dare speak to any of them but she sensed their pride and resentment. Northumbrians had never taken easily to being dictated to by London, and the recent crackdown by Parliament had been met with barely veiled hostility in this remote part of the country. Convinced that Northumberland was a 'lawless den of popery', the government had despatched Lord Lumley to bring the wayward population into line. As the new Lord Lieutenant of the county, Lumley had quelled the magistrates and raised a brutal local militia to suppress the Jacobite rebellion. Spies and informants were posted everywhere, searching out conspirators and anyone loyal to the Stuart cause.

The crackdown had backfired, resulting in strong popular support for the Jacobites. From the muted conversations and whispered exchanges on the market square, Mary gathered that the Jacobite rising was finally underway. The Northumbrian gentry had raised the Stuart standard in nearby Warkworth and proclaimed James III as the rightful King of England. Their army, led by Thomas Forster of Bamburgh, was camped on Lesbury Common to await the arrival of thousands of Scottish Jacobites; Northumbrians and Scots would lay aside their old enmities and unite in battle against King George's troops.

"Did you hear that, mother?" Lancelot hissed. "People are saying the Jacobite army is marching to Alnwick as we speak. They'll seize the town tomorrow."

"Aye, but your father is to be hanged today, laddie," Mary responded bitterly. "The rich men will have their war, but what difference does it make to us which king sits on the throne of England? What will become of us after your father's gone? Without a man's protection, we'll be cast out to die of cold and starvation."

"But you're wrong, Mother. Father spoke to me many times about the Old Pretender." Lancelot's boyish voice was fierce with passion as he repeated the words he had heard so often in his father's mouth. "King James is a Stuart and a true believer in the old faith. He was unjustly exiled to France, but even now, he is preparing to return to this country. When he's restored to the throne, all Catholics, rich and poor, will be able to worship in peace. Father said so."

Mary sighed but was too dispirited to argue with the boy. Didn't he understand that nothing would ever change for poor Catholics like the Robertsons? For as long as any of them could remember, they had lived apart from normal society, unable to practise their faith openly. Despised and rejected by the villagers of Embleton, they and the handful of other Catholic families in the area were forced to keep their heads down and survive on the outer fringes of the community.

She had voiced her anger and resentment so many times to James. Why must they live like hunted animals, always hiding their beliefs, always taking care not to draw attention to themselves? If theirs was the true faith, why did God punish them so? But her husband was outraged by such blasphemous thoughts and had beaten her many times for uttering them. A woman's place was not to ask questions, he reminded her, but to obey her husband.

"You and your addled woman's brain will be consumed by the fires of Hell," he would shout at her. "The Lord is testing our faith and will reward us in the afterlife for our devotion. God has ordained the station of every man, and mine is to be a humble shepherd. Yours is to serve and obey your husband. It's sinful to question His will."

And now, shivering in the cold on the market square, Mary silently wondered if it was God's will that James should be hanged for a crime he had not committed. He and the other eight men were no Jacobite conspirators; they had simply been caught and arrested for joining in a secret mass in one of the barns at Dunstan Manor. Someone – perhaps one of Sir Henry Thorburn's servants – had informed on them to the local militia, and the magistrates of Alnwick had seized the opportunity to make an example of these troublesome Catholics.

Suddenly, an excited murmur ran through the crowd as the nine convicted men were dragged out onto the square, their hands tightly bound and bodies roped together to form a single file. Mary and the three children strained to catch a glimpse of James, hoping he would spot them in the crowd and take some comfort in their presence. But as James stumbled forward with the other men, his head was bowed and he looked to neither left nor right. Mary gasped in horror at the sight of him. James had clearly been on starvation rations during his incarceration in Alnwick gaol, for his face was now positively gaunt and his lean frame emaciated. His matted fair hair, unkempt beard and filthy ragged clothes gave him the appearance of a madman.

She immediately recognised the other Embleton men. One of them was James's young cousin, Walter Robertson, and the others were Pattersons, Dunns and Hunters – all of them poor Catholics from Dunstan Manor or the neighbouring estate of Howick. The lives of these four families had always been woven together in a complex web of solidarity… and more often than not, marriage. As a young girl, Mary had always known that her choice of husband was restricted to the menfolk of these four families, each of them related in some way to the other. Now nine of their women were to be widowed and dozens of children would lose a father. How would they all survive in this cruel world? Was this God's will too?

In the end, Mary did not see the actual hanging, for as the men proceeded to the scaffold a violent wave of nausea swept over her and her stomach knotted in painful cramps. She clutched her swollen belly in panic, remembering that she was expecting a child and that she had eaten nothing since the previous day. But the last thing she wanted was to call attention to herself by fainting, or even worse miscarrying, on a market square in Alnwick. Chilled to the bone by the wind and rain and feeling her feet give way beneath her, she clutched her small son's shoulder frantically.

Lancelot took one look at Mary and immediately grasped the situation. Half-supporting his mother and grabbing his little sisters by the hand, he led them all away from the market square and down a quiet side street. Gasping for breath and willing herself to remain conscious, Mary collapsed onto the rough wet cobbles and propped herself up against the stonewall of someone's house. They all huddled together, Lancelot trying both to shelter his mother from the rain and comfort Jane and Susannah. The little girls were terrified, fearful they were about to lose not one parent but two on this horrific day.

It was some time before Mary felt the cramps lessening and her strength returning. Her mind cleared and she now realised it was futile to return to the market square. What purpose would be served by allowing three young children to watch their father die in agony, the noose tight around his neck and slowly squeezing the life out of him? Was it right for them to see James unjustly hanged like a common thief? She pulled herself clumsily to her feet and announced they must return immediately to Dunstan Manor. None of the children objected, but Lancelot felt they should pray for their father's soul before they left Alnwick. Soaked and bedraggled, the little group knelt on the cobbled street as young Lancelot led them in quiet prayer.

They kept their heads down as they left the proud walled city of Alnwick. Fearfully, they hurried through the narrow arch of Bondgate, one of four towers built long ago to guard the population from enemies and invaders. The Percy lion, carved into the stone of the gatehouse, looked down on the Robertson family as they passed.

The walk home seemed endless. It had finally stopped raining, but there was a cold wind blowing and they were all weary to the bone. They trudged northward along the muddy road in silence, stopping occasionally to let Jane and Susannah rest; Mary no longer had the strength to carry them. Lancelot's young face was pinched with exhaustion. They were almost beyond grief, their minds and hearts numbed by misery. The thought of James on Market Place, hanging from a rope like a common thief, was so unbearable that it was pushed temporarily from their minds. They needed every last ounce of energy to reach Dunstan Manor by nightfall.

As she plodded onwards, her long skirts heavy and sodden, Mary fervently hoped she would not lose the baby this time. She owed it to James to bear him a healthy child and prayed it would be a son. Although she was barely thirty years old, this was her eighth pregnancy; she had miscarried twice, and two other babies had died in infancy. She comforted herself with the thought that Lancelot looked hardy enough, although the two girls were so frail that she feared they would not survive another winter.

Mary's mind was racked with anguish. How were they to manage without a man to support them? Where would they live and how would she keep food in her children's mouths? She was ashamed to realise that these concerns were more pressing than her grief at losing a husband. Even worse, Mary wasn't convinced she had ever really loved James, although she had done her best to be a dutiful wife and mother. Although her husband had been an honest man and a skilful shepherd, he was also gloomy and inward-looking, not given to demonstrations of affection. Even when they were courting, he had not tried to hold her hand or charm her with sweet words.

She thought back to James's proposal of marriage – if it could be called a proposal, she mused. They had been strolling together along the beach towards Greymare Rock, with Dunstanburgh Castle looming high above them on the cliff top. It was a warm sunny day and also the first time, Mary had been alone with James, away from the suffocating proximity of parents and siblings. As was his wont, he made next to no conversation and looked almost as if he would rather be on his own. But the silence between them lay heavy in the air, and Mary instinctively felt this was a turning point in her young life. And she was not mistaken, although it took James a long while to finally clear his throat and mumble uncertainly: "I've been thinking that the time has come for me to take a wife."

Mary was a simple girl and had never expected artful compliments or grand declarations of undying passion from a suitor. Nevertheless, in her girlish dreams, she had imagined a young man expressing warm sentiments for her, promising he would always love and protect her. But James had clearly said all he had to say. Mary was simply expected to understand that the wife James intended to take was to be her. He looked at her questioningly and she nodded dumbly, feeling awkward and disappointed.

"I'll speak to your father," he said with an air of satisfaction, rightly concluding that his proposal had been accepted. "We'll be wed the next time a riding priest comes to Embleton." Although Roman Catholics were obliged by law to marry within the Church of England, Mary and James would not consider themselves truly married until a priest had sanctified their union. For this, they might have to wait weeks or even months, as the handful of priests still operating in Northumberland were all in hiding and lived in fear of their lives. Known as riding priests, they travelled in disguise from village to village, moving on before they could be caught and arrested.

Today Mary reflected sadly that the same riding priest who had married them in the true faith was also the cause of her husband's death. Father Andrew, who passed himself off as Sir Henry Thorburn's physician, occasionally stopped at Dunstan Manor and was invariably given food and lodging for a night or two. According to servant gossip, Sir Henry and his family still took mass privately, although it was many years since the Thorburns had professed their Catholicism in society at large. Those gentlemen who refused to espouse the Protestant faith had their lands seized, paid exorbitant taxes and were denied the right to vote or take public office. The price was simply too high to pay. As a result, Sir Henry was seen most Sundays at the parish church in Embleton and declared himself to be a staunch Anglican; in return, the authorities turned a blind eye to the occasional private mass, baptism or wedding at Dunstan Manor.

Two weeks ago, one of Sir Henry's men had discreetly spread the word to the poor Catholics in the area – the Robertsons, Hunters, Pattersons and Dunns – that Father Andrew would celebrate mass and hear confession that very evening in one of the barns at the Hall. At a time when the local militia were combing every corner of the county to root out Jacobite sympathisers, James and the other men would have been wiser to remain in the safety of their own homes. But they had responded to the call and gone to the barn as meekly as sheep to slaughter. Betrayed, arrested and now hanged, they had made the ultimate sacrifice for their faith.

"Mother, mother, take care!" cried Lancelot. Mary was abruptly jolted from her melancholy thoughts by her son clutching her arm and pulling them all to the side of the road. She had been so engrossed in raking over the past that she had not heard the loud clattering of a coach and horses approaching along the narrow potholed road, travelling in the same northward direction as themselves.

As the coach passed them at top speed, splattering mud over Mary and her three children, she instantly recognised the haughty profile of its passenger. It was Lady Catherine Thorburn, the hood of an elaborate brocade cape over her head and her plump body supported by velvet upholstery. She looked straight ahead, choosing to ignore the four bedraggled figures by the roadside.

Even if she had acknowledged us, thought Mary bitterly as the coach rapidly disappeared from view, *she would not have recognised us*. In the eyes of Lady Catherine and her like, people like them barely belonged to the human race; they had little more value than the horses pulling the coach. Their sole purpose in life was to serve those whom God had placed above them in the social order. Their reward would be in heaven, James Robertson had always believed.

"She must be going home to Dunstan Manor," remarked Lancelot. Mary nodded, wondering why Lady Catherine was in such haste to return to the estate.

It was well known to all that she disliked country living and generally contrived never to stay more than a week or two at the family home – and even then, only in summer. Unlike Sir Henry, who enjoyed hunting and playing cards with the local gentlemen, his wife spent most of her time at the Thorburn town house in Newcastle. According to servant gossip, she entertained there on a lavish scale, with or without her husband at her side. Mary surmised that there must be some pressing reason for Lady Catherine to abandon the city on this bleak autumn day. Did she think it too dangerous to stay in Newcastle without her husband, now that the Jacobite insurrection was underway? More than likely so, she concluded a few minutes later when a party of gentlemen on horseback, armed to the teeth, galloped past them in the same direction as Lady Catherine. Whatever was going on, Mary was determined not to expose her children to potential reprisals from the local militia. She urged them on impatiently, desperate to reach the safety of the shepherd's hut before nightfall.

There were no further encounters on the road back to Embleton, and the light was already fading as Mary and her three children trudged wearily into the village. Mary's first impression was that the winding main street, with its ragged line of cottages built in stone from the nearby quarry, appeared strangely deserted. The discovery filled her with relief rather than curiosity, for she wished only to pass through the village as unobtrusively as possible. Like all her fellow Catholics, she was used to being ignored when she ventured into Embleton. Although she rarely met with open hostility, she seldom received more than a curt nod from its inhabitants. But Mary's relief was short lived, for as the Robertsons approached St Cuthbert's church, they were faced with a large crowd of villagers, men and women alike, assembled outside the ancient edifice. The atmosphere was electric, and even from a distance, Mary could hear their jubilant cries.

"The Jacobites have captured Holy Island! Errington has raised the flag for the Old Pretender! The King's troops are defeated and are preparing to retreat south from Newcastle!"

Lancelot glanced up at his mother, his eyes flashing with hope despite the accumulated sorrows and hardships of the day. Mary too understood that if the news proved to be true, this was indeed a great day for Northumberland. Holy Island was only a short distance up the coast from Embleton and had a special significance for all Northumbrians, symbolising a bygone era of grandeur... an era centuries ago when Northumbria had been a mighty Anglian kingdom stretching north from the Humber all the way to the Firth of Forth. In those faraway times, the learned monks of Lindisfarne had made their monastery on Holy Island one of the foremost centres of learning in the Christian world.

Mary, intent only on remaining as inconspicuous as possible, tried to restrain her young son. But Lancelot had already broken from her grasp and was running eagerly towards the crowd, hoping to learn more. Mary had no choice but to keep Jane and Susannah close to her skirts and wait for the boy to return. She watched the crowd glumly, finding it almost unbearable to witness so much rejoicing and high spirits on the very same day James and the others had been unjustly hanged for their beliefs. No gallant Jacobites, she thought bitterly, had appeared today on the market square in Alnwick to save her husband. What did anyone care about a poor Catholic shepherd from Embleton?

Lancelot did not dare address any of the villagers directly but listened closely to their excited chatter. He ran back to his mother and sisters with even more momentous news. It was rumoured, he blurted out, that French troops were even now sailing for the Northumbrian coast to support the Jacobite rising. They would bring with them James Stuart, his exile in Paris finally over and eager to regain his rightful position as King of England and Scotland.

"No one knows for sure where the French will land, Mother. People are saying it might be at Dunstanburgh Castle, and we'll see James Stuart himself on the streets of Embleton!"

Mary could see no reason why the French army would choose to assail a ruined castle on a wild deserted bay, but at the same time she was loathe to dampen her ten-year-old son's high spirits. If such romantic notions could help him deal with the loss of his father, she was not about to squash them. She hugged him affectionately, feeling his thin body press against her swollen belly.

"Time will tell, laddie. Haway, we're nearly home now."

* * *

Next morning, Mary awoke with the first grey light of dawn. Lying still half-asleep on the rough straw mattress, she instinctively placed a hand on her rounded belly. Yesterday's cramps had abated, but she felt a strange ache instead and could not feel the baby moving inside her. The poor little creature must be as weary as its mother, she thought.

Inside the one-room hut, it was chilly and still damp from yesterday's torrential rain. She had done her best for the children the night before, lighting a fire and feeding them large bowls of the pottage that was their staple diet – a thick vegetable broth flavoured with the odd chunk of fatty boiled mutton. The three of them could hardly keep their eyes open and were asleep within minutes of the last spoonful.

As she gradually came to her senses, Mary had a fleeting vision of Lady Catherine. She imagined her sitting contentedly by a blazing fire in a pale silk dress, enjoying a dish of savoury roast venison and a glass of fine port wine. She had never set foot inside Dunstan Manor of course – or for that matter, any other habitation different from her own – but she had heard there were long polished tables, chairs cushioned in velvet and fine paintings on the walls. What impressed Mary most was that every member of the family had a separate bedchamber, with a soft feather mattress and thick brocade curtains at the window to keep out the cold.

She instantly pushed these idle ruminations from her mind, sparked off – she supposed – by the brief glimpse of her mistress in the carriage yesterday. In any case, it was pointless to compare Lady Catherine's existence with her own. Lady Catherine was not only rich and idle, she was secure and protected by a powerful husband, one of the foremost gentlemen in the county. Mary's future on the other hand was now precarious in the extreme; James may have been only a poor shepherd but at least until yesterday there had been a man to provide for the family. She was confident that the other Catholic families in the area – the Robertsons, the Hunters, the Pattersons, the Dunns – would offer support and comfort in her hour of need, but even so... from now on, she would need all her strength and determination in the battle for survival that lay ahead.

53

She propped herself up on her elbows and turned to look at her three children, asleep by her side on the mattress. Jane and Susannah were coughing sporadically in their sleep and even in the half-light looked alarmingly flushed and feverish. Mary prayed fervently that God would not take them from her as he had already taken two of her children. She knew there was nothing wrong with her little daughters that could not be cured by a warm home and regular nourishing food, but she was equally well aware that these small comforts would surely be denied them.

Lancelot was already up, Mary noticed with concern. Where on earth could the boy have gone at this early hour? She pulled herself clumsily to her feet, opened the door and made for the small copse behind the hut. Crouching down as best she could, she relieved herself on the thick wet carpet of autumn leaves. As she stood up and re-arranged her skirts, she suddenly guessed where Lancelot might be. Poor lad, she thought, wondering how she could bring some solace to her son in his misery and grief. A few minutes later, she set off to find him, striding swiftly across the vast expanse of moorland sloping down to the sea.

* * *

Mary had guessed right; she spotted Lancelot the instant she entered the stark, atmospheric ruins of Dunstanburgh Castle. The early morning mist had not yet cleared and a thin drizzle made visibility poor, but neither appeared to have deterred her son. He was standing looking out to sea, scanning the horizon in search of... what? She approached him quietly and squeezed his hand affectionately in hers.

"What in God's name are you doing at the castle, son? You'll catch your death with nowt but your shirt and breeches on your back."

"I'm keeping a lookout for the French ships, mother! Didn't you hear the villagers yesterday? They'll be landing somewhere on the coast anytime now, and it might be here at Dunstanburgh!" Lancelot was shivering in the morning chill, but his childish voice rose excitedly. "I want to be the first to welcome the Old Pretender on English soil! I'm sure James Stuart will avenge the death of my father and all the men who were hanged with him."

Mary sighed but chose not to argue. Lancelot's mind was still caught up in nonsensical dreams, but she understood too that this was his way of coping with James's death and the deluge of emotions it had brought on – shock, anger, grief and permeating them all, a strong sense of injustice.

"That's as may be, lad, and we'll know soon enough. But there's work to be done, and don't be forgetting you're the man of the house now that your father's gone. It's true you're only ten, but you're a good strong lad and you've got a canny head on your shoulders."

Lancelot glowed with pride at his mother's words and clasped her hand more tightly. His thin frame seemed to swell with a new sense of purpose.

"You need have no fear, mother, I'll never leave you or my sisters! Haven't I been helping Father tend the sheep since I could barely walk? You'll see, I'll be as good a shepherd as he ever was."

A wave of tenderness for her brave son swept over Mary. "I don't doubt it, lad. And that's why I have a very special gift to give you today. Something your father would have wanted you to have."

54

Without further ado, Mary delved a hand into her bodice and retrieved the small Celtic cross she had removed from its hiding place before she left the house. She handed it now to Lancelot and he stared transfixed at the crucifix gleaming in the palm of his hand. He had never seen it before.

"Your father held it very dear," Mary explained. "He was a man of few words, as you well know, but I'm sure he would have told you all about it if his life had not been taken from him so suddenly. All I can tell you is that this ancient crucifix came down to him through the Robertson line. It belonged to his grandfather, or maybe it was his great-grandfather – I can't say for sure. He did tell me the Robertsons came from over the border and fought for a Stuart king in Scotland long ago."

Mary's story clearly caught the boy's imagination. "So my forefathers were brave soldiers who fought to defend their faith!" He frowned as he tried to make sense of this distant past. "But why did they come here to Dunstan Manor, Mother?"

"I don't recollect, lad, I'm sorry. Maybe your father knew but he was never one to talk a lot, was he?"

Lancelot looked up, still clutching the cross and his eyes burning. "I swear to hold it as dearly as Father and hand it down to my son and my son's son after him. And I swear by all that is holy to avenge his death."

Mary was alarmed now. The last thing she wanted at this stage was more needless bloodshed. "Hush laddie, it's sinful to think of vengeance. Your father's death was God's will and it's not for us to question it. His suffering is at an end and he's surely in Heaven now with the angels. As for us, our lot is to endure as best we can on this earth and pray the Lord will keep us safe."

Lancelot made no reply but kissed the smooth dark wood of the crucifix and crossed himself. Hand in hand, they left the ruins of Dunstanburgh Castle and set off for home along the grassy path that hugged the cliffs and the wide sweep of Embleton Bay. The early morning sun was hidden behind heavy grey clouds and a fine drizzle continued to fall, but the mist was clearing. They had hardly covered more than fifty yards when they heard the pounding of horses' hooves behind them, heading in the same direction as themselves. Exposed as they were on the open moorland, there was nowhere for Mary and Lancelot to hide; they stopped dead in their tracks, filled with foreboding and waiting for the horsemen to reveal their identity. Was it the hated local militia on yet another anti-Jacobite rampage?

They had not long to wait, for a small party of five gentlemen soon came into view, riding at breakneck speed towards them. Mary was relieved to recognise two of the gentlemen: Sir Henry Thorburn himself and his eldest son Charles. She expected them to simply gallop past but instead was horrified to see Sir Henry raise a hand, bringing the horsemen to a halt by their side.

Mary curtsied deeply, both she and Lancelot bowing their heads low. As a humble shepherd's wife, she had never seen Sir Henry or any other fine gentleman at such close quarters and wondered what he could possibly have to say to them. Her mind flooded with anxiety as she raised her eyes to him. He was a thickset man with stout legs and a florid complexion, but the shrewd brown eyes looking down on her were not unkind. Sir Henry was thought to be a fair master by those who served him at Dunstan Manor, although his son Charles was heartily disliked. Aged around twenty, Charles took little interest in the estate and went out of his way to be rude and arrogant to servants and farmworkers alike.

"Are you not James Robertson's wife, woman?" Sir Henry began in stern tones. Mary nodded meekly, not daring to speak.

"I was sorry to learn of his hanging. May God rest his soul," Sir Henry continued. He coughed awkwardly and a short embarrassed silence ensued.

Charles Thorburn turned to his father impatiently, his pasty face and small beady eyes full of contempt. "Dammit, Father, why the devil are we wasting time talking to this miserable old hag and her ugly brat? We must make haste and reach Holy Island before the King's troops arrive. They're marching south from Berwick even as we speak, and every man will be needed to keep the island in Jacobite hands."

Mary kept her eyes cast down so that Charles Thorburn would not see the resentment she felt at his disrespectful words and careless insensitivity; her husband's death was obviously a matter of no importance to him. For a fleeting moment, she also wondered whether she really did look like an old hag. There was never any opportunity to see her reflection in a mirror and it had been many years since she had thought of her appearance. She remembered that not so long ago her thick dark hair had hung like a shining curtain down her back, her eyes had been clear and unlined and her body taut and lithe. Today, barely thirty years old, her face unwashed and her clothes filthy and shapeless, she saw herself for the first time in the eyes of a gentleman like Charles Thorburn... a miserable old hag.

But Sir Henry chose to ignore his son's outburst and looked steadily at Mary. "I'm putting Matthew Cresswell in charge of the sheep," he went on brusquely. "Your husband is dead and I cannot do without an experienced shepherd."

This was exactly what Mary had been dreading. So she and her children were to be turfed out of their cottage to make way for a new shepherd and his family; they would surely all starve to death before the winter was out. In spite of her fear of displeasing these fine gentlemen, she was determined to fight for her three children.

She joined her hands together and raised her eyes imploringly to Sir Henry. "For God's sake have pity on us, Sir, and don't cast us out of our home. My lad Lancelot is stronger than he looks and ready to do a man's work." She pulled Lancelot in full view of Sir Henry and placed her hands on his thin shoulders, willing the boy to stand as tall and straight as he could.

But Sir Henry's attention was not on Lancelot. He had noticed Mary's bulging stomach and now seemed to be contemplating a more merciful course of action. "I'll let you stay in the cottage until your child is born. After that, we'll see what is to be done. As for the lad, he must go this morning to see my bailiff Mr Dickson about a new position. Didn't you tell me we need another stable boy at the Hall, Charles?"

Charles Thorburn snorted disdainfully. Refusing to be detained further by such petty considerations, he deliberately pulled at his horse's bit in a show of impatience, making the animal suddenly rear up in fright and forcing the other riders to rein in their own horses. Sir Henry turned away from Mary and Lancelot, clearly losing interest in their predicament; the defence of Holy Island took precedence over the fate of a shepherd's widow. Without another word, he signalled to the men that it was time to resume their journey. Mother and son watched as the party galloped north along the coast and disappeared out of sight in the mist.

* * *

It was no more than a few weeks before the Rising was squashed. The high hopes of many Northumbrians were dashed as the early victories gave way to confusion and squabbling among Jacobite leaders. Lancelot was now working as a stable lad at Dunstan Manor but would race home across the moor after his chores to relate to his mother any news he picked up from the servants. Mary was sad to hear that the Jacobites had been forced to relinquish Holy Island. Without sufficient reinforcements to defend his troops' positions, the Jacobite commander Errington had no alternative but to surrender to the Hanoverian forces, hastily dispatched south from their garrison in Berwick.

The loss of Holy Island was a blow to Jacobite morale, made worse only a few days later when even more tragic news was reported at Dunstan Hall. Two of the long-awaited French warships had finally been sighted off Holy Island, and the French troops had signalled repeatedly to the castle. But it was too late; the Jacobite leaders were already languishing in Berwick gaol and the remaining Northumbrian troops were encamped inland. The French warships sailed on up the coast to Scotland, taking with them dreams of a Jacobite victory on Northumbrian soil.

In their imagination, Mary and Lancelot followed the Jacobite troops north, praying that every able man in the county would rally to the Stuart cause. Since the Northumbrian rebel army now numbered no more than three hundred men, their commander Thomas Forster realised that the only remaining chance of victory lay in joining forces with the Scottish Jacobites. For once, Northumbrians and Scots were united in their ambition to put a Stuart king back on the throne of England and Scotland. Drenched by pouring rain, Northumbrians, Lowland Scots and Highland Scots finally came together just north of the border in Kelso, the Highlanders playing their bagpipes as they marched into town.

By November, the entire Jacobite army had marched to Lancashire to engage King George's troops in battle. Sadly, the Northern rebels – poorly trained and outnumbered two to one – were no match for the disciplined professionalism of the Hanoverians. They were finally forced to surrender at the ill-fated Battle of Preston, where over a thousand Jacobite soldiers were taken prisoner. Forster and the other leaders of the Rising were captured and tried for treason.

Within a few short weeks, the Jacobite Rising had been brutally crushed. Those Northumbrians who had not been wounded, killed or imprisoned at Preston returned to their homes ragged and dispirited. Sir Henry Thorburn was not among them; when his son Charles finally rode into Dunstan Manor late in November, it was to announce to the family that his father had succumbed to injuries following the Battle of Preston. Servants and farmworkers alike genuinely mourned the death of Sir Henry but also looked to the future with apprehension, for Charles Thorburn was now sole master at Dunstan Manor.

Like the Jacobite cause, Mary's baby was stillborn. Since the day of her husband's hanging in Alnwick, Mary had sensed something was amiss, for she felt none of the fluttering movements and tiny kicks in her belly she had experienced during previous pregnancies. Her labour was mercifully short, but when the baby boy emerged, his tiny body was already discoloured and lifeless.

Mary was overcome by grief and then by a profound melancholy which she found herself unable to shake off. She named the baby James in memory of her husband and on November 14th – the same day the Jacobites surrendered at the Battle of Preston – buried the little corpse in a makeshift grave near the shepherd's hut.

Nick and Jenny (3)

"So poor old James Robertson came to a sticky end," said Nick. He felt an unexpected surge of sympathy for this distant ancestor. "It says here that he was hanged for treason – a very serious offence."

"But keep in mind that this was 1715, the year of the Jacobite Rising, and in Northumberland particularly there was widespread support for the Stuart cause. Many of the nobles and gentry in the county were opposed to the Hanoverian kings. In fact, they were secretly plotting to bring the Old Pretender, James Stuart, back to England and restore him to the throne." Again, Jenny felt it was vital for Nick to understand the historical context.

"But surely, a humble peasant like James wouldn't have been involved in such grand schemes?"

"We don't know if he played an active role or not," said Jenny with a shrug of her shoulders. "But think of the turmoil in the county at that time! London was determined to regain control of the wild, rebellious North. The government viewed Northumberland as a den of popery, and it's true that the county had one of the highest Catholic populations in England – perhaps around 15%. So in 1715, there was a brutal crackdown on Jacobite conspirators, and of course Catholics were first in the line of fire. There were government spies everywhere. Ordinary Catholics like James were simply rounded up by the local militia, jailed and hanged, whether guilty of conspiracy or not. It's very likely that James – and the eight other Embleton men hanged with him – just happened to be in the wrong place at the wrong time."

"And it was all for nothing in the end," sighed Nick. He turned his attention back to the Robertson family tree. "The aftermath can't have been easy for James's family," he remarked.

"That's putting it mildly," said Jenny, pointing to her inscriptions. "You only have to look at these dates. James's wife Mary dies shortly afterwards, aged 32. Their daughters, Susannah and Jane, die young too. Only their son Lancelot survives – a poor Catholic orphan in an incredibly hostile world."

"The Robertson dynasty was hanging by a thread at that point," Nick pointed out wryly. "Just think! If Lancelot hadn't continued the line, I wouldn't be here right now discussing my ancestors and wondering where to take you for dinner tonight."

Jenny glanced at her watch and laughed. "I didn't realise it was so late. But let's keep it simple, shall we? My favourite Italian restaurant is just down the road – we can walk there if you don't mind the rain."

"Sounds great." Nick was planning to make this dinner a turning point in their relationship. He always had the feeling there was some kind of invisible barrier between them, as if Jenny were keeping him at bay for reasons known only to herself. He desperately wanted to break down that barrier and get closer to her. He could only hope that Jenny's Italian restaurant would provide a suitably romantic setting for this.

"I'd like to go upstairs and change first, though," she added abruptly, getting to her feet. She bit her lip, unsure how to broach the subject which had been on her mind since Nick arrived. Well, there was no point in beating about the bush, she decided. "Have you booked a hotel for tonight?"

Nick was both amused by her frankness and more than a little disappointed by its implications. "Yeah, sure. Naturally, I didn't expect…"

"No, no, of course not." Overcome with embarrassment, Jenny fervently wished she had never asked such a leading question. What must he think of her? The idea of staying over at her place – much less sharing her bed – had obviously never crossed Nick's mind… And it was presumptuous of her to imagine that he might even want to. She reminded herself that although Nick was unfailingly pleasant and good mannered, he had never given any indication that he was attracted to her. It was a non-issue and she should never have raised the subject in the first place. He must be thinking she was some kind of delusional madwoman. "I just didn't want you to get the idea…"

"I didn't," said Nick, keeping his voice even. In point of fact, he had left London so hastily and had been so eager to see Jenny again that he had not thought to book a hotel. Well, she had certainly made it clear that she was not planning to go to bed with him tonight. The mutual spark of attraction he had sensed was just wishful thinking on his part. He only hoped the Newcastle hotel he had stayed in last time was not fully booked.

"Actually, I haven't checked in yet," he added, trying to sound casual. "Why don't I grab a cab and go over there now, dump my bag and then meet you at the restaurant… shall we say at eight?"

"Fine," said Jenny. She picked up the coffee mugs and started washing them at the kitchen sink. Anything to avoid looking into Nick's eyes…

* * *

Nick was first to arrive at Gino's, with its typical Italian-style décor and subdued lighting. Candles glowed softly at every table, which he took as a good omen. He asked for a quiet corner table and was relieved to see that neither the waiters nor the customers appeared to recognise him – a welcome change from London, where it was becoming difficult to go out incognito.

Jenny entered the restaurant a few moments later, looking poised and confident, and handed her coat to the waiter. As she walked towards him, he realised it was the first time he had seen her in anything other than jeans. The black long-sleeved wrap dress she was wearing accentuated her femininity, he thought, and the fashionable high-heeled shoes made her legs look toned and shapely. Her beautiful russet hair was styled in a loose, chin-level bob. Nick thought of Klara's bony frame and stick legs without regret.

"You look absolutely stunning," he said, getting to his feet. Jenny looked pleased at the compliment but not overly so, like a woman who was used to men falling over themselves to please her. Nick liked that look.

The conversation over dinner flowed naturally, both of them enjoying each other's company, chatting and laughing as if they had known each other all their lives. Family history was forgotten as Jenny pressed Nick for an update on the Tyneside colliery episode of *In Those Days*. Nick was only too happy to oblige; aside from her extensive knowledge of local history, he hoped involving her in the project would help bring them closer.

"I'd really like you to appear on the show, Jenny," he insisted. "You could set the scene, talk about your book, interview one or two local people…"

Jenny almost choked on her glass of wine. "No way!" she protested in mock horror. "I've never been on TV in my life, I'd be hopeless!"

"Nonsense!" said Nick briskly. "You'd be a natural – you're bright and articulate and gorgeous with it! The viewers will love you."

"You must be kidding," she said, although inwardly she was exhilarated at the prospect of being part of Nick's professional world. And the word 'gorgeous' had not fallen on deaf ears either.

"Actually, you remind me a bit of Dad," Nick went on. "He's retired now, but he used to be a teacher like you. You both have the knack of injecting passion into your subject matter – captivating your audience, just as you did with me when you talked about William and James earlier."

"Your Dad's an eminent professor, not a run-of-the-mill secondary school teacher like me," Jenny reminded him.

"You underestimate yourself, Jenny. Honestly, you'd have a lot in common with Dad – he'd absolutely love you!" He said the words without thinking and realised he was already imagining Jenny with him in London, introducing her to his family.

"Your mother wouldn't love me, though." Jenny was back on the defensive. Nick was putting out feelers, she knew, trying to draw her into his world. Why couldn't she simply accept the compliment graciously? In her mind's eye, she could see her friend Heather glowering at her in disapproval.

"What do you mean?" he asked with a quizzical smile.

"Well, I've read all about her online," she said, sounding more sarcastic than she intended. "The divine Nathalie Lambert, the glamorous style icon, the successful businesswoman… Your mother's the kind of woman who's had everything handed to her on a silver plate. She just glides effortlessly through life without ever having to fight for anything. Ordinary women like me just don't exist for her."

Nick was taken aback by this onslaught. Why did Jenny have to be so aggressive and resentful? He loved his mother and was not about to let her be put down in this way.

"That's totally unfair, Jenny," he said tersely. "Maman worked very hard to make InnerBeauty what it is today. She set it up from scratch, with next to no capital in the beginning. I remember when I was a kid, she used to work out of the kitchen."

"The kitchen in your posh town house in South Kensington," Jenny pointed out acidly. "And before she met your father, she no doubt lived in a similar posh town house in Paris."

Nick was incensed. How dare she cast judgement on his mother? And why did she always have to spoil their time together? "What is it with you, Jenny?" he snapped. "Is this some kind of inverted snobbery? Who do you think you are, laying into my mother like this? You don't know anything about her!"

"I don't need to, I only have to take one look at her!" retorted Jenny, determined to stand her ground.

"Well, let me enlighten you." Nick was glaring at Jenny now, his blue eyes ablaze. "Yes, she's smart and beautiful and elegant and I'm very proud of that. And yes, she comes from what the French would call a bourgeois background. Father made pots of money in Paris and escaped at the weekend to play golf in Normandy. Mother wore pearls and spent her husband's money and played bridge with other idle women just like her."

"There you are," drawled Jenny scathingly. "You've just proved my point."

"That's just it, there's no point to prove," said Nick icily. "You're pathetic, Jenny. You sound like you're on some kind of outmoded working class crusade! What do you want for God's sake – the return of the guillotine? Maman capitalised on her assets – her looks and brains and education – to turn InnerBeauty into one of the biggest skincare companies in Europe. She can't change where she comes from, just as you can't. Maman is as she is, just as you are who you are. End of subject."

There was a long, frozen silence. Nick's face was grim, his mouth set tightly in a hard line. Jenny, instantly overcome by a tidal wave of remorse, felt her heart contract painfully. She had deliberately provoked Nick, senselessly engaged him in a stupid and meaningless clash. He must think her petty and spiteful, and he would be right.

Nick signalled to the waiter to bring the bill and got out his credit card to pay, his expression wooden. Inwardly, he felt hurt and confused, although he instinctively sensed that Jenny had not really meant what she said. She had been brandishing those harsh words at him like a sharp sword to drive him away. And he still didn't understand why.

They left Gino's in silence and stepped out into the cold wet night. Jenny took a deep breath and turned towards him, her green eyes sparkling with tears.

"Nick," she said quietly. "I'm so, so sorry – that was unforgiveable. I behaved like a first class bitch." The chill wind blew her hair away from her face.

"Yes, you did," said Nick shortly. He kept his hands in his coat pockets, his shoulders hunched.

"The truth is that lashing out at your mother like that says far more about me – *my* hang-ups and frustrations – than about her." She was willing him to look into her eyes.

"I couldn't agree more," said Nick coldly, refusing to be mollified.

Jenny's heart filled with dread. She had deliberately tried to drive a wedge between Nick and herself, and she had succeeded. She realised she might be losing him... might have already lost him. If there had ever been anything to lose in the first place, she thought ruefully. She could not bear the idea of never seeing him again, letting him walk out of her life forever.

She cleared her throat and inched closer to him. "Oh Nick," she burst out, her voice choking with emotion. "I know I'm doing this all wrong but... I really like you. I mean, really, really like you. I couldn't stand it if... we weren't friends."

"Friends?" said Nick warily.

"More than friends, if you want," she said hesitantly. Her heart was pounding as she waited for his response.

"I do want," admitted Nick, his voice low. "But I just don't understand why you have to be so bloody-minded all the time. Why do you keep pushing me away? Am I really so mad, bad and dangerous to know?" Jenny saw a glimmer of humour in his eyes and hoped this was his way of reducing the tension between them.

"I'm the one who's mad, bad and dangerous to know," she quipped with a thin smile. "And I promise not to push you away any more. There are reasons why I've been acting this way, but they're stupid reasons – I can see that now. The thing is, liking you makes me feel vulnerable. But that's my problem, not yours. Do you think you could give me another chance, Nick?" She touched his arm gently and felt him respond to the pressure.

Their faces were very close now. They both sensed the kiss hanging in the air between them – an almost tangible presence, demanding to be admitted. Their lips met softly, tentatively. Then Nick took her in his arms and she nestled her head into his shoulder, overcome with relief and joy. They clung to each other silently for a long time, oblivious to the chill damp of the northern night.

Nick and Jenny (4)

The following Tuesday, Alan Robertson was tucking into what he called 'a proper English breakfast', which he prepared for himself every morning at seven o'clock sharp. Nathalie was not an early riser and in any case had decreed early on in their marriage that the sight and smell of so much fat and cholesterol made her feel sick. "*Ça me donne la nausée,*" *(1)* she would complain, shuddering in horror.

"Hi, Dad," Nick called out breezily as he entered the kitchen, freshly shaved and hair still wet from the shower. He made a beeline for the espresso machine and popped in a capsule; a coffee was all he had time for this morning.

"Have some toast," offered Alan, pushing the toast rack in Nick's direction.

"No thanks, Dad, I really have to be off *tout de suite,*" replied Nick, watching the coffee trickle into the small espresso cup. "By the way, I've been meaning to ask you – do we have any family heirlooms of any kind? You know... old photos, nick-nacks, things that have been handed down?" Jenny had told him that such artefacts were often useful in piecing together a family history.

Alan looked up in surprise from his bacon and eggs. "Family heirlooms? You must be kidding! What's put that into your head all of a sudden?"

"Well, I met a local historian in Newcastle whom I've earmarked for the show. It turns out she's a genealogist in her spare time – a pretty good one, actually. Anyway, the bottom line is she's researching the Robertson family for me." Nick had decided to keep his relationship with Jenny close to his chest for the time being.

"I doubt if she'll find out much, other than a long line of dirt-poor coal miners," remarked Alan. "As for heirlooms, the only thing I can tell you is that when your Grandma died, I helped clear out the house and brought a cardboard box of old stuff back to London with me. There's nothing of any interest, though, just bits and pieces I couldn't bring myself to throw out."

"Where exactly is this cardboard box?" asked Nick, sipping his espresso.

"Gathering mould in the attic." Alan glanced up curiously at his son. "What's she like, this genealogist?"

"Quite nice." Nick kept his voice casual. "I'm going up to Newcastle again this weekend, actually. I still have a few things to look into."

Alan raised his eyebrows. "Three trips to Newcastle in three weeks... I never knew pit villages could be so alluring," he said drily. "Or genealogists for that matter."

(1) It makes me feel nauseous.

* * *

64

Nick flew into Newcastle airport late on Friday evening – too late to meet up with Jenny, he decided. He had booked a return ticket back to London on the early morning flight on Monday, but other than that, he had no idea what was in store. Jenny had simply announced rather enigmatically that she was taking him away for the weekend.

"We're going on a magical mystery tour," she had told him on the phone, a note of mischief in her voice. "Let's just play it by ear, shall we?"

Nick wondered exactly what she meant by that. Since their parting kiss outside Gino's, Jenny had been constantly on his mind. She was in his thoughts as soon as he woke up in the morning and stayed with him all day at One Better Productions, however hectic his schedule. At night, he tossed and turned in bed, wishing she was there by his side and fantasising about making love with her. Whatever magical mystery tour Jenny was planning, he hoped it would involve holding her naked in his arms.

They had arranged to meet at eight the next morning at Jenny's little house in Jesmond. Nick wondered whether to take an overnight bag with him and decided against it, in case Jenny thought he was jumping the gun. He did however bring a small carrier bag containing the meagre findings of his search for 'family heirlooms' in the attic. Although he had not been hopeful of discovering anything of great significance, the contents of the cardboard box had nevertheless proved disappointing; most of it was memorabilia pertaining to his father. There were stacks of old school reports and a jumbled collection of photos – Alan as a baby in his pram, Alan at the seaside as a little boy, Alan on the school football team, Alan graduating from university, press cuttings about Alan's career later in life… His proud mother in Burnside had religiously kept everything. Nick had left all this at home but had taken the other items to Newcastle with him.

Jenny appeared at the front door as the taxi pulled up in front of her house, looking buoyant and excited. They exchanged warm hugs and kisses, as if confirming to each other that this was a new stage in their relationship, that the tensions of the past were gone forever. Nick handed over the carrier bag to Jenny.

"Slim pickings, I'm afraid," he said as he followed her into the living room. "But there may be one or two things of interest."

Jenny removed a brown manila envelope from the bag and emptied its contents onto the coffee table. There were a dozen or so old photographs, some of them more recent black and white snaps and others – brown-tinged and faded – from an earlier era. They sat side by side on the sofa while Jenny spread them out on the table.

"I expect Dad will know who they all are," Nick said, watching her as she studied the photos intently.

"Actually, I think I recognise most of the faces anyway," she said at last. "But I'd like to come back to them later, if you don't mind. It's important to do things in chronological order, don't you think?"

Nick nodded and felt in the bag for an object, which he took out with a meaningful smile and passed to Jenny for inspection. It was an ancient Celtic crucifix, carved in dark wood and covered in a thin layer of dust. Jenny turned it over and over in her hands, examining it from every angle. She looked up at Nick triumphantly.

"Well, if any further proof was needed of your Scottish Catholic origins, this is it!" she exclaimed. "Isn't it beautiful? It's obviously been lovingly carved by hand, although not necessarily by a professional. The figure of Christ is sculpted quite roughly, and the sides of the cross are slightly uneven in size."

"Yes, that's true," agreed Nick, leaning over to take a closer look at the crucifix. "But it does have a certain primitive resonance, doesn't it? You sense that generations of Robertsons have held this cross in their hands and prayed, that it was charged with significance for them…"

"That's exactly how I feel about it." Jenny's eyes were shining as they met his. As she had hoped, Nick was being drawn back into the past, letting its weight penetrate his being. His family tree, which he had initially seen as no more than an abstract series of names and dates, was becoming a tangible, organic entity. His ancestors were now real people who had lived and laughed and loved.

"I think I might have it looked at by an expert," he said musingly. "I don't expect it has any intrinsic value – other than sentimental – but it would be interesting to find out more about its age and provenance."

Their faces and bodies were almost touching as they pondered over the ancient cross together. At last, Jenny stood up decisively.

"Well," she said gaily. "If there's nothing else in that carrier bag of yours, I reckon it's kick-off time for the magical mystery tour!"

"Actually, there is one last thing." Nick retrieved another object from the bag and handed it to Jenny. "I haven't a clue who the hell this is – or for that matter whether he has anything to do with my family – but maybe you'll be able to enlighten me."

It was a miniature oil painting on canvas, only a few inches square and unframed, depicting a rather handsome young man. He stood with his back to the sea, his fair hair and white shirt ruffled by the wind. The dark shape of what appeared to be a castle was just visible in the background.

Jenny gasped and clutched her throat in excitement. She studied the painting for a long time, before turning it over and squinting at the faded inscription on the back. Finally, she turned to Nick, looking as thrilled as if she had just struck gold.

"Oh Nick!" she breathed. "I think this might be him! In fact I'm pretty sure it's him!" Seeing his mystified expression, she smiled and patted his hand. "I can't say more now, Nick. Just bear with me for a while, okay? All will be revealed, I promise."

Nick burst out laughing. "I take it this is part of your magical mystery tour?"

"It is now," Jenny told him. "Come on, it's time we hit the road!"

* * *

It was a cold, crisp day in early February, with a blustery wind and bright sunshine breaking through the clouds sporadically. As Jenny drove north up the Northumbrian coast, they soon left Newcastle and its suburbs behind. Nick was in an upbeat mood, as if setting off on a voyage of discovery. He had almost forgotten the unique beauty of the Northumbrian countryside – the wild moorland and wooded valleys, the hillsides dotted with sheep, the austere farmhouses and fields bounded by dry stonewalls, the feeling of space and freedom.

"Have you guessed where I'm taking you?" Jenny was watching with amusement as Nick kept turning his head to read the road signs along the winding country lanes.

"As I know you like doing things in chronological order, I reckon it must be Embleton!" laughed Nick.

Shortly afterwards, Jenny slowed speed as they drove into the picturesque village of Embleton and found a place to park. They got out of the car and looked around with interest, both of them bundled up in thick sweaters, quilted jackets and stout walking shoes. There were few people about as they strolled hand in hand through the village, breathing in its air of timeless tranquillity. They stopped to admire the ancient Church of the Holy Trinity with its imposing Norman tower; the church itself was built in the form of a cross and surrounded by crumbling old tombstones.

"Wouldn't it be wonderful if we came across some Robertson graves?" said Jenny excitedly, pushing open the church gate.

"Of course, but surely Catholics wouldn't be allowed a burial in an Anglican church?"

"Not necessarily, given the relative tolerance for Catholics in this area," mused Jenny. "And I know exactly how we can find out." She explained that inside the church was a plan of the cemetery and a list of the families buried there, each grave clearly identified. "I think the vicar must share my passion for genealogy!" she joked.

Sure enough, within minutes they had located two decaying tombstones side by side, the inscriptions barely legible in places. To their surprise and delight, the names and dates of the Robertsons buried there covered a long period, stretching from the mid-18th to the early 19th century. Nick recognised the names with a feeling of awe – the same Robertson men and women who appeared on his family tree.

"My God, Jenny, I can't believe it!" he exclaimed, bending down to decipher the faded inscriptions. "They're all here, every one of them!"

"Well, not all of them," Jenny pointed out. "And of course some of them aren't in your direct line – they're brothers, sisters and cousins of your Robertson ancestors. Even so, it's quite a find and also confirms that my research is correct."

"I think it's amazing!" enthused Nick, taking photos of the graves with his phone. He had come face to face with his Robertson roots and felt uplifted and enthralled by the discovery.

They returned to the car and drove on to Dunstan Manor. It was a gracious building, built in grey stone from the local quarry and surrounded by a well-manicured park. The imposing iron gates at the entrance were locked, but they peered through the bars and conjured up images of elegant carriages bowling up the sweeping drive leading to the house.

"I wonder what my humble ancestors made of Dunstan Manor," said Nick speculatively. "The Thorburns were their employers of course, but perhaps William and James and the others were secretly burning up with hatred and resentment at the sight of so much wealth."

"You're telling me how *you* would feel," commented Jenny. "But try to put yourself in their shoes instead. It's true that in those days, power and influence were concentrated in the hands of a small number of wealthy landowners like the

Thorburns. The vast majority of the population served these powerful landowners in one way or another – waiting on them in their homes, working on their estates and so on. And Northumberland was even more of a rural backwater than other parts of the country, still positively feudal in many respects. On the other hand, I don't think your Robertson ancestors back then would have viewed the Thorburns as their employers but as their masters. Don't forget they were uneducated and illiterate – many of them lived and died without ever setting foot outside the parish. The huge difference between their lives – the filthy hovels, the poor nutrition and backbreaking labour – and the lives of their masters was simply accepted as part of the established social order. And as the social order was ordained by God, it was hardly surprising that very few of them dared question it, much less openly rebel against it."

Nick put his arm around Jenny's waist and pulled her close. "I love the way you make everything come real for me," he said softly.

Jenny reached up to kiss him lightly. "There's one more place I want to show you before lunch," she said. "Dunstanburgh Castle."

Embleton and Dunstan Manor, Nick discovered, were about a mile inland from the coast. Grey clouds scudded across the wintry sky as Jenny drove them to the vast expanse of Embleton Bay and parked on the high rocky cliffs. There was no one else in sight as they got out of the car and took in the spectacular views. They huddled together, two lone figures battling against the wind, with the grey North Sea below crashing in huge waves onto the beach. Nick was stunned by the wild beauty of the vista before his eyes – the miles of wide sandy beaches, the rolling dunes and black, rocky outcrops.

"Is that Dunstanburgh Castle?" he said, pointing to the stark, massive ruin looming in the distance.

Jenny nodded. "It was built in 1313 and was once one of the greatest fortifications in England. Do you feel up to walking there?"

They set off at a brisk pace in the direction of the castle, its sprawling remains built on a rocky headland dominating the bay. The cold air stung their cheeks and whipped their hair around their faces. Nick felt he was following in the footsteps of countless Robertsons who had surely walked on this same grassy moorland, breathing in the bracing salty air. Had any of them taken refuge among the castle ruins? Had they used its remote location to plot the Jacobite uprising with other conspirators? Or had they simply met their sweethearts there in secret trysts, protected by its ancient walls?

They wandered hand in hand through the ruins as Jenny recounted the tumultuous history of the castle. Eventually, they decided to sit and rest on a massive flat stone, sheltered from the wind by the high crumbling wall behind them. Nick looked pensively out to sea.

"You know, this is the first time I've ever been here," he remarked at last. "But it's as if the places you've shown me this morning – the village, the church, Dunstan Manor – are all strangely familiar. I can't decide whether it's because you had already brought them alive for me before we set out this morning, or whether I truly sense the presence of my ancestors here."

"I suppose it doesn't really matter in the end, does it?" murmured Jenny, leaning her head on his shoulder. He pulled her tight, wishing he could make love to her there and then in the sheltered confines of the fortifications. Pity it was so damn cold, he reflected.

"Funnily enough, it's right here at Dunstanburgh Castle that the feeling is strongest," he went on, looking at her intensely. "Why is that, I wonder? This place is so wild and remote, and yet it's as if important events took place here in the past... events that changed the lives of my Robertson ancestors."

"Maybe that's exactly what did happen," Jenny whispered dreamily. She raised her eyes to his, and their lips met in a long, liquid kiss. They both felt the same sharp pull of desire, their arms locked around each other as if they could never be prised apart. They kissed over and over again, each kiss deeper and more languorous than the last.

"I wish you weren't wearing quite so many layers of clothing," he said ruefully, cupping her face in his hands. Jenny laughed softly and pulled away from him regretfully.

"My magical mystery tour includes lunch, you know," she reminded him. "I'm absolutely starving, aren't you?"

* * *

They ate in a quiet country pub nearby. The whitewashed walls of the lounge were lined with old photographs of the village and its inhabitants. "Very appropriate," remarked Nick as he looked up from a generous helping of homemade shepherd's pie. "You never know, there might be a Robertson or two gazing down at me!"

"That reminds me," said Jenny, pushing her empty plate to one side and adopting a more business-like manner. She rummaged in her capacious shoulder bag and retrieved her iPad.

"I left most of the documentation at home, but the Robertson family tree and most of the transcripts are in here," she explained as she clicked and scrolled through the records. Rays of winter sunlight shone through the lattice windows of the pub, lighting up her green eyes and burnishing her hair, making her skin look diaphanously pale. Nick longed to tell her how beautiful she was, but Jenny was clearly in professorial mode once more, looking every inch the teacher. She moved the iPad towards him, and together they poured over Nick's family tree. It was exciting to recognise Robertson names they had seen that very morning carved on gravestones in the churchyard at Embleton.

"Remember where we left off last time?" said Jenny, frowning at the screen. "We ended with Lancelot, the poor orphan whose father was hanged in Alnwick." Nick nodded.

"Well, here's the next generation," Jenny continued. "Your line is descended from Lancelot's son, William, who was born in 1748 and married a Phyllis Patterson at the age of twenty-one. William and Phyllis had eight children, the youngest of whom – James – was born in 1786 and is your direct ancestor."

"Yes, we saw inscriptions for them all on the tombstones this morning."

"That's right," mused Jenny. "All the fragments of the mosaic fit together very neatly – all except one. And if there's one thing I can't bear when I research family history, it's a missing piece, however tiny."

Nick peered more closely at the screen. "But James's life looks pretty straightforward to me. We have the BMDs – dates for his birth, marriage and death – and also for his wife and children."

"Yes," agreed Jenny, running her finger over the names. "But as you can see, James had an elder brother, John. We know John was born at Dunstan Manor in 1770, the first of William and Phyllis's eight children. But that's absolutely all we know! There's no trace of a marriage or children, and we have no idea when or where he died either. He just seems to have vanished in to thin air!"

"Maybe he never married," Nick suggested. "And you did say parish records were often unreliable."

"But not in this generation. As you can see, every single Robertson except John was duly baptised, married and buried in Embleton. At first, I thought John might have left the village and settled elsewhere, but I searched for him the length and breadth of the country and didn't find a single record for a John Robertson born in 1770 or thereabouts." Jenny sighed as she recalled the long frustrating hours she had spent online.

"So this distant uncle of mine is a missing piece in the mosaic," concluded Nick. "We'll never find out what happened to him."

Jenny smiled enigmatically. "That's what I thought too… until this morning."

III
John Robertson, May 1791

John led the horses and carriage from the stable yard to the main entrance of Dunstan Manor and waited patiently for Edward Felton to emerge from the house. He had spent hours that morning cleaning the carriage and grooming the two horses, meticulously picking their hooves to remove the mud and stones, brushing their coats until they gleamed in the warm spring sunshine. Percy Felton, the master of Dunstan Manor, was very particular about his horses being well cared for, especially those he used in hunting parties with the other local gentlemen. And John took pride in his work as a stable lad, although he often reflected ruefully that the horses were better fed and groomed than the men who tended to their needs.

Normally, it was the head groom, Jack Matthews, who acted as coachman for the Felton family, but that morning old Jack had complained his rheumatism was acting up again. So when word arrived that Edward Felton, a guest at the Manor, wished to be driven to Dunstanburgh Castle after luncheon, John volunteered his services. He had done his best to spruce up his own appearance, sluicing cold water from the horse trough over his face and hair and brushing the mud and dirt from his shirt and breeches.

It was a perfect spring day, and John had thrown back the hood of the landau so that his passenger could enjoy the sunshine and fresh air. It was no more than two miles from Dunstan Manor to the ancient ruined castle on the Northumbrian coast, but he was looking forward to the short ride. He was also curious to see Edward Felton for himself, for he had heard a great deal of gossip about him from the servants. The master's younger brother was reported to be a jovial character fond of fine food and wine, but also interested in scholarly and artistic pursuits. Today was the first day since his arrival a week ago that the weather was clement enough to tempt Mr Felton outdoors and indulge in his favourite pastime, painting.

It was over half an hour before two servants finally emerged from the Hall carrying an easel, canvas, folding seat, paint boxes and other artist's paraphernalia. Once everything was loaded into the carriage, Edward Felton himself appeared and was helped into the landau, nodding affably to John and the servants. He was a portly gentleman in his mid-forties with a fleshy face and florid complexion. In spite of the mild weather, he was bundled up in an enormous winter greatcoat of thick brown cloth, a wide-brimmed tricorne hat planted firmly on his bushy grey hair.

Without more ado, John jumped up into the coachman's seat and with a clicking sound to the horses, set off at a brisk pace in the direction of Dunstanburgh Castle. As they neared the hulking ruin, Edward Felton called out to

John to stop the carriage on the cliff top overlooking Embleton Bay. He appeared to have enjoyed the ride, and after stepping down from the carriage looked about him with an appreciative smile, taking deep breaths of the salty air and admiring the vast expanse of the North Sea sparkling in the sunshine.

"This is most certainly one of the finest prospects in all Northumberland! Wouldn't you say so, lad?" he exclaimed. Surprised to be addressed so cordially by a gentleman, John nodded in agreement and busied himself with lifting all the paraphernalia out of the carriage. Setting everything up to Mr Felton's satisfaction proved to be a lengthy process as the artist paced up and down, calling out orders to John as to the best position for his painting but then changing his mind again and again. The easel had to be placed at a precise distance from the castle, with the sun at a particular angle behind the artist and the paints laid out in a certain way. It was several minutes before Mr Felton was finally seated in the folding chair and ready to begin. John was then instructed to lead the horses and carriage far enough away to give the artist the privacy he needed, and wait until he was summoned for the journey back to Dunstan Manor.

John was more than happy to comply. He lay back on the grass, basking in the warm sunshine and enjoying this rare break from his endless chores in the Manor stables. A heavy stillness hung in the air, disturbed only by the sound of the waves lapping gently on the beach below and the occasional screech of a seagull. The young man glanced covertly at Edward Felton a hundred yards or so away, his stocky frame hunched over the canvas as he applied himself to his painting. Not for the first time, he wondered what it must be like to be a gentleman of leisure, to live in a secure comfortable world of privilege and wealth. He had felt uncomfortable earlier when Mr Felton had remarked on the fine prospect, because he had been struck by the realisation that it was the only prospect he had ever known. This jovial gentleman had the time and money to admire fine prospects the length and breadth of England if he so chose, whereas John had never even set foot outside the parish. More than anything else, John yearned to throw off his invisible chains, to find out for himself what else life had to offer.

It was late in the afternoon when Edward Felton signalled to John that it was time to leave. As John approached with the horses and started loading the artist's equipment into the carriage, he felt himself being watched. Mr Felton's eyes were on him, observing his every movement with a kind of studied concentration. And when John helped him into the carriage, the older man addressed him again.

"And what may your name be, young fellow?"

"John Robertson, sir."

"And what is your age, John Robertson?"

"One and twenty, sir," John answered confidently enough, although in truth he was unsure of his exact age. Like everyone else he knew, he could neither read nor write and his counting was shaky at best.

Mr Felton settled himself more comfortably in the open landau and continued his cross-examination, his tone of voice half-mocking but a kindly expression in his deep-set brown eyes.

"And have you been employed long at Dunstan Manor, John Robertson?"

Standing to attention at the carriage door, John wondered where this unexpected questioning was leading. Nobody of Mr Felton's station in life had ever before taken the slightest interest in him. "The Robertsons have served at

Dunstan Manor for as long as any man can remember," he answered proudly. "Our family has worked on Thorburn land for hundreds of years."

Instantly, he regretted his words, for Dunstan Manor was in fact no longer owned by the Thorburn family. Sir Henry Thorburn had died ten years ago, leaving behind four daughters but no male heir. Shortly afterwards, his eldest daughter Caroline had married Percy Felton, a wealthy middle-aged coal merchant from Newcastle, and now the estate had passed forever into Felton hands. John was afraid Edward Felton might be offended by his tactless remark, but the older man merely nodded.

"That's as may be, John Robertson, but the world is changing and Dunstan Manor must embrace change too. Those who refuse to adapt will be ruined – as ruined as the magnificent castle I have spent my afternoon painting."

John nodded grimly, not daring to express his thoughts. Whatever he said might be viewed as intolerable impertinence by a gentleman like Mr Felton, and the last thing he needed was to lose his position and be thrown off the estate. But as the carriage rolled and rattled its way back to Dunstan Manor, John reflected on Edward Felton's remark. It was easy enough, he thought, to talk of embracing change when a man had some degree of control over those changes taking place. But for the Robertson family and dozens of other local families like theirs, the world was changing for the worse... and there was nothing they could do about it. The poor had no control over their destinies, John concluded bitterly.

His mind turned to Percy Felton, the new owner of Dunstan Manor. It was common knowledge that the Feltons were not 'proper' gentry as the Thorburns had been. It was rumoured that Percy Felton's father had started life as a lowly tradesman, but he had amassed a huge fortune transporting coal down the river Tyne to Newcastle, ready to be shipped south to London and elsewhere. His business had expanded rapidly as the country's demand for coal increased in leaps and bounds, with more mines being sunk all over Southern Northumberland and Durham. His sons were now not only wealthy coal merchants but owners of several mines in the Newcastle area. In a single generation, the Felton family had become one of the richest and most influential in the county.

The recent arrival of Percy Felton at Dunstan Manor had had a profound impact on the families employed there. For generation after generation, the Robertsons and their like had served Thorburn masters who knew the names of every man, woman and child on their estate. The farmworkers were loyal to their masters and in return were granted at least a modicum of recognition and relative security. But ever since Percy Felton had taken over the running of the estate, the old customs and traditions had been mercilessly cast aside. Servants and labourers were treated with the same callous indifference as the hundreds of miners he employed in his Tyneside pits. It was clear to them all that Percy Felton cared nothing about the families in his employment and felt no particular responsibility towards any of them. Impervious to the ancient order of rural life, Felton had promptly introduced modern farming methods to Dunstan Manor and talked only of productivity and profit. Older labourers were being turned out of their homes along with entire families, forced to roam the Northumbrian countryside in search of casual labour on starvation wages.

The winds of change blowing at Dunstan Manor, John reflected, were icy ones indeed. And however affable and good-natured Edward Felton appeared, he was still Percy Felton's brother and could not be expected to sympathise with the plight of the farmworkers employed at the Manor. The Feltons could talk about embracing change as much as they liked, but John was expected to keep his opinions to himself.

* * *

Over the next few days, the weather continued to be exceptionally mild, and most afternoons John would be charged with driving Edward Felton to Embleton Bay. To his astonishment, Mr Felton had remembered his name and designated him personally as the coachman for these painting expeditions. The routine never varied from that first afternoon, and John soon learnt to anticipate the artist's many foibles and whims. Mr Felton was usually in fine spirits and often exchanged a few idle pleasantries with John about the weather or some other uncontroversial topic. However, John noticed that the older man's desultory manner was in sharp contrast to the piercing expression in his dark eyes. Occasionally, he caught Mr Felton staring at him with a strange intensity and wondered why he was the object of so much scrutiny.

Everything changed one breezy afternoon in the middle of May. John was stationed as always at a distance from Mr Felton, biding his time near the horses and carriage while the artist engrossed himself with his painting on the cliff top. Suddenly, a strong gust of wind blew in from the sea and overturned his easel; Edward Felton called out in horror, as his precious canvas was blown away, careering out of reach along the edge of the cliff. Clumsily, he heaved himself off the folding seat, visibly hampered by his thickset body in the bulky greatcoat.

John, however, was far fitter and nimbler; in a flash, he was on his feet and racing across the moorland in pursuit of the cartwheeling canvas. He managed to retrieve it just as it was about to escape his grasp and hurtle over the edge of the cliff. Gasping for breath and holding the precious canvas firmly to his chest, he walked briskly back to Edward Felton and handed it over. Miraculously, no damage had been done and the painting was intact.

The older man's panic-stricken expression gave way to overwhelming relief. "I can't thank you enough, young fellow. What would I have done without your help?" he continued in the same vein, as John cheerfully set about restoring the easel to its usual position and picking up the array of paint pots scattered about by the wind.

John felt almost embarrassed by Mr Felton's repeated expressions of gratitude; it was a feat any quick-minded young man could have accomplished. He felt even more awkward when the artist boldly held up the canvas for his appraisal, as if its rescue had broken down some unspoken barrier between them.

"Tell me, John Robertson, how do you find my little work of art? I should be interested to have your opinion!" There was a touch of irony in his voice, but there was also genuine curiosity in his merry brown eyes.

John was truly astounded. Why should this wealthy gentleman possibly care what a stable lad thought of his painting? Nevertheless, he set the canvas down on the easel and studied it carefully. John had lived close to this particular stretch of coastline since he was born and was familiar with all its changes of colour and light, the countless ways in which nature and the weather altered its contours. Although he had never seen a work of art before, his first thought was that Mr Felton's rendering of Embleton Bay was even more beautiful than the reality before his eyes. Dunstanburgh Castle occupied only part of the canvas, and its outline had been darkened and blurred to contrast with the huge expanse of water and sky it overlooked. The sea, which was blue-grey and choppy that day, had been enhanced in the painting with silver-tipped waves. The horizon had been given a faint pink tinge and was less sharply delineated than the real view before John's eyes.

"It's the finest painting I've ever seen, sir," he replied unhesitatingly.

"And how many other paintings have you seen?" Edward Felton's voice was almost playful now.

"None, sir," admitted John, feeling suddenly foolish.

To John's astonishment, the artist threw back his head and laughed heartily, obviously amused by the young man's frankness. "Well, if you had seen other paintings, you might not consider this one fine at all! I don't claim to be a great artist, you know, and I paint solely for my own diversion. But I should like you to look at it again and tell me what sentiment it arouses in you."

Edward Felton settled back on his folding chair and waited for a response, but then realised the phrasing of his question was too abstract for John. "I mean, what do you truly see when you look at the painting?" he added. "What do you feel?"

John turned back to the canvas. One word and one word alone sprang to his mind, and he could not help but blurt it out.

"Freedom, sir. I see freedom."

Mr Felton was both intrigued and moved by John's answer. He had expected some trite remark about the sea or the castle, but the young man had cut straight to the quick. John on the other hand was already wishing he had not spoken out; this was not an idle discussion between equals, and his honesty might well cost him his position at Dunstan Manor.

"I beg your pardon if I've spoken out of turn, sir," he mumbled awkwardly.

"Dammit, John Robertson, you must know you have nothing to fear in my presence!" exploded Mr Felton. "Now tell me truthfully, what does freedom mean to a young fellow like you?"

John had often turned over thoughts of freedom in his mind, but he was not used to expressing an opinion or even formulating his ideas in words. Nevertheless, he was determined that Edward Felton should not take him for an ignoramus.

"When I look at your fine painting, sir," he began falteringly, "I wonder what lies over the far horizon. The sea and sky stretch out as far as the eye can see, but I've heard tell there are foreign lands beyond. I ask myself if the men in these foreign lands have more freedom than I do."

"Freedom to do what?" Edward Felton leaned forward in his folding chair, obviously captivated.

In for a penny, in for a pound, thought John. Whatever Mr Felton thought of his foolish dreams, it was too late to back out now.

"I would like to live in a land where any man is as good as the next man, where all men start their lives on an equal footing. If I stay at Dunstan Manor, I can never be any more than I am now. My life will be exactly like my father's and my father's father before him. I often wonder whether there are other lands where a man can become whatever he chooses if he works hard – a farmer, a soldier, a merchant, a clergyman, even a learned gentleman like yourself, sir..." John broke off, afraid his speech must sound garbled and confused to an educated man like Edward Felton.

"I see," said Mr Felton slowly, leaning back in his chair and gazing at John thoughtfully. "But don't you think you're free to become whatever you choose in England?"

"Oh no, sir," answered John promptly. "I have no knowledge or learning, sir. I cannot even write my own name. So however hard I labour, however much I strive to better myself, what are my chances of living the life of a fine gentleman like yourself? None, Mr Felton, none at all."

"And would you like to live my life, John Robertson? Do you believe it to be so enviable?" There was a sardonic note in the artist's voice, but John was in no mood now to be mocked.

"I envy no man's life, sir. I merely wish for the freedom to make something of my own."

Edward Felton looked out to sea reflectively. "Well, lad, you've certainly given me food for thought. You know, I'm a member of several literary circles and philosophical societies in town. We hold political debates and converse on all kinds of spiritual and moral matters. Nevertheless, I must confess I have never meditated on the subject of freedom from the point of view of a young man of your condition. You give the word freedom an entirely different dimension."

John hardly knew how to respond to such elevated language and fell silent. He felt both elated by this strange conversation and at the same time anxious about its possible repercussions. After a moment, Mr Felton reached into the depths of his greatcoat pocket and pulled out a flask of what John thought must be ale. He took a short swig of its contents and held out the flask to John with a friendly smile. John was thirsty and accepted the flask readily enough, but after one gulp of the burning spirit, he was immediately reduced to coughing and spluttering.

Edward Felton burst out laughing. "I see you're not used to whisky, young man! I'm very partial to the stuff myself, but you must learn to sip it slowly at first until you become accustomed to its strength."

John grinned back, his face still red but enjoying the warm sensation of the whisky in his stomach. An easy mood of camaraderie enveloped them as they sat on the cliff top, Mr Felton in his folding chair and John on the grass at his feet. Together they admired the view of Embleton Bay, the spring sunshine warm on their backs.

Finally, the older man cleared his throat. "You spoke earlier of foreign lands beyond the horizon. What foreign land were you thinking of exactly?"

John had no knowledge of geography but gave the name of the only country he had heard of. "France, sir," he responded eagerly. "But I have no idea whether men there have any more freedom than in England."

Edward Felton snorted. He took a further swig of whisky and wagged his finger sternly at John. "Don't even think of going to France, John Robertson! The damned country is infested with Frenchmen and not one of them speaks a word of English!" He guffawed at his own wit before adding. "And there's not an honest Protestant among them, for they're all damned papists!"

Instantly. John rose to his feet, his blue eyes darkening as he looked down in anger at the older man. "Then maybe France is the right country for me, sir, for I'm a damned papist myself and not ashamed of it. The Robertsons have always defended the Catholic faith, and my father's grandfather was hanged in Alnwick for his beliefs. I will drive you back to the Manor now, Mr Felton, for there is nothing more to be said between us."

A heavy silence fell as Edward Felton's face betrayed a mixture of shock and disbelief. When he finally spoke, his voice was sombre, without a trace of his earlier flippancy and good humour.

"My dear young man, on the contrary there is a great deal more to be said between us. I had no idea you were a Roman Catholic, and I deeply regret speaking of your religion as I did. I have a habit of indulging in idle mockery and am sorry I did so in this case. It may surprise you to know that I believe all men should be entitled to practice their faith freely. And I'm ashamed to say that in this country, where we supposedly prize liberty above all else, Catholics do not have the same rights as other Englishmen. They are barred from voting, barred from public office, barred even from defending their country in the armed forces. Are you aware of these facts, John Robertson?"

"No, sir," answered John bitterly. "I have no learning as you do, so how can you expect me to know such things? All I know is that my family cannot worship openly in Embleton. There isn't even a Catholic church in the village. We keep ourselves to ourselves and do no one any harm, but we are scorned and despised by most of the villagers. Surely you cannot deny this, sir?"

The expression in Mr Felton's usually merry brown eyes was grave. "No, I don't deny it, lad. The cloak of your faith must lie very heavy on your shoulders." He attempted to haul himself out of the folding seat but the sudden effort was too much for him and he winced in pain. He held out his hand to John for help, and the young man pulled him to his feet.

"It's only my damned gout," he gasped in explanation but without relinquishing John's hand. He continued to hold it firmly in his own, so that the two men's bodies – one tall and slender, the other short and stocky – were almost touching. There was a strange expression in Edward Felton's eyes that puzzled the younger man, but he felt it would not be proper to pull away from his grip. After what seemed an eternity, the older man finally dropped John's hand and gestured that it was time to leave. Nothing more was said as John hastened to load the artist's equipment into the landau and harness the horses ready for departure. It was only when Mr Felton was comfortably ensconced and the carriage door was shut that he leaned out and grasped the young man's hand again.

"I meant it earlier when I said you should not think of going to France, young man. The French are in the midst of what they are calling a revolution, conducted in the name of the very principles we were speaking of. *Liberté! Egalité! Fraternité!*" Edward Felton waved his arms wildly in a grand gesture of Gallic exuberance. "But so far, the revolution has brought nothing in its wake but chaos and turmoil. The revolutionaries are intent on establishing a Republic and overthrowing their king. Is this what you want for England, John Robertson? Is this where your dreams of freedom must lead?"

"No indeed, sir."

John was dumbstruck by Edward Felton's impassioned outburst. But in one of his sudden changes of mood, the older man patted his hand and called out gaily,

"Let us be off, then! My brother and Lady Caroline will be most displeased if I'm not back in time for tea."

* * *

That evening, once he had fed oats to the horses and cleaned out the stables, John decided to have supper with his family. His parents and seven younger brothers and sisters lived a mile away from Dunstan Manor, in a one-room tied cottage which had been handed down from father to son for many years. The interior was dank and cramped, so much so that there was barely room for them all to lay their heads at night. His sisters slept together on one mattress and his brothers on another, while the youngest children slept alongside his parents. As the eldest, John often opted to stay at the Manor and bed down in the stables alongside the horses. But today was different. His mind was still buzzing from his conversation with Edward Felton, and he could hardly wait to share every word of their discussion with his father. As he strode along the narrow country lane, he constantly turned over in his mind the ideas they had exchanged. The talk of freedom, revolution and equal rights for Catholics excited and stimulated him, even though he had little hope that his own life would be changed as a result.

At the back of his mind, however, were disturbing memories of Mr Felton's attitude towards him, the way he had held John's hand, the emotion he was unable to conceal every time their eyes met. Was it simply a candid expression of fatherly affection for a younger man or was it… something else? John hardly dared put a name to the strange passion which this educated gentleman appeared to feel for him. He had occasionally heard whispered jokes and sniggering in the servant quarters about the wicked goings-on of the gentry, tales of depraved men fornicating with other men. John had no idea whether there was any truth in the jokes, for at the age of twenty-one he had little knowledge of the ways of the world. The only thing he was sure of was that such behaviour was a mortal sin and that these men would ultimately be damned to the eternal flames of hell. Yet how could John wish such a fate on the kind and amiable Edward Felton? He decided to push the disturbing memories from his mind, refusing to believe that Mr Felton's intentions towards him were anything other than manly camaraderie.

The tiny cottage came into view, looking as shabby and dilapidated as ever, but what struck John as he pushed the door open was the tense atmosphere inside. As always, the room was gloomy and ill-lit, but there was none of the chatter and banter his family generally engaged in at meal times. His younger brothers and sisters sat silently around the rough wooden table, glumly staring into the bowls of soup being ladled out for them by their mother. His father, Will Robertson, appeared not to have eaten at all and was sitting on a stool by the fire, evidently deep in thought, with a tankard of ale by his side. John noticed at once that he was holding the old family crucifix, turning it over and over in the palm of his hands, fingering it as if in silent prayer. The young man knew nothing about this ancient cross, except that it was a precious symbol of their faith and had been in the family for many years. It was kept in a safe hiding place and his father only brought it out on solemn occasions. His heart sinking, John immediately sensed that the Robertson household had received some bad news.

Will did not even look up as his son entered the cottage, but John's mother immediately turned and flashed him a warm smile of welcome. Phyllis Robertson was a stout homely figure, placid and even-tempered; John was her favourite child and she was always delighted to see him.

"Why, here's my bonny lad," she called out merrily. "Sit yourself down and have some of this good warm soup." She lowered her voice. "Your father's had some bad tidings and his spirits are right low, but maybe you already know why. You'll have heard up at the Manor what the master's got in store for us poor folks now. He's an evil man, that Percy Felton, an evil man."

John had no idea what the bad tidings could be. He glanced over at his father, still staring down despondently at the carved wooden crucifix. The thought crossed his mind that Will Robertson was roughly the same age as Edward Felton; both men were in their mid-forties but his father looked at least ten years older. His gnarled body and rotting teeth were in marked contrast to Mr Felton's fleshy florid face and portly well-fed frame. Gulping down his soup in a few mouthfuls, John stood up and moved his stool so that he could sit opposite his father.

Will Robertson was one of the most skilled and hard-working farm labourers at Dunstan Manor, but he was not a talkative man. It took John quite a while and much prompting and coaxing to hear the full story. It appeared that Percy Felton had now decided to spend most of his time in Newcastle and focus his energies on his highly profitable coalmining business. The estate at Dunstan Manor, which he had inherited through his marriage to Caroline Thorburn, increasingly bored him. He felt he had completed the process of modernisation in farming methods there and now wished to turn over the day-to-day management of his estate to tenant farmers. As of today, he had announced, his land was divided into four separate farms, each of them to be run by a different tenant. The farm labourers had brusquely been told that if they wished to continue working at Dunstan Manor, they were to apply to one of these tenant farmers and re-negotiate the terms of their employment.

Horrified, John immediately understood the full impact of this devastating news on the Robertson family. It was common knowledge that the whole of Northumberland was teeming with unemployed farm labourers, desperate to find work on any terms. His father would be in no position to bargain. Even worse, a new tenant farmer would feel no sense of obligation towards the workers at Dunstan Manor, however long their families had served there. His first priority would be to cut wages and keep only the youngest and fittest in his employment.

"Mark my word, John, we'll be cast aside and thrown out of this cottage. There'll be nothing but the hiring fair at Michaelmas for us now. We'll be treated like animals to be bought and sold."

John knew only too well that his father, like the other farmworkers in the area, lived in fear of being reduced to seeking work at the hiring fair in Alnwick, held twice a year. Dozens of destitute itinerant labourers looking for work were forced to stand on a platform and be looked over by potential employers. Landowners and farmers could pick and choose from an over-supply of men, forcing them to accept starvation wages in exchange for the promise of a roof over their heads. Work was usually contracted for a limited period – a year at most – after which the labourers had no alternative but to return to the hiring fair and look again for employment. It was a precarious existence in which entire families were shunted from farm to farm, uprooted forever from familiar villages and communities where they were known and respected.

John searched for words of comfort and reassurance. "There's not a man alive who knows more about working the land than you, Father. Whoever the new tenant farmer may be, he'll be lucky to have you in his employ."

Will refused to be cheered. "You don't know the half of it, lad. Our cottage is standing on land that's to be tenanted out to a man by the name of Benjamin Churnside. He lives at present not more than a few miles away in Ellingham, and they tell me he and his whole family have turned to the Presbyterian faith. They're worse than Cromwell's Puritans, that lot! Churnside won't give jobs to Catholics, I'm sure of it, when he can take his pick of other men."

"You don't know that for certain, Father," John protested. "This Benjamin Churnside may be a fair and honest man, for all he's Presbyterian. But it'll be first come first served from now on, so you shouldn't let the grass grow under your feet. You must walk over to Ellingham this very Sunday and speak to Churnside directly. And you won't be alone, Father, for I'm coming with you!"

"That's my boy!" exclaimed Phyllis, a beaming smile on her face. "Didn't I tell you, Will, that our John would know what's to be done? Let him do the talking with this Churnside fellow and everything will turn out for the best!"

* * *

John was as good as his word. The following Sunday, father and son set off early, Will wearing his thick smock and battered old farmworker's hat, John in a reasonably clean white shirt and breeches. On reaching the outskirts of Ellingham shortly before midday, they asked for directions to Benjamin Churnside's farm. As they drew near they saw at once that the house and outbuildings, although not grand or pretentious in any way, were tidy and well maintained; the whole property exuded efficiency and quiet prosperity.

A housemaid informed them that the family had not yet returned from the Presbyterian meeting house in Alnwick, where they attended service every Sunday. She added that they generally took their midday meal with the elders afterwards and would probably not be back before teatime. However, she was civil enough to direct them to one of the barns, where they were welcome to wait for the master's return if they had a mind. John and Will were grateful enough for the offer, for the fine spring weather of the past fortnight had broken and a chill drizzle was now falling.

As Ellingham's church bell struck four, a sturdy horse and cart finally clattered into the courtyard. The two men watched as Benjamin Churnside jumped down from the driver's seat, followed by a plump wife and three children. About forty years of age, he was a fine figure of a man, John thought; tall and well built, with curly chestnut hair and bushy whiskers, he wore a stern expression and had an air of quiet confidence. His Sunday suit was sober and unostentatious but cut in cloth of the best quality. He and his family disappeared into the house without further ado, leaving a stable boy to take care of the horse and cart.

It was another half hour before the maid appeared in the barn to tell John and Will that Mr Churnside was ready to receive them. To their surprise, they were shown into the front parlour, where the man they hoped would be Will's future master was sitting in a comfortable rocking chair by the fire, sipping a cup of tea. He beckoned to them to approach but did not offer them a seat, so father and son remained standing, their hair and clothes still damp from the continuing drizzle outside.

In spite of himself, John felt nervous, knowing that the next few minutes might determine the fate of his whole family. His father was relying on him to do the talking, and he had rehearsed over and over how he would persuade Mr Churnside to retain the Robertson family. If he was capable of conversing with a scholarly gentleman like Edward Felton, surely he could convince this stern-looking farmer without resorting to begging and pleading? Politely but confidently, he described his father's experience and skills. He emphasised that Will could sow, plough and harvest the crops but could also turn his hand to tending cattle and other livestock. He added that his mother found time to look after the vegetable plot, the older boys helped with weeding and trimming hedges and even the youngest, seven-year-old Jack, was adept at picking stones from the fields and scaring birds away.

"As far back as any man can remember, our family has worked at Dunstan Manor," he concluded. "We served the Thorburns well and now the Feltons. And you may be sure we'll serve you just as faithfully, Mr Churnside, if you'll be so good as to keep my father in your employ."

The farmer looked him up and down with interest. "John Robertson, did you say your name was? Aren't you one of the stable lads at the Manor? Upon my word, I've never heard a stable lad with so much to say for himself!"

John lowered his voice so as not to appear impertinent. "Aye, I work in Mr Felton's stables, sir, and hope to continue there. I'm here today only to assist my father and speak on his behalf."

"That's right, sir, that's right," interjected Will humbly, twisting his battered hat in his hands and wishing he could be anywhere but this neat, well-appointed parlour.

A long silence followed while Benjamin Churnside appeared to be weighing up the situation. When he finally spoke, his brusque words were not what John and Will were hoping to hear.

"Listen here, Robertson, I'm a plain farmer, not a rich man like Percy Felton. Mr Felton's overseer has told me how much he pays farm labourers – six shillings a week and a ration of ale, so I hear. Well, I can tell you straight I won't be offering the same wages. If you want to keep your position, it'll be a shilling less. Those are my terms and I'll brook no argument."

John looked at his father aghast. The family could barely scrape a living as it was, so how could they possibly manage on a shilling less? He was about to protest but Will spoke first.

"I'll take it, sir, I'll take it," he said meekly.

Benjamin Churnside nodded gravely, clearly satisfied that Will had accepted his terms so readily. But he had not finished with the Robertson men yet, for there was an even more crucial matter to be resolved. He pursed his lips tightly and positively glowered at them.

"The overseer has also informed me that your family are papists. I must tell you plainly that I don't hold with all that superstitious mumbo-jumbo, for no man needs saints and priests to intercede on his behalf with God. The means of grace are through prayer and the daily study of God's word in the Bible. We must all follow the path of righteousness by leading lives of virtue and edification. These are self-evident truths, do you not agree, Robertson?"

Will bowed his head submissively, at a loss for words. John on the other hand was frantically wondering how to respond in a way that would both appease Mr Churnside and allow his family to remain on the estate. He thought back to his discussion a few days ago with Edward Felton and suddenly remembered his exact words.

"I believe every man should be able to practice his faith freely, sir. Our family has always been Roman Catholic and we wish only to remain so. But I give you my word, Mr Churnside, you will never be troubled by our beliefs. You will never see or hear any sign of it while we serve on your land."

The farmer frowned and stroked his whiskers reflectively, clearly torn between his spiritual convictions and a desire to act fairly.

"I will not force you to recant your faith, for every man is at liberty to make his own choices in life. However, I believe that my duty is to instruct you in the will of God and lead you to eternal salvation. You'll come to understand for yourself the error of your ways. Therefore, I will only agree to employ your family on one condition…"

John held his breath, fearing the worst, while Benjamin Churnside took a sip of his tea.

"My family spends every Sunday evening after supper reading the Holy Bible and praying for God's divine grace. If you wish to remain in your present position, every man and boy in the Robertson household will be required to join us for these readings and prayers. In time, I have no doubt that each and every one of you will cast off papist cant and superstition and join our Presbyterian assembly."

John's pragmatic mind was working fast. The farmer was clearly determined to convert the Robertsons to the spiritual path he himself had chosen, but he would not actually force them to recant. In essence, Mr Churnside would allow them to practice their faith behind closed doors as long as they paid lip service to the Presbyterian religion once a week. If he agreed to Mr Churnside's terms, his family could stay on in the tied cottage and continue to work on the estate, albeit for reduced wages. That would have to suffice for now.

"We would be glad to join your family in worship on Sunday evenings, sir. We're always eager to listen to the word of the Lord," he replied, hoping he sounded suitably virtuous.

The farmer nodded approvingly. He rose to his feet and extended his hand to John and Will. "Let's shake on it, then," he declared.

A wave of relief swept over John as he and his father shook hands with Mr Churnside. The terrifying prospect of eviction and destitution, the humiliation of the hiring fair, had been – at least temporarily – averted.

* * *

"Say you'll marry me, John! Don't you want me as your wife, my love?" Jane Hunter rolled her half-naked body on top of John's, thrusting her breasts to his bare chest and spreading her legs invitingly as she nibbled his ear and pressed her lips to his.

It was not the first time by any means that they had snatched such secret moments together, usually in this dark corner of the stables at Dunstan Manor. Today they lay on the matted straw, Jane with her bodice unfastened and her petticoats bunched around her waist, John with his shirt off and breeches undone. Both of them knew that these brief physical encounters were a mortal sin, but the pleasure they both derived from them was proving irresistible. What had started innocently enough with smiles and stolen kisses had developed into ever more intimate caresses and furtive fondling; before they knew it, they had reached the point of no return and had long since ceased to wish for it. In fact, Jane was quite brazen in her desire for John and needed no persuading to join him in the stable; she was flirtatious and enticing, teasing him constantly into frenzies of passion.

John didn't answer the girl's question immediately, although he was well aware that for Jane these sexual interludes were simply a means to an end. Her ultimate goal was marriage, and she would not rest until she dragged him to the altar. He also realised he was taking unfair advantage of her, for the awful truth was that a wedding was the last thing on his mind. And although he enjoyed their lovemaking intensely, he was always fearful that he would forget to withdraw in time; if Jane became pregnant, he would be trapped into marrying her. This was no doubt exactly what she was hoping for, he thought ruefully.

In many ways, Jane Hunter would be an excellent match for John. She was eighteen years old and quite pretty in a coarse, buxom kind of way. She worked at Dunstan Manor as a milkmaid and was popular with indoor and outdoor servants alike. More importantly, she was from a Roman Catholic family, one of only a handful of such families living in the Embleton area. The Robertsons and Hunters were very close and had intermarried so often over the years that no one could remember exactly who was cousin to whom. John knew that both his parents and Jane's would be delighted if they married, although they would certainly not approve of these sexual romps in the stables.

He sighed pensively as Jane fell back on the straw, looking sulky at his half-hearted response. She started to re-arrange her skirts and lace her bodice over her round white breasts. What was holding him back? He felt guilty that he was not fonder of the poor girl; it was a simple case of out of sight out of mind. The physical attraction between them was undeniable, but John knew he would react similarly to any other attractive girl who threw herself at him as Jane did.

Yet it was the lack of choice rather than the lack of love that frustrated him most. Given his religion and station in life, he calculated there were probably no more than five or six local girls who would make suitable wife material. He had known them all for years, and none of them took his fancy. Nevertheless, it was expected he would marry one of these girls. Just as it was expected, he would work in the Manor stables all his life, his only prospect being advancement to head groom when old Jack Matthews died. John felt increasingly hemmed in, desperate to find out what lay beyond the narrow confines of Dunstan Manor.

"You do look grumpy today," Jane pouted. "I heard Mr Churnside is keeping your family on at the Manor. I thought you'd be content now."

"I am," snapped John and added to mollify her, "I just haven't been sleeping well these past two weeks. Can't for the life of me think why not."

This was not quite true. He knew exactly why sleep eluded him so often lately, why he found himself tossing and turning with his mind in turmoil; it was all because of Edward Felton. Their last encounter a fortnight ago had fired his imagination and unsettled him more than he cared to admit. Since then, John had not seen nor heard from the artist, except for brief glimpses when he emerged from the house with his brother and sister-in-law to call on neighbouring families. Jack Matthews drove the carriage on these outings, and John had not been asked again to take Mr Felton to Embleton Bay. The weather had turned cool and damp, so perhaps the artist was no longer inclined to pursue his painting of Dunstanburgh Castle. When John had made discreet enquiries in the servant quarters, he learned that the master's brother was often laid up with gout. According to one of the maids, Mr Felton invariably kept to his chamber with his books and whisky.

John sighed again. He felt as though his heated discussion with Edward Felton had opened a door in his mind. He had stepped out into bright sunshine, briefly glimpsing new ideas and a whole world of possibilities. Now that door had been slammed shut again, and he was back in a dark room where he was doomed to spend the rest of his life.

"You'd best get back to your duties, lass," he reminded Jane, planting a cursory kiss on her cheek. "There's no rush for us to get wed, is there? Just give me some more time to think about it."

Jane managed to hide her disappointment. Flashing him her most beguiling smile, she sprang to her feet and flounced out of the stable without a backward glance.

* * *

John was put out of his misery two days later when Mr Cartwright, the head butler, appeared at the stable door. Looking distastefully around him and even more distastefully at John, he informed him curtly that Mr Edward Felton wished to speak to him at once.

"You can't possibly set foot in the Manor with that filthy shirt on your back and stinking to the heavens of horse manure!" He gestured disdainfully in the direction of the scullery at the rear of the house. "Get yourself scrubbed down in there and then meet me in the entrance hall."

When John presented himself a few minutes later to Mr Cartwright, he realised he was shaking with nerves. It was the first time he had ever been inside Dunstan Manor and he was overcome by its grandeur. The thought occurred to him that his family's one-room cottage would fit into this magnificent entrance hall with ease. He looked around with awe at the impressive marble columns and sweeping stone staircase leading to the private chambers upstairs.

Mr Cartwright led him down a long corridor and knocked on one of the heavy oak-panelled doors. He heard a familiar voice calling out a loud 'Come in' and was shown into a room which he took to be the library. Mr Felton was sitting by a blazing fire in a high-backed armchair, dressed in a voluminous brocade robe and resting his feet on a stool piled with cushions. John was surprised to see the fire, for it was nearly the end of May and the room was stiflingly warm. He caught his breath again as he took in the magnificence of the library, with its high ceiling and large windows looking out onto the park. An ancient tapestry depicting a hunting scene occupied most of one wall, while two others were lined with row upon row of beautifully bound books. More books were piled haphazardly on a long table, its dark wood polished to perfection. Exquisite vases in silver and porcelain were displayed on smaller tables where they could be seen and admired.

"Well, don't just stand there, young man," said Mr Felton in kindly tones. "Sit down by the fire and share a whisky with me, for we have many things to discuss this afternoon."

Many things to discuss? John's heart was pounding but he did as instructed. Perching on the edge of an armchair directly facing Mr Felton, he watched as the older man took a long swig of brandy from a crystal glass and grimaced.

"This gout has been giving me misery for well-nigh two weeks now. The physician has attended me twice, but the damned fool merely tells me to eat and drink in moderation!" He snorted derisively.

"I'm sorry to hear it, sir."

Mr Felton waved John's sympathy aside. "Well, I haven't brought you here to listen to my woes. I wish to put an idea to you, a kind of proposition as it were. Before I do so, however, I will ask you a question and will require a truthful answer."

John had no idea where this strange conversation was leading, although he instinctively felt it might change the whole course of his life. It was as if he were out at sea and sailing towards an unknown destination. "I'll be glad to tell you anything you wish to know, sir."

Mr Felton leaned forward and gazed at John, his deep-set brown eyes intense. "Am I right in thinking you are neither married nor betrothed to be married, Robertson?"

"I am neither, sir." John thought briefly of Jane Hunter and squashed a faint pang of guilt. After all, he had made her no promises.

"That is just what I was hoping," remarked Edward Felton with satisfaction. "I myself am not married, you know. I have neither wife nor child and if the truth be known, I confess I was never much interested in either. Marriage and fatherhood are vastly overrated enterprises if you ask me!"

This revelation somehow came as no surprise to John. However, he was determined to clarify his own position, whatever Mr Felton's personal inclinations might be.

"I have every hope that God will grant me a good wife when the right time comes, sir."

Again, the older man made an airy gesture of dismissal. "That's as may be, young fellow, that's as may be. My point is merely that if you had been married or betrothed, it would have been an impediment to the plans I have been making."

John looked at him inquiringly but said no more. This was no impromptu exchange, he realised. Mr Felton had been weighing up what he would say and how he would say it. There was a short silence, broken only by the ticking of an elegantly ornate clock on a side table.

"I have taken a liking to you, John," Edward Felton suddenly blurted out. "I know it's an odd thing to say, but there it is. I believe you have a good head on your shoulders for a young lad of your station. I'm certain you could go far in life if you were only freed from the prison of your own poverty and ignorance.

What's more, you are very… very… well, let's just say I've taken a liking to you and leave it at that."

"I'm deeply honoured, sir." Overcome by embarrassment, John hardly knew how to respond. When he finally found the courage to meet Mr Felton's eyes, he saw that they were moist and full of tenderness. Quickly, he averted his gaze so that the older man could regain his composure.

Edward Felton coughed and cleared his throat. He took another swig of whisky before continuing in a more business-like tone of voice.

"I consider myself to be an enlightened man, one who has espoused modern ideas of liberty, progress and tolerance. As I told you, I'm an active member of a philosophical society where we discuss the works of the great Voltaire, Rousseau and others. Damned interesting even if they are French!" He gave a short laugh, amused as always by his own wit.

"Yet I have come to the conclusion," he went on solemnly, "that it serves no useful purpose to read such books, if one doesn't act on the noble principles they set forth. I, therefore, feel it is my duty as a man of fortune and learning to bring enlightenment to a deserving young man. In a nutshell, someone like yourself! You spoke to me of your aspirations of freedom, of your desire to improve your condition through your own merits, of your conviction that an opportunity to do so could not be found in England…"

John could scarcely breathe. A wave of excitement coursed through his body, but he forced himself to remain outwardly calm.

"Young man, I have decided to offer you the means to leave England forever and look for your fortune in America!"

America! John was as stunned as if Mr Felton had hit him over the head with a sledgehammer. He knew nothing of America other than a vague notion of a vast, virgin territory on the other side of the world. "Why sir, I hardly know what to say…" he stuttered. "Why do you wish me to go to America?"

Edward Felton proceeded to outline in greater detail his grand design for his young protégé. The United States of America, he explained, was a young nation which had gained its complete independence from Britain through revolution and war. The country was founded on ideals of personal liberty and religious freedom for all men, and these ideals were now guaranteed by a Constitution.

"Do you see that large brown book on the table there?" he interjected. "I should like to read you a passage which I feel sure will interest you."

John rose to his feet and passed the dusty tome to Mr Felton, who flicked impatiently through its pages until he found the words he was looking for.

"I know this will not mean much to a lad of your condition, but here are words which will be poetry to your ears: *All men are created equal and have an inalienable right to the preservation of life, liberty and the pursuit of happiness.*"

A right to happiness? John had not understood everything Mr Felton had so painstakingly tried to tell him about America, but this much was clear. In this faraway country called the United States all men, rich and poor alike, were not only free and equal but were even granted the right to look for happiness in their lives. It was a concept so foreign to John that he could barely grasp its implications.

"America must be a fine country indeed," he responded slowly, his mind ablaze with thoughts he was unable to formulate.

"But would you like to see it for yourself, John? Are you prepared to leave all that you hold dear to change your destiny, to forge a new life for yourself in a foreign land?"

John suddenly remembered Mr Felton's caustic comments about France in their previous conversation. "Do the inhabitants of America speak French?"

The older man guffawed. "I can assure you plain English is quite sufficient in America! You cannot begin to imagine how different the United States is from England. You'll not find the same social barriers or indeed religious intolerance as in this country. America welcomes new blood, new ideas! An intelligent, industrious young man with a will to work hard has every opportunity to get ahead and make his way in the world."

John felt his body and soul fill with a wild exaltation and could contain himself no more. "I've dreamed of such things, sir! I wish for nothing more dearly than to go to America!"

Edward Felton beamed at his enthusiasm. "Now listen carefully, John. I have a cousin, Walter Bell, who left England for America some time ago and has settled in the town of Philadelphia. He has amassed a considerable fortune there, both in land and in various business concerns. Judging by what he writes to me, my cousin is now a powerful man with a finger in every pie, as the saying goes."

John then discovered to his stupefaction that Mr Felton had already arranged every detail of his journey to America. He was handed travel documents for his journey by coach to the port of Liverpool, where he would board *HMS Voyager* and sail to the United States. He was told where to find Walter Bell on his arrival in Philadelphia and assured that he would be given work and accommodation there. Mr Felton had even written to his wealthy cousin, asking him to see to it that John learned to read and write in his free time.

Finally, Edward Felton handed John a large leather wallet containing a wad of banknotes. "This should be enough to get you to Philadelphia, young man. But it's a very long journey, you know, several weeks or more. You must use this money sensibly and spend only what you need to spend. No squandering it on gambling and women, mind you!"

Nothing could have been farther from John's mind. He had never set eyes on so much money, never in his wildest dreams imagined an adventure on this scale. Gradually, it was dawning on him that everything taking place in this magnificent library was not a figment of his imagination. In the space of little more than an hour, his life had changed forever.

John searched for words to express his gratitude to his generous benefactor, but his stammered thanks sounded woefully inadequate to his own ears. For Edward Felton, however, it was reward enough to see the young man's radiant face and shining blue eyes; his time and money, he felt sure, had been well spent. He thought suddenly of the opening lines of Rousseau's *Social Contract*:

Man is born free, and everywhere he is in chains. Those who think themselves the masters of others are indeed greater slaves than they.

* * *

Phyllis Robertson was alone in the cottage one morning when she heard the clattering of approaching hooves and a loud 'Whoa there' as a rider reined in his horse and stopped in front of her door. She had been listlessly sweeping the floor, lost in thoughts of John and wondering how he was faring on his long journey to America.

It had been three weeks since John had bade his family farewell and set off on his great adventure, and Phyllis missed her favourite son sorely. In one way, she was not surprised that this Mr Felton up at the Manor had taken him under his wing; there had always been something special about John. He was different from the rest of her brood – taller and more attractive, cleverer and more articulate too. Still, Phyllis was unable to shake off her grief. It was as if John had died, she felt, although in fact her son had left home in high spirits. He had also promised her faithfully to return to Northumberland one day and take them all back to America with him. This promise was all she had to cling to now.

Still holding her broom, Phyllis stepped out of the cottage and was surprised to see old Jack Matthews, the head groom at the Manor, dismounting his horse. What business could Jack possibly have with her? For a moment, her heart seized with sudden fear that he was bringing bad news about John. Her anxiety was instantly dispelled however when Jack greeted her with a broad smile.

"Good morning to you, Mistress Robertson," the groom called out cheerfully. "I've had orders to bring you this parcel directly. I'm to tell you it's a gift from Mr Edward Felton."

Phyllis's jaw dropped. John had of course told them all about his benefactor – his artistic leanings, his progressive ideas and more importantly the life-changing relationship that had developed between the two men. But privately, she had very mixed feelings towards Mr Felton, for it was this same educated gentleman with his foolish talk of freedom who had taken her son from her and sent him to seek his fortune in this foreign land called America.

Feeling flustered, she tried to keep her wits about her. "I know nowt about a gift, Jack. There must be some mistake."

But Jack was determined to carry out his instructions and simply thrust the parcel at her. "Hush, woman and open the damned thing, will you?"

Slowly and apprehensively, Phyllis removed the protective layers of paper and then gasped. Edward Felton's unexpected gift was a stunning miniature oil painting, no more than six inches or so in diameter. It showed John in a billowing white shirt, the wind ruffling his fair hair. He was standing on a cliff top with an expanse of grey sky and sea behind him, and Dunstanburgh Castle faintly outlined in the distance. He looked just as his mother remembered him – a handsome young man full of high hopes and dreams.

The old groom was almost as taken aback as Phyllis. Neither of them had ever seen a painting at such close quarters, much less received one as a gift. "By, it's a good likeness," he pronounced finally. "He was a canny lad, your John, and a great help to me at the stables. But I was forgetting something, Mistress Robertson – I have a message for you from Mr Felton himself. And now that I've seen his gift to you, I understand the meaning of it."

Jack cleared his throat and delivered his speech with great emphasis, as if trying to imitate Edward Felton's gentlemanly manners. "Mr Felton wishes you to know that John being already departed from the Manor, he was obliged to execute his gift from memory. He hopes it will bring you some small comfort in the absence of your son. There now, Mistress Robertson, those were his exact words and I haven't forgotten a single one."

"Please tell Mr Felton I give him thanks from the bottom of my heart." Phyllis was too overcome to say more. Clutching the painting to her ample bosom, she turned away abruptly and retreated into the cottage. She waited for Jack to mount his horse and ride off back to the Manor. Then she sat down heavily at the rough wooden table and stared hard at the portrait of her eldest son, as if by doing so John would somehow step out of the painting and walk into her kitchen.

Phyllis Robertson was not given to tears as a general rule. She had always viewed weepy sentimentality as a waste of time and energy, a luxury she simply could not afford. But now, she laid her head wearily on the table, almost touching the painting, and began to sob uncontrollably. "My bonny lad," she whispered softly as her fingers traced John's face on the canvas. "Will I ever see you again?"

Then she made the sign of the cross, for she had an ominous feeling that she would not.

Nick and Jenny (5)

Jenny turned over the miniature oil painting, where the name *John Robertson,* barely legible and written with a clumsy uneducated hand, was inscribed. "Don't you see, Nick?" she exclaimed, her face flushed with excitement. "This portrait is the key to the mystery!"

"But do you think John is the artist or the subject of the portrait?" asked Nick.

"I very much doubt that someone of John's station would have been such an accomplished artist. And even if he had been, he would have signed the painting, not scrawled his name on the back of it." Jenny turned the faded lettering towards the light streaming in through the pub window, her mind busily evaluating the various possibilities.

"Then who did paint it?"

"Well, unfortunately there's no signature on the canvas, which seems to suggest that it wasn't the work of a professional artist. Perhaps it was someone who took a fancy to John? He's rather gorgeous, don't you think?" She winked at him mischievously.

"Gorgeous men run in the family," said Nick jokingly. "Although to be honest, he doesn't look much like me. Still, he does have a definite Robertson air about him – not just the fair hair and blue eyes but something in the facial expression too."

Jenny did not reply, too absorbed in her study of the inscriptions on the back of the painting. "Look at these words below John's name – they're so faded I can barely make them out. *Filly Delfy*... whatever can that mean?"

"It doesn't seem to make much sense," agreed Nick. "*Filly Delfy* doesn't sound like the name of a person, does it?" They were both silent for a while, turning over the conundrum in their minds.

"Maybe it's the name of a place," said Jenny thoughtfully, saying the words out loud over and over. "*Filly Delfy, Filly Delfy, Filly Delfy*... Of course!" Her fist came down on the table so hard that the few remaining customers in the pub stared at them in alarm.

She grabbed Nick's arm impulsively, her green eyes wide and sparkling. "It's just dawned on me! We've been concentrating on the spelling of the words instead of their sound. But this inscription was clearly made by someone who was barely literate, someone who was trying to spell a word he had heard but never seen written down..."

"So..." Nick was now completely baffled.

"Philadelphia!" she blurted out. "That's the word he was trying to write! He was telling us where John Robertson went when he left Dunstan Manor. And that explains why there was no further trace of John in English genealogical records. I couldn't find him because he wasn't in England – he'd emigrated to America!"

Nick was speechless. "But… but… how can you be so sure?" he stammered.

"I'm not. But it's a hunch, and it gives me something to work on. When I get back home, I'm going to research every US record I can lay my hands on, every passenger list of every ship sailing to Philadelphia. I just have to find out what became of John Robertson, and I won't rest until I do!" Her eyes met Nick's with a look of steely determination.

"It would be brilliant if we could fit John into the Robertson mosaic," he agreed. "But the whole idea of him going to America doesn't sound very feasible to me. You're always telling me how poor and ignorant my Robertson ancestors were, how they hardly stepped outside the confines of the parish… Why should John have suddenly upped and emigrated to Philadelphia? And more importantly, where did he get the money for the passage out there?"

Jenny looked reflective, trying desperately to piece together the puzzle. "This painting is our only clue," she said earnestly. "John Robertson obviously didn't take it to Philadelphia with him, which is how it came to be handed down in your family for over two hundred years. That suggests the portrait was a kind of memento, perhaps given to a member of John's family by the artist."

"But who was the artist? And how on earth did he meet John?"

"Let's look at the facts," mused Jenny. "We know that John Robertson was born at Dunstan Manor in 1770 and almost certainly worked on the estate. But perhaps not as a farm labourer like the rest of his family… I'm just speculating here, but maybe he was a servant of some kind and came into contact with the artist – a guest or family member – at the Manor."

"Someone in the Thorburn family?" suggested Nick.

"Well actually, by the late 18th century, the Thorburn line had died out for want of a male heir. Dunstan Manor had passed into the hands of Percy Felton, thanks to a very advantageous marriage to the eldest Thorburn daughter." Jenny went back to her iPad and started clicking and scrolling through her records again.

"So by the time John came of age, the Robertsons would have been employed by Percy Felton?"

"Yes, although they probably didn't see much of their new master. You see, the Feltons weren't landed gentry like the Thorburns. They were upstart coal merchants from Newcastle, social climbers determined to buy their way into the old Northumbrian aristocracy. My bet is that Percy Felton wasn't much interested in his wife's estate." Jenny pointed to the screen, and Nick leaned over to look at transcripts of old Dunstan Manor records. "As you can see here, by 1793 the entire estate had been tenanted out to four farmers. John's father was then employed by one of these tenant farmers, Benjamin Churnside. Look, here's William's name on the list of labourers working for Churnside."

"Fascinating," said Nick, peering at Jenny's notes. "Judging by the number of horses and carts listed here, he must have been a man of substance."

"Yes, he was a prosperous Presbyterian farmer. You'll be hearing more about the Churnside family later… and the Felton family too, for that matter." Jenny smiled at him enigmatically. "But not just yet."

Nick gave her a quizzical look. "The suspense is killing me, but I promise to refrain from asking any more questions. I take it this is all part of our ongoing magical mystery tour?"

Jenny glanced at her watch. "Oh my God, is that the time? You're quite right – the magical mystery tour isn't over, and I'd like to get to Warkworth while it's still daylight."

* * *

It took them little more than half an hour to reach Warkworth. Jenny, hands on the wheel and speeding south along the coast through the wintry Northumbrian countryside, glanced covertly at Nick. He seemed lost in thought and had not said much since they left the pub, apparently content to let her guide him through the weekend. Was he mulling over the Robertson past, sifting through the succession of ancestors which she had brought to life for him? Was he stepping back through the centuries, examining the tiny fragments of his family mosaic – so insignificant at first sight – which made up the backdrop to the broad sweep of History? As for the miniature oil painting of John Robertson, she could hardly wait to start researching US records – in Philadelphia or elsewhere in America. Intuitively, she felt she was on the right track at last.

God, he was gorgeous, Jenny thought as she flashed another look at Nick in profile. With his languid elegance, wavy dark hair and patrician features, she guessed he must take after his French mother rather than the Robertson side of the family. Only the lean angularity of his face and the humorous glint in his clear blue eyes spoke of his Northumbrian roots.

She had planned this first weekend together carefully, to show him how the lives of past generations were not just a few short lines on parish records but real people and places. She had also wanted him to share her passion for Northumberland, to feel part of its turbulent history. And in her heart of hearts, she was hoping that this quest for his Robertson ancestors would bind Nick to her, help to intensify and deepen their relationship.

The initial spark of attraction they had felt was turning into something far more powerful. Ever since they had left Jesmond that morning, the tension between them – both sexual and emotional – had been building up. But unlike Nick, she knew precisely what lay ahead, for it was she who had arranged this first night together in Warkworth. She had decided to take control of her destiny, deliberately choosing to make the first move herself instead of playing some outdated game of seduction. She had understood that she would only overcome her fears by playing an active role. And if in the end the magical mystery tour turned out to be a disaster, she would have only herself to blame.

"Is this your first time in Warkworth?" she asked conversationally, determined not to dwell any longer on what might or might not go wrong tonight.

Nick, jolted back to reality, turned to her with a smile. "Sorry, I was miles away… Actually I haven't been to Warkworth for years, but Dad used to drive us up there in the school hols. I remember the fabulous sandy beaches and the endless dunes… and also how bloody cold the sea was!"

Jenny burst out laughing. "Well, it's not the Med, I grant you. But I learnt to swim in the North Sea – we're a hardy lot up here, you know."

By now, they were approaching Warkworth itself, nestled on the banks of the winding River Coquet, its ancient streets dominated by the massive castle at the top of the hill. "It's so peaceful and picturesque," remarked Nick. "Especially at this time of year, without the hordes of tourists."

"Yes, it's a charming rural backwater now," agreed Jenny. "But Warkworth was quite different two or three hundred years ago. It was twice the size of sleepy little Embleton for a start. In those days, Warkworth was a bustling town with woollen mills and corn mills along the river banks, not to mention stone quarries and the burgeoning coal mining industry nearby."

Nick flashed her a wry smile. "I assume you're giving me this crash course in local history for a reason."

Jenny slowed the car and started looking for a convenient place to park. "Well, I have to admit I have an ulterior motive for bringing you here. Quite apart from the fact that my own family originally came from this area. My Armstrong ancestors lived here for generations before they moved south to Tyneside."

Nick stared at her with renewed interest. "But that's wonderful! You must promise to tell me all about your family history instead of letting me hog the limelight with mine."

"It's all part of the magical mystery tour, you'll see," she said archly, backing expertly into a parking space and unlocking her seat belt. "But I don't want to divulge any more just yet. Shall we explore the village before it gets dark? I'd love to show you my favourite spots before we check in."

They walked hand in hand to the ancient stone bridge and paused for a while to gaze into the murky depths of the river below. Nick slipped his arm around her waist and pulled her towards him. "Did I hear you say check in?" he asked softly.

A wave of embarrassment came over Jenny. What if she was jumping the gun? What if she had misinterpreted the connection between them? "Yes," she muttered, feeling like an awkward teenager. "I've booked a room here in Warkworth, at the Hotspur Inn."

"Perfect." She felt his lips gently nuzzling her neck. "And did I hear you say A Room... in the singular?"

She forced herself to look up at him. The expression in his eyes – a mixture of desire and tenderness – was unmistakeable. "Yes... unless you'd rather change the booking to two rooms?"

"What do you think?" He took her firmly in his arms and kissed her. The tranquil, rippling sound of the Coquet flowing under the bridge filled their ears as they held each other tight in the waning February light.

* * *

A wave of panic swept over Jenny as she and Nick climbed the stairs to their room at the Hotspur Inn. She had drunk slightly too much over dinner, secretly hoping the wine would calm her nerves and boost her confidence. Yet as she turned the key in the lock and pushed upon the door to their room, she felt frustratingly sober. Not only sober but on the alert, as if about to face some kind of crisis.

It was too late to turn back now, though. She reminded herself firmly that she had planned this night together and even booked the room in which they were about to spend it. So this tense, edgy mood made no sense. After all, she was a grown woman of thirty-two, not some virginal bride on her wedding night.

The room was cosy and comfortably furnished, albeit in a slightly outmoded style. Nick strolled over to the window and looked down idly, hands in pockets, at the dimly lit courtyard below.

"I really like this place," he remarked. "It just oozes character, doesn't it?"

Jenny agreed. Although she had never had occasion to stay at the Hotspur Inn before tonight, she had often admired its solid stone-built exterior, the thick sandstone walls blackened with age.

"It was originally a coaching inn," she told him. "But I suppose it's not up to the standards you're used to." Instantly, she berated herself for sounding so abrasive. Why had she suddenly gone on the defensive again?

Nick refused to be goaded. "I think it's perfect," he said stoutly and moved towards the large four-poster bed. He flung himself onto the bedcovers and stretched out spread-eagled on his back. "I'm glad you chose a room with such a fantastic bed. Good thinking, Jenny!"

"I swear I had no idea," she protested with a girlish giggle, although she had in fact specifically requested this room. She turned away from him to hang up their quilted jackets in the wardrobe. Methodically, she set about unpacking her overnight bag, carefully arranging her change of clothing for the next day, laying out her toiletries in the adjoining bathroom. She felt Nick's eyes following her as she moved about the room; both of them were well aware that she was playing for time.

Finally, she rummaged in the bottom of the bag and pulled out a toothbrush, brand new and still in its plastic packaging. She turned to Nick and held it up with a triumphant grin. "I thought you might need one of these," she said.

Nick laughed. "Good thinking again." He patted the quilted bedcover invitingly with one hand. "Come here, Jenny," he added softly.

Almost reluctantly, Jenny lay down next to him on the imposing four-poster bed, feeling stiff and awkward. She had not made love with a man since her divorce over two years ago. Would the right moves and gestures come back to her naturally? Or would Nick – who had probably been to bed with countless women – find her pathetically inexperienced?

She turned on her side to face him, her body not quite touching his. "I think you should know... my sex life has been non-existent for quite some time," she began. This was the moment of truth, she thought, and there was no point in hiding her misgivings.

Nick looked at her disbelievingly before realising she was quite serious. He took her in his arms and drew her close. "We'll just have to make up for lost time, then," he murmured.

They were kissing passionately now, Nick's hands searching for her body under the thick sweater and jeans she was still wearing. Jenny longed to yield to him unthinkingly, to put aside the physical insecurity her ex-husband had instilled in her over the years. But as always, she was painfully conscious of her femaleness – her all too womanly curves, her large breasts, the soft flesh on her stomach and thighs. How could she possibly please a man like Nick? A man who could have his pick of fashionably thin it-girls with manicured nails and designer handbags? The photo she had seen on internet flashed uninvited into her brain – was he still dating that gorgeous Swedish model?

"I don't think I'm really your type," she said abruptly, pulling away from his embrace. The harsh words came out unbidden, although she knew they must sound absurdly childish to him.

Nick propped himself on one elbow and looked at her intensely. "How can you possibly think that, Jenny? What can I say to convince you how I feel about you? You're smart and funny and I love being with you. And you're the most stunningly beautiful woman I've ever met. Can't you see how much I want you?"

"Oh, I want you too, Nick," she burst out impulsively. "But what if… what if it's not good between us tonight? What if it's… a fiasco?"

"I very much doubt that," said Nick, a glint of humour in his blue eyes. "And anyway, there'll be other times."

It was at that precise moment that Jenny surrendered her heart to Nick, finally allowing herself to trust him and to trust herself. *There'll be other times...* They were simple words, uttered with the nonchalance of someone who found them self-evident. Yet their resonance in Jenny's ears was far stronger than any passionate declaration of love could have been. The emotional barrier she had carefully erected between them was broken down in an instant; her private fears and inhibitions, locked inside her for so long, fell away and crumbled. *There'll be other times...* Nick was telling her there was no hurry. He was reassuring her that they would learn to love each other and that they had all the time in the world in which to do so.

Jenny's whole body turned liquid with desire. She pulled him down towards her and pressed her lips to his. "I hope so," she whispered.

* * *

When Jenny opened her eyes next morning, she saw that Nick was already up – albeit still naked – and availing himself of the tea-making paraphernalia laid out on a tray in their room. She stretched out luxuriously, feeling refreshed and energetic in spite of the fact that she had barely slept. They had spent the night making love, unable to tear themselves away from each other.

Nick returned to bed with two cups of tea, and they propped themselves up comfortably against the pillows to drink it. Realising that it was already after ten, they decided to call Reception to order breakfast in their room and ask for a late checkout. Both requests were granted by the friendly landlady who had welcomed them to the Hotspur Inn the previous day.

Nick hung up the phone with a satisfied smile. "Ah! Now I can keep you in this four-poster bed for a while longer." They kissed again lingeringly, as if their lips had a will of their own. "We still have the rest of today, don't we? We don't have to go straight back to Newcastle?"

"Oh no," she said reassuringly. "The magical mystery tour isn't over yet. But I know you have an early morning flight back to London tomorrow, so we need to get back to my place by tonight."

Nick grimaced. "Let's not think about that for now. I want to make the most of today and also…" He hesitated briefly. "I want you to tell me what you've been keeping from me for so long… why you've been holding me at arm's length, acting so defensively. Last night, I felt I'd finally made a chink in your armour, but still… you've been hiding something from me and I need to know what it is."

Jenny sighed heavily and put down her cup of tea. Their night together had been so perfect, and the last thing she wanted was to cast a shadow over the weekend. Yet Nick's questions were understandable and legitimate; he had a right to know about her past. And in a way, she actually wanted to confide in him now; it would be a relief to unburden herself at last. After all, she no longer had anything to hide.

"Is there another man in your life?" he went on, and she could hear the anxiety in his voice.

"No," she responded slowly. "But there was. I was married, you see, although the whole thing ended in a very nasty divorce a couple of years ago." She looked squarely at Nick, seeing the stunned expression on his face.

"Married?" he stuttered. "I never thought… I mean, I just assumed…"

"His name was – is – Aidan Halsby. You've probably heard of him – he writes detective novels."

Nick looked dumbstruck. "Aidan Halsby? Of course I've heard of him! The guy's written a whole string of best sellers… I've even read some of them myself. How on earth did you two get together?"

"It was in my final year at Newcastle University. I went along to a book fair… Aidan was the guest star, autographing his latest novel. We got talking, and things just developed from there. I fell madly in love with him, although in hindsight it was probably more of a gigantic crush than anything else. It was my first serious love affair, you see, and I suppose I was bowled over… flattered that this successful writer could possibly be interested in me. He was twenty years older than me – mature, knowledgeable, stimulating…" She waited for Nick to react, but the expression on his face was unreadable.

"Aidan was born and bred in Northumberland," she went on steadily. "He lives in an old vicarage near Bamburgh – that's where he holes up to write his books. In the beginning, I used to drive up there occasionally to join him for the weekend – only when he asked me to, though. I was so captivated by him – so impressed, I suppose – that I never questioned why he didn't want to see me more often. He dictated the terms of our relationship from the outset. He told me he needed to cut himself off from the outside world for long periods, otherwise he couldn't concentrate on his work, and I completely respected that. And anyway, the arrangement suited me for other reasons…"

"What reasons?" said Nick sharply. She had feared she was boring him with her story but now realised he had been listening intently.

"Because of Mam." Her voice, which had been so controlled, now faltered with emotion. "You see, I had to stay at home in Burnside to take care of the family. When I was in my last year at school, Mam found out she had breast cancer, although sadly it was diagnosed two or three years too late. There was no way I could go away to university as I'd planned, so I opted to take my degree in Newcastle instead, where I could go on living at home and look after Mam. Dad was falling apart… he just couldn't cope with Mam's illness, much less keep house. My three little sisters were still at school, far too young to take charge of anything."

Impulsively, Nick took her in his arms. "My poor darling," he whispered as he smoothed strands of tawny hair away from her face. "I had no idea you'd been through such an ordeal. Did this guy – Aidan Halsby – help you through it?"

She smiled grimly. "Oh, Aidan is one of those totally self-absorbed geniuses who don't concern themselves much with other people's problems. He wasn't so much unsympathetic as oblivious. But at the time I didn't blame him, I was almost thankful for his indifference. You see, I needed time and space away from Burnside too. So whenever we were together in Bamburgh, I tried to cut myself off from all the worries and responsibilities at home, if only for a few hours." Jenny's expression was pensive as she thought back to her youth, those years of anguish when there had been little opportunity for fun and laughter.

"Now I understand what you mean about the relationship with Aidan suiting you," Nick mused. "You had no time for an ongoing, permanent relationship with a man... and in any case, Aidan wasn't offering you one."

There was a discreet tap on the door. Nick leaped out of bed and quickly donned a pair of jeans, while Jenny hastily pulled the bedcovers over her naked body. Her eyes followed Nick as he retrieved the breakfast tray from the landlady and laid it on a small table near the window.

It was still difficult for her to talk to anyone, even Nick, about the sheer hell of watching helplessly as her beloved Mam slowly died. The doctors at the hospital told her the cancer had turned metastatic and was gradually spreading to the lungs and liver and brain. Her once cheerful, capable mother lapsed into a debilitating cycle of constant pain, fatigue and depression. At the same time, her father – an amiable but ineffectual man – went into a state of denial. He took refuge in his job during the day and retreated to the pub after work – anything to avoid the heavy burden of responsibility. So it was left to Jenny, still in her teens, to care for her mother and take charge of the family. And although she managed to keep up with her studies and eventually graduate, she had never been part of the carefree, party-going student scene in town. Boyfriends, few and far between, soon lost interest in this overly serious girl who was hardly ever free to go out and have fun.

As a result, she was untroubled by the sporadic nature of her relationship with Aidan. He asked very little of her, while she in turn had neither the time nor the energy for an intensive love affair. It was only when her mother died – Jenny was twenty-five at the time and already teaching – that she was able to envisage a life of her own at last. And it was only natural that she turned to Aidan then, the man she loved. She longed for a stable, settled relationship with Aidan; she wanted a husband, a home and children. Still grieving from the loss of her mother, she poured out her heart to him one evening in the old vicarage. Had Aidan merely felt sorry for her at that moment or had he genuinely loved her? Whatever the reason, they were married three months later at a quiet registry office ceremony in Newcastle.

Despite her new status as Aidan's wife, Jenny's life changed very little. He wasn't cut out to play hubby, he warned her with a theatrical shudder, and the last thing he wanted was a woman fussing around the house all day. As a writer, he required solitude, silence and the freedom to sleep all day and work all night if he so chose. He encouraged Jenny to continue in her teaching career and offered to rent a flat for her near the school in Jesmond, so that through the week she could stay in town and lead her own life. Surely, he said, this was the ideal scenario for a cool, progressive couple? And Jenny, inexperienced and insecure, had agreed. In hindsight, she realised she had been afraid to ask for more, for fear of losing her brilliant, mercurial husband forever.

The marriage drifted on in this way for several years – and might have continued even longer, if it had not been for Graham. He always seemed to be around, even during school holidays when Jenny looked forward to spending more time with Aidan in the rambling old vicarage she tried to call home. He would pop in casually on his way to Bamburgh, appear unannounced just as they were sitting down to dinner, disappear with Aidan for hours on end on long country walks…

Graham, an attractive man in his early fifties, ran a local antique business and was Aidan's oldest and dearest friend. He had a sharp wit and spoke in a slightly condescending drawl. Although he was invariably courteous to Jenny, he made it clear from the outset that his relationship with Aidan was non-negotiable. At first, Jenny was friendly and welcoming, until she gradually realised that whenever Graham was present she was relegated to second place. The two men made her feel dull and intellectually inferior, putting her down if she tried to join in their conversations, or excluding her altogether and retreating to Aidan's study. They talked endlessly about people Jenny had never known and laughed at private jokes she didn't understand. As time went on, she became increasingly frustrated and resentful; it was as though she were in some nightmarish *ménage à trois.*

"Don't be ridiculous, my pet," Aidan would chide her whenever she dared broach the subject. "I can't bear tantrums. You're behaving like a spoilt child, and it's time you grew up."

In desperation, Jenny finally turned to her best friend – sensible, down-to-earth Heather. It was the first time she had voiced her misgivings about her marriage; she had thought she would be betraying Aidan by implying their relationship was anything other than perfect. Heather listened without interrupting while she confided how troubled and unhappy she was.

"How's your sex life with Aidan?" she asked bluntly.

Jenny was forced to admit that she and Aidan rarely made love; even when they did, it was usually she who made the first move. But their relationship was based on a meeting of minds, she added staunchly. She had always loyally made allowances for Aidan when it came to the physical side of their marriage. He was no longer a young man after all, he was often engrossed in his work, he generally came to bed late… The lack of sexual passion, she stressed, was not an issue.

"Are you kidding?" an astounded Heather retorted. "You're still in your twenties and sex isn't an issue? What planet are you on, Jenny?"

Heather was making her see Aidan in a new, colder light. Reluctantly, Jenny told her friend that she always felt sexually inadequate with Aidan, that she was afraid he found her physically distasteful. Aidan was often critical of her appearance and repeatedly urged her to go on a diet, to take more exercise… He would pinch the soft flesh on her stomach and thighs and laughingly tell her to 'get rid of all that flab'.

"But that's crazy!" Heather protested fiercely. "You're a lovely, attractive woman, Jenny – most men would fall head over heels for you! Can't you see what's behind all this?"

And at last, Jenny did see. The truth had been staring her in the face for years, but she had refused to confront it. She had fallen under Aidan's spell as a vulnerable young girl and allowed herself to be deluded and lied to for years. How could she have been so blind?

After a sleepless night, she set off early next morning for Bamburgh, leaving a garbled message at the school about coming down with flu and needing to take the day off. She felt guilty about pretending to be sick, but this was an emergency. It was a Wednesday, and she knew Aidan would not be expecting to see her; she always spent her working week in town. She wanted to catch him unawares, while at the same time dreading the outcome.

She reached Bamburgh shortly before nine, leaving her car at the bottom of the lane instead of driving straight up to the vicarage. As she approached on foot, she saw immediately that Graham's car was parked in front of the house. Noiselessly, she let herself into the hall and tiptoed upstairs to the master bedroom. Her chest felt so constricted that she could hardly breathe.

Even before she pushed open the door, she knew she would find them in bed together. It was like some comic scene in a farce, she thought afterwards – Graham shrieking in horror, an incredulous Aidan leaping out of bed naked. She had not planned what her own reaction would be, but now she found herself unexpectedly incensed with rage. She yelled and screamed at them both, giving vent to the fury and resentment bottled up inside her for so long. There was a terrible scene, all three of them shouting insults at each other. In the end, Jenny stormed out and slammed the door on her husband and his lover.

Much later, Jenny and Aidan managed to meet and have a more civilised conversation, although Aidan never apologised for his behaviour. He and Graham had been lovers for many years, he revealed, although he thought of himself as bi-sexual rather than gay. There was no reason, he argued, why Jenny should react so unreasonably in today's liberated society. Surely, they could work out a modus operandi which would suit everyone?

But for once, she refused to be manipulated. Aidan had tricked her, lied to her from the start about his homosexuality and his longstanding love affair with Graham. He had hurt her deeply, but worse still, he had humiliated her. How could she have been so gullible and naïve? How could she have let herself be taken in and made a fool of?

Eventually, the divorce went through, leaving Jenny alone to lick her wounds. Since then, she had found it impossible to trust any man; there was no way she could believe anything they said. What game were they playing? What were they hiding from her? At the ripe old age of thirty-two, she had convinced herself that she was not cut out for men, that she was far better off on her own… until she fell in love with Nick Robertson.

***

"So that's the whole sorry tale," said Jenny with a rueful smile. Now that she had told Nick everything about her past, she felt as if a heavy burden had been lifted from her shoulders.

But Nick still looked horrified. "I could kill the bastard," he blurted out, "for putting you through all that."

"No point," she said crisply. "I really don't care about Aidan Halsby anymore. But ever since the divorce went through two years ago, I just couldn't bring myself to trust another man. As soon as a man started showing signs of interest, I always wondered if he would betray me too. I wasn't prepared to risk being hurt and lied to again. But I've finally realised it was myself I didn't trust, because I had no faith in my own judgement."

"And now you do have faith?" Nick moved closer and took her hand in his.

"You can't fall in love without taking risks," she said with a wry smile. "And the fact is, I'm in love with you."

"It's mutual. And I promise I have no other lovers, gay or otherwise, hiding in the closet." He pulled a funny face and she laughed in spite of herself.

"Not even that blonde Swedish model?" She had not intended to ask, but the question popped out nevertheless.

"Klara, you mean? No, that's all over," he assured her. "Seriously, my love," he added more earnestly, "I won't let you down, ever." He kissed her gently and Jenny's heart flooded with joy.

Nevertheless, she forced herself to be honest about her marriage. "I hope I haven't painted a one-sided picture of my relationship with Aidan," she said. "You must understand that he wasn't entirely to blame. I think he was genuinely fond of me to begin with. He probably saw me as some kind of personal experiment in bi-sexuality. I don't think he would ever have married me, though, if I hadn't forced his hand when Mam died." She stretched her arms luxuriously above her head. "Anyway, it's all water under the bridge now. And I have to give Aidan credit for one thing…"

"What?" Nick's tone was suspicious.

"It was Aidan who got me interested in local history and genealogy. He was very knowledgeable himself and had several books on Northumberland in his library. It was Aidan who encouraged me to write *The Rise and Fall of the Tyneside Pit Village.* He probably hoped it would keep me occupied on the long winter nights in Jesmond, while he and Graham cosied up together behind my back." Jenny's laugh was light-hearted, but there was a flash of bitterness in her green eyes.

She heaved a sigh. "Oh Nick, I'm tired of talking about Aidan. Let's move on, shall we?" She began to briskly clear away the remains of their breakfast, making room on the table for her iPad. "We're still in the middle of our magical mystery tour, you know. We need to go back to your family tree for a few minutes before we check out of the hotel."

Nick sensed her change of mood. "Of course," he agreed. "As I recall, we'd come as far as John Robertson, my distant uncle several times removed who apparently ran off to a weird place called Filly Delfy."

Jenny grinned. "Yes, but as I explained, your direct line doesn't actually descend from John Robertson but from his younger brother James, born in 1786." She pointed to his name on the family tree which had just appeared on the screen of her iPad. "I think he was known as Jack rather than James, because he's listed as *Jack Robertson, Labourer* on the Dunstan Farm register. As you can see here, in 1809 Jack married a girl called Agnes Ridley, and they had nine children."

"The Robertsons all seem to breed like rabbits," remarked Nick drily.

"Large families were the norm in the labouring class in those days. Children were seen as an additional source of income for the family and put to work at a very early age. The problem in Northumberland at the turn of the 19th century, as in many other parts of rural England, was that there was simply not enough work on the land for this burgeoning population. Agriculture was becoming increasingly mechanised too, so there was no need to employ as many farm labourers as in the past. Times were hard in Northumberland for the likes of Jack Robertson. Hundreds of unemployed labourers – with their families in tow – were reduced to roaming the countryside looking for work." A born teacher, Jenny was already warming to her subject.

"So poor old Jack had a precarious existence back then?"

"No, he seems to have been one of the relatively lucky ones," said Jenny, scrolling through her notes. "He lived and worked all his life on Dunstan Farm – pretty uneventful, really. But things changed radically for Jack's eldest son, Henry – here he is on the family tree, born in 1810. Henry's your direct ancestor."

"Am I right in thinking you brought me to Warkworth because of Henry?"

Jenny nodded. "I reckon Henry must have been quite a rebel in his youth. Just look at these transcripts…"

IV

Henry Robertson, February 1828

Henry could not remember a time when he hadn't been in love with Eliza. He had always taken great pains to conceal his adoration and was certain nobody suspected. This was because everyone at Dunstan Farm would find the very notion of Henry Robertson loving Eliza Churnside preposterous; they would laugh in his face and then tease him mercilessly about his 'sweetheart'. Although Henry was only seventeen years old, he had his pride and was certainly not about to let himself be turned into a figure of fun. Worse still was the thought of Eliza overhearing jokes about him and dismissing him in her mind as a pathetic fool.

Eliza was an only child. Her father, Matthew Churnside, was the master of Dunstan Farm and ran it with a rod of iron, tempered somewhat by a strong sense of justice. His labourers, including the Robertsons, respected him unreservedly but occasionally wished he were not quite so virtuous. Matthew Churnside had made it clear that he didn't hold with drinking and merrymaking; he was an elder at the Presbyterian meeting house in Alnwick and took his role of spiritual guide very seriously. Only his beloved daughter could bring a smile to his face and a softness to his voice. It was universally acknowledged that Eliza Churnside was the apple of her father's eye.

"They do say Miss Eliza is all set to make a fine marriage." The entire family – Jack and Agnes Robertson, their nine children and Jack's elderly mother Phyllis – were sitting around the kitchen table eating supper one bleak Sunday evening in February. Henry had been daydreaming as usual, but his ears pricked when he heard his mother mention Eliza's name. "They say she's been educated to hold her own with any of the young ladies in the county. She can sing and play the piano and even speak French, so they say."

"Stop your tittle-tattle, woman," Jack Robertson retorted tersely. "They do say this and they do say that, do they? Much you know about fine marriages! And anyway, it's nowt to us who the hell she marries. It won't put another crust of bread in our mouths, will it?"

Agnes shrugged her shoulders and snorted, but she knew better than to argue with her husband on a Sunday evening. In a short while, he and his four sons would be obliged to leave the warmth of the cottage, as they did every week, for an hour of prayers and bible study at Dunstan Farm.

"We've committed no crime, and our faith is nobody's business but our own!" he would protest irritably every Sunday. "Why can't the master leave us in peace?"

But Jack's question was purely rhetorical, for he was well aware of the unspoken agreement between himself and his employer. Like his father Benjamin before him, Matthew Churnside disapproved of Catholicism and felt it was his moral responsibility to show the Robertsons the error of their ways. So for well over thirty years, Robertson men and boys had dutifully trooped to Presbyterian prayer meetings at the Churnside residence. They had no alternative if they wanted to keep their cottage and go on working at Dunstan Farm.

It was time to go. Jack stood up wearily and signalled to his mother, whom he had taken in when old Will Robertson had died fifteen years ago. Phyllis was now well over seventy years old but still surprisingly hale and hearty. She did much of the cooking and cleaning in the cottage, thereby enabling Agnes to work most days on the farm and earn a few extra shillings

At Jack's signal, Phyllis got to her feet without a word. She went to retrieve the old wooden crucifix from its hiding place under her mattress and handed it reverently to her son. With Jack holding the crucifix high, the whole family – except Phyllis who was too old to do so – got to their knees and chanted a Hail Mary in unison, ending with the sign of the cross. This Sunday ritual, in the privacy of the rundown labourer's cottage, was the Robertsons' way of reaffirming their faith. As for the intricately carved crucifix, they had no idea how it had come into their family but it held deep meaning for them all. When Jack left for the weekly prayer meeting, he always slipped the crucifix into his pocket as a small gesture of rebellion. Its presence there strengthened his resolve; the Presbyterian sermonising he was forced to endure would have no effect on him or his beliefs.

It was a bitterly cold evening with driving sleet and an icy wind blowing in from the sea. As Henry trudged across the sodden fields with his father and three younger brothers, he pretended to share their disgruntled mood. No one must guess how happy and elated he really felt; the weekly prayer meetings were his only chance to see and admire Eliza Churnside at close quarters.

Half an hour later, they were all assembled in the spotlessly clean farmhouse parlour. Matthew Churnside, dressed soberly in black as usual, sat at a highly polished table with his wife and daughter. Facing them as if in church were three rows of hard wooden chairs occupied by the men and boys of two Catholic families – the Robertsons and their longstanding friends and neighbours the Hunters.

The opening prayer session – conducted in authoritative tones by Mr Churnside – always seemed endless to Henry, mainly because it was impossible for him to look at Eliza with eyes closed and head bowed. What he really looked forward to was the bible reading, which the farmer always entrusted – as he proclaimed proudly every week – 'to my dear daughter whose reading never fails to bring us all comfort and joy'.

Henry listened rapturously to Eliza's clear mellifluous voice, free at last to gaze at her openly and study every detail of her face and bearing. At twenty, Eliza was three years older than him and exuded an air of quiet confidence. She was taller than most girls and held herself very straight and erect – just like a princess, Henry always thought. Her heart-shaped face with its upturned nose and sparkling green eyes was a constant source of delight to him, but it was her hair he loved most. A shining chestnut colour, it tumbled down her back in wild cascading curls in total contradiction to her demure demeanour. Henry tried to concentrate on her reading, wondering not for the first time how such stern words of sin and damnation could be uttered by those soft lips that he dreamed every night of kissing.

Oh, how he yearned to be alone with Eliza so that he could pour out his feelings to her. Ever since he was a child, he had watched her from afar, all too conscious that she was unaware of his existence and never so much as glanced in his direction. Why should an accomplished young lady like Eliza Churnside be even remotely interested in a scruffy labourer's son in ragged clothes? But Henry refused to give up, could not bring himself to believe there was no future for them. He racked his brains constantly, searching for ways to become a legitimate part of Eliza's life. How could he get to know her without being summarily booted off the farm by her ever-watchful father?

The answer suddenly flashed into his mind as Eliza came to the end of her bible reading and looked up. She smiled impersonally at the rows of men and boys seated in front of her, but for some reason, her eyes rested on Henry and met his. The look they exchanged lasted no more than an instant, but for the first time, Henry thought he had caught some small sign of recognition in Eliza's clear green eyes. His heart started hammering against his chest and he felt his face flush red. At the same time, a plan began to form at the back of his mind.

Henry had just realised that the key to a relationship with Eliza was right there, staring him in the face. Matthew Churnside's sole objective in holding the Sunday evening prayer meetings was to convert his Catholic labourers to the Presbyterian doctrine. The Robertsons were duty-bound to attend but had always stubbornly refused to pay more than lip service to a religion that was not their own. And yet these same prayer meetings were the only time he and Eliza Churnside came face to face on a regular basis. What if Henry were to express an interest in Presbyterianism and request further spiritual guidance from Mr Churnside? He was certain the farmer would be gratified but equally certain that his responsibilities at Dunstan Farm would leave him no time to instruct Henry in the Presbyterian faith. That being the case, wasn't there a chance that he would entrust Eliza with this important task? It was a slight chance admittedly, but Henry was desperate enough to clutch at straws. And even if Mr Churnside insisted on overseeing Henry's instruction himself, Eliza would be bound to hear of it and look on him in a favourable light, as a deserving young man eager to better himself.

It only remained for him to persuade his father. Jack Robertson was a slow-witted man but put great store by his Catholic faith; he would be outraged at the very idea of Henry taking an interest in Presbyterianism. Nor must he ever suspect Henry's real motive; any mention of Eliza's name was to be avoided at all cost.

Best to strike the iron while it's hot, thought Henry, as the Robertsons emerged from the sprawling Churnside farm. The sleet had abated and the wind had dropped too, but there was a thin layer of snow lying in the fields and the icy air cut through their bodies like a knife.

"There's something I want to talk to you about, Father," began Henry with as much confidence as he could muster. As he had feared, he had hardly uttered more than a few words before Jack exploded with rage, ranting at him and accusing him of forsaking the faith of his forefathers. "I'm ashamed to have such a turncoat for a son!" he shouted, his voice ringing in the stillness of the winter countryside.

"Listen to me, Father, for God's sake! Surely, you don't believe I would ever give up my faith? Don't you see that if I can make Mr Churnside believe that one of our family wishes to receive spiritual instruction, he will think more highly of us? And that means he won't turn us off his land and our position will be safe here.

Who knows, perhaps the master will grow to favour me and hand over some of the running of the farm in a few years? Mr Churnside's not getting any younger and hasn't been blessed with a son of his own. He might be glad of a trustworthy lad by his side to assist him. But it would have to be one who shared his beliefs, wouldn't it? Surely, you can see all I want is the good of our family?"

Henry wondered whether Jack would swallow his line of reasoning, some of which he had made up as he went along. The main thing was to keep Eliza out of the picture, he repeated to himself as he continued in the same vein for some time, knowing that his father's brain was slow to adjust to new ideas. He needed his father's agreement before he could broach the subject with Mr Churnside and was prepared to argue relentlessly with him for as long as it might take to get it.

In the end, Jack not only capitulated but even started to sound genuinely convinced. It was Jack who explained to the rest of the family – repeating his son's arguments verbatim as if they were his own – how they would all benefit by Henry's receiving religious instruction. He even urged Henry to approach Mr Churnside on the subject without delay. Henry was inwardly jubilant, overjoyed that his ploy had worked.

Only old Phyllis Robertson, his grandmother, looked sceptical. She made no comment but gave him a long baleful look as if she could see right through him. Early next morning as Henry left the cottage in fine fettle to start his day's work, he found the old woman lying in wait for him by the chicken coop.

"You can't pull the wool over my eyes," she began tartly. "I know you're mooning over that Eliza Churnside, and I'll tell you straight no good can come of it. She's got her sights set higher than the likes of you, lad! If it's a sweetheart you're hankering after, there's plenty of other young lasses that would have you at the drop of a hat."

"You're losing your mind, old woman," retorted Henry, panic-stricken that Phyllis had uncovered his secret passion.

"I've lost many things in me time, lad. I've lost a husband, I've lost a dear son, I've even lost me teeth. But one thing I haven't lost is me mind!"

Henry laughed in spite of himself and Phyllis's eyes softened. "Eh Henry, every day that passes you remind me more and more of your Uncle John. He was a fine-looking lad like you, and clever with it. Not like that numbskull father of yours who hasn't got a brain in his head!"

Phyllis never had a kind word to say about her youngest son, and not for the first time, Henry was struck by his grandmother's ingratitude. It was Jack after all who had taken her in when she was widowed. But Phyllis's love was exclusively reserved for John, the eldest son who had run off to America as a young man. It had all happened long before Henry was born, but he knew everything about this legendary uncle who had been befriended by a rich artist at Dunstan Manor and given the means to seek his fortune in the United States. Phyllis even had a miniature portrait of Uncle John which she kept safe under her mattress along with the ancient wooden cross. Most evenings, she would bring out this painting of her son and stare at it lovingly, wiping away the odd tear. John had promised her faithfully that he would return to Embleton one day, but over thirty years had elapsed since his departure. Was he still alive? Had he been shipwrecked and drowned at sea during the long voyage to America? Or had he died from some strange sickness to be found in that faraway land? Phyllis steadfastly refused to believe the worst and clung to the hope that she would be reunited with John before she went to her grave.

Henry decided honesty might well be the best policy with Phyllis. "You won't let on about Eliza, will you Grandma? You mustn't mention it to a living soul!"

Phyllis gave him a withering look but shook her head. "No, I won't tell, lad. But take it from me, no good can come of it, no good at all."

* * *

Henry felt as if he had died and gone to heaven. He could scarcely believe that he was actually sitting next to Eliza at the massive dining table, breathing the same air as her. He was close enough to see the delicate shadows under her green eyes, the gleam in her chestnut curls, the down on the nape of her long white neck. Eliza was wearing a sober grey dress with a demure lace collar at the neck, but in Henry's view, her natural beauty shone through her plain attire like a beacon.

In the end, everything had gone according to plan, almost miraculously so. As Henry had hoped, Matthew Churnside was pleased by Henry's respectful request to further his religious education and equally regretful that he had no time himself to take on such a task.

"But if you come up to the house one hour before the prayer meeting on Sunday evening, I dare say my daughter will be delighted to instruct you. She is as well versed in our faith as myself and will be eager to bring spiritual enlightenment to all those who sincerely seek it."

Henry was astute enough to realise that Matthew Churnside would never have made such a suggestion if he had considered him a threat to his daughter's virtue in any way. To Mr Churnside, it was inconceivable that Eliza, universally admired as an accomplished young lady of twenty, would see Henry as anything but a puny, uncouth boy of seventeen, a social inferior employed by her father. But Henry didn't care one jot about Mr Churnside's poor opinion, for his very insignificance was proving to be an advantage. Here he was, alone in the parlour for a whole hour with an unchaperoned Eliza. Henry was determined to play his cards right and make the most of it.

"Before we begin the study of Presbyterian doctrine," began Eliza solemnly, "I thought it would be useful for you to learn about the history of our religion and how it differs from Catholicism. For this, we must go back all the way to the 16th century and the Protestant Reformation. Have you ever heard of John Knox, Henry?"

Henry snapped out of his reverie and looked into Eliza's earnest face. It suddenly occurred to him that if he wanted to win Eliza's affection, these sessions in the farmhouse parlour would have to take place on a regular basis. And Eliza would only be willing to devote her time and energy to his education if he genuinely applied himself, impressing her with his aptitude for serious study. This, he felt sure, was the way to Eliza's heart.

"No, Miss Churnside," he answered meekly.

"John Knox was a Scotsman who studied in Europe – in Switzerland to be precise – with Calvin and brought his teachings back to this country. Oh, but I'm forgetting, first of all I need to explain who Calvin is…"

Henry focused his attention on Calvin, and as the lesson progressed found himself captivated by Eliza's words. His own faith had always been instinctive and unquestioning; he had never heard religion discussed in this reasoned manner, nor ever met anyone who thought it worthwhile to converse with him at all. Eliza was a born teacher, not only kind and patient but eager to make the lesson interesting and informative.

"Presbyterian… it's a strange word, isn't it, Miss Churnside?" remarked Henry as their allotted time together drew to a close.

"Oh Henry, I'm delighted you're asking me such questions! Curiosity is the key to true understanding, you know. Yes, it is an odd word, I suppose. It denotes the form of government within our community. You see, Presbyterians don't worship in a parish church like the one in Embleton and we don't have a priest or vicar. We gather at the meeting house in Alnwick, and our congregation is governed by an assembly of elders, all of them upstanding God-fearing men. It's a great honour to be an elder, you know, and my father is proud to have been elected as one of them."

At that very moment, Matthew Churnside opened the door and entered the parlour with an affectionate smile to his daughter. "I'll have to interrupt your lesson, Eliza. The farmworkers have arrived for our prayer meeting and I don't wish to keep them waiting outside in the cold. But tell me, my dear, does young Henry Robertson have the makings of a good scholar?"

"Yes indeed, Father. In my opinion, Henry would benefit greatly from regular instruction. I should like him to return next Sunday at the same time – that is, if you agree, Father."

"What do you say to that, lad?" enquired Mr Churnside, turning to Henry.

"I'm most grateful to you and Miss Churnside, sir. I can't think of anything I'd like better."

* * *

In the weeks that followed, Henry continued his Sunday evening classes with Eliza. His love for her was becoming almost obsessional, for she occupied his thoughts constantly – her graceful movements, her dainty white hands resting on the bible, the earnest expression in her clear green eyes as she selected a suitable passage. At night, his thoughts of Eliza turned into passionate dreams in which she lay naked in his arms, yielding with wild abandon to his caresses. Henry would awake from these dreams aroused and drenched in sweat. He knew such fantasies were sinful but was unable to prevent them, although he prayed every night for God to purify his soul.

Henry was indifferent to everything that was not Eliza – the blustery winter weather, old Phyllis complaining about the pain in her back, his mother railing at the shortage of food as she struggled to provide for a family of twelve. As for his work on the farm, Henry performed his duties mechanically, oblivious to his father berating him for his carelessness.

Although the lessons themselves had initially been a mere pretext to spend time with Eliza, he found himself enjoying them more and more. Through the week as he carried out his chores, he repeated under his breath what he had been taught the previous Sunday, eager to please Eliza and win her approval.

"You're coming along in leaps and bounds, Henry!" she exclaimed one evening in April. "A fountain of knowledge, I do declare!"

Henry had never heard the expression before and was instantly captivated. "That's true, Miss Churnside, knowledge is like a fountain. When you teach me, I can feel your words flowing through my mind like cool water, making everything clear and clean inside me."

"Why, what a beautiful thing to say, Henry!" Eliza blushed with pleasure.

"How did you come by so much learning, Miss? You know so much and I so little."

"I have Mr Metcalfe to thank for almost everything I know, Henry. Mr Metcalfe is an elder at our meeting house and a dear friend of my father's. He has three grown children of his own and I have always been close to his youngest, Jane. Mr Metcalfe is a progressive thinker and a great believer in education for females. He arranged private tuition for us all, and Jane and I took our lessons together. As a result, I am acquainted with the classics, the arts and history... even French, although my accent leaves much to be desired!" She giggled, giving Henry a tantalising glimpse of a less serious, more girlish Eliza.

Henry realised with a thrill that for the first time, Eliza was actually confiding in him, treating him as an equal. He was determined, however, to find out more about this Mr Metcalfe, instinctively wary of any male presence in Eliza's life.

"Are you fond of Mrs Metcalfe too?" It was a leading question, but Eliza appeared not to notice and rattled on merrily.

"Oh, poor Mrs Metcalfe passed away many years ago, and since then, Mr Metcalfe has devoted himself entirely to his work. He's a physician in Alnwick, you know, and keeps himself abreast of the most advanced medical practices in the country. His patients are fortunate indeed to be in the care of such an eminent doctor."

And fortunate indeed to be able to pay for one, thought Henry in spite of himself but kept this subversive thought to himself. "Is he a kind man?" he continued.

"Outwardly, he looks stern but he has a kind heart, I'm sure of it. He has always looked on me as a daughter... until quite recently, that is..." Eliza's brow suddenly furrowed and her voice trailed away.

There was an awkward silence in the parlour. Henry was tempted to press Eliza further but sensed that she would say no more on the subject. He must keep his wits about him and try another tack.

"I wish I could read and write like you, Miss Churnside," he said wistfully. "Then I could read the Bible every day, even when you aren't there to instruct me."

Eliza's eyes widened as she was struck by a sudden revelation. She patted Henry's hand impulsively. "I should have thought of it myself, Henry! Of course you must learn to read and write and I shall be the one to teach you!"

Henry's hand was tingling from the warmth of Eliza's fleeting touch, but the pleasure was short-lived. She jumped quickly to her feet and snatched a sheaf of paper and a quill pen from a side table. "We'll start with your name, Henry Robertson. Look, I'll write it for you..."

Henry watched fascinated as Eliza wrote in flowing copperplate, taking care to make the letters larger and plainer than usual.

"Henry begins with the letter H. In the alphabet, we pronounce it *aitch* but it denotes the *huh* sound. *Huh* for Henry, do you see?"

Henry did see. The bible next to Eliza caught his eye and he pointed to the ornate gold lettering on the cover. "It's the same letter as this one here, Miss."

"Precisely!" exclaimed Eliza triumphantly. "What you see are the words *Holy Bible. Huh* for Henry and *huh* for holy… oh Henry, how clever you are! I'm sure you'll learn to read and write in no time at all."

* * *

Later in life when he looked back on that time, Henry always thought that learning to read and write marked a turning point in his relationship with Eliza. He found mastering these new skills far more stimulating than the rigorous religious instruction he had been following since February. He realised he was no longer simply anxious to please Eliza but genuinely motivated to learn. On her side, Eliza seemed relieved to broaden the scope of her teaching beyond strictly spiritual matters.

The atmosphere of the Sunday evening classes grew more and more informal as Henry quickly progressed from the alphabet to deciphering short words and simple phrases. They laughed together as Henry made his first clumsy attempts to imitate Eliza's copperplate. The heavy Presbyterian bible was pushed to one side and replaced by discussions on more entertaining topics, such as the latest novel or poem Eliza was reading. He never dared ask whether she had informed her father of these changes but was only too happy to leave the question unanswered.

Initially, Henry had been too dazzled by the sheer physical presence of Eliza to wonder how she herself felt about their weekly lessons. But gradually, Henry came to understand that the time they spent together was a welcome diversion in Eliza's dull routine. As a respectable young lady, her freedom was restricted by the puritanical morality of her family and the strict codes of conduct in society at large. She was in effect mostly confined to the four walls of Dunstan Farm, where the long days were occupied in sewing, reading and playing piano in the parlour. Occasionally, she would mention visits from fellow Presbyterians in the neighbourhood, but none of them seemed to bring her much amusement.

The highlight of Eliza's week was the Sunday morning outing with her parents to attend service at the meeting house in Alnwick. Henry followed her to Alnwick in his thoughts, racked by irrational fears and speculation about what might be happening there. He imagined dozens of smartly dressed, well-mannered young men pursuing Eliza and begging for her hand in marriage. And at the back of his mind was the shadowy figure of Mr Metcalfe, whose attentions – as Eliza had hinted – were now becoming less fatherly. But surely, Eliza could not be interested in a dried-up old widower with a bald pate and a paunch?

More than ever, Henry yearned to win Eliza's love, but it was a different kind of yearning now. After several months in her company, he no longer viewed Eliza as an unattainable object of adoration. She had become a real person who smiled and laughed, whose upturned nose was slightly too large and whose teeth on closer inspection were crooked. His desire for this new, less than perfect Eliza was all the fiercer and his wild passionate dreams all the more vivid.

As the months passed, Henry sensed that Eliza enjoyed his company and even appeared to be quite fond of him. Although he was certain her feelings were far less intense than his own, he had the impression more than once that she was flirting with him, testing her powers of seduction on him. As he practised writing the letters of the alphabet, she would pull her chair a little too close to his, placing her hand over his own to guide the quill pen. He could feel her breath on his face, the warmth of her body against his; once he even felt the tip of her breast brushing his arm. He would hold his breath, not daring to move, torn between the exquisite pleasure of the moment and the frustration of holding back.

There were changes in his appearance too. The awkward gangly youth who had presented himself to Eliza Churnside on that first Sunday in February was fast becoming a young man. In the space of a few months, he had shot up in height and was now slightly taller than Eliza. His shoulders were broader, and the fair down on his cheeks was thick enough to need shaving. Henry wondered whether Eliza had noticed these changes and was now coming to see him in a different light. He was struck by a new, teasing expression in her green eyes and the coquettish way she tossed her chestnut curls, only too well aware of the effect she had on him and inwardly enjoying every moment of it. She knew she was safe in the parlour of her own home, above reproach and out of Henry's reach.

The cool, wet spring finally gave way to an exceptionally warm July, lifting Henry's spirits and flooding his mind with fanciful hopes and dreams. However hard he had been labouring on the farm during the day, sleep still eluded him in the long hours of daylight after supper. Most evenings, he would sit outside the cottage on a low stool, using a long stick to write Eliza's name in the dust. He wondered what she was doing at that precise moment. Was she reading her favourite volume of Shakespeare's sonnets? Or had she opened her bedroom window to let in the balmy summer air and was now brushing her luxuriant curls, her feet bare and only a light chemise covering her slender white body? Henry's heart was ablaze with love, but at the same time, a steely determination was starting to form at the back of his mind. *I must have Eliza Churnside,* he thought, *and have her I will.*

* * *

Their ordered lives at Dunstan Farm changed one Sunday evening in late August. As was his wont, Henry approached Mr Churnside's house from the rear and came in by the kitchen door. He usually received a warm welcome from the cook, Betsy Hunter, but today she greeted him with a dismayed expression. "Miss Churnside said I was to tell you she can't give you instruction today."

"But why ever not, Betsy? Is she ill?" A wave of panic swept through Henry, for Eliza had never before cancelled a lesson.

"I don't know as she's ill, bonny lad, but she's right downcast and not her usual self at all."

"Where is she? Can I at least speak to her?"

Betsy Hunter heard the note of desperation in Henry's voice, confirming what she had suspected for quite some time. She hesitated, debating whether she should say more. But the Robertson and Hunter families had always been close; Henry's mother was her cousin and they often enjoyed a good gossip together.

"Well, she's not in the house and that's a fact. I saw her go off with her book an hour ago, and I wouldn't be surprised if she's not down by the castle. She's fond of walking there when the weather's fine." There was a mischievous glint in Betsy's eyes as she revealed Eliza's whereabouts.

It was no more than a mile to Embleton Bay and the massive ancient ruin of Dunstanburgh Castle. Without even pausing to thank Betsy, Henry turned on his heel and ran out of the kitchen. It was a sultry summer evening and the sky was overcast, as if a storm were brewing. Henry broke into a sweat as he quickened his pace, wondering whether some disaster had befallen Eliza. What other explanation could there be for her behaviour?

As the sea came into view and Henry strode purposefully across the broad sweep of moorland towards the castle, he saw no sign of Eliza.

In fact, there was not a soul in sight as far as the eye could see, either on the headland itself or the rocky outcrops below. The sea lay calm and pearly grey in the early evening light. The air was cooler here than at the farm, and a light salty breeze filled Henry's nostrils. He entered the precincts of the castle and began to wander within its strong granite walls, hoping to come across Eliza at every turn.

He caught his breath as he spotted her at last, sitting on a grassy verge at Castle Point and looking out to sea. Her back was turned to him, and the book she had brought with her had been cast aside unopened. She was dressed in a light summer dress of cream muslin and sat perfectly still, lost in thought and oblivious to Henry's approach. When he sat quietly beside her, she started slightly and looked up at him, unsmiling yet unsurprised. It occurred to him that she might have been expecting him to come after her all along? He wondered whether – consciously or unconsciously – she had wanted them to meet here, alone and unsupervised at last.

"Please tell me why you're so downcast, Eliza." Henry made no pretence at formality and simply took her hand gently in his. It was the first time he had not addressed her as Miss Churnside, but she seemed not to notice.

Eliza left her hand listlessly in his. She bowed her head, as if weighed down by a heavy burden she could not throw off. Eventually, she heaved a sigh and turned her distraught, heart-shaped face to Henry's, tears glinting in her green eyes.

"Oh Henry, I'm at my wit's end. You see, I feel it's my duty as a daughter to please Father, and I know he wants only the best for me. He insists it would be a most advantageous match..." Eliza's voice broke and to Henry's astonishment, she burst into tears. Could this vulnerable girl be the same demure, composed Miss Churnside he had worshipped from afar for so long? Without thinking, Henry put his arm around her waist to comfort her, and just as spontaneously Eliza laid her head on Henry's shoulder. He felt her whole body shaking with anguish.

"What advantageous match do you mean, Eliza?" Yet even before the words were out of his mouth, Henry had guessed the answer to his question.

"It's Mr Metcalfe, Henry." Eliza's words were muffled, for she had burrowed her face into his chest and was sobbing openly now. "He has declared his love for me and asked for my hand in marriage... I know I should feel honoured... everyone holds him in such high regard... he's a physician of great distinction... but... oh Henry, I don't like the peculiar way he looks at me... and however hard I try, I simply don't love him at all!"

Henry's worst fears were proving to be well founded. As he held a tearful Eliza in his arms, he was filled with loathing for the saintly Mr Metcalfe and at that precise moment would gladly have murdered him. Yet at the same time, he felt

111

exultant and strong, for Eliza had just confessed she did not love Mr Metcalfe. Better still, she was opening her heart to him for the very first time.

He waited a while until Eliza's weeping abated, then he turned her tear-stained face up to his and spoke urgently. "Surely, you must know how much I love you, Eliza. I would lay down my life for you if you asked me to. I feel I've been waiting for this moment all my life, waiting to tell you... although there are no words to describe what is in my heart."

Eliza's eyes widened in alarm, like a startled fawn, and she pulled away from him slightly. Henry had neither planned nor rehearsed what was happening between them on this sultry summer evening, but the passion locked inside for so long flowed out of him and gave him the courage to go on.

"Come away with me, Eliza, come away! We must go to a place where no one knows us, we can be wed there and start a new life together... We could go to Newcastle, I hear it's a big town and there's work to be had there... Say you'll marry me, Eliza, and I'll make you the happiest woman in England!"

Eliza stared at him as if he had gone mad, although her eyes betrayed the tenderness she felt for him. "Why Henry, I'm very fond of you to be sure, fonder than I should be... but surely you must realise that what you're suggesting is impossible! Leave my home, my family and everything I hold dear for a penniless boy of seventeen? How can you imagine I would even contemplate such a wild scheme?"

Her response was not what Henry had hoped for, but he was undeterred. He must make Eliza understand how much he loved her, in a way that words could never express. Instinctively, he drew Eliza tightly into his arms and bent his head to kiss her. This time, Eliza did not pull away. The art of kissing was one in which neither of them was practised, yet they both felt the same intense pleasure as their lips met and their bodies locked together. Waves of excitement were coursing through Henry. He continued to kiss her passionately, moving his lips across her face and down her neck. He could feel Eliza responding, the tension draining from her body as she abandoned herself to his caresses. His hand slid down to fondle her breasts, squeezing them through the thin muslin of her dress. Eliza moaned softly and arched her back, yielding to his lovemaking and clinging to Henry as if she would never let him go.

They fell back as one onto the grassy bank, exploring each other in a way neither of them could have imagined only a few seconds before. As Henry impatiently unfastened her bodice and then pushed the layers of petticoats up around her waist, Eliza's slender white body – the body he had possessed so many times in his dreams – was revealed to him at last. The sweet scent of the lavender water she used intoxicated his senses, and her skin was irresistibly soft to his touch. Strangely, neither of them felt any embarrassment or false modesty as their naked bodies came together at last. They were alone in their private world and free of all constraints beyond their own desire. The long shadow of the ancient Northumbrian castle protected them, and there was no sound except the waves below lapping gently onto the sands of Embleton Bay.

It was all over very quickly, Henry thrusting inside her and Eliza crying out; whether in pain or pleasure they hardly knew. Afterwards, they lay entwined for a while, Henry's face buried in her mane of chestnut curls. The air had cooled, and a stiff breeze began to chill their naked bodies. Henry tried to pull Eliza closer and

112

kiss her, but her mood had suddenly changed. She pushed him away from her and sprang to her feet, snatching at her clothes and dressing in frenzied haste.

"What have we done, Henry?" She sounded on the verge of hysteria, her face flushed and fearful. "We've strayed from the path of virtue and committed a mortal sin. God will surely punish us and we will burn in Hell for all eternity!"

Still naked, Henry stood up and grasped her by the shoulders in an attempt to calm her. "If we were wed, there would be no shame in what we've done, Eliza. You're mine now, you have given yourself to me. If you marry me, our sin will be forgiven."

"Marry you? Marry you?" Eliza shrieked. "Have you taken leave of your senses, Henry? Do you think for one moment that my father would allow me to marry the likes of you? How could I bring such a disgrace on my family? Why, we'd be the laughing stock of the county!"

Henry recoiled, cut to the quick by her hurtful words. He was only too well aware of his station in life and the social chasm that separated them. Even so, he had not expected such hostility from the girl who only minutes before had given herself up so eagerly to his lovemaking.

Eliza had backed away from him now, clutching her book to her chest as if for protection. Her mouth was set in a hard line and her voice was harsh. "No one must know of this, Henry, do you hear me? We must carry this shameful secret to our graves. From now on, I forbid you to come to the house or approach me in any way. It's an order, Henry, and if you don't obey, I'll have you thrown off the farm."

Henry was too shocked to respond. So Eliza had already effaced their fleeting moment of passion from her memory… The beautiful naked girl he had held in his arms had metamorphosed into the stern figure of a social superior, Miss Eliza Churnside. Without another word, she swung abruptly away from him and set off at a brisk pace over the moorland, brushing grass from her skirt and rearranging her hair. Henry watched dejectedly until she had disappeared from view, then he sat down on the patch of grass where they had made love. His hands smoothed the blades of grass, still flattened by the weight of their bodies. He stayed there motionless until it was so dark that he could barely make out the outline of the castle ruins. He wished he could stay there forever.

* * *

For the next two weeks, Henry forced himself to go about his duties as usual, hoping against hope that Eliza would have a change of heart and send word for him to come to her. Although she had expressly forbidden him to do so, more than once he appeared discreetly at the kitchen door of Dunstan Farm. He was desperate to have news of Eliza, and the cook, Betsy Hunter, was his only source of information. But Betsy was not forthcoming, and the response was always the same: Miss Churnside had come down with the fever and was keeping to her bedchamber. Was Eliza really ill, Henry wondered, or was she simply avoiding him?

Summer turned into autumn and the weeks turned into months, with no news of Eliza to break the drab monotony of Henry's existence. Eliza no longer appeared at the Sunday evening prayer meetings, and no one was surprised when he announced that she was too sick to continue instructing him. In fact, Eliza had not been seen outside the farmhouse at all since that fateful August evening, not even to attend Sunday service at the Presbyterian meeting house in Alnwick. Yet Henry could not resign himself to losing her and thought of her constantly. At night, he dreamed over and over again of making love to her as he had done before, his dreams so vivid that he could smell the scent of lavender on her skin and feel the imprint of her body against his.

Henry was completely unprepared for what happened next. One wet evening in the middle of November, Matthew Churnside burst unannounced into the cottage just as the twelve members of the Robertson family were sitting down to enjoy a well-earned mutton stew for supper. His face like thunder, the farmer glowered at them all before striding over to Jack Robertson and hauling him from his stool by the scruff of the neck. "On your feet, man, this instant!" he barked.

The entire Robertson family gaped uncomprehendingly. Jack stood up shakily to face his irate master, racking his brains as to what he could have possibly done wrong. Henry was filled with foreboding, immediately sensing that this unexpected visit had some connection to Eliza and himself.

"Is it true, man?" shouted Mr Churnside, spluttering into Jack's face.

"Is it true that your swine of a son has seduced my daughter?"

Jack was speechless, stunned by this virulent accusation. In utter bewilderment, he looked over at Henry, who rose instantly to his feet. "I'm old enough to speak for myself, sir," he said with as much confidence as he could muster.

Matthew Churnside's face turned scarlet with rage. "How dare you speak to me in this manner, you depraved beast? Can you deny that you have defiled my daughter, abused her virtue and brought disgrace on us all? Can you deny that you have committed the mortal sin of fornication?" The Robertsons, all on their feet now, huddled together in silence by the hearth as the farmer continued to rant in the same vein. Only Henry faced him squarely, waiting for him to take breath so that he could respond.

"I don't deny that we've committed a mortal sin, Mr Churnside, and for this I beg God's forgiveness and yours. But you must believe me when I tell you I didn't seduce Eliza, I swear I didn't."

Matthew Churnside was almost apoplectic by now. "How dare you call her by her Christian name? Do you expect me to believe that a young lady of my daughter's rank, who has followed the path of righteousness all her life, would stoop to consort with a papist pig like you? You have violated her purity and taken advantage of her innocence!"

A fleeting memory of Eliza's tongue in his mouth and her searching hand in his breeches flashed through Henry's mind, but he thought it wiser to keep such things from her father. "Did Eliza actually say I seduced her?"

Mr Churnside looked taken aback and even slightly discomfited. "Well no, not in so many words... But your vile behaviour has resulted in... Eliza has just revealed to me that she is with child!" He blurted out the words accusingly, glaring at Henry with open hostility.

Strangely enough, the possibility of Eliza becoming pregnant had never occurred to Henry until that moment. Although he was shocked by the news, he also felt perversely proud. When he spoke, there was no mistaking his sincerity. "I love Eliza from the bottom of my heart, sir, and my dearest wish is to marry her and make her happy. Surely, God will forgive our sin if we're wed."

"This is preposterous!" Matthew Churnside looked as if he were about to explode. "Have you gone mad, you brute? Love my daughter? What impertinence! And you dare to speak of marriage? Do you imagine for one moment that I would consent to such a scheme? My only daughter married to the lowest of the low, to a family of filthy papists breeding like rabbits!"

To Henry's surprise, Jack Robertson, usually so humble and slow-witted, spoke out sharply. "There's no call to talk about my family like that, sir. We're not animals!"

Mr Churnside slumped onto a vacant stool and buried his face in his hands. A heavy silence fell over the tiny cottage, broken only by the crackling of the log fire in the grate. The Robertson family stood as still as statues, knowing their fate was hanging in the balance. Eventually, the farmer raised his head, and they all saw he had regained his composure. His expression was now grimly calm and his tone of voice measured as he turned back to Jack Robertson.

"Jack, I have no wish to see you or your bairns turned out of your home to starve on the roads in winter. You, and your father before you, have served my family well. And it's plain to see that you knew nothing of your son's depraved conduct..."

"No sir, he knew nowt," interjected Henry quickly.

Matthew Churnside rounded on Henry in annoyance. "Shut your mouth, lad, and don't open it again in my presence!" He made a visible effort to control his nerves as he reverted to Jack. "So I will allow you to retain your position at Dunstan Farm, providing you agree to my terms..." Jack Robertson breathed a sigh of relief but waited to hear more.

The farmer adopted his sternest demeanour. "Firstly, your despicable son will leave my farm by first light tomorrow and will never return to these parts again. I never want to see him or hear his name spoken as long as I live. Secondly, he must swear by all he holds sacred never to approach Miss Churnside again, nor the child when it's born." Henry's heart sank, although he instantly understood that this harsh sentence meted out to him was the only way to save his family from eviction and disgrace.

"Thirdly, what has passed between him and my daughter will remain a secret. No one in this room will ever speak of it to a living soul. Is that absolutely clear?" Jack nodded mutely.

"Finally, my daughter will be sent north to my wife's family for the entire duration of her confinement. She will leave as soon as suitable arrangements can be made." To everyone's surprise, he suddenly turned to Agnes, casting his shrewd eyes over her stout shapeless figure. "How old is your youngest child, Mistress Robertson?"

Agnes, looking flustered, pulled her toddler protectively to her skirts. "Little Joan is just gone eighteen months, sir."

"And how old are you, woman?"

"I hardly know for sure, sir," stammered Agnes. "Seven and thirty or thereabouts, I reckon."

Mr Churnside nodded in quiet satisfaction and turned back to Jack. "Here's what I propose, Robertson. You will make it known that your wife is with child.

She will keep to the cottage as far as possible and tell everyone that her confinement is a difficult one. When Eliza's baby is born, we will bring him to you, and he will bear your name. You will raise him with your other children as if he were your own."

Agnes gasped but Jack shot her a warning look. "I understand, sir."

"I wish my grandchild to be properly fed and clothed, Robertson," the farmer added testily. "You'll have an extra two shillings a week on your wages for your... trouble. Those are my terms, Robertson, and I trust they're acceptable to you. Take it or leave it."

Jack nodded mutely. The whole family watched transfixed as the two men shook hands firmly, almost as if this strange pact were nothing more than a business transaction. Without further ado, Mr Churnside turned abruptly on his heels and left the cottage, slamming the door behind him. They heard his horse whinny as he rode off through the driving rain.

* * *

It was still raining heavily the next morning as Henry prepared to leave the rundown cottage which had been his home for the past eighteen years. His world had been turned upside down in the space of a few minutes, and he still could not quite take it all in. He felt numb and empty inside, on the verge of tears yet unable to cry.

After Mr Churnside's visit, the rest of the evening had been spent preparing for Henry's departure. When Agnes broke down in tears at the prospect of losing her eldest son, Jack had told her sharply to pull herself together. Henry had done wrong, he reminded them all, and brought shame on the family. It was only right they should all pay the price for his sin. Under the circumstances, Mr Churnside had been more than fair, allowing them to remain in his employment and even putting an extra two shillings on Jack's wages. God had already blessed them with nine children, he added, and it would be no hardship to raise another child – Henry's child – as their own.

It was decided that Henry would go south to the village of Warkworth, where Agnes's cousin, Becky, was married to the local blacksmith. Becky would surely not turn a relative away, and at least Henry would have a roof over his head while he was looking for work. "It's no more than ten miles or thereabouts to Warkworth," Agnes assured her son. "You'll be there well before it turns dark." Henry swore he would not breathe a word to Becky's family about the real reason he was leaving home; he was simply to say there was no longer enough work for them all on Dunstan Farm.

Now it was time for Henry to leave, with nothing but the clothes he was standing in. Agnes had given him half a loaf and a generous slice of home-cured ham, which he carried in a makeshift sling under his jacket to keep them dry. He hugged his younger brothers and sisters in turn, painfully aware that he would probably never see them again. He embraced Jack and Agnes, all three of them choking back their tears.

"It's all for the best, lad, believe me," murmured Jack.

It only remained for Henry to say goodbye to his grandmother. Old Phyllis was standing by the door, clutching a small bundle of sacking to her chest. "Didn't I tell

116

you no good would come of all this?" she reminded Henry sharply. But she hugged him tightly all the same and said she would pray for him every day, just as she prayed for her son John. She handed the small bundle to Henry. "I want you to have this, bonny lad, and may God keep you safe."

When Henry peered into the rough sacking, he started in surprise. Phyllis had entrusted him with her two most precious possessions: the ancient Celtic crucifix and the miniature portrait of her son John. Instinctively, he glanced at his father, who was scowling resentfully.

"That cross has been in this family for as long as anybody can remember, Mother," Jack protested. "It's only right it should come to me when you're gone, not our Henry."

"It belonged to your father," Phyllis reminded her son icily. "And God knows I'll be in me grave next to him soon enough! But for now, that cross is mine to give to whoever I choose. Surely, you don't begrudge your poor son some comfort and protection? Our Henry's going away from us all forever, and the cross will keep him from danger."

Jack said no more but could not help feeling bitterly disappointed. He had taken care of his mother all his life, yet old Phyllis had never shown him any consideration or affection. Her love and devotion had always been reserved for John, the elder brother Jack could hardly remember. And now, she was giving the crucifix and the portrait of John to Henry.

"The cross will be my greatest treasure, Grandma; I'll keep it with me always." Henry put both his hands on Phyllis's shoulders and looked down at her fondly. "But I can't let you give me the painting. I know how much it means to you, and you'd have nothing left to remind you of John."

"I'm giving it to you for a reason," replied Phyllis firmly. "You see, there's something you have to do for me. As soon as you've saved up enough money, I want you to sail to America and find your Uncle John. You can show him this painting as proof you're his nephew, and I know he'll take you under his wing. He told me America was a land of freedom and opportunity, even for poor people like us. You can make a better life for yourself there and live with your uncle until you find yourself a wife. Not an uppity little madam like that Miss Churnside, mind you, but a nice lass of your own kind!"

Henry was moved to tears. His grandmother had obviously given a great deal of thought to his future and had concocted a plan, however unrealistic, which she felt was in his best interests.

"But Grandma, Uncle John might be dead for all we know! And even if he isn't and I had enough money to travel to America, which I never will, how would I find him? Eliza showed me the map of America in Mr Churnside's atlas, and the whole of England is a tiny place compared to the size of America. Searching for Uncle John would be like looking for a needle in a haystack!"

Phyllis was undaunted. "John told me the name of the town he was to go to." She thought back frantically to the last conversation she had had with her son more than thirty years before. "It's a place called… Phila… Phila… Philadelphia!" She flashed a toothless but triumphant smile at Henry.

"Philadelphia," repeated Henry slowly. "I'll make sure to write the name on the back of the painting so as not to forget. And don't worry, I'll take good care of it, I swear."

Phyllis nodded and patted his arm affectionately. "God bless you, bonny lad, and go with you always."

Henry placed the small bundle in the sling, alongside the bread and ham. Phyllis stood aside as her eighteen-year-old grandson stepped out into the rain on that grey November morning. She waved several times at his receding figure, but Henry never looked back.

He followed the old coastal path south, pausing in spite of the inclement weather to admire the beauty of Sugar Sands and Marden Rocks. As he approached the vast expanse of Almouth Bay at low tide, the cold wind whipping his cheeks, he was suddenly filled with a strange exhilaration and sense of adventure. He continued south towards Warkworth, walking with renewed vigour and his mind buzzing with plans for the future.

Henry, true to his word, was never seen again at Dunstan Farm. Friends and neighbours were not particularly surprised when Jack put it about that Henry had taken it into his head to visit relatives in Warkworth and look for work there. Everyone knew that young men were deserting the countryside in droves to seek employment in the stone quarries or the burgeoning coal mines of southern Northumberland.

Eliza's hasty departure from Dunstan Farm aroused little interest either. Matthew Churnside simply announced to all that his wife had received bad news from her family in Bamburgh. Mrs Churnside's elderly aunt, they had heard, was seriously ill and Eliza had been summoned to nurse her. There was no saying how long she might be away, he added, as if to forestall any queries about her return home.

No one appeared to make any connection between the two departures, simply because it was unimaginable that a labourer's lad of eighteen could be linked to the accomplished young lady at Dunstan Farm. If Betsy Hunter, the Churnsides' cook, had her suspicions, she was careful to keep them to herself.

As instructed by Mr Churnside on that fateful evening, Agnes Robertson seldom ventured out of the cottage in the months that followed. Jack spread the word that his wife was expecting another child and suffering from all manner of ailments. "I'll be right glad when the bairn's born and she stops moaning and groaning and making me life a misery," he joked to a sympathetic audience of other men.

The only event to disturb the predictable pattern of life at Dunstan Farm was Phyllis Robertson's death at the ripe old age of seventy-seven. Henry's departure had affected her spirits badly, bringing back memories of her son John leaving many years earlier. On Christmas Eve, she took to her bed after supper and could not find the strength to get up again. She spent her days praying and refused to eat or drink, in spite of Jack and Agnes's constant pleading. She grew frail and weak, begging to be allowed to die in peace.

One morning at first light, Agnes bent over Phyllis's hunched figure and announced to her husband that the old woman had passed away in her sleep. They both crossed themselves and knelt down together to pray for her soul. "She's had a good run for her money," commented Jack philosophically. "We all have to go some time." He would miss his mother more than he cared to admit, even though he had never been her favourite son.

Winter turned to spring, the months slipping by uneventfully while Jack and Agnes waited apprehensively for news of Henry and Eliza's baby. Towards the end of May, Jack heard that Mrs Churnside's sick aunt in Bamburgh had passed away and that both the master and mistress had left the farm for a few days to attend the funeral. He immediately guessed the real reason for their departure.

"The baby's come," he whispered to his wife as soon as he stepped through the cottage door that evening. "They've gone to fetch the child and bring him to us."

"Maybe Miss Eliza will want to keep her baby once it's born," said Agnes speculatively. "It's unnatural for a mother to give up her child to strangers."

"We're not strangers," retorted Jack. "The bairn may be a bastard, but he's Henry's child after all. We have a duty to do the best we can for the little mite.

We'll bring him up alongside our other bairns, and he must never know he's not one of them."

"You keep on saying he this and he that... it might be a little lass for all we know!"

But Agnes was mistaken, as the Robertsons discovered a few days later when Matthew Churnside and his wife rolled up at dusk in a large horse-drawn cart. Jack noticed that Mrs Churnside was holding a tiny bundle protectively to her bosom and that the back of the cart was piled high with luggage and various personal effects. The master had evidently decided to stop first at the cottage before returning home to Dunstan Farm, intent on delivering the tiny bundle to the Robertsons before it came to anyone else's attention.

Inside the cottage, Jack and Agnes's children looked on in amazement as Mrs Churnside removed her cape and carefully placed the baby in Agnes's arms. "He's a bonny wee lad," she said softly, as if reluctant to part with her grandchild.

"There'll be no mawkish sentimentality, Mrs Churnside," barked her husband. "We both know this is the right and proper thing to do, so I'll not have you crying over spilt milk."

The Robertson children clustered around their mother to admire this puzzling new addition to the family. He was indeed a fine baby, plump and healthy, and Agnes loved him instantly. She realised that the presence of Henry's son in their family would help make up for the loss of Henry himself.

Matthew Churnside glowered menacingly at the children. "If you tell a single soul what you've seen today, you'll live to regret it. One word out of any of you and I'll have you beaten to a pulp and thrown into the poorhouse in Alnwick!" They nodded in fright and cowered behind their mother.

Mr Churnside took a seat at the head of the kitchen table and signalled to Jack to join him. "There are a number of details to be discussed," he began curtly. "Firstly, the child has already been baptised at St Aidan's church in Bamburgh. I couldn't find it in my heart to tell a lie in the house of God, so I had no alternative but to declare the true identity of both mother and father. However, Bamburgh is a good distance away, and I'm confident this matter will never reach the ears of anyone in Embleton. I've made a generous donation to St Aidan's, generous enough for the vicar to assure me of his absolute discretion."

Jack nodded sagely. "What name has been given to the child?"

"Thomas Robertson."

"Thomas!" exclaimed Jack in bewilderment. "There's never been a Thomas in our family!"

"Nor in mine," replied Matthew Churnside tersely. "That's the whole point, man. Surely, you've brains enough in that thick head of yours to understand."

Jack looked sullen but decided to overlook his master's sharp words. "You need have no fear, sir, the understanding between us is clear. The bairn must always believe I'm his father, and he must never know of his... errr, connection... to your family."

Matthew Churnside sighed pensively. "Aye, that's how it must be for the foreseeable future, Jack. But I've been thinking long and hard about this matter, praying for the Lord's guidance. I've come to the conclusion that it would be morally reprehensible on my part to disown the child completely. He's my grandson when all is said and done, and may well be the only one I'll ever have. I feel I have an obligation towards him, if only for Eliza's sake."

Jack and Agnes glanced at each other in confusion, wondering whether Mr Churnside had had a change of heart. Did he mean to acknowledge Henry's child after all?

"Here's what I propose, Robertson," went on Matthew Churnside earnestly. "The bairn will be in your charge as we agreed, at least in his infancy. But I'll keep my eye on him and make up my mind as to whether the lad shows any promise. If he does, I will take it upon myself to ensure he receives an education of sorts. I've promised as much to Eliza, but I'm not prepared to make any commitment at this stage. We must wait and see whether the boy has enough Churnside blood in his veins to warrant my attention."

Jack felt annoyed at Mr Churnside's high-handed attitude but was in no position to argue. It was in the master's power to throw them all off the farm whenever he chose. The shameful prospect of his family roaming the countryside, destitute and starving, was one to be avoided at all costs.

"Aye, sir," he murmured meekly. "But won't Miss Churnside want to have a say as to what's best for the bairn, she being his mother and all?"

"Miss Churnside has entrusted me with any decision which may or may not be made with regard to Thomas's future." Matthew Churnside spoke sharply but avoided looking directly at Jack. "There's something else you need to be informed of, Robertson. My daughter is to be wed in Bamburgh next week."

Jack and Agnes gasped. Eliza getting married barely two weeks after giving birth to Henry's child! And who could the husband possibly be? What man would be prepared to take on a fallen woman like Eliza?

"You're not acquainted with her future husband, Jack, nor will you be," Matthew Churnside went on firmly. "Suffice to say that he is a professional gentleman of learning and distinction, an elder in our assembly. He has recently accepted an important position in Edinburgh and will take up residence there with Eliza immediately after the wedding. Under the circumstances, I can only be grateful that such a respectable man, in a true spirit of Christian forgiveness, would consider marrying my daughter despite the mortal sin she has committed. However, he has only agreed to do so on condition the child be banished from his sight and never spoken of again. So there you have it, Jack. Eliza has sworn never to see her son as long as she lives, and any decision regarding his future is mine and mine alone."

A heavy silence followed these chilling words. *Poor little Tom,* thought Agnes, as she gazed tenderly at the baby sleeping so peacefully in her arms. Little did he know how much strife and heartbreak he had already caused in his brief existence… Henry forced to leave home in disgrace, Eliza married off to a man she didn't love, and neither of them permitted to love and care for their child. She looked up and was surprised to find Mrs Churnside looking at her with a wistful expression. The two women exchanged a sympathetic smile, united in an understanding which their menfolk could never share.

Nick and Jenny (6)

Nick narrowed his eyes as he scrolled through the documents on Jenny's iPad. "I don't get it," he said in bewilderment. "These transcripts appear to contradict each other. Nothing makes any sense."

"Only at first sight," Jenny interjected. "I started to see the light when I looked more closely at the 1841 census report for the Robertson family. You see, before that date all we genealogists have to work on are parish records and local registers. But in 1841 for the very first time, the government decided to conduct a nationwide census, and thereafter every ten years. Census reports are a treasure trove of information because they provide details about every member of a particular household – their names and addresses, when and where they were born and even better, their occupations. That's why I can tell you far more about your family history from 1841 onwards than before."

"But looking at the 1841 census for the Robertson household, everything looks perfectly normal," Nick argued. "Here they all are at Dunstan Farm. We have the head of the family, Jack Robertson – aged fifty-five – and his wife Agnes, followed by the names of their numerous offspring. Henry – my direct ancestor – doesn't appear on it, but it's hardly surprising he didn't live under the same roof as his parents in 1841. He would have been over thirty by then, with a family of his own."

"Quite," agreed Jenny. "Henry actually appears on the 1841 census here in Warkworth, which is why I brought you here. But we'll come back to Henry later."

"So what did you mean by seeing the light?"

"Well, if we go back to the Robertson household, the youngest child – Thomas Robertson, aged twelve – is declared as Jack and Agnes's son. But what puzzled me was that – unlike every other member of the family – there was no trace of his birth in the Embleton parish register. I did some research and finally found a record of his baptism ten miles to the north – in Bamburgh, as it happens. And the record quite clearly states: *Thomas Robertson, illegitimate son of Henry Robertson and Eliza Churnside.*"

Nick let out a long breath as the truth began to dawn on him. "So Jack and Agnes Robertson were passing Thomas off as their son, when in fact they were his grandparents... And Thomas, who turns out to be Henry's son, is my direct ancestor, right? Which makes me..."

"The descendant of an illegitimate line," confirmed Jenny with a smile. "Although little Tom wasn't technically a bastard, since his father acknowledged his paternity. Still, in the early nineteenth century, children born out of wedlock were rejected and stigmatised in respectable society. We think nothing of it nowadays, but in Henry and Eliza's era, people took a very different view of such matters. Extra-marital sex was tantamount to fornication, and fornication was a

122

mortal sin. It's hard for us to imagine, but a child like Tom would have been scarred for life by his birth."

"Easy to see why Jack and Agnes chose to pretend he was one of their own children, then, rather than expose him to that kind of trauma."

"Precisely," said Jenny. "And in Tom's case, his illegitimacy, if it had been made public, would have been particularly shameful and shocking. After all, his father Henry was only eighteen at the time, and Eliza Churnside—"

"Weren't the Churnsides the masters of Dunstan Farm?" interrupted Nick.

"That's right. In socio-economic terms, Henry and Eliza were worlds apart. Eliza Churnside was not only three years older than Henry, but more importantly, she was the cherished only child of a prosperous middle class farmer. Henry on the other hand was just a penniless young lad, the son of an ignorant Catholic labourer who worked for Eliza's father. The very idea of them marrying would have been unthinkable in those days. And what made matters worse – much worse – was that the Churnsides were Presbyterian. I've checked their records at the Alnwick Meeting House, so I'm sure of that. They most likely looked down on the Catholic Robertsons as both socially and morally inferior. Eliza would have been brought up very strictly, according to a puritanical code of morality. So for a respectable girl like her to be seduced – or raped for all we know – by a rough, uncouth lad like Henry..." Jenny raised her eyebrows in mock horror.

Nick looked aghast. "I certainly hope Henry didn't rape her – I prefer the seduction scenario. So if I understand you correctly, Eliza not only brought disgrace on her family but was also forbidden from marrying Henry. Still, that doesn't explain why the baby was baptised in Bamburgh?"

"Aha!" said Jenny triumphantly. "This is where I had to do a bit of detective work. I assumed that Eliza must have been banished from Dunstan Farm until the baby was born – her parents would have wanted to conceal the scandal of her pregnancy. But why did she choose Bamburgh for her confinement? Well, I checked the Churnside family history and discovered that Mrs Churnside, whose maiden name was Fenwick, was actually born in Bamburgh and still had close relatives living there. One of them must have been persuaded to take Eliza in for the duration of her pregnancy."

"My clever little Sherlock Holmes," quipped Nick, planting a kiss on her nose. "So Henry and Eliza were separated by their families until the baby was born... Wouldn't it be nice to think they were reunited later? But we know Thomas was brought up by his grandparents, so it doesn't look that way."

"No, I don't think Henry and Eliza were ever re-united. It looks as though Eliza simply washed her hands of the baby and palmed him off on Jack and Agnes. Henry was sent away in disgrace to Warkworth and – as far as I can make out from existing records – never went back to Embleton again. My guess is that the Churnsides and Robertsons came to some kind of discreet arrangement – maybe a financial one – whereby the baby would be passed off as Jack and Agnes's."

"And what became of Eliza? Was she left ruined and broken-hearted? Did she spend the rest of her life pining for her sweetheart Henry?" Nick's tone of voice was playful, although in fact he felt himself being drawn into the drama of Henry's life.

"It certainly doesn't appear so," said Jenny drily. "Judging by my records, she probably wasn't the romantic type. You see, shortly after the baby's birth, Eliza got married in Bamburgh to a man called Tobias Metcalfe. My research tells me that he was thirty years older than Eliza, a widower and a prominent local physician."

Nick's jaw dropped. "Wow, this girl certainly didn't let the grass grow under her feet! I must say I don't like the sound of Eliza Churnside and her marriage of convenience – she must have been a conniving little so-and-so. I wonder if she told her husband about the baby?"

"That's something we'll never know… And I don't think we should judge Eliza too harshly. For all we know, she might have spent the rest of her life feeling guilty and remorseful about letting her baby go. And maybe if she'd been born in today's world, she would have kept the baby and tried to make a go of it with Henry. But we have to look at their lives in context and take into account the huge social and religious pressures of the times."

"I suppose so," said Nick grudgingly. "And what became of Eliza and her rich old husband?"

"All I can tell you is that soon after they were married, Eliza and Tobias Metcalfe moved to Edinburgh. On subsequent census records, they appear as a married – but childless – couple. It's sad to think that the baby Eliza gave up was the only child she ever had. What's more, Tobias Metcalfe died only six years after the wedding, leaving Eliza a widow at twenty-six. She never remarried and died in 1860, at the age of fifty-three."

There was a long silence as Nick tried to digest the details of this strange episode in his family history. "It's so frustrating not knowing what was going on in their minds," he said at last. "We know the basic facts about what happened. We can speculate and make assumptions about the rest, but we can never get inside their heads or feel what they were feeling."

Jenny heaved a sigh. "I couldn't have put it better myself. That's the worst part of being a genealogist, I'm afraid. You can only go so far."

"It's little Tom Robertson I feel sorry for," he mused. "His mother abandoned him for the sake of respectability, while his father ran off to Warkworth and wanted nothing more to do with him. I wonder whether the poor kid ever found out who his real parents were…"

Jenny gave him the benefit of one of her enigmatic smiles. "There's every indication that he did," she said softly.

V

Tom Robertson, Christmas 1841

Night was falling fast on that bitterly cold Christmas Eve. Tom and the other quarry workers laid down their tools and set off home to their families. In spite of the freezing temperatures and icy wind, they had been working since dawn, for the days were short in winter and they were paid by the quantity of stone they managed to produce. It was lucky there had been no snow so far this winter. When a blanket of snow covered the bleak landscape of Embleton Quarry, work had to be suspended and the quarrymen's families went hungry.

Tom had been working at the quarry for almost a year now, by default rather than choice. Although old Jack was still employed at Dunstan Farm, as generations of Robertsons had been before him, many other families were being driven off the land. There was simply not enough work available for the hundreds of farm labourers swamping the market. The older Robertson boys had already left home and were now working at the nearby colliery in Shilbottle. But old Jack Robertson stubbornly refused to let Tom follow suit – "it's heathen to crawl on all fours like an animal in the bowels of the earth," he would say. Nevertheless, every penny was needed to keep the wolf from the door in the Robertson home, so Tom had been glad of the chance to earn the odd shilling or two at the quarry – the finest limestone quarry in Northumberland, as his fellow workers assured him proudly.

Tom was only twelve years old and not yet strong enough for the hard physical labour quarry work entailed, forcing the stone from the rock beds with the most rudimentary of tools. However, he made himself useful by fetching and carrying for the stonemasons, loading carts with scrap stone and other menial tasks. Several times a day, he would set off up the steep inclines with a cowhide bucket, collecting the masons' blunt tools and bringing them back to the quarry blacksmith for sharpening. It was a harsh brutal existence for a young boy, but the taciturn quarry workers always had a kind word for Tom and made sure he was seated next to the stove when they all stopped work at midday for their bait and brew.

Tom trudged wearily up the narrow lane leading to Dunstan Farm, looking forward to an extra hour in bed next morning. He had been coughing all day and prayed he would not be laid off, for there was no pay for sick workers. At any rate, the quarry would be closed for Christmas Day, to enable all the workers to attend church with their families. Tom was looking forward to celebrating Christmas mass, along with the other Catholic families in the area, at Our Lady of the Rosary Chapel in the nearby village of Ellingham. Although he was not deeply religious by nature, he took comfort in the ornate beauty of the chapel, the soft glow of the many candles, the heady scent of incense and the sonorous voice of the priest as he chanted strange words in Latin.

As he approached the entrance to the farm, Tom was startled to see Matthew Churnside there, leaning against the wide gate and puffing on a clay pipe. Why on earth was the master lurking in the gloom, as if lying in wait for him? Tom had had little to do with Mr Churnside in his short life and felt embarrassed to come across him now, covered in stone dust from head to toe and clad in his dirty moleskin jacket and iron-shod clogs.

"So there you are, Tom Robertson. I thought I'd catch you on your way home," said the farmer gruffly. "I want to have a word with you, lad. Are you going to that damned mass of yours tomorrow?"

Tom nodded, his mind racing. He wondered whether he had done something wrong or offended Mr Churnside in some way, for there could be no other reason for this odd encounter.

Matthew Churnside sighed and shook his head disapprovingly but made no comment. He had long since given up trying to convert the Catholic families in his employment to Presbyterianism. When emancipation laws had been passed twelve years earlier, giving equal rights to Roman Catholics and finally allowing them to practise their faith freely, he realised that he too must conform to the new spirit of religious tolerance in Britain. So although he was still convinced that the Robertsons and their like had strayed from the path of righteousness, he no longer tried to force his own beliefs on them.

"Come to the farmhouse after mass and we'll talk then." The farmer swung the gate open and let Tom through.

Tom did his best to sound self-assured. "Aye, sir. I'll be there, sir." He set off across the field, leaving Mr Churnside standing by the gate and feeling the farmer's eyes boring into his back as he made his way home to the cottage. Pushing the door open, his nostrils were filled with the fatty pungent smell of roast goose – a rare treat reserved for their Christmas Eve supper. Famished after the long cold hours at the quarry, Tom's mouth watered at the prospect.

Jack had just returned home himself and was sitting placidly by the fire, his muddy boots off and his legs stretched out in a relaxed pose. Now in his mid-fifties, he suffered increasingly from rheumatic pain in his joints and found it difficult to straighten his back after a hard day's labour on the farm. His wife Agnes, stout and florid, was sitting gossiping at the kitchen table with her cousin Betsy Hunter, Mr and Mrs Churnside's cook.

Tom immediately related his strange encounter with the farmer. "The master wants to speak with me tomorrow at the big house. I don't understand, Dad, what can it mean?" But instead of giving him the simple explanation he had been hoping for, Jack's face took on a wary expression.

Betsy Hunter sniggered maliciously. "By, and it's taken him long enough to get around to it!" She smirked knowingly at Tom, making him feel stupid and inadequate.

"Hold your tongue, woman!" Jack's voice rang out sharply. He got to his feet and crossed the kitchen to where Tom stood in bewilderment, putting his hands reassuringly on the boy's shoulders and smiling at him with forced jollity.

"If Mr Churnside wants to see you tomorrow, then you must do as he says, lad. There's nowt more to be said on the matter tonight, and you'll know soon enough what it's all about. It's Christmas Eve, Tom, so let's forget the master for now and get cracking on that roast goose!"

The maid showed Tom into the parlour and bobbed a curtsey to her master and mistress before retreating to the kitchen. The room was poky and dimly lit but spotlessly clean and tidy. Mr and Mrs Churnside were sitting peacefully by the fire drinking tea, the farmer with a heavy bible in his lap and his wife embroidering a linen napkin. Looking up from her work and seeing Tom, Mrs Churnside immediately gathered up her sewing and left the room without a word. She had evidently been forewarned by her husband that he wished to speak to Tom alone.

"Come in, lad, and a Merry Christmas to you," the farmer called out brusquely. "Let me have a good look at you. Come over here and turn around slowly."

Astonished by this bizarre request, Tom nevertheless did as he was told. He felt the older man studying him closely, his eyes running over Tom's bony frame, taking in his unruly mane of chestnut curls and the clear green of his eyes.

"My word!" exclaimed Mr Churnside. "There's no denying you have the look of your…" His voice trailed off and he took a sip of tea as if to assemble his thoughts. "Sit yourself down by the fire, lad, you look blue with cold." Tom was only too glad to take a seat in the rocking chair just vacated by Mrs Churnside; his cough was worse than the previous day and he was starting to feel feverish and shivery.

"I hear you've found employment at Embleton Quarry, Tom. What are your duties there?"

Tom did his best to describe his work, even more baffled. Why on earth should Mr Churnside be remotely interested in the details of his humdrum existence? "When I'm older and have mastered all the skills of the trade, I hope to be a proper stone mason, sir," he finished proudly.

The farmer's reaction was surprisingly harsh. "A quarryman! What kind of an occupation is that? Surely, you must want something better from life than working yourself into an early grave? Do you know how many men die of silicosis from all the stone dust in their lungs? And some of them are maimed for life when their limbs are crushed under heavy blocks of stone! Is this all you aspire to, lad?"

Tom was dumbfounded. What other life was he supposed to aspire to? And why should Mr Churnside care whether he worked in a quarry or not? He knew better than to be impertinent however. "There are worse things than being a quarryman, sir," he said tentatively.

Matthew Churnside frowned and pursed his lips, steeling himself for what was to come. For the past twelve years, he had been both dreading but also perversely looking forward to this moment. Eventually, he looked Tom straight in the eye and cleared his throat. "Look here, Tom, there's something I must reveal to you and there's no easy way to say it. I will therefore disclose what you must know in as few words as possible. The fact is that Jack Robertson is not your father, but your grandfather. Your real father is Henry Robertson, whom you will have thought of until now as your elder brother."

Mr Churnside's blunt words hit Tom like a sledgehammer. He could scarcely breathe, and his heart started hammering in his chest like a wild butterfly. Henry! He had heard of this elder brother of course, but Henry had left home before Tom was even born and was hardly ever mentioned in the Robertson family. Although

Tom had always sensed that a cloud of disgrace hung over this mysterious brother, there was an unspoken understanding in the family that no questions were to be asked about him. And now, Mr Churnside was telling him that Henry was his father and that everyone in his family had been lying to him since he was born!

"I don't understand, sir," he stammered. "Why is it you telling me all this and not my own..." He couldn't bring himself to pronounce the word father.

Matthew Churnside took a deep breath. "Because your other grandfather is me, Tom. Your mother was... still is... my daughter, Eliza."

Tom heard the words but could hardly take them in. It was as if this conversation were taking place with another person, someone who could not possibly be himself. His whole world had been turned upside down by a few short sentences; they seemed to hang in the air of this stuffy parlour as if they were living things.

Could his mother really be this woman, Eliza Churnside? Tom tried to think straight but could make no sense of this strange notion. He had not even known that the master had a daughter at all; she had certainly never been seen at Dunstan Farm.

"Are Henry and your daughter married, then?" he asked faintly, trying to fit the pieces of this nightmarish puzzle together.

"They most certainly are not." Mr Churnside's voice rang out stern and disapproving. "I would never have given my consent to such an unsuitable match, as you may well imagine. Eliza and your father were separated once and for all before you were born."

Tom felt his eyes welling with tears and fought hard to keep them back. "Then I'm a bastard, sir, nothing but a bastard!"

The farmer felt a surge of pity for the boy he had finally acknowledged as his grandson. "Strictly speaking, you're not a bastard, lad, for your father's name appears on the church register. You're illegitimate for sure in the eyes of the law, but not a bastard."

The technical nature of Mr Churnside's explanation was incomprehensible to Tom, for the horrific fact remained that his parents were not married. He was well aware how bastards were treated in Embleton. Scorned and despised, the very existence of such children was a constant source of shame to their families. It was unbearable for Tom, only twelve years old, to discover that he was one of them... a social outcast, unwanted and rejected by all, living proof of the sin committed by his genitors.

"What about my mother, sir? Doesn't she wish to see me?"

Matthew Churnside heard the pleading tone in the boy's voice and knew he must put an end to any illusions in that quarter. "You must put all thought of your mother from your mind, Tom. She's made it quite clear she wants nothing more to do with you. She married a highly respectable gentleman and lives many miles away in Scotland. I can assure you the last thing she wants at this stage is to be reminded of your existence."

Tom was devastated. The harsh words sank into his brain like a heavy stone and hurt him even more than the discovery of his illegitimacy. So his mother cared nothing for him and rejected him absolutely. He was a blemish on the face of the earth. It would have been better for them if he had never been born and better for him if he had never been told.

128

"And my father?"

Mr Churnside sighed heavily. "You must speak to Jack on that score, lad, but I warrant you'll hear no different from him. Henry's made no attempt to get in touch with you these past twelve years, has he?" Tom shook his head sorrowfully. "Well then, isn't that sufficient proof of his indifference? Instead of worrying your head about Henry, you should be grateful to your grandfather Robertson for giving you a home all these years."

And lying through his teeth to me all these years, thought Tom miserably. A tight knot of anger was starting to form in his stomach, and with it a steely determination to leave all this behind him. He would get out of Embleton and have nothing more to do with these adults who had tricked and betrayed him.

Tom's face betrayed every conflicting emotion churning inside him at that moment; his pinched face and burning eyes revealed only too clearly a mixture of hurt, unhappiness and resentment. Matthew Churnside wondered if he had been rather too direct and now searched for a way to comfort this boy of twelve.

"It's not as bad as it sounds, Tom," he began reassuringly. "I've come to realise that as your grandfather, I have a moral obligation to secure your future, to see to it that you have better prospects in life than being a quarryman. A proper education will provide you with such prospects, and I therefore wish to ensure you're sufficiently schooled to choose a more fitting occupation. A clerical position in Alnwick, perhaps, or even..." Mr Churnside paused as he caught Tom's startled expression but pressed on, hoping the opportunity he was being offered might make up for the devastating blow he had received earlier.

"Or even take over Dunstan Farm when I'm gone," he continued, realising as he blurted out the words that deep down this was what he truly wished for. "God knows I'm not getting any younger, and I have no son to assist me. It's true I have a nephew over in Ellingham, but there's no saying whether he'd be interested in this farm. At any rate, Tom, it's not something that needs to be decided now. We'll discuss the matter again when your education is completed."

Tom shot the farmer a hostile look, inwardly seething with rage. Matthew Churnside, who had taken no interest in him for the past twelve years, had suddenly remembered he was his grandfather. He now imagined he could simply pick Tom up like a parcel and dispatch him wherever he chose. "I'll have none of your charity, Mr Churnside," he spat out. "And I have no need of an education."

The farmer, who had expected gratitude, was taken aback by Tom's stubborn resentment. "You'll see things differently when you've had a chance to think about it, Tom. I'm offering you an opportunity any lad of your station would be overjoyed to take. Now listen to me, boy. Next month you'll be leaving for Newcastle, where I have obtained a place for you in a reputable institution. You will board at the school and remain there for the next five or six years, depending on your ability. I don't think it wise for you to come back to Embleton at all during this time... far better for you to dedicate yourself entirely to your studies."

I won't go, I won't go, thought Tom rebelliously. He said nothing however, knowing it would be useless to argue with Mr Churnside.

The farmer took Tom's silence for acquiescence. "So you see, Tom, this is a grand opportunity indeed." He cast his eyes disparagingly over Tom's ragged, dust-covered clothes. "Naturally, you'll have to be properly attired in Newcastle,

129

so my wife will take you to be measured for suitable clothing and see to any other requirements."

"Aye, sir," said Tom meekly, although he had no intention of following any part of Mr Churnside's scheme. His head was throbbing badly, and the shivering sensation in his limbs had not abated.

"Now run back home and tell Jack what's been decided, lad. He'll be right proud when he hears of my plans for you."

* * *

"You're all liars, the lot of you! I hate you, I hate you all!" yelled Tom, flinging the cottage door wide open. The entire Robertson family was crammed into the kitchen for the Christmas festivities, including Jack and Agnes's elder children who were already married and had children of their own. The chatter and laughter died away as all eyes turned to Tom standing in the doorway, his face livid with rage and his fists tightly clenched.

Jack immediately moved towards Tom, guessing what Matthew Churnside had revealed and understanding how shocked the boy must be feeling. "Now lad, don't get yourself so upset. What did the master tell you exactly?"

"You know what he told me! You all know, the lot of you! I bet everyone for miles around knows what I am... a bastard!"

Agnes leaped to her feet and attempted to give Tom a comforting hug. "It makes no difference to me, bonny lad! I've loved and cared for you as well as any mother. And I'm still your grandma, aren't I?"

Angrily, Tom pushed Agnes away and stared at the gaping faces in the room. How had he never noticed that he didn't look like them? The Robertsons were like peas in a pod, with their wiry frames, sandy-fair hair and blue eyes. It dawned on him for the first time that his own appearance was very different from theirs. How could he have been so stupid?

"I want nowt to do with any of you – you're all liars and cheats! I only want to know where my father is! I have a right to see him and hear the truth from his own lips." Tom glared accusingly at Jack and Agnes, refusing to be appeased.

"Our Henry was only seventeen when it all happened, lad," said Jack quietly. "He was turned off the farm and went to Warkworth to stay with your mother's... I mean, grandmother's cousin. We've had no word from him since he left home. We don't know if he's still in Warkworth – he could be anywhere at all, anywhere. Don't try to find him, Tom, it'll only make more trouble. If Henry had wanted to claim you as his son, he'd have found a way by now. Let sleeping dogs lie, lad, there's no use crying over spilt milk." Jack was known to be a man of few words, and this long speech astonished everyone present.

"That's for me to decide, not you!" shouted Tom, choking as his whole body was suddenly racked by a fit of coughing. The sickness in his chest and head was worse, he knew. He was burning with fever and felt as though his legs were about to give way.

Agnes put her arm around his bony shoulders. "You're in a bad way, Tom. You need to rest and get your strength back before the quarry tomorrow morning. We'll talk about all this later, when you've calmed yourself and you're feeling better. Haway over here and lie down, bonny lad."

Tom allowed himself to be led to a mattress in the corner of the room. Agnes went on talking to him soothingly as he curled up with his back to the assembled family. He had learned all he needed to know about his father's whereabouts, and a plan was gradually unfolding in his mind. He realised he had not told Jack and Agnes about Mr Churnside's scheme to send him away to school, but they would find this out for themselves once he had gone.

The prospect of finding his father shone like a beacon in Tom's fevered brain. Henry had been banished in disgrace from Embleton, but he had surely never intended to abandon his son. Tom was certain that if his father could only see him, he would love him and take him in. Father and son would be reunited at last.

* * *

Tom lay sleepless all through that Christmas night, staring into the dark and trying to suppress his coughing fits as far as possible. His face and body were burning up with fever, yet at the same time he was shivering with cold and excitement. The next morning, he forced himself by sheer willpower to rise at dawn as usual, assuring Jack and Agnes that he felt much better and quite fit enough to resume work at the quarry. Agnes prepared his bait and brew can, relieved that the boy seemed to have calmed down and was adjusting to the traumatic revelations of the previous day. The past was past and couldn't be undone, she reflected. What sense was there in stirring up painful memories and making trouble for them all?

Tom called out a casual goodbye to the Robertsons, hoping he sounded more normal than he felt, and set off across the fields towards the quarry. He had no intention of going there however, just as he had no intention of ever returning to Dunstan Farm. His entire life prior to Mr Churnside's fateful words now struck him as a cruel masquerade. Everyone had known the truth except himself, he thought bitterly. He imagined them all – Jack and Agnes, the numerous siblings who now turned out to be uncles and aunts, the dozens of neighbours and friends, the Churnsides and their servants – gossiping and sniggering about him behind his back. He flushed with shame and humiliation just thinking about it.

As soon as he reached the narrow lane at the far side of the farm, Tom turned south in the direction of Warkworth. He was unsure where Warkworth was exactly and also whether Henry was still living there. However, he thought it must be no more than a few miles down the coast and reckoned he would reach his destination before nightfall. As for what he would do if it transpired Henry had left Warkworth, he had no clear idea but hoped that someone in the village would know of his present whereabouts. He brushed aside the pangs of guilt he felt about Jack and Agnes; he could well imagine how worried and fearful they would be when they discovered he had run away from home. They would guess where he had gone of course, but Tom was confident they would not try to come after him. They would assume his quest for Henry would prove fruitless and that he would come back to Dunstan Farm in due course, his tail between his legs. *But that's where they're wrong*, thought Tom defiantly, *that's where they're wrong.*

It was a dank freezing morning, but Tom noted thankfully there was still no sign of snow. Heavy, grey clouds scudded across the sky and the icy wind from the sea howled around him, ringing in his ears and making every step forward a battle against the elements. He forced himself to walk briskly at first, trying to ignore how ill he was feeling, but after an hour or so, his pace slowed despite all his efforts. Taking shelter with his back to a dry-stone wall, he decided to sit down for a few minutes and eat his bait, hoping the food and rest would give him the renewed energy he needed to press on. He did indeed feel better with a full stomach, but his hands and feet were still numb with cold. Even his brain seemed to be numb, making it hard for him to think straight. *Perhaps it's just the fever*, thought Tom, cursing himself for falling ill just when he needed every ounce of strength.

There was hardly a cart or carriage on the road as Tom trudged slowly southwards. He realised that for the first time in his life, he was truly alone, a tiny human form in the emptiness of the dismal winter countryside. Gradually, he lost all track of time and only knew he must keep going, however exhausted and sick he felt. At times, he staggered and thought he was about to faint, but he knew he would freeze to death if he allowed himself to succumb.

What little light there was in the sombre wintry sky was already fading by the middle of the afternoon. As darkness fell over the moors, Tom started to panic; there was still no sign of Warkworth, or indeed any human habitation at all. Desperately racking his brains to devise some plan of action for the night ahead, he suddenly heard a large horse and cart clattering along the road behind him. He turned expectantly and waited for the driver to draw level, signalling for him to stop. In the dim light, he could barely make out the outline of a burly farmer, bundled to the neck in a thick winter greatcoat and a battered old hat clamped firmly over his ears.

"Am I on the right road for Warkworth?" he called out, instantly breaking into a prolonged fit of coughing. His whole body doubled up with the pain in his chest.

The farmer peered at him curiously through the gloom. "Aye, but you'll never get there tonight by the look of you. How old are you, lad?"

"Fourteen," lied Tom, pulling himself to his full height. "Can you tell me how long it'll take me to get there?"

"Well, you're not far from Alnmouth Bay at present," replied the farmer laconically. "But it's still a fair stretch to Warkworth from there. And you can't walk in the pitch dark, now can you?" Tom shook his head dismally.

"You look right poorly to me," the farmer continued brusquely. "You need a good night's rest if you ask me. What business have you in Warkworth anyway?"

"I'm going to see me father." Tom could not keep a hint of defiance from his voice.

The older man made no comment but felt a surge of pity for this poor boy, his face as pale as a ghost, roaming the countryside in the middle of winter. "Well, I reckon your father will still be there in the morning, lad. Climb in with me and I'll give you some supper. You can bed down on the kitchen floor for the night."

Tom could hardly believe his good fortune as he clambered gratefully into the cart. The gruff farmer was as good as his word, taking Tom back to his rambling old cottage and instructing his wife to 'get the lad a proper supper'. After a hearty meal, he bedded down with an old blanket on the hard kitchen floor. He tossed and turned for hours, too ill to sleep, but the embers of the fire kept the kitchen warm for most of the night and at least he had not been reduced to sleeping outside in the freezing cold. The next morning, fortified by a hunk of bread and a cup of milk still warm from one of the farmer's cows, Tom bade farewell to his kind hosts and set off on the final stage of his journey.

* * *

Still racked by coughing fits and too weak to walk at a normal pace, it took Tom longer than he had hoped to reach his destination. Nevertheless, his heart lifted when he caught sight of the magnificent castle in the distance, silhouetted against the leaden sky. Surely, this must be Warkworth! Approaching the small town, he was struck by how much larger and busier it looked than the sleepy village of Embleton. The castle itself, ancient seat of the mighty Percy family, sat majestically on top of a hill which sloped down to the winding river Coquet below. Between the castle and the river lay Castle Street and the town itself, humming and bustling with every imaginable kind of tradesman and vendor.

Tom walked slowly down the length of Castle Street, feeling suddenly nervous and wondering how he should go about finding his father. He reached a sturdy two-arched stone bridge spanning the river and gazed into its depths for a while. A constant flow of villagers crossed the bridge in both directions, but Tom could not pluck up the courage to accost any of them. Eventually, he wandered off in the direction of an ancient church of grey stone. He was starting to feel weak and dizzy again and prayed he would not pass out. He paused by the iron gate at the entrance to the graveyard, coughing and spitting out phlegm in turn.

"No beggars allowed here!" snapped an authoritative voice in his ear. "Move along, you ruffian!"

Tom looked up to see the vicar coming through the gate and slamming it firmly behind him. He was a lanky gaunt man with a thin humourless face, set now in a forbidding expression.

"I'm not begging!" protested Tom indignantly. "I'm here to visit my... a relative of mine, by the name of Henry Robertson. Do you know where I might find him, sir?"

The vicar looked the scruffy boy over from head to toe, from his unkempt matted hair to his frozen bare feet, encased in heavy clogs. "Of course I know Henry Robertson, although I can't imagine what business he could have with the likes of you. He's one of my parishioners and you may find him at the Hotspur Inn..." The vicar indicated a sizeable building at the bottom of Castle Street and strode off without another word.

So my father works in an inn, thought Tom as he crossed the busy market square towards the Hotspur. It seemed an odd occupation for his father, and even odder to imagine him as one of the vicar's parishioners. Jack and Agnes would not be happy if they knew Henry had abandoned the faith of his forefathers to join the Church of England.

The inn's courtyard was deserted, except for a sullen old man standing by the stables and puffing on a pipe. Cautiously, Tom approached the solid oak door leading into the bar and opened it a fraction. Peering through the smoke-filled gloom, he saw that the room was packed with men drinking ale, some of them sitting at small tables and playing cards. But just as he was about to go in and make enquiries, the door was yanked wide open and he found a stout arm barring his way. Another stout arm pushed him roughly back outside into the courtyard.

"What do you think you're doing here, you little bugger? Had away with you, lad, before I get me broom to your backside!" Stumbling backwards and startled out of his wits, Tom was confronted with a woman of indeterminate age, not much taller than himself and enormously fat. She had greasy black hair and an ugly bad-tempered face, with close-set brown eyes and a mean mouth.

"Sorry, missus," stammered Tom. "I'm looking for me... I mean, I would like to see Henry Robertson, if you please."

"Would you, now?" retorted the woman aggressively. "Who the hell do you think you are, you dirty rat? And what makes you think Mr Robertson wants to see you?"

Tom had not expected such a hostile reception, but for some inexplicable reason, he thought it wiser not to mention the real reason for his visit. What could he say to this fearsome woman that would induce Henry to step outside and speak to him? "I've come with an important message from his family," he ventured finally. "I must speak to Henry Robertson, and him alone."

The fat woman glared at him suspiciously and jabbed a stern finger into his chest. "Don't you dare move an inch from where you're standing, or you'll feel the back of me hand! I'll tell him you're here." As she limped back into the inn, Tom noticed that she had a clubfoot.

Tom stayed rooted to the spot for five minutes or more, desperate now to see his father at last. The old man had not moved away either and was clearly enjoying the scene. He chuckled into his pipe and his gnarled face cracked into a toothless grin. "She's an old witch, that one! Ugly as sin and a temper to drive any man to his grave!"

"Who is she?" asked Tom curiously.

"That's Sally Rutherford, lad. I've been working here for nigh on thirty years and never seen a smile cross her evil face. I reckon she's so sharp she'll cut herself one of these days. Her father owns this here inn, but he's nowt like his daughter. He's a good man, is Ben Rutherford."

"And do you know Henry Robertson?" Tom was avid for any information he could gather about his father.

"Course I do, lad. Henry's been helping Ben Rutherford run the Hotspur for a good ten years. And all set to take over the place when old Ben dies, for he's getting wed to Sally next month. He knows which side his bread's buttered on, does Henry, he's no fool. But you wouldn't catch me bedding down with that old witch for all the tea in China!"

Tom was stunned into silence. How could his father even consider marrying this fierce loud-mouthed harridan? What could possibly have induced him to take on a woman like Sally Rutherford? Five minutes turned into ten as Tom stood his ground, shivering uncontrollably in the cold. And yet he would have waited there all day if necessary, for this, he felt sure, was the most important moment in his short life.

Eventually, the door to the inn opened and a man of about thirty emerged. He was of medium height and fairly nondescript in appearance, neatly dressed in a clean white shirt, waistcoat and thick woollen breeches. His fair hair was already thinning, and his broad shoulders were hunched in a defensive attitude. There was

134

no mistaking the blue Robertson eyes, however, and Tom recognised his father instantly. He stepped eagerly towards him. "I'm…" he began.

But Henry instantly cut him short. Raising a warning finger and glancing apprehensively at the old man, he drew Tom to one side and looked at him coldly.

"I can see who you are, dammit. How the hell did you know I was here?" he hissed.

Tom was taken aback by his father's harsh words and struggled to gather his thoughts. "Well, I found out about you from Mr Churnside," he gabbled incoherently. "And then when I got here, the vicar said you were one of his parishioners. But I don't understand, are you—"

"That's all in the past," Henry interrupted. "I've no time for that papist claptrap these days." Again he cast a wary look at the old man before turning back to Tom and lowering his voice.

"Now listen to me, lad. You had no call to come here making trouble. I want nowt to do with you, and the sooner you get back to Embleton, the better. I've done well for meself in Warkworth, I'm going places here. Soon enough, I'll be master of this inn, and I'm not letting you or anybody else stop me. I may have made some mistakes in the past, but I'm not going to pay for them for the rest of me life. Make no mistake, I won't let a bairn like you get in the way of me plans. Nobody in Warkworth knows anything about… what happened all those years ago, and that's how it must stay. If Sally or her father ever found out…"

Henry's words cut into Tom's heart like a knife; they left him in no doubt of his father's feelings. He felt his whole being, body and soul, freeze over at this ultimate rejection. Ever since his Christmas Day encounter with Matthew Churnside, he had deluded himself into believing that Henry must surely love him and want to be reunited with him. Now he could no longer shield himself from the unbearable truth. He meant nothing more to Henry than a foolish mistake in his past, an embarrassing impediment to his father's personal ambitions. His mind went blank with misery and he could think of nothing to say, nothing which might change Henry's mind.

Henry delved into the pocket of his breeches, took out sixpence and thrust the coin into Tom's hand. "Take this, lad; it should be enough to get you back to the farm. Now had away with you and don't come darkening my door again." And without more ado, he turned on his heel and disappeared into the gloom of the inn.

Tom was devastated. The waves of humiliation and sheer misery coursing through his being were so powerful that it was as if his very soul had been annihilated. He stared dejectedly at the cobblestones of the courtyard, his mind numb with pain.

"Not much of a welcome, eh?" The old man ambled over to Tom and put a sympathetic arm around his thin shoulders. "I reckon you'd best go home like Henry says."

The man's kindly words had an unexpected effect on Tom. His eyes burned with rage and his whole body tensed in defiance. "I won't go home! I'll never go back there! Nobody wants me, nobody!" He looked down at the sixpence in his hand and turned to the old man. "I need to earn me keep. Please mister, is there any work to be had in these parts?"

The stable man scratched his head and pondered for a while. "They're hiring men by the dozen at Radcliffe colliery, so I hear. They say there's enough coal in that pit to keep every hearth in the country burning!"

"Where's Radcliffe, mister?" Tom asked eagerly.

"Follow the river along to the harbour at Amble – it's no more than a mile at most. Then all you have to do is keep south along the waggonway until you get to the colliery."

A tiny glimmer of hope shone in Tom's eyes. *I'm twelve years old now,* he thought, *old enough to fend for myself and make my own way in the world. I'll show them, I'll show them all!*

* * *

Later in life, Tom could never remember the last, seemingly endless, leg of his journey. By the time he arrived at Radcliffe, however, he was conscious that he was very ill indeed. The cold had seeped into every bone in his thin body, yet at the same time, he felt feverish and his limbs were trembling. His mind had ceased to function coherently, other than to force him forward step by step along the waggonway leading to the colliery. More than anything, he longed to lie down and sleep, while knowing that doing so might prove fatal in such bitterly cold weather.

Radcliffe itself was different from anywhere he had ever seen before, nightmarishly so. The gloomy grey of the winter sky hung over the colliery like a dark shroud, sucking any colour or light from the grim scene. The natural beauty of the Northumbrian countryside seemed unable to penetrate Radcliffe; coal dust permeated the air and had settled on every building and blade of grass.

It was the first time Tom had been to a pit village, and he looked up in awe at the massive engine houses flanked by two tall chimneys, the huge wheels and winding machinery. A few dozen hovels, laid out in rows and all adjoining, huddled in the shadow of the colliery; the rows were separated by narrow, foul-smelling lanes. One or two women with small children were to be seen picking their way gingerly through the mud and refuse, but for the most part the cold weather was keeping the inhabitants indoors. As for the menfolk, he guessed they were all at work underground.

Tom made his way to the colliery itself, where high iron gates barred the entrance like a prison. A notice board was affixed to the gates, announcing in large lettering: *WANTED, at Radcliffe Colliery, hewers, putters and other boys. Applications to be made to Mr W Appleby at the Colliery Office. Colliery houses now available for Workmen.* Being illiterate, Tom was unable to decipher the words but silently prayed that the thick black print above his head was to do with job vacancies.

Suddenly feeling dizzy and faint, he clutched the iron railings for support. He realised he would have to rest before going through the gate and applying for a job, for no colliery manager would hire a boy who looked so weak and sickly. *I'll sit down for a few minutes,* Tom thought, *just long enough to get my strength back.* He sank to the ground and closed his eyes.

* * *

When Tom finally awoke, he found himself lying on a hard mattress in a dark windowless room. The room was unfamiliar, and his first reaction was one of panic. Throwing back the thin blanket, he tried to jump to his feet but the effort was too much for him and he sank back groaning onto the mattress. The noise alerted the woman in the next room, and she rushed in immediately to check on Tom. She was middle-aged, wan and drably clothed, but Tom was comforted by her kindly expression as she held her hand to his brow.

"Thank the Lord, the fever's gone!" she exclaimed with a smile. "Eh, you gave us a right fright, lad. We all thought you were a goner. You've been delirious these past three days and weak as a kitten and all."

Three days! Tom could hardly believe the woman's words and struggled to recall what had happened and how he came to be here. The woman turned her head and called out to someone in the next room. "Annie! Warm some milk for the lad, he's coming to."

The kind woman continued to talk soothingly to Tom, smoothing his hair and gently patting his arm, until a girl of about his own age entered with a cup of milk. She wore a shapeless pinafore dress falling almost to her ankles and a thick brown shawl knotted tightly across her chest. She had big brown eyes and long dark hair pulled tightly away from her face. Smiling shyly at Tom, she stood waiting with the cup of milk while her mother helped Tom into a sitting position. When Tom had taken a few sips, the older woman spoke to him again, her voice gentle.

"What's your name, lad?"

"Tom Robertson," croaked Tom.

"And what were you doing at the colliery gates?"

"Looking for work, missus."

The woman heaved a sigh and held Tom's hand in hers. "Well, you were in no fit state for work, I can tell you. It was me husband and our two lads that found you after the shift. You would have frozen to death if they hadn't picked you up and carried you back here."

Tom tried to express his gratitude, but the woman barely listened to his faltering words. "Hush lad, there's no need for thanks. Just lie back and rest for now. You can talk to me husband when you get your strength back."

Within three days, Tom was well enough to get up, although he still felt feeble and shaky on his feet. His coughing fits had not abated but came at less frequent intervals. He discovered he was in one of the back-to-back houses he had noticed on arriving in Radcliffe. The entire family was crammed into two poky rooms; the door opened directly onto the front room, which served as both kitchen and parlour, with sleeping quarters in the windowless room at the rear. The house had neither drains nor privy, but this came as no surprise to Tom for his home at Dunstan Farm lacked the same amenities.

Here in Radcliffe, however, the squalor and close proximity of so many families created an all-pervasive, unbearable stench which he had never experienced before. He thought nostalgically of the Robertsons' freestanding cottage at Dunstan Farm, surrounded by rolling green fields and a glimpse of the sea sparkling in the distance. At the farm, the air was fresh and bracing, he remembered. They were not holed up like rats, as were the inhabitants of Radcliffe. Well, all that was in the past, he reminded himself sternly; he had to look to the future now.

137

Gradually, Tom got to know the family who had taken him in and saved his life. The master of the house was George Armstrong, a big burly man of about forty with massive shoulders and strong sinewy arms; it was his wife Hannah who had cared for Tom throughout his sickness. There were three children in the Armstrong family. The two eldest boys, Dan and Bobby, were two or three years older than Tom and already working at the colliery alongside their father. Eleven-year-old Annie was clearly her father's favourite however, and George always had a smile and a hug for her when the men of the family came home after their shift.

It was through Annie that Tom learned there had been three younger children in the Armstrong family – a boy of ten and two little girls – until the previous summer when they had died in one of the recurring cholera epidemics at Radcliffe. "Dad says it's the filthy water from the Bondicarr burn that gave them the sickness," she told Tom sadly. "He says the pit owners couldn't care less whether we live or die."

Tom waited until the following Sunday – the only day the men were not at work – to approach George Armstrong on the subject of a job at the colliery.

"Are you sure you're strong enough to go down the pit, lad?" enquired George sympathetically. "You still look right poorly to me."

"I'm as right as rain now," lied Tom. "And I can't keep taking food from your table like this. You've been so kind to me, and I want to pay you back."

"How old are you, Tom?"

"Twelve."

"Well, you're too young to sign the Bond by yourself. You'll need your father to come to the colliery and give his permission."

This was a problem Tom had not anticipated, but his mind worked quickly to find a way around it. He had resolved to put his past behind him and was therefore unwilling to confide in George. If the older man found out he had run away from his home in Embleton and that his father lived only two or three miles away in Warkworth, he would send him packing immediately.

"I'm all alone in the world," he blurted out finally. "My family are all dead and buried. They died…" He remembered his conversation with Annie earlier that week. "They died of the cholera."

George frowned and gave him a shrewd look. He was not entirely convinced Tom was speaking the truth, but the boy was evidently desperate to escape from someone or something in his past. Who knows what suffering the lad's had to endure, he thought. He felt a surge of pity for him, and something else besides. Tom's youthful vulnerability reminded him of the son he had loved so dearly, the son he had watched die in agony only a few short months before.

"Right, then," he said decisively. "I'll tell you what we'll do, Tom. Tomorrow morning, I'll take you to see the overman, Mr Appleby, at the pit. I'll say you're me nephew come down from the north and that you'll be lodging in my house. After all, you'll have to live somewhere, won't you? You can stay with us and hand over your pay, just like me other lads, for your board. How would that suit you, Tom?"

Tom's face lit up with happiness. George Armstrong was offering him a solution to all his problems, a way to start afresh and efface the heartbreak of the past from his memory. He reminded himself that no one in Radcliffe knew he was a bastard, ignored by his mother and rejected by his father. He would make sure no one ever found out.

"What's the Bond?" he enquired eagerly.

An embittered look came over George's face. "The Bond!" he spat out. "The damned Bond is our contract to work for the colliery. It's little more than a bond of slavery, for the owners set the terms and the pitmen must accept or see their families starve. When a man signs the Bond, he pledges to work for the colliery for one year... but the colliery doesn't pledge to provide him with work. If the overman thinks the men are getting ideas above their station, he can close the pit down and starve every family in Radcliffe."

"But surely you could just leave the colliery and find another job somewhere else?"

George's laugh was humourless. "That's known as absconding, lad, and any man caught breaking the Bond is sent straight to jail. There's no way out, Tom! They treat us like bloody animals, and if we dare speak out against our conditions, they evict us from our homes and bar us from working elsewhere."

Tom's heart contracted with fear, but he forced himself to look unconcerned in case the older man thought he was not up to the challenge. "I don't care! I want to go down the pit, and that's flat."

"You might feel differently this time next week," replied George grimly.

* * *

"Thomas Robertson, did you say his name was?" Mr Appleby's voice was brusque.

"Aye," said George. He and Tom stood in silence, caps in hand, while Mr Appleby carefully inscribed Tom's name on the massive colliery register. The overman was short and rotund, with a shiny red complexion and beady grey eyes.

"Place your mark here, Armstrong," he ordered curtly. George took the quill pen and signed with a cross, as did all the men at Radcliffe.

"You know the conditions for putters, Armstrong," continued Mr Appleby, obviously thinking it below his dignity to speak directly to Tom. "Fourteen hours a day Monday to Friday, nine hours on Saturday. Eleven pence a week if he brings up enough corves."

"Aye, I know the conditions all right, Mr Appleby," said George sullenly. "I was hoping you could start Tom off as a *marra* to our Bobby. That way, they'll work together and Bobby can show him the ropes."

The overman glared at George in annoyance. "That's for me to say, not you. And I'm warning you, Armstrong, I'll not stand any more impertinence from you. Don't think I don't know what you get up to in the village. I keep myself informed! You're a troublemaker, Armstrong, and you give the men dangerous ideas. Any more of it and I'll have you behind bars!"

"I hear you, Mr Appleby," said George tersely. "Thank you, Mr Appleby, I'll be off now." He bowed respectfully and steered Tom gently out of the overman's office.

* * *

At the quarry in Embleton, Tom had been used to working long hours in all weathers, but his first weeks at Radcliffe colliery were infinitely worse than anything he had experienced before in his short life. Going down the pit was like descending into the bowels of hell, a stifling nightmarish place where armies of black-faced men and young boys toiled ceaselessly in its cavernous depths. In those first bleak weeks of winter, he hardly saw the light of day, for it was dark when he started his shift and dark when he finished.

He discovered he was not the youngest worker at Radcliffe pit by any means, for boys as young as six were employed as trappers. Tom was thankful he was too old for such work, as it meant sitting alone for long hours in the darkness, operating the trap doors which were vital for the ventilation of the pit.

His job as a putter required every ounce of his physical strength. He and two other boys spent fourteen hours a day loading coal into corves, large tubs which then had to be pushed and pulled on wooden rails along the long narrow tunnels to the surface. Sometimes he was attached with a rope to the front of the corve, pulling the heavy load behind him like a beast of burden; sometimes he had to push with all his might from the rear. A token identifying the three boys was affixed to every tub, for they were paid according to the number of corves they managed to load and bring up in a day.

"You'll soon get the hang of it," Bobby kept telling him encouragingly. If Tom had not had George's younger son as his *marra*, he felt sure he would never have survived those first weeks. Bobby showed him how to navigate through the low narrow tunnels, bent almost double, without hurting his back. He warned him of the dangers which might injure or kill them at any time, in particular the dreaded firedamp explosions which occurred when the naked candles used by the miners met with foul gaseous air.

At the end of every working day, Tom was so exhausted that he could barely eat the supper Hannah prepared for them all; he wanted only to sleep. Every muscle in his body ached, and his eyes were red and sore from the coal dust and darkness. "Mam says it's always like that in the beginning, but it soon goes," pronounced little Annie as she gently bathed his swollen eyelids in warm water. She squeezed his hand comfortingly and planted a kiss on his brow.

Tom soon realised that George Armstrong was a man to be reckoned with in Radcliffe. The other miners looked up to him and asked his advice when they needed support at the colliery. George was acknowledged by all, including the colliery management, to be one of the best hewers at the pit, using both skill and strength to undercut and dislodge coal from even the most difficult seam. Tom watched him labouring at the coal face in every imaginable position – standing, sitting, kneeling, crouching and even lying on his side.

Considering that hewers were paid by the quantity of coal they produced, George should have been one of the best-paid pitmen at the colliery, yet he seldom earned more at the end of the week than any of the other men. On Saturdays, when he came off his shift weary to the bone and handed his meagre pay over to Hannah, he would rant and rage at the injustice of his situation.

"Appleby and the *keekers* have got it in for me!" he would complain, banging his fist on the kitchen table. "They've branded me as a trouble-maker because I stand up for the men to the management. So what do they damn well do? They find fault with nearly all me corves at the laying-out. They take shillings off me pay every week, and there's nothing I can do about it because I'm chained to the bloody colliery with that damned Bond!" A hushed silence would follow these tirades, while Hannah made him a cup of tea and tried to calm his nerves. Eventually, George would storm out of the house, slamming the door in his wake, for a pint or two of ale with the other men at the Radcliffe Arms.

At twelve years old, Tom didn't dare question George, but Bobby was only too eager to explain how the system worked. "The problem is the laying-out," he began. "When the corves of coal get pulled to the surface, every one of them is inspected by a *keeker*. The corve has to be full right to the top, otherwise they forfeit sixpence from the hewer's pay. But Dad says the lighting in the tunnels is so dim that the men can't always see properly and there might be a tiny corner of the tub less full than the rest. It's the same if the *keeker* finds any shale or stones in the corve – he docks sixpence from the pitman's pay. Dad's sure they look out for his token on the corves and deliberately find fault with his work so as to cut his wages. Mr Appleby's got him down as an agitator, you see."

"What's that?" Tom asked, his eyes as round as saucers.

"An agitator is what the management calls men who stand up for their rights," Bobby replied stoutly. "There's more goes on at the Radcliffe Arms than drinking ale, you know. Dad and some of the other men have started a movement to defend the workers. Sometimes they go to Amble on Sundays to meet with miners from other collieries. They've formed a union to demand the abolition of the Bond and better working conditions for every pitman in Northumberland. You'll see, Tom, things will change for the better if all the miners unite together."

The months slipped by however with no improvement in sight for the colliery workers. Occasionally, Tom wondered how he managed to survive the harsh treatment, the backbreaking labour and squalid poverty of his life at Radcliffe. Yet never before had he felt such a sense of belonging, as if he were a tiny piece of an organic whole. It wasn't simply that he was grateful to the Armstrongs for taking him in. He actually felt part of their family; with George and Hannah he was surrounded by the same easy warmth and affection he had known at Dunstan Farm. He also felt part of a larger family – the tightly knit mining community of Radcliffe.

* * *

Sunday was the day everyone in the village looked forward to, the one day of the week when the men and boys escaped the stifling darkness of the pit. Many of the Radcliffe families walked to Amble to attend church service in the morning, but the Armstrongs and a growing number of others did not. Tom, brought up in the unquestioning Catholic faith of the Robertson household, was secretly shocked by George's scathing remarks about religion.

"Religion suits the rich folk all right, but it keeps men like us in poverty! The preacher tells us to be meek and mild, to know our place in the world and not try to rise above it. Blessed are the poor, the Bible says, for theirs is the Kingdom of God. Aye, us poor folk are sure to go to heaven when we're dead, so they tell us, but what proof do we have there's a heaven at all? And how come the rich aren't worried about not getting to heaven themselves? They're happy enough to keep their money and finery and leave us to wallow in filth like pigs."

"Surely, it's blasphemous to talk like that," ventured Tom, thankful that he had never confided anything of his Catholic past to George.

"Blasphemous is a word the rich use to prevent a man from using his brain. We're told God is merciful, Tom, and that He will answer our prayers. But if this is so, why does God not intervene to end the evils and injustices the poor folk in this hellhole must endure? A hellhole where men are treated like beasts of burden, coughing their guts out day after day down the pit, with nothing to hope for but an early grave! A hellhole where the bairns drop dead like flies from the cholera… aye, and the ones who survive are so worn out from their work that they barely have the strength to lift a spoon to their mouths! No Tom, believe me, there's no merciful God up there listening to the poor man's prayers. What has God ever done for the likes of us? We must help ourselves, lad, that's the only way!"

The more Tom thought about George's radical views, the more logical they sounded. He came to no definite conclusions, but his interest in George's political activities grew in the same measure as his faith waned. In one way, it was a relief not to attend church service on Sundays, for it left more time to sleep and rest after his arduous week's work as a putter.

Most Sundays, the Armstrong family walked along the waggonway to Amble, to visit George and Hannah's numerous relatives there. The waggonway was deserted on Sundays, in marked contrast to the other six days of the week when packhorses pulled carriage after carriage of coal on its wooden rails to the harbour, for shipment to London and elsewhere. Amble itself was no longer the sleepy fishing village it had once been. The harbour had been enlarged to accommodate the dozens of vessels needed to transport coal from the local collieries, and as a result, people were flocking in from the surrounding countryside to find work there.

Tom found Amble rough and raucous compared to sleepy Embleton. Nevertheless, he revelled in the bracing sea air and spent hours strolling among the noisy jostling crowds at the harbour or roaming around the teeming streets. Sometimes he would be in the company of George's sons, or a handful of other boys and girls from Radcliffe. More often, he would manage to shake them off and escape, with Annie by his side.

There was an unspoken bond between Tom and Annie which they both recognised but never spoke of aloud. They had always been easy in each other's company, but as time passed, their friendly familiarity changed in nature. Both young people realised that their happiest moments were when they were alone together, whether simply engaged in idle banter or sharing their private hopes and dreams. Often it was so easy to guess each other's thoughts that no words needed to be uttered at all.

As they left childhood behind, Tom and Annie became inseparable. Their attachment did not go unnoticed in Radcliffe, and they were subjected to more than their share of crude jokes and lewd insinuations from the other boys and girls in the village. Tom and Annie laughed good-naturedly and continued to walk out together as usual, until eventually their friends tired of mocking them and accepted them as the village sweethearts.

On Sunday afternoons, when the weather was fine, Tom and Annie walked the short distance to the coast to admire the endless miles of wide sandy beaches at Druridge Bay. It was their private paradise, a magical place where they could forget the dreary vista of the colliery and enjoy the fresh air and spectacular views by the seashore. They would search for a sheltered spot in the dunes and bask in the warm breezy sunshine, their bare feet luxuriating in the soft sand.

Tom was never quite sure whether the rest of the Armstrong family realised how close he and Annie had grown. At home, the young couple took pains to keep their exchanges casual, and in any case, George and Hannah correctly assumed that their time together was spent innocently enough. As time passed and Tom felt new urges in his own changing body, he tried to keep his eyes away from the small breasts developing under Annie's shabby pinafore dress, the way her skirts revealed hips that were softer and more rounded than before. In spite of himself, his mind strayed to forbidden territory. He kept wondering how Annie looked naked and longed to hold her scrawny young body in his arms.

There was no chance of that in the Armstrong household however. Although all six of them slept side by side on mattresses in the small back room, the three boys slept on one side of George and Hannah, with Annie on the other side. Every night after supper, Hannah and Annie disappeared into the back room to undress, shutting the door firmly and making sure they were already in bed before the men were allowed to enter. The same strict ritual was observed in the morning in reverse. Tom's dream of seeing Annie naked would have to wait.

* * *

"Tom, why don't you ever want to walk out to Warkworth on Sundays?" Now fifteen years old, Tom and Annie were at Hadston Carrs, sitting on the flat black rocks which jutted far out into the North Sea. The salty water lapped around their feet, and the spring sunshine glinted on the long sandy stretch of Druridge Bay. Tom had rolled up his shirtsleeves, while Annie had removed her coarse linen cap to let her long dark hair blow freely in the sea breeze.

Tom had been dreading this question. The village boys and girls had invited them countless times to join them on the long walk to Warkworth. So far, Tom had always found an excuse not to go, but he was aware that Annie was puzzled by his obduracy. Yet how could he tell Annie that he would rather die than set foot again in Warkworth? How could he risk a chance encounter there with his father? Henry Robertson presumably knew nothing of his presence in Radcliffe and no doubt imagined he had long since returned to Embleton. And what if Annie discovered he was a bastard? Tom was certain she would want nothing more to do with him, and he would lose the person he loved most in the world.

He stared out to sea, pretending he had not heard her question, but Annie was persistent. "Everyone says there's no finer walk than along the Coquet River. And Warkworth has a massive ancient castle we could explore. I just don't understand why you won't take me there, Tom."

"I have me reasons, Annie, but I can't tell you. You would despise me if you knew."

"That's not fair, Tom! You know everything there is to know about me, and yet you hardly ever speak of your own life before you came to Radcliffe. Is there some secret you're keeping to yourself? Is it to do with Warkworth? Whatever it is, you should trust me enough to tell me… and you know I could never despise you, Tom, never!" Annie squeezed his hand persuasively.

143

Torn between his fear of losing her and his need to unburden himself, Tom's mind was in turmoil. "Annie, if I tell you—"

"I swear on my life I'll never repeat it to a living soul," Annie interjected solemnly.

Tom searched for the right words but could find none. "Well, the truth is… me father's in Warkworth!" he blurted out. Annie started but said nothing, waiting for him to gather his thoughts and explain in his own good time. The words did eventually come, flowing out of Tom's mouth in an unstoppable stream. He told her everything – his childhood in Embleton with Jack and Agnes at Dunstan Farm, their Catholic faith, the Presbyterian Churnsides who were their masters, Henry and Eliza's sin and its tragic consequences for them all.

"So you see, Annie," he concluded, his voice barely audible now. "Everybody lied to me for years and years, they all betrayed me. In the end, I'm nowt but a bastard and an unwanted one at that, for both me mother and father have cast me out and want nothing to do with me. And neither will you, now that I've told you the truth!"

Annie's heart filled with tenderness for the boy by her side, his face a picture of misery and despair. She seized his arm and forced him to look into her eyes. "Oh Tom, hinny, it makes no difference to me! If anything, I love you all the more for this terrible misfortune in your life. Remember you have a new family now and more than that, you have me. Tom, you must know I would do anything for you, anything at all!"

It was the first time Annie had expressed her feelings so openly, and her words moved Tom so deeply that he could not speak. He tilted her face to his and kissed her fiercely on the mouth, hugging her so tightly to his chest that she could scarcely breathe. They had exchanged shy kisses before, but this one was more intense, more meaningful by far. Tom felt his heart would burst with love for this sweet girl and her unswerving loyalty.

"Annie, we both know we were meant for each other. I'm certain God guided my steps to Radcliffe and your family so that we could be together always. If I have you by my side, I can face any hardship on this earth." Locked in each other's arms, they continued to whisper soft words of love.

"And you know, Annie," Tom reminded her, "in a few years I'll be a hewer, and then we can afford to…"

"Be married," breathed Annie. "I want to be your wife more than anything else in the world, my dear."

Tom took her hand and brought it to his lips. "We're still too young to be wed, Annie. I can't speak of this to your father yet. But you have my pledge and I yours. And mark my words, Annie…" The expression on his face darkened slightly. "There'll be no child of mine born from sin, for I know only too well the pain that comes of it. So we'll wait until we're properly wed before we… have any bairns."

Annie was about to acquiesce when Tom was suddenly seized by a protracted bout of coughing. The girl's heart contracted with pity and the familiar underlying fear she tried to ignore. "It always grieves me when you cough so badly, hinny. It's as if your sickness when you came to us never really left you. Mam says your chest is so weak you shouldn't be working down the pit at all."

Tom refused to dwell on a subject which might spoil the happiness of the day. "It's just a cough, Annie, nowt more."

* * *

That Sunday evening, George came home in high spirits from a Miners Association meeting in Amble. "Every pitman in the county is coming out on strike!" he announced jubilantly. "If we all stand united, the colliery owners will be forced to accept our demands and every man and boy will reap the benefits. Justice will be done at last, I'm sure of it!" He slammed his fist on the kitchen table, not in anger for once but in steely resolve.

A shock wave of excitement ran through every member of the Armstrong family, although there was apprehension on Hannah's face too. The miners would not be paid while they were out on strike, she knew, and how long could she continue to put food in six mouths before they all starved to death? She kept these fears to herself however, for George and the three boys were clearly thrilled by the prospect of a face-off with the unscrupulous Radcliffe management.

George explained that the miners in County Durham and Tyneside were already on strike, and the movement was spreading north like wildfire to every colliery in Northumberland. They were unanimous in their demands: the abolition of the yearly Bond, an end to excessive and unfair laying-out and a twelve-hour working day for men and boys alike. They were also calling for higher wages and the appointment of mines inspectors to improve ventilation and other safety measures. Even to George, it seemed a tall order to achieve all these goals in the short term. Still, the strike leaders hoped that by drawing attention to the miners' plight nationwide, the colliery management would have no alternative but to negotiate and yield to at least some of their demands.

"First thing tomorrow, I'm going with a few of the lads to see Mr Appleby and tell him the Radcliffe pitmen will be on strike until further notice. The other men will all stand outside with the banners." Seeing the family's baffled expression, George added proudly that sympathetic tradesmen in Amble had helped them concoct makeshift calico banners, painted over in black lettering with their demands. "We have to make sure every newspaper in the county writes about our strike."

"But what good will that do, Dad? We can't read newspapers," objected Bobby.

"No we can't, more's the pity. But rich people read them, people with schooling read them, members of Parliament read them and even Queen Victoria reads them!"

The boys burst out laughing, and George went to fetch them all a jug of ale as a special treat.

The following morning at first light, Tom and the other Radcliffe miners – well over a hundred of them – massed in the courtyard outside Mr Appleby's office with buoyant hearts and resolute faces. Tom and Bobby proudly carried a banner which they were unable to read but which they knew supported the miners' cause. George Armstrong and two other miners' delegates had just stepped inside the colliery building to inform Mr Appleby of the strike.

The two boys, standing at the forefront of the expectant crowd, could hear most of what was being said inside the office, for the spring weather was fine and the window half open. They could also see Mr Appleby's face quite plainly, and it was not a reassuring sight. The overman's expression was apoplectic with rage.

145

"How dare you come into my office with such preposterous demands?" he bellowed. "You're nowt but the scum of the earth, you and the other ignorant pigs outside!"

The three men stood their ground without flinching. "There's no call for disrespect, Mr Appleby," warned George. "We're only claiming what's right and fair, and if you hadn't refused to listen to us all these years, there wouldn't need to be a strike at all."

"Damn it! Don't think for one minute you'll get the better of me, you rabble rouser," roared the manager in menacing tones. "The owners will have you hanged for such insubordination! You'll be sorry for this, the lot of you."

"We're not afraid of your threats, Mr Appleby," said George grimly. "Well, it seems there's nothing more to be said for the present. The strike will continue until you and the pit owners give us satisfaction. Good day to you, now."

Without waiting for a response, the three men turned on their heels and strode out of the office, leaving Mr Appleby fuming at his desk. As they emerged grinning into the pale spring sunshine, every miner present threw his cap into the air and cheered. The men's exuberant chanting – "Strike! Strike!" – rang around the courtyard and could be heard in every house in Radcliffe.

* * *

The euphoric mood in the village soon faded as the weeks passed and the strike dragged on; the initial enthusiasm was fast giving way to doubt and despair. The pit owners had shut down the colliery and obstinately rejected all offers of negotiation or compromise. The inhabitants of Radcliffe were no strangers to poverty, but the hardship they endured during the strike surpassed anything they could have imagined. "We'll starve the men back to work," Mr Appleby predicted confidently.

With no wages coming in and meagre savings long since spent, the villagers battled on with empty stomachs and grim determination. For the first week or two, a handful of sympathetic tradesmen in Amble agreed to give them credit for food and provisions, but most of them – intimidated by threats from the colliery management – refused. Many of the pitmen were reduced to begging for food from relatives and friends in neighbouring villages. Others tried to earn a few pennies by roaming the countryside looking for odd jobs, or pushed handcarts around farms asking for leeks, turnips or anything else that could be had. The old and the sick, too weak and frail to withstand such deprivation, simply died.

Tom came into his own during the strike, for as a child at Dunstan Farm, he had learned how to snare rabbits and hares, bag pheasants and partridges or nose out the eggs of birds in hedges and fields. Armed only with sticks and a makeshift catapult, he would set off in the morning with Bobby on his quest and rarely came home without a killing. As soon as he spied his prey, he would lie down flat and creep stealthily through the grass, raising his head at intervals. Then at the crucial moment, before the unsuspecting animal had time to take flight, he would stretch the catapult and let fly.

"Without our Tom, there'd be no food on the table tonight," Hannah would declare.

"He's a grand lad and that's a fact," agreed George with a wry smile. George himself was often away in Amble; his brother Joe was a fisherman, and when George helped him unload his catch at the harbour he was always given fresh fish to take home for supper.

One evening in June as Tom and Bobby were trudging wearily through the village, taking turns to carry a sizeable hare across their shoulders, Annie rushed out of the house to meet them half way down the lane. Tom's stomach was hollow with hunger, for he had had nothing to eat since a crust of bread that morning. As Annie approached, he was struck by her pitiful appearance, as if the strike had drained all colour and life from her wan face and emaciated body.

"There's a man to see you, Tom," she announced breathlessly. "He's come on horseback and calls himself Milburn. He's in the house waiting for you."

"I know no man by that name." Tom was puzzled but hastened his step, noticing a sturdy horse standing placidly enough in front of George's house. With a mixture of curiosity and foreboding, he pushed the door open to find a gnarled old man sitting at the kitchen table, puffing on an ancient pipe. Hannah hovered anxiously behind the unexpected visitor, evidently unsure how to deal with the situation.

"By, you've grown since I last saw you," said the old man, looking Tom over calmly. "It must be all of three years now. Don't you remember me, lad? The name's Milburn, I'm the stableman at the Hotspur Arms." Tom's heart lurched violently and his body tensed. He suddenly recognised Milburn as the man who had witnessed his devastating encounter in Warkworth with his father; the stableman had watched as Henry rejected him and banished him from his sight forever.

Hannah sensed that the old man had not come to Radcliffe on a social call. Taking Annie and Bobby firmly by the arm, she announced they had to pop out on an errand in the village. Tom and the stableman found themselves face to face, alone at last.

"I didn't know whether you'd be in Radcliffe or not, but I came anyway on the off chance," continued Milburn. "You'll recall it was me told you about jobs going at the colliery. As soon as I got here, though, and said I was looking for a Tom Robertson, I found you easily enough."

Tom's mind flashed back to the scene in the courtyard at the Hotspur; he had completely forgotten about asking the stableman where he could find work in the area. "I remember you now, Mr Milburn," he said cautiously. "But I don't understand what brings you here. Does me father wish to see me?" He instantly regretted his words and cursed himself for even allowing himself to think them. Had he still not accepted his father's rejection? Was there still a foolish, tiny corner of his heart hoping against hope for Henry's love?

Milburn shook his head mournfully. "I've come with bad tidings, lad. Your father's passed away, God rest his soul."

Tom was too stunned to respond. A great swell of emotion, grief mingling with disbelief, swept through every fibre of his being. "But I... how..." he stammered inarticulately.

"Aye, I had a feeling Henry was your father that day," the stableman went on. "But I wasn't sure until Henry told me himself on his deathbed. He called for me near the end and said I was to find you after he was gone."

"But me father was still a young man," protested Tom incoherently. "How could he have died so suddenly?"

Milburn puffed on his pipe reflectively. "I reckon old Henry lost the will to live. You see, he fell off a ladder and injured his back a while ago. He was bedridden for months, could hardly move for the pain. And not a word of comfort from that ugly witch he married! You remember her, lad, Sally Rutherford the innkeeper's daughter?"

Tom nodded mutely. How could he ever forget the ferocious harridan with the clubfoot, her spiteful aggressive behaviour? He remembered how appalled he had been to think his father could marry such a woman simply for money and security.

"Oh aye, Henry was out to feather his nest, wanted his feet under the table at the Hotspur," continued Milburn dolefully. "I knew from the start he'd live to rue the day. Sally did nowt but nag him day in and day out, made his life a misery. But when he hurt his back and had to keep to his bed all those months, a change came over him. He took to the drink in a bad way – God knows how many bottles of rum he got through in a day – and wouldn't eat a thing. In the end, he fell into a kind of melancholy. He took no interest in anything, just lay there week after week drinking and saying as how he deserved to go to hell for all the bad things he'd done."

Tom was dumbstruck at Milburn's description of Henry, so unlike the terse, short-tempered man who had driven him out of the Hotspur.

"One day, he sent for me," said the stableman with a sigh. "The poor bugger was in bed, delirious with the rum and the pain in his back. He talked and talked, saying the same things over and over again. Told me he was a bad son and was sorry he'd never sent word back to his family in Embleton to tell them where he was. Told me there'd been trouble up there with some lass called Eliza when he was just a lad. Told me she was the only lass he'd ever loved. Told me he should have gone to the ends of the earth to find her after they were torn apart. Told me you were their son and that he'd treated you as no father should."

Tom's heart was thudding so painfully against his chest that he was sure it must be audible to Milburn. Despite the harsh reality of his father's death, Milburn's words seemed to loosen the tight knot of hurt in his stomach. There was an odd kind of comfort in the knowledge that in the end Henry had recognised him as his son, that he had been consumed by remorse at the end of his life. If only Henry had called for him, thought Tom with yearning, he might have been saved. He would have rushed to his bedside and assured him of his forgiveness and love.

"Can you tell me when the funeral will take place, Mr Milburn?"

"I'm sorry, lad, Henry was buried last week. I was under strict instructions from Sally Rutherford – Mrs Robertson as she is now – that you were to stay away. She didn't want a bastard son bringing disgrace on the family, she said."

Seeing the dejected look on Tom's face, the stableman instantly regretted his words. "Take heart, lad, for your father left something for you – his most precious possessions, he said." Milburn gestured to a plain wooden box on the kitchen table which Tom had been too upset to notice until now. He suddenly felt dizzy and sat down heavily, although he was unsure whether his weakness stemmed from hunger or the shock of Milburn's news.

The box contained two objects, neither of which Tom recognised. The first was an old, simply carved crucifix, obviously a relic of Henry's Catholic past. He turned the smooth wooden cross over in his hands, wondering what significance it might have had for his father. Henry had made it clear that since settling in Warkworth he had discarded the old faith in favour of the more conventional Church of England. Yet if his father valued the crucifix so highly, Tom supposed it must have been handed down through the Robertson family. Perhaps Henry had taken it with him when he left Embleton.

The other object in the box was even more puzzling. It was a miniature oil painting on a canvas frame, portraying a young man in a white shirt with the sea in the background. Tom studied the young man's face closely, wondering if it depicted his father. Aside from the fair hair and lean face so prevalent in the Robertson family, there seemed little resemblance to the Henry he had seen in Warkworth only three years ago. And surely, only rich men owned portraits and paintings? How had a man of Henry's station in life come by such a possession? He turned the canvas over and discovered lettering in a rough scrawl on the back. At that moment, he wished with all his heart that he could read and write.

"Did me father tell you anything about these things?" he asked the stableman curiously.

"Sorry, lad, I couldn't make anything out, he was that delirious towards the end. But he said over and over they were precious to him and that you must hold them dear." Milburn rose to his feet and pulled on a battered old hat. "Well, I reckon I've done me duty to old Henry and I'd best be going now. Goodbye and God bless you, Tom."

Tom watched as the stableman hauled his old frame into the saddle and rode off down the row of colliery houses. He put the crucifix and painting back into the small wooden box, his mood more pensive now. Then he carried the box carefully into the dark recesses of the back room and tucked it under his mattress. He needed time to reflect on the momentous events of the day before discussing them with anyone, even Annie.

* * *

To Tom's relief, the Armstrong family did not dwell on the stableman's visit. Sensing that he was reluctant to discuss the matter, they simply chose not to pry. As for Annie, she had no doubt Tom would confide in her in his own good time. In any case, the entire episode quickly faded into insignificance when George made his appearance late that evening.

George's drawn face and haggard expression filled them all with dread. Impatiently, he pushed away the bowl of watery soup which was all Hannah had managed to provide for supper.

"I've heard a rumour going around the Miners Association in Amble," he announced ominously. "They're going to bring blackleggers in, to mine the coal in our place! Lead miners from the Pennines, so they say." He explained to his horrified family that colliery owners and managers throughout Northumberland, determined to break up the strike and start operating the pits again, were paying lead miners handsomely to travel north and supplant the men on strike.

"You understand what this means," George warned them darkly. "The strike will peter out when the blackleggers arrive, for the men will have no option but to go back to the pit. They'll be afraid to be kicked out of their jobs if other men have been found to do the work in their stead. It grieves me to see all our suffering come to nowt. We've endured so much hardship these past few weeks, with our families wasting of hunger before our very eyes... and all to no avail!" He burrowed his face in his hands in despair.

"You mean you're calling the strike off, Dad?" asked Bobby in anguish. "You told us over and over we must be steadfast and hold out for our demands. Surely you're not giving in now?"

"The strike will end anyway when the blackleggers force the men to go back to work," said George bitterly. "Who can blame them for wanting to put food in their children's empty bellies? And they won't want to run the risk of eviction either."

Eviction! The enormity of the word filled them all with horror. Surely, the colliery managers would not turn poor hungry families out into the street? George rose to his feet and paced restlessly around the tiny room.

"Look, you may as well know, there have been hundreds of evictions already on Tyneside. The stories are enough to make your blood run cold. Whole families dragged by the neck from their homes at a moment's notice... not a shred of pity for the old, the lame, sick bairns, women with newborn babies. I don't know exactly what Appleby has up his sleeve for the Radcliffe pitmen or when the evictions will start – tomorrow, the day after, next week maybe? But I'm damned sure of one thing – I'll be at the top of his list! The colliery owners have the names of every man in the Miners Association, and they'll want to make an example of the strike leaders. The constables will be coming for us soon, breaking down our doors and arresting us, just as they've been doing all over the county."

A shiver of fear ran down their spines; none of them had imagined the strike would have such dire consequences. "But what does this mean, George?" Hannah cried out. "What's to become of us all?"

"We have to face facts," said George soberly. "I'm done for in Radcliffe. When the men go back to work, Appleby won't take me on again – me or any of the other strike leaders. And he'll make sure the men know what happens to so-called trouble makers who stand up for their rights. But I'm damned if I'm going to wait here as meek as a lamb to be thrown into jail! I'm leaving Radcliffe with a few of the other men at first light tomorrow."

A tumult of voices greeted this announcement. Where was George going? Were they going with him? How could he desert his family and leave them all to be evicted? To Hannah, the very idea of leaving Radcliffe was unthinkable. She and George had grown up in Amble, their families had lived in the area for as long as anyone could remember. This was the only place they had ever known.

George raised his hand for silence and tried to reassure them as best he could. "I know it's hard, but it won't be for long and I believe it will all turn out for the best. I've heard tell there's a new colliery just been opened a few miles north of Newcastle, in a village by the name of Burnside. They're crying out for good hewers, hiring dozens of men every week and laying on housing for them. I reckon we can all make a fresh start there if we play our cards right. Now here's what I want you to do..."

George's instructions were crisp and crystal clear. He would slip out of the village at dawn and make his way south to Burnside; the three boys were charged with protecting Hannah and Annie until such time as they were all reunited. They were to prepare themselves for eviction by loading a handcart with the bare necessities they would need when they left Radcliffe. If and when the eviction took place, they would set off for Burnside immediately, where George would hopefully have found employment and be waiting for them all. Their new home was no more than a twenty-mile walk from Radcliffe, George added encouragingly, although this piece of information did little to cheer them. The months of strike action and reduced food rations had weakened all their constitutions; Hannah wondered anxiously if her children would have the stamina to cover the distance to Burnside.

"What if we're not evicted?" put in Tom optimistically. "After all, the talk of blackleggers coming might be nowt but idle gossip. Maybe Appleby will leave us all in peace."

"I doubt it," George answered grimly. "But if you're not turned out, wait a week and then join me in Burnside anyway." He tried to dispel the heavy weight of gloom and foreboding which had descended – almost palpably – on his family. "These are hard times, but we'll come through. They won't get the better of us, we won't let them!"

Tom and Annie's eyes met in quiet understanding. Whatever this new life in Burnside might hold in store for them, they would face it together.

Nick and Jenny (7)

The terraced streets of Amble were almost deserted on that Sunday afternoon, for the crisp sunshine of the previous day had turned to huge banks of leaden grey clouds and an icy wind was blowing off the sea. The sleepy little town lay at the mouth of the Coquet, only a short distance from Warkworth, although in Nick's view it had none of Warkworth's picturesque charm. He found it hard to imagine Amble as Tom Robertson would have known it in the 1840s. Jenny had described it as a boomtown with a thriving fishing industry and a busy port which shipped coal from the local mines to London and beyond. Sadly, Amble had long since fallen into decline.

Nick and Jenny strolled hand in hand to the old harbour, where countless seagulls circled and screeched overhead and dozens of brightly painted boats bobbed on the water. The wind cut through their quilted jackets like a knife. They looked out at the choppy grey expanse of the North Sea, uplifted by the sense of space and the sharp salt air.

"What a fabulous end to the magical mystery tour," he said. "But there's so much I still need to get my head around. This whole period was clearly a major turning point in my family history."

"Yes," she agreed. "Just as it was for millions of other people all over the country. Until the nineteenth century, all the Robertsons had ever known was the old rural way of life in Northumberland. But with the dawn of the Industrial Revolution, men and their families were leaving the countryside in droves, looking for work in the mines and factories and mills. Henry Robertson was the first to leave Dunstan Farm, albeit under the cloud of Eliza Churnside's pregnancy. And he did well for himself in Warkworth, at the Hotspur Inn."

"You're a little minx, Jenny Armstrong," he teased her. "We spent last night in the very same inn where old Henry had lived and worked for years. For all we know, we might even have been sleeping in his bedroom! And you never said a word!"

"I meant to," she said archly, remembering their blissful night of lovemaking. "But we were rather busy with other things, as I recall."

She was still mulling over the strange twists and turns in Henry's life. "Remember the 1841 census record I showed you? Henry, who was still single and just over thirty at the time, is listed as a lowly servant at the Hotspur Inn. His employer, the innkeeper, was a man called Benjamin Rutherford. It looks as if Henry was quite an ambitious young man, because the following year he married Rutherford's only daughter, Sally. Quite a catch for a penniless nobody like Henry... I bet he had his sights set on taking over the inn himself after Rutherford's death."

"Maybe he genuinely loved the girl," protested Nick, preferring not to think of his ancestor as a cold, calculating upstart.

"I have my doubts," said Jenny drily. "Sally Rutherford was eight years older than Henry – an old maid pushing forty. There were no children from the marriage, and Henry himself never lived to become innkeeper at the Hotspur. He died very young, at thirty-four."

"So neither Henry nor Eliza had any more children after Tom," mused Nick. "If it hadn't been for their illegitimate son, my particular branch of the Robertson family would have died out and I…"

"Wouldn't be around to tell the tale," she finished. "The Robertson dynasty was hanging by a thread back then! So thank heavens for Tom Robertson." She slipped her arm through his and squeezed it affectionately.

"And you say Tom worked in a colliery in these parts?"

"Yes, at Radcliffe. I didn't think it was worth taking you there today – the pit has been disused for many years and there's nothing much left of the village. But I was thrilled when I found Tom's name on the 1842 Radcliffe colliery register, employed as a putter. Poor lad, he was only thirteen at the time. You know, Nick, we've all read books about the inhuman working conditions for coal miners in the Victorian era. But however much we know about their lives intellectually, we still can't come close to imagining how appalling it really was. Men and boys were worked and exploited to within an inch of their lives." Jenny paused for breath, fiercely indignant as she always was when she thought of everything their ancestors had endured.

But Nick was still baffled by the story of Tom Robertson. "Surely, it can't be just coincidence that Tom worked at Radcliffe, hardly a stone's throw from his father in Warkworth? Don't you think the poor lad must have left Dunstan Farm in search of him? And if that's the case, why did Henry – who was after all living in relative comfort at the Hotspur Inn – let the boy go through hell at the colliery instead of taking him in?"

"That's the one missing piece of the mosaic," Jenny agreed. "As far as we know, Tom and his father were never reconciled, and yet…"

"And yet?"

"Somehow the old crucifix and the painting of John Robertson were handed down, generation after generation, to you. So either Henry or Tom – and I would guess Henry – must have taken them as mementoes when they left Dunstan Farm. Which leads me to believe that at some point father and son must have communicated, otherwise the family artefacts wouldn't have ended up in Tom's possession." They pondered the various possibilities, desperately wishing they could lift the veil of mystery shrouding Henry and Tom's relationship.

"The other thing that puzzles me," Nick continued, "is how young Tom survived when he arrived at Radcliffe. After all, he was only twelve or thirteen at the time – he couldn't possibly have afforded to rent lodgings on his own."

"Aha!" Jenny exclaimed, her green eyes lighting up. She had been looking forward to this moment ever since she had met Nick. "It's time to let you in on a little secret."

"Oh no, not another secret!" he groaned. Arm in arm, they walked slowly away from the harbour and back into town.

"Remember I told you yesterday that my own family originates from this area?" she began. "The Armstrongs were fishermen by trade and lived in and around Amble for centuries. But by 1830, some of them had turned to the local collieries for employment, among them my ancestor George Armstrong. The 1841 census shows him living in Radcliffe with his wife Hannah and three surviving children. Their other children had died in infancy, probably of cholera – there were several terrible cholera epidemics in those years."

Nick's jaw dropped. "That's fascinating! Tom Robertson lived in the same village as your ancestors."

"Yes, but that's not all," Jenny went on. "You see, on the 1842 colliery register, Tom is recorded as George Armstrong's nephew."

Nick gasped in astonishment. "Tom was related to your family! And you've been keeping it from me all this time!"

"No," corrected Jenny with a meaningful look. "I can certify that Tom wasn't George Armstrong's nephew. As you can imagine, I know every nook and cranny of my family history and there's no trace of a Robertson before then. So George lied to the colliery about Tom being a relative, which suggests that he was protecting him in some way. Perhaps he simply felt sorry for the lad and took him under his wing – and very likely into his home. My guess is that during Tom's years at Radcliffe, he actually lived with George Armstrong and his family."

Nick stared at her in disbelief. "I'm gobsmacked! But how can you be so sure?"

"I'm not absolutely certain," she admitted. "But there's another clue. You see, at some point between 1842 and 1848 – I can't tell you the exact date – Tom moved with the Armstrongs to Burnside. There was a strike at Radcliffe colliery in 1844, so maybe that was what sparked the decision to migrate south. Further down the coast on Tyneside, coal mines were springing up like mushrooms. The population of Newcastle more than doubled in the first half of the 19th century, and the demand for labour in the new pit villages was huge. People were flocking to Tyneside from all over Britain to find work, not just in the mines but in metal-working, rail and shipbuilding too."

"What an adventure it must have been!" mused Nick, his imagination fired as he visualised Tom and his adopted family taking to the roads of Northumberland to seek a new life in Burnside.

"We'll never know the exact circumstances of their move to Burnside. But what we do know for sure is that they were all settled there by 1848, because that very year, there's a record of Tom's marriage in the local church – to Annie Armstrong, George's daughter. They were both still in their teens – childhood sweethearts, I suppose. And three years later, in the 1851 census, the whole clan is registered as living under the same roof in Burnside... George and Hannah Armstrong, their two unmarried sons, Tom Robertson and his wife Annie – and their two-year-old son, James." She tugged at his arm, her heart welling with emotion. "Oh Nick, isn't it wonderful?"

Nick stopped dead in his tracks as Jenny's dramatic revelation sank in. "Oh my God, this is incredible! Our families are actually related! Two of our ancestors were husband and wife... How long have you known about this?"

"Well, to be honest, I guessed who you were as soon as you told me you were Geordie Robertson's grandson. But I wanted to complete your family tree first, so as to be absolutely sure. And also…" She put her arms around his neck and kissed him lightly. "I wanted to see how our relationship would develop – or not."

He held her tightly and returned the kiss with passion, oblivious to the cold and the curious glances from passers-by on the Amble streets. He looked down at her, a flicker of amusement in his blue eyes. "So it's fair to say we're kissing cousins, then?"

Jenny gave him a flirtatious smile. "That just about sums it up. I quite like the idea, don't you?" They kissed again, finding it almost impossible to stop.

"And now," she said after a while, "the magical mystery tour is finally over. We're going to head back to Newcastle – down the same road Tom and Annie Robertson travelled to start their new life in Burnside."

"I like that idea," he said softly. "I like it very much."

Nick and Jenny (8)

It had been three long weeks since that last weekend in Northumberland, when Jenny had taken Nick on a magical mystery tour which had proved magical in more ways than one. After so many years of playing the field – flitting from one air-brained girl to the next like some half-crazed butterfly – Nick had never expected he would fall in love so easily nor so deeply. No wonder the French called the experience a *coup de foudre,* he mused. Jenny Armstrong had indeed struck him like the proverbial thunderbolt with her supremely womanly mix of beauty, charm and intelligence.

Had the thunderbolt struck by mere chance or had it been propelled by the hand of fate? After all, their love affair would never have started had it not been for the new series of *In Those Days.* Their paths would never even have crossed if his assistant Evie had not urged him to meet an unknown local historian and set up a subsequent meeting with her in a Newcastle hotel. He remembered with a smile their first brittle exchanges, two strangers warily sizing each other up; the relationship might easily have gone no further. It was Nick's discovery of his family history that had forged a special bond between them. Jenny had woven an intricate tapestry of the past, drawn him into the fascinating mosaic of his Northumbrian heritage. She had shown him that his Robertson ancestors were not simply names on a family tree but real people, men and women whose lives were embedded in some mysterious way in the deepest recesses of his being.

It was strange to think that their families had been entwined for almost two hundred years, he reflected, ever since a young lad by the name of Tom Robertson had married little Annie Armstrong. Had Tom loved Annie as intensely as he loved Jenny? He suspected that Tom and Annie, crushed by the weight of grinding poverty back in the 1840s, had had little time or energy to devote to passion. The frivolities of romantic love were luxuries they simply could not afford. And yet the invisible magnet of attraction between a man and a woman, the powerful combination of emotion and desire which bound them together, must have been the same. When Nick conjured up thoughts of Jenny in his mind's eye, he visualised more than her thick mane of tawny hair, the startling green of her eyes, the pale translucency of her skin, the way she walked and smiled. He actually sensed her being as tangibly as if she were physically present. He could feel the liquid warmth of her kisses, the velvety softness of her body, the unique scent of her skin… If Tom Robertson had truly loved Annie Armstrong, he must surely have experienced the very same feelings.

The frustration of not seeing Jenny on a daily basis was unbearable for Nick, but he simply could not spare the time to travel north. He had been working almost around the clock to prepare the forthcoming series of *In Those Days.* The mounting pressures of planning and preparing each programme in detail had prevented him from returning to Newcastle, even for a flying visit. For the last three weeks, every waking moment had been spent in the glass-partitioned offices of One Better Productions. The only upside was that falling in love seemed to have activated his creative juices, sparking a constant flow of new ideas and angles for each programme in the series. He knew now that Jenny and his father had been right to criticise the clichés and superficiality of the previous shows. This time, he was determined to inject authenticity and depth into every theme, from Tyneside collieries to Scottish crofts, from Liverpool dockyards to Cornish fisheries.

Nick glanced at his watch and saw that it was just after seven in the evening; Jenny must be home from school by now, he thought. In spite of his hectic work schedule, he and Jenny managed to communicate constantly. Several times a day, they exchanged phone calls, e-mails and text messages – some of them funny, some romantic and others unabashedly erotic. He was just about to call her when he saw a text message from Jenny flash up on his smartphone.

It took me a while but I finally cracked it! I found John Robertson! Isn't it exciting? Jenny x

Jenny was like a dog with a bone, Nick thought fondly – or more accurately, like a particularly dogged detective. She had been intrigued from the start by the portrait of the fair-haired, young man in his billowing white shirt, Nick's distant uncle who had mysteriously disappeared from the parish records in the 1790s. And if there was one thing a keen genealogist like Jenny could not bear, it was a gap in the family tree.

Very. Did he emigrate to Philadelphia as you suspected? he answered immediately.

It was another five minutes before Jenny's next message came through, as if she had been debating how to respond. *Would rather you heard it from the horse's mouth. Let me know if no message from a Robertson in the next day or two.*

Nick wondered what she meant by the horse's mouth, given the fact that John Robertson had been dead and buried for two hundred years. Did she expect John to rise from his grave and grab the nearest phone? But he had discovered on their magical mystery tour that Jenny enjoyed keeping him in suspense, so he refrained from pressing her with further questions.

* * *

Next morning, Nick almost jumped out of his skin when he opened his computer to find an e-mail from a man called John Robertson with a United States address. His eyes widened still further as he feverishly read through the message on the screen.

Hi Nick, it began with typical American familiarity.

I hope you don't mind me reaching out, but your friend Ms Armstrong and I have been corresponding for a while and she gave me your details. I was truly overwhelmed when she told me that our family founder and my namesake, John Robertson, was born in Northumberland, England. Here in Philadelphia, we're proud that our Robertson dynasty can be traced back over two centuries, although we were never able to find out where our earliest ancestor, John Robertson, had originated. Thanks to Ms Armstrong, we now know he came from Northern England and that his line goes back many generations there.

Jenny had surpassed herself this time, Nick thought admiringly. True to her word, she had actually succeeded in tracking down one of John Robertson's descendants. He read on with mounting excitement.

Ms Armstrong has informed me that John Robertson came from a poor family who worked on the land. You may not know, however, that he didn't stay poor for long when he arrived in Philadelphia in 1791. He taught himself to read and write and always put great store by education. He worked hard to achieve success and by the time he died had become one of Philadelphia's leading businessmen and foremost citizens. I guess that's what we Americans mean when we talk about the American Dream.

Nick suppressed a grimace. The American Dream was the kind of corny expression he disliked, although he had to concede that in this particular case there was some truth in it. From humble beginnings serving his wealthy masters at Dunstan Manor, John Robertson had apparently metamorphosed into a successful self-made man in the more egalitarian society of the United States.

At that time, Philadelphia was the largest port in the US and a busy trading centre. We know for sure that John started work in the employment of Mr Walter Bell, who owned a thriving textile business in the city. In 1797, he married Mr Bell's daughter, Margaret, and took over the business after Mr Bell's death. We have reliable records of the births of John and Margaret's five children. We also have a record of John's death in 1835 at the age of 65.

The Robertson family business has continued to grow and prosper ever since those early days. We gradually moved out of textiles and started to invest in property development and real estate management. I guess our common ancestor John Robertson would be proud if he could see what the Robertson Realty Corporation has become today.

Never having heard of the Robertson Realty Corporation, Nick clicked impulsively on the link to its US website. On the home page was a photo of the company's Chairman, John Robertson, the man whose e-mail he was now reading. The photo showed a bald middle-aged man with heavy jowls and several chins, wearing a dark suit and a jovially bland expression. He looked very different, Nick thought in amusement, from the good-looking young fellow in the miniature painting. On closer inspection, however, he thought he detected a slight resemblance to his own father, Alan Robertson, although the American had no beard and was several stones heavier. Was he just imagining it or could there be a genuine family likeness?

The website presented what was clearly a multi-million dollar corporation in the United States. Clicking on the section *About the Company,* Nick nearly fell off his chair as he read that *The Philadelphia-based Robertson Realty Corporation is one of the oldest family-run commercial and real estate companies in the US.* Nick could hardly take it all in. John Robertson's American descendants were now millionaire business tycoons!

The last paragraph caught his eye. *The John Robertson Foundation currently donates $250.000 in scholarships every year, to enable deserving students from under-privileged homes to study at the finest universities in the United States.*

He found himself inexplicably moved. An illiterate country lad from Northumberland who – as emphasised in the e-mail – put great store by learning had given his name to a modern-day foundation promoting higher education. Resolving to read more about the scholarship fund later, Nick closed the website and reverted to the e-mail message.

If you or Ms Armstrong ever travel to Philadelphia, my wife Ruth and I would be honoured and delighted to welcome you to our home. It would be our pleasure to present you with a copy of the American branch of the family tree, dating back to our common ancestor John Robertson.
Sincerely yours,
John Robertson IV
Chairman of the Board

Nick sat back in his swivel chair and spun it around several times, his mind whirling as fast as the chair. The missing fragment in Jenny's 18th century mosaic had been found on the other side of the Atlantic Ocean, and with it a hitherto unknown chapter in his family history! Without thinking, he grabbed his phone, hoping to catch Jenny before she set off for school. She answered immediately.

"I've just had an e-mail from the States!" he yelled in excitement. "This is incredible, Jenny!"

"Quite a turn up for the books, eh? I must say I'm pretty chuffed to have tracked our John Robertson down. And what a man he must have been, to go from rags to riches in the space of a lifetime!"

Nick suddenly remembered the last paragraph of the e-mail. "How would you like a holiday in the States this summer?" he blurted out.

Jenny laughed. "Starting with a guided tour of Philadelphia, I suppose? Oh Nick, I'd love to but…" Her voice trailed off.

"But what?"

"Summer's still months away. I miss you so much…"

He made a snap decision. "I'm coming up to Newcastle this weekend," he told her firmly.

"But I thought you were totally snowed under at the moment?" The eagerness in her voice belied the words.

"I am but I'm coming anyway. I'm going insane without you, darling. I'll let you know what time the flight gets in."

* * *

That Saturday morning, Jenny took Nick to Burnside. It was the beginning of spring, although there was still little sign of it; a cold, blustery wind was blowing and a fine drizzle fell intermittently. They stood in the middle of the village on the hump-back bridge, overlooking the rather unimpressive stream which gave Burnside its name. A continuous flow of traffic passed them on what had once been known as the Great North Road, the old coaching route from London to Edinburgh. Nick had a sudden vision of Tom Robertson arriving here with the Armstrongs in the 1840s, wearily pushing a handcart down this very road.

"I was hoping to shoot part of the Tyneside colliery programme in Burnside," he remarked disconsolately. "But there doesn't seem to be much left of a Victorian pit village. I'm not getting any sense of atmosphere."

"It does look a bit nondescript, doesn't it?" Jenny agreed. "Burnside today isn't much more than a suburb of Newcastle. The rows of back-to-back colliery houses were demolished ages ago, replaced by these sprawling council house estates. The village school, the church, even the working men's club, were all pulled down over the years. The colliery itself closed in 1975 and as you can see, everything's been cleared and grassed over as if it had never been. The old slag heaps have been turned into these green and pleasant little hills."

"No doubt it was a great improvement for the people living here," sighed Nick. "I just wish there had been a more authentic feel about the place."

"Don't worry," said Jenny reassuringly. "I can suggest several suitable locations in the area for *In Those Days*. And I've put together a whole list of interesting local people you can interview for the programme. Old people who have vivid memories of the way life in a colliery village used to be, and also descendants of mining families who take an interest in their heritage."

"Well, one of those people is going to be you," Nick said emphatically. "You've put forward so many brilliant ideas for the show… I don't know what I'd have done without you. And I think you'd be a natural on TV!"

Jenny's hand flew to her throat in panic. "You must be kidding!" she squealed. "I've never been on the telly in my life!"

"There's always a first time," he insisted. "Trust me on this one, Jenny, you'll be great."

They strolled on hand in hand through the village to the modest semi-detached house Nick always thought of as Grandma's. He did not linger long, for another family had moved in after his grandmother's death ten years previously and everything looked different. The pocket-size front lawn had been concreted over and there was a new, rather showy front door. Guessing how he felt, Jenny squeezed his hand sympathetically.

"Why don't you come and meet my Dad?" she suggested unexpectedly. "It's not far from here, and I'd really like you to see the house I was brought up in." Despite her casual air, Nick suspected she had been planning this visit all along. If she had, he was delighted. It proved that Jenny wanted him to be part of her life, to meet the people who were important to her.

He realised they were expected as soon as he walked through the kitchen door. The house was abnormally spick and span, every available surface cleared and polished to perfection. He remembered that Jenny had described her father as a rather weak, ineffectual character and guessed that one or other of her three sisters had been commandeered to do some serious housework prior to their visit.

They found Dave Armstrong sitting in the front room watching football results on television. He got to his feet with alacrity, a large amiable-looking man in a grey tracksuit and sneakers.

160

"Pleased to meet you, lad," he said, hand outstretched to shake Nick's as Jenny introduced them. He gestured towards the sofa, where a pretty woman and a little girl were sitting, both of them beaming up at him expectantly. "This is our Kim and our Emma – they've been dying to meet you. In fact, half the street would have been in here if I'd let on Nick Robertson was coming."

Jenny and her sister, Kim, promptly disappeared into the kitchen to make coffee while five-year-old Emma continued to stare at Nick in star-struck admiration. "Are you the man on that programme Mammy and Auntie Jenny watch?" she finally ventured.

"I wouldn't be surprised," Nick responded with a wink. He turned to Dave in an effort to make conversation. "Have you ever watched *In Those Days,* Mr Armstrong?"

Dave snorted derisively. "Why no, man. The only thing I watch on the telly is football. I'd never heard of you before our Jenny told me who you were. But I knew your Grandma well enough. Aye, she was a canny woman, your Grandma. Everybody around here liked her."

"Yes, my sister and I always had a great time when we came up here to stay with her," said Nick as the two women returned, bearing mugs of coffee and biscuits.

Dave looked balefully at the coffee and stood up. "Fancy something stronger, lad?" He left the room to get two cans of beer out of the fridge and handed one to Nick. "Now, about the match today – United will have a hard job winning, I reckon. What do you think, eh?"

Nick, who was not an avid football fan, was thrown off balance for a moment by the question. However, he instantly realised this was a subject dear to Dave's heart. Summoning up every scrap of knowledge in his possession, he managed to conduct a reasonably articulate conversation with Jenny's father about Newcastle United's prospects in the Premier League that season. Jenny looked on approvingly, evidently delighted that Nick's first foray into her family circle was going so well. When eventually the conversation moved on to other topics, the ice had been well and truly broken.

"You were brilliant," Jenny said warmly as they got back into her car afterwards and waved goodbye to the small group clustered at the front door. "Dad really took to you, I could tell. I know you two don't have much in common, but you found a way to connect with him and I loved that."

"And I love that you loved it," he responded lightly, leaning over to peck her on the cheek as she started the engine of her small car. "After all, didn't you tell me we're kissing cousins? The Robertsons and Armstrongs have always stuck together, haven't they? Well, that's the way I want it to stay."

* * *

Half an hour later, they were back at Jenny's house in Jesmond, intending to have a light lunch and then spend the afternoon picking up the threads of Nick's family history. Both of them were now busy in Jenny's cluttered kitchen, Nick making French dressing for a salad while Jenny beat eggs in a bowl for an omelette.

"By the way," he said casually, reaching over for the olive oil. "I wonder if you could get away for a few days at the end of May?"

"Sounds great," she responded cheerfully. "The end of May coincides with the half term holiday. What did you have in mind?"

"Well, I have an old friend from my Lycée days, Philippe, who's getting married then and has roped me in to be best man. I'd really like you to come with me to the wedding." Nick had in fact received a formal invitation several months earlier and had initially toyed with the idea of taking Klara. He hoped Jenny would not suspect as much and take things the wrong way.

Jenny's heart missed a beat. So far, she had met no one in Nick's inner circle, and she was both thrilled and daunted by the prospect. She stopped beating the eggs and swung around towards him excitedly. "I'd love to, Nick. Where's the wedding being held?"

"Oh, it's in France, on some wine estate in Saint Emilion… Château something or other. I've never met Philippe's fiancée but apparently her family are quite prominent in the wine business. Don't worry about travel arrangements – I'll book the flights to Bordeaux and hire a car for us. Philippe says they can put us up at the château – plenty of bedrooms apparently – so we won't need a hotel. After the wedding, I thought we might take off together and explore the area, maybe go further south to Biarritz. It should be fabulous at that time of year." He smiled at her expectantly.

Jenny fought back mounting panic. It was one thing to meet Nick's inner circle but quite another to take centre stage as the best man's girlfriend at what sounded like a very grand, glamorous wedding. Her heart missed another beat as she mentally rifled through her wardrobe upstairs. "Oh my God," she groaned. "I've got absolutely nothing to wear. Will it be very formal?"

"Well, I've been instructed by Philippe to dig out my morning suit and look reasonably smart on the day." He put his arms around her waist and hugged her. "And as for you, I'm sure you'll look gorgeous whatever you wear."

Jenny ignored this last comment, her mind already grappling with possible outfits for a smart spring wedding in the south of France. It was a special occasion and she wanted Nick to be proud of her. Another somewhat scary thought suddenly occurred to her. "But Nick, my French is practically non-existent. I'll be out on a limb with nobody to talk to, looking totally ridiculous…"

Nick, still holding her tightly, was kissing the soft skin of her throat and neck. "You can talk to me," he murmured softly. He drew away from her slightly so that he could look into her eyes. "Seriously, my love, you'll have plenty of people to talk to. All my Lycée friends are bi-lingual for a start, and you can chat to my parents and my sister Charlotte too."

Jenny's green eyes widened in alarm. "So your Mam and Dad are going to the wedding too?" she blurted out, her voice rising and the Geordie lilt more prominent. She realised it was not Nick's father that she dreaded meeting but his formidable mother, the ultra-stylish Nathalie Lambert. What would Maman think when she saw a frumpy, overweight maths teacher hanging onto her beloved son's arm? In her mind's eye, she could already see Nathalie examining her from head to toe, with a disapproving shrug of her bony French shoulders.

"Yes, my parents and Philippe's are great friends," Nick was telling her, apparently unaware of her nightmarish imaginings. He cupped her face gently in his hands, forcing her to meet his eyes. "Look Jenny, I'm sorry to spring this on you at such short notice, but it'll all go fantastically well, you'll see. And from now on, I want you to be part of my life, darling, to meet the people who are important to me. I just know they'll all love you as much as I do." He gave her a searching look, sensing her hesitation. "You will come to the wedding with me, won't you?"

She was about to jump off at the deep end, thought Jenny, and it was sink or swim. A French society wedding, where she would be expected to mix with Nick's high-powered cosmopolitan friends, was way out of her comfort zone. It was not that she felt inferior in any way, it was just that their codes and patterns of behaviour were wholly unfamiliar to her. How long would their love last, she wondered, when Nick finally saw her as she was – a fish out of water, a provincial nobody? She reminded herself that she had already been married to a celebrity of sorts, but Aidan was an eccentric recluse whose small group of friends were arty intellectuals. Nick's world was a million miles away from Aidan's.

And yet Jenny was well aware that she and Nick could not hide away indefinitely in their private love nest. It was one of the reasons she had introduced him to her father and sister earlier that day. Equally, she knew she would lose Nick eventually, if she shied away from getting to know the people who made up the fabric of his life when they were apart. She told herself firmly that if Nick had not been serious about their relationship, he would not have invited her to the wedding in the first place. "Oh Nick, of course I'll come," she burst out. "But I've only got two months left to shop for that dress!"

* * *

It was just like that very first evening, thought Nick as he watched Jenny bustling about the kitchen. Mugs of coffee at the ready, family tree spread out flat on the table, files and transcripts neatly stacked, laptop open… this girl certainly took her genealogy seriously.

"There's one thing I'd like to show you before we get started," Jenny began, opening the search engine on her computer and typing her request. Seconds later, several images flashed onto the screen of an imposing Victorian mansion in grey stone, complete with gables, turrets and bow windows. "This is Felton Hall," she announced meaningfully. "The place is just a couple of miles outside Burnside, but I decided it wasn't worth taking you there this morning. The Feltons sold it off years ago, and it's since been converted into a golf club."

"Felton? The name sounds familiar," he said thoughtfully. He suddenly remembered the connection. "Of course! Didn't you tell me the Robertsons worked for generations on the Felton family estate at Dunstan Manor?"

"Exactly. By a curious twist of fate, when Tom Robertson moved south to Burnside in the 1840s, he found himself with the same employer as his family back in Embleton. By that time, the Feltons had amassed a huge fortune in coal mining, and Burnside was just one of the many collieries they owned. The family was one of the driving industrial forces on Tyneside, mega-powerful and mega-wealthy – although of course their prosperity came from exploiting thousands of dirt-poor miners like Tom Robertson." Jenny grimaced in disgust and closed the image of Felton Hall on her computer.

"Yes, poor Tom was just a cog in a gigantic wheel," Nick mused. "I wonder whether he was aware of the huge transformations taking place in Victorian society, the new industrial economy springing up in cities all over Britain."

"Tom was almost certainly illiterate, so I doubt he would have phrased it quite like that," said Jenny wryly. "And he wouldn't have read this newspaper article either." She picked up a battered leather-bound book and turned to one of the pages she had earmarked. "According to this report in the Newcastle Journal, *Newcastle is making more strides in wealth, population and importance than perhaps any other city in the Empire.*"

"But did Tom know that?" Nick persisted. "After all, the fact that he was illiterate and ignorant doesn't mean he was unintelligent. On the other hand, how much time and energy did he actually have to think about the big picture, the larger issues? Maybe he and the other half-starved families in Burnside simply accepted grinding poverty as their lot. Poor sods, what grim lives they all led."

"Yes, but it wasn't all grim," Jenny argued. "It's true that pit villagers rarely set foot outside the confines of the colliery, that their mental horizons were very limited by our standards. Even so, they could take some measure of comfort and consolation in the pit village culture all around them. Burnside was a tightknit community where people stood together in good times and bad. There was a strong sense of identity and a true spirit of solidarity, if only from necessity."

"Necessity?" queried Nick.

"Absolutely. One of the reasons for the team spirit and camaraderie among miners was that their work was not only exhausting but dangerous. It was vital to pull together underground, each man relying on the others for his safety. It was the same above ground with their wives and families. There was always somebody to lend a hand, to help out in times of trouble. So I would argue that in that sense, miners like Tom were better off than factory workers in the big cities, where the social fabric was harsher and more impersonal."

"You're probably right," Nick agreed. "I must say you describe the pit village culture very well in your book." He picked up a copy of *The Rise and Fall of the Tyneside Collieries* and brandished it proudly. "You'll be glad to hear I've now read it cover to cover. Well done, darling – it's very thoroughly researched and makes absolutely fascinating reading."

Jenny felt herself blushing and quickly changed the subject. "Well, in many ways, Tom and his family were typical of the culture I set out to analyse in the book. He and Annie married very young and had a large family. They all lived cheek by jowl in the rows of squalid back-to-back houses that employers like the Feltons provided for their workforce—"

"Tom was unusual in one way, though," Nick interrupted. "He was Roman Catholic."

"He certainly had been, that's true," she acknowledged. "But then he married into the Armstrong family, who were C of E. It looks as though Tom simply abandoned his faith once he arrived in Burnside. There's no trace of a Catholic wedding or christening in the Robertson family from the 1840s onwards – not in Tom's branch at any rate."

"It's hardly surprising," Nick said reflectively. "I suppose poor Tom felt he'd suffered enough from dogma and prejudice. After all his very illegitimacy was the result of religious intolerance. His father Henry had been barred from marrying Eliza Churnside, not least because he was Catholic and she was Presbyterian."

"I'm sure that was a major factor," Jenny nodded. "And maybe Tom just wasn't a particularly religious person. By that time, religious fervour was waning in England, particularly in the working class. A survey conducted in 1850 claims that only 40% of the working class population attended church regularly."

But Nick, whose attention had turned once more to his family tree, was eager for more personal information. "Tell me more about Tom and Annie," he insisted. "I see here they had six children…"

"Yes," she responded, pulling out the relevant files and transcripts. "You're directly descended from Tom's eldest son James – known as Jim – born in 1849. The youngest child is Ellen, born in 1862, and there might well have been more children if Tom Robertson hadn't died two years later."

It was strange, thought Nick, but he felt genuinely sad, as if an old friend had just passed away. "How tragic… he was still a young man, only thirty-five. What do you think caused his death?"

Jenny sighed sympathetically. "If only we knew. Pit accidents were a common occurrence of course. Sometimes the pitman was killed outright, sometimes he was maimed or injured or died from lack of medical treatment. Also, some miners didn't have the physical stamina to survive more than a few years underground and died from sheer exhaustion and poor nutrition. Then there was lung disease, not to mention outbreaks of cholera and typhoid…"

Nick wondered which of these scourges had got the better of Tom Robertson, a man scarcely older than himself. "So Annie was left a widow with young children on her hands?"

"Yes," said Jenny, leafing through the transcripts. "God knows how they survived without a man's wage coming into the house. Jim, the eldest son, was only fifteen at the time – he couldn't possibly have earned enough to feed a family of seven. But nobody was ever left to starve in Burnside… The pit village culture of solidarity would have kicked in, with friends and relatives rallying around to help until they were back on their feet again."

"And what happened to Annie?"

Jenny showed him the record of Annie Robertson's death in 1882. "Annie was quite young herself when she died, only fifty-two. I don't think we realise how difficult life was for wives and mothers in villages like Burnside. Historians have tended to focus on the miners themselves and their terrible working conditions, but I feel sorry for the women too – constantly scrimping to feed their families on wages that were barely subsistence level."

"Yes, you describe it very well in your book." Nick turned to the chapter on colliery wives. "*The women were condemned to a life of permanent drudgery, confined to overcrowded houses with no running water or indoor plumbing.*" He flicked over to the next page. "And I was horrified to read this description of Burnside, written in the 1860s by a gentleman passing through the village… *Burnside would win a contest for abomination. The connected dwellings are stifling with foul air and so cramped that the inhabitants are forced to store coal on the bare earth under the beds. As for sanitation, the entire village makes do with six earth closets, having no doors, with ashpits attached. Consequently, the streets are ankle deep in a sea of mud and open sewage.*"

"But what other choices did these poor, illiterate women have?" said Jenny indignantly. "Marriage and children were the only option for a respectable young girl. It was vital to find a husband as soon as possible, because men were the sole breadwinners. Of course, many girls worked in factories or went into service until such time as they got married, but the pittance they earned in these occupations was just a stopgap solution until a husband came along. Very few women managed to break out of the mould… unless you count Ellen of course…"

"Ellen?" Nick's curiosity was aroused.

"Yes, Ellen Robertson – Tom and Annie's youngest child." She opened a slim file by her side.

"Well, there doesn't seem to be much of a story to tell," he remarked drily. "There are only four transcripts in your file."

"Yes, the first is the record of Ellen's birth in 1862," she said. "But the record of her death is far more interesting. Ellen managed to break out of the mould all right, but she paid a very high price for doing so…"

VI
Ellen Robertson, November 1880

Ellen rushed into the huge kitchen at Felton Hall and picked up the silver tea tray prepared by the cook.

"Get a move on, you daft numbskull!" urged Mrs Bolam irritably. "Mrs Felton rang the bell for tea ages ago, and she doesn't like to be kept waiting."

"Sorry, Mrs Bolam," murmured Ellen meekly enough but scowled as soon as her back was turned to the housekeeper. Battleaxe Bolam, as the maids referred to her, ruled over Felton Hall with a rod of iron. However hard she tried, nothing Ellen did ever seemed to meet with the housekeeper's approval.

As Ellen walked briskly along the long dark corridor of the servant quarters and then climbed the steep stairs to the drawing room, her knees almost buckled under the weight of the massive tray. As well as the heavy silver teapot, milk jug and sugar bowl, the tray was laden with delicate cups and saucers, egg and cress sandwiches cut into dainty triangles, freshly baked scones with butter and home-made jam and Mrs Felton's favourite sponge cake. It's all right for some, muttered Ellen under her breath, thinking of the plain starchy food served with monotonous regularity in the staff kitchen.

Ellen had been in service at Felton Hall ever since leaving the village school in Burnside at the age of twelve, and she had hated every minute of it. For the first five years, she had worked as a scullery maid, 'the lowest of the low' as Mrs Bolam had frequently reminded her – sixteen hours a day scrubbing floors on her hands and knees, emptying chamber pots and washing mountains of dirty dishes. Now aged eighteen, she had 'moved up' to the position of second housemaid and was finally allowed to show her face above stairs.

Although Ellen grudgingly conceded that her duties were less gruelling than before, she was still as exhausted as ever when she finally collapsed into bed at the end of her backbreaking day. And no wonder, she thought, when she was up at six every morning cleaning grates, filling heavy coal buckets, lighting fires and carrying hot water upstairs for the Felton family and their frequent guests. The only thing that alleviated the endless drudgery of her life was her friendship with Maud and Gladys, the two young maids who shared her unheated attic room at the Hall. They always managed to cheer each other up, giggling and gossiping and making fun of Battleaxe Bolam.

Mrs Felton always took tea with her sister, Mrs Charlotte Swift, on Thursday afternoons, so Ellen was not surprised to see them both engrossed in conversation as she entered the drawing room with the tea tray. It was an imposing room, decorated in the cluttered ornate style of the day and filled to bursting point with heavy Victorian furniture and expensive ornaments. The two sisters sat facing each other in high-backed brocade armchairs on either side of a blazing coal fire. After bobbing a curtsey, Ellen set about arranging the contents of the tray on the spindly mahogany side tables, trying to be as quiet and unobtrusive as possible so as not to disturb the two ladies.

Emily Felton, a haughty woman in her early fifties, emanated smug self-satisfaction from every pore of her fashionably dressed body. Her husband, Alfred Felton, was one of the wealthiest men in Northumberland; the Felton family not only owned the colliery in Burnside but a string of pits all over the county, as well as holdings in various other industries on Tyneside. Mrs Felton had urged him to purchase the ancient sprawling manor near Burnside twenty years earlier. She had promptly renamed it Felton Hall and transformed the ramshackle property into one of the finest homes in the north of England. Although the family owned other properties, including a grand town house in Newcastle and a large country estate further north in Embleton, Mrs Felton was inordinately proud of Felton Hall and spent most of her time there.

"It's all new money, though," Mrs Bolam would pronounce balefully. "Oh aye, they give themselves airs and graces but they'll never be top drawer." The housekeeper had previously been in service to 'proper gentry', and although she never failed to treat her employers with the utmost respect, she privately thought that Mr and Mrs Felton were not 'real quality'. Ellen was baffled by all the hair-splitting. Who cared whether the money was old or new when there was so much of it?

As Ellen poured tea into the rose-patterned china cups, she could not help but follow the animated conversation in the drawing room. The housekeeper had warned her repeatedly that servants were paid to be deaf, but Ellen liked to pick up the odd snippet of gossip as she went about her duties.

"I'm in such a tizzy, my dear," exclaimed Mrs Felton's sister. "We'll be moving into our new house in Jesmond next month and I'm at my wit's end! So much to do and so little time!"

Ellen already knew from previous afternoon teas that Charlotte Swift and her husband had decided to sell the family estate in Morpeth and move into a modern, purpose-built home in the fashionable Newcastle suburb of Jesmond – 'so much more convenient for Percy's offices in town', as she pointed out. Mrs Swift, having made a less advantageous match than her sister, was acutely conscious of the difference in wealth and status between them. Percy Swift was a partner in a highly successful firm of Newcastle solicitors, but the family fortune was no match for the Felton millions.

"Is something particularly troubling you, Charlotte?" enquired Mrs Felton.

"Oh, mainly the servants. Now that the children have all left home and are nicely settled, we won't need to keep such a large staff in the new house. I've already told a number of them that we're letting them go, but the problem is that some of the very servants we wish to retain are reluctant to leave Morpeth and accompany us to Jesmond. One of the housemaids announced this morning as bold as brass that she's walking out with some young man in the village and flatly refuses to move to Jesmond. It's all such a muddle, Emily, whatever shall I do?"

"Servants are so inconsiderate these days," declared Mrs Felton, shaking her head disapprovingly. "After everything we do for them, they could at least show more gratitude!"

Ellen would normally have stored this last remark in her mind, to be gleefully repeated for Maud and Gladys's amusement in the attic that evening. Today, however, she barely registered it, for she had just heard something of far greater interest. Mrs Swift needed a new housemaid in Jesmond! And Jesmond was no more than a stone's throw from the hustle and bustle of Newcastle! Although Ellen had only been to the big city twice in her life, she had loved its grand buildings and fashionable shops, the stylish carriages rattling down its wide streets, the noisy crowds thronging the pavements. And now, she glimpsed a way to be part of this urban excitement, to escape from the rigid discipline of Felton Hall and the dreary squalor of her home in Burnside. This was an opportunity she must not let pass.

"That will be all, Ellen," said Mrs Felton dismissively. Ellen realised she was still hovering – quite unnecessarily – over the tea tray and hastily retreated from the drawing room. Determined now to waylay Mrs Swift before she left Felton Hall, she slipped into the dining room and set about polishing the silver, leaving the door slightly ajar so that she could see through to the grand entrance hall. Eventually, she heard Mrs Swift emerge from the drawing room and be helped on with hat and coat by a solicitous Mrs Bolam. After escorting her courteously to the private carriage waiting at the door, the housekeeper disappeared downstairs to the servant quarters. This was Ellen's chance!

As the carriage started to pull away from the house and gather speed on the long gravel driveway, Ellen darted out of the dining room in pursuit of Mrs Swift. She ran alongside the carriage waving her arms and calling to the driver to stop. The horses were promptly reined to a halt and Mrs Swift pulled down the carriage window, a startled expression on her plump middle-aged face.

"Have I left something behind in the drawing room?"

"No, ma'am," said Ellen, slightly out of breath. Levelling her brightest smile on the woman she hoped would be her future mistress, she launched straight into the opening gambit she had prepared in her mind. "Begging your pardon, ma'am, I didn't mean to eavesdrop, but I couldn't help overhearing that you were in need of a housemaid."

Mrs Swift, although slightly taken aback by such impertinence from a servant, responded affably enough. "I am indeed in need of a housemaid, but if you're proposing to fill the position, I must decline immediately. I couldn't possibly remove you from Mrs Felton's service. Surely you're not dissatisfied here at the Hall?"

"Oh no, ma'am," lied Ellen. Racking her brains frantically for a convincing argument, she said the first thing that came into her mind. "It's just that me uncle lives in Newcastle and his wife passed away last month. He's been right poorly and he's getting on in years, so I know it would be a comfort to me Mam if I were living close by and could call on him now and then." Ellen had no such uncle but hoped her story might soften Mrs Swift's heart.

"Well, of course this puts the matter in an entirely different light." Mrs Swift pursed her lips and looked at Ellen more closely, taking in her rosy-cheeked young face and neat appearance. "What's your name, girl?"

"Ellen Robertson."

"Well, I can't promise anything, Ellen, but I'll have a word about you to my sister. What are your wages at Felton Hall?"

"Thirteen pounds a year and me room and board, ma'am."

"My present housemaid earns no more than twelve pounds," retorted Mrs Swift crisply.

"I don't mind, ma'am," interjected Ellen. "I'd do anything to… to be near me uncle."

"I see," said Mrs Swift thoughtfully and instructed the driver to continue on his way. Ellen watched the carriage until it disappeared from sight at the end of the driveway, hands behind her back and fingers firmly crossed for good luck.

***

Ellen tried hard to conceal her jubilation when Mrs Bolam informed her tersely that Mrs Felton had consented to her departure. Ellen was to take up the position of housemaid in Mrs Swift's new home in Jesmond.

"She's only agreed as a special favour to her sister," added the housekeeper. "And also because of your ailing uncle, a widower in Newcastle."

"That's right, Mrs Bolam."

The housekeeper narrowed her eyes and scrutinised Ellen suspiciously. "It's the first I've heard of this uncle," she remarked tartly.

Oh, but Ellen no longer cared whether old Battleaxe Bolam believed her or not! Her heart was bursting with happiness, she felt like waltzing around the kitchen. At last, she would be free of Mrs Bolam's iron grip, free of the grinding poverty in Burnside. Style and sophistication awaited in fashionable Jesmond! She did not delude herself that her work would be any less arduous in Mrs Swift's household, but on her days off she would be able to take the tram into town and watch the passers-by, admire the displays in the shop windows… Things were looking up for Ellen at last, and who knew what the future might hold? Perhaps some up-and-coming young man would come courting and take her dancing or to the music hall? With an effort, she forced her attention back to Mrs Bolam who was issuing instructions about the practicalities of her departure.

"So you'll be starting in your new position on January 1st, and Mrs Swift is very kindly sending her carriage over to fetch you and take you to Jesmond. You must make sure you've packed and prepared all your belongings well in advance."

"Yes, Mrs Bolam."

"And a word of warning, Ellen," concluded the housekeeper frostily. "You're a flighty young lass, if you ask me, and too clever by half. Don't be daft and let yourself be led astray, with all them wicked goings-on in Newcastle. Remember your conduct must be above reproach at all times."

Ellen bit her lip and suppressed a giggle. "Yes, Mrs Bolam," she said meekly.

***

On her next Sunday off, Ellen walked the two miles from Felton Hall to visit her family in Burnside and tell them the momentous news. Burnside was a thriving pit village, only a few miles from Newcastle and spread out on either side of the Great North Road. The mountainous pit heap and hulking colliery machinery loomed over rows and rows of identical back-to-back houses. Although there was not a blade of grass to be seen in the dreary grey terraces, the owner of the mine Mr Felton had had the whimsical idea of naming each street after a flower – roses, lilies, violets and so forth. The Robertson family lived on Lilac Street, and it was there that Ellen now hastened.

She tripped down the street in high spirits, carefully avoiding the open *middens* of mud and sewage running down the middle. She was greeted with friendly smiles and greetings on all sides, for in Burnside everyone knew everyone else. She also received a gratifying number of admiring glances from its male inhabitants. Although Ellen had always been told that vanity was a sin, she was well aware she was one of the prettiest girls in the village and could take her pick of any of the local lads. Yet to her own surprise and everyone else's, she had declined all invitations to 'walk out' so far. It was as if she were holding out for something better, as if life had more in store for her, although she had no idea what this might be. She only knew she was in no hurry to marry young and settle into the life of endless drudgery that would be her inevitable lot as a miner's wife. She only had to look at the wives and mothers of Burnside to see what would become of her – women with lined, drawn faces who looked old before they were out of their twenties, women whose bodies were worn out from relentless childbearing and household duties, women dressed in coarse, cast-off clothing. *No,* thought Ellen, *there's plenty of time before I need to choose a husband.*

It came as no surprise to Ellen to see so many male heads turn as she sauntered down Lilac Street. At eighteen, in her best Sunday jacket and ankle-length skirt, a matching bonnet pinned firmly to her head, Ellen made an attractive sight. Although she was no great beauty in the conventional sense, she was fresh-faced with rosy cheeks and sparkling blue eyes. Her long brown hair was thick and glossy, easy to pile up and style in different ways. What she lacked in height she made up for with an enviably small waist and trim figure perfectly suited to the hourglass fashions of the day. No amount of strict corseting could entirely conceal the high, rounded shape of her large breasts and curvaceous hips. Her plump thighs, she knew, were not her best feature but were in any case hidden from view by voluminous petticoats and long skirts. All in all, Ellen was well pleased with her appearance as she pushed open the door of number 24, Lilac Street.

Like all the others in Burnside, it was a drab two-room house – one up, one down – with neither ventilation, water nor privy. As she entered the dingy front room, Ellen was struck as always by the all-pervading smell of boiled bacon and cabbage. Surprisingly, only two members of the family were at home. Her mother was scouring pots at the kitchen sink, and her eldest brother Jim was sitting on a cracket stool, filling his pipe with *baccy* by the smoking coal fire. They both looked up at Ellen with a welcoming smile.

"Eeh, it's our Ellen here already," said Annie. "Want a cup of tea, hinny? And there's some leftover suet pudding an' all if you fancy it."

Ellen accepted both offers and plumped down in the one and only comfortable chair in the house – a rocking chair Jim had made with his own hands. "Are you keeping any better, Mam?" she asked, although she was not expecting a positive response. Barely fifty years old, Annie looked at least ten years older with her frail, stooped body and sparse, straggling grey hair. And no wonder, thought Ellen, after everything she's been through to keep hearth and home together all these years.

Ellen had no recollection of her father, Tom Robertson, who had passed away when she was still a baby. Her mother said he had died of the *black lung*, a terrible

171

disease which afflicted countless miners constantly exposed to the coal dust of the pit. "Poor Tom, he always had a weak chest," Annie would tell them sorrowfully. She had been left with six children on her hands, the eldest of whom, Jim, was barely fifteen at the time and still too young to earn a man's wage. How they had managed all those years Ellen hardly knew, but her mother had sacrificed herself to somehow keep food on the table for them all. When Ellen had left school at twelve to go into service at Felton Manor, the only reaction in the Robertson home had been one of relief. It was one less mouth to feed and a few extra shillings coming into the house.

But the years of grinding poverty had taken a toll on her mother's health, not only physically but mentally. Once Jim had grown up and become head of the household, Annie's vitality seemed to gradually drain away. She talked more and more of the past, looking back wistfully to the time when she and Tom were young. She recalled how they had moved south to Burnside from Radcliffe colliery in the aftermath of the Great Strike of 1844. She spoke yearningly of their long walks together on the beach at Druridge Bay, breathing in the fresh salty air. More than anything she longed to see the Northumbrian coast again, but there was little hope of that in Burnside. Although it was no more than a few miles to the seaside, there was never enough time to give up a whole day to walking there and back. "And anyway, what would we do when we got there?" Jim would ask her in bewilderment. None of them except Annie had ever seen the sea.

Annie had only two mementoes of her old life with Tom, which she kept in the bottom drawer of the huge oak dresser. Both had been handed down through Tom's family, she said with pride, although Ellen could see little appeal in either. There was a strange-looking wooden crucifix, and also a miniature portrait on canvas of an unknown young man who was apparently a Robertson. Yet whenever Annie was questioned about her late husband, she was invariably vague and unforthcoming. She would only say that Tom had not been born at Radcliffe colliery but in a place to the north by the name of Embleton. None of it was of any interest to Ellen in any case. The Robertsons were dirt poor, they had always been dirt poor and that was an end to it as far as she was concerned.

"Ted Anderson's been around again, asking after you," remarked her mother as Ellen – ravenous as usual – tucked into the suet pudding. "I just don't understand why you won't walk out with him, Ellen. He's a canny lad and he's always been sweet on you. He'll make a good husband for some lass."

"Oh Mam, give over," protested Ellen. "I've told you, I'm not interested in courting yet. I'm saving meself!"

Jim snorted loudly at this last remark. "Who are you saving yourself for – Prince Charming?" he quipped. "If you save yourself too long, all the lads in Burnside will be taken. You'll end up long in the tooth and an old maid."

"Hardly," snapped Ellen. "I'm only eighteen, for God's sake."

But Jim persisted. "What kind of a future is there skivvying all hours at Felton Hall? Waiting hand and foot on them idle buggers who wouldn't know a hard day's work if it hit them in the face?"

This was her chance to show them, thought Ellen. "As it happens," she said coolly, "I won't be at the Hall much longer. I've found meself a much better position in Jesmond. It's a lovely place near Newcastle where all the rich people live!" She told them about Mr and Mrs Swift but refrained from mentioning the story of her non-existent uncle in town.

Ellen was gratified to see that both her mother and brother were suitably impressed. "But it's all of six miles to Newcastle!" wailed Annie. "It's bad enough you being in service at Felton Hall, but if you move to Jesmond, we'll never see anything of you at all."

Ellen hugged her mother comfortingly and assured her that thanks to the new horse-drawn omnibus service, she would be able to visit them on her days off. "But not as regular as I do now, Mam," she warned. "I want to make new friends in Newcastle... and see the streets and the shops and the theatres... Eeh Mam, isn't it exciting?"

"Aye, it's exciting all right," replied Annie dubiously. "But it's dangerous for a young lass all by herself in the Toon. And easy to fall by the wayside with no father or brother to watch out for you."

"Oh Mam!" exclaimed Ellen scornfully. "You're cooped up in this house day in and day out, so what the hell do you know about dangers and falling by the wayside? You've never set foot outside of Burnside for thirty years and more!"

Annie's mouth set in a stubborn line. "Aye well, I know what I know," she muttered darkly.

Jim jabbed a warning finger in Ellen's direction. "Any more lip from you, you little madam, and you'll get a clip around the ear," he growled.

* * *

Charlotte and Percy Swift's new residence in Jesmond was everything Ellen had hoped for. Oakdene House was an imposing grey stone house set in a leafy suburban avenue, far from the ceaseless noise and polluted air of the town. Long sweeping lawns and a well-tended rockery garden fronted the property. The interior was spacious and elegant, although cluttered with the same massive furniture and abundant bric-a-brac to be found in most Victorian homes of the time. Felton Hall, with its vast draughty rooms and endless corridors, had always felt chilly even in the height of summer, so Ellen was delighted to discover that Oakdene House was both eminently functional and well heated.

The Swifts' new residence also boasted a pumped water supply, and they had spared no expense in installing the most up-to-date indoor plumbing. Ellen gawped in admiration at the luxurious copper bathtub with its ornate taps and claw feet, and the decorative washstands in every bathroom. She gasped at the sight of the mechanical water closet complete with a modern flush system. Felton Hall, despite its grandeur, had no indoor plumbing at all, and Ellen shuddered now as she remembered the sheer hard work involved in satisfying the needs of an entire household. At the Hall, she had spent hours every day filling heavy buckets of water, heating gallons and gallons of it in the kitchen, then lugging it up steep stairs and along endless corridors so that family and guests could wash and bathe. Of course, Ellen herself was not allowed to use the modern facilities at Oakdene House – her own room was almost as spartan as her previous attic accommodation. Nevertheless, she was overjoyed; from a housemaid's point of view Oakdene House was a vast improvement on Felton Hall.

The other thing she appreciated about her new position in Jesmond was the more congenial, informal atmosphere which prevailed. Mrs Swift was generally good-humoured and undemanding; her three children were all married with families of their own, and Ellen saw little of them except for the occasional visit when lunch or tea had to be prepared and served. In fact, it seemed Mrs Swift was not given to entertaining at all; she preferred going out, calling on other ladies in town or engaging in what she referred to as good works. As for Percy Swift, Ellen saw even less of him than she did of his wife. He left early each morning for his solicitor's offices in Newcastle and often dined out in various gentlemen's clubs. Master and mistress appeared to find little pleasure in each other's company, and Ellen was not surprised to discover that they slept in separate rooms.

The housekeeper at Oakdene House, Mrs Watson, was a plump motherly woman who quickly took a shine to Ellen and treated her almost like a daughter. Although she could not shorten Ellen's long hours of work nor make her duties any less arduous, she did her best to give her as much time off as she possibly could.

"You're only young once," she would say affectionately. "A bonny lass like you should be making the most of life, not stuck in this house all the hours God sends. Now then, I know for a fact that Mr and Mrs Swift are both out for the afternoon, so you can finish dusting the parlour later and have a couple of hours to yourself in the Toon. But mind you're back for supper, pet!"

Ellen was only too happy to oblige and hop on the next tram into town. Oh, she loved Newcastle! It was now one of the largest cities in England, a veritable powerhouse of industry, prosperity and affluence. With its entrepreneurial pioneering spirit, Newcastle had embraced modernity wholeheartedly. Mosley Street, Ellen was told, was the first in the world to be lit by incandescent lightbulbs. The High Level and Swing Bridges spanning the mighty River Tyne were magnificent feats of engineering admired all over the country. And the city's architects had built a neo-classical centre with some of the finest streets and most modern buildings in England.

Ellen could almost smell the energy and opportunity in the air. In spite of the dirt, the smoke and the thousands of poor people crowding its streets, there was a palpable sense of progress and the promise of a better life. How stultifying her old existence in Burnside seemed now – she could never go back to living in a pit village!

Within a few weeks, Ellen had fallen in with a group of local girls of her own age, whom she met by chance one afternoon in a tea-room on Grainger Street. They had begun by exchanging a few pleasantries over a cup of tea and soon became fast friends. Lily, the ringleader, was a fat blowsy girl with a loud voice and raucous sense of humour; Ellen thought she was great fun and laughed at all her jokes.

She knew that neither her mother nor Mrs Watson would approve of her new friends. They would take one look at Lily and brand her instantly – 'rough as the roads', 'a brazen hussy' and similarly damning epithets. But it was thanks to Lily and her friends that Ellen was discovering everything there was to see and do in Newcastle, and for that she was very grateful. She learned that the girls were employed as seamstresses in Black Gate – the old part of town – but she never went down there on her days off. It was much more fun for them all to meet in the city centre, to saunter down the stylish streets, peer into shop windows and admire the latest fashions on display. On her meagre pay, Ellen couldn't afford to actually buy anything, but she enjoyed every moment nevertheless. How lucky I am to have made new friends so quickly, she thought as she caught the tram back to Jesmond.

* * *

It was a stiflingly hot Thursday afternoon in August, and Mrs Watson had set Ellen to cleaning the bedrooms upstairs. A heavy stillness lay over the house, for Mrs Swift was out for tea with her sister at Felton Hall and Mr Swift was at his offices in town. Ellen had left the master's bedroom until last, knowing that it was a relatively easy room to dust and clean. The solicitor had spartan tastes, and his chamber was devoid of the drapes, flounces and ornamental clutter in his wife's room. Ellen kneeled down to blacken the grate, feeling rather faint from the heat. Perspiration was streaming down the inside of her arms and between her breasts.

It's like an oven in this room, thought Ellen, cursing her heavy housemaid's uniform which she wore year-round regardless of the weather. Despite the suffocating heat, she was dressed as usual in a thick black dress, buttoned tightly to the neck and falling in cumbersome folds to her ankles. Underneath the dress were the usual layers of calico underclothes – chemise, drawers, corset and petticoats, with black stockings held in place just above the knees by garters. Completing the outfit was a long white apron, a mobcap and stout black shoes.

Finding the atmosphere unbearably close, Ellen stood up and opened the sash window to allow a breath of air to enter the room. As she did so, she felt suddenly dizzy and faint. She mopped her brow with a handkerchief and breathed deeply in an attempt to pull herself together. *I'd feel better if I could only lie down and rest for a minute,* she thought, gazing longingly at Mr Swift's comfortable feather bed. It was strictly forbidden of course; Mrs Watson would have a fit and dismiss her on the spot if she caught a housemaid taking such liberties. But if she was quick, Mrs Watson would never know, Ellen told herself. All she needed was to take the weight of her feet for a moment.

Casting caution to the winds, Ellen removed her stout shoes and apron and collapsed onto the blue satin eiderdown. Oh, it was bliss to feel the plump pillows under her head and the cushioned comfort of Mr Swift's soft mattress! She lay flat on her back with her arms and legs spread, relishing the moment. Without moving from her horizontal position, she managed to cast aside her mobcap and shake out her mane of brown hair, damp with perspiration. She clumsily undid the buttons of her dress to the waist and yanked the bodice apart to let the summer air from the open window fan her neck and chest. Impatiently, she pulled her skirts up as far as her knees. I'll just cool off for a minute, Ellen promised herself, already feeling less faint. The warmth and comfort were making her drowsy, and in spite of herself, her eyelids drooped…

Ellen didn't know how long she had been dozing but something – perhaps the faint smell of eau de cologne in the air – brought her to her senses. Opening her eyes, she nearly jumped out of her skin at the sight of a man standing over the bed, staring down at her reclining body with interest. The man was in his late fifties, nondescript in appearance but smartly dressed in a dark suit with starched wing collar and necktie. Ellen took in his mottled red complexion, bushy moustache and side whiskers. *Oh my Lord,* she thought with horror, *it's Mr Swift! What in heaven's name is he doing at home at this time of day?*

In a flash, she sat up and pulled her skirts back over her ankles. She was about to spring to her feet but was stopped by Mr Swift's firm hand on her shoulder. He continued to tower over her, making her acutely aware that the bodice of her dress was open. It was a most improper situation for a housemaid, Ellen knew. Overcome with shame and embarrassment, she wondered what excuse she could possibly make for her conduct. Mr Swift would quite rightly consider that taking a nap on his bed was an unforgiveable transgression. This, she feared, was the end of her short career as a maid in the Swift household.

"Eeh sir, I'm so sorry," she began, flustered. She attempted to pull her hair back into some semblance of order. "It was that hot, you see, and I was feeling a bit wobbly. Oh please, Mr Swift, don't dismiss me. I swear it'll never ever happen again!"

To her surprise, she saw that the solicitor, eyebrows raised in amusement, did not appear to be annoyed in the slightest. "On the contrary, I sincerely hope it *will* happen again," he remarked coolly. "You make a very pretty sight indeed. What a fine looking girl you are... Ellen, isn't it?"

"Yes, sir," said Ellen humbly, still sitting on the bed and turning her blue eyes up to him.

"Naturally, your little... rest, shall we say, must never come to the attention of Mrs Swift. I'm not convinced she would regard your behaviour with the same benevolence as myself."

Ellen was distraught. "Oh, please, please sir, don't tell the mistress! Or Mrs Watson either, she'd never forgive me."

Percy Swift made no reply but sat on the bed beside Ellen. He was perspiring heavily, Ellen noticed, and his breathing was short. "I'm sure that can be arranged, my dear," he said at last. "It can be our little secret."

Ellen felt weak with relief. "Eeh, thanks very much, sir! I don't know how I can ever repay you for your kindness."

The older man clamped his hand firmly on her arm. "Well now, as a small token of your gratitude, I was hoping you would allow me a peek at..." His eyes rested on Ellen's open bodice. "You have nothing to fear, my dear, and... I'd make it worth your while."

Nothing in Ellen's young life had prepared her for this moment. Totally ignorant of what her mother would call 'the ways of the world', she knew practically nothing of men or sexual matters. In Burnside, the subject was never openly discussed. She knew there was a connection between 'men's needs' and childbirth, but any allusions to such subjects among the women were always made in hushed whispers. Now, with Mr Swift sitting on the bed by her side, her stomach was churning and her mind was in turmoil. She wished with all her heart that she had not lain down on the master's bed.

Ellen was astute enough to understand that what Percy Swift was proposing was highly improper and that she was effectively being blackmailed. Yet the alternative – being dismissed on the spot and then going home to Burnside in disgrace – was equally unthinkable. And if Mr Swift only wanted a quick look inside her bodice, surely no real harm would be done? Too ashamed to speak, Ellen nodded mutely.

Mr Swift smirked in quiet satisfaction and carefully pulled away her chemise so that he could peer into the dark depths of her bosom. Evidently appreciating what little was on view, he then slid a hand underneath her chemise and delicately fingered her breasts, patting them with almost clinical precision as if he were testing the quality of goods he was about to purchase. After a few seconds, he removed his hand and stood up, leaving Ellen feeling both soiled and mortified.

"My word, Ellen, I must say you're extremely... well endowed!" he exclaimed, pulling at the collar of his starched shirt as if overcome by his exertions. "I came home early to change for a formal dinner at the Town Hall this evening, and I'm damned pleased I did." A wily expression suddenly appeared on his florid face. "In fact, my dear," he added. "I do believe I shall need to come home early at the same time next Thursday. Isn't that the day Mrs Swift always calls on her sister? So we shall be quite undisturbed, Ellen. Won't that be nice?"

Without waiting for Ellen's response, he took a silver coin from his pocket and tossed it on the quilted eiderdown. "Buy yourself something pretty, my dear," he said with a faint smile. Nodding politely in her direction, he left the room and closed the door quietly behind him.

Ellen picked up the coin – half a crown! In a few seconds, she had earned what she made in a week as a housemaid. What had just happened was sinful and immoral, she knew. But after all, she thought in spite of herself, Mr Swift's hand in her bodice had been a small price to pay if it meant keeping her position at Oakdene House. She wondered whether all masters were entitled to such favours from their housemaids. Perhaps Mr Swift had thought her ignorant and unsophisticated? Her heart still thudding, Ellen fastened the buttons of her dress with shaking hands and slipped the coin into her apron pocket.

* * *

The next two Thursday afternoons followed a similar pattern to the first. Ellen lived in fear that Mrs Watson would take it into her head to come upstairs on some pretext or other and catch them both red-handed – or red-faced in Ellen's case. But the still summer afternoons passed without disturbance of any kind, and Ellen hardly knew whether to be glad or sorry. At night, however, anxious and remorseful, she tossed and turned in her tiny attic room at Oakdene House. She would awake from strange dreams drenched in sweat, dreams in which she was sinking in dark murky waters, out of her depth and unable to swim. Would she be damned for all eternity as a result of her goings-on with Percy Swift? She prayed constantly that she would not.

The amazing thing was that Mr Swift wanted nothing more than to re-enact – over and over again – that first afternoon when he had caught her dozing in his room. He would begin by arranging her on the bed in the exact pose he desired, although with considerably more of her body on view than the first time. Her chemise was now pushed down so low that it barely covered her nipples, while her housemaid's skirts were pulled high to her thighs. When Ellen was reclining to his satisfaction, pretending to be asleep, the solicitor would leave the room and then stealthily reappear. Ellen was instructed to keep her eyes closed while the long minutes ticked by and she sensed Mr Swift's strange presence in the room. Eventually, he would start stroking her breasts, his fingers feathery-light. This was

177

her signal to 'awake' and gaze at him rapturously. The older man would then sit on the bed and pull her onto his lap – like a doll, thought Ellen – and pet her for a while, although he never kissed her on the lips. When he tired of this, he would push her away almost dismissively, place half a crown on the bedside table and take his leave.

Ellen was increasingly racked by guilt but forced herself to remain silent, for it was clearly out of the question to confide in either her family in Burnside or the kindly housekeeper, Mrs Watson. She could well imagine their outraged cries of shock and horror if she ever confessed her misdeeds. In the end, she decided to talk the situation over with Lily and the other girls in town. Lily had a good head on her shoulders, she thought, and was bound to know what to do.

* * *

On her next Saturday afternoon off, Ellen stood at the foot of Grey's Monument, where she had arranged to meet up with her new friends. She stared up admiringly at the magnificent statue of Earl Grey, former Prime Minister and the son of a prominent Northumbrian family. What a grand place Newcastle is, she thought as she waited contentedly in the bright September sunshine, and how right I was to move away from Burnside!

Lily and the girls arrived, arm in arm and full of chatter as usual. Ellen couldn't help noticing their cheap garish clothes – far from ladylike, she was forced to admit – and their raucous laughter as they walked along the streets of Newcastle. She knew it was not proper behaviour for respectable young women, but they were good friends and had been so kind in taking her under their wing. Ellen waited until they were all comfortably installed in Betty's Tea Room – the best cuppa in the Toon, according to Lily – before broaching the subject of Mr Swift. She recounted – hesitantly and blushing to the roots of her hair – everything that had occurred.

"I know it's wrong," ended Ellen miserably. "But I can't see how to get out of it now without losing my job at Oakdene House."

"Bloody hell!" breathed Lily softly. "You're a sly one, Ellen Robertson, and no mistake. You look as if butter wouldn't melt in your mouth, but you're getting paid half a crown just for showing your titties. By, you're a lucky duck!"

Ellen was appalled by Lily's reaction. "But surely you must admit it's not right, Lily. I'm only doing it because Mr Swift might tell if I didn't give him his way, and then I'd be out of a job."

Lily waved her hand airily. "For God's sake, Ellen, don't talk so daft! This is no time to go all straight-laced. You're onto a very good thing with this Mr Swift and getting handsomely paid for it an' all. Does he…?" She made a lewd gesture and the girls – all except Ellen – burst into giggles.

"You mean… The Act?" stammered Ellen, for this was the only term she had ever heard used in Burnside. Even then, discussions about The Act were restricted to married women.

"Aye, The Act," said Lily sardonically.

"No, no… nothing except what I told you."

Lily grinned from ear to ear. "Even better, hinny. Your Mr Swift's nowt but a slavering old fool – all he's interested in is play-acting! And that's not much to ask, is it? Keep your head screwed on, lass, and you'll find there's plenty more than half-crowns to be had. If you play your cards right, Ellen Robertson, you could end up making a fortune without so much as breaking into a sweat. Now you listen to your friend Lily, pet, I'm going to give you a few tips…"

The girls huddled together in the tea-room as Lily gave them the full benefit of her experience in the art of seduction. Ellen, with a mixture of horror and fascination, learned more about sex in those few minutes than in the previous nineteen years of her existence. She also received – in no uncertain terms – explicit advice on how to take her relationship with Percy Swift to what Lily referred to as 'the next step'.

"So…" ended Lily in a long drawl. "If I heard you right, you've got seven and six in your purse at the moment, just waiting to be spent?"

"Aye," admitted Ellen.

"Well, us lasses are going to help you spend it!"

Oh, but it was grand to stroll down Grey Street and spend her three half-crowns on frivolous things! Ellen had never worn anything that wasn't either ill-fitting, homemade or cast-off. She was almost crazed with excitement as she realised she could actually afford to buy something pretty for herself, something that didn't need to be plain and sensible. In the end, Lily and the girls helped her choose – amidst whoops of delight and much laughter – a pair of exquisite black lace gloves and a new hat. The hat, which she wore perched high on her head, was a tiny but extravagant affair in blue taffeta with matching streamers down the back. Ellen stood in the milliner's shop holding a mirror, turning her head this way and that to admire her reflection from all angles. The hat was irresistible, and so was she! Pushing the last shreds of guilt from her mind, she paid the milliner with a radiant smile.

* * *

In the weeks that followed, Percy Swift could not help but notice the change in Ellen's attitude towards him. She was fast losing her inhibitions and – as he pointed out delightedly – 'entering into the spirit of things'. Previously, Ellen had been painfully shy when forced to undress or expose any part of her flesh. Now she was learning to make their little games more entertaining, pouting mischievously and casting him seductive glances as they acted out the same old routine. Ellen had come to understand that Mr Swift enjoyed the process more than its culmination. More often than not he was content to sit in an armchair, puffing on a cigar and watching her avidly as she – oh so slowly – unbuttoned her dress, bared her shoulders and gave him tantalising glimpses of her breasts. She also understood that her beauty and desirability in Mr Swift's eyes gave her a certain power over him, a power which Lily had instructed her to exploit to the full. "Make sure you've got the old fool wrapped around your little finger and then… strike while the iron's hot, lass!" she had urged.

"My dear, you're becoming more alluring by the day," the solicitor declared with a beaming smile at the end of one of their afternoon sessions. "How old are you, Ellen?"

"Just turned nineteen, sir."

"And tell me, my sweet, are you walking out with a young man at the moment?"

"Oh no, Mr Swift, I'm a good girl." Ellen gave him a flirtatious look as she sat on the edge of the bed, delicately pulling on her black stockings.

"You mean no young man has ever courted you, Ellen? I'd have thought a pretty girl like you must have dozens of admirers!"

"Oh aye, admirers," replied Ellen, tossing her thick mane of brown hair so that it fell in fetching disarray over her bare shoulders. "But I don't give a toss for any of them. I'm keeping meself pure." She stretched out her shapely legs in the stockings but did not pull her skirts down, well aware that Mr Swift was captivated by the view.

The older man's eyes lit up. The idea of Ellen's purity was obviously one which both gratified and excited him. "And so you should, my dear," he replied earnestly. "God forbid you should let some callow lad – an ignorant dock labourer or a filthy coal miner – get his rough hands on you and defile your beauty. I couldn't bear it, Ellen! I want you to keep yourself for me, and me alone." He squirmed restlessly in the armchair, his face flushed with passion.

This was her chance at last, Ellen realised, thinking back to Lily's words of advice. She heaved a dramatic sigh and moved languidly across the room to Mr Swift, swaying her hips as she did so. With a wistful smile, she arranged herself on his lap and nestled her face into his shoulder.

"There's nothing I'd like better than to stay as we are, sir," she murmured softly. "All I want is to go on pleasing you." She wrapped her arms around his neck and pressed her body to his with as much ardour as she could muster. "But we can't go on much longer like this. We'll be caught out soon, I know it! I'm sure the housekeeper smells a rat, she's been giving me funny looks lately. And what would Mrs Swift say if she knew about our little games, under her own roof an' all?" Seeing the thoughtful look on his face, Ellen pressed on. "In any case, I'll have to find meself a husband one day if I'm not to stay a housemaid forever. What choice do I have?" She knew it was a leading question and held her breath as she waited for the solicitor's reaction.

Percy Swift did not respond immediately. He pursed his lips and squeezed Ellen's waist possessively, weighing up the options in his mind. "You're a good girl, Ellen," he told her at last. "I've grown rather fond of you these past few weeks. You and I understand each other perfectly, don't we? You know..." He cleared his throat in embarrassment. "You know what I like."

"Oh I do, sir, I do." Ellen, making the most of her position on his lap, tickled his whiskers playfully.

The older man's eyes rested hungrily on her soft milky skin and half-revealed breasts. "You deserve to be protected, my sweet," he said thickly. "By a man of substance who can take good care of you." Ellen held her breath, hardly daring to believe her ears.

"I'm prepared to offer you an advantageous arrangement, Ellen," he went on solemnly. "One which will benefit us both. But you must give me your word that your... favours... will be reserved exclusively for me."

Ellen kept her expression meek and demure as the older man outlined his plans for her, although she could barely contain her excitement. What Mr Swift was

180

proposing exceeded her wildest expectations. Lily and the girls would be green with envy when they heard!

Percy Swift coughed awkwardly. "By the way, my pet, I have a little hobby which I hope you'll indulge when we're properly settled."

Ellen raised her brows quizzically; she had absolutely no idea what the solicitor could possibly mean. But now was not the time to ask, she told herself… better not rock the boat.

"I can't wait to find out what it is, sir," she whispered teasingly.

* * *

Just two weeks later, Ellen informed an astounded Mrs Watson that with Mr Swift's permission, she was leaving her job at Oakdene House with immediate effect. The very next day, she moved into rented rooms in Newcastle, situated conveniently close to Percy Swift's offices on Grainger Street. She gasped with delight at the sight of her new accommodation, hardly able to believe that she would actually be living there. Although the parlour and kitchen were neat and comfortable enough, the *pièce de résistance* was the plush bedroom with its flocked floral wallpaper, crimson velvet furnishings and huge four-poster bed. She particularly loved the elegant chaise longue, too short to lie on but just long enough to recline gracefully. Leading off the bedroom was a modern bathroom containing a massive tub, and even a dressing room fitted out with a full-length mirror and wardrobes to hang her clothes. Never in her wildest dreams could Ellen have imagined this would all be hers!

And her good fortune did not stop there, for the elderly solicitor not only paid the rent on the rooms but also gave her – in cash – a not ungenerous monthly allowance for personal expenses. He always sent word before he called on her and in any case was too taken up with work to visit her rooms more than twice a week. The rest of the time, Ellen was free to do as she chose, as long as she remained discreet and behaved decorously. She was a lady of leisure at last, she thought exultantly as she stretched out luxuriously in the huge bed every morning. She would never go back to skivvying again! True, she was a kept woman, the mistress of an eminent Newcastle solicitor… but was that really such a bad thing? Ellen managed to persuade herself that it was not. She was young and pretty and alluring. Was it her fault if Mr Swift was – in his own words – bewitched by her charms?

She spent many happy hours in her small parlour pouring over the latest fashions in ladies gazettes and periodicals, carefully noting all the subtleties of style and cut. She realised with a wild surge of elation that she could now afford some of these gorgeous creations. Newcastle suddenly became a veritable treasure trove of modistes and milliners, hosiers and shoemakers. Ellen roamed the town's busy streets in a haze of happiness, purchasing anything she fancied… gloves, purses, fans, perfume, soft kid boots to show off her ankles. She ordered dresses in taffeta and velvet, exquisitely cut to flatter her tiny waist and feminine curves, with skirts gathered elegantly at the back and cascading to the floor in graceful loops and drapes. She chose the dresses in extravagant, impractical colours – parma violet and almond green, cyclamen pink and cornflower blue. Just looking at them hanging in her wardrobe gave Ellen a thrill – what fun it was to be frivolous!

Her favourite haunts were Newcastle's ultra-modern department stores, Bainbridge's and Fenwick's, where she was free to wander and pick up items that caught her eye. In the smaller shops, she couldn't help noticing that certain tradesmen and sales assistants looked down their noses at her and treated her with barely concealed disdain. Although nothing was ever said to her face, it was as if they could see right through her and recognised her for what she was – a housemaid from a pit village with a broad Geordie accent. But there was no such snobbery in the town's department stores and Ellen felt more at ease there. Bainbridge's was a vast sprawling edifice with four floors and hundreds of employees; it had been one of the first department stores in the world and was still at the forefront of innovative retailing. And now, Fenwick's had just opened its doors and was all set to rival Bainbridge's as the finest store in the North East.

Percy Swift was entranced by Ellen's transformation. "My dear, you're quite the young lady now," he exclaimed jubilantly as she twirled in front of him in one of her new dresses. "I only wish I could show you off as you deserve." They were both well aware, however, that the solicitor could never be seen in society with Ellen. If they were ever caught together at the theatre or dining out, the news would spread through town like wildfire and reach the tree-lined avenues of Jesmond in no time.

Ellen discovered that the hobby her protector had alluded to before she left Oakdene House was photography. Mr Swift was the proud owner of a very expensive contraption which he had delivered to her rooms and installed in the bedchamber on a tripod. It was a cumbersome wooden view camera with what looked to Ellen like a leather concertina in the middle and glass plates which the solicitor assured her were the very latest technique. Ellen was not much interested in the bizarre apparatus, but she listened patiently enough as Percy Swift expounded at length on his 'pride and joy'.

Their relationship took on a whole new dimension with the arrival of the camera, for the solicitor's visits were now exclusively occupied in taking photographs of Ellen. The preparation and setting-up of these pictures was time-consuming, laborious and – in Ellen's view – tedious in the extreme. Mr Swift could happily spend hours fussing over his camera, adjusting the lighting and arranging Ellen in the exact pose he had in mind. Although she was not averse to showing off her shapely figure to advantage and enjoyed the atmosphere of theatricality in the bedchamber, she found Mr Swift overly fastidious in his quest for perfection. Her arm must be draped gracefully over the back of the chaise longue 'just so', her head must be turned towards him at a precise angle, the folds of a silk robe must fall faultlessly to her feet. Eventually, when the solicitor was satisfied with the result, his head would disappear under a heavy black cloth draped over the camera and the photograph was taken.

Over the next few months, Percy Swift photographed Ellen in an infinite variety of poses. He had encouraged her to replace her old calico underclothes with expensive lingerie and now took great pleasure in exploring the artistic possibilities of embroidered lace camisoles, fine satin drawers and black silk stockings. As he grew more proficient and confident technically, he urged Ellen to pose for him naked, missing nothing of the elaborate show she put on for him as she slipped sensuously out of her garments. Even in the nude pictures, however, Ellen's voluptuous figure was never entirely on view, for the solicitor was more interested in artistic effect than blatant eroticism. When, for instance, she was instructed to bare her magnificent breasts – a sight her elderly admirer never tired of – one breast would be artfully concealed by a cascade of tumbling brown hair. If her legs were parted in a mock display of wild abandon, Mr Swift would painstakingly drape a long silk scarf between her plump thighs. Ellen pandered to his every whim with good grace, well aware that satisfying the solicitor's voyeuristic obsessions was vital if she was to remain his mistress.

* * *

"Saucy pictures? Is that all he's interested in, then?" Lily enquired inquisitively. Ellen allowed her – and occasionally the other girls – to call at her lodgings from time to time, although she made sure these visits never came to the attention of Percy Swift. She felt instinctively that the solicitor would not approve of her consorting with the likes of Lily. This afternoon, they were sitting comfortably in Ellen's cosy parlour and had already managed to get through the better part of a bottle of gin. She was fast discovering that a shot of gin picked her spirits up in a way tea never had.

"Well, practically all," said Ellen hesitantly. "He doesn't really touch me that much, and when he does…" Her voice trailed away in embarrassment.

"You mean he's still not performing The Act, then?" Lily broke into hysterical giggles and helped herself to more gin.

Ellen turned the question over in her mind, for in truth she was not quite sure how to respond. She thought back to the rare occasions when her more provocative poses had aroused Percy Swift sufficiently to push her onto the four-poster bed and heave his portly body on top of hers. Face scarlet and gasping for breath, he would thrust half-heartedly between her legs for a while and then collapse by her side in utter exhaustion. Ellen was both amused and irritated by these episodes.

"I wouldn't call it The Act exactly," she finally admitted. "Everything sort of… peters out."

Lily roared with laughter at this but then leaned over and grasped Ellen's hand, her round face suddenly serious. "Petering out or not, lass, you'd better watch out for yourself anyway. You don't want a bun in the oven, do you?" Seeing Ellen's bewildered expression, she realised she would have to be more explicit. "Eeh, they don't come more gormless than you, Ellen Robertson! Listen pet, if you ever get pregnant with Mr Petering Out, come to your friend Lily straightaway. I know a woman down by the quayside that's good at getting buns out of ovens. She's a dab hand with the old knitting needle and she charges a fair price."

Ellen shuddered in horror. "Lily, surely you don't mean you've actually…?" She couldn't bring herself to say the words.

"Once or twice," replied Lily matter-of-factly. "All of us lasses have to sooner or later, you know how it is."

But Ellen didn't know how it was. Of course, she had long since realised that Lily's job as a seamstress occupied very little of her time. Lily herself often alluded to 'making a bit of extra on the side' when she needed to. But today her crude talk of buns and knitting needles forced Ellen to face up to a shocking truth she had carefully avoided so far. Her funny, cheerful friend was nothing but a common prostitute, as were the other garishly dressed girls whose company she so enjoyed.

A shiver ran down her spine at the thought, followed by a stab of cold fear. If Lily was a whore, a harlot – and all the other insults thrown at her kind by respectable God-fearing people – then what did that make Ellen? She could no longer hide from reality. She too was selling her body to Percy Swift for money, and therefore in the eyes of society, she was as much a 'fallen woman' as Lily. For the first time since she had started her new life in town, Ellen felt deeply ashamed, as if she had been physically tarnished and corrupted by her wrongdoings with Percy Swift. But at the same time, she knew there was no going back.

"Ta Lily, I'll let you know," she managed to say in a strangled voice, "but I'm sure it won't come to that."

* * *

One Sunday in May 1882, Ellen finally made up her mind to pay a visit to her family in Burnside. Her conscience had been preying on her for quite some time, for it was several months since Percy Swift had settled her in Newcastle as his mistress and not once had she made the journey home. The Robertsons would naturally assume she was still in service in Jesmond, while on her side, she was afraid to break the news of her departure to them, to face the inevitable questioning that would follow. Luckily for Ellen, none of her family were given to writing letters – they had neither the time nor energy and her mother was illiterate in any case – but she knew her prolonged absence must worry them nevertheless. She also knew they would be horrified if they found out what she had become. In Burnside, people didn't beat about the bush, and she could well imagine the words they would fling at her – trollop, slut, tart…

Well, they don't need to know, thought Ellen defiantly as she walked to the omnibus station in the Haymarket. She had been careful to dress more plainly than usual, although she couldn't resist wearing one or two fancier items to impress them all. She had also bought a large beribboned box of bonbons and chocolates as a conciliatory offering. She clambered into the horse-drawn omnibus – which now provided a daily service to the Tyneside pit villages – and sat as inconspicuously as possible in one of the back seats, arranging her skirts neatly about her. Six miles separated her from Burnside, and Ellen needed to rehearse in her mind what she would say to her mother, her brother Jim and the dozens of other siblings and relatives who would be bound to pop into the house in Lilac Street when they heard of her visit.

The omnibus clattered up the Great North Road, stopping along the way to allow passengers to descend. Ellen was the only person to get off in Burnside. She paused for a moment on the old stone bridge that crossed the filthy burn running through the village and looked about her. The coal dust in the air, the hulking colliery machinery, the drab back-to-back houses, the grimy pitmen in their flat caps, the shabby harassed-looking women, the ragged children playing in the streets… it was all so familiar to Ellen. And yet to her surprise, a surge of happiness flooded through her and she felt her spirits lift. Ellen Robertson had come home to the only people in her life who truly loved her.

The whole of Lilac Street flocked to No 24 when news of her visit spread through the village. Friends and family packed into the tiny front room to greet the local lass who was doing so well for herself in Jesmond. In the end, the chatter and gossip rose to such a pitch that Ellen was spared from having to explain why she had not paid a visit home for so long. With a careless smile, she simply said she didn't get much free time and had made new friends in town. She regaled them all with descriptions of Oakdene house, the elegant streets of Jesmond, the amusements and amenities on offer in the Toon.

The box of bonbons was passed around with squeals of pleasure. "By, these must have cost a pretty penny," Jim commented drily. "I didn't know housemaids made that much money." Ellen told him tartly not to be such a sour puss, and everyone in the room laughed merrily.

All the young women exclaimed at Ellen's fancy new clothes, in spite of the fact that she had deliberately played down her appearance before she set off from town. They swooned over her lace gloves, took turns trying on her frothy little bonnet and lifted the hem of her skirts a fraction to admire her satin-trimmed petticoats. As for her dainty kid shoes with the elegant button fastening at the side, they were ecstatic. They had never seen such shoes except on the feet of fine ladies.

"But how can you afford all this, Ellen?" asked her sister-in-law Rose in awe. "It would take our Jim three months wages to pay for this lot, and there wouldn't be a penny left over either."

"Things are different in Newcastle," replied Ellen with an airy wave of her hand, selecting a marshmallow from the box of bonbons. "You just have to know the right places to shop." She was enjoying her moment of glory in Burnside, basking in their adulation and her own superiority. No harm in that, she told herself, pushing any remaining pangs of guilt firmly to the darker recesses of her mind.

Her mother, Annie Robertson, had kept unusually quiet throughout Ellen's visit. She had busied herself all afternoon brewing endless cups of tea for the stream of visitors calling in at No 24 but otherwise had not joined in the enthusiastic reception for her daughter. When everyone had departed however and Ellen announced it was time to catch the omnibus back to town, Annie offered to walk with her as far as the bridge.

For the first time, Ellen noticed how frail her mother had grown, her skin translucently pale and her cheeks hollow. "Oh Mam, don't bother yourself," she said, feeling suddenly remorseful. "You look as if you're on your last legs, and I can easily catch the omnibus by meself."

But Annie was quietly insistent. "I know you can, lass, but I want to come." She took Ellen's arm and clung to it tightly as they made their way slowly down Lilac Street. Ellen sensed that her mother had been biding her time all afternoon and hoped Annie was not about to sermonise her and spoil her visit.

The older woman did not mince her words. "I've been watching you today, Ellen Robertson, and I don't like what I see. Oh aye, you've got everybody else fooled with your airs and graces and your la-di-da manners, but you can't pull the wool over your Mam's eyes. You're getting above yourself, lass, prancing around as vain as a peacock! How in heaven's name did you come by all that finery, eh? Answer me that!"

Damn it, thought Ellen, this was exactly the kind of scene she had wanted to avoid. "I told you," she pouted sulkily. "I know where to buy on the cheap."

"Rubbish! And is that rouge you've got plastered on your cheeks? Painted and powdered like some fancy woman... you look as common as muck, Ellen!"

Ellen decided attack was the best form of defence. "All the lasses in Newcastle wear rouge, Mam! And anyway, what would you know about the latest fashions? You haven't been out of Burnside since the year dot!"

Annie stopped dead in her tracks. "Oh, I know you think I'm nowt but an ignorant pitman's wife, lass. You look down on us all, it's plain to see. Well, you can think again! I'm no fool and I can see you're being led astray. You were brought up proper and to know right from wrong. But you've fallen by the wayside, Ellen. There's an air of sin about you – I can smell it, I can smell it!"

To Ellen's horror, Annie's chest was heaving, and tears had started to roll down her sallow face. "Mam, Mam!" she cried desperately, hugging her mother tightly in an attempt to comfort her. "You're getting yourself worked up about nowt! I'm a grown woman now, Mam, and I can look after meself. There's no call to worry about me, Mam, no call at all."

Annie pushed her daughter away gently and drew herself up with dignity. "I don't think I can walk as far as the bridge after all, lass, I'm feeling a bit done in," she said in a low voice. "I won't press you further if you won't tell me the truth. But one last word, Ellen... if things get bad, you can always come back to Burnside. You'll always have a home here, hinny."

"Don't be so dramatic, Mam, I don't know what you're on about. Eeh look, here's the omnibus coming down the road, I must run." Ellen hurriedly pecked Annie on the cheek, and the two women parted company at the bottom of Lilac Street.

* * *

It was high summer now, and Ellen had not seen Percy Swift for five weeks. As the solicitor had always called on her with clockwork regularity, Ellen noted his continuing absence with growing anxiety. Had he tired of her already and found some other fresh-faced girl to his liking? Was he taking a summer holiday with his family and had forgotten to tell her? Or was he sick in bed? This last possibility seemed most likely, for Mr Swift was getting on in years – Ellen guessed he must be close to sixty. She also knew he disliked warm weather because it made him sweat heavily and brought on what he called his 'palpitations'.

Still, the situation was becoming critical. This month's rent had not yet been paid, and the landlady was demanding her due – a figure that made Ellen gasp in disbelief and which she was quite incapable of paying herself. She had, she realised, been wildly extravagant, spending all her allowance on frivolities but saving nothing. Now she was down to her last few shillings. She badly needed Percy Swift to shore up her finances and appease the irate landlady.

Ellen didn't dare make direct enquiries, well aware that her place in Mr Swift's life was illicit. Her elderly lover would be furious if she emerged from the shadows of his existence and exposed them both to the crude light of discovery. So day after day, she hung around the entrance to his offices on Grainger Street, hoping to catch him going in or coming out. But the elusive Percy Swift was nowhere to be seen.

In desperation, Ellen finally made up her mind to go to Oakdene House. There must be some way to find out if he was at home, perhaps ill in bed, or away travelling with the family. She caught the tram to Jesmond and hovered on the pavement fifty yards or so from the grand house where she had been a housemaid only a few short months before. She waited for an hour or so, pacing slowly back and forth at a safe distance, but to no avail.

In the end, there seemed to be no alternative but to present herself at Oakdene House and discreetly ask what had happened to Mr Swift. Steeling her nerve, Ellen decided to walk around to the rear of the house and knock on the kitchen door. With any luck, she could have a quick word with the cook or a housemaid and be on her way before anyone else noticed.

But to her consternation, it was the housekeeper, Mrs Watson, who opened the kitchen door. Ellen recalled all too well the suspicious disapproval in the housekeeper's eyes when she had handed in her notice, and how flustered and awkward she had felt. Trying to appear composed now, she smiled brightly at the older woman. "Good afternoon, Mrs Watson. Remember me – Ellen Robertson? Hope you don't mind, like, but I was just passing in the neighbourhood and thought I'd drop in to see how you all are."

The housekeeper did not return her smile, nor did she invite her in. "I've nowt to say to the likes of you," she snapped and tried to shut the door in her face.

Ellen jammed her foot in the door and made her voice more plaintive. "I'm sorry, Mrs Watson, I meant no harm. I was just wondering if Mr Swift... was keeping well."

The housekeeper flashed her a venomous look. "By, you've got a nerve showing your face here, you brazen hussy! Oh aye, I cottoned on straightaway what you were up to with the poor gentleman – seducing him bold as brass under his own roof and then setting yourself up as his fancy woman. You should be ashamed of yourself, fornicating with a man old enough to be your grandfather!"

Ellen was speechless. Was this how it looked to the world? She had a sudden vision of Percy Swift's persistent overtures in the early days, his constant wheedling and her own innocence and embarrassment. It seemed profoundly unjust that the tables had been turned and she was now the guilty party. This was no time to argue her case with Mrs Watson however.

Ignoring the housekeeper's tirade, she did her best to keep her voice even. "I hope Mr Swift isn't poorly? I haven't seen him for a while."

"Aye, you haven't seen him because the poor man passed away three weeks ago!" There was a gleam of triumph in Mrs Watson's eyes as she saw Ellen's shocked expression. "The whole family's gone into mourning, and the mistress hasn't even the strength to leave her bedchamber. And it's all your fault he's gone, Ellen Robertson! You must have known the master had a heart condition and was on doctor's orders not to exert himself. Poor Mr Swift, you finished him off with your wicked ways! You'll burn in hell for your sins, you trollop!"

The housekeeper's vindictive accusations seared through Ellen's soul. Incapable of thinking clearly, much less responding, she turned on her heel and fled. Her mind was in turmoil and her heart was pounding fit to burst. She ran blindly through the quiet Jesmond streets in a state of sheer panic, oblivious to the curious looks of passers-by.

Percy Swift was dead! Despite his obsessive voyeurism and bizarre tastes, he had always been kind to her in his way. But Ellen could feel neither pity nor grief for her wealthy protector. No, her thoughts were entirely taken up with her own predicament. What was to become of her now? Her lodgings, her regular monthly allowance, her comfortable new lifestyle… all this had evaporated in the blink of an eye, leaving her alone and penniless. She cursed herself for carelessly squandering her allowance. If she'd had any sense at all, she would have saved a few pounds for the proverbial rainy day. Now the rainy day had arrived, and Ellen could barely afford to buy a tram ticket back into town. How naïve and foolish she'd been!

Incoherent thoughts swirled around in her mind. She remembered her mother's parting words after that last fateful visit to Burnside… If things get bad, you've always got a home to come back to, Annie had told her, almost as if she had foreseen today's disaster. Yet the idea of returning to Burnside in shame and disgrace was unthinkable, for Ellen was far too proud and stubborn to eat humble pie. And in any case, she had no desire to go back to her old pit village life. She had grown up, had a taste of something better, a glimpse of other possibilities in life. No, she must find her own way out of this mess.

How was she to make a living, then? It would be difficult to find another position in service without a reference, even if she had wanted to. And in any case Ellen felt, however irrationally, that any prospective employer would instinctively turn her away. Tarnished by her affair with Percy Swift, she would be branded as a domestic temptress, a loose woman who led respectable men astray. But the alternative – working her fingers to the bone in a factory – was equally unappealing. Did she really want to join the ranks of those haggard women with their threadbare clothes and sad, hopeless faces? No, she thought defiantly, she was young and pretty and had acquired a veneer of gentility through her association with Percy Swift. Surely, she could put these assets to use in a way which would ensure her livelihood?

* * *

"Oh Lily, Lily, what am I to do?" Head in hands, Ellen sat on her friend's dilapidated old sofa and for the first time that day gave in to soft tears.

Lily put a comforting arm around her shoulders. "You have a good cry, pet," she said kindly.

On returning to her lodgings in Newcastle after the disastrous visit to Oakdene House, Ellen had not wasted any time. Quickly and efficiently, she had packed her personal belongings – as many as she could carry – and unobtrusively slipped out of the building and into a passing hansom cab. The landlady would be furious that she had absconded without paying the rent but no doubt would manage to recoup her due somehow by applying directly to Percy Swift's offices.

The hansom cab had dropped her down by the quayside, at the entrance to Lily's lodgings in Black Gate. Ellen found herself in a maze of narrow alleys and crumbling old buildings – a far cry from the affluent town centre where she had been living. Oddly enough, this was the first time she had actually visited Lily, and she was shocked to discover the harsh reality of her life. A pall of polluted air hung over the slum tenements of Black Gate, and the stench of sewage and detritus permeated its streets. The whole area was like some nightmarish rabbit warren, seething with the countless poor of Newcastle – the ragged army whose labour fuelled this powerhouse of a city. Black Gate extended as far as the murky depths of the river Tyne, with its shipbuilding and engineering works. Lining the riverbanks were dozens of staithes, where ton after ton of coal was loaded and then shipped to all four corners of the Empire. Ellen had been no stranger to poverty in Burnside, but at least the pit villagers stood together in mutual support and solidarity. The hopeless squalor of Black Gate was an entirely different kind of poverty.

When Ellen's tears had subsided into occasional hiccups, Lily rose to her feet and retrieved a half-empty bottle of gin from behind the sofa. Pouring a generous measure into two smeared glasses, she proffered one to Ellen. "Get this down you, hinny, it'll do you the world of good. Everything looks better after a nice nip of gin!"

Ellen downed the gin and felt its warmth spread through her stomach. "Who would have thought Mr Swift would die so suddenly?" she mused forlornly, her face still wan and tear-stained.

"Swift to come and swift to go!" chortled Lily, replenishing Ellen's glass. "Well, there's plenty more fools where he came from… Take it from me, pet, with your face and figure you'll find yourself another Mr Swift before the week's out."

"But how am I to live in the meantime, Lily?"

"Well, you're welcome to bed down with me for a few days, just till you get yourself sorted. And if you're short of a few bob, you can always flog some of your fancy clothes." She fingered the heaps of lace and taffeta and velvet flung carelessly over the back of the sofa. "This fur jacket must be worth a pretty penny for a start!"

Ellen sighed heavily. Lily was putting into plain words unpleasant truths which she already knew but had been unwilling to confront. There was only one way she could get back on her feet and make a living in her present situation. There was a name for what Lily was proposing but Ellen could not say it, even in her own mind. She reassured herself with the thought that it would simply be a temporary expedient until her prospects improved.

Sipping her gin more calmly now, she looked around Lily's dreary little room with distaste… the tiny window with its cracked pane and cobwebs, the filthy mattress and grubby sheets, the threadbare mat on bare boards. There were no cooking facilities whatsoever, and the privy was in the courtyard at the rear of the building, shared by all sixty tenants according to Lily. The small washbasin on a stand by the door had to be filled with water from a pump at the bottom of the street. Ellen was appalled to see her friend living this way. She thought of her mother, who scrubbed and scoured every day to keep their house in Burnside spick and span. Her years as a housemaid had also taught her the virtues of cleanliness and order. She kept these disloyal thoughts to herself however, for Lily was kind in her rough and ready way and at this particular moment, the only person she could turn to.

"Well, maybe just to tide me over," she conceded, still refusing to acknowledge openly what lay ahead. "But I don't know if I'm cut out for it, Lily, I've never… you know…"

"Oh, don't make such a meal of it, man!" Lily snapped impatiently. "Who do you think you are, the Virgin Mary? You'll soon learn the ropes, hinny, there's nowt to it. Shake that lovely figure in their faces and the men will be queuing up for you!" She emptied the remains of the gin bottle into their glasses and proceeded to initiate Ellen into what she euphemistically called the tricks of the trade.

* * *

The very next afternoon, Ellen positioned herself at the entrance to Bainbridge's department store, her mouth dry and her heart pounding. She was dressed in one of her most flamboyant outfits – selected for her by Lily – and pretending to admire the display in the shop window while waiting for an imaginary friend. She could still not quite believe that she was doing this, touting for customers on the street like a common tart. But as usual, she managed to push this unpleasant thought to the darker recesses of her mind and concentrate on her immediate goal.

After almost an hour of hovering uncertainly at the store entrance, Ellen was feeling both foolish and frustrated. What was she doing wrong? Dozens of men had walked past her on the street without so much as a glance in her direction. She willed herself to do better, trying to remember some of the tips Lily had shared with her the previous evening – something about catching the eye of one particular man and holding his attention.

Ellen scanned the crowd appraisingly and spotted a man about fifty yards down the street, walking in her direction. Quickly, she took in his appearance – burly, middle-aged, but not a gentleman judging by his clothes. He looked like a prosperous farmer in town for the day or a well-to-do tradesman. Steeling her nerve, she stepped out from the shadows of the store entrance and planted herself in his direct line of vision. When she was sure the man had noticed her, she placed a hand on one hip, tilted her head to the side and flashed him an alluring look before swinging around again to gaze at a dress in the shop window. She held her breath, torn between hope and fear, as the man drew near. Suddenly, she felt his presence at her side, smelling strongly of beer, his body almost touching hers. "Nice frock, eh?" he said gruffly, gesturing to the window display.

This was exactly the cue Ellen had been hoping for. She turned towards him with a winning smile, casually brushing her breast against his arm as she had learned to do with Mr Swift. "Eeh, it's a lovely frock! But I could never afford it these days. We've fallen on hard times, you see, and I have to care for me sick mother…"

The man barely listened to Ellen's well-rehearsed lines. "Well, we'll have to do sommat about that, won't we?" he interjected, his voice pleasant enough but his eyes hard. "How much do you need?"

Ellen slipped her arm in his and whispered in his ear. The man nodded, and together they walked off down the busy Newcastle Street.

* * *

The man was the first of many customers for Ellen over the next year. Oh, she had learned the tricks of the trade soon enough, but it was a harsh and humiliating existence. For the first few weeks, she had assumed she would find another Percy Swift – a rich, well-mannered gentleman who would keep her in style and require very little in return. Now she understood how naïve she had been.

The men she consorted with day after day were very different from the elderly solicitor and his elaborate games. Unlike Mr Swift, most of her customers barely looked at her; they were rough, brutal and unconcerned about anything but their own immediate sexual needs. These men saw Ellen's body as nothing more than a commodity to be used as they pleased; they paid for what they wanted and made sure they got it. Ellen discovered that when her customers were sexually engaged with her, she simply ceased to exist as a human being. Some would proffer a kind word as they left, but they were the exception. Others enjoyed hurling insults at her – slut, harlot, whore. More than once, she had been slapped, punched and beaten up by men who thought such gratuitous violence was normal and that she deserved nothing better. One man had even forced her to submit to unspeakable acts and then had run off without paying.

Ellen tried to put on a brave face with Lily and the other girls, carefully concealing the tight knot of misery in her soul. They would not have understood such niceties in any case. For Lily, there was no shame in prostitution, it was simply a way to make a living. And she would rightly point out that Ellen was no better than any of the other girls working the streets. Like them, she rented sordid rooms in Black Gate, 'received' her customers in the same grubby sheets, drank as much gin as they did.

When Ellen looked back on the course of events since she had left Burnside, she could not put her finger on the precise moment it had all gone wrong. She had somehow been caught in a dizzying downward spiral and at every turn had ignored her scruples, and more importantly her common sense. Hadn't she always known that an unmarried woman who flouted the strict code of morality imposed by society was bound to pay a heavy price? How could she have imagined the rules would not apply to her? How could she have been so wayward, so frivolous, so thoughtless? Ellen tortured herself constantly with these thoughts, but she knew too that there was no turning back. In her mind's eye, she saw the Burnside Ellen she used to be, fresh faced and rosy cheeked, tripping down Lilac Street with a spring in her step. She barely recognised the hardened, embittered, empty shell of a woman she was now.

Before she became one herself, Ellen had never noticed how many prostitutes there were in Newcastle. Now she saw them at every turn – hundreds of loud, aggressive women fighting to survive by flaunting their bodies on the city streets. Competition for customers was so fierce that she was often reduced to selling her services for a pittance, just to keep herself fed and the rent on her miserable lodgings paid. It was simply a question of supply and demand. She consoled herself with the thought that she was still young and desirable, but she had seen the filthy old hags on the quayside, copulating with sailors in dark alleys for a few pence. She was chilled to the bone by the realisation that they too had once been as young and desirable as she was now. Yet there seemed no way to extricate herself from the dark, bottomless pit into which she had fallen.

Ellen's only comfort was that no one in Burnside knew of her degradation. Her family would assume she was still in service in Jesmond, even though she had not paid them a visit or written home in many months. They might think badly of her for being undutiful and uncaring, but this was infinitely preferable to the searing shame she would feel if they ever found out the truth.

* * *

Ellen felt a tentative hand on her arm and swung around eagerly towards the man who had appeared by her side. She was in dire need of a customer that Saturday afternoon and had been standing at her usual corner on Pilgrim Street for well over an hour, shivering in the chill wind and drizzle.

She looked up into the man's face and drew back in horror. It was Ted Anderson, her old flame from Burnside! The shy gangly youth who had been so keen to walk out with her had turned into a strapping young man with a forthright, angular face and clear grey eyes.

"Ellen? Is it really you?" he asked hesitantly. "By, I hardly recognised you... have you changed your hair or sommat?"

Ellen laughed awkwardly. She had dyed her hair blond a few weeks ago and the result was disastrous; her glossy brown curls had turned a brassy yellow colour and now looked as dry and lifeless as straw.

"Eeh Ted, fancy seeing you here in the Toon!" She tried to look pleased, although Ted Anderson was the last person she wanted to run into. She had been dreading someone from Burnside catching her hustling on the city streets, and now the cat was well and truly out of the bag.

"Why don't we find somewhere to sit and talk, Ellen? I'll treat you to a cup of tea if you like," offered Ted, indicating a teashop opposite. Unable to think of an excuse not to, Ellen followed him across the road. A few seconds later, they were seated at a corner table.

Ted removed his cloth cap and scrutinised her closely, making no attempt at polite conversation. Ellen squirmed with embarrassment, for there was no mistaking the effect of her dyed hair, garish make-up and plunging neckline. Eventually, he leaned across the table and gently took her hand, his frank grey eyes boring into hers. "Oh Ellen, Ellen... What's happened to you, lass?"

Ellen looked down at his big pitman's hand enveloping her own with its warmth and comfort. "Oh, this and that," she said carelessly, hoping she sounded more nonchalant than she felt. "I had enough of skivvying, so I left service and since then I've been... living on me own. I always liked me independence, you know."

Ted absorbed this information without comment but relinquished her hand, knowing it was a lie and also disappointed that she would not speak plainly. But how could she possibly confide in him, Ellen asked herself in anguish, when the truth was so unspeakable! She did not dare meet his eyes, toying with her cup of tea to fill the awkward silence between them.

Desperately, she tried to change the subject. "So tell me, Ted, what brings you to Newcastle?"

Ted's eyes were still boring into hers. "I came in to buy an engagement ring. I'm getting wed next spring."

"Eeh, fancy that! And who's the lucky lass, then?" Her flippant tone belied the unexpected sinking feeling in her stomach.

"Mabel Green. You remember Mabel from Rose Street, Ellen? She was in the same class as you at school."

192

"Of course I remember her," snapped Ellen, surprising even herself by her sharpness. Surely, she wasn't jealous?

"You know I always had me heart set on you, Ellen," said Ted softly. "I waited a long time for you an' all, but you wouldn't have me no matter how hard I tried. So me and Mabel..." His voice trailed away, almost apologetically.

Ellen looked into the young miner's kind, honest face and wondered why his words caused her so much pain. She had never been in love with Ted Anderson, so it was ridiculous! She could have had him if she'd wanted him, but she'd been so sure she could do better than marry a pitman. There was no reason at all why he shouldn't marry Mabel Green instead. Nevertheless, an unexpected wave of nostalgia for Burnside brought unwanted tears to her eyes, for the sight of this straightforward young man reminded her of the simplicity of her old life and the innocent, young girl she had once been. She remembered what her mother had said about Ted back then: "He'll make a good husband for some lass." Ellen had been dismissive and scornful, but how right Annie had been!

She swallowed hard and searched for another topic of conversation. "How are they all at home, Ted? Is Mam keeping well?"

"I'm sorry to be the one to tell you," said Ted gruffly. "Your Mam passed away last December, just a few days before Christmas as I recall. Your Jim sent a telegram to the address in Jesmond where you worked, but there was no reply. He was hoping you'd be there for the funeral, but you never came."

The news cut through Ellen like a knife. It was not only the grief of loss she felt but shame and guilt too; she was a selfish, unworthy daughter who had neglected a loving mother. *I'll never forgive myself for not being with her at the end,* she thought sorrowfully.

"A few days after the funeral, your Jim and me, we went to seek you at that posh house in Jesmond," continued Ted earnestly. "But they said they never wanted to hear your name mentioned again and slammed the door in our faces. So we went into the Toon to see if we could find you there. Your Jim said he felt responsible for you, what with both your Mam and Dad in their graves. We must have combed every street, Ellen, asked dozens of people passing by if they knew your name. But nobody had ever heard of you. Your Jim reckoned you must have moved to another town."

Now it was her turn to clasp Ted's hand in hers. "Oh Ted, that's exactly what they must all go on thinking! I'm sorry for all this, if you only knew how sorry I am... sorry for so many things. But if you can still find it in your heart to show me some kindness, please do one thing for me. Don't tell them at home you ran into me today, don't tell them... what I am now."

He squeezed her hand sympathetically. "Don't worry, pet, I won't. Your Mam would turn over in her grave if she could see you now, and your family... well, I think it would break their hearts if they knew..." He rose awkwardly, laid a few coins on the table and put his cap firmly back on his head. "Well, I doubt if our paths will cross again, Ellen, but I wish you all the best." He gazed down at her, his eyes full of pity. "Ta-da, hinny," he said softly.

"Goodbye, Ted. Good luck to you and Mabel." Ellen watched as the young miner strode briskly down Pilgrim Street and disappeared from view. She sat motionless for a long time in the tea-room, feeling empty and weary beyond belief.

Like a mirror, she had seen reflected in Ted's eyes the full magnitude of her shame. How he must have despised her! How could she have let herself sink so low?

* * *

Ellen opened her eyes blearily, head throbbing and stomach empty. For some reason, she had been dreading today: May 4th, 1887. Although nobody knew it but herself, it was her 25th birthday. She lay in bed in her shabby little room in Black Gate and tried to imagine how today would have been if she had stayed in Burnside. She would be married to a kind-hearted pitman, probably with three or four children by now, surrounded by the affection of relatives, neighbours and friends. She visualised herself making love with Ted Anderson, and the words of tenderness he would have whispered in her ear.

Instead of which, she was a woman with neither husband nor friends, eking out a living as a whore in one of the roughest areas of Newcastle. And there was certainly no place for children in her lonely, precarious existence. In fact, Ellen was not sure whether she was still capable of child-bearing at all. In the past five years, she had been obliged to call on Lily's woman 'down by the quayside' three times – three pregnancies and three painful abortions conducted by a drunken hag with knitting needles. The last had been four months ago and she had almost bled to death. The woman had warned her in a matter-of-fact way that there might be some damage to her 'organs', adding with a cackle that it was 'just as well in your trade'. Ellen had still not regained her strength and had felt in low spirits ever since. In any case, nobody cared if she lived or died, she thought miserably. Even Lily, who had fallen in with a gang of ne'er-do-wells and been jailed a year ago for petty pilfering, had deserted her.

You're going soft in the head, she said out loud, although there was no one to hear. Stop feeling so sorry for yourself! Supporting herself on one elbow, Ellen reached out for the bottle of gin on the rickety bedside table and took a deep swig. Gin had been her only comfort for a long time now. She needed it first thing to face the day, she needed a flask in her pocket while she was hustling for customers on the streets, she needed a shot after every customer to forget the way they treated her and she needed a bottle at her bedside to send her into a dreamless, alcohol-soaked sleep. Food was now of secondary importance, and what little she ate she bought from market stalls and street vendors.

She roused herself sufficiently to crawl out of bed and walk unsteadily to the window. She opened it wide and took deep breaths of the sharp spring air. She tried to work out the time of day and concluded it must be late afternoon already; she had spent nearly twenty-four hours in bed. Increasingly, Ellen preferred bed and a bottle of gin to standing on street corners touting for trade; sometimes two or three days elapsed before she found the courage to leave her room. This was a slippery slope, she knew, for she earned less and less money as time went by.

In any case, she no longer had the looks to command a high price for her services. Twenty-five years old, Ellen mused, as she took a long hard look at her reflection in the cracked old mirror. She looked much older, and she knew it. Her brassy dyed hair was falling out in tufts, her skin was pasty and blemished, and the sparkle had gone from her bloodshot eyes. Her buxom figure had thickened and coarsened, her legs were swollen and veined. As for the voluptuous breasts so admired by Percy Swift, they now sagged almost to her waist.

Well, this was no time for moping, Ellen reminded herself sharply. She badly needed to shore up her finances and had heard a naval ship would be docking on Tyneside that evening. There were bound to be dozens of brash sailors swarming through the quayside, out to get drunk and desperate for female company. Still, she felt too weary to fetch a bucket of water from the street pump and carry it back up three flights of stairs to her room. Instead, she put aside all thought of washing and applied a thick cake of powder and rouge to her face. Turning her attention to the two shabby dresses in the cupboard, she selected the red one with the cutout bodice. It was mud-spattered and stank under the armpits, but sailors were not known to be choosy. The red one would have to do, she decided.

Ellen left her room and descended to the rear of the tenement building, pushing open the door to the privy. She couldn't put it off any longer, she really had to go. A wave of nausea swept over her as the overpowering stench from the privy hit her. The cesspit was partially covered by a wooden bench with a large hole in it. Ellen lifted her skirts gingerly, sat on the bench and urinated as quickly as she could. Then she walked down to the quayside in search of her first customer.

She positioned herself at the entrance to a dark alley, hoping she would not have to wait too long. She was wearing a black jacket over the red dress but had left the bodice undone so that whenever a man walked by, she could open the jacket and flash her breasts at him invitingly. She was just about to do this for the umpteenth time that day when a burly constable loomed in front of her and grabbed her by one arm.

"Get moving, you fat slut. I'm taking you in for testing."

Ellen's response was instantaneous. Trying to escape his grip, she pushed the constable away and kicked him hard in the shin; her one thought was to make a run for it, to disappear down the alley before he could catch her. But the policeman had obviously anticipated this move and kept his balance, while yet another policeman appeared on the scene. Grabbing her firmly before she could duck out of their reach, they yanked her arms behind her back. She felt the click of handcuffs on her wrists. Together they prodded and pushed her along the narrow streets, Ellen screaming protests, until they arrived at the police station.

"Name and address," the officer at the desk said laconically, barely looking at Ellen. She spat out her particulars and watched as he laboriously inscribed them in a thick leather-bound register. "The test's tomorrow morning. You're going in the clink for the night," he informed her. Without further ado, Ellen was flung roughly into a bare cell alongside a handful of other prostitutes; she heard the door clang shut behind her. It had taken no more than fifteen minutes for her worst nightmare to come true.

Until now, Ellen had been lucky enough to escape testing, unlike many of the prostitutes she knew. Syphilis had reached such endemic proportions in the big cities and ports of Britain that a law had been passed, authorising the police to arrest prostitutes and check them for infection by subjecting them to a genital examination. If a prostitute was found to be infected, she was confined to a Lock Hospital for an indefinite period. Ellen knew only too well that there was little or no chance of survival for these women, since no effective cure for syphilis had been found.

She spent the night shivering on the cold stone floor of the prison cell, ignoring the raucous shouting and brawling of the other women. She was starting to feel weak with exhaustion, for she had drunk all the gin in her hip flask and had eaten nothing for two days. Everything seemed so unreal, as if she were in the middle of a bad dream; she longed to shake off the dream and wake up as usual in her bed in Black Gate. Could this really be happening to her? Her mind was numb with sheer terror.

* * *

Ellen was aroused from a fitful sleep by a constable kicking her roughly in the shins. Dizzy and still half-asleep, she was pulled unceremoniously to her feet and dragged down a long corridor into a bare, windowless room. She saw that there were four constables – but no female presence – in the room. The officer who appeared to be in charge of the proceedings had removed his jacket and was rolling up his sleeves. "Get your clothes off and lie down there," he ordered brusquely, pointing to a bare wooden table in the middle of the room.

Ellen, still cowering by the door, realised there was no escape from the dreaded test. She reached under her skirts to take off her drawers and clambered clumsily onto the table. Even as she did so, there was a tiny flicker of rebellion at the back of her mind. It was all so unfair, she thought. Why did the police never bring the prostitutes' customers in for testing? Why did the men always get off scot-free and it was only the women who were subjected to such humiliation?

The four men sniggered as she lay down fully dressed on the table. "I said, get your clothes off and I meant all of them," barked the officer in shirtsleeves. "We want to have a look at every square inch, for medical purposes of course." More sniggering followed this remark.

Ellen exploded with rage. "You can't force me to do that, you bastards! I know me rights, I'll report you to the authorities!" She jumped off the table and tried to make for the door, but the four policemen were too quick for her. She was pushed backwards so violently that she lost her balance and fell, hitting her head against a corner of the table.

"Little Miss Modesty, eh? Who do you think you are, you fat trollop? Get your clothes off or I'll have you locked up for more years than you've had hot dinners!"

Ellen complied, her hands trembling as she removed her clothing. It was all too plain that if she did not obey the officer's orders, he and his men would strip her forcibly. Naked and shaking like a leaf, she hoisted herself back onto the table. She squirmed helplessly as the four constables spread-eagled her and tied her arms and legs tightly to the table legs with ropes. "She's a right little tartar, this one, Sergeant," commented one of the men jokingly, and they all laughed.

The sight of the sergeant in shirtsleeves, looming over her with a collection of large metal instruments, made Ellen shut her eyes tightly. She clenched her fists, praying for the strength to endure the examination. The pain as she felt one instrument after another penetrating her was unbearable. The sergeant clearly had no medical expertise, pushing and prodding unnecessarily over and over again. Ellen groaned in agony but was too tightly bound to move. She had been reduced to a mere slab of meat in the hands of a brutal butcher. She was no longer a human being.

"Well, that's that," pronounced the sergeant dismissively after what seemed like an eternity. Ellen opened her eyes, hoping she would be allowed to dress now and put this excruciating experience behind her. But the men were in no hurry to relinquish their prey.

"Aw come on, Sarge, we haven't had any fun yet," protested one of the constables, while the others grinned inanely. Ellen's eyes moved wildly from one to the other, trying to make sense of what was happening.

"Go on, then," said the sergeant. "But don't take all day. There's eight more tarts we have to get through this morning."

The ordeal was not over yet. Ellen felt the three men's hands on her flesh, pinching and squeezing her breasts, her nipples, her stomach so hard that she cried out in pain. She moaned and begged them to stop, but the men were too busy guffawing and exchanging lewd comments to care.

After a while, the sergeant, intent on getting back to the business in hand, ordered the constables to stop and instructed them to untie the ropes binding Ellen. With a supreme effort, she managed to haul herself into a sitting position on the table, so ashamed and humiliated that she could not meet the eyes of her tormentors. Her skin was raw and bruised, and she felt a searing pain inside her vagina. She felt as though she had fallen to the bottom of a deep dark well, crushing her soul beyond repair in the process.

The sergeant, busy filling in a form now, looked up at her briefly. "Well, the test was positive," he stated impassively. "You've got the pox all right."

Contracting syphilis had always been one of Ellen's worst fears. Every prostitute in Newcastle knew it was a painful, incurable illness; it brought on fevers, blindness and dementia before an almost certain death. Yet today, shaking uncontrollably in this cold bare room, she no longer had the strength to care. She wanted only to curl up in a corner and blot out this cruel world. She understood now why the three constables had stopped short of sexual penetration; the sergeant must have signalled that she was infected, and they had not wanted to put themselves at risk.

The sergeant, unfazed by Ellen's lack of response, turned to one of the policemen. "She'll have to be taken away today and put straight into confinement at the Lock Hospital."

"Begging your pardon, Sergeant, but we received a report yesterday from the Chief Registrar at the hospital. All the wards are full to overflowing, and there's no room to take on more patients. They're instructing all constabularies in the area to send women infected with syphilis to the workhouse infirmary until further notice."

Ellen broke down at the mention of the workhouse. She moaned and wept and begged the men for mercy, although she knew that none would be forthcoming. This would be her fate, she understood now, to die in a waking hell alongside the dregs of society. She thought briefly of her honest, hard-working family in Burnside and thanked God they would never know how low she had sunk. She had never felt so utterly alone.

"Is there any person you wish to be informed?" asked the sergeant, pen poised and obviously keen to get through the official procedure and be rid of this hysterical woman.

Ellen, still naked, stepped down from the table and answered with as much dignity as she could muster. "There's nobody." Her eyes were lowered and her voice barely audible.

"What? Speak up, lass, I can't hear you," barked the sergeant irritably.

Ellen turned her sore, bruised body towards the four men and faced them squarely. There was a fierce, blazing light in her eyes that gave her the look of a caged animal. "There's nobody!" she screamed. "Nobody at all!"

Nick and Jenny (9)

Nick stared in horror at Ellen's death certificate. "It says here she died in the workhouse infirmary in Newcastle," he gasped, hardly able to believe his eyes. It was one thing to read about workhouses in history books but quite another to learn that a family member had ended up in one. "The date is September 1887, so she'd have been no more than—"

"Twenty-five," Jenny interjected. "Poor Ellen came to a very sorry end. Everyone knows the workhouse was the last resort for the destitute – the old, the sick, the drunkards, the tramps…"

"But this transcript gives Ellen's profession as *none*," he went on, frowning at the small print on the certificate.

"*None* was just a euphemism for prostitute in workhouse vocabulary, I'm afraid. Ellen was what the Victorians piously referred to as a fallen woman. And in those days, once a girl strayed from the straight and narrow, there was no turning back. She was branded for life and cast out of conventional society forever."

"But you keep talking about the culture of solidarity in colliery villages," Nick protested indignantly. "So how come her family left her to die in the workhouse?"

"I doubt whether they even knew she was there. Ellen was probably too ashamed to tell her family how low she'd sunk." Seeing his shocked expression, Jenny pressed on with her explanation. "Oh, the Robertsons would have rallied around if she'd lost her job or fallen on hard times. They'd even have forgiven an illegitimate child, although the scandal would have brought disgrace on the entire family. But we must remember that Ellen came from the respectable working class – decent, hardworking people who abided by the strict morals of the day. For them, prostitution was an unforgivable sin, literally a fate worse than death."

"But it all seems so harsh," Nick insisted. "We all know there were hundreds of thousands of prostitutes in Britain in that era."

"Oh yes," Jenny agreed. "It was the fourth largest female occupation in Ellen's day. And of course the vast majority of prostitutes came from the working class, girls who had previously been in dead-end jobs – laundering or charring or suchlike."

"Is that what happened to Ellen?"

"We have very little information about her life." Jenny leafed through the slim file by her side. "Apart from her birth and death certificates, all we have are two census reports. In the 1871 census, Ellen is nine years old and her father, Tom Robertson, long since in his grave. The head of the family is Ellen's elder brother Jim, aged 22, who by then is already married with a baby son. The census shows Ellen, her mother Annie and Jim's family all living under the same roof."

"Well, that confirms what you told me earlier. But what about the 1881 census? Ellen would have been nineteen then."

"Yes, this is where things get interesting. Like many working class girls, Ellen was in service at the time. She was apparently employed as a housemaid by a Mr Percy Swift, a well-established Newcastle solicitor residing in Jesmond." Jenny looked up from the 1881 census report, a gleam in her green eyes.

"Jesmond!" exclaimed Nick. "How strange to think Ellen should be living so close to this very house…"

"Isn't it?" Jenny nodded meaningfully. "But I did a little homework on this Percy Swift and discovered that his wife Charlotte was none other than the sister of Emily Felton – the lady of the manor, so to speak, of Felton Hall in Burnside!"

Nick let out a long breath. "Those Feltons again!"

"There seems to be no getting away from them! And the connection with Felton Hall may explain why Ellen left Burnside to go into service at Oakdene House, Jesmond." Jenny intuitively felt the move could not be pure coincidence, although as so often in genealogical research there was no formal proof.

"Yes, but it doesn't explain why Ellen became a prostitute," Nick said flatly.

Jenny sighed. "Oh Nick, let's try to put ourselves in Ellen's shoes for a minute. Here she is, an innocent girl of nineteen, perhaps a very pretty one. She manages to escape from the poverty and squalor of a pit village, and for the first time in her life, she feels free at last! She has a steady job with a well-to-do family in a pleasant and very fashionable residential area. And what's more, she's just a short tram ride away from all the excitement of a big city!"

Nick raised his eyebrows quizzically. "Is this Newcastle you're talking about?"

"Yes!" snapped Jenny, feeling defensive about her hometown. "At the time, Newcastle was reaching the peak of its prosperity, heaving with new money and modern, progressive ideas. Just imagine how a simple girl fresh from Burnside would have been drawn to the bright lights and fancy clothes…"

"So you think Ellen wanted a piece of the action? She was lured into prostitution by the prospect of easy money?"

"Like millions of other poor, ignorant girls before her," said Jenny wistfully. "The temptation must have been too hard to resist. She was young and frivolous, away from her family's supervision and longing for all the good things money can buy. The real question is, what tipped the balance? What particular event pushed her over the edge?

What triggered her fall into prostitution? If only we knew… but all we can say for sure is that six years later, she died in the workhouse infirmary."

"If she was in the infirmary, she must have been ill," mused Nick.

"A common cause of death in those days was tuberculosis, or consumption as it used to be called. Or she might have died from alcohol abuse – cheap gin was the prostitute's best friend. But given the appalling levels of hygiene in her profession, it's more than likely that Ellen died of syphilis – known as the pox or the clap at the time. We must remember there was no cure for syphilis before the discovery of penicillin, and what treatments were available sometimes did more harm than the disease itself. Terrible skin rashes, blindness, dementia…" Jenny lapsed into silence and carefully closed the slim file which was all that remained of Ellen Robertson's short life.

Ellen's was a chilling tale, thought Nick. It occurred to him that in her own way, Tom Robertson's youngest daughter was just as much a product of Victorian society as the colliery workers in Burnside. He had barely noticed her name on the family tree at first. Ellen had been no more than a tiny piece in the mosaic of his family history, so tiny as to be almost invisible because she had never married, never had children and had therefore left no trace of her passage on earth. Yet now Ellen seemed very real to him, real enough for her screams of misery to rent the mists of time shrouding her life. In fact, he was surprised by how quickly the mists had cleared, as if the past was now drawing ever closer to the present. The Victorian era Ellen had known was beyond living memory, but only just. He had needed all his powers of imagination to tread the paths of ancestors who had lived centuries ago. But he did not have to walk far to find Ellen Robertson.

"I wonder if there are any photos of Ellen," he said, sifting through the small pile of mementoes he had salvaged in the attic. "I'd love to see her face, to know what she looked like."

"I'm afraid there aren't any," said Jenny. "Photography existed in the 1880s of course, and it was quite a status symbol in the middle and upper classes to have a family portrait done. But it was the kind of superfluous expense working class people simply couldn't afford. The next generation was different, though. By the early twentieth century, even poor families had a treasured photo or two – taken for a wedding or some other special occasion."

Nick was still scrutinising the blurred, faded images of bygone Robertsons. "Maybe you can help me work out who's who here?"

"Of course, but I have another photo I'd like to show you first." Jenny reached out for a manila envelope containing a handful of photographs from her personal collection. She handed one of them to Nick, and he examined it curiously. It was a large photograph, obviously taken by a professional, under which were inscribed the words *Burnside Colliery, 1913*. It depicted a dozen or so miners lined up in a row, with the pit-head wheel of the colliery towering behind them in the background. The men were in their working clothes – flat caps, heavy jackets, waistcoats and collarless shirts. Nick's first thought was that they looked surprisingly clean and spruce, as if the photo had been taken before their shift or perhaps to mark some kind of holiday. What struck him even more forcibly was their proud, erect bearing and the frank, fearless way they looked at the camera.

"You can see these men had a real sense of their own worth and identity," he remarked.

"They did," Jenny agreed with a smile. "And if any further proof was needed, just listen to this." She flicked through the book she had written, *The Rise and Fall of the Tyneside Collieries,* until she reached the page she was looking for. "Here's what a visitor to Burnside wrote at roughly the same time this photo was taken: *The miners employed at the colliery bear a high character in the coal trade. There is little mixture of men from different districts, and the people are somewhat proud of their Northumbrian descent."*

"Wow," Nick exclaimed, feeling a sudden surge of pride in his own Northumbrian descent.

Jenny pointed to one of the miners in the photo. "This is my great-grandfather, Charlie Armstrong." Her finger moved to the man standing next to him. "And this is his best friend, Bill Robertson. As far as I know, this is the only existing photo of your great-grandfather."

Nick's heart lurched as he peered at the blurred figure in the picture, the first ancestor in his family tree to have left a photographic record of his physical appearance. His great-grandfather was of average height, with a wiry frame and a good-natured expression on his angular face.

"Just to clarify, Bill was Tom Robertson's grandson," Jenny explained. "His father was Jim Robertson and his aunt – although I doubt if he ever met her – was Ellen. Bill was born in 1874, so at the time this photo was taken he would have been in his late thirties." She pointed to a tall, broad-shouldered young man standing next to Bill. "And this gorgeous guy," she said meaningfully, "is Alex McCulloch."

Nick looked blankly at Jenny; the young man was indeed very handsome and had a devilish twinkle in his eye, but the name meant nothing to him. Jenny stared back at him in astonishment. "Don't tell me you've never heard of Alex McCulloch," she protested disbelievingly.

Nick shook his head in bewilderment, and Jenny suddenly decided to keep this particular card up her sleeve for now. "Well, you'll be hearing a lot more about him soon," she remarked mischievously. "But for now, let's go back to your great-grandfather, Bill Robertson."

She turned to Nick's small collection of photos and carefully selected one of them. It had been taken in a Newcastle studio called Jerome's, and the solemn-faced group of women it depicted were all in formal poses. At the centre of the group was a middle-aged woman looking stiff and severe; she was seated on a high-backed chair with a small child on her knee. Her long, black dress was high-necked and tightly corseted, and her hair was uncompromisingly scraped back from her face.

"This is Hannah Robertson, Bill's wife," Jenny pointed out. "And the little boy on her knee is your grandfather, Geordie Robertson. He doesn't look more than three or four, so I would guess the photo was taken shortly after the First World War."

"Who are the two girls?" Nick indicated the shy figures in pinafore dresses posing awkwardly at Hannah's side.

Jenny quickly consulted Nick's family tree. "They must be Hannah's two daughters, Violet and Mary Jane. The eldest child was a boy called John, but as you can see, he's not in the photo. To be honest, I can't find any trace of John after the 1911 census. What is it with these disappearing John Robertsons? It took me ages to find the first one, who turned out to have emigrated to Philadelphia! And now this one... But nil desperandum, Nick, I'm still working on the case of your great-uncle. I'll track this John down if it's the last thing I do!"

"I bet you will!" Nick laughed. He turned back to the photo and pointed to a young woman standing behind Hannah, one hand resting on the chair. Unlike Hannah, though, she was wearing a modern, loose-fitting dress, the skirt short enough to reveal her ankles. She had very blond hair cut in a bob, framing a face which would have been unremarkable if it had not been for the young woman's expression – quietly confident and undeniably intelligent. "Surely this can't be one of Hannah's daughters too?"

"No, it's her younger sister Alice." Jenny flashed him a meaningful look. "Actually, Alice is my great-great aunt."

Nick looked puzzled. "Don't you mean she's *my* great-great aunt?"

"It so happens that her name is Alice Armstrong," laughed Jenny, pausing for effect before making her announcement. "So that makes her my great-great aunt and yours too!"

Nick tried to get his head around this unexpected family connection. "So that means there was yet another Robertson-Armstrong wedding!" he groaned as the penny finally dropped. "I hope there aren't too many more of them, otherwise we'll be arrested for incest..." He leaned over and kissed her playfully.

"No, I promise this is the last," said Jenny. "So... as you've just worked out, your great-grandfather Bill Robertson married a local lass by the name of Hannah Armstrong. But I have to admit at this point that the star of the show for me is her sister, Alice. I have a very soft spot for Alice Armstrong." She gazed fondly at the dignified young woman with the blond hair in the photo.

"What's so special about Alice?"

"Oh, my great-great aunt has always been a source of inspiration to me," said Jenny. "Not just because she was a teacher – although obviously that's something we have in common – but because of how hard she had to fight to become a teacher in the first place. In fact, Alice was the antithesis of poor Ellen Robertson. She was living proof that a woman – and a working class woman at that – didn't have to be a victim. She showed that there were other choices for a woman besides marriage and children, that a woman could be strong and independent. Just imagine, Nick, a poor pitman's daughter from Burnside who pulled herself up by the bootstraps and rose to be an educated professional woman... That was really something in Alice Armstrong's day!"

"She must have been quite a woman, like another formidable Armstrong female I could mention," said Nick wryly. He watched as Jenny opened a thick file marked *Alice Armstrong*. "I see you've done quite a bit of research on her."

"Oh yes," said Jenny eagerly, her eyes lighting up with enthusiasm. "Alice Armstrong was an important figure in the local community. She also played a key role in my family... and yours."

VII
Alice Armstrong, May 1916

Hannah Robertson closed her eyes wearily and tried not to doze off; it must be well past midnight, she reckoned. The little colliery house on Lilac Street was still and dark, for the entire family was fast asleep upstairs. Hannah had been up as usual breast-feeding little Geordie, only six weeks old. She was now sitting in her favourite rocking chair, gently cradling the baby and smiling down in amusement at the expression of satiated contentment on his little face.

Hannah had mistakenly assumed that her child-bearing days were over and was initially none too pleased when she had found herself pregnant again at the age of thirty-eight. After their three older children were born, she and Bill had always been careful to restrict their lovemaking to what they hoped were 'safe times'. Unlike most pitmen in Burnside, Bill was a sensible man in that respect. No point in breeding like rabbits, he would say, if you can't keep your bairns decently fed and clothed. Yet to her own surprise, as soon as little Geordie was born, she had instantly bonded with him, far more intensely than she ever had with her other children. He was a beautiful baby too, placid and good-natured – a blessing from heaven, Bill would say fondly.

Hannah debated whether to go back to bed but decided it was hardly worthwhile. Bill was working the fore-shift today and had to be at the colliery by two o'clock in the morning. In another few minutes, at most Little Archie, the Burnside *knocker*, would be rattling at windows with his long pole to make sure all the miners on the shift were roused from their slumbers. And she still had to prepare Bill's tin box of *bait* too, although he never took more than jam sandwiches and a flask of cold tea to the pit; like most miners, he preferred to work on an empty stomach. After the shift, though, he would come home ravenous and wolf down whatever dinner she had ready for him. Reluctantly, Hannah laid the sleeping baby in his crib by the fire and set about her chores.

Sure enough, she soon caught the familiar sound of the *knocker* making his way down Lilac Street. She heard Bill groan upstairs as he forced himself out of his warm bed. Within a few minutes, he joined her in the tiny front room, dressed for work in a long jacket with large side-pockets, a waistcoat, a flannel shirt, stout trousers, worsted stockings, hobnail boots and a flat cap. Keeping her husband's clothes clean and dry was a constant challenge for Hannah. She spent long hours beating them against the back wall to remove the coal dust, fetching buckets of water from the stand-pipe down the street, heating the water on the kitchen range, scrubbing the filthy blackened clothes by hand in the *poss-tub* and then drying them out in front of the coal fire. Bill's boots had to be scraped and polished daily too, although she usually assigned this arduous task to one of her daughters.

"How's our little Geordie, then?" said Bill cheerily as he collected his *bait* from the kitchen table.

"Good as gold. Just look at him, Bill, he's a picture. Eeh, have you ever seen such a bonnie bairn?"

"Never! He must take after you, pet." They both laughed, and Bill pecked her cheek lightly before making for the door.

"How's your back this morning?" Hannah called out after him.

"Right as rain, man, couldn't be better," declared Bill stoutly and stepped out into the dark street. "Ta-da, hinny," he said softly as he shut the door behind him.

Hannah sighed as she went upstairs, undressed and climbed back into bed. Bill was not a man to complain, and she suspected he was simply attempting to reassure her. As a stoneman, Bill spent long hours cutting stone to find coal and then shot-firing to blast through the seam; he worked crouching or lying on his belly, often soaking wet in water inches deep. At forty-two, he was a lean, wiry man, tough and resilient like all the Burnside colliery workers. Yet Hannah couldn't help but notice how exhausted he had looked lately, worn down by back pain, bouts of bronchitis and recurrent headaches from inhaling the shot powder.

Hannah lay awake, unable to sleep although she knew she badly needed to rest. Bill always told her she was a born worrier and should count her blessings instead of fussing and fretting. She reminded herself that she had many blessings to count… a roof over her head, a dependable husband, a steady wage coming in and four healthy children. And since the onset of this terrible war, Hannah thanked God that Bill was too old to be called up. So many young men in Burnside had enlisted in the Army in the first wave of patriotic fervour, but how many of them would return safe and sound to their families? Yes, Hannah realised, there were many in Burnside far less fortunate than herself.

She had been married to Bill Robertson for sixteen years and had never had cause to regret it. Although neither of them was romantically inclined, their relationship lay on a far more solid foundation of longstanding familiarity and affection; they had grown up in the same street and their families were very close. She had been Hannah Armstrong before her marriage, and it wasn't the first time by any means that a Robertson had wed an Armstrong in Burnside. It was common knowledge that the two families had even moved to the area together many years before, although Hannah was unclear about the details. People in Burnside had neither the time nor the inclination to dwell much on the past.

As for Bill, he was a quiet, unassuming man with an even temper and a dry sense of humour. Unlike some of the Burnside pitmen, he was not given to bragging and brawling, nor was he a heavy drinker. Oh, on Saturday nights, he would go down to the Miners Arms and get drunk with the rest of the men, but that was only natural. It was universally acknowledged that a working man needed to relax and let off steam at the end of a backbreaking week's labour. But the rest of the week, not a drop of alcohol passed Bill's lips, and he handed over every penny of his pay packet to Hannah. These were great virtues in any wife's eyes.

* * *

A few hours later, Hannah was on her feet again, serving up breakfast – bread and dripping washed down with tea – to the three older children sitting at the kitchen table. She barely listened to Violet and Mary Jane, aged ten and seven respectively, chattering at the top of their voices as usual. Girls were unimportant to Hannah's way of thinking, at least until they married and could settle into their allotted role of wife, mother and homemaker. And once married, a woman's needs and opinions should always come second to her husband's, in Hannah's view, for men were the protectors and wage-earners. Only they could provide for a home and family.

Hannah had always placed her hopes and dreams in her eldest son, John, but she had to admit that so far he was proving to be a disappointment. She watched him shovelling down his bread and dripping as if he hadn't been fed in months and wondered what would become of him. At thirteen, John would be leaving school in a few weeks but had been dragging his heels at the prospect of following in his father's footsteps and signing on at the colliery. A wayward boy with a wild streak and a fierce temper, he had already been in trouble several times with the local constable. Still, Hannah was confident that a hard week's work at the pit would soon knock some sense into him.

As soon as the three children had left for school and she had checked on little Geordie, awake but gurgling peacefully for now, Hannah decided to scrub the front doorstep. It was a beautiful, spring morning, and it would do her good to breathe in the cool fresh air and feel the sunshine on her back. Like most miners' wives, Hannah took great pride in keeping her house spick and span; a well-kept doorstep was recognised as the sign of a well kept home. Kneeling down outside the door, she scrubbed the step energetically and then set about whitening it with donkey stone. Lilac Street was fairly quiet at this time of day, except for the cries of small children too young to go to school and women out in their back yards, exchanging friendly gossip with neighbours. Yet the distant familiar sounds from the colliery workings were always there – the buzzers and hooters and bells, the constant drone of the ventilation fan and the rumble of coal wagons on the Tyne railway.

The peace of the spring morning was shattered forever in the space of seconds. A deafening blast emanating from the mine – three massive explosions one after the other – shook the very ground Hannah was kneeling on. Leaping to her feet, her hand flew to her throat in anguish, as she instinctively understood the enormity of the disaster. Pit accidents, although mercifully rare, were something every villager in Burnside feared. She looked around her in panic and saw dozens of women, screaming and wailing, already racing in the direction of the colliery. Snatching little Geordie from his crib, she wrapped him in her shawl and ran as fast as she could to the pit workings, where one of the shafts was blasting out flames and clouds of coal dust. The scene was one of utter confusion, a suffocating hell in which Hannah found herself calling out her husband's name, clutching hysterically at anyone in her line of vision. Bill, Bill… dear God, where was Bill?

The first miners who had survived the accident began to emerge from the second shaft, which fortunately was still intact. Coughing and spluttering, they told the assembled crowd that shot-firing in one of the seams had caused a firedamp explosion. The crowd of women started to moan and sob, but Hannah's heart froze with dread as she realised that her husband, as a stoneman, would be at the very nucleus of the accident. Clasped tightly to her bosom, little Geordie started to wail in fright but Hannah ignored the baby's cries. Her whole being reached out to Bill, trapped in the bowels of the mine. On this fine spring morning, tragedy had come to Burnside, and the nightmare of every miner's wife was unfolding before her very eyes.

The hours passed with agonising slowness as every able pitman descended the shaft again and again in a desperate effort to rescue their fellow workers, although they were often driven back to bank by the foul air underground. Bands of miners began to arrive from neighbouring collieries, knowing that every pair of hands would be needed to clear the wreckage and save the trapped miners below. Dozens of men were hauled to the surface, some maimed or injured, others almost suffocating to death from the poisonous fumes. Their wives and children clustered around them, weeping with relief to see them still alive. Heart pounding and stomach churning, Hannah paced up and down near the entrance to the shaft, praying with every fibre of her being that Bill would be next to emerge. At one point, a woman advised her kindly to breastfeed her howling baby, and she did so distractedly. To her relief, Geordie stopped wailing afterwards and fell asleep in her arms.

As the day dragged on and light began to fade from the sky, the men continued the rescue operation with unswerving determination, tirelessly striving to save as many pitmen as possible. Corpses were being brought to bank too, but Hannah could not bring herself to look at them. She choked with grief when she was told that her fifteen-year-old nephew, little Bobby Armstrong, had not survived severe burns to his face and body. She heard that most of the dead had succumbed to chokedamp, some of them found with their caps in their mouths in a desperate attempt to avoid inhaling carbon monoxide gas. Among these were Bill's cousins, Andy Robertson and his brother Lance, found dead in each other's arms.

Bill was the last corpse to be dragged out of the shaft. With absolute certainty, she knew it was her husband, even before she heard horrified voices all around her whispering his name. Two black-faced miners, their eyes startlingly red-rimmed, approached with grave faces and stood on either side of her, holding her up by the arms. "You'll have to identify the body, lass," they murmured gently.

Shaking uncontrollably from head to toe, Hannah was led to the forefront of the crowd and made to look down at Bill, lying stretched out on the bare earth. Her husband's face and body were barely recognisable, for he had been crushed by a fall of stone from the shot-firing and then badly burned by the explosion. He must have died almost instantly, Hannah realised. She nodded mutely to the two men and then felt her legs buckle beneath her as a wave of shock and grief swept over her. One of the men took the baby from her arms and the other caught her as she collapsed fainting to the ground.

***

The following Sunday afternoon, Alice Armstrong arrived in Burnside to find blinds drawn, streets deserted and the entire village in mourning. The toll from the pit accident earlier that week was horrendous: nineteen men had died in the explosion and another seven were seriously injured. Having travelled all the way from County Durham, Alice had missed the funeral service that morning. Still, she was here now and could at least offer some much-needed sympathy and support to her sister Hannah.

At twenty-four, Alice was the youngest of the Armstrong brood and a full fourteen years younger than Hannah. Although she was not particularly tall and her figure was unremarkable, she exuded a natural authority and dignity unusual in such a young woman. She could not be described as a pretty girl; her long face was too narrow, while her light blond hair – her one outstanding feature – was rather severely cut and bobbed in the new modern style. Today, as always, she was immaculately turned out. She walked down Lilac Street with the erect carriage of a woman confident of her own worth and her place in the world.

Alice entered Hannah's house without knocking – nobody in Burnside ever knocked on doors – and was surprised to find her sister bustling about the small front room, emptying drawers and piling various possessions on the kitchen table. She had expected Hannah to be distraught with grief and was disconcerted to find her so composed, an expression of icy resolve on her wan face.

"I'm so sorry, my dear," said Alice, giving her sister an affectionate hug. "Such a tragedy, such terrible news about Bill. I can't imagine what you must be going through, but I came as soon as I could and I mean to help in any way I can."

Hannah did not respond, afraid that if she did she would break down and give way to her emotions. She had not shed a tear since the accident, her sorrow pent up inside her like a hard tight ball. She was terrified of letting go, terrified that she would lose her mind and find herself unable to cope with the grim future ahead.

"Where are the bairns, Hannah?" Alice had noticed that the house was empty except for little Geordie in his crib by the fire.

"They're sleeping over at Mam and Dad's for a few days. We thought it was best, so that I can clear the house in time." Hannah's voice was strained, and she swallowed hard in an effort to control the flood of misery welling up again inside her.

"Sit down, my dear," said Alice firmly. "I'll make us both a cup of tea, and then we can talk things over properly." She busied herself at the kitchen range and produced two cups of strong tea, placed one in front of her sister and then sat down facing her. "What do you mean, Hannah, clear the house?"

"The bailiff came around the day after the accident. I've been given a week's eviction notice. He said he was sorry but rules are rules and I'm not entitled to a colliery house now that Bill's... gone." Hannah slumped despairingly over the kitchen table, burying her head in her hands.

Alice was appalled. She knew as well as anyone that colliery houses were reserved for working men and their families, but the decision to evict Hannah so soon after the disaster at the pit was both callous and grossly unfair. Bill had worked for thirty years at the colliery and had just lost his life at the coalface. Did his wife and children not deserve better treatment than this?

She tried to keep calm for Hannah's sake. "Have you received any compensation so far?"

"Oh aye," said Hannah bitterly, indicating a buff envelope lying on the kitchen table. Alice opened it and took out a few pound notes, along with a typewritten letter of condolence signed by Sir Reginald Felton, the owner of the mine. She fingered the notes indignantly, knowing the money would not cover Hannah's needs for more than a few weeks at best. But this was no time for protestations of social injustice, she reasoned; just now her sister was more in need of constructive advice than commiseration.

"It's little enough, that's for sure. But Hannah, I'll be able to help you out a little. I'm making a steady wage now, and I've already got some money saved."

"I couldn't take money from a woman," declared Hannah stoutly, drawing herself up with pride.

If the situation had not been so tragic, Alice would have found her sister's stubborn refusal comical. Hannah disapproved of her quest for independence, as did most of the inhabitants of Burnside. In their view it was 'not right' for a woman to show some ambition, to break through the barriers of social class and gender, to educate herself and rise above her allotted station in life. But Alice had ignored their caustic comments with quiet determination and persevered in her chosen path. Recognised by all from an early age to be exceptionally bright, she had managed to further her education by winning a place at a pupil teacher college, where she had been boarded, educated and prepared for the teaching profession. She was now a fully-fledged elementary schoolteacher and currently working in the colliery village of Cornhill in County Durham. She was not the first woman to qualify as a teacher by any means, but teachers from a working class background – whether male or female – were few and far between. No wonder they all thought of her as a social misfit, she mused.

"Don't be silly, Hannah. It's hardly the moment to turn down help, even if it does come from a woman," she remarked drily, patting her sister's hand to soften her words. "But we must plan ahead too and find a place for you to live… and think how you can make a living for yourself and the bairns."

Hannah's eyes took on a wild, desperate expression. "Make a living? Work in a factory in Newcastle, you mean? Or go into service? How do you expect me to do that, for God's sake? The baby's only a few weeks old, Alice, how could I possibly leave him and the other bairns?" She paused to think. "Our John's all set to leave school. Once he starts earning at the pit, there'll be some money coming in."

"It'll be a few shillings at most, Hannah. Your family can't survive on the wages of a thirteen-year-old lad." But an idea was starting to germ in Alice's sharp brain, one which she decided to keep to herself at present. "Let's not worry about that for now, though. Listen Hannah, I don't know if this is the right time to tell you, but I have some good news – news that will let me help you even more."

"Are you getting wed?" asked Hannah eagerly.

Alice tried not to show her exasperation. Was a wedding the only possible good news for an unmarried woman? Couldn't she aspire to more than being permanently confined to the home as a wife and mother, subordinate in every way to her husband? No, Alice was determined to be part of the wider world, to play an active role in society and express her own views as to how it could be bettered. Teaching was providing her with a way to do so, enabling her to stand on her own two feet and carve out a life of her own.

"No, I'm not getting wed," she answered with a wry smile. "The Education Board bars female teachers from marrying, and I'd never give up my position in any case. I've worked so hard for it, Hannah, and I love teaching. I feel I can really make a difference, you know, broadening children's minds. I want to show them how education can lead to opportunities in life, open up new perspectives."

"You'll end up an old maid," remarked Hannah sourly.

"I probably will, and that's fine with me!" Aware that her tone was too abrasive, Alice decided to try a different tack. "My good news is much better than finding a husband, Hannah. You see, I'm coming home to Burnside for good!"

Alice explained enthusiastically how Mr Carr, the headmaster of the village school and her own former teacher, had written to the Education Board and specifically recommended her for a new position opening up in Burnside. With the colliery expanding so rapidly and dozens of men moving with their families to work there, the number of school-age children was fast increasing and an additional teacher was desperately needed. Both Alice and Mr Carr had been delighted a few days previously when the Board sent confirmation that her transfer from Cornhill to Burnside had been approved.

"So you see, Hannah," went on Alice reassuringly. "You won't be alone. I'll be here from now on to help you find your feet and take care of the bairns."

Hannah nodded, although she doubted whether her sister truly understood her predicament. Alice was so young and fearless. What did she know about looking after a home and four young children, counting pennies and making ends meet on a pitman's pay? Hannah was fourteen years older than Alice, and a part of her resented being dependant on her sister in any way. Yet her spirits lifted in spite of herself. Alice was so clever and capable, so eminently sensible. She would know what was to be done now that Hannah's world had fallen apart.

"What's this, my dear?" Alice was sifting through the jumble on the kitchen table – untidy piles of bed linen, Bill's pit clothes, pots and pans – and had come across a plain wooden box.

"I don't really know." Hannah's voice was disinterested. "I found it at the back of a drawer. Something handed down through Bill's family, if I remember rightly. He showed it to me once when we were first married. I doubt if it's worth anything, so I reckon I'll just throw it out."

Alice opened the box curiously and held up its contents to the light: an old, intricately carved wooden crucifix and a miniature portrait which looked as if it had been painted long ago.

"I wonder who this young man was," she mused. "He has a look of Bill about him, don't you think?"

Hannah studied the painting and laid it to one side indifferently. "I can't see any resemblance," she said finally. "And I don't like the look of that cross; you'd take it for one of those Catholic crucifixes. But the Robertsons have never been Catholic as far as I know, so I can't make out how Bill came by such a thing."

"Well, don't throw any of it out whatever you do," instructed Alice firmly. "I'll try to find out more when I have a moment." Hannah shrugged her shoulders, in no mood to argue about such trivialities. At that moment, the baby started to cry, and Alice picked him up from his crib and cradled him gently in her arms.

"Your Geordie is a beautiful baby, my dear, but you must remember that the poor little lad will never know his father. You owe it to him to pass on Bill's family heritage, however little it means to you."

Hannah nodded and placed the box carefully on top of the envelope containing the pound notes.

* * *

Alice's next port of call was her parents' home in neighbouring Rose Street. As always whenever anything important happened in Burnside, be it cause for celebration or cause for mourning, the villagers gathered in each other's houses – and today was no exception. Joe and Bella Armstrong's front room was packed with family and friends, all dressed in black and engaged in muted conversation about the disaster at the mine. Plates of homemade scones and cups of strong sugary tea were being served to all. It was not often that Alice managed to get away from her job in County Durham and pay a visit home, so her arrival was like a breath of fresh air from the outside world. Joe and Bella embraced her warmly, glad of the diversion from the unremitting gloom and despair in Burnside.

"I've just come from our Hannah's," she told her parents. Everyone in the room shook their heads in commiseration, murmuring that it was disgraceful to turn a poor widow with four children out of her home. "I'm sorry I couldn't be back in time for the funeral," she added apologetically. "How was it?"

Alice learned that hundreds and hundreds of people had turned out – not only from Burnside but from other pit villages – to pay homage to the nineteen men killed in the explosion. The vicar had given a moving speech, not forgetting to praise the courage and devotion of the dozens of miners who had taken part in the rescue operation.

"Did Sir Reginald and Lady Felton attend?" she enquired.

"Lady Felton came with her younger bairns," Bella replied. "She was very kind and had a word with all the miners' families. She said Sir Reginald's going to erect a stone memorial in the village, with the names of all the pitmen who were killed."

"What we need are better safety measures, not a blasted memorial," spat out Joe Armstrong bitterly. "Old Felton is like all the colliery owners, dragging his feet to stop mines inspectors coming in and telling him what should be done to protect the men. Any money spent on safety would come out of his profits, and we all know profit is the only thing the bugger cares about."

Alice was heartened to see her father in such a feisty mood. A squat man in his early sixties with the miner's bandy legs and brawny arms, he was still remarkably hale and hearty in spite of over fifty years of service at the colliery. "I think it's shameful of Sir Reginald not to attend," she commented.

"Lady Felton said he had to go to London on short notice," scoffed Joe. "But we all reckon he didn't dare show his bloody face here in case the pitmen turned on him and strung him up by the balls! It would have served the bugger right and all. Colliery workers are killed every year in Northumberland, but them fat-cat owners couldn't give a damn." A murmur of approval went around the tiny front room from men and women alike.

"As it happens, I'm planning to pay a call on Lady Felton tomorrow and introduce myself," announced Alice with a hint of pride in her voice.

"Introduce yourself as what?" demanded Joe.

"As the new schoolteacher in Burnside!" exclaimed Alice triumphantly. She explained the circumstances of her new appointment and told her astounded parents that after the summer holidays, she would be returning to the village on a permanent basis. Looking around the familiar faces in the front room, she was gratified to see their looks of admiration and respect.

"Eeh, she's a clever lass, our Alice," proclaimed her father. "I've always said she's got a man's brain in a woman's body." Although clearly meant as a compliment, this remark never failed to irritate Alice. Was it so inconceivable that her woman's body might contain a woman's brain – but one equal to a man's? She bit her lip, knowing it was useless to argue the point.

"You'll never get a man now, hinny," sighed her mother. "No man wants to be saddled with a clever lass." The other women in the room nodded smugly; there was no point in Alice being educated if she ended up an old maid, deprived of the only things that mattered in life – a husband and children. Alice smiled grimly, feeling as always like a freak of nature.

"Have you heard from our Eddie?" she asked. Her brother was serving in the Northumberland Fusiliers and – she guessed from reading the papers – most likely preparing for a decisive battle on the Somme in France.

Bella perked up at the mention of her son's name and retrieved a black-and-white postcard from the mantelpiece. "We got this three weeks ago. Here pet, you can read it if you like."

Alice perused the card, which had been sent from the Channel port of Boulogne-sur-Mer and bore a short laconic message in Eddie's untidy scrawl: "Dear Mam and Dad, we have got a two day leave here. Everything is fine and there is nothing to worry about. Your loving son, Eddie."

Alice's eyes pricked with tears. She knew of course that cards and letters from the front were censored if they carried too much information, but nevertheless it was typical of Eddie to make light of his situation. She followed the progress of the war avidly in the press and was well aware that trench warfare was very far from being a 'fine' experience. Clearly, her brother's one thought as he put pen to paper had been to reassure his family back home in Burnside. Still, at least he was still alive.

Her eyes darted to Don and Peggy McCulloch, sitting morosely in one corner of the room. The McCulloch family lived next door, and it was unlike them to look so glum. As a general rule, they were high-spirited and humorous, living proof that Scottish Presbyterians were not necessarily dour. Having moved from the Ayrshire mines twenty or so years previously, Don and Peggy had quickly settled into Burnside and adopted the accent and customs of their Geordie neighbours. Their eldest son, Alex, and Alice's brother, Eddie, had been *marras* at the colliery before the war and had volunteered together to serve in the Northumberland Fusiliers.

"Have you had a card from your Alex?" enquired Alice, suddenly concerned.

Peggy McCulloch shook her head, her eyes betraying the constant tension and anxiety she was going through. "There's been no word for two months now, pet. We can't help but worry, our Alex has always been so good about writing home."

Alice's heart contracted, but she tried to sound more sensible than she felt. "The postal service is sometimes disrupted, you know, and some letters take a long time getting through. No news is good news, so they say. I'm sure you'll be hearing from Alex soon, Mrs McCulloch." The older woman smiled faintly, desperately wanting to believe her.

Dear God, let's hope I'm right, prayed Alice. The conversation in the room resumed and she let it wash over her, lost in thoughts of Alex but making sure her face gave nothing away. No one in Burnside must ever find out her true feelings for Alex McCulloch.

She and Alex were the same age and had always been part of each other's lives. They had sat next to each other in school and over the years had developed an easy camaraderie. They had shared all their hopes and dreams and talked endlessly about every topic under the sun. Alex was every bit as intelligent as Alice, although he had none of her dedication to academic excellence. Nevertheless, he had understood her ambition to become a teacher and was thrilled when she won a place at the pupil teacher college.

After Alice left home to live in County Durham, she and Alex saw very little of each other but corresponded regularly. There was no trace of romance in these long letters, however, for theirs was a meeting of minds. Alex, like all the other Burnside lads, had started work at the colliery at the age of twelve and was now a hewer – the most respected and best-paid job at the mine. Yet he had lost none of his intellectual curiosity and devoured every book available at the Miners Institute, particularly those dealing with history and politics. He had developed a keen interest in the trade union movement and the budding Labour Party, sharing his idealistic vision of the future in long impassioned letters to Alice. She responded in the same vein, writing of her conviction that education was the key to the emancipation of the working classes.

Yes, it was a true meeting of minds, thought Alice ironically – at least on Alex's side. Alice was all too aware that he didn't think of her as a woman at all; she was merely a comrade-in-arms, a plain Jane, a blue-stocking whose activism and ambitions were on a par with his own. Alex on the other hand was the tallest, most handsome, most charismatic man she had ever met and could have his pick of any girl he chose. Every unmarried female for miles around was setting her cap at him.

Alice reminded herself sternly that her romantic dreams of Alex McCulloch would have to remain in the realm of fantasy. She was not about to sacrifice her career in the teaching profession for any man, even him. With a great effort, she pushed Alex temporarily to the back of her mind; she needed to order her thoughts and prepare a plan of action before she called on Lady Felton the next day.

* * *

Winifred Felton spotted Alice from her drawing room window as she walked purposefully up the long tree-lined drive towards Felton Hall. Judging from the fact that she was on foot and that she was smartly but plainly dressed, Lady Felton guessed that the unknown young woman approaching must be the new schoolteacher. Old Mr Carr, the headmaster of Burnside School, had written to her recently to announce this new appointment. So this is Miss Alice Armstrong, she thought, slightly irritated to hear her ringing as bold as brass at the front door instead of going around to the tradesmen's entrance at the back of the house. She debated whether to tell the butler she was not receiving that afternoon, but in the end decided it might be quite diverting to meet her.

Two minutes later, Alice was shown into the drawing room, looking as poised and unflustered as if grand houses like Felton Hall were her natural habitat. Winifred Felton took in her charcoal grey, simply cut suit; the new calf-length skirt showed off her trim ankles but also revealed sensible laced-up shoes. She wore a small felt hat with a flat brim over her decidedly modern blond bob. A rather unconventional young woman, surmised Lady Felton as they exchanged greetings and Alice was offered a seat in a comfortable armchair opposite her own. In fact,

Alice was feeling more intimidated than she looked, although she was determined not to show it. Sir Reginald and Lady Felton – he had been knighted twenty years ago for outstanding services rendered to British industry – were among the richest and most influential families in Northumberland. Nor had Alice ever been inside a house as impressive as Felton Hall. Oh, how she loved this drawing room, so elegant and perfectly proportioned! The expensive furniture and lamps, with their curved lines and decorative motifs, were in the distinctive Art Nouveau style; Lady Felton was obviously a woman of refined taste. Alice's eyes travelled to the vibrant watercolour painting displayed on one wall, depicting a glorious Mediterranean scene.

Winifred Felton instantly caught the young woman's admiring gaze. "It's a Signac," she said. "My husband and I purchased it at an exhibition in Paris two years ago. Unfortunately, our journeys to the Continent have been curtailed since the onset of this terrible war."

"How inconvenient for you," said Alice crisply.

Lady Felton visibly stiffened. "My two eldest sons are serving king and country in the Royal Navy," she announced in icy tones.

Oh dear, thought Alice, this wasn't an auspicious start to the conversation; she realised she must have sounded very rude. "You must be so proud of them both," she responded warmly. "My brother Eddie is serving in the Northumberland Fusiliers. It seems we women spend our lives these days constantly worrying about the safety of our loved ones. We can do nothing but wait and pray for their safe return home."

Looking somewhat mollified, Lady Felton turned the conversation to her new appointment. Alice, feeling on far safer ground now, spoke enthusiastically about her ambitions for the village school. "I would so like to expand our small collection of books, Lady Felton. It's so important for children to develop a love of reading at an early age, don't you agree? And I strongly believe they should have a proper playground too, a place where they can exercise in the fresh air and engage in sporting activities. *Mens sana in corpore sano.*"

The older woman was impressed in spite of herself by so much energy and drive. "Quite so, Miss Armstrong. I shall be pleased to make a donation to the school when your plans have progressed."

Alice thanked her effusively, hoping she had found an ally in this grand lady. "It means a great deal to me to be teaching at the school where I was a pupil myself."

Lady Felton could barely conceal her astonishment when Alice added that she had been born in Rose Street and that her father worked at the colliery. Could this ladylike, articulate young woman really be the daughter of one of the uncouth, ignorant pitmen employed by her husband? She certainly didn't speak in the Geordie dialect, and even her Tyneside accent was not too broad.

"Then you must know of the terrible accident which occurred at the colliery a few days ago, Miss Armstrong. No doubt, you've heard that Sir Reginald intends to erect a memorial in honour of the miners who lost their lives."

This was the cue Alice had been waiting for. "The memorial will be most appreciated of course, Lady Felton. However, it won't help the widows of Burnside feed and clothe their children, nor put a roof over their heads once they're evicted from their homes."

Winifred Felton bristled with annoyance. How dare this upstart teacher put her on the defensive and imply that her husband's management of the colliery was at fault in any way? And why on earth should she be made to feel responsible for the plight of these people?

"All the widowed women have received adequate compensation," she pointed out frostily. "And surely, their families will rally around and come to their aid. I'm certain the parish or the Board of Guardians will provide relief for the most needy too. You must understand, Miss Armstrong, that Sir Reginald has done everything that is required of a colliery owner in such unfortunate circumstances."

Thinking of her sister Hannah and all the other destitute women in Burnside, Alice pressed on regardless, refusing to be put in her place. "Everything that is required from a legal point of view, perhaps. But don't you see that these women feel humiliated at the prospect of begging for charity? Or taking money from relatives who can barely make ends meet themselves?"

Lady Felton listened to this tirade in stony silence, but Alice was determined to have her say. "Take my sister Hannah, for instance, whose husband, Bill Robertson, was killed in the accident. She and her four children will soon be cast out of their home, with nothing but a few pounds compensation between them and the workhouse. She's desperate to find work of some kind, so that she can take responsibility for her children and bring them up decently."

It was the first time Winifred Felton had been forced to think about the colliery disaster in human terms, to consider its consequences for the women left behind. Poverty was an issue she avoided as a general rule; it made her uncomfortable to realise how pampered and sheltered her own life was. But she was not an insensitive woman by any means and now found herself wondering how she would have coped if she had been one of the Burnside widows, penniless and homeless through no fault of her own. It suddenly occurred to her that mourning their husbands was a luxury these pitmen's wives could not afford. The struggle for survival took precedence over such sentimental considerations.

"Did your sister have an occupation before she married?" she asked, feeling cornered yet unable to extricate herself from the drift of the conversation. She could see only too well where Alice was leading her.

"She was in service as a laundry maid."

The two women sat for a while in silence while Lady Felton's mind ran through the possibilities and Alice mentally crossed her fingers.

"Well, naturally she couldn't go back into service," remarked Lady Felton reflectively. "She would need to go back home to her children after work."

"Yes indeed. My sister's youngest child is only a few weeks old. But it's barely two miles from the village to Felton Hall, easily within walking distance." Alice was leading her horse to water, but could she make the horse drink?

"You must understand, Miss Armstrong, that I can't possibly be expected to provide employment for all the widowed women in Burnside," Lady Felton blurted out defensively. Alice nodded reluctantly.

"Nevertheless, there's plenty of work in the laundry here, as you might imagine in a household of this size. If you can vouch for your sister's character and she can be utterly relied upon to be present at the Hall from eight in the morning to six in the evening…"

"Oh, she can, she can!" exclaimed Alice, unable to contain her excitement. "You've been most kind, Lady Felton, Hannah will be so grateful. Shall I instruct her to arrange the details with your housekeeper?"

"Please do, Miss Armstrong." But now that her attention was focused on the plight of the Burnside widows, another possibility crossed Lady Felton's mind. "I may have a solution to the problem of housing, at least for some of the women," she began hesitantly. "Naturally, I would have to speak to my husband, and I'm not sure at this point whether it's even feasible…"

Alice's plan, carefully elaborated before today's visit, seemed to be succeeding beyond her wildest expectations. She thought it best to say nothing, however, in case Lady Felton suddenly backed away from this new idea, whatever it was. She looked expectantly at the older woman, willing her with every fibre of her being to continue.

"When you walked over here today, Miss Armstrong, you may have noticed – about half way between Burnside and the Hall – a row of disused farm labourer's cottages. I believe there are six or seven of them, and they must be in a sorry state of disrepair, for they haven't been occupied for years. There's no water supply either, although I seem to remember there's a well nearby which might be made to work again. If you think that some of the families in need would be interested…"

"I know they would," Alice assured her without hesitation. "The cottages are dilapidated of course, but I'm sure everyone in Burnside would be happy to give a hand in repairing them and making them fit for habitation. It would be a godsend to widows like my sister."

"Well, in that case," said Lady Felton with a smile, "I'm sure I can persuade Sir Reginald to let the families live there rent-free."

A jubilant Alice beamed back at her. "What you have offered to do today, Lady Felton, will be of far more benefit to these women than any grand memorial. On their behalf, I thank you from the bottom of my heart."

* * *

In the autumn of 1916, Alice threw herself into her new job at Burnside School with her usual enthusiasm. Mr Carr and his wife kindly offered her two chilly rooms on the top floor of the schoolhouse for a very modest rent. It was a convenient arrangement, and Alice was happy enough to take her meals with them while still retaining some privacy when she wanted to be alone.

The elderly headmaster was delighted to have his former star pupil teaching alongside him. "You have a fine mind, my dear, and I'm so proud of what you've accomplished," he told her. "If we were living in a fair and just world, by all rights you should have gone to university."

"It's too late for me now," said Alice. "But times are changing, and one day working class children – boys and girls alike – will have the chance of a university education. It won't be for many years perhaps, but my mission is to make sure these children make the most of their abilities in today's world."

Alice had neither the time nor the inclination to give much thought to her personal circumstances that year. With so many men away at the front and the war dragging on inconclusively month after month, she felt duty-bound to devote all her energies to her work. Qualified professional women like Alice were proving invaluable at a time when thousands of male teachers had left their jobs to enlist in the army, many of them never to return. The absence of so many men was undeniably creating opportunities for women in general and teachers in particular. Women all over Britain were playing a vital role in the war effort, keeping the home fires burning in factories, offices and schools. Alice was confident that when the war was over every woman in Britain would be given the right to vote. It was outrageous, she felt, to prevent women from playing an active role in public life, to bar them from university, to keep them legally and financially in a state of inferiority to men.

But Alice was in no mood for political activism during that autumn of 1916, for morale was low in Burnside as the number of British casualties at the Western front reached horrendous proportions. Thousands of young men were being injured or killed daily, their lives destroyed before they had barely begun. In September, Alice was shocked to see Danny Moore, one of her old classmates, back in Burnside after being invalided out of the army; he had survived the bloodbath of the Somme but had come home with both legs amputated and blind in one eye. Two weeks later, a telegram was delivered to Alice's parents on Rose Street; her brother Eddie had been killed in action at the Battle of Morval.

Yet even as she mourned her brother and tried fruitlessly to comfort Joe and Bella, Alice's thoughts turned continually to Alex McCulloch. She felt guilty that her grief for poor Eddie was diluted by her anxiety for Alex, but she couldn't help herself. Although she had never been an assiduous churchgoer, she was surprised to find herself praying every night for Alex's safe homecoming. It was a thankless task, for he never wrote to her and nor did she expect him to; she wasn't his sweetheart and was certain she never would be. It was just that she simply couldn't face the prospect of a world without Alex. However tenuous his place in her life, it was a place which no one else could fill.

Life was very hard for her sister Hannah too, although without Alice's timely support, she would have been destitute. Dozens of Burnside men had volunteered to help repair the disused labourers' cottages which – again thanks to Alice – Lady Felton had offered rent-free.

Holes in roofs were fixed, panes were installed in windows, walls and floors were consolidated. The village women scoured and scrubbed every square inch of the filthy, rat-infested interiors to make the houses habitable. Hannah and other widows like her were grateful enough to move into these poky, damp cottages devoid of even the most basic facilities. At least they were not separated from their children and had a roof over their heads, however dilapidated.

Winifred Felton had been as good as her word, and Hannah was now employed as a laundry maid at Felton Hall. At first light every morning, she left little Geordie, the baby, in her mother's care and walked the two miles to the Hall. She came home exhausted after ten hours of washing, scrubbing and ironing mountains of clothes, towels and bed linen. Her hands were swollen and red raw, her back ached constantly, and sometimes she was so weary she could barely stand. But Hannah told herself it could have been worse; the baby was healthy and easy to care for, while her daughters Violet and Mary Jane helped with the cooking and household tasks when they came home from school.

John, the eldest son Hannah had counted on to start work at the colliery and help shore up the family finances, had let them all down. There had been long bitter arguments, with Hannah begging him to get a job at the pit and John adamantly refusing to do so. He was only fourteen years old, Hannah reminded herself, and who could blame him when his father had been killed in that same pit only weeks before? Even so, he was the man of the house now and must take responsibility for the family. Although John had always had a selfish streak, surely he wouldn't abandon them all in their hour of need?

But John didn't want to be tied down to a lifetime of supporting a mother and three siblings. One day, Hannah came home to find him gone for good; he had packed his few belongings into a knapsack and left a scribbled note announcing he was off to join the Merchant Navy. A distraught Hannah waited month after month for news of her son, to no avail. John Robertson was never seen or heard from again in Burnside.

"You're well rid of him, Hannah," declared Alice firmly. "John's always been a bad penny and he'll come to a sticky end, you mark my words."

"But how could he do this to me?" wailed Hannah. "How can I feed us all with what I earn as a washerwoman at Felton Hall? It was hard enough making ends meet when Bill was alive, but at least he was bringing in a man's wage."

"Oh Hannah, my dear, you know you can always depend on me." Alice was well aware that her elder sister was too proud to accept money directly from her, but in the weeks and months that followed, she made it her business to come to the aid of the Robertson family. She bought the children new shoes in winter and warm clothes for school, passing the purchases off as birthday or Christmas presents. She came to eat with them once a week but always arrived with a laden basket of food. With Alice's help, sympathy and advice Hannah Robertson and her children managed to scrape by, unlike so many others in Burnside.

* * *

When little Elsie McCulloch, ten years old and the youngest of the McCulloch brood, filed into Alice's class with the other children on that cold February morning in 1919, she could hardly wait to announce the news.

"We've had a letter from our Alex, he's on his way back home!" she proclaimed to everyone within earshot, her round face lit up with excitement.

"That's nice, Elsie," responded Alice with a smile. "Your Mam and Dad must be thrilled."

Oh, but Alice was thrilled too! Heart thudding and not wanting to betray her feelings to a classroom full of pupils, she turned her back and busied herself in wiping the blackboard. Ever since the Armistice had been signed three months earlier, she had thought of little else but Alex McCulloch's return. She thanked God every night that he had survived this horrific war, supposedly the war to end all wars. There had been no communication between them for almost five years now, so he could have no idea how ardently she longed to see him again. But Alice, her fierce unrequited love for Alex McCulloch blazing inside her, didn't care.

From various reports she had been reading in the newspapers, Alice was not surprised that Alex was being demobilised relatively soon after the Armistice. The Army was giving priority discharge to men who had volunteered for service at the outset of the war, and also to men who were needed in vital industrial occupations such as mining; Alex met both criteria. But she knew it might be days or even weeks before he was back in Burnside, for the logistics of organising the return of hundreds of thousands of men were laborious to say the least. Alex would have to wait in a transit camp on the French coast before he was allocated a place on a Channel crossing. Then there would be another wait in a Disbursement Centre in the south of England while the administrative formalities of his discharge were processed and a railway warrant was issued for his journey north to Newcastle. Alice burned with impatience as her imagination followed him through the various stages of his demobilisation, although she knew such agitation was entirely irrational. What on earth did she expect to happen once Alex was back in Burnside? Nothing, she reminded herself sternly, nothing at all.

As it happened, Alice did not have long to wait. Five days later, as she was preparing to leave the empty classroom after school, Alex McCulloch turned up unannounced, a broad grin on his face and still dressed in his army uniform and greatcoat. Her heart lurched, colour flooded her face and – for once in her life, throwing caution to the winds – she ran straight into his arms.

"Oh Alex, I'm so happy to see you home at last!" she cried, standing on tiptoe and looking up into his eyes.

"Not as happy as I am to be here," he said cheerfully as he enveloped her in a brotherly hug. "I never thought I'd be so glad to see a pit heap again, I can tell you. Foreign travel isn't all it's cracked up to be!" He released her and stepped back. "Teaching suits you, Alice. You're looking well."

"So are you," said Alice, blushing and struggling to regain her composure. "I see you're still wearing your uniform." She hardly knew what to say now that he was finally here in the flesh.

"Aye, but not for long. I'll get a pound from the Army if I turn my greatcoat in."

"I see." Her heart still pounding and her throat dry, Alice searched desperately for a topic of conversation. Luckily, Alex, clearly less perturbed by their reunion, took her out of her misery by squeezing her hand and offering his condolences for the death of her brother Eddie. They talked about him quietly for a while, although Alice found it hard to focus. She was overwhelmed by Alex's sheer physical presence.

Oh, she had forgotten how handsome he was! Over six feet tall, Alex McCulloch stood out from the other Burnside miners with his broad frame and long, muscled legs. He had a strong, virile face with a chiselled jaw, unruly dark hair and slate grey eyes that glinted when he smiled. He looks every inch the hero of a romantic novel, thought Alice. But it was not only Alex's masculine good looks that made him so attractive. He seemed to exude a natural charisma – a combination of keen intelligence, innate self-confidence and quiet authority – felt by everyone, men and women alike, in his presence. He was a man people instinctively trusted, a man admired by men and adored by women.

Caught up in the flow of conversation, they sat down at the same school desks they had occupied so many years ago. Alice bombarded him with questions about his years in the trenches, but Alex – usually so articulate and keen to share his experiences – held back. He needed time, he said, to put his thoughts into perspective and try to make some sense of the horror and bloodshed he had witnessed almost daily.

"I'm not trying to keep anything from you, Alice," he added with downcast eyes. "I'm just not ready yet, and I don't know if I'll ever find the words to describe the sheer savagery of it all. Ever since I left France, I keep asking myself, what was it all for? Nine million men from all over Europe were slaughtered, but what were they fighting for?"

Alice was shocked. "You mustn't think that way, Alex. Our soldiers didn't die in vain; they gave their lives for king and country."

"Oh aye, the British and French have won the day for now. But how will that benefit the ordinary working men of Europe? The fat cats who started the war will expect us all to buckle down and go back to our jobs as if nowt had happened."

Alice was thrown off balance by his cynical reaction; she had been so sure that Alex would come home proud of the part he had played in Britain's victory. She sensed that the war years had radicalised his thinking. Alex was a grown man now and would no longer be satisfied with abstract ideas.

"Look at the Russians, Alice!" he went on, his eyes lighting up with enthusiasm. "They didn't wait for the end of the war to stand up to oppression. They've overthrown the Czar and are creating a new socialist society. Revolution is a reality in Russia."

"But surely, you don't want a revolution in this country?" protested Alice. "The Czar was a despot and kept the Russian people in virtual serfdom. But Britain is a democracy, and if we want to bring about change and improve the lives of ordinary people, we must use the machinery of government. Socialist reform must be implemented gradually and peacefully, by winning a majority in Parliament. As far as I can see, revolution is bringing little to Russia but anarchy, starvation and violence."

Alex mulled over her words and gave her the wry smile she found so irresistible. "Aye, I suppose you have a point. You know, the one and only good thing about the war was that it gave me a chance to talk with men from all over the country – men of all classes and trades I'd never have met if I'd stayed here in Burnside. Dockers from London, mill workers from Lancashire, farm lads from Devon… we're all in the same boat! What the coal miners must fight for on Tyneside is part of a nationwide battle for justice that concerns every working man in Britain. I know now that if all us workers unite, we'll be an unstoppable force for change."

Alice was elated to see that the trenches had not quelled Alex's spirit, or his fierce passion for political ideas and social causes. Nevertheless, his convictions had hardened, and his old youthful idealism was now overlaid with a new maturity and determination. It occurred to her that even if Alex never returned her love, she could still play a vital role in his life… as an ally, a sparring partner and a friend. She could hardly wait to find out what the future held in store for them both.

* * *

Alex went back to his old job as a hewer at Burnside colliery, but every moment of his spare time was dedicated to local politics. He joined the Northumberland Miners Association and soon made a name for himself as a union activist. He gave impassioned speeches in Newcastle, calling for the mines to be removed from private ownership and nationalised. This, he insisted, was the only way to secure across-the-board improvements in the coal industry – the regulation of coal prices, a decent minimum wage, an eight-hour workday and stringent measures for the miners' safety.

Soon acknowledged as a born leader and talented public speaker, Alex's reputation spread through Tyneside like wildfire and soon reached the ears of Sir Reginald Felton, his employer at Burnside colliery. But Alex was a first-rate hewer and immensely popular with the men; Sir Reginald had no desire to make a martyr of this rebellious young man by firing him. He decided to bide his time for now and instructed his colliery manager to keep a watchful eye on the activities of Alex McCulloch.

Alice and Alex resumed their old relationship as easily as if the intervening years had never been. She could not accompany him to union meetings, well aware that her presence would almost certainly meet with hostility in this tough, exclusively male environment. But there were many other opportunities for them to spend time together, for they had both joined the Labour Party and attended regular meetings and conferences at the local chapter in Newcastle.

Once again, Alex was quickly singled out as a young man with the potential to play a key role in the fast-expanding Labour movement, but this was an arena where Alice could shine too. In political meetings, she was unafraid to stand up and have her say when she felt strongly about something, as she did about women's suffrage.

"Is it fair," she would demand boldly, "that every man in this country has the right to vote while most women are still barred from participating in public affairs? Yes, the government has granted suffrage to women who are over the age of thirty and own property, but what about the millions of women like myself who fall into neither of these categories? We refuse to be relegated to second-class citizenship. We reject absolutely this disgraceful state of affairs, and I call on the Labour Party to pledge unstinting support for our cause." Alice sat down amidst loud applause and was gratified to catch a look of pride and admiration in Alex's eyes.

Her favourite times were the bus journeys into town, when she had Alex entirely to herself. Although they were always surrounded by other passengers and there was nothing improper about the situation, these bus rides provided a kind of intimacy that Alice looked forward to immensely. It was true they rarely discussed personal matters, but every minute was filled with heated debate – and often fierce arguments – about the political issues of the day. And as they talked, Alice secretly basked in the warmth and closeness of his body next to hers. She breathed in his clean, manly scent and pretended – however irrationally – that they were just another courting couple on a night out.

This private fantasy, which persisted in spite of her better judgement, was dashed forever when Alex announced in the spring of 1920 – barely a year after his return to Burnside – that he was engaged to be married.

"I'm nearly twenty-eight, Alice," he pointed out soberly. "I reckon it's about time I settled down, don't you?"

Alice forced herself to smile, to look surprised and delighted, to make all the right noises. Alex must not notice that his words had caused her heart to contract and her soul to freeze over. "Congratulations Alex, what wonderful news! And who's the lucky bride-to-be?"

The question was deliberately flippant, for she already knew the answer. Gossip about Alex and Kate Malone had been rife for weeks, but Alice had chosen to ignore it. People were always linking Alex's name romantically to one girl or another, and she had hoped the latest rumours would prove to be as unfounded as the rest.

Alice was well aware that this particular courtship met with widespread disapproval in the village. The McCullochs were strict Scottish Presbyterians and looked down on Irish Catholics with righteous scorn, while the Catholic Malone family was already up in arms at the prospect of Kate marrying outside her faith. Even though there was a far greater degree of religious tolerance than in previous generations, the vast majority of pit villagers still tended to marry within their own religious community. Still, Alice speculated, if anyone could pull this one off it was Alex. There wasn't a living soul strong enough to stand in the way of Alex McCulloch once he had set his heart on something.

"I'm sure you've heard I've been courting Kate Malone," he went on eagerly. "And I know what you must be thinking, Alice. But it's not Kate's fault if she was brought up a papist. Her grandfather was a survivor of the Great Famine, and it's only natural for the Irish to cling to their history and their faith. I've talked to Kate about it all, and now she sees the error of her ways. She understands that Catholicism is a force of oppression and has kept the poor down for centuries with all that superstitious mumbo-jumbo. She's already promised to convert to the Church of Scotland."

I'll bet she has, thought Alice. Little Kate Malone wouldn't give religion a second thought if it meant getting her hands on Alex McCulloch. Why, every female for miles around would be green with envy. Perhaps it was unkind – and unfair to Kate – to harbour such thoughts, she reasoned, but at that precise moment she didn't care. "I see," she murmured, her jaw aching with the effort of smiling.

"It wasn't easy talking Mam and Dad around to the idea," said Alex. "And the Malones were none too pleased either. But they'll get over it in time, Alice, they'll have to. Eeh, I can't wait for you to get to know Kate properly, I'm sure you'll like her. She's the sweetest, bonniest lass I've ever met. You will come to the wedding, won't you Alice?"

"Of course I'll come," said Alice brightly. "Wild horses couldn't drag me away."

* * *

Alice rifled through the racks of summer dresses in the Ladies Fashion department of Fenwick's, trying to find something suitable to wear to Alex's wedding. She was determined to look her best on the day, if only to conceal how she would be feeling inside. Faced with such a bewildering choice of colours and styles, she felt flustered and out of place; she had never been much interested in clothes or her own appearance. If only she could be more like the other women out shopping in Newcastle today, squealing with delight over the latest fashions and comparing material and cut as if their lives depended on it.

Luckily, a young shop assistant came to her aid. "What about this one, Miss?" she suggested helpfully, pulling out a dress from the rack. "It's all the rage this season and it comes in two colours, either lilac or pearl grey."

"Perfect, I'll try them both on." Alice grabbed the two dresses and disappeared into the changing room, the shop assistant hard on her heels and still chattering nineteen to the dozen.

She undressed hurriedly, tried on the lilac dress and took a long hard look at herself in the full-length mirror. The dress fit reasonably well, although the new fashions with their loose lines and dropped waists did little to flatter Alice's slender figure. The bodice of the dress flattened her bust, while the skirt bagged over her small waist. As for the solemn face – pale and devoid of make-up – reflected in the mirror, it was unlikely to turn male heads, Alice thought critically. No wonder Alex McCulloch didn't find her attractive, or even notice she was a woman at all... The mirror revealed exactly what she was: a dowdy blue-stocking, a straight-laced schoolteacher well on the way to spinsterhood.

Alice had always despised women who relied on flirtation and feminine wiles to catch a man's eye; she had never learned to smile coyly, pout and flutter her eyelashes, sway her hips as she walked. She had always supposed that intelligent men would not be fooled by such behaviour, that they would appreciate a woman whose brain and personality were a match for their own. Yet today, she realised that her uncompromising attitude to physicality had merely resulted in making her invisible in the eyes of a man she was madly in love with. And it was too late now, much too late... Alex McCulloch was lost to her forever.

Tears pricking at the back of her eyes, she removed the dress carefully and put her own clothes back on. She emerged from the changing room to find the sales assistant still hovering nearby, a bright smile on her pretty young face.

"I'll have this one, please," said Alice abruptly, thrusting the pearl grey dress at the girl. Grey, she had decided, was a more serviceable colour and could be worn on numerous other occasions.

"Oh, what a shame," exclaimed the sales assistant, looking genuinely disappointed. "That lilac shade suits your blond hair and colouring really well, Miss. All you need is a bit of powder and lipstick to set off your complexion."

"I really don't think so," snapped Alice. She had no intention of arguing the merits of lilac or pearl grey with this silly shop girl.

"There's a matching hat to go with the dress," persisted the girl, presenting Alice with a grey felt tam o'shanter. "And this lovely rope of jet beads would look just perfect at the neckline."

"Fine, I'll take everything." Alice no longer cared about the wedding outfit and was simply desperate to pay and get out of the store. What did it matter anyway, she thought bitterly. Alex McCulloch would look straight through her whatever she wore, blind to any woman except Kate Malone.

* * *

The wedding day in early July dawned bright and sunny, the first really warm day that summer. Alice, smartly turned out in her new pearl grey dress, sat at the back of Burnside Presbyterian Church; her sister Hannah and the three children, all of them spruced-up for the occasion, sat next to her. The church was packed with Burnside miners and their families, all waiting expectantly for the appearance of the bride. Alex could be glimpsed standing by the altar, his back turned to the congregation and conversing with the minister.

The Malone family had reluctantly given their consent to the marriage but adamantly refused to attend the wedding service. They and the rest of the Irish Catholic community would not set foot in a Presbyterian church, although they had agreed to attend the reception which was to follow in the village hall. So, Kate Malone would not be given away by her father but by one of his *marras* at the colliery, a close friend and – more importantly – a Protestant.

When she thought back to the wedding service in later years, Alice's memories were always blurred and confused. All she could remember was that her stomach was churning throughout and that she was choked by an emotion she hardly knew how to define – passionate longing mingled with resentment and frustration. She fought hard not to betray her feelings, to maintain a pleasantly neutral expression. She was thankful that everyone around her was too absorbed in the ceremony to pay attention to the village schoolteacher at the back of the church.

Only Hannah noticed that her face was unusually flushed and that she was perspiring heavily. "Are you all right, hinny?" she whispered sympathetically.

"Yes," hissed Alice fiercely. "It's just so hot in here with all these people. I wish it was all over, don't you?" Hannah gave her a quizzical look but patted her hand gently and said no more.

The reception afterwards began decorously enough but soon turned festive as the drink flowed freely and the wedding guests entered into the spirit of the occasion. Huge platters of ham sandwiches were devoured and equally huge quantities of beer consumed. The drab village hall was filled with noise and laughter as the people of Burnside seized on this opportunity to forget their cares and celebrate.

Alice hung back, sipping a small glass of sherry near the door and making desultory conversation with her mother. She wondered how soon she could possibly escape without looking rude. She had barely spoken to Alex, other than pecking him on the cheek and proffering congratulations outside the church. Friends and relatives swarmed around him now, chattering and joking as the atmosphere in the hall reached fever pitch. She watched him, standing head and shoulders above the other men and looking almost unbearably handsome in his new suit, a white carnation in the buttonhole and his unruly hair smoothed down for the occasion.

"I hope you're enjoying yourselves." Alice started in surprise and found herself looking into the beaming face of Kate Malone, or Kate McCulloch as she had just become.

"Aye, we are that. It's been many a year since we had such a grand wedding in Burnside," piped up Bella Armstrong.

"What about you, Miss Armstrong? Can I get you another glass of sherry?"

"Oh, please call me Alice – Miss Armstrong makes me feel so ancient! No more sherry just now, Kate, but it's a lovely reception. Thank you so much for inviting me."

"Alex would have been right disappointed if you hadn't come. He puts great store by your opinion, Miss. He always says what a sharp mind you've got." Kate, her face glowing and her eyes sparkling with happiness, gazed adoringly across the crowded room at her husband. "Eeh, Miss Armstrong, I'm the happiest lass in the world today. Alex could have married anyone he wanted and yet he picked me!"

Yes, and I can't help wondering why, mused Alice, chiding herself at the same time for harbouring such thoughts. She forced a polite smile and watched the girl appraisingly as Kate drifted off and circulated among the wedding guests. What on earth did Alex see in her? Kate was a mere slip of a girl, barely nineteen and almost a decade younger than her husband. Self-effacing and uneducated, she had been employed as a seamstress until she had met Alex at a village hop. Oh, she was pretty enough in her way, Alice conceded, with her tiny delicate figure and porcelain complexion – a frail little sparrow of a girl. But what in heaven's name could she and Alex possibly have in common, what did they find to talk about?

She cursed herself for her stupidity as it suddenly dawned on her that Alex McCulloch didn't expect meaningful discussions or fierce political debates from his wife. Intelligent conversation was an area reserved for his male cronies... and Alice herself of course. She surmised that he had mentally classified her in some grey indeterminate zone, neither fish nor fowl and certainly not a woman. Oh, Alex held progressive views in many ways and enthusiastically espoused ideas of female emancipation. But clearly when it came to choosing a wife, Alex had looked for traditional womanly virtues... gentleness, submissiveness, abnegation. There would be no life for Kate beyond the domestic sphere. She would devote herself exclusively to cooking, cleaning and making a comfortable home for her husband and their children, always putting his interests and concerns before her own. In return, Alex would provide material protection and financial support – the age-old marital pact, thought Alice grimly.

She realised she had been naïve to imagine that Alex would seek out an equal partner, a companion on the road of life, as his wife. No, he was perfectly happy with a woman like Kate – a woman who acknowledged her intellectual inferiority and was content to play second fiddle to her husband for life. But what about love, what about passion? How could little Kate, so incapable of understanding the workings of his mind, possibly love Alex as much as she did? It just wasn't fair, thought Alice miserably as so many unanswerable questions flooded her brain.

"Haway over here, bonny lass," called out Alex. "It's time for a toast to my lovely bride." Kate flitted eagerly across the hall towards her husband and stood proudly at his side in her ill-fitting bridal gown and cheap lace veil. Next to Alex's broad masculine frame, she looked tiny and almost waif-like. By now, Alex – bolstered by several pints of beer – was in fine fettle, elated and sentimental. Putting a protective arm around Kate's thin shoulders, he looked down at her misty-eyed and indulged in a long rambling speech about the bride's beauty and his own good fortune in marrying her.

Alice knocked back the remains of her glass of sherry and joined in the wild applause and cheering of the other guests, but her ordeal was not yet over. Alex beckoned to someone in the crowd, and old Davy McCracken promptly appeared at the groom's side armed with a fiddle.

"And now," Alex boomed to the assembled guests, "I'm going to sing a rendering of one of the greatest love poems ever written, by the greatest Scottish poet who ever breathed – Robert Burns."

With Davy scraping on his fiddle and Kate blushing furiously, Alex's strong baritone voice filled the village hall.

O, my love's like a red, red rose
That's newly sprung in June.
O, my love's like the melody
That's sweetly play'd in tune.

As fair art thou, my bonnie lass,
So deep in love am I.
And I will love thee still, my dear,
Till a' the seas gang dry...

Alice could endure no more. Unable to wait for the song to end, she pushed brusquely past her mother and made for the door. "Sorry Mam, I'm feeling a bit poorly," she gabbled incoherently to an astounded Bella. The exit was blocked by the overflow of guests, spilling out into the street and enjoying the summer sunshine. She started to elbow her way through them but was detained by a firm hand grabbing her by the arm. She swung around wildly and was promptly pulled to one side by her sister Hannah.

"For God's sake what's wrong, Alice?" she hissed in alarm.

"It's nothing, Hannah, I just need..." Alice tried to wriggle out of her sister's strong grip, but Hannah refused to release her. She knew how dishevelled she must look, her cheeks burning and tears rolling unchecked down her face. Looking into her sister's eyes, she saw that Hannah had intuitively understood why she was so distraught, had guessed the source of her misery.

Hannah put a warning finger to her lips to silence her. "Not another word, pet, people are starting to stare. Now pull yourself together, lass, or there'll be gossip. Go home if you must, but for God's sake don't make a spectacle of yourself." She pulled a handkerchief out of her pocket and dabbed lightly at Alice's tears, making it look as though she were removing a speck in her eye.

Alice, her heart still pounding, realised that Hannah had come to her rescue in the nick of time. Her reputation would be irreparably damaged if there was the slightest suspicion in Burnside of anything untoward in her relationship with Alex McCulloch. She couldn't run the risk of becoming an object of pity and ridicule in the village. Salvaging the last remnants of her pride and squaring her shoulders, Alice made a supreme effort to look composed.

"See you later, then," she said to Hannah in as near a normal voice as she could muster and moved quietly away. Extricating herself calmly from the jostling crowd, she even managed to casually wave goodbye to one or two of the wedding guests. She walked at a deliberately slow pace down the empty, sun-drenched streets of Burnside, her body feeling curiously weightless but her soul as heavy as lead under the clear blue summer sky. She let herself noiselessly into her rooms at the schoolhouse, peeled off the serviceable pearl grey dress and folded it neatly over the back of a chair. Kicking off her shoes, she lay down on her narrow bed and waited for the tears to come, now that she could shed them freely. But no tears came.

* * *

Life went on for Alice, as it always did, and to all outward appearances she had every reason to be content with her lot. The headmaster of Burnside School, Mr Carr, was in poor health and more than happy to entrust Alice with ever more responsibilities. She threw herself with a fierce intensity into these fresh challenges, if only to take her mind off the gnawing pain inside her whenever she thought of Alex McCulloch… and Kate.

Yet there were genuine satisfactions and occasional moments of elation too. Over the last few years, she had managed to build up a sizeable collection of children's books, some donated and others picked up for next to nothing at second-hand sales. These were kept under lock and key in a small room adjoining the headmaster's study, which was rather grandly referred to as the School Library. The pupils had free access to the books after school hours, and nothing pleased Alice more than to peek into the room and catch one of the girls absorbed in *Little Women* or a boy engrossed in *Treasure Island*. Reading, she told the children constantly, was like pushing a door open and discovering the world in all its amazing diversity – different people, different countries, different civilisations both past and present. Not all the children were receptive of course, but it was immensely rewarding for Alice to encourage those who were. It gave meaning to her life and chosen vocation, convinced her that her work as a schoolteacher in Burnside was worthwhile.

Lady Felton had kept her word too, and thanks to her generous donation Burnside School was now endowed with a proper playground and sports field, together with all the equipment needed to play cricket, rounders, netball and football. In fact, to her great surprise, Alice's relationship with her wealthy benefactor had developed into something resembling friendship. She was regularly invited for tea at Felton Hall, and although their different stations in life prevented the two women from becoming truly intimate, they nonetheless enjoyed each other's company and spent many happy hours discussing art and literature. By unspoken agreement, the subject of politics was studiously avoided, for Winifred Felton sensed that Alice's views were far more radical than her own. On her side, Alice – grateful for the donation to the school and hopeful for further donations in years to come – refrained from mentioning that she was an active Labour Party member. Nor did she ever allude to her friendship with Alex McCulloch, which would have been akin to waving a red flag to a bull as far as the Feltons were concerned. Sir Reginald Felton looked on Alex as a leftist firebrand and revolutionary rabble-rouser of the worst kind.

Unsurprisingly, the hostility of the wealthy owner of Burnside colliery had no effect whatsoever on Alex himself or his commitment to improving working and living conditions for mining families. Although he rarely discussed Kate or his personal life with Alice – except to inform her with quiet pride a few months after the wedding that she was expecting their first child – he confided in her unreservedly when it came to his political ambitions. Alice was thrilled to learn that Alex had been asked to stand as a Labour candidate in the forthcoming county council elections.

"I think we have a real chance of winning this time," he told her eagerly. "And if enough Labour men are elected, we can force the colliery owners like Felton to clear the slums and improve housing conditions in pit villages like Burnside. It's a disgrace the way pitmen and their families are made to live like animals in this country, while capitalist bastards like Felton are filling their pockets with the profits of their hard labour. If I'm elected, my goal is to make sure every miner in Northumberland has electricity, indoor plumbing and a proper bathroom in his home."

Alice was unconvinced. "But isn't that an unlikely scenario, Alex? After all, why should Sir Reginald and others like him surrender a share of their profits to improving housing for their employees? What's in it for them?"

"If the mine owners were more enlightened managers, instead of shamelessly exploiting the miners as they do now, they'd understand that a healthy, motivated workforce would be more productive and ultimately generate more profit. Oh, I know you think I'm just dreaming, Alice, but the housing issue is crucial. I believe the time is ripe! If we all pull together, decent housing for pitmen will be achieved faster than you think."

As always, Alice was impressed by his drive and determination. She was also gratified that Alex continued to share his political aspirations with her, for she guessed that this was an area from which Kate was excluded. She consoled herself with the thought that the bond of friendship between them was indestructible. And she had finally come to accept, albeit painfully, that romantic love would never be part of the equation.

By an odd twist of fate, it was only a few months after Alex's wedding that Alice discovered she had a male admirer of her own. His name was Walter Barnes, and ironically, it was Alex himself who introduced them at a Labour Party meeting in Newcastle. At subsequent meetings, she noticed in amusement, Walter never missed an opportunity to sit next to her and engage her in conversation. Unused to male attention, Alice was both embarrassed and intrigued by the young man's unconcealed admiration.

On the bus journeys home to Burnside, Alex teased her mercilessly about what he referred to as her new romance. "Don't be so standoffish with the poor fellow, Alice," he pleaded with her jokingly. "The looks you give him would freeze a volcano! He's not a bad bloke either, so why not give him a chance?"

And why not indeed, thought Alice. Even if she was an old maid of twenty-eight, it might be rather pleasant to be courted by a respectable man like Walter Barnes. Somewhat piqued by Alex's unrelenting mockery, she decided to discreetly signal to Walter at their next encounter that she was willing to take the relationship further.

And so, the courtship began in earnest, and Alice discovered that in many ways Walter Barnes was an eminently suitable match for her. Still single at thirty, he was employed as a bank clerk in Gateshead, on the south bank of the Tyne. Like Alice herself, he had clawed his way out of poverty by dint of hard work and self-education. Alice appreciated his sensible, if rather humourless, approach to life and his determination to progress in his chosen profession. They had much in common and spent long enjoyable hours browsing in Newcastle bookshops and discussing the political issues of the day in sedate tearooms.

After several months had passed in this fashion, Alice sensed that things were coming to a head. Alex had long since stopped teasing her about Walter but never questioned her directly about this new man in her life; perhaps he thought it would be invading her privacy to do so. As for her sister Hannah, she was clearly overjoyed that Alice had finally found a prospective husband.

"There's plenty of fish in the sea," she would say archly. "And not all of them are called Alex McCulloch." It was as far as she ever came to alluding to Alice's breakdown at Alex's wedding, but there was no need to say more. Hannah obviously hoped that Walter's attentions would help to eradicate any lingering thoughts of Alex from her mind.

Oh, if only she could! Yet, however hard Alice tried to convince herself of Walter Barnes's worthiness, he paled into insignificance when compared to Alex. Walter was undeniably kind, generous and her equal in intelligence, but he had none of Alex's charisma and high spirits. Privately, she found his steadfast devotion rather off-putting and wished he could bring more lightness and laughter to their courtship. As for Walter's physical appearance, she found him not unattractive in a burly, masculine sort of way; yet at the same time, she was forced to admit her complete indifference to him. She was happy enough to let him take her arm or hold her hand occasionally but had no desire whatsoever for any closer bodily contact.

Once when they had been sitting in the dark at the Odeon, watching the flickering images of a motion picture on the screen, Walter had put an awkward arm around her shoulder and attempted to kiss her. Alice recalled how repelled she had felt, how quickly she had averted her face and pretended not to notice his overtures. But how would she have reacted if it had been Alex McCulloch pulling her close in the cinema and brushing his lips against hers? She knew the answer and it didn't bear thinking about.

The moment of truth arrived towards the end of May, 1921. Walter had invited Alice to dinner that Saturday evening at the Mayfair Hotel in Newcastle – an unheard-of treat for both of them under normal circumstances. Guessing that Walter intended to propose over dinner, she realised she had been remiss in allowing the courtship to continue unchecked for so long. It was wrong of her to lead Walter on in this way, to let him believe she would accept an offer of marriage. With a sudden pang of guilt, Alice wondered if she had merely been using Walter to flatter her own vanity, or worse still to make Alex jealous. Well, she had failed on both counts!

As she dressed for the fateful dinner in her rooms above the schoolhouse, Alice resolved to end the relationship as gracefully as possible that very evening. She was not quite sure how she would go about it, but the subject must be broached before Walter got around to popping the question. Still reflecting on her plan of action, she checked her appearance before leaving to catch the bus into town. She was smartly dressed in the same pearl grey frock, tam o'shanter and jet beads that she had worn to Alex's wedding less than a year before. Her blond hair was newly washed and crimped for the occasion, and as a concession to the Mayfair Hotel, she had even powdered her nose and applied a touch of crimson lipstick.

Less than an hour later, Alice was walking purposefully through the elegant splendour of the hotel foyer towards the restaurant. Her ladylike bearing gave the impression, she hoped, that such fashionable venues were a normal part of her existence. The obsequious *maître d'hôtel* at the door instantly led her to a corner table, where Walter nervously awaited her in his best dark suit and starched collar. He reeked of eau de cologne and his thinning hair was sleekly oiled for the occasion.

Feeling uncomfortable and somewhat overawed by the unaccustomed grandeur of their surroundings, they sat facing each other across a table set with immaculate white linen, heavy silver and glowing candles. The hushed atmosphere in the restaurant was not conducive to easy conversation, and they spent the first part of dinner in almost total silence, nibbling at the *hors d'oeuvres* and pretending to enjoy a horrendously expensive bottle of claret.

As the main course arrived, Alice searched for a way to broach the subject on her mind. "It's so kind of you to invite me here," she began with a smile. "I really appreciate it, although I must tell you that…"

But Walter too was determined to say his piece. "I wanted us to be somewhere special for what I have to ask you tonight, Alice. You see… I had a conversation recently with the director of the bank, Mr Jenkins. He's very pleased with my work, more than pleased in fact. My wages have just been raised quite substantially, and he even gave me to understand that in the next few years, I have every hope of being promoted to deputy branch manager." He sat back triumphantly in his chair, waiting for her reaction.

"But that's marvellous, Walter! I know how hard you've worked to get on at the bank, and I'm truly delighted for you."

"So you see, Alice…" Walter leaned earnestly towards her across the table and clasped her hand in his. "Now that my prospects are assured and my earnings are more than sufficient to keep a wife and family, I feel the time has come to tell you… how fond I've grown of you." He gazed into her eyes expectantly.

She had not managed to stave off the proposal in time, she realised. And it was hardly the most romantic of declarations either. Yet how could she blame Walter for his lukewarm feelings when she didn't love him either? There was a long pause while Walter waited for her to respond.

She cleared her throat hesitantly. "Well, of course I'm fond of you too, Walter, but…"

Walter breathed a visible sigh of relief. "Well, that's settled then. You know, Alice, I reckon we'll make a great team once we're married."

She was completely taken aback. Wasn't a young man supposed to propose marriage in the interrogative form? Yet here was Walter jumping the gun, smugly assuming she would be overjoyed to accept his offer. And although she had always thought marriage should be a union of equal partners, she was perversely irritated by Walter's businesslike approach. A great team indeed! She thought fleetingly of Alex's passionate rendering of the Burns poem at his wedding and bit her lip.

"I don't think you understand, Walter," she stammered. "You know as well as I do that the Education Board strongly disapproves of married women teachers. I'd almost certainly lose my position if we…"

"Well, naturally I thought that once you had your own home and family – I do want us to have children, Alice – you'd be quite content to… you know, keep house."

Alice bristled with annoyance. Walter would give up nothing by marrying her; on the contrary, his social status and professional standing would be enhanced by having a respectable wife, a well-run home and children. She on the other hand was expected to sacrifice everything she had worked so hard to achieve – her work, her autonomy, her financial independence.

"What makes you think I'd be – as you put it – quite content to keep house, Walter?"

Walter flushed, perspiration gleaming on his brow. "Well, you know… because… well, because—"

"Because I'm a woman," Alice interrupted, her voice sharper than she had intended. She realised this disastrous conversation must be ended in a way which would allow Walter to save face. "Look," she continued in more conciliatory tones. "I'm very flattered by your proposal, Walter, but I'm afraid I can't accept. If I led you to believe I wished to marry you, it was unintentionally done and I'm sorry. Teaching means the world to me and I couldn't possibly give it up."

Walter stared at her woodenly, stunned and confused by her rejection. What could she say to soften the blow and help the poor man swallow such a bitter pill?

"I've really enjoyed your company these past few months, Walter. You're a decent man, and I'm sure dozens of young women would jump at the chance of marrying you. When you find one, as I know you will, I hope we can remain friends."

Walter looked crestfallen, like a small child whose favourite toy has suddenly been snatched away. A haughty waiter saved them from further embarrassment by appearing at their side with a large menu and enquiring whether they were ready to order dessert.

"No dessert, thank you," they chorused and laughed nervously. Walter asked for the bill and they sat in tense silence, both of them longing to be gone and out of each other's company.

"Let me pay for my half of dinner," Alice blurted out. It seemed so unfair that Walter should eat into his hard-earned savings for an evening which had proved such a failure.

Walter was genuinely shocked at the suggestion. In his mind, it was clearly out of the question for a woman – even one who had just turned him down – to pay her own way in a restaurant. "I'll not hear of it," he declared indignantly. Alice watched as he perused the bill, took out an alarming number of pound notes from his wallet and laid them flat on the table.

Two minutes later, they had left the Mayfair Hotel and stood facing each other in the street. They shook hands solemnly, as if they were now total strangers to each other.

"No hard feelings, then?" Alice asked tentatively.

"Why no, man," said Walter with a shy smile, his Geordie accent coming unexpectedly to the fore. "Ta-ta, Alice, and all the best."

As she travelled back to Burnside on the bus and went over the evening in her mind, she felt both relieved and slightly peeved. Relieved that Walter, who had sounded almost offhand when they parted, was sensible enough not to let his heart be broken… and slightly peeved that the only proposal of marriage she was likely to receive in her life should have been so disappointing.

She was even more dashed a few days later when she confided to Alex that she had broken off her relationship with Walter Barnes. He gave a short dismissive laugh, as if her personal life was of no concern to him at all.

"Well, it's probably all for the best," he proclaimed breezily. "If you'd married the poor sod, you'd have had to move to Gateshead! And who in his right mind would want to live south of the Tyne, eh?"

Alice forced a smile and blinked back her tears. There would be plenty of time for crying later, in the safety and solitude of her bedroom.

* * *

The General Strike began in May 1926. The intervening years had been largely uneventful for Alice, but not for Alex McCulloch who was now a man to be reckoned with, not only in Burnside but all over Tyneside. At thirty-four, he not only served as county councillor but was also recognised as one of the key figures in the Northumberland Miners Association. He and other militant union leaders had been urging the pitmen to take action for quite some time, arguing that a nationwide strike was the only way to rally public opinion to their cause, make people aware of the unfair treatment to which miners were subjected. Colliery owners like Sir Reginald Felton, faced with a drop in coal prices and exports but intent only on maintaining their own profits, had forced colliery workers over and over again to accept lower wages and longer working hours. The situation had become untenable, for in seven years the average miner's pay had dropped from £6 to under £4.

"How much longer will you keep giving in to Felton and his kind?" thundered Alex to an angry audience of miners in Burnside. "They're bleeding the last ounce of strength from us, exploiting honest men to increase their own wealth! Now is the time to unite and demand our due! Now is the time to nationalise the British coal industry!"

So coal miners all over the country voted for the strike, rallying to the militant union slogan: *Not a penny off the pay, not a minute on the day.* They were heartened when the powerful TUC decided to back them by calling on workers in other industries to join the strike. There was now a nationwide movement to force the British government to put a stop to wage reductions and worsening conditions.

The strike began in Burnside in a spirit of jubilation, for the pitmen were convinced Sir Reginald would not want colliery operations to be stopped for more than a few days. Nor, Alex added, would the government want the entire national economy to grind to a halt.

But they were proved wrong, for the government succeeded in maintaining essential services by bringing in the army and enlisting the support of middle class volunteers. Barely a week later, most of the strikers in other industries were back at work, leaving the coal miners to battle on alone. The mood in Burnside was now less buoyant but – as they always did – the resilient pit villagers rallied together in a spirit of mutual support and camaraderie. Hard-earned savings were depleted, and the Co-op store gave limited credit for food and other staples. Local farmers were persuaded to donate potatoes and turnips, while the unemployed men of Burnside combed the countryside for whatever edible takings they could find.

As the weeks went by with no end to the strike in sight, Alice could only look on in dismay as hunger and deprivation cut ever deeper into the population. Although it was the height of summer, the ragged barefoot children in her class looked pale and sickly, their little faces pinched and drawn. Their mothers looked even worse, for colliery wives always put the needs of their husbands and children before their own. Alice tried to help by serving on the local Board of Guardians. At first, the colliery families had been too proud to apply to the Board for relief, but as the strike dragged on day after day the women of Burnside were forced to put aside their dignity and beg for food and clothes for their families.

One day in late July as she set off to pay a call on her sister Hannah, Alice ran into Kate McCulloch walking down Bluebell Street with her two sons – five-year-old Robert (named after the famous Scottish poet) and little Angus, aged three. She had not seen Alex's wife for some time and was horrified by the change in her appearance. Although Kate had always been waiflike, she now looked positively ill. Her face had taken on an unhealthy grey pallor with huge dark shadows under her eyes, while her tiny frame looked shrunken and emaciated... except for the prominent bulge revealing that a third pregnancy was now well underway.

"Oh aye, I'm keeping fine," she reassured a genuinely concerned Alice. "Once the baby's born, I'll be right as rain again. It's just that this strike seems never-ending, doesn't it?" Her expression was suddenly wistful. "If only Alex was at home more often, the bairns hardly ever see him... but he and the other union men are doing their best to pool resources in the pit villages, so he's out all the hours God sends helping them as needs it."

Alice privately thought Kate needed some help herself. She wondered whether Alex, caught up in his unstinting crusade for the working class, had even noticed his wife's condition. Poor little Kate, she thought, her heart no longer filled with envy and resentment but only pity and commiseration for her plight.

More bad news awaited her when she arrived at Hannah's crumbling old cottage to find her sister distraught, wringing her hands in desperation. The housekeeper at Felton Hall, she learned, had slashed the staff's working hours. How were Hannah and little Geordie to survive on a laundry woman's half pay?

"You'd think Sir Reginald was out to punish us because the miners are on strike," cried Hannah bitterly. "The housekeeper says they can't afford to pay us full wages any more, but how can that be true? They've got millions in the bank, millions, and what have we got? Nowt, that's what!"

Alice could only sympathise and murmur words of comfort, promising to come to Hannah's aid with a share of her own wages. Her sister finally calmed down and set about making a fresh pot of tea; they sat drinking for a while in companionable silence.

"It's a blessing there's only me and our Geordie to feed these days," Hannah sighed. "At least the lasses are off me hands, now that our Violet's in service and Mary Jane's working at that factory in the Toon. If only our John..." She broke off abruptly and to Alice's surprise suddenly produced a flimsy envelope from the drawer of the kitchen table.

"Hannah!" she exclaimed. "You didn't tell me you'd had word from John." She quickly calculated that Hannah's eldest son, who had run away from home ten years ago and never been heard from since, must be all of twenty-three by now.

"Aye, the letter came last week, but there's no need to look so pleased, lass," retorted Hannah grimly. "Wait until you've read it." Alice picked up the envelope curiously, noticing it was postmarked from Australia. She drew out a single sheet of cheap lined notepaper on which John had scrawled a few short lines. She was amused to see that his handwriting and spelling had not improved since his departure from Burnside.

Dear Mam,

You mite be surprised to resieve this. I am not in the merchant navy any more. I have emigraited to Australia and got a job as a mechanick, erning good money. I got married this year as well. She is called Dot and is eckspecting our first. We live in a town called Brisbane and are doing all right.

Hope your well and all the best,

John

"So he's in Brisbane," breathed Alice in amazement.

Hannah snorted in disgust. "Aye, but that's all the address he's seen fit to give me. That way, I can't write back and ask him for help."

"Maybe his conscience has been preying on him all these years, and he doesn't want you to worry about him anymore," said Alice tactfully.

"I've long since stopped worrying about him, selfish bugger that he is! I've had more than enough worries of me own, working me fingers to the bone and trying to put food on the table for three bairns. Little Geordie and me could starve to death for all he cares!"

"Well, you can put him out of your mind once and for all now," concluded Alice firmly. "But speaking of Geordie, it's high time we had a chat about further education…"

"What further education?" Hannah's tone of voice was instantly suspicious. "As soon as the law allows I want him out of school and earning his keep down the pit. I can't go on like this much longer, Alice, I'm weary to the bone. There's days I wake up so tired I can hardly drag meself out of bed. Just look at me hands! The pain in the joints is so bad it keeps me awake at night."

She spread her red-raw hands on the kitchen table, the joints in her fingers swollen and bent from the mountains of laundry she washed and ironed every day. Again, Alice was quick to give her the sympathy she so obviously craved, for nobody knew better than she how harsh her sister's life had been since Bill's death in the colliery accident ten years before. And it was undeniable that Hannah, with her worn lined face and iron-grey hair, looked far older than forty-eight. The long years of drudgery and penny-pinching had taken their toll on her health. Yet privately, Alice wished that her sister were not quite so relentlessly negative, so determined to drape herself in the heavy mantle of martyrdom at every turn.

"I know how tired you must be feeling," she began. "But at least you still have your family around you. I'm sure Violet and Mary Jane would be happy to lend a helping hand if you asked them."

Hannah sniffed dismissively. "They're just lasses, man! And it won't be long before Violet and Mary Jane are married with bairns of their own. You can't depend on daughters, Alice, they're neither use nor ornament! No, the only person in this world who'll look after me in my old age is Geordie, and you can't tell me any different."

"Well, that's precisely why you must give him the chance to have the best possible education," Alice persisted. "I know Geordie's still only ten, but I've been watching his progress at school lately. He's a quiet lad but clever, with good marks in all subjects but particularly arithmetic and nature studies. I believe he'd do well in grammar school, and you know I'd be happy to pay the fees. Please let me do this for him, Hannah, and for you! If he passes the Matric, he may go on to university, and even if he doesn't, he'll be sure to find a steady, well-paid job."

Hannah's face darkened, her eyes flashing with rage. "Grammar school? The Matric? University? Have you gone stark raving mad, Alice Armstrong? I don't want our Geordie getting ideas above his station, turning into a toffy-nosed snob and forgetting where he came from! There's nowt wrong with working at the colliery as his dad and granddad did before him... And I need the money, Alice. I can't wait another eight years until he passes some posh Matric exam, I'll be in me grave before then!"

How could Hannah be so shortsighted, thought Alice in frustration. Every time she broached the subject of grammar school, she met with the same point-blank refusal. Her sister's unspoken fear, she knew, was to lose her only remaining son, to face old age alone and destitute after a lifetime of sacrifice. It was understandable of course, but there was something unhealthy about her fierce possessiveness. Why couldn't she see the obvious benefits of a proper education for the son she professed to love so dearly? Why was she holding him back, dragging him down into the trap of poverty that awaited him in Burnside? And why, thought Alice despairingly, must Hannah always reject every kind offer out of hand?

"You always said after Bill was killed in the accident that you didn't want Geordie working at the colliery," she reminded her sister.

"I've made him swear he'll get a job above ground." Hannah's face hardened, her mouth a thin stubborn line. "He's my son and I know what's best for him. So you can stop interfering in his life and stirring things up with your fancy notions! Oh aye, you think you know it all with your grand ideas about education, but you don't know what it's like to be a wife and mother. Eeh, when I think you could have had that nice Walter Barnes and all... I just don't understand you, Alice. You're neither fish nor fowl and that's a fact!"

Hannah's final thrust was needlessly cruel and they both knew it. But once again, Alice was made painfully aware that in Burnside – and indeed in conventional society at large – she was perceived as some kind of misfit, a dried-up old maid devoid of normal womanly feelings. Oh, the villagers looked up to her of course, but in their eyes, she would always be incomplete, unfinished in some mysterious way, simply because she had never known the vastly overrated – in her view – satisfactions of matrimony and motherhood. And yet, most unfairly it seemed to Alice, the same rule did not apply to unmarried men. Bachelors were never objects of pity and ridicule as spinsters invariably were. She bit her lip but said nothing; Hannah's sharp tongue had hurt her more than she cared to admit.

* * *

At the beginning of September, as the miners' strike entered its fifth month, Kate McCulloch went into labour. Sixteen long hours later, tended only by the local midwife, she gave birth to a healthy baby girl.

The ordeal was too much for Kate's frail constitution however, and she passed away as dawn broke the next day. Although it was not a rare occurrence for working class women to die in childbirth – such tragedies were grimly accepted as another of life's injustices – everyone in Burnside was shocked by the sudden death of Alex McCulloch's sweet, young wife.

Alice was one of the many mourners to call at Alex's home on Bluebell Street but could do little more than offer her condolences; the house was in total confusion, packed with weeping relatives and an endless stream of visitors come to pay their respects. The Malones were insisting on a Catholic funeral for Kate, having learned from the midwife that Kate had begged for extreme unction on her deathbed. Clearly, her conversion to the Presbyterian faith had been a sacrifice she was prepared to make for Alex's sake, but one that only went skin deep. Alex relented, too overwhelmed by grief to argue. Since there was no Catholic church in Burnside, the funeral, therefore, took place in a neighbouring village but Alice chose not to attend. There was nothing she could do to help Alex by going, and she had never felt comfortable with the endless chanting and pomposity of Catholic rites.

Yet thoughts of Alex occupied her mind constantly as the enormity of his situation began to sink in. He had loved Kate dearly, she knew, however much it still irked her to admit it. But over and beyond the tragedy of her death, Alex now had to face huge practical problems. How could an ordinary working man be expected to cope with a home and three children – two of them under five and the other a baby – on his own? Not to mention the fact that Alex was not just an ordinary working man. It would be well-nigh impossible for him to continue as a leading political figure without a wife to run his home and family. Worse still, his future prospects would be inevitably compromised; rumour was rife within the Labour party that Alex would be selected as one of the candidates for Tyneside in the next General Election. What chance did he have of becoming a Member of Parliament now? Alice's heart went out to him – surely, there must be something she could do?

She waited until Saturday evening to pay another call at Alex's house on Bluebell Street, fully expecting him to be surrounded by relatives and friends as he had been last time. But she arrived to find the house deathly quiet and the back door closed – a surprising occurrence in itself for doors were always left open in Burnside when the weather was mild. She knocked two or three times but there was no response, although she sensed the house was not empty. Pushing the door open, she walked through the untidy kitchen – neglected since the funeral and strewn with unwashed dishes – and peeked around the door into the front room.

There he was in the gloom, oblivious to her presence, sitting bowed and head in hands on the battered horsehair sofa. The fire was unlit, and an empty bottle of whisky stood on the floor by his side. Hearing the door click shut behind her, he looked up morosely but did not greet her at first. Alice noticed that he had lost weight since the start of the strike; his face was gaunt and unshaven, his eyes bleary and red-rimmed. Without a word, she sat next to him on the sofa and patted his shoulder sympathetically, not wanting to intrude but hoping Alex would turn to her for comfort.

"Oh Alice," he groaned miserably. "Thank God you've come."

She squeezed his arm and spoke to him softly. "I know how bad you must be feeling, Alex. I'd do anything to help you, anything at all."

Her words triggered an outpouring of emotion, a torrent of grief. Alice let him talk until he had talked himself out. His thoughts were incoherent and disjointed, and he wept unashamedly at intervals. She suffered in silence as he told her over and over again how much he adored Kate, how sweet and gentle she had been, how dearly she had loved her children. More than once, he ranted against God's cruelty in taking her from him.

"It's just not right," he cried out bitterly. "The poor lass was only twenty-five and never hurt a soul in her whole life. And it's all my fault, she wouldn't have died if it hadn't been for me."

"Don't talk that way, Alex, you're not to blame for any of this," protested Alice.

"Oh aye, I am, make no mistake. I called the doctor in after our second was born, Kate was in such a bad way. He told me she had consumption and needed proper care. A long period of rest convalescing in a warm climate, nourishing food and medical supervision, he said. What chance of that is there in Burnside, for God's sake? How could I afford to send her abroad?" He buried his face in his hands again, his shoulders shaking uncontrollably.

"It was cruel of the doctor to say that. He knew full well it was out of the question."

"But I haven't told you the half, Alice. He also said another baby might kill her and we must refrain from… you know… marital relations. And we did try, Alice, I swear we did! But a man has needs, as you must know, and I'd never have gone to another woman while Kate was with me. So one night—"

"Alex, please stop." This was forbidden territory, a dangerous minefield that Alice refused to enter. It wasn't a question of being prudish. It was simply that such unbridled confessions conjured up images she wanted to block out of her conscience… images of Alex making love to his wife. At the same time, she was deeply moved by his vulnerability; he had never before poured out his heart to her like tonight. It was their first moment of real intimacy.

Nevertheless, she felt duty-bound to make him see reason and face the future, however bleak. "I do understand, Alex, truly I do. But there's no sense in raking over all this now and blaming yourself for something you couldn't help. Poor Kate's gone, and there was nothing you or anybody else could do about it. Listen to me, now! You must try to pull yourself together for the sake of the bairns; your duty is to them now. Where are they tonight, by the way?"

"They're with Mam. She said she'd take them in for a few days until… I get sorted." Alex's tears had dried and he was starting to look more composed. He picked up the nearly empty bottle of whisky at his feet and raised it in her direction. "Here's to us, Alice," he proclaimed with a grimace and took a last swig. "Wha's like us?"

"Damn few." Alice's response to the old Scottish toast was automatic, although she refrained from adding the traditional 'and they're a' deid'.

Seeing her eyes drifting to the empty bottle, Alex unexpectedly flashed a rueful smile. "Don't worry, Alice, I haven't drunk it all tonight. There were a few drops left over from Christmas, that's all." She smiled back, relieved to see him looking more his normal self.

"You're quite right, Alice, enough of this maudlin self-pity! Those three motherless bairns are all that counts now, and I must do the best I can for them." There was a long pause as he leaned back on the sofa and stretched his legs, his arms folded and his expression reflective. "Well, they can't stay with Mam forever,

237

that's for sure. She's pushing sixty now and has enough on her plate without taking on three wee bairns. No, there's only one solution, Alice, I'll have to find a housekeeper – a good woman who'll cook and keep house and look after the bairns while I'm at work. Ideally, I'd like her to live here with us, but I reckon that's out of the question. There are only two bedrooms upstairs and in any case… there might be talk in the village if people thought—"

"No, it wouldn't be proper for her to live in," Alice agreed. She thought over Alex's suggestion and realised it was the only viable solution, although she guessed that paying for a full-time housekeeper would make a sizeable dent in his wages.

Another thought occurred to Alex and he turned towards her eagerly. "Alice, I've just had a brainwave! How would your sister Hannah feel about being my housekeeper? After all, she's a respectable widow and has brought up four bairns of her own. Her little Geordie is old enough to take care of himself and anyway, I'm sure you'd keep an eye on him if need be, wouldn't you? Oh Alice, would you have a word with her about it? I'd pay her the same wages she gets working for that bugger Felton… at least I will when the strike's over and I'm earning again at the pit—"

He broke off in amazement as he saw that Alice, always so calm and sensible, had suddenly burst into tears; she was sobbing as helplessly as a child. Alice herself could not have explained in rational terms why the idea of Hannah becoming Alex's housekeeper should be so unbearable, but it was. Oh, she didn't imagine that her middle-aged sister would tempt Alex romantically… but all the same, Hannah would be sharing his life in a way that she never could – washing his clothes, making his bed, cooking meals for him, caring for his children. The very thought of it was unendurable! Even so, under normal circumstances Alice would never have broken down in Alex's presence. It was just that by sharing his own deepest feelings with her that evening, he had unwittingly opened the floodgates of her own long-concealed emotions.

Feeling foolish and embarrassed, she hastily brushed her tears away and tried to regain her composure. "Sorry, Alex," she said softly, her voice still hoarse in spite of herself. "I'm sure Hannah will be thrilled, and of course I'll have a word with her on your behalf. I don't know why I reacted so stupidly. I'm just… tired, that's all."

Alex put his arm around her shoulder and pulled her towards him affectionately. The unaccustomed closeness, the warmth and strength of his body next to hers, intoxicated her senses. "It's not just about being tired, though, is it?" he murmured gently. "I think everybody takes you for granted, Alice – your sister, your pupils, the entire population of Burnside, and me of course… especially me. You're such a strong capable woman, you see, and we all forget that you need to be loved and cared for as much as anyone else."

The tenderness in his voice unleashed another wave of emotion in Alice. It was the first time Alex – or any man for that matter – had truly spoken to her as a woman. Without warning, he had entered the unplumbed depths of her innermost self and released the well of yearning and need in her heart. She nestled against him and turned her face up to his, unsure how to express the rush of love she felt for him at that moment.

She blurted out the words before she had time to think. "Oh Alex my dear, please love me! Just this once, please love me!"

Alex drew away from her sharply as the words seemed to reverberate around them in the quiet front room. His grey eyes widened in bewilderment. "Alice, have you lost your mind? You don't know what you're saying!"

But it was too late to unsay the words, and in any case she no longer wanted to unsay them. Another Alice – a fearless, passionate woman she hardly knew existed – had momentarily replaced the old, rational Alice. For once in her life, she would be true to this new Alice, regardless of the consequences.

She rose clumsily from the horsehair sofa and kicked off her shoes. Silently, she unbuttoned her serviceable dress and pulled it roughly over her head. Alex's jaw visibly dropped, as she stood solemnly before him in her plain camisole, long bloomers and thick, sensible stockings. It was not a seductive pose, for Alice had no experience of men and her knowledge of sex was theoretical at best. But her desire for Alex swept away any residual feelings of modesty or embarrassment. Nor was there any need for words; her silent plea was almost audible in the room. She was asking him to take her, to love her, to make her his own.

He got to his feet and stood over her, placing his big hands squarely on her narrow shoulders. "Alice pet, you're upset this evening, out of sorts… Believe me, you don't understand what you're doing…"

"I do understand." She stood on tiptoe and put her arms around his waist, letting her hands slide up his broad back and pressing her body against his. She tilted her face upwards, searching for his mouth. For an interminable moment, she was afraid he might push her away; then to her delight she felt Alex's arms enveloping her tightly and his lips forcing hers apart in a long searching kiss. How glorious it felt! Her whole body seemed to melt into his, and she thought she would surely die of happiness then and there.

He loosened his embrace and looked deep into her eyes. "Are you sure, Alice?" he whispered.

She nodded mutely, not daring to speak. Alex drew apart from her and taking her hand, led her upstairs to the bedroom. It was the same bedroom he had shared for six years with Kate, but at that moment Alice cared nothing about Alex's past and even less about the future. Her whole being was concentrated on the present, this moment in time she was sharing with him. She was oblivious to the peeling wallpaper, the unmade bed and grubby sheets. She felt herself transported into another, wholly unfamiliar world, an enchanted place where she was free at last to love Alex and be loved by him in return.

They made love all night, constantly finding new sources of excitement and pleasure. Alice revelled in his masculinity and shivered with ecstasy as he ran his strong hands over her tingling skin. She had no way of knowing whether he was skilled in the art of lovemaking or not, but his mixture of undiluted passion and tenderness fulfilled her in a way she could never have imagined before that night. Oddly enough, she felt no pain, even at the moments when she most expected it. She simply gave herself to him gladly, holding nothing back, and for the first time in her thirty-four years, she felt whole, intensely and completely happy.

They dozed off in the early hours of the morning but were roused by the grey light of dawn penetrating the tiny bedroom; in their haste, they had forgotten to draw the curtains the night before. Alex leapt out of bed and peered out of the window into the narrow back alley.

"Thank God it's Sunday, there's not a soul up and about yet," he remarked. "If you slip out now, nobody will be any the wiser."

Reality hit Alice like a splash of icy water to her face, although Alex was right of course. There would be a huge scandal if it was known they had spent the night together. A respectable spinster and a widower in deep mourning... it didn't bear thinking about! But she badly wanted to hang on to the bliss of the night before just a little while longer. The words *I love you* rang out in her mind and were screaming to be said. She smiled up at him and patted the place next to her invitingly. "I'll be gone in a minute, I promise."

Alex perched on the side of the bed and searched for his pack of cigarettes. He lit one and puffed on it contentedly, sitting propped up against the pillows. Alice raised herself on one elbow and looked up at him with shining eyes. "Before I go, I must tell you how much you mean to me... and always have. Tonight has brought it home to me in a way I never thought possible. I..."

"Don't say things you'll be sorry for later, hinny." Alex's voice was kind, but the expression on his face was suddenly guarded. "I think the world of you, Alice, you know that. You're the cleverest woman I've ever met, an example to us all. But..."

Her heart sank like a lead weight inside her and her stomach knotted. Alex was talking to her exactly as Walter Barnes had done. He was fond of her, he respected and admired her... but he didn't love her and never would. She had strayed into dangerous territory by baring her soul, for in doing so she had altered the mood between them, created tensions where there had been none before.

Alex drew her towards him with his free arm, and she buried her head into his chest, deliberately hiding her face from view. Stubbing out his half-consumed cigarette, he turned towards her.

"Look at me, Alice, and listen. What passed between us last night was wonderful. Like a moment of madness, something disconnected from ordinary life. I never realised you were so beautiful, my dear... and you are beautiful, believe me. But we both got carried away, didn't we, although for different reasons. It was wrong of me, very wrong, to take advantage of your... innocence."

She raised her head to protest, but he silenced her with a brief kiss. "Truth be told, Alice, I'm ashamed of meself. My poor Kate is barely cold in her grave and look how I've just spent the night... How could I have put her from my mind so soon, how could I have defiled her memory? In the eyes of the world, what we did was more than a moment of weakness, Alice; it was sinful. We must forget it ever happened, put it behind us forever. You do understand what I'm saying, don't you?"

And of course Alice did understand, although every word felt like a hard stone lodging in her soul. She was too proud to plead with him however. She would not burden him further by making a scene, however much her heart was breaking. "You're right. I was just about to say the same myself," she said crisply.

The old Alice was back now, acting the part he expected of her, cloaking herself in the familiar mantle of responsible, self-reliant schoolteacher. "I really must be off," she added and started looking for the camisole and bloomers she had discarded so wildly the night before. Pulling on her underclothes, she ran downstairs and picked up her dress from the floor beside the horsehair sofa. She slipped on her shoes and patted her blond bob into shape.

Alex had followed her and was watching her dress with an anxious frown on his face. "Before you go, Alice, I hope you know that… Look, you will tell me if there's been… an accident, won't you?"

"You mean if I get pregnant?" said Alice briskly. "Yes, I'll let you know." Alex nodded and cautiously opened the back door to make sure the coast was clear. He gave her a thumbs-up sign, beckoned her to come through the tiny back yard and opened the gate noiselessly. Not even pausing to say goodbye as she passed him, she slipped into the narrow alley separating the rows of colliery houses. Feeling like a criminal on the run and praying she would not be caught, she flitted like a shadow through the dim, silent streets of Burnside. Luck was on her side, and a few minutes later she was safely back in her lodgings at the schoolhouse, panting and dishevelled but her reputation intact.

* * *

Alice spent the entire day in her rooms, relieved that it was Sunday and she didn't have to face her pupils – and the world at large – until the following morning. At breakfast time, she slipped briefly downstairs to inform a sympathetic Mrs Carr that she was indisposed and needed to rest, although in reality she had never felt more alive in her entire life. She simply wanted to be alone, to take stock of what had happened the night before and try to make some sense of it.

She made herself the occasional cup of tea during the course of the day but otherwise felt too restless and agitated to eat. Hour after hour, she lay on her bed staring at the ceiling, reliving those magical hours with Alex McCulloch. Every word, every look, every embrace they had shared shot through her fevered brain and made her skin tingle with pleasure.

Eventually, she calmed herself sufficiently to turn her mind to what lay ahead for them both, to the days and weeks and years that would somehow have to be lived through. She knew there was no question of a future together and didn't delude herself into hoping that last night's unbridled passion would ever be repeated. Alex had made all that perfectly clear, and she herself could see no other course of action, however much she loved him with every fibre of her being. The sad truth was that Alex didn't love her in return and had no intention of allowing their friendship to develop along romantic lines. But they were both mature adults, Alice reminded herself, and would hopefully – in the fullness of time – be able to regain some semblance of normality in their relationship. They would learn to behave in each other's company as people had always seen them behave. It was up to her to show Alex that she had no other expectations, that she laid no claim on his affections beyond the easy camaraderie they had always shared.

Still, she felt no regret for what had passed between them. Her heart soared anew as she recalled the sheer joy of those brief hours with Alex. Nobody could ever take that experience away, it was hers to keep for the rest of her life – stored away in her soul like a hidden treasure, to be taken out and cherished whenever she chose. Alex had made a woman of her at the ripe old age of thirty-four, casting out forever the dried-up old maid she had been before. Alice understood at last what it meant to be fulfilled, to have been – even if only for one night – intensely and unreservedly loved by a man.

On an impulse, she sprang to her feet and took a long appraising look at her reflection in the dressing table mirror. She smoothed her hands over her dress and peered curiously at her face, tidying strands of blond hair as she did so. Was it her imagination or did her figure look more rounded and feminine? And her face seemed to glow with an inner radiance too, softening her skin and lighting up her eyes. Oh, but it was ridiculous to have such fanciful ideas! Alice chastised herself for this fleeting moment of vanity. She was the same plain Jane she had always been, she told herself sternly.

And yet... Alex had told her she was beautiful, had spent all last night proving it to her. Just for today, Alice wanted to believe it, wanted to keep that inner radiance for a while longer. She smiled at her reflection and turned away from the mirror, her mind already occupied with the busy week ahead at Burnside School.

* * *

Two months later, in November 1926, the strike finally came to an end as the coal miners were driven back to work out of sheer economic necessity. Morale in Burnside was low, for in the end the pitmen had been forced to accept longer hours and lower wages. Nothing had been achieved, they felt, after the long months of deprivation and hardship.

This was not entirely true however. Public opinion was now largely sympathetic to the miners' cause, and in a few short years, Alex and Alice rejoiced as the government introduced a raft of new measures to improve conditions in the coal industry: minimum wages, unemployment insurance, more generous old age pensions and stricter safety regulations.

In Burnside itself, Sir Reginald Felton was finally persuaded to improve housing conditions for the pitmen. The rows of slums – Lilac Street, Rose Street, Bluebell Street and others like them – were demolished and replaced by new colliery houses with electricity and indoor plumbing. It was a major victory for Alex and the other Labour county councillors.

Hannah Robertson was overjoyed to leave her laundry job at Felton Hall and work as a housekeeper for Alex McCulloch and his three motherless children. As a result, ten-year-old Geordie stayed on after school most days with his Aunt Alice, who continued to further his education with her usual enthusiasm but never managed to persuade Hannah to let him go to grammar school.

Alice's sexual encounter with Alex did not result in what he had termed an 'accident'. Yet the initial relief of realising she was not pregnant was followed by deep disappointment and recurring bouts of melancholy. She and Alex never made love again.

Nevertheless, there were other satisfactions in Alice's life. A few short months after the strike Mr Carr, her mentor and the headmaster of Burnside School, passed away. To Alice's surprise and delight, she received a letter from the Education Board, informing her that Mr Carr had sent glowing reports of her work over the years and had expressly recommended her as his successor. Alice Armstrong, the miner's daughter with a passion for education, was barely thirty-five when she took over the running of the school as headmistress.

Nick and Jenny (10)

By the middle of May, panic was setting in. Half-term and the dreaded wedding in France were drawing ominously near, and Jenny was still searching for The Dress. Although she had never been obsessive about clothes, she was determined to look her absolute best in Saint Emilion. She wanted Nick to feel proud when he introduced her to his friends and family. So that Saturday morning her old friend Heather had been commandeered to help in the quest for what was beginning to look like the Holy Grail. The plan was to methodically search every shop, store and boutique in Newcastle until a suitable outfit was found. Yet after two frustrating hours of frantically dressing and undressing in stifling changing rooms, Jenny was still no closer to that elusive dress.

"You don't even know what you're looking for," protested Heather in exasperation.

Jenny mentally reviewed the dozens of dresses she had tried on so far. Too short, too frumpy, too tight on the hips, too tarty, too casual, too much cleavage on show, too juvenile… none of them were just right.

"I'll know when I see it," she said firmly. She paused to consider her options. "I suppose I could always look on internet, but I'm a bit of a stick in the mud when it comes to shopping for clothes. I like to feel the material, hold the dress up against me before I try it on…"

"I hear there's a little shop just opened, with lots of smart clothes for special occasions," Heather put in helpfully. "I've never been so I don't know if it's any good, and it's right on the other side of town but—"

"What have I got to lose?" Jenny countered. "Let's go!"

The little shop in question was tucked away down a side street and from the outside looked unimpressive. A bell tinkled discreetly as they entered. The shop was empty except for the sole shop assistant, a well-groomed older woman who greeted them with a friendly smile.

Jenny, still frazzled from the morning's fruitless exertions, started rifling through the racks of clothes. Her spirits lifted as she realised that although limited, the selection of dresses on display was both original and stylish. Instinctively, she took one out and held it up by the hanger to the light.

"Ooh," Heather enthused. "That's gorgeous!"

Even without trying it on, Jenny could see that the dress was expertly cut. It was a tailored wrap-dress in a lustrous ivory silk, overlaid with a bold graphic print in waterlily green. Without a second thought, she dived into the changing room to try the dress on, feeling it slide over her body like a light caress. She emerged to survey her reflection in the shop's full-length mirror. The dress, she saw instantly, was stunning – artfully draped and designed to flatter every curve.

Heather raised both her thumbs in approval. "That's the one!" she pronounced emphatically.

The shop assistant nodded. "The colours are just right for your hair and skin tone."

"Well, it's definitely the best we've seen so far," Jenny conceded, turning this way and that in front of the mirror.

"You're going to knock 'em dead at that fancy French wedding," Heather asserted.

"Oh, it's for a wedding, is it?" The shop assistant began rifling through the racks of clothes. "You'll be needing the matching jacket, then?"

The jacket was of course equally perfect – collarless with elbow-length sleeves and sleekly tapered at the waist. She gasped as she glanced down at the price tag.

"You can wear the jacket separately," the shop assistant said smoothly. "Dress it down for work with jeans and flats."

Jenny raised her eyebrows, trying to imagine herself in the classroom wearing this divine creation. Still, she told herself firmly, this was no time for nit-picking.

"Ooh look, Jenny!" Heather had been roaming around the little shop and now held up a pair of high-heeled sandals in the same waterlily green as the dress. "You must try them on!"

Unsurprisingly, the sandals – tied with a soft nappa bow at the ankle – were irresistible too. Jenny admired her new, flawless silhouette in the mirror, noticing how the shoes instantly made her legs look longer and slimmer. The shop assistant smilingly handed her a clutch bag and broad-brimmed ivory silk hat to complete the ensemble.

Jenny groaned inwardly. "How much for the whole outfit?" she asked the shop assistant, trying to keep a faint note of hysteria from her voice. The woman tapped on her pocket calculator and announced a figure which would make a sizeable dent in her monthly salary.

"Stop counting pennies, girl," Heather said, guessing her thoughts. "Go for it!"

Minutes later, the two friends were out in the street again, weighed down by several glossy shopping bags containing Jenny's purchases. Jenny was giddy with excitement and at the same time, she realised, hunger; it was now well past lunchtime. She looked about her and noticed they were walking towards the same smart, four-star hotel where she and Nick had first met.

She turned impulsively to Heather. "Let's go and celebrate with a slap-up lunch. My treat."

***

The bar adjoining the restaurant was packed with Saturday shoppers relaxing over drinks. As they made their way through the chattering crowd, Jenny spotted the table where she had waited for Nick to arrive on that first encounter. It was only a few short months ago, she mused, and yet so much had happened since then. She noted with amusement that the table was now occupied by a trendy young couple, apparently too busy tapping messages on their respective smartphones to speak to each other.

The two women were ushered to the only remaining table in the restaurant and sat down thankfully, feet surrounded by shopping bags. Jenny promptly ordered champagne for them both, and they clinked glasses together with triumphant smiles.

"Thanks, Heather; you've been a saint for putting up with me, trekking around Newcastle week after week. Now I can finally relax and maybe even start looking forward to this wedding." Jenny took a sip of champagne, savouring the delicious sharpness of the bubbles in her mouth.

"I don't know what you're so uptight about," sighed Heather. "I'd go like a shot if anybody asked me." She leaned forward conspiratorially. "And I'll tell you one thing, Jenny Armstrong. When Nick sees you in that outfit, it won't be long before you're out shopping again – for your wedding dress!"

"Don't be daft," Jenny scoffed, her cheeks colouring slightly nevertheless. Had the idea of marrying Nick been lurking unseen in the dark recesses of her mind? Even so, she was not about to indulge Heather's romantic fantasies.

"I've only known Nick since January," she pointed out. "Our relationship is only just starting. Marriage is definitely, repeat definitely not on the cards." She spoke crisply, as she did in the classroom when she wanted to assert her authority.

Heather threw up her hands in mock defence. "Okay, okay, have it your own way." She gave Jenny a meaningful look. "But you can at least admit you're in love with him, can't you? It's written all over your face every time you say his name. And nobody's happier than me to see you like this. To be honest, I'm quite surprised you finally managed to put Aidan behind you."

"Not as surprised as me," said Jenny wryly. "Aidan was a fiasco from start to finish, and afterwards I just wanted to hide away and nurse my wounds. I bottled up my feelings for so long – the resentment, the anger, the fear of being hurt again…"

"Until you met Nick," Heather reminded her.

Jenny fought back the emotion welling up inside her. "It's true, I feel like a different woman since I met him. In fact, I feel more truly myself, more complete, than at any other time in my life. Nick somehow managed to break through all my fears and inhibitions. He unlocked a part of me I never even knew I had. What happened with Aidan suddenly seemed insignificant, a distant memory. I finally looked in the mirror and said – get over yourself, girl, stop snivelling about the past. All I want now is to give myself up absolutely to whatever it is Nick and I have together. And even if it doesn't work out in the end and I get hurt again, it doesn't matter. It'll always be something precious, something I'll keep with me for the rest of my life." Her voice was resonant with passion, so much so that a couple at a neighbouring table stopped talking and stared at her curiously.

"So you do love him, then?" Heather prompted gently.

"Oh yes," Jenny admitted, her voice so low it was barely audible. She drained her glass of champagne and was relieved to find the waiter at her side, back to take their orders for lunch. She engrossed herself in the menu and enquired about the various specialities on offer, trying to regain her composure.

Heather, having succeeded in getting Jenny to pronounce the L word, tactfully steered the conversation to more neutral topics until their starters – seared scallops and asparagus – were served.

"By the way, you still haven't told me how the filming went," she said. Nick and the crew of One Better Productions had been in Newcastle the previous week to shoot *In Those Days*. The programme on Tyneside collieries was scheduled to go on the air that autumn.

"Well, we had to work to a very tight schedule," Jenny began hesitantly. "It was all pretty stressful and confused. Nick says there's still a lot of editing to do, but overall he's really pleased with the way the show's shaping up. In fact..." She paused, wondering whether to disclose the rest of her news.

"In fact, what?" Heather looked up inquisitively from her scallops.

"Well, when Nick originally said he'd like to interview me for the show, I imagined it wouldn't be more than a fleeting appearance. But in the end, he asked me to co-present the programme with him. Incredible as it sounds, he keeps telling me I'm telegenic. And to be honest..." She paused again, not wanting to appear conceited.

"To be honest, what?" Heather pressed her eagerly.

Jenny looked as if she herself could hardly believe what she was about to say. "Well, to be honest... I enjoyed every minute! After the first take, I didn't feel nervous at all in front of the camera, I just focused on what I had to say and how best to say it."

Heather sat back and folded her arms appraisingly. "So now it turns out my best mate is a glamorous television star with a celebrity boyfriend!"

They both burst out laughing. "Don't be daft, man," said Jenny in her best Geordie accent.

* * *

It was perfect weather for a spring wedding, thought Jenny, as she and Nick drove through the rolling countryside and well-tended vineyards towards Saint Emilion. They had left Bordeaux airport and the city traffic behind, and now she rolled down the window of their hired car, breathing in the soft balmy air and warm sunshine.

"Do you realise this is the first time we've been away together?" she said. "I mean, properly away."

"What about that dirty weekend of ours up north?" he quipped. "Or doesn't that count as properly away?"

Jenny laughed. "This is entirely different," she told him emphatically. "And much nicer too!"

Nick glanced down at the car's satnav. "I think we should be at Château d'Estissac in the next ten minutes or so."

"Oh my God!" Jenny sat up in alarm, closed the car window and began to pull a comb through her tousled hair. "You still haven't told me anything much about this wedding. I need a detailed brief on the who, what, where and why right now!"

"Okay, here goes," he replied with a quizzical smile. "Philippe, as you know, is one of my oldest friends. I was really pleased when he asked me to be his best man. But today is the first time I'll be meeting his fiancée Marie-Laure. She's the personification of perfection according to Philippe, but I suppose he's somewhat biased in her favour. Anyway, it's Marie-Laure's parents who own Château d'Estissac, where the wedding reception is to be held tomorrow evening."

"After the church wedding?"

"Yes, the church wedding will be tomorrow afternoon in Saint Emilion, although in fact Philippe and Marie-Laure were legally married yesterday."

Jenny looked puzzled. "What do you mean, legally married?"

"Well, in France a civil wedding is compulsory – it's the only ceremony which is legally binding," explained Nick. "But for Philippe and Marie-Laure, the civil wedding was just a formality, which is why only close family attended and we weren't invited. The big event is the church wedding tomorrow, and I hear there'll be over three hundred guests at the reception afterwards."

Jenny swallowed hard at the prospect of trying out her shaky French on a swarming crowd of Gallic socialites. "What about your parents and sister? Didn't you tell me they'd been invited?"

"Yes, they're close friends of Philippe's parents. They're here already, actually, staying at a hotel in town. But Philippe was adamant we should stay at the château – privilege of the best man, he said." He peered through the window as they approached huge wrought iron gates, beyond which stretched countless neat rows of vines. In the middle distance stood a sprawling mansion flanked by twin towers, its smooth pale stone gleaming in the sunshine.

Vous êtes arrivés, (1) the satnav informed them unnecessarily. Nick stopped the car at the gates, and they looked up to see an elegantly engraved sign confirming their arrival at *Château d'Estissac.*

"Wow," breathed Jenny. "Is your friend marrying into royalty or something?"

"Not bad, eh?" Nick remarked drily and started up the car again. They drove down the wide gravelled drive towards the château, which appeared to be surprisingly deserted apart from a few cars parked haphazardly at the entrance.

"Are you sure this is the place?" whispered Jenny as they got out of the car and stood looking about them for some sign of human life.

Nick was just about to ring the ancient bell hanging by the entrance, when the heavy wooden doors were abruptly pulled open to reveal a rather dishevelled girl. She was wearing faded cropped jeans and a scruffy tank top.

"I thought I heard a car pull up," she said with a friendly grin. "Hi, I'm Marie-Laure. You must be Nick and Jenny. I'm so pleased to meet you both." She proceeded to kiss them warmly on both cheeks and ushered them into the vaulted hallway of the château, furnished with antique side tables and upholstered armchairs. "Philippe," she called towards the rear of the house. "*Tes amis sont là!"(2)*

The bridegroom-to-be appeared seconds later, unshaven and even more dishevelled than his bride. "*Salut!"* he greeted Nick, and the two old friends exchanged affectionate hugs. More cheek-kissing and friendly banter followed as he was introduced to Jenny.

"I'm sorry things aren't more organised," he apologised in slightly accented English. "There's still loads of last-minute stuff to sort out, but we've managed to enlist most of Marie-Laure's relatives to help. Come through and see for yourselves."

Nick and Jenny were led through the hall and then outside to the rear of the château. It was here, they realised instantly, that the wedding reception was to be held. Acres of immaculate lawn stretched before them, in the centre of which stood an enormous white marquee. Beyond the lawns, they glimpsed the glinting turquoise water of a stunning infinity pool. A small army of cheerful helpers scurried about the grounds, fetching and carrying accessories for the wedding. A few children were setting out tea lights and candle lamps.

The décor inside the marquee was a stylish reproduction of the classical French style. Immaculate white linen cloths covered dozens of meticulously laid round tables, surrounded by spindly gilt chairs. Ornate candelabra served as centrepieces to the place settings and rows of sparkling crystal glasses.

"It looks so beautiful," Jenny exclaimed. "Just like Versailles!"

Marie-Laure smiled her agreement. "That was the general idea. There'll be lots of flowers too, but they're being delivered tomorrow morning. And the plan is to have cocktails before dinner around the pool, although we still haven't quite finished setting everything up there."

Various people entered the marquee to be introduced to the newcomers. There seemed to be a bewildering array of aunts, uncles and cousins whose names Jenny knew she would never remember. However, she and Nick had clearly been adopted as members of the family, at least for the duration of the wedding, and several more rounds of enthusiastic cheek-kissing ensued. Jenny was particularly charmed by Marie-Laure's father, a debonair man in his late fifties with the exquisite manners of the French aristocrat.

"Ravi de faire votre connaissance, Mademoiselle," he pronounced as he took her hand and bowed. *"J'espère que vous passerez un agréable séjour parmi nous."(3)*

Not for the first time since arriving in France, Jenny silently resolved to brush up her French. It was painfully obvious that almost everyone at Château d'Estissac – with the notable exception of its owner – was making an effort to speak English, however poorly, for her sole benefit. She on the other hand had not even attempted to try out her schoolgirl French. And as Nick launched into an animated conversation with Philippe and Marie-Laure, she noticed how they spontaneously reverted to French when they were not speaking directly to her.

She knew all about Nick's English side of course. They had spent months together happily exploring his Northumbrian ancestry, the long line of Robertson farm labourers and coal miners who made up his family history. But Nick, she realised more acutely now, was also French on his mother's side. He had been educated at a French *lycée* and had a wide circle of French friends and relatives. He was in fact just as intrinsically French as he was English, so she could not simply shut out one-half of him and pretend it was not there. She recognised more clearly now that being part of Nick's life would also involve understanding and embracing his French heritage. And at the wedding tomorrow, when she finally met his formidable mother, Nathalie Lambert, she would have a golden opportunity to do just that.

Marie-Laure suddenly remembered her duties as hostess. "I'm so sorry, you must be exhausted. I'll show you both up to your room now, and you can freshen up. Then we'll have something cool to drink and afterwards… well, I was hoping you might help to place the name cards on the tables." She pointed to a large box of tightly packed cards, next to which was spread a huge table plan indicating where each guest was to be seated.

"Marie-Laure, *chérie!*" exclaimed Philippe in tones of mock chastisement. "Nick and Jenny might have made other plans. They'll probably want to meet up with Nick's family and go sightseeing in Saint Emilion."

"Oh no," protested Jenny rather too hastily, preferring to put off the dreaded encounter with Nathalie Lambert as long as possible. "We'd much rather help out here, wouldn't we, Nick?"

"Absolutely," said Nick. "Let's get changed into something more comfortable, and then we can get cracking on those name cards."

(1) You have arrived.
(2) Your friends are here!
(3) Delighted to make your acquaintance, Miss. I hope you'll enjoy your stay with us.

* * *

Nick held the car door open for Jenny while she gingerly eased into the passenger seat, taking care to keep her wide-brimmed hat in place and simultaneously avoid creasing her silk dress. They were in plenty of time for the wedding, but as best man Nick preferred to get to the church early. As soon as she was comfortably settled, he slammed the door shut and sprang into the driver's seat, looking resplendent in full morning suit attire.

"I know I've told you this a dozen times already," he remarked as they drove out of the château grounds, "but you look absolutely beautiful today. In fact I'm fast running out of adjectives – beautiful, gorgeous, stunning, sexy..."

"Keep going," said Jenny mischievously. "I can supply you with more adjectives if need be." She gave silent thanks to Heather and the sales assistant in Newcastle for their powers of persuasion. Her wildly expensive outfit had proved to be just right for a wedding which – since arriving at Château d'Estissac – she had realised would be very smart indeed. And knowing she looked her best gave her the confidence she needed to face the fray.

A few minutes later, they parked the car near the remains of the ancient city ramparts which had protected Saint Emilion for centuries. Jenny took Nick's arm as they walked towards the medieval church where the wedding was to be held. It was a gracious building, complete with cloisters and tall stained glass windows, set high up over the town's network of steep winding streets. Dozens of well-dressed guests were already clustered at the entrance to the church, while at a respectful distance stood a scattering of curious onlookers. The wedding of Marie-Laure d'Estissac was clearly not an event to be missed in Saint Emilion.

Nick had been scanning the guests in search of his family and was now boisterously waving to three people standing on the fringes of the crowd. "Come on, darling," he told Jenny. "It's time for you to meet the Robertson clan."

Any awkwardness Jenny might have felt at that moment was instantly dispelled by the animated buzz of conversation all around them; they had to almost shout to make themselves heard. As expected, she was immediately drawn to Nick's father, Alan Robertson, and looked forward to a quiet moment when she could get to know him better.

Nick's sister, Charlotte, was exactly as she had imagined – a brilliant, talented doctor dedicated to her humanitarian work with the French Doctors. Poor Charlotte had inherited none of her mother's looks, however, and was dressed for the occasion in a frumpy navy blue suit which did nothing for her stocky figure. She greeted Jenny with an engaging smile and a frank, forthright manner.

"Just look at them all!" she exclaimed, gesturing at the crowd of chattering guests. "I can't wait for it to be over!"

Meanwhile, Nathalie Lambert's eyes had been flickering discreetly over Jenny, taking in every detail of her appearance. Unlike the introductions at Château d'Estissac the previous day, there was obviously going to be no cheek-kissing in this instance. Nathalie merely shook Jenny's hand with languid grace.

"How lovely to meet you, dear," she said coolly and immediately turned to Nick, slipping her arm possessively through his. *"Nicolas, mon chou,"* she murmured. "You must take us in and show us to our places. Bridegroom's side, I imagine?"

As the family made their way into the church with the rest of the guests, Nathalie leading the way and still arm in arm with Nick, Jenny had no alternative but to follow on behind. They proceeded slowly down the aisle, Nathalie occasionally blowing kisses to various acquaintances and promising to catch up with them later. She certainly knows how to put on a show, thought Jenny, trying not to feel resentful.

Still, she had to admit that Nathalie certainly lived up to her image. She was every inch the glamorous businesswoman, a real-life advertisement for her own Inner Beauty brand. Tall and slender with sleek dark hair, poise oozed out of every pore of her flawless skin. Today she was wearing a daring jumpsuit in lace the colour of latte coffee; its palazzo pants fell in fluid lines over her gold sandals, and a wide sash belt cinched her tiny waist. The jumpsuit was almost backless, held together only by long satin ribbons. Jenny stared at Nathalie's lithe, tanned back, the chains of a tiny gold bag with the unmistakeable Chanel logo dangling from her bony shoulders, until they reached their allotted pews.

As best man, Nick left them to join Philippe, who was hovering by the altar looking jittery. Jenny, seated between Nathalie and Alan, swelled with pride as she watched the two men quietly discussing arrangements for the wedding ceremony; she had never seen Nick look as handsome as he did today.

The last of the guests trickled through the packed church, looking for spare seats. An attractive couple with two small sons murmured apologies as they squeezed their way along the row of pews in front of theirs. Nathalie unexpectedly sprang to her feet and tapped the young woman on the shoulder.

"Sophie! *Quelle surprise!"* she exclaimed as the two women embraced affectionately. Alan and Charlotte got to their feet too and joined in the cheek-kissing and excited chatter. Since no one remembered to introduce her, Jenny remained seated and observed the vivacious young woman. Petite and slim, with an elfin face and huge dark eyes, Sophie was wearing a brightly coloured dress which showed off her girlish figure. She exuded the kind of effortless chic that always made Jenny feel inadequate. Could she possibly be the mother of those two small boys clinging to her skirts?

Everyone sat down abruptly as the strains of organ music, announcing the bride's arrival, filled the church. "Who was that?" Jenny whispered to Nathalie. "A friend of the family?"

Nathalie's smile was faintly condescending. "Sophie? Didn't you know, dear? That's... that was..." She paused for effect. "Sophie and Nick were almost engaged. We were all so sad when they split up." She heaved an exaggerated sigh. "*C'est la vie,* I suppose."

Jenny was spared the need to reply as everyone in the church turned to watch Marie-Laure d'Estissac commence her slow walk down the aisle on her father's arm. Jenny gazed unseeingly at them, her heart beating painfully and feeling sick to the stomach.

"Doesn't she look adorable?" hissed Nathalie, seemingly unaware of the impact of her revelation.

Jenny cleared her throat and swallowed hard. "Yes," she said dully.

The rest of the wedding ceremony passed in a haze for Jenny. She was oblivious to everything except Nick, standing straight-backed at the altar as he diligently fulfilled his duties as best man. At one point, he half-turned in her direction, obviously trying to catch her eye, but Jenny merely stared back at him stony-faced.

Her mind was reeling as she tried to come to terms with what she had just heard. So Nick had been in a long-term relationship with another woman, he had been in love with this woman and perhaps still was... Why had he never told her about Sophie, why had he kept it from her? She had poured out her heart to him, telling him everything about Aidan. She hated herself for letting her defences down and trusting Nick so absolutely. She had been so happy with him, so sure this time it would be different. Yet he had lied to her, betrayed her just as Aidan had. Once again, she realised bitterly, she had been stabbed in the back.

* * *

There was no opportunity to confront Nick after the church ceremony, for they were instantly caught up in the general atmosphere of excitement and celebration. Nick was constantly surrounded by a circle of old friends who were clearly overjoyed to see him again. He tried repeatedly to draw Jenny into these babbled exchanges, but they were mostly in French and she understood very little of what was being said. In any case, she was no longer in the mood to play the role of sociable girlfriend to the best man. She felt as if several buckets of icy water had been thrown in her face. The day was ruined and there was no way she could pretend to enjoy it. Nick noticed how taciturn she had suddenly become, but she told him brusquely she had a headache. Looking puzzled, he wandered off by himself to mix with the guests, leaving Jenny in the company of his sister.

"What a circus!" Charlotte exclaimed sarcastically. "All these shallow people with their silly designer clothes... I ask you, what's the point of it all?"

Jenny sighed heavily and Charlotte, mistaking this for a sign of agreement, continued in the same vein for some time. Jenny barely heard her, lost in brooding speculation about Nick and the attractive girl she had just met, with her huge eyes and slim figure. She was so eaten up with jealousy that she could hardly bear to look at Sophie, but at the same time, her eyes were irresistibly drawn to her. She watched covertly as Sophie, in her brightly coloured dress, circulated among the guests, looking as if she was having the time of her life.

In a tiny corner of her mind, she knew it was absurd to be so obsessive. Nick was a grown man of thirty-one, and it was senseless to imagine he had never been involved with other women. Yet for some reason, it had been far easier for her to envisage him with glamorous, empty-headed bimbos like the Swedish model he had dated before meeting her. Jenny could dismiss these relationships as meaningless, wholly disconnected from the love they shared now. Sophie on the other hand was painfully real. She had suddenly been confronted with a bright, pretty girl whom Nick had cared for and made love to for years. And what made it even more unbearable was that he had deliberately concealed this longstanding affair from her.

The afternoon wore on, followed by the poolside cocktail party at Château d'Estissac. For once, the constant flow of champagne did nothing to lift Jenny's spirits. She stood glumly nursing her glass, oblivious to the soft spring evening and the exquisite beauty of her surroundings. When dinner was announced and the guests began making their way towards the huge marquee, Nick and Jenny took their seats at the table of honour with the bridal couple and their close friends. She was relieved to note that Sophie and her husband had been placed elsewhere.

To Jenny, the dinner seemed interminable. She responded in monosyllables to all attempts at conversation and barely tasted the succession of delicious dishes being served. Nick, torn between concern and mounting exasperation, put his arm solicitously around her shoulders. "What's wrong, darling?"

"Nothing," snapped Jenny. "I told you, I've got a headache."

Nick searched for another topic of conversation. "Did you know that the Château d'Estissac wine we're drinking tonight is a 1987 vintage, the year Marie-Laure was born? That's really something, isn't it?"

Jenny refused to be humoured. "I couldn't care less," she said coldly. "It's just wine at the end of the day."

Nick shrugged his shoulders irritably and turned away. As if the atmosphere between them was not tense enough already, Sophie chose that precise moment to wander over to their table, glass in hand, and tap Nick playfully on the shoulder. Jenny's heart contracted as Nick scraped back his chair and got awkwardly to his feet to greet her.

"Nicolas! I haven't had a chance to catch up with you all day! I'm dying to hear all your news and of course…" She paused and smiled engagingly at Jenny. "You must introduce me to your friend."

Nick looked as if he wished the earth would swallow him up. "Yes, of course. Sophie, this is Jenny Armstrong. Jenny, this is Sophie Deschamps, or rather Sophie Laroque as she is now. Sophie's an old friend of mine."

Jenny remained seated and looked up at Sophie unsmilingly. "Hi," she said flatly and deliberately turned her back on them both. She knew she was expected to go through the motions of speaking to Sophie, but her whole body seemed to have turned to water. She toyed with her plate of wedding cake and tried to follow what they were talking about in French. The conversation was subdued and lasted for quite some time.

Eventually, Sophie drifted back to her own table and Nick sat down again next to Jenny. "You were unforgivably rude just now," he hissed. "What the hell's gotten into you?"

Jenny glared back at him, seething with resentment. "I'd rather be rude than a lying bastard like you."

Nick drew away from her. "A lying bastard?" he stuttered uncomprehendingly.

"You kept it all from me, didn't you?" Jenny burst out, waving an accusing arm in Sophie's direction. "How many other women have you been hiding away? Dozens of them, I suppose. You might be married with ten kids for all I know!" Even to her own ears, the words sounded petty and childish, but she was ablaze with anger.

Nick's eyes widened as the penny suddenly dropped. "Sophie? Is that what this is all about? Is that why you've been sulking all day?" He buried his face in his hands. "Oh my God, what did you hear? Was it Maman?"

"Oh yes," sneered Jenny. "Your beloved Maman thoroughly enjoyed spilling the beans. She was just thrilled to fill me in on your great love affair with the adorable Sophie. Patronising bitch! She ridiculed me, she humiliated me..." Her voice had risen and she was almost shouting now. A hushed silence fell over the table as everyone stared in consternation at her.

"You're hysterical, Jenny. Keep your voice down and stop making such a scene," Nick barked. He forced himself to keep calm and took her hand. "Listen, darling, you're getting this all wrong..."

She wrenched her hand away and stood up abruptly, toppling the spindly gilt chair as she did so. "Oh, so now it's my fault, is it? Well, you won't have to put up with me any longer, I'm leaving!" She turned on her heel and flounced off, oblivious to the hundreds of guests in the marquee.

"Please yourself," Nick called after her.

* * *

Jenny lay hunched up in bed in the darkness, feeling emotionally drained and utterly miserable. Why had she made such a spectacle of herself? Everyone must have thought she was some kind of madwoman, and as for Nick... She wondered whether he felt ashamed of her, whether he was sorry he had ever brought her to Saint Emilion. It would be perfectly understandable if he wanted nothing more to do with her. After all, she reminded herself bitterly, hadn't she told him she wanted nothing more to do with him?

And yet in some proud, stubborn part of her heart she felt her anger had been justified. She loved Nick Robertson with every fibre of her being, but she was not about to take him on any terms. He had treated her badly, and she deserved more than that.

Music drifted up to her room from the marquee. A live band was playing the usual golden oldies guaranteed to get everyone on the floor. Now that the formal dinner was over, the dancing and partying had begun in earnest. The bursts of laughter from the guests below made Jenny feel even more forlorn. What was Nick doing now? She shut her eyes tightly as horrific visions flooded her tired brain. Nick dancing with Sophie, holding her tight, telling her he had never loved anyone but her...

She tossed and turned as the hours dragged by. Just before four in the morning, she heard footsteps in the corridor, followed by the sound of the door creaking as Nick let himself into the room. She lay absolutely motionless while he quietly undressed and got into bed. Her back was turned to him and her whole body felt rigid with tension. She prayed he would fall asleep immediately; there was no way she could face any more quarrelling tonight.

Long minutes of silence followed, both of them lying awake in the darkness. Then she felt Nick turn towards her and touch her shoulder gently. "Jenny," he whispered. "I know you're not asleep."

She did not respond, although her heart was pounding and brimming over with love for him. "Jenny, darling," he repeated softly, his voice hoarse with emotion.

She sensed his warm nakedness next to her and moved slightly, unable to resist the surge of desire she felt. Suddenly, as if of their own volition, their bodies locked together in a tight embrace. They made love fiercely and silently, united in a mutual passion that transcended language. Speaking would have been superfluous at that moment, for their hands and lips expressed what they really felt. Nick was telling her that he truly loved her, that nothing and nobody must come between them. Jenny was telling him that whatever had happened in the past was unimportant, that all she cared about was this moment in time with him.

Much later, they lay quietly in each other's arms, relaxed and totally fulfilled. They had still not spoken, but now Nick switched on the small bedside lamp. The light cast a dim glow over their nakedness.

"We have to talk," he said tenderly. "I don't want to go to sleep with this bad feeling between us. Just hear me out, all right? Give me a chance to explain?"

"You don't have to," she reassured him. "It really doesn't matter."

"It does," he said firmly. He pulled her into a sitting position and propped them both up comfortably against the soft pillows. "First of all, it was wrong of me not to tell you about Sophie before we came here. I should have guessed she'd be invited to the wedding. And I know I should have told you about her in any case, but honestly, there never seemed to be a right moment. You can put it down to male thoughtlessness if you like, but I didn't think there was that much to tell. It was just a teenage romance at the end of the day. And I thought if I said anything about Sophie, you would make it into more than it actually was. You do have a tendency to go over the top, you know."

"I know," Jenny admitted ruefully.

"Okay, here goes. Sophie and I have known each other since we were kids. We were at school together and she was my first serious girlfriend, the first girl I slept with. We were only sixteen at the time, and I suppose I was flattered she'd zeroed in on me. She could have taken her pick of the guys – she was so pretty and bright and fun to be with. Our mothers were over the moon. They were great friends – still are – so in their eyes, this was a match made in heaven."

"So I gathered," said Jenny drily.

"Anyway, Sophie and I let the relationship drift on. We even chose to go to the same university and shared a flat together, like some staid married couple. I can see now that we wanted totally different things from life back then, so right from the start it was a disaster waiting to happen. Sophie was sweet but she lived in some kind of fantasyland. The scenario she'd written for us involved romance and true love and wedding bells. She had cast me as her Prince Charming, but it wasn't a role I was willing to play. I was still in my teens, and all I wanted was to go out and party and lay as many girls as I could get my hands on."

Jenny repressed a smile. "I presume that's what you did, then?"

"In a nutshell, yes. Don't get me wrong, I was very fond of Sophie. I suppose I even loved her in my own selfish, immature kind of way. But I can't deny I behaved badly during those student years. I saw other girls on the side and went out boozing with my mates instead of spending cosy evenings at home with her. Things were going from bad to worse between us, but Sophie kept hoping we could patch it up and I... well, as usual I didn't have the guts to break off the relationship. Anyway, it all came to a head one Valentine's Day."

"Oh-oh," said Jenny wryly, guessing what was coming.

"Sophie had planned a candlelit dinner at home for the two of us. When I went off to a lecture that afternoon, she even reminded me about it. But to my eternal shame, I just clean forgot. I ran into two or three of the guys in the student bar, not to mention a girl I fancied like mad at the time. The bottom line is I came home totally blasted in the early hours to find Sophie packing her bags. She told me in no uncertain terms that she'd had enough of me and was moving out. THE END was written in large capital letters all over her face. I didn't argue or try to stop her." He glanced at Jenny, who was listening attentively. "I suppose I was secretly relieved to be let off the hook. That's all really," he finished lamely.

"How old were you at the time?"

Nick made a swift calculation. "Just turned twenty, I guess. Ridiculously young to be shacked up with somebody on a permanent basis."

"And what happened afterwards?"

"Well, our mothers were devastated, needless to say, and tried to convince us to make up. But Sophie and I knew it was over between us. Things were awkward for a while of course, and we avoided running into each other as far as possible. Then I met her at a party in Paris about five years ago. She was with Arnaud, the guy who's now her husband, and looked blissfully happy. We ended up talking for a long time – really talking for once – and made our peace. I was pleased she'd found what she wanted – love, marriage and now two lovely children, as you saw today."

Jenny felt the tight knot of pain and jealousy inside her unravel and dissolve. "Oh Nick, I'm sorry I made such a fuss about it all. And I wish I hadn't been so rude to everyone all day. I'll have a lot of apologising to do tomorrow."

Nick kissed her softly. "Don't worry, it'll all come right."

Jenny nodded. "But just tell me one more thing, Nick, before we close this chapter once and for all. Are there any more Sophies I should know about?"

Nick burst out laughing. "I promise there aren't. After Sophie and I split up, I suppose you could say I sowed my wild oats, as if I were making up for lost time. But I never met a girl I really cared for. Maybe I didn't allow myself to care." He drew her into his arms. "But all that's changed now."

"Has it?" said Jenny archly.

He looked deep into her eyes. "Read my lips, Miss Armstrong," he whispered. Slowly, he mouthed the words, "I... love... you."

"I... love... you... too," she mouthed back.

* * *

They slept late next morning, and when Jenny awoke, shafts of sunlight were already penetrating the room through the half-closed shutters. She felt utterly carefree and ridiculously happy. Glancing at Nick and finding him still fast asleep, she got quietly out of bed and tiptoed, naked and barefoot, to peer through the window.

255

Down on the vast lawns below, dozens of people were still milling about, although less formally dressed than the previous day. Jenny remembered that a morning-after brunch was being served in the marquee for the wedding guests and suddenly felt ravenous.

She heard a muffled groan behind her. "It's far too early to get up, Jenny," mumbled Nick. "My head's splitting, darling. Close the shutters and come back to bed."

Jenny smiled inwardly, recalling that Nick had been partying until the early hours. She on the other hand was not even remotely hungover, in spite of all the wine and champagne she had consumed at the wedding. In fact, she felt remarkably clear-headed and brimming with energy. She padded back to Nick and planted a sympathetic kiss on his brow.

"I'm desperate for a cup of coffee," she whispered in his ear. "I'm just going to pop down to the marquee for a while. You can always join me later if you feel up to it." There was no response from Nick. He lay spread-eagled on his back, eyes closed and mouth slightly open. *Just like a baby,* thought Jenny fondly.

She showered quickly and slipped into a simple cotton dress and flat sandals. As quietly as possible so as not to disturb Nick, she left the room and descended the wide stone staircase to join the other guests outside in the château grounds. The warm June sunshine caressed her bare arms as she strolled across the grass to the marquee.

A buzz of subdued conversation filled the marquee as the remaining wedding guests enjoyed brunch before setting off home. Jenny picked her way through the tables and chairs towards the sumptuous buffet laid out in the centre of the marquee. She poured herself a glass of fresh grapefruit juice and stepped back from the buffet table, almost colliding into a young woman as she did so. She realised with a shock of recognition that the young woman was Sophie. Well, it was now or never, she told herself firmly.

"Sophie! How lovely to see you again!" she exclaimed with a radiant smile.

"Hi, Jenny," said Sophie cautiously, looking slightly bewildered. As well she might, thought Jenny, remembering how sullen and ungracious she had been at dinner.

She drew the young woman to one side. "Look, Sophie, I really want to apologise for last night. You must have thought me very rude, but it was just… I was feeling a bit out of sorts."

A look of relief appeared on Sophie's face. "Oh, no need to apologise. Weddings are always a bit of an ordeal, aren't they, especially when you don't know anybody. I just hope it wasn't anything to do with me. I mean…" She hesitated briefly. "I hope Nick's Mum hasn't been filling your head with nonsense," she blurted out.

Jenny grinned wryly. "Well, now that you mention it…"

"I knew it!" Sophie looked exasperated. "Listen, Jenny, I don't know why Nathalie still has a bee in her bonnet about us. Nick and I are ancient history, as I'm sure he told you himself. We were just kids at the time, barely out of school for heaven's sake. I'll always be fond of Nick of course, but we were never right for each other. In fact most of the time we were at uni together, he acted like a—"

"Like a right bastard," finished Jenny. "So I gather."

Sophie burst out laughing. "Yes, I'd say that's a fair description. Of course, I always knew there was a nice sensitive guy lurking inside Nick somewhere, but in the end I got tired of waiting. The bottom line is he messed me around for years, and I finally decided it was time to move on."

"I don't blame you." They exchanged a look of mutual female understanding.

"But now, the nice sensitive guy has emerged," Sophie continued. "Nick's finally grown up! And I can tell by the way he looks at you that the new Nick is very much down to you. In fact, he told me last night how much you mean to him. He said he felt a different man since meeting you. I'm very happy for you both, I really am."

Sophie's sincerity was unmistakeable. "Thanks," said Jenny awkwardly, feeling all the more ashamed of her own petty, spiteful behaviour. She spotted Sophie's husband, Arnaud, making his way towards them with the two small boys in tow.

"I'm sorry to break things up, darling," he began. "But it's a long drive back to Paris, and I really think we should be making tracks now."

Sophie nodded agreement and pecked Jenny affectionately on the cheek as everyone said their goodbyes. "I'm so glad we had a chat and cleared the air. You and Nick must come and stay with us in Paris, if you don't mind our noisy little monsters!" She bent down to the boys' level and clapped her hands playfully. "*Allez les garçons, on rentre à la maison!*" (1)

Jenny stood and watched as the family walked towards the exit, Arnaud with his arm around Sophie's waist and the two children running excitedly ahead. How could she have been so foolish as to imagine that Sophie and Nick were still in love? It was patently obvious that Sophie loved no one but her husband.

Still mulling over her own insecurities, she helped herself to a cup of coffee and heaped smoked salmon and eggs benedict onto a plate. Holding both precariously, she started to weave through the crowded tables, hoping to find an unoccupied seat. Then she heard someone call her name and turned to find Alan and Nathalie both on their feet, waving wildly in her direction and indicating the empty chair next to them. Gratefully, she joined them and set her plate down on the table, noticing as she did so that Nathalie's idea of brunch appeared to consist of nothing more substantial than fresh fruit and a bite-sized brioche.

"We were wondering where you both were," Nathalie greeted her. She looked as immaculately groomed as the day before, thought Jenny, feeling instantly inadequate in her chain-store cotton dress. Nathalie was wearing a cream linen suit and an exquisite necklace of turquoise and amethyst beads. The short skirt showed off her long tanned legs.

"I'm afraid I came down on my own," Jenny explained. "Nick's feeling a bit the worse for wear this morning."

Alan gave a loud guffaw. "Well, we can guess why that is! And how are you, my dear? We noticed you were a bit under the weather yesterday."

Out of the corner of her eye, Jenny caught Nathalie's sharp, watchful expression. She looked steadily back at Alan, refusing to be thrown off balance. "I'm much better, thanks. Everything's fine now. I only hope my little upset didn't spoil your day."

To her surprise, Nathalie leaned forward and clasped her hand. "I'm so glad," she gushed. "Alan thought I might have made some dreadful *faux pas*. I do hope I didn't?" She fluttered her eyelashes, clearly expecting to be told the very idea was preposterous.

Jenny surmised this was as close to an apology as she was ever likely to get from Nathalie Lambert. "Of course not," she said sweetly. "I just had a headache, that's all."

Nathalie gave a faint smirk of satisfaction and popped a strawberry into her mouth, levelling an unmistakeable I-told-you-so glare at Alan.

(1) Come on, boys, we're going home!

* * *

Half an hour later, there was still no sign of Nick, and Nathalie had long since drifted off to gossip with her circle of smart friends. Alan and Jenny, left to their own devices and armed with cups of coffee, moved out of the marquee to find a quiet spot to talk. They sat on the grass in the shade of a giant chestnut tree bordering the lawns, admiring the majestic façade of Château d'Estissac.

Jenny studied Alan covertly as they exchanged small talk for a while. He looked far more relaxed today than he had done in his formal suit at the wedding. His greying fair hair and beard were distinctly less groomed, while his baggy trousers and faded shirt had both seen better days. Apart from the Robertson blue eyes, she saw no resemblance between father and son; Nick had been lucky enough to inherit his mother's height and colouring. Yet looking more closely at Alan's face – the long nose and high forehead, the jawline and set of the chin – she was forcibly reminded of the photos she had seen online of John Robertson, the President of the Robertson Realty Corporation in Philadelphia. The similarity between the two was uncanny. Strange, thought Jenny, how one young man who had crossed the Atlantic in the late 18th century had passed on Robertson traits, generation after generation, right down to the present day.

"I've been looking forward to having you to myself," remarked Alan eventually. "Nick's told me all about the exciting research you've been doing into the Robertson family history. Funnily enough, it never occurred to me to delve into it myself. And even if I'd asked, I don't think anyone in the family knew much about it."

"That was often the case in working class families. In pit villages like Burnside, life was too hard to give much thought to family trees and ancestors. I'm glad you're interested in our project, though. Nick's become quite an amateur genealogist, you know."

"So it seems." Alan looked at her frankly, taking in her mane of tawny hair, creamy skin and huge green eyes. "Although I suspect he may have an ulterior motive for this sudden passion for genealogy... But tell me, my dear, what have you managed to uncover so far? Nick refuses to talk much about it, strange to say. He insists he wants to have the whole project completed before he reveals all."

"Well, it's pretty much wrapped up," Jenny told him. "And we've made quite a few unexpected discoveries along the way, as you'll find out in due course. Your earliest documented ancestor, William Robertson, dates back to the mid-17th century." She was gratified to hear Alan's gasp of surprise. "Starting with William, Nick and I have been travelling down the line, one generation after the other. So far we've reached the early twentieth century and your great-aunt Alice, a woman who also happens to be my great-great-aunt." She flashed him a triumphant smile, waiting for his reaction.

Alan stared at her in stupefaction. "Dad's Aunt Alice? But I don't see how..." His expression cleared as he pieced together the puzzle. "Of course! She was an Armstrong, wasn't she, just like you? How silly of me not to make the connection! So that means we're related, then?"

"Distantly," Jenny rectified. "It's hardly surprising when you think about it. There isn't a Robertson in Burnside not related in some way to an Armstrong. But being a bit of a feminist, I'm particularly interested in Alice Armstrong. I only wish I'd met her, but she died in 1981 at the ripe old age of eighty-nine... before I was born, unfortunately. She's quite a legend in Burnside, as you know, and of course the old folk who were her pupils still remember her. But you, as her great-nephew, must have known her well..."

Alan's mind flashed back to his faraway childhood in Burnside. His life had changed so radically since then that the boy he had been seemed like a different person. "Oh, I have vivid memories of Aunt Alice. She was the kind of person who never went unnoticed. A bit of a tartar of course, rather stern and forbidding, as I recall. But she was an exceptional woman for her time, with a razor-sharp mind and a burning desire to help her pupils get ahead in life. She believed in education, you see, as the path to social progress and personal fulfilment."

"She must have been very proud of you, then?" Jenny interjected. "A grammar school boy, the first lad for miles around ever to win a place at university... not to mention your brilliant career as a university professor. It must have given her great satisfaction to witness all your achievements."

Alan nodded thoughtfully, suddenly seeing his great-aunt in a new light. "Yes, I suppose in her eyes, I was living proof that her dream was attainable. I was part of that first baby-boom generation – one of the working class kids up and down the country who managed to get out of places like Burnside, who were given the chance of a free university education..." He mused for a while and then laughed out loud. "What I remember best about Aunt Alice was the way she would nail me as I was walking home from primary school. I had to go past her house, you see, and she would drag me inside and grill me relentlessly. Multiplication tables, spelling tests, the kings and queens of England... quite a daunting experience for a young lad, I can tell you. No wonder I was always top of the class, I wouldn't have dared face her otherwise!"

"It obviously worked," Jenny pointed out with a smile. "But what about your father, Geordie Robertson? Surely, Alice must have had plans for him too when he was young?"

Alan heaved a sigh. "I'm sure she did, but you see, Dad never really had a chance. He was just a baby when his father was killed in a mining accident, as I'm sure you know from your research. So he grew up both poor and insecure, with a widowed mother working her fingers to the bone up at Felton Hall to put food on the table. Hannah Robertson was a real dragon by all accounts..."

"You never knew your grandmother, then?"

"No, she died in 1948, the year I was born. Sadly, I never knew either of my Robertson grandparents."

"These dead ends in genealogy are so frustrating," Jenny said pensively. "When I'm researching generations within living memory, I always try to flesh out the bare bones of a person. You know what I mean, glean information about them from people who knew them well... their character, their foibles, their interests in life. But in this case, it's quite difficult to link up the Robertson family chain, because you have no memory of your grandfather, Bill Robertson, and Nick has no memory of his. As you know, Geordie died before he was born."

"Oh, I'll be happy to fill you in on Dad," said Alan. "What is it you want to know?"

"Well, of course I have the bare bones," Jenny explained. "His birth in 1916, his job at Burnside colliery, his service in the Second World War, his marriage... but what kind of man was he? What made him tick?"

Alan scratched his beard reflectively. "Actually, that's a damn good question – and one I've never really given much thought to. You see, to me Dad was just Dad – a quiet, unassuming sort of bloke, as many men of his generation were. It was hard to know what thoughts were going through his mind, and as for emotions... they were rarely expressed in our house, or shown for that matter. The word love, for instance, was totally absent from our vocabulary, even when it was present in our hearts." He grinned at her. "In those days, touchy-feely was an unknown concept in Burnside."

Jenny burst out laughing. "Touchy-feely was certainly never part of pit village culture," she agreed. "People thought it was soft – a kind of self-indulgent weakness – to talk about their emotions. And yet your Mam and Dad were married for many years, so at some stage, they must have fallen in love, been rocked by passion..." She gave him a playful look.

Alan raised his eyebrows. "Mam and Dad rocked by passion, are you kidding me? But you're right, of course. The thing is, as a child you always see your parents as permanently middle-aged, staid and settled. You can't imagine them young and fancy-free, and even less being rocked by passion. As for having sex, the very idea is unthinkable!"

"Well, unless your birth came about by immaculate conception, sex must have come into the equation at some point," Jenny laughed. "Didn't they ever talk about how they met?"

"Not really. They were just married and that was that." He shrugged his shoulders. "Oh dear, Jenny, I'm not being very helpful, am I? You've set me off wondering now, wishing I could step back in time and see Mam and Dad as they were before I was born..."

Jenny sighed. "I know the feeling," she said.

VIII
Geordie Robertson, March 1946

Geordie's heart lifted as the Flying Scotsman rumbled over the Tyne Bridge and ground noisily to a halt, brakes screeching and hissing steam, at Newcastle Central Station. The train was packed with servicemen like himself, chain-smoking and cracking jokes, all of them freshly de-mobbed and eager to get home to their families.

"This is Newcastle Central Station!" a loudspeaker boomed out quite unnecessarily. The familiar Tyneside lilt in the man's voice brought a smile to Geordie's lips. There's no place like home, he thought, as he grabbed his kit and jumped out of the carriage onto the station platform.

He spotted his mother immediately, leaning on her walking stick and looking anxious; she looked older than he remembered, and somehow smaller too. Hannah Robertson was in her late sixties now, but her lined face and stooped shoulders made her appear years older. Well, she's had a hard life, he reminded himself, working her fingers to the bone for us all. It's up to me to make sure she wants for nothing in her old age.

"Mam!" he called out, arms outstretched as he strode towards her. Hannah's expression lightened when she caught sight of him. He enveloped her in an affectionate hug but received no more than a cursory peck on the cheek in return. Well, his mother had never been the demonstrative sort, he thought wryly. Nevertheless, she tucked her arm into his as they made their way through the raucous, jostling crowd.

"By, I'm right pleased to see you, lad," she said when they could finally hear themselves speak. "I can hardly believe you're back safe and sound. I thought they'd never let you out of that blasted Army!"

"I'm one of the lucky ones, Mam. The government wants to step up coal production, so mining's been classified as a vital industry. All the servicemen who were colliery workers before the war got priority status for de-mobbing."

"But you don't even work underground," objected Hannah.

Geordie grinned. "I told you I was one of the lucky ones, and even luckier to have a job to go back to. There are thousands of other lads leaving the forces now who can't say as much."

Once outside they caught a tram to take them through the centre of Newcastle as far as the Haymarket bus station, which served Burnside and dozens of other pit villages to the north of the city. Geordie looked out of the window with interest, revelling in the familiar sights and sounds of his hometown. The sky was grey and leaden, with an icy wind gusting through the streets. He was faintly disappointed to see the passers-by, bundled up in thick overcoats and home-knit mufflers, looking

261

so morose. However irrationally, he had expected his own mood of elation to be reflected in their faces. Didn't these people realise the war was over? Didn't they understand that the strict rationing and scarcity of consumer goods in Britain was a small price to pay, compared to what millions of civilians were enduring all over Europe? Geordie vividly remembered the horrific scenes of devastation he had witnessed in the last year of the war, garish images he kept trying – unsuccessfully so far – to eradicate from his mind.

"How's Aunt Alice?" he enquired, determined to keep his homecoming cheerful. "I was expecting to see her with you at the station."

"You're my son, aren't you?" snapped Hannah. "I wanted you all to myself for a few hours."

Geordie repressed a sigh. He knew how devoted his mother was to him, how much he owed her, but he wished she were not quite so possessive.

"She's coming around for supper, so you'll see her then," Hannah added grudgingly. "It won't be much of a spread with so little in the shops, but I've done the best I can. I haven't forgotten it's your birthday, you know!"

Geordie gave a mock groan. "Don't remind me, Mam! Thirty years old and what have I got to show for it, eh?"

Hannah glared at him. "You've been fighting a war for your country, and winning it too – that's what you've got to show! I couldn't be prouder of you and that's a fact, even though I've had to get by on me own for the past six years. And anyway thirty isn't old, man – you're in your prime, Geordie, in your prime!"

* * *

It was the first time Geordie had been inside their new house on Hawthorn Terrace, and he was impressed. It was a far cry from the old cottage on the outskirts of Burnside, with its leaking roof and primitive amenities, where they had lived before. And ironically, they had the Germans to thank for their new accommodation! During one of the many air raids on Tyneside, launched from German bases in occupied Norway, Burnside had been hit – accidentally, it was thought – by a stray bomb. Luckily, no one had been killed or seriously injured, but among the houses which had taken a direct hit was Hannah's. After retrieving the few belongings not destroyed in the raid, she had moved in with her sister Alice at the schoolhouse for the remainder of the war. And now, they had been allocated this brand new council house with two bedrooms, electricity and a proper bathroom – they had never known such luxury!

Geordie went upstairs, threw his army kit on the bed and surveyed his room with satisfaction. The floorboards were still bare and it was empty apart from a single bed and built-in cupboard, but it was light and airy and clean. He would have his own private space at last.

Aunt Alice arrived for supper with a beaming smile and a bottle of sherry she had been keeping for the occasion. Hannah had used all her ingenuity to make Geordie's homecoming as festive as rations would allow. After a small glass of sherry each, they sat down to a nourishing meal of cottage pie with plentiful helpings of turnips and carrots. Having diligently saved her margarine, sugar and egg coupons, Hannah had even managed to make a small – very small – fruit cake for dessert. Not a crumb was left on the plate now as Geordie puffed contentedly on a Woodbine and Hannah placed a fresh pot of tea on the table.

"Not much of a party, is it, Geordie? Celebrating your birthday with two old fuddy-duddies like us!" Aunt Alice's eyes twinkled as she handed a cup of tea to her favourite nephew.

"I wouldn't have it any other way." Geordie responded in the same bantering tone as his aunt but at the same time realised he was simply telling the truth. Who else in the world really cared whether he lived or died, when all was said and done? Oh, he had two elder sisters of course, but Vi and Mary Jane no longer lived in Burnside; they had married miners from neighbouring pit villages and had families of their own to worry about. He also knew there had been a much older brother, John, although his mother rarely alluded to him except to complain that he had 'buggered off to Australia and left us all in the lurch'. As for the other men in the family, both his grandfathers had long since passed away, while his uncles and male cousins in Burnside had never come close to replacing the father he had never known.

For most of his life, he had desperately tried to imagine what kind of man Bill Robertson had been. His father had died when Geordie was still a baby, killed along with eighteen other men in the horrific colliery accident of 1916. Unfortunately, there were no photos of Bill, although Hannah often told her son he was the 'spitting image' of his father; he had inherited the wiry frame, sandy hair and clear blue eyes of the Robertson side of the family. This was solace of a kind, for it gave Geordie a feeling of belonging, a sense of continuity. Even so, he longed to give more substance to the shadowy figure who had been his father. Unfortunately, Hannah, being neither articulate nor imaginative, had never been able to find words to describe her husband to Geordie's satisfaction. He had, she merely said, been a good man and a good worker who had provided for his family. Geordie fought back his frustration for her sake; it always upset Hannah to rake over the past, to recall a time when her life had been happier and more secure.

The only memento he had of Bill Robertson was the old wooden box Hannah had given him on his sixteenth birthday. "I know nowt about it," she had told him. "I just know it came down through your Dad's family and he would have wanted you to have it."

Geordie was a grown man now and hadn't opened the box for years. He had all but given up trying to pierce its mysteries, for it offered no answers to the questions that haunted him. What was the significance of the carved crucifix, for instance? "If you ask me, it's one of them Catholic crosses," Hannah had said disapprovingly. "Funny, that. Your Dad never set much store by religion, but he was no papist."

As for the miniature portrait, what possible connection could there be between the fellow depicted in the painting and his family? As a boy, Geordie had been captivated by the image of this handsome young man from a bygone era, with his ruffled fair hair and white shirt billowing in the wind. There was something romantic about him, standing on a cliff-top with the grey sky and sea behind him, and the blurred shape of a castle just visible in the distance. Even more mysteriously, the young man was identified on the back of the canvas, in an uneducated scrawl, as '*John Robertson Filly Delfy*'. Geordie presumed he was an ancestor of some kind but could make neither head nor tail of *Filly Delfy*. Oh, if only he knew how his father had come by the portrait!

"Wakey wakey!" Geordie was jolted from his reverie by Aunt Alice leaning across the table and lightly tapping his arm.

"Sorry, Aunt Alice," he mumbled apologetically. "It's been a long day, I'm feeling a bit done in. What were you saying?"

"I was just asking if there was a young woman waiting for you to come home. Now that you're out of the army, I expect you'll be thinking of getting married and settling down?"

A tight-lipped Hannah intervened before Geordie had time to respond. "Why should he be thinking of getting married?" she demanded tartly. "Haven't I looked after our Geordie all his life? He's got everything he needs under this roof!"

"Well, surely not quite everything, Hannah," murmured Aunt Alice mischievously, well aware she was on dangerous ground. Any mention of girls and marriage was like waving the proverbial red flag to a bull as far as Hannah was concerned. She simply couldn't bear the thought of another woman in Geordie's life, much less the possibility of him leaving home… and her.

"Sorry to disappoint you, Aunt Alice. There's no young woman waiting for me." Geordie kept his voice light-hearted, unwilling to be drawn further into a discussion he knew might turn acrimonious. He deliberately refrained from answering the second part of Aunt Alice's enquiry however, for he *was* thinking of getting married and settling down. Surely, that was only natural for a single man of thirty?

Aunt Alice refused to be fobbed off. "Well, there's a village hop on next Saturday, you should go. The girls will all be standing in line to dance with you!"

"I doubt it," said Geordie drily.

"There's no call for our Geordie to go gallivanting," Hannah decreed firmly. "He'll have plenty on his plate when he goes back to the colliery on Monday. He won't want stupid lasses setting their caps at him at some hop!"

Geordie yawned and got to his feet. "Sorry, but I really am dead beat tonight. I think I'll turn in if you don't mind." He winked slyly at his aunt and bent to peck both women on the cheek.

"Good night, Mam. Good night, Aunt Alice."

* * *

The following Monday morning at 8:30 sharp, Geordie was back in the red brick Administration building at Burnside colliery.

Mr Harbottle, the office manager, clapped Geordie on the back and beamed at him as if he were the proverbial prodigal son. "By, it's grand to see you back at the pit. Since the war ended, we've been working flat out – we need every pair of hands we can get."

"Aye, I'm glad to be back. There's worse places in the world than Burnside, I can tell you, and I saw quite a few of them in the army."

Geordie's boss was clearly not much interested in hearing about them. He waved a hand at a desk piled high with buff files and unopened mail. "I don't need to show you the ropes, lad, so you can get cracking on that lot straightaway."

"Right you are, Mr Harbottle."

Geordie sat down at his desk – the same one he had occupied before the war – with a faint smile of amusement. One of the things that had struck him most forcibly since returning to Burnside was that most people, entirely taken up with their own lives, showed a distinct lack of curiosity about what he himself had been through over the past six years.

Geordie had spent these years in the Durham Light Infantry and seen action in North Africa, Italy, France, Holland and Germany. He had come within an inch of his life on several occasions and killed more German soldiers than he cared to remember. Their faces – many of them no more than young lads, enlisted soldiers like himself – were still vivid in his mind. Perhaps those faces would fade from his memory in time, but what could never be erased – and nor did he wish to do so – were the faces of his comrades-in-arms killed in action. These were men who had been as familiar to him as his own family; they had served together, fought the enemy together, shared the same barracks and laughed at the same jokes. He knew their names and often the names of their sweethearts, their wives, their children.

Geordie had been stoic and courageous in active combat; as a soldier, he accepted the inherent risks and dangers of war. Everyday life in the army on the other hand had always been abhorrent to him. What people at home didn't realise, he mused, was the sheer discomfort and stultifying boredom of it all – the abysmal food, the extreme heat or cold, the endless waits and delays, and worst of all the constant lack of privacy. The enforced promiscuity of army life – sharing quarters with dozens of other men – had been a heavy cross to bear for someone as quiet and introverted as Geordie. Still, he was lucky enough to have come through the war unscathed; so many men had not.

And if people were uninterested in the experiences of returning servicemen, perhaps that was only to be expected. For five and a half long years, they had been fed a daily diet – on the radio and in the papers – of news from the front. They had spent those years fearing for their loved ones in the armed forces, praying they would survive the latest attack, the latest manoeuvre, the latest bombing raid. Now that the country had finally emerged victorious from the war and peace had returned to Europe, they simply wanted to pick up the pieces and get on with the business of daily life.

True, winning the war had so far not alleviated the drabness of their lives or put an end to the strict rationing they had endured for so long. And yet in Geordie's view, the future in post-war Britain looked far brighter for ordinary working people than it had ever done in the past. Following the landslide victory of the Labour Party the previous year, Clement Attlees's government was taking measures which would have been considered revolutionary not so long ago – redistribution of wealth by means of a cradle-to-grave welfare state. Geordie wholeheartedly supported the new National Insurance scheme which would provide the entire population with free health care, unemployment and sickness benefits and an old-age pension. These were radical measures for which political activists like Aunt Alice and Alex McCulloch had been fighting for decades; now they were to become reality. The lives of millions of working class people would be changed for the better by the new legislation.

By the middle of the day, Geordie was still ploughing through the backlog of paperwork on his desk, interrupted occasionally by grimy-faced miners at the end of their shifts who had heard he was back at the colliery and called in to greet him.

Although Geordie had been promoted to senior clerk shortly before the war, the pitmen still considered him as 'a Burnside lad' – a Robertson on his father's side and an Armstrong on his mother's. And Geordie himself wouldn't have had it any other way; having a clerical job instead of a manual one gave him no right to feel superior.

Nevertheless, he was painfully aware that he had not lived up to Aunt Alice's high hopes for him. As headmistress of the village school, she had always been passionate about education as a means of social advancement. He recalled the fierce arguments with his mother as Aunt Alice pleaded with her to let Geordie attend the local grammar school. But Hannah had always stubbornly refused. "I don't want our Geordie getting above himself," she would say. It was the refusal of a blinkered, ignorant woman, but Geordie could not find it in his heart to feel resentful. Instinctively, he understood that what she really feared was losing him. By keeping him tied to Burnside, Hannah kept him tied to her.

So Geordie had left school at fourteen and started work at the colliery as an apprentice screener, learning to pick stones and other debris out of the coal as it arrived at bank. He still remembered the bowler-hatted inspectors who supervised the screeners' work, making sure that only the highest-grade coal left the colliery. It was tiring, monotonous work but Geordie was proud to be a wage-earner at last. He knew that every shilling he brought home would help to lighten the load for his mother.

Aunt Alice, however, had other plans for him. One day, she took it upon herself to call on Lady Felton, whose husband owned Burnside colliery and with whom she was on cordial, if not intimate terms. Over a pot of Earl Grey and a slice of battenberg cake, she voiced concern that the colliery management was failing to provide proper training for young men with potential. Young men, she added pointedly, like her nephew, whose father had been so tragically killed in 1916 while in Sir Reginald Felton's employment. Her nephew, she insisted, was wasted as a screener; he was a bright, industrious boy with a good head for figures. The message did not go unheeded, for Lady Felton had a high regard for the formidable Miss Armstrong; that very evening she made it her business to broach the subject with her husband. A week later, Geordie was taken off screening and being trained as a junior wages clerk.

As Aunt Alice had foreseen, he was far more suited to clerical work than manual labour. Since those first months counting out pay packets for the hundreds of miners working at Burnside, he had gradually mastered all the aspects of administration at the colliery, from staff management and training to complying with health and safety regulations. In 1940, a month before he was called up, Geordie Robertson was promoted to the position of senior clerk.

It was up to him to advance his career still further, as Aunt Alice frequently reminded him. Over the years, she had urged him repeatedly to leave Burnside and look for opportunities elsewhere. But Geordie had always felt his first duty was to his mother. He was Hannah's only remaining son and she depended on him entirely, not only financially but emotionally too. His heart ached as he thought of everything she had endured during those long years of poverty. As a child, he had watched helplessly as his widowed mother struggled day after day, year after year, to keep the proverbial wolf from the door. With no father at home to provide for the family, Geordie had grown up feeling anxious and insecure. But he was a grown man now and earning a decent wage; surely he owed it to his mother to support her in her old age?

It was well past eight o'clock when Geordie decided to call it a day. He stacked the remaining files neatly on his desk and got to his feet. Yawning and stretching his arms over his head, he looked up to see the familiar face of Fred Eliot in the doorway. Fred, recently de-mobbed like himself, was an old school friend and a trained colliery electrician.

"Still here, are you?" said Fred jovially. "You know what they say, all work and no play and all that…"

"Aye, but it was my first day back and there was a lot to get through. How about you?"

"Never stopped for breath since I came on shift this morning. I'm off home now but just thought I'd pop in to see if you're going to the hop on Saturday night? I'm taking your cousin Jean, you know." There was a satisfied smirk on Fred's face.

Geordie raised his eyebrows meaningfully. "Oh, you're courting Jean now, are you? No flies on you, eh?"

"Strike while the iron's hot is my motto!"

Geordie laughed. "And the best of British, Fred! I'm not sure about the hop, though. I've got two left feet at the best of times, so what lass would want to dance with me?"

"Don't be daft, man! They'll all be running after you…"

"You must be kidding," said Geordie wryly. "Still, I might look in and have a pint with the lads."

* * *

The hop, held in the assembly room at the back of the Miners Arms, was in full swing as Geordie ordered his second pint of beer. The hall was packed with young people from Burnside and the surrounding villages, dressed up for Saturday night and out to enjoy themselves. The noise level was deafening as dozens of couples danced energetically to swing music from a live band – a band, thought Geordie, which was making up in enthusiasm what it lacked in professionalism.

Standing next to Fred and Jean and a few other old acquaintances, he sipped his beer and surveyed the hall with interest. He realised he hardly recognised most of the boisterous youngsters on the dance floor, who had grown up while he was in the army. At the same time, many of the young men and women of his own age, now married with children, were not there. He felt like a fish out of water, a staid thirty-year-old in a room full of immature, raucous lads and silly, giggling girls.

Snap out of it, he told himself sternly. If he didn't want to end up a crusty old bachelor, it was high time he found a nice girl and settled down. He had no idea who this nice girl might be however, or where she could be found. And his experience of women so far, he thought ruefully, could best be described as sporadic. Oh, he had walked out with a few local girls before the war, but none of these budding romances had gone very far – his mother had seen to that. Hannah had viewed them all as scheming females out to trap him into marriage, and more importantly lure him away from her. For Geordie, it had been easier to give the girls up than face Hannah's constant carping; he had not been in love with them in any case.

Later, during the war, there had been a few sexual adventures, all of them short-lived; some had been paid for in hard cash with women Geordie thought of as 'ladies of the night'. All in all, his sex life had been like North Africa, he thought sardonically... an arid desert with the occasional welcome oasis.

Still, Geordie was a man who had few expectations of life and was consequently never disappointed when little was forthcoming. He was lucid enough to know he had neither the looks nor the charm women seemed to look for in a man. In social gatherings, he was too quiet and unassertive to attract their attention or interest. On the other hand, he mused, he was neither ugly, stupid nor destitute... surely there must be a girl out there somewhere for him!

"What do you think of the talent, then?" said Fred, one arm around Jean's shoulders and the other digging him in the ribs.

Geordie studied the dancing couples, trying to think of some witty response. It was then that he suddenly caught sight of a girl, flushed and laughing, dancing the jitterbug with a lanky youth in an ill-fitting suit. She was petite and very pretty and easily the best dancer on the floor. The girl was wearing a wartime utility dress, dark blue with polka dots and a short straight skirt; in spite of the unflattering boxy style, Geordie saw she had the kind of curvy, feminine figure he found attractive.

"Not bad." His eyes followed her as she twirled and twisted with the lanky youth. "Who's that lass over there?" he asked, nodding casually towards the girl.

Fred gawped at him. "You need your eyes tested, man! Don't you remember her? That's Meggie McCulloch!"

Geordie gasped in disbelief. Meggie McCulloch! He barely recognised her, although he had known her all his life. For many years, his mother had been Alex McCulloch's housekeeper after he was left a widower with three young children – one of them, Meggie, just a baby at the time. Geordie had only been ten years old when Hannah went to work for the McCulloch family, but he had always avoided spending time in their home. He instinctively felt there was no place for him in a house where Hannah worked as a paid employee. Instead, he stayed with Aunt Alice after school and had his tea at the schoolhouse until his mother had finished her chores.

When he had joined the army six years ago, Meggie was still a scrawny schoolgirl, someone he might greet with a friendly wave if he passed her in the street. She had turned into a real stunner, he thought in amazement. He tried to work out how old she would be now, making a few quick calculations in his mind. She must be at least ten years younger than himself, probably no more than nineteen.

Geordie stood watching her for the next half hour, unable to take his eyes off this new grown-up Meggie. She was without doubt the belle of the ball that evening, dancing with one young man after another but always returning to her giggling group of girlfriends when the music stopped. He noted with amusement that her two elder brothers, Robert and Angus, were keeping a close watch on her in case any of the young men stepped out of line.

Geordie was not fond of dancing, particularly boisterous dances like the jitterbug. He decided to wait for the band to play a slower number so that he would not look too ridiculous if he asked Meggie to dance. Eventually, the musicians struck up the first notes of an old-fashioned waltz. It was now or never, he told himself.

Fred, who had obviously picked up on his interest in Meggie, was prodding him in her direction. "Haway man, what are you waiting for? Get stuck in!" he urged. Geordie steeled his nerve, crossed the hall with as much confidence as he could muster and approached the gaggle of girls.

"Can I have this dance, Meggie?"

She took his extended hand with a coy smile and followed him onto the floor. As they began to waltz, Geordie noticed how light she was in his arms, graceful and quick-footed; he hoped he didn't look too clumsy by comparison. He glanced down into her face and found she was even prettier at close quarters. Her dark brown hair fell almost to her shoulders, elaborately waved in the Veronica Lake style. He took in her delicate complexion, sparkling hazel eyes and crimson lipstick. She smiled up at him, revealing a perfect set of pearly white teeth.

"Geordie Robertson! Fancy seeing you here… I heard you were back in Burnside but I wasn't sure if it was you. You look so different!"

"Older, you mean." He returned her smile and slid his arm a further inch or two around her waist so that her body was drawn closer to his. The heady perfume she was wearing – acquired somehow despite the rationing – intoxicated his senses. "It's nice to see you again, Meggie. What are you doing these days?"

She grimaced. "I've been working at the local Co-op ever since I left school, but I can't stand it any longer. Selling fruit and veg and tins of corned beef to the same old crones, day in and day out… I've had it up to here!" Her hand flew to her neck in a knife-like gesture.

Geordie laughed. "I'm sure you could find another job."

"I'm going to," Meggie retorted. "The Co-op doesn't pay much, but if I can make more money elsewhere I can leave home and get away from that spiteful old witch."

Geordie knew exactly whom she meant. His mother had lost her housekeeping job with the McCullochs when Alex, to everyone's surprise, had re-married ten years previously. Alex's second wife, Nancy, was a middle-aged widow with no children; they had met at the county council offices where she worked as a typist.

"I take it you don't get on with your stepmother," he said drily.

"I'm fed up to the back teeth of her! Old misery guts, I call her. It was bad enough when I was little – she was always coming between me and Dad, making trouble and trying to keep us apart. But it's even worse now! She's on me back all day – nag nag nag! I spend me life trying to keep her face straight." Meggie tossed her hair and pouted.

The dancers were applauding the band as the waltz came to an end, but Geordie kept his arm around Meggie's waist. "How about a drink to cool off, eh?"

He took her hand and led her to the bar. "What are you having, Meggie? Sherry? Gin and tonic?"

"Just lemonade, please. I'll get stick from Robert and Angus if I have anything stronger."

Lemonade! So little Meggie had not even reached the legal drinking age of twenty-one… Geordie felt like a baby-snatcher, cavorting on the dance floor with a girl still in her teens.

Although the loud music and laughter around them made it hard to exchange more than pleasantries, Meggie seemed to be enjoying his company. Geordie found her fun to be with, vivacious and high-spirited. As the evening drew to a close, he offered to walk her home and was thrilled when she agreed.

"I'll have to ask me brothers, though," she added, running across the hall like a schoolgirl to ask permission. Geordie watched as Robert and Angus glanced in his direction and nodded, evidently judging she would be in safe hands with him. And she would be, for he was not the kind of man to take advantage of a respectable young girl.

* * *

He did not attempt to hold her hand as they strolled through the dark lamp-lit streets of Burnside; there would be plenty of time for holding hands in the future, he hoped. For the time being, he was more interested in getting to know her.

"So what do you like doing in your spare time, Meggie?"

He was not surprised to learn that she went dancing once a week, usually at the Savoy dance hall in Newcastle. "Dad doesn't mind as long as I'm back home on the last bus," she added hastily. Geordie made a mental note to improve his dancing skills and pressed her for more.

"Oh, and I love going to the pictures," Meggie said excitedly. "Especially romantic films."

"What's your favourite?" Geordie was drawing her out, letting her do the talking.

"*Gone with the Wind.* I just love the story… and Rhett Butler of course, he's gorgeous! It's beyond me how it took Scarlett so long to realise she loved him all along. She fooled herself into thinking she was in love with Ashley, but Rhett was definitely the right man for her."

Geordie was amused to hear anyone get so carried away by a film. "I've never seen *Gone with the Wind*," he admitted.

Meggie stopped dead in her tracks. "Not seen *Gone with the Wind*? I can't believe it! Well, you can catch it this week; it's showing again at the Royalty."

Geordie recognised an opportunity when presented with one. "That's a grand idea – why don't you come with me, Meggie? Unless you'd be bored seeing it again, of course."

"Oh no, I've seen it five times already. I'm practically word perfect!"

Geordie laughed. They arranged a date for the following week and continued chatting until they neared Meggie's house on Holly Street. But there was to be no prospect of a goodnight kiss, for standing at the front gate in the chill darkness was the towering figure of Meggie's father, Alex McCulloch.

As the pair approached, Alex recognised Geordie and shook his hand affably. "Well, if it isn't Geordie Robertson! Thanks for walking our Meggie home, lad. I can't help worrying about her when she goes to these dances, you know."

"I don't blame you, Mr McCulloch. Well, I'd better be off now. See you next week, Meggie." Geordie raised his hand in a gesture of farewell, not wanting to prolong the conversation until he had thought the situation through.

As he walked home, his mind was whirling. He wondered whether Alex McCulloch would object to him taking Meggie out, whether he would be considered good enough to court his daughter. Geordie had always been somewhat in awe of Alex, a larger-than-life character who had all the drive and ambition he himself lacked. Meggie's father was nothing less than a local legend, a working class hero whose union activism had earned him respect and admiration in every pit village on Tyneside. It was largely thanks to Alex's efforts that Burnside miners and their families had finally been given decent housing. It was he who continually campaigned for better conditions at the colliery – adequate lighting underground, hard hats for the men, pithead baths with hot water for miners coming off their shifts. Mining was still an arduous occupation of course – hard, dirty work at the best of times. Nevertheless, men like Alex McCulloch had made fairer wages, shorter hours and a safer working environment a reality for millions of British pitmen. He was a man of integrity, someone the villagers looked up to as 'a grand man'.

There were few men who could measure up to Alex McCulloch, thought Geordie, and he certainly didn't count himself as one of them. Did Meggie expect to marry a charismatic hero like her father? He sincerely hoped not.

* * *

Geordie took Meggie out regularly during that spring of 1946, although not as often as he would have liked. It was not even a proper courtship, for Meggie had made it perfectly clear that she was not interested in a steady boyfriend. She wanted to play the field, she said, and have a good time. Geordie bided his time and accepted her terms with good grace. Life had been dreary for girls like Meggie during the war, and it was hardly surprising she wanted to spread her wings now.

He made a conscious decision not to force the issue, to wait for their relationship to mature slowly, like a ripening fruit. He was lucid enough to see her as she was – frivolous and extravagant and somewhat shallow – and yet he was drawn to her like a moth to a candle flame. He loved her gaiety and optimism; he loved the gold glints in her hazel eyes when she laughed. He loved the way she crossed her legs seductively and then demurely smoothed her skirt over her knees. Most of all, he loved her capacity for enjoyment, her ability to take pleasure in the smallest of things.

His physical desire was almost unbearable at times, although thankfully she was unaware of his longing for her. Like many girls her age, Meggie was truly innocent; her head was filled with romantic fantasies but she had no real knowledge of sex itself. Her behaviour with men was strictly codified according to an unwritten book of rules for respectable girls. She was expected to play hard to get, to keep both herself and her boyfriend in check, to avoid any real physical intimacy. Geordie was not surprised by Meggie's behaviour; he himself would not have wanted to marry a girl who had 'been around'. If anything, it made him feel more protective towards her; beneath the flirtatious exterior was a vulnerable nineteen-year-old girl.

The only place Geordie managed to hold Meggie in his arms was on the dance floor. When they were dancing, he could feel her rounded body close to his, he could lean towards her to whisper something in her ear and brush his lips against her soft cheek. So he was quite happy to take her to the Savoy dance hall in Newcastle, although accompanying Meggie never guaranteed exclusivity. Popular and vivacious, she was invited to dance by a seemingly endless stream of young men. In fact, thought Geordie in quiet amusement, it was rather like a scene from *Gone with the Wind*... Scarlett surrounded by beaux at a ball in the Old South, with himself cast in a secondary role!

Spring gave way to summer, by which time Geordie's dancing skills had improved considerably. Keen to look his best at the Savoy, he invested in an expensive new suit – dark brown with a fashionable chalk stripe. The jacket was double-breasted and the wide-legged trousers had turn-ups.

"That suit must have cost a pretty penny," remarked his mother acidly as he was leaving the house one Saturday night. "It's a right waste of money, a get-up like that."

"Well, it's my money so I'll do what I want with it."

Hannah sniffed disapprovingly. "I suppose you're going out again with that little flibberty-gibbet."

Geordie glared at her. "If you mean Meggie McCulloch, the answer is yes. And what's more, you shouldn't talk about her like that."

Hannah glared back unrepentant. "Everybody in Burnside's talking about her. Lady Muck, they call her! Who the hell does she think she is anyway? All dolled up and flaunting herself at every man for miles around!"

"Mam!" Geordie was genuinely shocked. "That's really unfair. Meggie's just a young lass, all she's after is a bit of fun. And times have changed since your day, you know. Girls want a bit of breathing space before they get married."

Hannah snorted derisively. "Is that what she calls it? Well, I won't have some pea-brained lass like Meggie McCulloch taking advantage of my son. She's making a right fool of you, if you ask me."

Geordie's eyes flashed with anger. "But I'm not asking you, Mam. I'm bloody well old enough to know what I'm doing, so just mind your own business for once, will you? I'll see Meggie McCulloch if I feel like it, and that's flat!" He turned on his heel and deliberately slammed the back door on his way out. This was one relationship he would not allow his mother to wreck.

* * *

It was the beginning of August, and the evening air was soft and balmy as Geordie knocked at the door of Meggie's house on Holly Street. He was holding a bunch of dahlias, carefully picked from his allotment just outside the village, and was looking forward to taking Meggie to the local cinema. But it was Nancy McCulloch, Meggie's formidable stepmother, who opened the door. She looked him up and down suspiciously.

"Evening, Mrs McCulloch," said Geordie pleasantly. "Is Meggie at home?"

"You must be Geordie Robertson. Your mother used to keep house here, didn't she? Well, I suppose you'd better come in." Nancy knew perfectly well who he was of course, which made her greeting all the more spiteful. He followed her silently into the front room and stood there awkwardly, waiting to be offered a seat. Nancy indicated an armchair by the fire and jerked her head upwards at the ceiling.

"She's still upstairs, tarting herself up as usual. That's all she's fit for, though. She never lifts a finger in this house, I can tell you. Expects to be waited on hand and foot! I don't know what the world's coming to, with lasses like that."

Nancy's recriminations, as Geordie well knew, were grossly unfair. Meggie was always complaining about the arduous household chores her stepmother gave her when she came home from work. He said nothing, praying for Meggie to be ready soon. He could hardly wait to escape the clutches of this old battle-axe with her pinched face and dour expression.

He was rewarded a minute later by the sound of Meggie's high heels clattering down the stairs. She burst into the room with a beaming smile.

"Sorry to keep you waiting, Geordie, I had to wait for me nails to dry!" She raised both hands to indicate the bright scarlet varnish. She was looking particularly lovely, Geordie thought, hair newly washed and lying on her shoulders in soft waves. She was dressed in a flimsy cream blouse and a tan-coloured skirt with box pleats. The outfit, simple though it was, showed off her curvy figure to perfection.

"You'll catch your death in that blouse," remarked Nancy disapprovingly. "It's so thin; you can see your petticoat through it."

Meggie scowled and Geordie suppressed a smile; he had no objection to the transparency of the blouse. "I've brought you some dahlias from the allotment," he said, tactfully changing the subject and handing the flowers to Meggie.

"Oh, aren't they beautiful! Come into the scullery while I put them in a vase." They both hastily retreated to the kitchen, thankful to be out of Nancy's sight. Meggie stood on tiptoe to retrieve a glass vase from the top shelf of a cupboard.

"It's been a grand year for dahlias." Geordie was genuinely proud of his small plot on the outskirts of Burnside. Like many colliery workers, there was nothing he enjoyed more than pottering about in the fresh air at the allotment on Sundays. Most of the miners grew vegetables – potatoes, leeks and cabbages to feed their large families. Geordie on the other hand preferred to cultivate flowers; he enjoyed the vibrant splashes of colour they brought to his garden.

"The hydrangeas have been coming on really well too," he went on conversationally as Meggie filled the vase with water and began to arrange the flowers. "How would you like to walk up to the allotment with me this Sunday and have a look?"

Meggie rolled her eyes despairingly. "Walk to the allotment? What would I want to see an allotment for? They all look the same to me!"

Geordie made no further attempt at persuasion; this was clearly yet another area where they had nothing in common. But Meggie was grabbing his hand eagerly now and pulling him towards the back door.

"Haway, man! I've got some really exciting news to tell you, much more exciting than your old allotment!"

As soon as they were out in the street and walking to the bus stop, Meggie could contain herself no longer. She had found a new job as a shop assistant at Bainbridge's department store in Newcastle, she announced triumphantly, working on the haberdashery counter. She had handed in her notice at the Co-op and would be leaving at the end of the week.

"I'm over the moon!" Meggie turned towards him, her hazel eyes sparkling and cheeks glowing. "Do you realise what this means? As soon as I start earning enough, I'll be able to leave home. You know I think the world of Dad – and our Robert and Angus of course – but I can't take any more of that mean old sourpuss. You saw how she treated me just now, didn't you?"

Geordie nodded sympathetically. "But do you think you'll like selling buttons and ribbons all day? It sounds a bit dull to me."

Meggie laughed. "Oh, it's a bit more than that, you know, there'll be dressmaking patterns too and suchlike. But once I'm properly settled, I'm hoping they'll move me to the beauty counter – that's what I'm really interested in! And in any case, it'll be much more exciting to work in Newcastle. I'll meet all kinds of people, make new friends…"

Geordie tried to look enthusiastic, although the prospect of Meggie caught up in a social whirl – with a fresh crop of male admirers – was not one he relished.

"Well, I'm afraid I won't be around for your first week at Bainbridge's, Meggie. I'm off on holiday on Saturday, remember?"

Meggie shuddered in mock horror. "Well, you're welcome to it, that's all I can say! Why anybody would want to spend a whole week cycling and birdwatching on their own is beyond me…"

Geordie had been interested in nature studies ever since he was a schoolboy and over the years had developed a passion for birds. Before the war, he had saved up to buy a bicycle, and subsequently good-quality binoculars, so that he could explore the countryside around Burnside. When the Holidays with Pay Act came into force in 1938, granting all workers one week's paid leave a year, Geordie had gone on a cycling holiday – his first ever – in the northern part of the county around Bamburgh. That week had stayed with him all through the war, engraved in his memory as the best time of his life. He had spotted puffins, grey seals and dolphins at Stag Rocks. He had taken a boat trip from Seahouses to the Farne Islands to view the vast seabird colonies there – the arctic skuas, terns, eider ducks and other species. Now he could hardly wait to visit the area again.

Geordie sighed in resignation. He had tried to interest Meggie in his hobby, had attempted to describe the thrill of spotting a rare bird after waiting patiently for hours, binoculars at the ready. She would stare at him in disbelief, as if conversing with an amiable lunatic; to her birdwatching sounded unimaginably dull. Meggie's idea of going to the seaside was a day trip to Whitley Bay, where she could stroll along the promenade with an ice-cream and then take a ride on the roller-coaster at the Spanish City.

"Well, I'll be back soon and you can tell me all about your new job then," he said forbearingly. "I'll miss you, you know," he added without thinking.

They were standing at the bus stop by now, and for once, they were completely alone. Geordie put his arm around her waist and pulled her close. "Will you miss me too, Meggie?"

Meggie moved away slightly, forestalling any further intimacy. "Oh aye," she said carelessly, with a toss of her long dark hair. "But it's only a week, isn't it? I'll hardly notice you've been away!"

* * *

The day after Geordie came back from holiday, he decided to call in on Aunt Alice after work, instead of going straight home to Hawthorn Terrace. He was looking forward to telling her all about his Northumbrian cycling trip, knowing that – unlike Meggie – she would be genuinely interested. In fact, if the truth be told, Geordie enjoyed Aunt Alice's company more than any other woman he knew. His mother had become so embittered and sharp-tongued over the years that it was hard to have a meaningful conversation with her. Aunt Alice on the other hand, besides being a good listener, was always ready for discussion and debate; her astute observations made her a stimulating sparring partner.

From long habit, he walked into the schoolhouse without knocking and caught his aunt reclining on the sofa with her eyes closed, listening to classical music on the wireless. The sound of the sitting room door closing behind him roused her from her reverie, and her eyes lit up with pleasure.

"Geordie, what a nice surprise! I was just about to make myself a cup of tea, but now… let's treat ourselves to a glass of port, shall we?" He greeted her with a peck on the cheek and watched as she opened the drinks cabinet and selected two crystal glasses from the neatly aligned rows.

"You're looking well, Aunt Alice," he remarked. There was no denying she had aged well. By his reckoning, his aunt must be in her mid-fifties by now, but she had retained her trim figure and ladylike demeanour. And although her silky blond hair had recently taken on a silvery sheen, the years had added both character and a certain softness to her face.

"I can't complain, my dear, although I must admit the summer holidays came as a welcome respite this year." She handed him a glass of port and disappeared into the kitchen to find the biscuit tin.

Geordie surveyed the tastefully appointed sitting room with pleasure; everything was so orderly and tranquil. Over the years, Aunt Alice had purchased some good-quality furniture, mostly antiques from Newcastle auction houses, as well as a few fine etchings and delicate ornaments. It was a far cry from the rows of colliery back-to-backs where she had grown up, but in his view, his aunt deserved every single item and more. Her position as headmistress and everything she owned had been earned through hard work, dedication and the pursuit of excellence. She was living proof of what a working class woman with brains and ambition could achieve.

Aunt Alice listened avidly as he recounted his holiday. He showed her the notebook he had kept throughout, listing the various birds he had sighted and their exact location. This year, he had not cycled as far north as Bamburgh, preferring to explore the wild coastline of Druridge Bay instead. In Amble, he had even persuaded a local fisherman to take him for a boat trip around Coquet Island to view the puffins.

"All in all, it was a smashing holiday, but… I had a strange feeling at times, Aunt Alice," he confessed at last. "One I didn't have on that last holiday before the war when I headed up to Bamburgh and the Farne Islands."

"Whatever do you mean?" Aunt Alice leaned forward, her curiosity aroused.

"Well, I know it sounds daft… but it was as if I'd been there before, to Druridge Bay and Amble. I stayed a couple of nights in Warkworth as well, at an inn called the Hotspur. I've never been to any of these places in my life and yet they seemed familiar somehow…" Geordie gave her an embarrassed smile, convinced she would find such whimsical ideas ridiculous.

But Aunt Alice merely looked thoughtful. "Druridge Bay, Amble, Warkworth… anywhere else?"

"Yes, as a matter of fact. Towards the end of the week, I cycled a few miles further up the coast and stopped at a little village called Embleton. It was a pretty little place, and I managed to find a room above the local pub. In the bar, they told me there was a ruined castle nearby, Dunstanburgh Castle, and I thought I'd take a look. It was by the sea and so beautiful, Aunt Alice – wild and deserted. I had that feeling of familiarity again, but even stronger this time. It was sort of eerie but not frightening, if you see what I mean. In fact I felt very peaceful, as if I belonged there in some way."

"Perhaps you were experiencing *déjà vu*, Geordie. Do you believe in supernatural phenomena of that kind?" Aunt Alice gave him one of her piercing looks.

Geordie scratched his head in bewilderment. "I've never thought about it until now, but the feeling was very real. It was the first time I'd been to any of these places, and yet in some strange way I recognised them instantly, as if they were a part of me."

Aunt Alice frowned, as if trying to recollect something important. "I did hear that our families – on both the Robertson and Armstrong sides – originated in the northern part of the county. But I was never told exactly where from… However, perhaps on your cycling trip, you accidentally discovered the birthplaces of your ancestors, and that's why you had this impression of *déjà vu*. It's a possibility, don't you think?"

Geordie nodded and they both laughed awkwardly. They sat for a while in companionable silence, each of them mulling over Geordie's experience. Eventually, Aunt Alice topped up their glasses with more port.

"And what about your social life, my dear?" she enquired. "I hear you've been seeing a lot of Meggie McCulloch lately?"

Geordie grimaced. "Aye, I have, although some might call it an exercise in futility."

"Don't be flippant, Geordie, it doesn't become you," said Aunt Alice crisply. "Just say what you mean, for heaven's sake."

"Well, I don't seem to be getting anywhere with Meggie, that's all. She's out on the town every chance she gets, and she doesn't like me one jot more than the other lads who chase after her. It's only natural, I suppose – after all, she's ten years younger than me and not ready to settle down yet. The thing is, she's just not interested in a serious relationship."

"And I take it you are?"

There was no fooling Aunt Alice, thought Geordie, although he was almost grateful for the opportunity to unburden himself. "I suppose I am serious, yes. I've fallen in a big way for Meggie, but I don't kid myself she feels the same. And there are days when I wonder what I see in her at all. She's not the only bonny lass in the world, is she?"

He paused, but his aunt maintained a neutral expression and waited for him to go on.

"We never talk about anything serious," admitted Geordie eventually. "And what worries me even more is that we don't even seem to have much in common. I don't blame her for not being interested in my job or my allotment or birdwatching or any of the other things I like, but still…"

"What about books? Doesn't she read at all?"

Geordie gave her a wry smile, thinking how typical it was of Aunt Alice to ask the question. "Reading? The only books Meggie reads are those Mills & Boon novels – she loves all that romantic rubbish."

"Ah yes, I know the books you mean." Aunt Alice raised her eyebrows sardonically. "They all follow the same pattern – handsome dashing hero holds beautiful helpless girl in his masterful embrace…"

Geordie burst out laughing. "Aye, that's the general drift."

"It doesn't sound likely she'll follow in her father's footsteps, then? No passion for the bigger issues? No political crusades or campaigning for social justice?"

Geordie shook his head, suddenly remembering that Alex McCulloch and his aunt were both active Labour party members. "She couldn't care less about all that, although she's very proud of her Dad of course. She's been told since she was a bairn how much he's done to defend the miners' cause. But to her, Alex McCulloch isn't a hero, he's just her Dad."

"That's understandable, naturally." Aunt Alice was clearly at pains not to voice any criticism of Meggie.

"And she's not very happy at home, Aunt Alice," continued Geordie, now in full flow. "She's just started this new job at Bainbridge's, and she's hell-bent on leaving home as soon as she can afford to. It's her stepmother, you see, she just can't stand her."

"I'm not surprised," Aunt Alice snapped with uncharacteristic venom. "I've never met such a grasping, mean-spirited woman in all my life. It's beyond me what a man like Alex McCulloch could have seen in her. Men can be such fools when it comes to women."

Geordie was taken aback by this unexpected onslaught; it wasn't like Aunt Alice to be so vindictive. "Aye, and I suppose you think I'm one of them," he retorted drily.

Aunt Alice immediately leaned over and patted his hand. "Oh no, my dear, I didn't mean that. I was thinking of something else entirely… And I don't think you're foolish to fall in love with Meggie – the McCullochs have always had more than their fair share of charm, haven't they? It must run in the family!"

The quip was light-hearted but sounded strange to Geordie's ears. What on earth could a staid spinster like his aunt know about charm, whether McCulloch charm or otherwise? It wasn't the kind of observation she usually made. But he was too immersed in his own woes to give the matter further thought.

"Well, fool or no fool, there's nothing I can do about it, even if I wanted to. I think about Meggie day and night, I can't seem to get her out of my mind. And I want her more than I've ever wanted any woman…" Geordie broke off in despair and buried his head in his hands; it was the first time he had expressed his true feelings to anyone, even to himself. He bit his lip in an effort to repress the tidal wave of emotion inside.

Aunt Alice put an affectionate arm around his bowed shoulders, waiting for him to calm down. When she finally spoke, her voice was low and compassionate.

"You mustn't think I don't understand, Geordie my dear. I know exactly how you feel, believe me. But falling in love is never a rational choice, is it? Passion, desire, the endless longing… there's no logical explanation as to why we have these feelings for one person in particular. And sometimes that person may be unsuitable, or simply unable to return our love…" Aunt Alice's voice trailed off.

Geordie had never heard his aunt talking like this... almost as if she were a normal woman! Here she was this evening, a dried-up old maid in her fifties, words like passion and desire tripping easily off her tongue. For the first time, it occurred to him that his aunt might have had a romantic attachment in her past. He suddenly saw her in a new light, imagining a youthful Alice in love with some young man who had never returned from the Great War.

Feeling sorry for her, he raised his head and looked into her eyes. "Aunt Alice, I didn't realise you—"

But she was already back in control and cut him short instantly. "It was all a long time ago, and a great deal of water has flowed under the bridge since then. I'd really rather not discuss it." She retrieved her glass of port and drained it swiftly.

"The situation is quite different in your case, Geordie. Meggie's feelings may not be as strong as yours at present, but there's every chance she'll return your love eventually. She's just a young girl, as you said yourself. But when she grows up a little and gets to know you properly, she'll realise what a fine, steady young man you are."

"Dull and dependable, you mean," said Geordie with a short laugh.

"You know perfectly well that's not what I mean," replied Aunt Alice emphatically. "Don't give up, my dear, you must be patient. Mark my words, one day she'll see you as the handsome dashing hero of her dreams... just like in those silly books she reads!"

* * *

But even Aunt Alice could not have foreseen what was to come, Geordie reflected disconsolately; he was soon to regret his cycling holiday and curse himself for having left Burnside at all. Something had happened to Meggie during that short week he was away, something more than just her new job at Bainbridge's. Whatever it was, her attitude towards him changed; she became brittle and evasive, almost aggressive at times. Whether by chance or design, she was always too busy to go out with him. She had to work late, she said, or she had already made arrangements for that particular evening. Although Geordie had always known he had no exclusive claim on Meggie's affections, these days she seemed to be slipping through his fingers altogether.

As the cool crisp days of September gave way to chill winds and rain in October, Geordie grew increasingly desperate. Every time he called at Meggie's house in the hope of catching her in, he was greeted either with a sympathetic 'Sorry lad, you've just missed her' from Alex McCulloch or a tight-lipped 'She's out again' from Nancy. They probably felt sorry for him, he thought miserably. Even worse, he felt he must cut a pathetic figure in the village; the whole of Burnside was probably making fun of him behind his back. Nothing was more ridiculous than a spurned lover mooning over a girl whose indifference was plain for all to see.

"That minx is making a laughing stock of you," his mother observed tartly. The words stung Geordie's pride and bruised his male ego. Even so, he refused to admit defeat, to give up all hope of Meggie. He had to find out what was going on, however painful the discovery might be.

The following Saturday night, Geordie caught a bus to Newcastle and went to the Savoy dance hall on his own; he felt sure he would find Meggie there. He moved as unobtrusively as possible through the crowd and climbed the stairs to the balcony, where he could look down on the dancers below. Anxiously he searched for Meggie among the dozens of couples dancing to the big band music which had become so popular since the war.

His heart missed a beat as he suddenly caught sight of her, gliding effortlessly around the dance floor in a smooth foxtrot. His first thought was that he had never seen her looking so beautiful. She was dressed in a powder blue gown with a sweetheart neckline, and her glossy brown hair was swept up in a sophisticated chignon. He saw her radiant expression as she looked up adoringly at her partner, and his eyes shifted to the man who held her so confidently in his arms.

Although it irked him to admit it, Meggie had found a dancing partner as skilled and graceful as herself. They were easily the most stylish couple on the floor and made the other dancers look amateurish in comparison. The man she was dancing with was no callow youth either, but a grown man roughly the same age as Geordie. He was tall and well-built, with dark hair Brylcreemed to perfection and a raffish smile. His suit was flashy and his tie rather loud, but there was no denying how attractive he was. So Meggie has met her Rhett Butler at last, he thought sardonically.

Knowing how Meggie liked – as she put it – to play the field, Geordie expected her to take leave of the man when the foxtrot ended. But as the band struck up another number and the pair launched into an energetic quickstep, Geordie realised with a sinking heart that Meggie and this unknown man were clearly no strangers to one another. Their bodies were wholly in tune, arms and legs moving together so naturally that they seemed to belong to one and the same person.

Unable to pull himself away from the balcony, Geordie watched transfixed for almost an hour as Meggie and her dashing partner danced their way through the evening. Meggie seemed to be having the time of her life, laughing at the man's jokes and hanging on tightly to his arm between dances as she made a show of being out of breath. Geordie's stomach knotted as he saw how the man kept pulling her close, letting his hands slide caressingly up and down her back and over her hips. Geordie himself had never dared treat Meggie with such familiarity, had never shared that kind of physical intimacy with her. He was aflame with jealousy.

Eventually, he made his way discreetly to the bar and ordered a beer, wanting only to steady his nerves and return to the balcony unnoticed. He cursed inwardly as he spotted Fred Eliot, hand in hand with Jean, only a few yards away. He tried to move off before they caught sight of him, but it was too late. Waving frantically to attract his attention, Fred and Jean were already weaving their way towards him.

"Geordie, Geordie!" Fred called out in an embarrassingly loud voice. "Have you gone blind, man? Didn't you see us standing over there? And what are you doing at the Savoy on your own, lurking like a thief in the night?"

Geordie laughed awkwardly, already wondering how soon he could escape from their company without appearing rude.

"I see you're not out with Meggie tonight, then?" queried Fred, as blunt as ever.

Geordie shook his head ruefully. "No such luck." It occurred to him that Fred might know Meggie's dance partner. "I've never seen that fellow she's with, have you?"

"Oh aye, she introduced us when me and Jean bumped into them here a few weeks ago. His name's Harry Walker, travelling salesman by trade apparently.

He's a bit of a cocky bugger, if you ask me – I wouldn't trust him an inch. Comes from somewhere down south, judging by the accent."

This last remark told Geordie very little, since to people in Newcastle 'down south' meant anywhere south of the Tyne. In any case, it was immaterial to him where the man came from. He turned instead to his cousin Jean.

"What do you think of him, Jean?" he asked, trying to sound offhand.

"Eeh, he's a right charmer, I'll give him that," said Jean with a knowing smirk. "I bet he gets away with blue murder with all the lasses. We call him Handsome Harry, don't we Fred?" The couple burst out laughing at this private joke, leaving Geordie feeling foolish. He smiled blandly, attempting to conceal the conflicting emotions raging inside his mind. Hopelessness, jealousy, blind rage…

"Handsome Harry, eh?" He gave a short laugh, forcing himself to make desultory conversation with the pair for another minute or so before excusing himself. But the prospect of taking up his observation post on the balcony again was suddenly unbearable. Feeling sick to the stomach, Geordie collected his coat from the cloakroom and caught the bus back home.

* * *

It wasn't long before everyone in the village knew about Meggie and her whirlwind romance with a handsome travelling salesman. Meggie herself, having dropped her other male suitors like the proverbial ton of hot bricks, made no secret of it. She regaled the girls in Burnside with tales of her glamorous nights out with Harry Walker.

"I've got nothing against colliery lads," she would say to her female audience with a condescending smile. "But once you've been out with the likes of Harry – a man with proper manners who's been around and knows what's what – there's no going back."

Gossip about Meggie and Harry Walker spread like wildfire through the village, although Geordie did his best to shield himself from it all. As the weeks passed, he retreated into his shell, trying to shut out lurid visions of Meggie and Harry together. And yet he couldn't bring himself to believe that his dreams of a future with her were dashed forever. He noted that Meggie had not yet brought Harry Walker to Burnside and introduced him to her father; this fact gave Geordie a tiny glimmer of hope. Perhaps she was simply infatuated with the fellow and the affair would blow over like a summer storm.

Geordie no longer called at the McCulloch house; there was simply no point. Occasionally, he would run into Meggie on the streets of Burnside, but their exchanges were always stilted and strained. Meggie never explicitly told him their relationship was over, nor did Geordie press her for an explanation. On his side, he would rather not hear the brutal truth, and on her side, she seemed embarrassed to tell him. She was only twenty, he reminded himself, and clearly had no idea how to manage the situation. Neither did he for that matter; he knew he was in a state of denial but preferred its dull ache to the searing pain of reality.

He threw himself into his work to take his mind off Meggie. Even the colliery manager, Mr Harbottle, thought he was overdoing it and made cryptic comments about 'all work and no play'. His free time was mainly spent in solitary pursuits, tending his allotment or cycling to the coast when the weather was fine. Aunt Alice tried to persuade him to accompany her to Labour Party meetings in town, but he refused to be coaxed.

"You really should involve yourself more," she chided him. "This is a very exciting time for the coal mining industry, you know. The collieries are about to be nationalised, and eight hundred thousand workers will benefit. You'll be one of them, Geordie – don't you care?"

"I read the papers, Aunt Alice. I know what's going on, and of course I'm all in favour of nationalisation. I just don't feel like going to political meetings, that's all."

Aunt Alice shook her head in disapproval but said no more. She knew the real reason for her nephew's low spirits and felt powerless to help.

The only person who rejoiced in Geordie's misfortune was Hannah. His mother tactfully refrained, however, from mentioning Meggie by name, knowing that any hint of 'I told you so' on her part would be counter-productive. As autumn turned to winter, she noted with delight that Geordie was avoiding female company of any kind. Once bitten, twice shy, she surmised. Hannah fervently hoped that Geordie, having been unceremoniously thrown over by Meggie McCulloch, would be content to lick his wounds at home for the foreseeable future. In fact, she was determined to keep him with her at Hawthorn Terrace… for good.

Geordie knew he should be making an effort to see other girls, if only to show Meggie he wasn't moping because of her. One or two young women in Burnside had been dropping heavy hints in that area, apparently rating him as excellent husband material – still single at thirty, with a steady well-paid job and good prospects. But eligible bachelor or not, Geordie was simply not interested in any of these girls. None of them measured up to Meggie. None of them had her gaiety, her vibrancy, her zest for living… and none of them had her soft skin, her sparkling hazel eyes or womanly figure.

Geordie was inflamed with rage whenever he imagined Harry Walker charming Meggie with his smooth talk. In his mind's eye, he saw Harry's hands exploring her voluptuous curves, expertly undressing her… Geordie shut his eyes tightly to block out the excruciating vision of everything the bastard might do to his sweet innocent Meggie. How could he think of courting another girl when his feelings for Meggie McCulloch were so obsessional?

He would never love anyone else, never. Over and over again, he kicked himself for keeping his cards close to his chest, not telling her how much she meant to him. Perhaps it might have changed the course of events if he had spoken out. But Geordie was not an expansive man, and his natural reserve had held him back. In that respect, he was no different from most men in Burnside – or elsewhere on Tyneside for that matter. Overt demonstrations of affection were not part of the local culture. Even for married couples, gestures of love and tenderness were restricted to the privacy of the bedroom.

Did Harry Walker genuinely love Meggie or was he simply leading her on… or even worse, leading her astray? Geordie's worst fears were confirmed in Newcastle one evening when he called in at a pub on Percy Street for a quick pint of beer. To his surprise, he caught sight of Harry Walker in a corner booth, accompanied by another man and four boisterous females. Knowing he would not be recognised by

Harry, Geordie was not overly anxious. He ordered a drink and stood at the bar, where he could keep the man in his line of vision without appearing to stare.

Harry looked as if he had already had more beer than was good for him, and so did the girls screaming with laughter at his jokes. They were definitely not what his mother would call 'nice girls'; they wore too much make-up and were showing far too much leg and cleavage for that. Harry, wearing the same cheap suit as at the Savoy, had loosened his tie and was sitting with his legs sprawled wide. Two of the girls had their arms draped over his shoulders, while Harry's roving hands were around their waists. Harry Walker was evidently not the perfect gentleman Meggie thought him to be. In Geordie's view, no man who loved a respectable girl would spend his evenings getting drunk with these raucous tarts.

Christmas 1946 was spent at home with his mother and Aunt Alice – the two women who loved him most, thought Geordie sardonically. He felt he was fast turning into the crusty old bachelor Hannah wanted him to be, especially when he opened her Christmas present – a hand-knitted jumper in a particularly dreary shade of grey. He put it on dutifully and tried to inject some enthusiasm into his voice as he thanked her.

Aunt Alice gave him a new book by George Orwell, the much-acclaimed *Animal Farm.* "Orwell's style is satirical," she explained. "But nevertheless, it's an excellent critique of the Soviet system. It shows how brutal dictators like Stalin have corrupted the original ideals of Socialism." Aunt Alice was a fervent admirer of the left-wing writer and continued to expound at some length on the book's message. Not for the first time, Geordie envied his aunt's passion for politics, her belief in the force of ideas to change society for the better.

"It's a shame you weren't born a man, Aunt Alice," he quipped. "I bet you'd be running the country by now!"

"Maybe I would at that," said his aunt crisply. "Well, it's too late now for women of my generation, but I'm convinced Britain will have a female Prime Minister one day. You mark my words!"

On New Year's Eve, Geordie forced himself to go out, having decided to celebrate the advent of 1947 by getting blind drunk at the Miners Arms. He downed pint after pint, although the festive spirit at the pub only made him feel more morose. There was no sign of Meggie, who was presumably out on the town living it up with Harry Walker. At closing time, he staggered home to Hawthorn Terrace in a state of utter despair. His head spinning, he managed to climb the stairs to his unheated bedroom. The room was so cold that icicles were forming inside the window, but Geordie was too drunk to care. He collapsed fully clothed into bed and slept around the clock until Hannah roused him next day with a cup of tea.

* * *

When Geordie went back to work in the New Year, he found a long-awaited notice at the entrance to the colliery: "*This colliery is now managed by the National Goal Board on behalf of the people.*" Union activists and Labour Party leaders had fought for many years for nationalisation, and now eight hundred thousand coal miners all over Britain would benefit from the legislation passed by Clement Atlee's government. At the sight of the notice, Geordie and every pitman in Burnside whooped and cheered. It was an unforgettable and immensely exhilarating moment.

Geordie had read in the Newcastle *Evening Chronicle* that Sir Reginald Felton and the other shareholders in the South Northumberland Coal Company had received compensation from the government '*for an undisclosed amount*'. He wondered wryly how many thousands of pounds Sir Reginald had made from the deal, but in the end, he decided it no long mattered. At long last, the miners had broken free from the Felton family and all the other wealthy colliery owners up and down the country. Social justice had finally prevailed.

"By, it's a grand day for the miners," remarked Fred as they stood side by side at the colliery entrance with the other men. "I'm glad Alex McCulloch has lived to see this day."

Geordie agreed enthusiastically, not knowing how poignant Fred's words would prove to be. Just ten days after the nationalisation of the coal mining industry, Alex McCulloch was felled by a massive heart attack and died shortly afterwards at the age of fifty-four.

Everyone in Burnside was stunned by the news of his sudden death. Alex was such a fine figure of a man, still in his prime and as active as ever in the service of his fellow miners. Few people had known Alex had a weak heart, although it later transpired that he had been discreetly consulting a doctor for chest pain for quite some time.

Burnside and the surrounding villages went into deep mourning, for the name of Alex McCulloch was known and respected all over Tyneside. Burnside had lost its most famous son, a man of true conviction and integrity. But to the colliery workers and their families, Alex was also a loyal friend, kind-hearted and humorous.

The miners went to work wearing a black armband. "He was a grand man," they all agreed. There was no need to say more.

Hundreds of people came to Alex's funeral in Burnside Presbyterian Church. The crowd massed quietly outside, for it was impossible to seat everyone inside the church. Aside from family and friends, places were reserved in the front pews for the many dignitaries who arrived by motorcar to pay their respects to one of Northumberland's great men.

Afterwards, Geordie followed the hushed crowd to the cemetery. The men held their caps in their hands while the minister intoned the words of the burial service. As he stood motionless between his mother and aunt, he was struck by the intensity of their grief. Hannah, he knew, had been Alex's housekeeper for ten years, but it was unlike her to be so emotional. She sniffed and dabbed her eyes repeatedly as she remembered the long bleak years of poverty before the war.

"Alex McCulloch kept the wolf from our door, and I'll always be grateful to him for that," she whispered to her sister as the coffin was lowered into the ground.

But Aunt Alice was incapable of responding; her shoulders shook uncontrollably, and hot tears flowed freely down her face. Feeling sorry for her, Geordie tucked her arm into his and patted her hand comfortingly. It was the first time he had ever seen Aunt Alice in such a state. True, she and Alex had been comrades-in-arms in the Labour movement for decades, but his aunt's reaction today was nevertheless disconcerting. It crossed his mind fleetingly that her feelings for Alex were far, far deeper than any of them had guessed…

Craning his neck and standing on tiptoe to see over the heads of the assembled mourners, Geordie caught a glimpse of Meggie standing by the open grave. Head bowed and flanked on either side by her two elder brothers, Robert and Angus, she looked tiny and dejected. She was bundled up against the January cold in a black coat several sizes too big for her. Knowing Meggie's love of fashionable clothes, Geordie guessed the coat had been loaned by a relative for the funeral. His heart went out to her, and he longed to rush to her side and hold her in his arms.

Surprisingly, Harry Walker was nowhere to be seen. Geordie felt that a man who genuinely cared for Meggie would have found time to support her in her hour of need. On the other hand, if Meggie hadn't invited Harry to the funeral, surely they couldn't be on very intimate terms? Funeral or no funeral, Geordie was slightly cheered as he considered this possibility.

* * *

The weeks following the funeral were dull and frustrating ones for Geordie. He felt stifled and oppressed, his mood shifting between apathy and restlessness. Although he had been out of the army for almost a year, he felt he had not advanced one iota in building a future for himself in this new post-war era. He was still working at Burnside colliery, he was still living at home with his mother, he was still single. There seemed to be no purpose to his life, no mountains to climb or bridges to cross. He thought about starting over in another part of the country – even emigrating to Canada or Australia – but his sense of duty towards his mother always held him back.

He had called at Holly Street the day after the funeral to offer his condolences to the McCullochs, but soon realised he had chosen the wrong time to do so. A dozen or more visitors were crammed into the front room, where Nancy was holding court and playing the part of inconsolable widow to the hilt. As for Meggie, she sat listlessly in a corner of the room and seemed hardly to notice Geordie's presence.

There had been no further contact between them since then, although he heard she was in very low spirits and stayed at home every night. Of course, it was only natural she should grieve for her father, he thought. Meggie had always clung to Alex for emotional security, all the more dependent on his love because she had never known her mother. Alex had been her rock of Gibraltar, as Geordie well knew, and now that rock had been prised away from her.

Even so, he couldn't help wondering what had happened to Harry Walker. Did he and Meggie still see each other in Newcastle now and then? Or had she told Harry she wasn't ready to resume her social life for a while? Well, she had been head over heels in love with the damned fellow for months, Geordie thought, so it was unlikely she had broken off the relationship, and even more unlikely that Harry had given up on a beautiful girl like Meggie.

In the middle of February, Aunt Alice invited Geordie to tea one Sunday afternoon. Usually, he popped in to see his aunt whenever the fancy took him, so he was somewhat puzzled by this formal invitation. As soon as he stepped into the drawing room at the schoolhouse, however, the reason became apparent. Perched nervously on the edge of the sofa was an unknown young woman with frizzy hair and owlish spectacles. So that was it… Aunt Alice was playing matchmaker. She was trying to set him up!

"Oh Geordie, my dear, do come in," trilled Aunt Alice. "Let me introduce you to a charming young friend of mine, Edith Slater, whom I met recently at a Teachers Union meeting. Edith, this is George Robertson, the nephew I've told you so much about."

Geordie smiled politely at Edith and they shook hands. Edith, he discovered, taught at a school in Gosforth, a prosperous Newcastle suburb not far from Burnside. She was slightly taller than Geordie and looked a few years older too. As the afternoon wore on, however, he realised that what Edith lacked in looks she made up for with conversational skills and a sharp sense of humour. No doubt, Aunt Alice had decided this bright young teacher was an eminently suitable match for her favourite nephew.

It was only when Geordie stood up to take his leave of the two women that Aunt Alice played her trump card.

"By the way, Geordie," she said casually. "Edith and I have tickets to go to the theatre on Friday, but I'd completely forgotten it's my night to help out at the local library. Silly me!"

"Don't worry, Alice, I'll try to find someone to come along in your place," interjected Edith, as if the ideal replacement was not right there before her eyes. "Such a shame, though. It'll be a wonderful evening, a brilliant production of Ibsen's *Doll's House* at the Theatre Royal…"

Aunt Alice looked pointedly at her nephew. "I wonder if you'd like my ticket, Geordie? I wouldn't like poor Edith to go to the theatre on her own."

Geordie realised with mild amusement that he had been cornered. There was no way he could turn the offer down without appearing churlish. He accepted the ticket with as much good grace as he could muster and arranged to meet Edith the following Friday in the foyer of the Theatre Royal.

In the end, he enjoyed the evening immensely. It was only the second time in his life he had been to the theatre, and he was captivated by the atmosphere at the famous Newcastle venue – the plush crimson seats and tiered, gilded balconies, the smartly dressed audience and buzz of anticipation before the show. He had never heard of Ibsen and had no idea what to expect, but the acting was superb and he found the theme of the play challenging.

In the interval, he bought drinks for himself and Edith at the bar, and they launched into an animated discussion about the characters in the play.

"I can see now why two single women like you and Aunt Alice were so keen to see the play," remarked Geordie drily. "This fellow Ibsen doesn't seem to rate marriage very highly, does he? You must be glad to be well out of it."

"Oh no," protested Edith, perhaps fearing Ibsen's message might put Geordie off her. "I mean, it's true the play is a critique of the traditional roles of men and women in marriage, and our male-dominated society in general. Nora, the main character, feels oppressed and unfulfilled as a wife. But the worst of it is that *A Doll's House* was written over sixty years ago and so little has changed since."

"That's a bit of an exaggeration, isn't it?" Geordie argued. "After all, women have the vote these days. They're free to lead independent lives, like you and Aunt Alice. And when all's said and done, if living with a man is so unbearable, why do the vast majority of women still want to get married?"

"Most women want children," said Edith soberly. "And society has decreed that children must be born in wedlock. Many women marry for financial reasons too. A husband provides a level of material security and income most women still can't earn for themselves."

Geordie had never considered married life from the female standpoint; he certainly hoped Meggie's views on the subject were less cynical than Edith's. "So what's in it for the husband, then?" he countered with a quizzical smile.

"A family, of course… and a comfortable, well-kept home… and legal sex on demand." Most of the women Geordie knew would have been embarrassed by the mere mention of the word 'sex', but Edith looked him squarely in the eye as if they were discussing the weather.

She was right in a way, he conceded. He longed to make love to Meggie but knew that she – or any other respectable girl for that matter – would never consent to a sexual relationship unless there was a wedding ring on her finger. Nevertheless, his dreams of Meggie were very different from Edith's notion of legal sex.

"Aren't you forgetting love?" he said quietly.

Edith flushed and averted her gaze. Geordie realised she was more comfortable discussing sex than love; he suspected that in reality she had no experience of either.

He moved the conversation to more neutral topics, and they finished their drinks in a more relaxed mood. Edith was excellent company, he had to admit; in fact in many ways she was easier to talk to than Meggie, whose grasp of most subjects was limited at best. But there was no spark of attraction between them at all, at least on his side. He surveyed Edith's frizzy hair and plain, earnest face, trying unsuccessfully to imagine her in his arms. Whereas, the mere thought of Meggie was enough to quicken his desire…

When the play ended, they left the theatre in high spirits and parted company in the Haymarket, where Edith was to catch a trolley bus home to Gosforth. He had offered to accompany her, but Edith insisted she would be perfectly safe.

"There's absolutely no need, and it's miles to Burnside from the trolley terminus," she pointed out cheerfully. "It's been a lovely evening. We must do it again."

This was obviously Geordie's cue to arrange another meeting, but he had no intention of giving Edith false hopes. He shook her hand firmly, in a way which could not possibly be construed as a romantic overture.

"Aye, that would be very nice. See you around, Edith." She smiled bravely as he turned away in search of his own bus home. They both knew they would never see each other again.

"No more matchmaking," he admonished Aunt Alice with a grin on his next visit to the schoolhouse. "I can manage that sort of thing by myself."

"I just feel you need to get out more, dear. And Edith is such an interesting young woman, don't you think?" It was a lost cause, but Aunt Alice was loath to admit defeat.

"She could be the most interesting young woman in England for all I care. I just don't want to be fixed up, with Edith or anybody else."

* * *

286

Geordie could bear it no longer; he was desperate to see Meggie. Several weeks had elapsed since Alex McCulloch's death – a decent interval, he decided. That Sunday afternoon – plucking up his courage and steeling himself for a rebuff – he walked over to her house and knocked firmly on the door. To his relief, it was Meggie herself who appeared, bundled up in a shapeless old jumper and skirt. Her hair was lank and unwashed, and her face was pale and drawn; Geordie barely recognised the fun-loving girl he had courted only a few months before. Seeing her like this made him feel tender and protective.

"Hello Meggie, I was wondering if you fancied a bit of fresh air? It's a lovely day, so I thought we might take a stroll along the burn." Geordie had rehearsed these words on his walk over to the house, although he had no idea how they would be received.

Meggie nodded unsmilingly, like a child obeying the instructions of a solicitous parent. "All right, then," she said in a low voice. She reached out for her coat, which was hanging from a hook behind the door.

They walked in silence through the streets of back-to-backs, around the colliery and then down to the burn whose murky polluted waters flowed out into the countryside. It was a cold, wintry afternoon, although rays of wan sunshine warmed their backs and hinted at the spring to come. Seeing that Meggie was not in a talkative mood, Geordie waited until they were well clear of the village before he spoke to her.

"I haven't had a proper chance to get you on your own, Meggie, but I'm really sorry about your Dad. I know he meant the world to you."

"Thanks, Geordie," she responded dully.

"How's Nancy bearing up?" Geordie doubted whether relations with Meggie's stepmother had improved, but he wanted to draw her out.

"Oh, she's not really bothered deep down, she just pretends. You know what she's like – playing the drama queen as usual." Meggie's voice was bitter. "I can't stand living in that place much longer. And now that me Dad's gone…" She bit her lip and lapsed into a tense silence.

"What's keeping you, then?" It was a leading question, but Geordie had to find out whether Harry Walker was still in the picture. If Harry really cared for Meggie, wouldn't he have proposed by now?

Meggie stiffened visibly and turned her face away. They walked on side by side in silence, Geordie's unanswered question hanging ominously between them. Meggie was clearly struggling to keep her emotions in check, although her eyes sparkled with tears. By now, they had left the burn behind and were nearing the village again from the far side, passing through the small recreation park known as the Welfare. The park was almost deserted on this cold afternoon, aside from two or three boys aimlessly kicking a football. Geordie indicated a bench next to the children's swings and took Meggie's arm. "Let's sit down for a minute, shall we?"

Meggie nodded mutely in the childlike way Geordie found so endearing, and he put his arm comfortingly around her shoulder. She was shaking uncontrollably now, trying not to release the pent-up feelings inside. He had never seen her so distraught.

"Sorry if I upset you, pet, talking about your Dad like that," he said softly.

There was a long pause before Meggie finally turned to him. "Oh Geordie, it's not just me Dad. Well, it is of course, but it's much, much worse than that." She buried her face in her hands. "I can't tell you, Geordie, you or anybody else."

Gently, he prized her fingers away from her blotchy, tear-stained face and cupped it with his hands. "There's nowt you can't tell me, Meggie. It'll go no further, I promise. And maybe it's not as bad as you think and I can do something to help."

Meggie stared back at him, as if weighing up his words and deciding whether she could trust him. Finally, she wrenched his hands from her face and turned away.

"I'm pregnant," she said flatly, letting the words fall from her lips like two heavy stones.

As much as he despised Harry Walker, Geordie had never imagined this eventuality. His heart was thudding and every muscle in his body had tensed, but he tried to keep calm for Meggie's sake. "Tell me about it," he said.

"It was Harry," she began. *As if it could possibly be anyone else,* thought Geordie grimly. Having summoned up the courage to make her confession, Meggie was in free flow now, the words spilling out so fast that he could barely follow her.

"It was only the once, Geordie, I swear. I'm ashamed to even think of it now. Harry took me to a nightclub on New Year's Eve, and we were having such a grand time. He kept buying me gin and tonics, and in the end me head was spinning so much I could hardly think straight. When I started feeling sick, we left the club. Harry said we should go back to his lodgings and I could lie down until I felt better. So that's what we did, although I can't remember how we got there."

Geordie knew what was coming next. He could feel the anger seething inside him like a wild animal straining to be unleashed. "Go on, pet," he said.

"It's all in a kind of haze now. I felt so dizzy I thought I was going to pass out, so Harry helped me into bed. He kept saying he loved me, over and over, and that it wouldn't be wrong to... you know, go all the way. And then suddenly... he was on top of me. Oh Geordie, it hurt so much..." Meggie retrieved a handkerchief from her coat pocket and blew her nose.

Geordie could imagine the sordid scene all too vividly. He was convinced Harry had deliberately set out to get Meggie drunk and have his way with her. And sweet unsuspecting Meggie, just turned twenty and unused to alcohol, had walked straight into his trap. The bastard presumably thought there was nothing wrong in taking advantage of a silly young girl. But he had forced himself on her... and in Geordie's book, that was tantamount to rape.

"That's all, really," she continued miserably. "When it was over, Harry told me to get dressed, and then he put me in a taxi home. I hated meself afterwards, for getting drunk and letting him... do that. But then, me Dad died and nothing else mattered. I felt so lonely – cut adrift with nobody to watch out for me anymore. So I pushed Harry and New Year's Eve to the back of my mind, I tried not to think about what had happened. It was only when I didn't get the curse..." She glanced fearfully at Geordie. "You must be thinking what a slut I am. I wouldn't blame you if you wanted nowt more to do with me."

The thought had never crossed Geordie's mind. "Don't be daft, lass," he said stoutly. "We have to be practical now and see what's to be done. Are you absolutely sure you're expecting?"

"Yes, I reckon I'm two months gone."

"And what does Harry say about all this? Surely he's going to stand by you?"

Meggie stared at him desperately. "But that's the problem, Geordie, don't you see? I haven't seen him once since New Year's Eve! I didn't worry at first… he's a travelling salesman, so I was used to him being away now and then. But this time… well, it's been weeks now. I've been to his lodgings time and time again, but he's never in and I don't dare ask the landlady. I've been around the pubs too, but nobody seems to know where he is. I'm at the end of me tether, Geordie!"

Geordie sighed. He wished he could take Meggie in his arms and tell her how much she meant to him; he would have gladly married her on the spot. But the time for that had passed. Meggie was expecting a baby, and the man responsible must be found and made to marry her. There was no alternative in Geordie's view; rules were rules, and his own feelings were irrelevant in this particular situation.

"I'll find him for you, pet, even if I have to travel the length and breadth of the country. I'm not going to let the bastard get away with this."

"Oh, Geordie! Would you really?" Meggie's eyes shone with renewed hope. As if he were the proverbial knight in shining armour, he reflected sardonically. He resented being cast in the role of go-between, hated the idea of searching for a man who would take away the only girl he had ever loved. But for Meggie's sake, Harry Walker must be found.

***

Geordie lost no time in acting on his promise to Meggie. That very evening, he took the bus to Newcastle and made his way to the address she had given him. To his surprise, Harry Walker's lodgings turned out to be in a seedy boarding house, down an alley off Percy Street. It was distinctly at odds with the image of sophisticated man about town Harry had been at such pains to project.

Geordie rang the bell and waited with steely determination. He had rehearsed what he would say to Harry when he came face to face with him, if only to take his mind off what he really wanted to do, which was to beat the bastard to a pulp. Eventually, the door opened to reveal a stout, middle-aged woman in bedroom slippers, wearing an old housecoat with a faded floral pattern. Her hair, tightly rolled up in curlers, was concealed by a lime-green nylon turban. Arms folded defensively over her ample bosom, she surveyed Geordie warily.

"Evening, missus," he began politely. "Are you the landlady here?"

"I am. And who are you when you're at home?"

Not an auspicious start, thought Geordie. "My name's George Robertson, and I've come to see one of your lodgers, Harry Walker. Is he in?"

The woman snorted dismissively. "A bit late, aren't you? He's been gone since the New Year. The bugger sneaked off one night without so much as a by your leave and left me with a month's rent unpaid. I knew from the start he was a nasty piece of work, that one." She gave Geordie a sharp look. "What's your business with Harry Walker anyway?"

"It's not business exactly," he said. "I don't even know Mr Walker. I've come on behalf of… my sister. She needs to see him urgently."

"Your sister, eh?" the landlady sneered. "Well, she's not the first lass come looking for him and she'll not be the last. I could have told them what he was like.

289

That man went through more women than I've had hot dinners. Up and down them stairs at all hours, keeping me awake at night with the commotion..."

Geordie had suspected Harry was a womaniser ever since he had come across him in the pub a few weeks before, but this was even worse than he had feared. It was crystal clear now that Harry had never been serious about Meggie. She was just one of a long line of adoring females, to be used and abused as he saw fit. Nevertheless, he owed it to Meggie to give the man a chance to do the right thing.

"I'm sorry to hear it, but my sister still needs to speak to Mr Walker. Have you any idea at all where I might find him?"

The landlady smirked triumphantly, enjoying having the upper hand in the exchange. "Oh aye, I know where you can find him all right." She paused for dramatic effect. "Behind bars, that's where!"

Geordie was speechless. He stared at the woman, wondering if he had heard her correctly. "You mean he's in jail?" he stammered.

"Aye, that's right. The coppers came looking for him shortly after New Year, but he'd already scarpered. Turns out, he was quite a Tricky Dicky and no mistake. Involved in burglaries, fraud, embezzlement, you name it... Well, they caught up with him in the end, and I read all about his trial in the paper. He was sentenced to ten years in the nick – and serves him bloody well right!"

Geordie had seen nothing in the local press about Harry Walker's arrest, but on the other hand, he had not been on the alert for such news. In any case, it hardly mattered now. His heart sank as he thought of Meggie and how devastated she would be when she found out the harsh truth about the man who had seduced her. He was already dreading being the one to tell her.

"Well, thanks for your time, missus," he said, his brain still trying to digest everything he had been told. Harry Walker was nothing more than a common criminal!

He took his leave of the landlady and set off towards Percy Street. She called after him in a strident voice, determined not to let him go before she had played her trump card. "And you can tell that sister of yours not to bother waiting for him either! The coppers told me he's got a wife and three bairns in Doncaster." She went back inside and slammed the door.

Geordie walked on without answering, but his mind had suddenly cleared; he knew exactly what needed to be done next.

* * *

The very next day, Geordie stood leaning on a lamppost near the staff exit of Bainbridge's, the big department store in Newcastle where Meggie worked. It was Monday evening, and he had left the colliery early so as not to miss her when she finished her shift.

He spotted her at once among the dozens of chattering shop girls pouring out through the staff door. He noticed that she had made an effort with her appearance and was looking more her normal self. She had washed her hair and was wearing her favourite red lipstick, although there were still huge dark shadows under her eyes. She seemed unsurprised to find him waiting for her and agreed at once when Geordie suggested having a bite to eat at a nearby café.

As Geordie had hoped, the café was almost empty except for an elderly couple huddled over cups of tea. He chose a table as far away from them as possible and ordered steak and kidney pie with chips for Meggie and himself. He was dreading having to dash whatever illusions she still had about Harry Walker, but he was excited too. He had a plan of action now.

She looked at him expectantly. "Did you find him, then?"

"No," said Geordie. He took a deep breath and recounted what he had learned from the landlady, keeping to the basic facts. He avoided giving details – Harry's womanising, for instance – which would only hurt Meggie unnecessarily. On the other hand, he told her about the wife and three children in Doncaster, for this was information Meggie needed if any decisions were to be made.

Meggie did not weep or make a scene, as Geordie had feared she might. She stared down at the rapidly cooling plate of pie and chips and sighed heavily.

"I was expecting something like this, Geordie. Deep down, I knew I was only fooling myself that he still cared for me. In fact, I'm not sure he ever cared for me, he was just putting on an act. The warning signs were staring me in the face, but I ignored them."

"You mustn't blame yourself, Meggie."

She raised her eyes to meet his, with a resolute expression he had never seen before. "Oh, but I do blame myself. I was stupid and naïve, and it's high time I grew up. And I have the baby to consider now."

Geordie reached across the table and squeezed her hand sympathetically. "You must think carefully about what's best for both of you. But remember… people don't look kindly on unmarried mothers and illegitimate children, however unfair that may be. You'll never be able to lift your head in Burnside again. And surely you don't want to go through life with nobody to look after you and the bairn?"

She shrugged her shoulders helplessly, and he pressed on. "I can give you a way out of this mess, Meggie," he said urgently. "All you've got to do is marry me." He wished he had phrased his proposal more romantically, but it was too late now.

She gasped in shock; the possibility of marrying him had clearly never crossed her mind. "Geordie, you must be mad! I wouldn't even hear of such a thing. I'd never let you throw your life away on me, never mind take on a bairn who's not your own. It's very kind of you to offer, though."

Geordie found this last remark so incongruous that he burst out laughing. "Kind! Do you think I'm being kind, Meggie? Don't you know how much you mean to me, sweetheart, how much I've wanted to marry you ever since I met you?" It was the first time he had dared call her sweetheart, and he was thrilled by the sound of the word on his lips.

Meggie looked taken aback by the intensity of his feelings. "How much I mean to you?" she repeated slowly. "No, I can't say as I do. You never said anything like that before." She cleared her throat in embarrassment. "I mean, you never told me you loved me or anything."

"But I do, Meggie, you know I do." Why did those three little words – I love you – always stick in his throat? Why was it always so difficult for him to express his innermost feelings? He cursed himself for being so wooden, so inhibited. He racked his brain for convincing arguments to sway her decision in his favour.

"I know you don't love me, Meggie…" He paused but she was honest enough not to contradict him. "But you might learn to love me in time. And you do like me, don't you?"

She gave him a faint smile. "Oh aye, I'm very fond of you. You're a really nice man, and everybody in Burnside thinks highly of you…"

Quite an endorsement, thought Geordie drily. "Well then," he continued reassuringly. "That's a good enough start, I reckon. There's no time to lose, though. We should get married as soon as the bans are published, all right? And Meggie, you mustn't worry about the bairn, I'll bring him up like my own. You'll see, I'll be a proper father to him and he'll never know the difference."

Meggie's expression was pensive as she turned over in her mind this unexpected proposal of marriage. "But Geordie, the baby would be born just a few months after the wedding, so everybody would know…"

Geordie grinned. "Well, we wouldn't be the first couple in Burnside to marry in a hurry. By the time the bairn comes, you'll be a respectable married woman, and the rest will be forgotten soon enough."

"What if there's gossip? What if people ask… who the real father is?"

"They won't dare," said Geordie emphatically. "Once we're married, the bairn will be ours, end of story. They'll soon find something else to gossip about."

Meggie lapsed again into a thoughtful silence, although Geordie sensed he was bringing her around to his point of view. He decided to try another tack. "And just think, pet, after the wedding, you can leave home at last and get your stepmother off your back."

Meggie brightened visibly at the prospect. "By, I can hardly wait!" she exclaimed. "But Geordie, where would we live?"

"Why, at Hawthorn Terrace, of course. With Mam." As soon as he uttered the words, he realised his mistake. Meggie's face froze as if he had suggested moving in with a two-headed monster.

"Oh Geordie, I couldn't face it. It would be a case of out of the frying pan into the fire. I know what your Mam's like, remember? She kept house for us for ten years. Oh, she cleaned and cooked and washed and ironed all right, but… she's as hard as nails, Geordie. She never had a kind word for me and me brothers when we were little, and she was always so sharp-tongued. I couldn't live under the same roof as your Mam, and that's flat."

Geordie knew his mother's character well enough to recognise the truth in Meggie's words. But he refused to let Hannah stand between him and a future with the woman he loved. What could he say to allay Meggie's fears?

"She's had a hard life, pet, try to make some allowances for her. And we wouldn't be living in the same house for long. I've been saving up, you know, and in a year or so, I reckon I'll have enough put by for a deposit on a house of our own. Wouldn't that be grand, eh?"

Seeing Meggie's expression lighten, he pressed her again. "Marry me, Meggie. I'll do everything I can to make you happy, I promise. Say yes, sweetheart, say yes."

To his delight, she gave him a shy smile. "Yes," she said finally. "I'll marry you, Geordie. I just hope we can make a go of it, that's all."

***

"I won't have it, Geordie! I won't let you ruin your life with a lass who's not fit to shine your shoes! And I won't have that little trollop under my roof!"

Hannah was incandescent with rage. Geordie had not expected her to jump for joy at the news, but he had at least hoped to make her see reason. Once again, he had underestimated her fierce possessiveness, her icy determination to keep him all to herself. But this was one battle his mother was not going to win. He let her rant and rave at him until she was so hoarse that she started to splutter and cough.

"For God's sake, Mam, sit down and pull yourself together." He guided her to an armchair and went to fetch a glass of water in the kitchen. She drank it, gasping for breath, and he waited patiently until she had recovered her composure. "I was hoping you'd have the good grace to be pleased for me, Mam. Most mothers are happy to see their sons find a nice lass and get married."

Hannah jerked her chin resentfully. "I might be, if she was a nice lass," she said tartly. "But she's not. I could tell you a few things about Meggie McCulloch—"

"I don't want to hear them," Geordie interrupted. "And let me tell you one thing, Mam. It's not for you to judge the woman I've chosen to marry. I don't want to hear another word against Meggie from now on, do you understand?"

Hannah looked sullen and pursed her lips. Geordie stood over her with a dogged, glowering expression she had never seen before. "And let me tell you another thing, Mam. You're welcome to live in this house with Meggie and me, but in case you hadn't noticed... I pay the rent. I decide who lives under this roof, not you."

They were harsh words, he knew, but there would be no peace at Hawthorn Terrace if he didn't put his foot down from the outset. Hannah grimaced, looking trapped and defeated. Where on earth could she go if she refused to share her home with Meggie? She realised bitterly that she was in no position to argue.

"But why do you have to rush into things?" she pleaded. "Why don't you have a proper engagement like other people?" Her eyes suddenly narrowed in suspicion. "Is there something you're not telling me, lad?"

Geordie sensed danger; this was a potentially explosive area to be avoided at all costs. He straightened his shoulders and drew himself upright. "Meggie and I will be getting married as soon as the bans are published. It's what we both want, and I don't have to explain the ins and outs to you." He gave her a long warning look. "I don't want any trouble with Meggie, Mam. Is that clear?"

* * *

In the end, the wedding date was set for the Easter weekend. Geordie was determined to spare no expense. He wanted everything done properly for Meggie's sake, to start their marriage on the right footing. He splashed out on the best engagement ring he could afford and arranged a wedding breakfast in the village hall, to be held after the church service. Over eighty friends and relatives were invited for the occasion; it would be a grand day in Burnside.

At Meggie's request, they were married at Burnside Presbyterian Church, much to his mother's disapproval. "They're a funny lot, these Presbyterians," Hannah complained huffily. "We've always been Church of England in our family." Geordie's mind turned briefly to the ancient wooden crucifix which had been handed down to him by generations of Robertsons and wondered privately whether this was true. But he was not about to argue with his mother about such minor details. He would gladly have married Meggie in a cowshed if it made her happy.

Very few brides could afford a white wedding in the austere economic climate of 1947, and Meggie was worried in any case about her pregnancy starting to show. Thanks to a generous employee discount from Bainbridge's, she selected instead a pearl grey suit with a pale pink blouse and matching hat. As he watched her walk down the aisle, eyes sparkling and smiling demurely, on the arm of her brother Robert, Geordie's heart swelled with pride. It was immaterial to him that this beautiful girl was expecting another man's child. Meggie McCulloch was about to become Meggie Robertson; she was his and his alone.

"Congratulations, my dear," said Aunt Alice warmly as she pecked him on the cheek after the ceremony. "Didn't I tell you everything would come right in the end? Love conquers all!"

In later life, when Geordie looked back on his wedding day, his memories were always rather blurred. The only thing he clearly recollected was the feeling of dizzy euphoria he could scarcely conceal, and Meggie's glowing face as she looked up into his. In a wild surge of optimism, he believed at that moment that Meggie was learning to love him.

* * *

As soon as the wedding breakfast was over, Geordie and Meggie travelled by train to North Yorkshire for a week's honeymoon in Scarborough. Geordie was hoping that a holiday alone together – away from the drabness of everyday life in Burnside – would help them forge a more intimate relationship and help Meggie see him as her husband rather than – as he feared – a useful expedient in her time of need.

He had booked one of the best rooms in the aptly named Grand Hotel. Meggie's face lit up with excitement as she gazed at the massive Victorian building set high on the cliff top, with its spectacular views over South Bay. Unlike Geordie, who had moved around the country during his long years of army service, it was the first time Meggie had been south of the Tyne. She was enchanted by Scarborough, even though it was only April and the popular seaside resort was still fairly quiet. She could hardly wait to explore its elegant streets and discover the many tourist attractions on offer.

To all outward appearances, the honeymoon was a success. Anyone who saw them walking arm in arm along the promenade that week would assume they were a young couple in love. Day after day, they took leisurely strolls in the spring sunshine, they sat in cafés devouring fish and chips when it rained, they went boating on the lake when it was fine, they rode on the miniature railway and took in all the sights. Meggie never tired of the amusement arcades and the shops. She spent hours avidly watching the other holidaymakers, all so carefree and smartly dressed. It was a far cry from Burnside, and a welcome break from the strain of the past few months.

But it was all a sham, as they were both well aware. Their laughter was brittle, and the endless bright chatter was forced. The image of happy honeymooners they presented to the outside world was merely a façade.

The tension and bad feeling had started on their wedding night. Geordie could hardly wait to make love to Meggie; he had fantasised about this moment for so long. Even so, he was prepared to be gentle and patient, knowing that Meggie was still a novice in sexual matters despite her pregnancy. She had been in a drunken stupor when Harry Walker had seduced her. Geordie wanted to show her that making love with him would be different.

He ordered two glasses of brandy to be brought up to their room as a treat, although Meggie was patently nervous and refused to take even a sip. She pulled aside the drawn curtains and looked out into the Scarborough night.

"Look at all the bright lights, Geordie! Oh, I just love Scarborough!" She turned towards him eagerly, and Geordie went to join her at the dark window. He took her in his arms, but she drew away when he bent to kiss her.

Pretending not to notice, he stroked her hair and whispered softly in her ear. "Let's go straight to bed, sweetheart." He started to unfasten the buttons of her blouse, instantly aroused by the soft swell of her breasts visible through the flimsy pink silk.

Meggie clutched the blouse defensively to her throat. "I'll be back in a minute, Geordie. I have to get ready first." She started rummaging in her suitcase for her night attire and toiletries, then disappeared into the bathroom without a backward glance. Geordie heard the key turn in the lock of the bathroom door.

He undressed quickly and put on his pyjamas. He climbed into the large double bed, leaving the room in darkness except for the soft glow of a bedside lamp. It had been a long day, and in normal circumstances, Geordie would have wanted nothing more than a good night's sleep. But tonight was different. His physical desire for Meggie was so intense that sleep was the last thing on his mind.

It was fully half an hour before Meggie emerged from the bathroom, dressed in a white cotton nightgown with a high beribboned neckline and long sleeves gathered at the wrists. Almost reluctantly, she lay down next to Geordie and immediately turned out the bedside lamp.

"Goodnight, then," she said in a muffled voice, turning her back and keeping a safe distance between them.

It was not what Geordie had expected on his wedding night. He pulled her towards him and enveloped her in his arms. "Meggie, for God's sake! We're husband and wife now." He tried to kiss her in the darkness and ran his hands gently down the soft curves of her body. He felt her large breasts – slightly swollen now from pregnancy – pressing against his chest and longed to feel her naked skin under his fingertips. Impatiently, he started to pull up her nightgown, realising as he did so that she had not even removed her underwear. Her girlish modesty only made him want her more.

"I can't, Geordie, I can't! Don't make me, please!" He could barely see the outline of her face in the darkness, but her voice was shrill and hysterical. She yanked down her nightgown and turned away from him again.

Geordie propped himself on one elbow and touched her hunched shoulder. He could feel her whole body shaking and guessed that she was crying. "Meggie, what's the matter? Surely you know there's nowt wrong with a husband and wife coming together in bed?" He could not comprehend why Meggie was behaving like this. She had agreed to marry him and must have known that sex would be part of the equation in their future life together.

Meggie sat up abruptly and switched on the bedside lamp. Her face was set in a stubborn, pinched expression that Geordie had never seen before. "It's not fair, Geordie, you can't force yourself on me like this. You've got no right to put the baby at risk. I read all about it in *Woman's Own.* Couples have to stop... you know, doing it... when the woman's expecting. So you'll just have to wait until the baby's born."

Geordie was so astounded that he burst out laughing. "Listen to me, Meggie! You're talking rubbish, pet. You're barely three months gone, and there's no risk to the baby at all at this stage." He reached out to her again and cupped one of her breasts through the thick cotton of the nightdress. "I promise you, I'll be gentle. I've wanted you for so long... please don't spoil our first night together."

Meggie pushed him away roughly and folded her arms defensively across her chest. "Don't you dare lay a finger on me. I've told you already, I have to protect the baby."

Geordie had never imagined he would be confronted with this humiliating scenario on his wedding night. He had never tried to take advantage of Meggie when they were courting. He had played by the rules and tried to do everything right. Tonight he felt cheated, annoyed with Meggie for depriving him of his rights.

Again, he tried to contain himself. "Surely, I'm at least entitled to kiss my wife," he said in a wheedling tone of voice which he resented having to adopt. "And I want to see what you look like without that blasted nightie. I want—"

"No, I can't let you," Meggie replied flatly. "Men are all the same, and if I let you get away with one thing, you'll be wanting to do the next. I'm not putting up with any hanky-panky until the baby's born."

Geordie's heart froze. Getting away with it... putting up with it... was this her idea of marital relations? He had been prepared to cope with Meggie's sexual ignorance. Like many girls of her age, what little she knew about sex was gleaned from romantic Hollywood movies and Mills & Boon novels. But her open hostility tonight was a different matter entirely. It was as if she now saw all men as ruthless predators, bent only on their own sexual satisfaction. Perhaps her traumatic one-night stand with Harry Walker had left an indelible scar.

"So you think I'm like that bastard who got you pregnant," he protested in exasperation. "The one who ditched you, Meggie. The one who turned out to be a common criminal, and a married one at that. You're forgetting who got you out of that bloody mess and made a respectable woman of you." He had not intended to lash out at her, but he was boiling with rage.

Meggie turned bright scarlet. "Oh, you're going to throw that in my face at every turn, are you? I'll be hearing that for the next forty years, will I?" Her voice rose shrilly. "You know what, you're forgetting something and all. I never came running after you, I never asked you for nowt. You were the one swearing undying love and begging me to marry you! What makes you think you're entitled to a damn thing?"

The harsh words seemed to reverberate around them in the silence of the dark room. Neither of them could ever unsay what had just been said. The wedding night was ruined, and their marriage had got off to the worst possible start. Geordie felt rejected and utterly humiliated.

"Have it your own way, Meggie," he said coldly. "You won't catch me begging you again."

* * *

After the honeymoon, Meggie moved into Hawthorn Terrace to start her married life with Geordie… and her mother-in-law. Aunt Alice jokingly referred to them as a *ménage à trois*, although Geordie was unamused. He had known from the outset that it was far from an ideal scenario, but the reality was even worse than he had imagined.

Hannah had grudgingly consented to give up her bedroom – the only one which could accommodate a double bed. However, she complained constantly about being relegated to Geordie's old room, which was north-facing and cramped. As for Meggie, she tiptoed around the house like an unwanted guest overstaying her welcome. This was of course exactly how Hannah wanted her to feel.

Geordie had persuaded Meggie to give up her job at Bainbridge's. She was expecting a baby now, and in any case, Geordie believed a married woman should not work outside the home unless her husband was unemployed or otherwise unable to support her. The result was that Meggie became bored and irritable. Although she never said so in so many words, she clearly blamed Geordie for this new life of dull domesticity.

Household chores were a constant source of conflict. Hannah, now nearly seventy years old, was willing enough to let Meggie take over the dusting, polishing, scouring and scrubbing. Initially, Meggie tried her best to please her mother-in-law but soon came to resent the way her work was inspected and invariably found wanting.

"She treats me like a bloody maid," she would complain to Geordie when they were alone. "Except a maid gets paid and I don't."

But the main bone of contention between the two women was Geordie himself. Any task which – directly or indirectly – related to him personally remained Hannah's exclusive domain. Meggie was expected to wash the dishes after every meal, but his mother continued to buy the groceries and do all the cooking. She claimed that only she knew how Geordie liked his tea mashed, his eggs fried and his potatoes roasted.

"Why don't you show me, then?" protested Meggie not unreasonably. But Hannah obstinately refused to give an inch, despite Geordie's assurances that he was not a fussy eater.

It was the same when it came to the laundry. Meggie washed all their clothes and bed linen, but only Hannah was allowed to starch and iron Geordie's shirts.

"But I used to iron shirts for me Dad and our Robert and Angus," argued Meggie, brimming over with resentment.

"Aye, that's as may be," retorted Hannah. "But they were just pitmen. Our Geordie's a senior clerk at the colliery, and he has to look smart."

Time and again, Geordie pleaded with his mother to be more amenable, to accept Meggie as her daughter-in-law and make her feel at home.

Hannah shrugged her shoulders. "I never wanted a daughter-in-law in the first place. I warned you she'd be nowt but trouble, but you foisted her on me anyway. And here she is, hardly got her feet through the door and expecting already!" She narrowed her eyes and shot Geordie a sharp look. Hannah had her suspicions about Meggie's pregnancy, although she didn't dare question her son directly.

The endless domestic strife resulted in Geordie spending as little time as possible at Hawthorn Terrace. Every morning, he breathed a sigh of relief when he set off for work at the colliery, and every evening he dreaded coming home to face the two women, glaring at him as if he were the guilty party in some unspecified court case. Most evenings, they would sit in the small front room after supper, Hannah knitting and listening to the wireless, Geordie and Meggie reading on the couch. The tension in the air was palpable, each of them harbouring grudges against the other two.

Geordie made sure his weekends were fully occupied too. He tended his allotment or went out cycling into the countryside to spend an hour or two bird-watching. On the Saturday afternoons when Newcastle United was playing at home, he joined the crowd at Saint James's Park and cheered on Jackie Milburn. Everyone on Tyneside was proud of 'wor Jackie', the man who had helped turn the Magpies into one of the top football teams in the country.

On Friday and Saturday nights, Geordie escaped to the Miners Arms and downed a few pints – sometimes more than a few – with the other Burnside men. Hannah was usually in bed by the time he came home, but an irate Meggie would invariably be waiting up for him.

"It's all right for you!" she would yell at him. "You're out enjoying yourself as free as a bird, but what about me? I'm stuck here night after night with that miserable old bag upstairs!"

In one way, Geordie sympathised with Meggie. After all, she was only twenty and used to being out on the town, dancing and having fun. But in another way, he felt she was being unfair, for his behaviour was no different from any other married man in Burnside. Going out was fine for courting couples, but a husband was not expected to take his wife out. Married men went to work and brought the wages home, so they were naturally entitled to enjoy themselves at weekends. It was only right that married women should stay home and take care of the children. Geordie therefore saw nothing wrong with the way he occupied his free time, although he wished the baby was born. Once Meggie had a baby to look after, she would surely realise that her dancing days were over for good.

There was still no physical contact of any kind between them. Geordie was still smarting from his rebuff on their wedding night and had made no further overtures. Meggie would allow herself to be pecked on the cheek when Geordie came home from work, although he suspected that even this minimal display of affection was more for Hannah's benefit than his own. When they went upstairs to bed at night, they undressed with their backs turned to each other. Once under the covers and the lights out, they slept as far apart as possible, making sure their bodies never touched.

And yet in spite of everything, Geordie still loved Meggie. It was just that he felt he was looking at her through a pane of glass, unable to reach out to her or touch her. It was as if he could see her moving about on her side of the glass partition, but she never looked in his direction. She never heard him when he tapped on the pane and called out to her. Strange to think they lived under the same roof and even shared a bed, for in reality they were worlds apart.

* * *

Meggie was almost five months pregnant when she had a miscarriage. It started one morning shortly after Geordie left for work, when she began to experience severe pain and heavy bleeding. Recognising the symptoms immediately, Hannah rushed down to the schoolhouse so that she could use Aunt Alice's telephone. Geordie was duly alerted at the colliery, and an ambulance was summoned to transport Meggie to the local cottage hospital.

Frantic with anxiety, Geordie had to wait for six agonising hours before he was finally allowed to see Meggie. He followed a plump, middle-aged nurse through the busy ward and pulled aside the cubicle curtain to find her lying there, looking wan and weary. Her face was drained of colour and had an unhealthy waxen sheen.

"Meggie, pet," he said gently, bending to kiss her cheek. "I'm so sorry you've lost the baby."

Meggie's eyes instantly filled with tears. "It serves me right," she croaked. "It's God's way of punishing me for doing wrong. He didn't want me to keep the baby."

Geordie was appalled. "That's nonsense, Meggie," he said firmly, determined she must not fill her mind with such gruesome thoughts. "Nobody's punishing you for anything. Millions of women have miscarriages, and yours is no different from anyone else's."

She was too weak to argue. "You can have another baby, Meggie," he whispered, his heart leaping at the prospect. "I mean, we can have our own bairn. Yours and mine."

Meggie closed her eyes and grimaced. "You don't understand, Geordie. I wanted this baby." She started to sob, while Geordie helplessly stroked her hair.

The nurse promptly reappeared in the cubicle. "Your wife's been through a terrible ordeal, Mr Robertson," she said briskly. "She needs to rest now. You can come back again tomorrow when she's feeling better."

But when Meggie was eventually discharged from the cottage hospital, it seemed to Geordie she was not getting better at all. And as the weeks passed, he watched in dismay as she sank into a worrying state of lethargy. She picked at her food and – unusually for Meggie – took no interest in her own appearance. Day after day, she drifted aimlessly about the house in her dressing gown and slippers. She refused to go out or even sit in the back garden and enjoy the early summer sunshine. Most of her time was spent in bed, dozing or listlessly flicking through women's magazines.

Geordie found it difficult to empathise with her distress; he understood why she was grieving but not why it was taking her so long to recover. He was at his wit's end, afraid that Meggie might be having a serious nervous breakdown but not knowing how to console or help her.

To her credit, Hannah proved more sympathetic than Geordie had expected. She refrained from her usual caustic comments about Meggie and treated her with surprising patience and forbearance.

"Men don't know what a woman goes through at times like these," she told Geordie. "I had two miscarriages meself, you know. But even so, she should have come through the worst by now. I think she needs to see a doctor."

In spite of Meggie's feeble protests, Geordie made an appointment with old Doctor McGregor, who had been treating the families of Burnside for over thirty years. He even walked her to the surgery himself to make sure she kept the appointment. It was half an hour before she finally emerged from the consultation, her face as pale and expressionless as before.

Doctor McGregor beckoned to Geordie. "Can I have a quick word with you, Mr Robertson?" Meggie took a seat in the waiting room while Geordie followed the doctor into his office.

"Is it serious, Doctor?" he began, already dreading the answer.

The bluff old doctor was quick to allay his fears. "Not at all, Mr Robertson. I've given your wife a thorough examination, and I can assure you there's nothing physically wrong with her. However, you must understand she's been through a lot of grief this year – first losing her father and now the baby." Geordie nodded, mentally adding Harry Walker to the list.

"Time's a great healer in cases like this," continued Doctor McGregor. "Nevertheless, it's been over two months now since the miscarriage, and it's time Meggie got over her loss. I would advise you both to try for another baby as soon as possible."

If the doctor only knew that he and Meggie had still not consummated their marriage, thought Geordie wryly. "There's nothing I'd like better," he responded. "But Meggie won't hear of another baby."

"She will now," said Doctor McGregor, his voice kind but firm. "I've had a long chat with Meggie and convinced her it would be for the best. I think you'll find her quite amenable now."

* * *

Thanks to Doctor McGregor and his timely advice, Meggie finally consented – although never in so many words – to having sex with her husband. It certainly could not be called lovemaking by any stretch of the imagination in Geordie's view. On the other hand it was better than nothing at all.

Their physical encounters in bed – once or twice a week at most – were brief and unsatisfactory for them both. Reluctantly, Geordie had accepted Meggie's conditions. The room had to be in complete darkness, they had to be under the bed covers and she would not remove her nightdress. She allowed herself to be kissed and caressed, but her body remained tense and unresponsive throughout. Geordie knew she clenched her fists when he penetrated her.

Afterwards, Geordie would lie on his back, listening to Meggie's breathing change as she drifted into sleep. He stared into the darkness and wondered if this was how things would always be. Did Meggie hate him for trapping her into marriage? She had only accepted him to avoid the disgrace of being an unmarried mother, but the miscarriage had changed everything. There would be no baby after all, yet Meggie was still locked in marriage to a man she had never loved.

Geordie recalled his evening at the Theatre Royal with Edith Slater, and her sarcastic remarks about marriage and 'legal sex'. So this is what she had meant, he thought miserably. This furtive, joyless coupling was all he could expect from his wife.

He was astute enough to realise that nothing would change while Meggie and his mother lived under the same roof. When they were in bed together and Geordie tried to make love to her, Meggie was obsessed by the idea that Hannah – supposedly asleep in her room next to theirs – could hear everything.

"She's listening, I know she is," she would hiss whenever the mattress springs creaked. "I bet she's got her ear glued to the wall. Oh, I hate all this!"

And so their enforced cohabitation continued, with Meggie nagging him relentlessly about getting a council house of their own.

"Meggie, you bloody well know there's no chance of that!" he lashed out in frustration. "There's a nationwide housing crisis, for God's sake! Millions of people have their names on council waiting lists. People who were bombed out of their homes in the war, whole families living in overcrowded slums and desperate for a house… You don't know how lucky we are to be in Hawthorn Terrace, in a brand new council house. Shut up and stop whining, for God's sake!"

Meggie burst into noisy tears. "I can't stand it in any more, living with your Mam!" she moaned. "What kind of a life do you think I have here, day after day, with her breathing down me neck?"

Geordie couldn't bear to see her so unhappy. Awkwardly, he put his arms around her and let her cry on his shoulder. "I've already told you, pet, I'm saving up for a place of our own. It won't be long now, I promise."

* * *

One rainy morning in September, Geordie was surprised to receive a telephone call at the colliery from his eldest sister. He and Violet rarely saw each other, for Violet lived a few miles away in the colliery town of Ashington with her husband and five children. Geordie instantly guessed there must be some emergency; why else would she need to use a telephone?

Violet sounded agitated. "Sorry to bother you at work, Geordie, but we had a telegram this morning from Ernie's family in Carlisle. His mother's passed away, and we need to leave as soon as possible for the funeral." Geordie vaguely recalled that Violet's husband Ernie was a Cumbrian by birth.

"That's bad news, Vi," said Geordie sympathetically. "Is there anything I can do?"

"Not you exactly, but I need you to tell Mam what's happened. The thing is, we can't afford train tickets for all seven of us. I was hoping Mam could come over here and look after the bairns for a day or two while Ernie and me go to Carlisle for the funeral."

Geordie lost no time in relaying the news, and a few hours later Hannah was boarding a bus to Ashington, clutching a large leather bag containing a change of clothing, a book and her knitting. She was not looking forward to taking care of Violet's five boisterous children. "They wear me out, them bairns, screaming and fighting all the time," she complained as Geordie helped her onto the bus. "I only hope Vi and Ernie won't be gone too long."

There was a spring in Geordie's step as he walked back to Hawthorn Terrace. Perhaps this break from Hannah's constant presence would help cheer Meggie up and put their relationship on a better footing? He suddenly remembered it was Meggie's twenty-first birthday that Friday and decided to make it a truly special occasion.

He broached the subject that very evening over supper. "It's not every day you turn twenty-one, is it? I thought you might fancy going out for a slap-up dinner in Newcastle? Or maybe you'd rather have the McCullochs over here at our house for a bit of a party?"

Meggie, who had always been so fun-loving in the past, shook her head. "Thanks for offering, Geordie, but I'm just not in the mood. Why don't we have a nice supper at home instead? If you like, I'll make you some Lancashire hot pot, I know it's your favourite. And jam roly-poly for pudding, eh? With your Mam away, I'll have the kitchen to meself for once!"

Geordie could not have been more delighted. On Friday evening, he came home from work carrying a bottle of red wine in one hand and a box of Meggie's favourite Milk Tray chocolates in the other. Her face lit up with pleasure at the unexpected treat.

"And that's not all," Geordie announced with a grin. "I've bought you a little something for your twenty-first." With a proud flourish, he produced a small box tied with red ribbon from his coat pocket.

Meggie squealed with glee and snatched the box from his hands. She caught her breath as she took out a pair of pearl earrings set in gold. "Eeh Geordie, you shouldn't have!" she protested, although her excited expression told a different story. "They're absolutely gorgeous!" She hurried over to the mirror above the mantelpiece and tried them on, turning her head this way and that to admire the effect.

"What do you think, then?" she asked coyly, spinning around to face Geordie.

"You look smashing!" He was pleased to see that Meggie was wearing his favourite dress too. It was one she had made herself, in lilac poplin with three-quarter length sleeves, cinched at the waist with a belt of the same material. She had even made an effort to style her hair; it was swept back from her face and fell in glossy curls to her shoulders. It was months since he had seen her look so pretty.

Meggie's hot pot was delicious, although even if the food had been burnt to cinders Geordie would have eaten it gladly. What really gave him pleasure was to see Meggie so animated and relaxed. They spent the evening chatting and laughing in the same way they used to when they were courting. This was the kind of togetherness husbands and wives were supposed to have, Geordie thought. As they lounged at the table after the meal, enjoying the last of the wine and dipping into the Milk Tray, he felt they were just like any other young married couple.

Meggie started to clear the table, stacking the dirty plates and cutlery. Geordie followed her into the kitchen, where she was already running water into the sink to wash up. Her back was turned to him as he moved to put his arms around her waist and nuzzle the nape of her neck.

"Let's give the dishes a miss for once, eh?" he whispered in her ear.

Meggie turned to face him, giggling mischievously. "What would your Mam say if she found out? I'd never hear the end of it!"

"Well, she'll never know, will she?" Geordie pointed out drily. "Listen, Meggie, I've been meaning to tell you something. Don't worry, it's good news. There's nothing finalised yet, but…" He drew away and leaned against the stove.

Meggie turned off the tap and dried her hands hurriedly on the tea-towel. "Haway, Geordie, out with it!"

"Well," began Geordie, savouring the moment. "I don't know whether you've heard, but there are plans to build a new housing estate – private houses – to the south of Burnside. I've had a word with the developers, and the first houses should be finished in a year or so…"

For once, Meggie was speechless, hardly daring to believe where Geordie was leading the conversation. She stared at him expectantly, the tea-towel dangling forgotten in her hand.

"I've been to see the bank manager and all. I can use my savings for the deposit, and we'll have to take out a mortgage for the rest," he explained. But he could no longer contain his excitement. "Oh Meggie, we'll have our own home at last! Just imagine that!"

Meggie rushed towards him and threw her arms ecstatically around his neck. "I can't believe it! Oh Geordie, this is the happiest day of my life!"

He held her tightly in his arms. "Mine too. Don't get too carried away, though, there's nowt in writing yet. But I'm pretty sure it'll all go through as planned."

He bent to kiss her and for the first time felt her respond to the pressure of his lips. He was not sure whether it was thanks to the pearl earrings, the effect of the wine or the prospect of a new home, but he didn't care. He was overwhelmed by love and desire for Meggie. He wanted her tonight more than ever before.

* * *

He led her – still giggling and unsteady from the wine – up the stairs and into their bedroom. It was not quite dark yet, and Meggie moved to the window to draw the curtains.

"Not tonight, sweetheart. Just this once I want to see my lovely wife." He pushed her gently onto the bed and lay on top of her, feeling her warm softness pressing against him. For once, she did not resist or go tense.

Geordie began to unfasten the buttons of her dress, his fingers clumsy with excitement. Meggie lay passively, neither obstructing his efforts nor helping him. Undressing her was no easy task, he discovered as he struggled to remove the dress, only to be confronted with a petticoat, a sturdy bra, an unyielding corset and waist-high panties.

"Fighting Rommel was a piece of cake compared to getting your clothes off," he muttered under his breath. Meggie suddenly burst out laughing and wriggled from under him into a sitting position. Expertly, she unhooked her bra, revealing high firm breasts. She pulled off her corset and panties, then leaned forward to deftly undo her suspenders and roll down her nylon stockings. "There!" she exclaimed triumphantly, tossing the stockings to the floor and lying back on the bed again. She looked up at him expectantly, as if uncertain what to do next.

Geordie was transfixed at the sight of her. She was naked at last, and even more beautiful than he had imagined. Her skin was pearly-white and flawless, her limbs rounded and delicate; she seemed to ooze femininity from every pore. He undressed quickly and lay down again next to her, running his hands lingeringly over her body. He prayed that for once she would not tense up. He didn't think he could bear being rejected yet again.

303

Their lovemaking was cautious and laborious, far from the earth-shattering fusion Geordie had dreamed of. Meggie relaxed sufficiently to put her arms around him but otherwise hardly moved. Still, it was a step in the right direction, he reflected, a huge improvement on their previous times together. There was hope now that – given enough time and patience – she might actually learn to enjoy making love.

Afterwards, Meggie lay quietly in his arms, her head cushioned on his shoulder. The peaceful silence was broken only by the alarm clock ticking on the bedside table. The room was in darkness now, and they felt the night air chilling their naked bodies. He pulled the bed covers over them both, and they snuggled down again together. He felt himself drifting contentedly into sleep.

"Geordie?" Meggie's voice was low.

"Mmm?"

"I've been meaning to tell you something."

"What?"

There was a long pause before she spoke again. "I know I don't deserve you, Geordie. You've always been so kind and gentle with me, and I… well, I haven't always treated you right—" She broke off, her voice choking.

"Don't be daft, hinny," murmured Geordie in genuine embarrassment.

"No, it's true. And since we got married, I haven't been much of a wife to you either, have I?" He did not respond and she pressed on. "Well, from now on, I've made up me mind to do better. I'm going to try, really try, to change things between us. And I have to start by making the most of what I've got instead of moaning about what I haven't got."

He pulled her closer and smiled in the darkness. "We'll both try, Meggie. There's plenty of time, we have our whole lives ahead of us."

He suddenly remembered that Sunday afternoon the previous summer when he had poured his heart out to Aunt Alice. At the time, he had been in despair, sure that he had lost Meggie forever. His aunt had told him that one day Meggie would grow up and learn to appreciate him as… what were her exact words? Ah yes, a fine steady young man. He chuckled quietly to himself.

"What's so funny?" piped up Meggie.

"Nothing, pet," said Geordie softly. "Nothing at all."

Nick and Jenny (11)

"Sorry I couldn't make it to Newcastle this weekend, darling," said Nick into the phone. "I miss you." It was one week after the wedding, and he was standing by the window of his den in South Kensington, looking down on the Sunday morning joggers below. He watched the first drops of rain patter against the window pane and thought nostalgically of the balmy sunshine in Saint Emilion.

"I miss you too, but I understand – honestly," Jenny assured him. "I know you're up to your neck in post-production at the moment. You're putting in far too many hours at One Better."

"And when I'm not there, I'm away on location shooting the other episodes of *In Those Days*. Next week, it's Scottish crofters and we haven't even finished the script. We're working to a ridiculously tight schedule."

"Don't forget where your priorities lie," said Jenny teasingly. "The show on Tyneside collieries is the only one that interests me."

Nick laughed. "Don't worry, the editing is almost done. I've had to cut a lot of the raw footage, I'm afraid. The programme's only forty-five minutes long and choices had to be made. Still, Mark's ecstatic about what he's seen so far."

"Mark Goodwin, your boss?" breathed Jenny. "That's brilliant!"

"He was particularly ecstatic about you," Nick added drily. "I'll have to make sure you two never meet." He heard Jenny giggle and suddenly longed to be with her, to see those deep green eyes shining into his. "We can't go on this way, darling. I mean, not being together all the time."

He had blurted out the words without thinking, and there was a short silence over the phone. "I know," she said softly.

His train of thought was interrupted by Alan's voice calling from the foot of the stairs. "Nick, are you ready?"

"I'm coming, Dad," he called back and then reverted to the phone. "I'll have to go, Jenny. The Red Lion awaits." He had already told Jenny about this Sunday morning ritual with Alan. When they were not otherwise occupied, father and son liked nothing better than to walk to the local pub and enjoy a quiet pint together.

"Don't let me keep you," said Jenny, and he heard the fond amusement in her voice.

"Love you," he said.

"Love you too."

***

Comfortably ensconced at their usual corner table in the pub, Alan was flicking through the wedding photos on Nick's phone. He paused to look more closely at a full-length shot of Jenny, posing rather self-consciously at the entrance to Château d'Estissac.

"She's a smasher," he pronounced.

"Yes, she's quite a woman," Nick agreed. "Funny, I feel as if she's always been part of my life, even though we only met a few months ago."

"Serious, is it?" Alan tried to sound casual as he took a sip of beer.

"Very."

Alan nodded in understanding. "Life's strange, isn't it?" he remarked. "I mean, out of all the women in the world you could have fallen for, you've picked a Burnside lass – and an Armstrong at that."

Nick smiled. "You know, when I first met Jenny I had no idea we would become so close. In fact, we got off to a pretty bad start! It was researching the family history that brought us together. Initially I thought of it as a bit of lark – digging up my Robertson roots with a girl I rather fancied. But it gradually became something much more meaningful and we really started to connect. By helping me find the past, Jenny also helped me find myself."

Alan pondered his words, savouring this rare opportunity of a heart to heart with his son. "You've been on a voyage of discovery, one I should have made too and never did. But my point of departure was very different from yours, Nick. When I was young, I was hell-bent on putting Burnside and all it represented behind me. Going to university was part of my escape route. I couldn't wait to break free, throw off the past like a shabby old coat." He wondered whether Nick, whose existence had always been so cushioned and privileged, could relate to the teenage Burnside lad he had been. Even to himself, it seemed like a different world.

"But kids like me were lucky," he went on. "For the first time in history, it was actually trendy to be working class! I didn't have a posh accent or middle class manners… but all that was suddenly okay in the Sixties. Still, in hindsight I realise how selfish I was, how uncaring. The truth is, I was never around in Burnside when they needed me."

Nick looked puzzled. "Needed you?"

Long-forgotten memories flooded back into Alan's mind. "I'm thinking of your grandfather, Geordie Robertson. He was pushing sixty when Burnside colliery closed in 1975 and he was made redundant. I remember the headline in the Newcastle Journal saying the pit had been shut down with 'indecent haste', that it could have been made more productive and profitable. Dad felt as if he'd been kicked in the teeth – he was so angry and resentful—"

"But surely they all got redundancy pay, didn't they?" interjected Nick.

Alan smiled grimly. "That was exactly my thinking too at the time. I even told Dad it would be nice for him, at his age, to be unemployed. But being Dad, he searched high and low for another job and then felt so humiliated when he couldn't find one. He kept saying he was good for nothing but the scrap heap. To be honest, I was too self-centred at the time to listen to him properly. I didn't realise that he was heartbroken, you see, that a part of him had died with the mine. And that he was also grieving for the death of Burnside."

"It was the end of an era, I suppose," said Nick gravely. "The death of the pit village."

"It was. But at the time, I wrongly assumed that most people would welcome its passing with open arms. I envisioned a brave new world waiting for them out there – progress and prosperity for all. But of course as Dad was well aware, the closure of the colliery wasn't just an economic issue but a cultural – almost spiritual – one." Alan was in full flow now, the lecturer in him coming to the fore as he tried to explain the events of forty years ago.

"Your Jenny, of course, understands all this," he continued, draining his glass. "The miners didn't only lose their jobs, they lost their community. When the colliery closed, the thread of continuity suddenly snapped – the spirit of camaraderie among the men, the solidarity of village life. The slag heaps were cleared and grassed over, the young men left Burnside in droves to look for jobs elsewhere, strangers moved into the village… And within a decade, the last traces of a local culture – built up over generations – had all but disappeared."

"How did Grandma feel about it all?" asked Nick curiously.

"Oh, she tried to cheer Dad up, make him look on the bright side of things. But it was just as much a blow to her as to everyone else. I remember her saying she was only glad her father hadn't lived to see the pit close."

Nick thought of Meggie's father, Alex McCulloch, and his lifelong battle to defend the miners. "You know, Dad, until I met Jenny I didn't realise I had such an impressive great-grandfather on the McCulloch side of the family. I knew Grandma was proud of her father of course, but she never talked about his political involvement. Neither did you, for that matter."

"You're right, I've been very remiss." Alan felt a pang of guilt that he had passed down so little information to Nick about his Geordie roots. "Alex McCulloch was a grand man, as they say on Tyneside. He was a heroic figure in his way, a local legend for miles around. Thanks to Jenny, you know now what a huge impact he had on the lives of ordinary working people."

There was a discreet ping as a new message arrived on Alan's phone. He consulted it briefly and showed it to Nick. *Are you two coming back for lunch?* Nathalie wrote. The two men's eyes met, reluctant to relinquish this precious moment of intimacy.

Nick leaned over and retrieved a menu from the unoccupied table next to them. "Let's have lunch here," he said decisively. "Tell Maman we'll be home later."

* * *

When they finally emerged from the Red Lion, the drizzle had stopped and a watery sun shone down on the London streets. They were both in an excellent mood, having demolished a copious lunch and a bottle of Beaujolais Villages.

"Feel like stretching your legs?" said Nick. Alan nodded, and the two men set off at a leisurely pace in the direction of Kensington Gardens. The park, with its well-tended lawns and vibrant flowerbeds, was tranquil on this June afternoon. They strolled as far as Kensington Palace and sat on a stone bench near the Round Pond.

"I hope I'll get to read the family history, once the research is completed," Alan remarked. "It's quite an accomplishment, what you two have done. Coming full circle, as it were."

"Not quite full circle." Nick's tone of voice was playful. "We still have one more ancestor to research." He jabbed a finger at his father. "You!"

Alan burst out laughing. "Well, that shouldn't take long. You already know everything there is to know about me."

"Most of it," Nick rectified. "Your childhood in Burnside, your academic career, your professional achievements… and your family life since you married Maman, of course. But you were in your mid-thirties when you met her, and what happened before that is a bit of a mystery to me. For instance, I gather you lived with another woman before you and Maman got together?"

"Ah, you mean Liz," said Alan expansively, his mind drifting back almost half a century. "Yes, we were together for all of fifteen years, although as you've probably noticed, it's a taboo subject at home. Your mother goes ballistic if I so much as mention her name. For some reason, she's still jealous of Liz, even after all these years."

"Fifteen years with a woman is a long time," mused Nick. "You must have really loved Liz."

Alan did not respond immediately; love was not a word he and Liz had used much. "In a way," he conceded finally. "But it wasn't the kind of love I have for your mother. Liz and I saw ourselves as free spirits, too cool for bourgeois notions like love and fidelity."

Nick was taken aback; he found it difficult to imagine his father as anything other than a middle-aged pillar of respectability. Then he remembered the old photos of Alan in his twenties – the shoulder-length hair and unkempt beard, the flower-patterned shirts and bell-bottoms. His father certainly hadn't looked like a pillar of respectability back then.

"How did you meet Liz?" he asked curiously.

"We met at a party in our first year at university. Liz was a fine art student, and I fancied her immediately. She had a unique style that made her stand out from the other girls. Short, spiky hair, eyes made up all dark and sultry… and she wore weird, vintage dresses she picked up second-hand. She was a dead ringer for Julie Driscoll."

"Julie who?"

"You mean you've never heard of Julie Driscoll? I'm appalled by your ignorance." Alan grinned sardonically before picking up his train of thought again. "Back then, in the Sixties, we didn't realise how lucky we were, what a great time it was to be young. The best of times, I still think, at the risk of sounding like an old fuddy-duddy. British society was being turned on its head, swept away on a tidal wave of great music, great fashion, the Pill. They were golden years of freedom and opportunity where we truly believed the world could be changed for the better. We were spared much of the ugliness, the senseless violence and brutality in today's society. We had peace and prosperity, with the assurance of a well-paid job when we graduated. Liz and I were very much a product of those hedonistic times. We went to rock concerts, we smoked pot, we believed in free love…"

Nick found himself feeling almost envious of his father's generation. "Sex, drugs and rock 'n roll!" he proclaimed with a laugh.

"Absolutely!" Alan thought nostalgically of his carefree, unstructured existence in those days. "After we graduated, Liz and I stayed together, moved into a place in Notting Hill which I eventually bought. But there was still no commitment between us, no plan to make a life together. And naturally, we were both free to have sex elsewhere if the fancy took us. The arrangement suited us very well for many years. Don't get me wrong, though, we genuinely cared for each other. We just didn't want an exclusive relationship."

Nick was discovering a different side to his father today, a side Alan had never previously shed light on. His father's self-confessed swinging lifestyle unsettled him for some reason, threw him off balance. "And this went on for fifteen years?" he said incredulously. "Neither of you ever wanted to get married and have a family?"

"God, no! Liz and I prided ourselves on rejecting that whole bourgeois scene. Our place in Notting Hill was a kind of bohemian open house, always full of people drifting in and out. There were lots of wild parties, endless debates on the political and artistic issues of the day. Liz could never have coped with having a baby in any case. She'd always been into alcohol and drugs, but over the years things went from bad to worse. She could hardly function without them in the end."

"What did she do for a living?" Nick was intrigued in spite of himself.

"The fact is, she did bugger all," Alan responded bluntly. "Liz fancied herself as a great artist, you see. She tried her hand at everything – painting, sculpture, pottery, jewellery design – but never managed to sell any of it. Somebody had to bring the bacon home, though, and that somebody was always me. So I completed my PhD and then started lecturing, publishing my research and earning a decent income. Liz thought it was all drearily conventional, although she was glad enough to spend my money. That's what tore us apart in the end."

"She felt the relationship was no longer on an equal footing?"

Alan heaved a sigh. "Who knows what she thought? She was prone to wild mood swings because of the booze and dope. She used to rant and rave at me that I was turning straight, becoming totally uncool. I knew in my heart it was the end of the line between us, but I couldn't bring myself to just walk out after all those years and leave her to fend for herself. In the end, the problem was taken out of my hands."

Nick was horrified. "You don't mean she…?"

Alan shook his head. "Oh no, nothing so dramatic. One day, Liz simply announced that a great-aunt had passed away, conveniently leaving her a substantial amount of money and a huge property on the Devon coast. In the same breath, she informed me she was ditching me and moving to Devon with Simon."

"Who the hell was Simon?" said Nick sharply.

"Simon used to sleep on the couch at our place from time to time. He was an art student, barely out of short pants as far as I could see. I knew they were lovers of course, but I never dreamed she would dump me for some puny adolescent like Simon." Alan's voice was clipped and dismissive. "It dawned on me then that Liz had been using me for years. She'd never earned a penny of her own, but as soon as she came into some money, she dropped me like a ton of hot bricks. Once she moved out, though, indignation gave way to relief. I felt as if a great weight had been removed from my shoulders and I was free at last to live my own life."

"When did all this happen, then?"

Alan made a quick mental calculation. "I reckon it must have been 1981. Yes, that's it. I remember we were both thirty-three at the time."

Nick let out a low whistle. "Now I see why you married so late. Did you meet Maman soon afterwards?"

"Oh, a few months later. I was perfectly content in the interim period, though. It was wonderful to be able to focus on my work at last, instead of constantly dealing with Liz's manic ups and downs. And then, out of the blue, I was asked to give a series of lectures at Sciences-Po in Paris."

Nick was back on familiar ground now. He knew his mother had been a student at Sciences-Po, the elite French school which like the LSE was specialised in political science and economics. But he had never quite grasped how the two had managed to meet and fall in love. A beautiful Parisian student of twenty-one and a rather unprepossessing English lecturer twelve years her senior... it seemed an unlikely match.

"So tell me how you and Maman got together," he urged.

Alan was instantly on his guard. "No way," he said curtly. "Your mother and I have always protected our *jardin secret,* as she likes to call it. What's in the garden is nobody's business but ours."

Nick felt dashed, although he knew his father too well to try to change his mind. Still, he wished the discussion had not been terminated so abruptly. The mood of intimacy between them was dispelled, and Alan's face had taken on a wooden, withdrawn expression.

The expression was misleading however, for at that precise moment Alan's mind was in turmoil. His thoughts were racing back to those momentous days in Paris over thirty years ago. His memories were still so sharp that he could almost breathe the crisp winter air on the Boulevard Saint Germain. He had a sudden vision of himself – younger and slimmer, dressed in a shabby brown corduroy suit – striding purposefully to the lectern in the dusty amphitheatre of Sciences-Po. As he briefly surveyed the assembled students before starting his lecture, one of them caught his eye. A solemn girl with long dark hair and a vivid orange scarf draped at the neck...

IX
Alan Robertson, January 1982

Standing at the lectern preparing to begin his lecture, he noticed her at once. She was sitting on her own in the third row of the amphitheatre, notepad and pen at the ready. Initially his eye was caught by the orange silk scarf tied at her neck, but then he noticed the perfect oval of her face and the rather solemn expression in her huge dark eyes. The girl stood out from the sea of chattering students in their jeans and thick sweaters. She sat quietly, gazing up at him expectantly. Their eyes met briefly, impersonally, and then the girl ran a slender hand through her long dark hair. It was a graceful, exquisitely feminine gesture.

Well, it wasn't the first time he had been distracted by an attractive female student, Alan thought sardonically. And he had made it a golden rule since he began his academic career to avoid all personal – and especially sexual – involvement with them. Some of his male colleagues at LSE, he knew for a fact, were not above the odd dalliance with a pretty student, but in Alan's view the risks of such affairs outweighed the benefits. It was not that he was averse to casual sex – a long line of liberated young women had found their way into his bed over the years – but his own students were strictly off limits. And he was not about to make an exception to the rule in Paris.

When Alan had been asked to give a series of six lectures – in English, mercifully – at the prestigious Ecole de Sciences Politiques in Paris, he had felt intensely gratified. It proved that his reputation as an expert on European affairs was spreading and that his research was now recognised well beyond the confines of the LSE. He had entitled the course *What Future for Europe?* and had broken it down into six modules, each of them approaching the topic from a different angle – institutional, political, economic, financial, military and cultural. Today he was about to cover the first module.

Sciences-Po, as it was more commonly known in France, was located just off the Boulevard Saint Germain on the fashionable, arty Left Bank. Arriving in Paris the night before, Alan had been delighted to discover that the modest hotel room provided by Sciences-Po for the duration of the course was within walking distance of the school and a good number of the city's many attractions. He was determined to make the most of his stay in Paris and brush up his somewhat rusty A-Level French.

Alan's carefree mood continued as time passed and he settled into his new routine. His academic obligations at Sciences-Po were not overly demanding, leaving him ample free time to explore the city. He spent many happy hours visiting the Musée d'Orsay or simply peering through the windows of the art galleries and antique shops on the Rue des Saints Pères. He enjoyed wandering idly through the Jardin du Luxembourg, the trees bare and leafless in the winter sunshine. Most of all, he liked to stroll along the crowded city streets, breathing in the cold frosty air; he would stop at the first café that took his fancy and order hot chocolate or mulled wine. To Alan, it felt more like a holiday than a professional assignment.

* * *

The thought-provoking lectures on Europe gave rise to heated debate among the politics students who regularly filled the amphitheatre. Alan, who had always revelled in argument and contradiction, was delighted. Some of the students would even come to speak to him personally after the lectures, and he enjoyed the cut and thrust of their questions. But the dark-haired girl with the vivid orange scarf never approached him, although Alan was always acutely aware of her presence. When the lectures were over, she would simply gather up her belongings and leave without a backward glance. Alan would watch her retreating silhouette – tall and slender – with a mixture of fascination and disappointment. He wondered why such a beautiful girl was always alone.

He gave his final lecture one Friday afternoon, having booked a return flight to London for the following day. That evening, he had dinner with François, a young French lecturer and single like himself, at the famous Brasserie Lipp. The restaurant was packed to the rafters with the usual crowd of journalists, politicians and the odd showbiz personality. Over the *blanquette de veau* and an excellent bottle of Brouilly the two academics exchanged views – almost shouting to make themselves heard through the din – about the French government and the likelihood of Mitterrand being forced to backtrack on his most radical left-wing policies.

"Pity I won't be here to see what happens," said Alan. "Tomorrow at this time, I'll be back in London with Margaret Thatcher." The waiter arrived with two coffees and the bill. "I'll be sorry to leave Paris, I must say, but I'm planning to make the most of my last day here. I was thinking of visiting the Musée Rodin, actually. Is it far from here, do you know?"

"No, you can get there on foot." François proceeded to sketch a rough itinerary on a scrap of paper. "I'd have come with you, but I've got a lot on this weekend." Alan voiced regret but was secretly relieved; he had been looking forward to admiring the works of the great sculptor on his own.

* * *

After a leisurely breakfast at the hotel, Alan set off for the museum, armed with the scribbled street map he had pocketed the night before. Walking briskly to fight off the bitter cold, it took him only a few minutes to reach the Rue de Varenne, where the Musée Rodin was situated. The weather was dull and leaden, with an icy wind whipping through the city streets, so he was not surprised to find the museum gardens almost deserted. He wandered for an hour among the monumental sculptures exhibited in the frosty grounds. His hands and feet were numb with cold, and he wished he had not left his gloves behind at the hotel.

Eventually, he went inside, feeling his body gradually relax in the sudden warmth. The various rooms of the museum overflowed with Rodin's masterpieces, so familiar to him from photos and books and yet even more impressive in reality. He stood transfixed in front of *Le Baiser*, and then began to circle slowly around the sculpture so as to view the world's most celebrated kiss from different angles.

"It's very beautiful, isn't it?" said a low voice from behind him. He swung round, starting in surprise as he came face to face with the dark-haired girl from the amphitheatre.

"Yes, it's one of my favourites," he responded automatically. It seemed pointless to pretend he didn't recognise her. "Aren't you one of the students at Sciences-Po?" he continued, pointing to the brightly patterned silk scarf at her neck. "I recognise the orange scarf," he added jokingly.

"It's Hermès," she rectified, clearly objecting to her beautiful scarf being referred to as orange.

Alan burst out laughing. The girl gave him a blank look, obviously wondering what he found so amusing. "But you're right, I'm at Sciences-Po," she went on. "My name is Nathalie Lambert. And yours is Monsieur Robertson."

"Alan, please." He smiled at her and they shook hands formally, as if meeting for the first time at a smart dinner party. "Have you seen *Le Baiser* before?" he asked conversationally.

"Oh yes, I come to the museum quite regularly." Their eyes reverted to the fluid, powerful lines of the white marble sculpture, portraying a naked man and woman entwined in a sensual embrace. "I find it very moving, both erotic and romantic. I mean, their bodies are so natural and relaxed. You can tell they've made love together many times." She gazed at Alan intently, totally unembarrassed. "*Vous ne trouvez pas?"(1)*

Alan nodded, and their eyes locked together. He wished he were less English, less inhibited; she must be expecting a response in the same vein. Instead, he made a few pedantic comments about Rodin's inspiration for the sculpture – the adulterous lovers from Dante's Divine Comedy.

The ice was broken nevertheless. They walked on together side by side, exchanging the occasional remark about the various exhibits. It was just a chance encounter between strangers, thought Alan, and yet anyone watching them might imagine they had come to the museum together. Now that he could see the girl at close quarters, he was almost overcome by her physical presence... her slender figure and graceful gestures, her dark eyes and aristocratic features. He made a conscious effort not to look at her too often, in case she guessed his thoughts.

Alan's mind was whirling as they emerged from the museum. In spite of the alarm bells ringing loudly in his head, he was loath to part from Nathalie. Would she take it the wrong way if he invited her to lunch? In the end, it was she who took charge of the situation.

"*Oh là là,* it's so cold!" she exclaimed, buttoning up her long, military-style overcoat. "I know a nice café near here where we can warm up." He smiled his agreement, once again struck by her poise and confidence.

Sitting at a wobbly round table in the café, they ordered bowls of steaming *soupe à l'oignon* and took off their coats. "So what did you think of my lectures?" he asked, genuinely curious.

She paused before replying, running long fingers through her dark hair in that familiar gesture Alan found so alluring. "Oh, I enjoyed the course immensely, although I'm not sure your ideas are realistic. Your premise is that in twenty or thirty years the Soviet Union will have collapsed, Germany will be reunited and a new federal Europe will extend from the Atlantic to the Urals. You envisage a Europe with its own constitution, its own currency, its own *force de frappe*... But it's a purely speculative premise, and therefore necessarily subjective." She sat back in her chair and scrutinised him, waiting for his response.

"Subjective?" Alan protested. "Speculative? The indicators underpinning my research are anything but speculative!" As he began to expound his views in more detail, he was nevertheless impressed by this bright, articulate girl and the attentive way she listened to him. Nathalie's English was near perfect, he realised, but her intonation and phrasing remained very French. He found the combination quite irresistible.

"How come you speak such good English?" he asked in an attempt to steer the conversation to more personal topics.

"*Oh là là!*" she sighed. "My mother had an old school friend who married an Englishman and went to live over there. Manchester, can you imagine?" She rolled her eyes dramatically, her tone of voice implying a fate worse than death. "Every summer, my parents would send me to Manchester to improve my English... I hated every minute! Their horrid suburban home, their disgusting children, their boring friends, the atrocious weather..."

"You're forgetting the ghastly food," he said drily and was gratified to see her smile at last.

"Okay, okay, maybe I'm exaggerating just a little," she conceded. "But if I ever have to go back to England, I won't set a foot outside of London. *Jamais, jamais!*"

Alan wondered briefly what Nathalie would make of a Tyneside colliery village like Burnside. It didn't bear thinking about. "I take it you're a true *Parisienne*, then?" he teased her.

She gave him a long, appraising look. "Why don't you come to my place and see for yourself?" she said abruptly. "I mean, if you don't have anything better to do this afternoon. This café is so uncomfortable, don't you think? *Chez moi* we can talk and have a drink and..." Her voice trailed off uncertainly.

Whatever Nathalie intended by this invitation, Alan knew immediately he wanted to find out. "I'd love to," he said emphatically.

(1) Don't you think so?

* * *

His mind was churning as they travelled on the *métro* to Nathalie's flat. What the hell was he doing on his last day in Paris with this beautiful young girl? She couldn't be much more than twenty, he reckoned, and he was breaking every rule in the book by consorting with one of his students. Even so, he was caught up in the thrill of the unknown. And after all, what did he have to lose? They would have a drink and chat, and then he would get back to his normal life in London. In a few days, he would have forgotten about the whole episode. Knowing he would never see Nathalie again both unnerved and excited him.

Nathalie's *chez moi* turned out to be in Neuilly, an exclusive residential district on the fringes of Paris and home to the city's well-heeled elite. The low-rise building was stylishly modern and overlooked the manicured woods and lakes of the Bois de Boulogne. When Nathalie unlocked the door to the top-floor flat, Alan discovered a vast lounge with French windows running along its entire length. The décor was contemporary – a designer's dream of shiny parquet floors, expensive cream leather sofas and glass tables. He took in the jungle of huge potted plants and the splashy abstract paintings on the walls. Thinking of his untidy terraced house in Notting Hill, Alan was struck by the pristine neatness of Nathalie's home. The only personal touches in the flat were the glossy magazines on the coffee table and a few formal photographs in silver frames on the grand piano.

Nathalie took Alan's coat and removed her own, revealing a black polo neck sweater and jeans. She threw both coats on the cream leather sofa and turned to him. "I could show you the rooftop terrace," she remarked casually. "But I think it's too cold to go out there today."

"Surely, you don't live here on your own?" he asked in amazement. He had been expecting student digs, not this elegant penthouse flat.

For the first time, Nathalie looked discomfited. "No, it belongs to my parents. I suppose you're thinking someone my age should have moved out by now, but it's comfortable and convenient and…" She gestured airily at the empty lounge. "We all lead very separate lives. This weekend, my parents are at our second home in Deauville. Riding and golf and dinner parties with friends… you know the scene."

Alan didn't know the scene. This affluent, bourgeois lifestyle was worlds away from his own somewhat bohemian existence in London. He picked up one of the photographs on the piano, instantly recognising a slightly younger Nathalie posing with her parents and an older brother. Her father, tall and distinguished, had the same dark hair and eyes as Nathalie. He also had the self-satisfied air of a wealthy, successful man who was rarely crossed. He stood behind his wife, who was seated like a queen on her throne, ankles neatly crossed and wearing what looked like a Chanel suit and pearls.

Nathalie glanced at the photo disparagingly. *"Et voilà ma petite famille!"(1)* she said sarcastically. "The perfect family, don't you think?" She pointed to her father. "This is Papa. He's an investment banker, a total workaholic… and practically never at home. Julien, my brother, is following in his footsteps – he lives in Hong Kong and doesn't keep in touch. As for Maman…" She took the photo from Alan's hands and put it back in place on the piano.

"Well?" Alan pressed her.

Nathalie looked again at the elegant woman in the photo with her hard, contrived smile. "Oh, there's not much to say about Maman," she said dismissively. "Except that she's spoilt and pampered and completely divorced from reality. She leads a busy life, though. Beauty salons, shopping, gossipy lunches with friends… you get the picture?"

"The picture I'm getting is that you're not overly fond of your mother."

Nathalie caught his look of faint amusement and gave a short laugh. "I don't have strong feelings for her either way. All I know is that she's the antithesis of the woman I want to be. She's frittered away her life, totally dependent on Papa for money and status, forced to turn a blind eye to his mistresses because she can't cope on her own…" She flashed Alan a defiant look. "I won't let that happen to me. I won't let a man use his power to oppress and manipulate me."

He was slightly irritated by the note of strident feminism in her voice, although paradoxically he found her even more desirable in this mood of righteous indignation. His eyes flicked over her long slim legs in the tight jeans, the shape of her small breasts under the black polo-neck sweater. "Not all men are tyrannical monsters," he pointed out mildly.

She stared at him appraisingly, as if debating whether to pursue the discussion. "Perhaps not all," she conceded. "Let's go through to the kitchen."

Alan followed her into a spacious, ultra-modern kitchen, gleaming with stainless steel and the very latest in electrical gadgets. He sat on a high stool at the counter while Nathalie took a bottle of Krug out of the fridge and found two tall crystal champagne glasses.

"It's one of the advantages of living at home," she remarked cheerfully. "You never run out of champagne." She perched on a stool next to him and watched as he opened the bottle and filled their glasses. "*Santé,*" she said, raising hers.

"Cheers," said Alan. They sipped the champagne, their eyes meeting over the rim of the glasses. He wondered again why she had invited him here. Students sometimes developed crushes on their professors, he knew, but she wasn't that kind of girl. And he found it hard to believe that Nathalie would find him even remotely attractive.

She gave him a forthright look. "Are you married, Alan?"

This girl certainly doesn't beat about the bush, he thought. "I'm not, as it happens. Are you?" His tone was facetious.

"Of course not," snapped Nathalie. "I'm only twenty-one, whereas you must be at least—"

"Pushing thirty-four."

"Precisely." Nathalie continued to scrutinise him. "And are you in a long term relationship?"

"I was."

"What was her name?"

"Liz."

"How long were you together?"

"Fifteen years. We split up a few months ago."

Nathalie gasped in horror. "*Oh là là,* fifteen years! Like being in prison, *non?*"

"Actually, it wasn't." Alan decided to put an end to this one-way interrogation. "Look, Nathalie, this is really none of your business. We've only just met after all."

Nathalie looked crestfallen. "You're right. You must think me very… what's the right word? Pushy, I suppose. It's just that I don't know the etiquette, I'm not sure what happens now."

She was disarmingly unsophisticated, Alan realised, behind the self-confident façade. He noticed that her hands were trembling slightly. "The etiquette for what?"

Nathalie swallowed hard and took a gulp of champagne. "I mean, what's the next step? Do we keep talking and finish the champagne and then go to bed? Or would you rather go to bed right now?"

316

Alan could hardly believe his ears. He was no novice with women and had sensed the sexual tension between them since they arrived at the flat. But he had always preferred to let such situations evolve naturally. This blatant propositioning was both unnecessary and off-putting.

"I don't recollect having said I wanted to go to bed with you at all," he teased her. "Do you think I'm some kind of sex fiend? That I jump on any pretty girl who plies me with champagne?"

Nathalie looked unamused. "I suppose not. But I did think you might jump on me."

Alan burst out laughing. "Look, Nathalie, I'm sure jumping on you would be a very pleasurable experience, but really—"

"Oh, please don't say no," Nathalie interrupted. "Look, I'm obviously doing this all wrong, but the thing is I'd really like to go to bed with you. You look like the right sort of man." She got down from the bar stool and faced him squarely. "I mean it."

To Alan's astonishment, she bent down to remove her boots and woollen socks. Barefoot now, she pulled her black sweater over her head, revealing tiny, pointed breasts and no bra. He watched mesmerised as she unzipped her jeans and eased them over her narrow hips and long legs. Stepping out of the jeans, she took off her panties and cast them nonchalantly on the kitchen floor. She had smooth, pale gold skin and was the most beautiful creature Alan had ever seen.

She shook her long dark hair over her shoulders and raised huge brown eyes to his. "Are you sure you won't change your mind?"

Alan was no longer sure of anything. What man in his right mind would turn down this gorgeous French girl clearly intent on getting laid? What did he know about Nathalie Lambert anyway? Maybe she made a habit of picking up strange Englishmen and luring them to her flat. He felt a surge of reckless desire, unable to take his eyes off her body, subjugated by her beauty. He was no longer in control, nor did he want to be.

He stepped down from the bar stool, enveloped her in his arms and attempted to kiss her. She pulled away from him and grasped his hand, leading him out of the kitchen towards the rear of the flat. She pushed open the door to her bedroom, gloomy in the waning light of this January afternoon. Still holding his hand, she lay on the bed and pulled him down with her.

"*Viens, viens,*" she whispered in his ear.

(1) *And this is my little family!*

***

Afterwards, they lay together on the bed in a loose embrace. It had not exactly been an earth-moving experience, Alan reflected. After the strip-tease seduction scene in the kitchen, he had been expecting sexual fireworks but instead had found Nathalie tense and surprisingly passive. She had simply followed his lead, almost as if she were venturing into unknown territory. He felt disconcerted and puzzled by her behaviour.

He planted a kiss on her brow and pulled away from her to check the time. "Christ, Nathalie, I really have to go!" he exclaimed in sudden panic. "I'm flying

317

back to London tonight, and I need to get back to the hotel to pack my bags." He jumped off the bed and began to hurriedly pull on his clothes.

Nathalie switched on a bedside lamp and watched him dress, a forlorn expression on her face. "It wasn't very good for you, was it?"

Alan caught the vulnerability in her eyes. He leaned over and brushed her lips. "You're a very beautiful girl," he reassured her. "Look, I hate to just run off like this but…"

"*Tu files à l'anglaise,*" *(1)* quipped Nathalie, forcing a smile. As he made for the lounge in search of his coat, she padded after him, still naked. She stood at the entrance to the flat while he put it on.

Alan's mind was already on his return trip to London, calculating the time he would need to go back to the hotel and take a taxi to the airport. He deliberately did not offer to leave his phone number, and to his relief, she did not ask for it or give him hers. There was no point in pretending they would ever meet again.

"Bye, then," he began awkwardly. "Thanks for the—"

"Champagne," said Nathalie crisply. She stood before him, graceful and statuesque, as naturally as if she had been fully dressed. She opened the door and let him through. "*Au revoir, Alan,*" she murmured softly.

(1) You're taking French leave.

* * *

Alan gave a start when he heard the doorbell ring and automatically glanced at his watch. It was already after nine and he was not expecting any visitors this evening. He had been marking essays at his desk at home for the past two hours and was looking forward to an early night. In the three months since he had returned from Paris, early nights had become the norm. It was not a conscious decision on his part. He simply found himself increasingly bored with his old circle of friends and the predictability of their libertarian, progressive views. He was also, more surprisingly, tired of being sexually promiscuous. Since his strange encounter with Nathalie Lambert, he had gone out of his way to avoid casual sex. It was not that he missed Nathalie or had any thought of seeing her again; it was just that the episode seemed to mark some turning point in his life. Maybe he would end up a crusty old academic after all, he thought sardonically.

He removed his horn-rimmed glasses and headed for the front door. To his astonishment, the visitor turned out to be Liz, whom he had not seen or spoken to since she had walked out on him a year ago. It was a damp April evening, and she looked wan and bedraggled. She was holding a carrier bag from the off-license down the street.

"Hi, Alan." She thrust the bag at him, as if making a peace offering, and sidled past him without waiting to be invited in. "Long time no see. I had to come up to London for a few days and thought it would be nice to catch up."

He shut the door carefully to collect his thoughts and reluctantly followed her inside. After the initial surprise of seeing her again, he already wished she had not come. He had long since mentally filed their fifteen years together in a box marked The Past and had no desire to open that particular box again.

Liz surveyed the untidy front room and turned to him with a beaming smile. "Oh Alan, everything looks just the same! It feels so great to be back ho—" She stopped just short of pronouncing the word home. "To be back in London," she amended hastily.

"You might have called first instead of just turning up out of the blue," said Alan, not caring if he sounded ungracious. He gestured towards his small study and the essays stacked on the desk. "I've got a load of stuff to finish tonight."

"If I'd called, you'd have only put me off," Liz retorted. "But to make amends, I've brought you a bottle of your favourite wine." She pointed to the carrier bag he was still clutching. "Why don't you pour us both a glass instead of doing your grumpy old professor act?"

Alan relented and went to find two glasses in the kitchen. He returned to find Liz curled up on the sofa, lighting a cigarette. "Got any grass?" she asked casually.

"No." He handed her a glass of wine.

"Okay, okay, no sweat." She smiled beguilingly and patted a place next to her on the sofa. "Take a pew and tell me what you've been doing with yourself all this time."

He sat opposite her, deliberately avoiding the sofa, and began to talk about his university work. His personal life, such as it was, was no longer any business of hers. She listened distractedly, chain-smoking and splashing more wine into her glass at intervals.

"What about you?" he countered. "Where's your teenage lover-boy?"

She laughed awkwardly. "Simon, you mean? Oh, he ripped me off for every penny I had and then scarpered."

"So your aunt's inheritance is all spent?" Alan sensed he was about to find out the real reason for this unexpected social call.

"Practically all." She gave a self-deprecating grimace. "You know me, baby, I've never been much good with money. The bottom line is I'm pretty broke right now." She drained her glass and looked at him in a way he saw was meant to be flirtatious. "I've still got that huge house in Devon, though. In fact I've come to offer you a deal."

"A deal?" he spluttered. "Look, Liz, whatever deal you have in mind, there's no way I—"

"Just hear me out, will you?" There was an unmistakeable hint of desperation in her voice. "I want to give you the house in Devon, sign over the property to you. You'd know how to manage it better than I ever could. We could always rent it out or keep it as a holiday home or—"

"We?" He had already guessed what was coming next.

"Well, I was hoping you'd let me move back in here with you." She stared at him imploringly, her eyes glistening with tears. "Oh Alan, I'm no good without you. I've missed you and I've missed our life together. I know you were pissed off when I dumped you. And who can blame you? It was all my fault for screwing everything up. I made a mistake, a really stupid one. But I've had time to think since then, and I want us to get back together like we used to be. It'll be better this time, I promise you. I'm going to start rehab, kick the booze and dope..." She was pleading with him now, desperate to crack his armour.

"Rehab? I'm glad to hear it," he said soberly, although he doubted she really meant it. He scrutinised her for the first time since she had arrived, taking in her thin, lined face and sinewy neck and arms. She looked a wreck, he thought, far older than thirty-three. "But it's all immaterial to me now. I've moved on, Liz, and it's high time you did too."

To his horror, she actually threw herself at his feet, her head resting on his knees and her arms clutching his shins. "Surely those fifteen years must mean something to you, baby?" she sobbed. "We had such a cool thing together, everybody said so. Remember all the good times, the laughs, the parties…"

He extricated himself from her embrace and got shakily to his feet. Liz had always known how to twist him around her little finger, he recalled; she would try every trick in the book to get her own way. He was determined not to be taken in this time. "Don't make a spectacle of yourself, Liz. There's no point, and you'll hate me later for doing it. Look, I'm going to have to spell it out to you. There's no way you're moving back into this house, or into my life either."

"Why not?" she wailed, still slumped on the floor. "There's nobody else living here, is there? And I know you're not seeing anybody special – I asked around before I came tonight."

"For God's sake, Liz, I'm perfectly happy living on my own." His embarrassment was fast turning into irritation. How could he get her to calm down and – more crucially – leave? "Come on, Liz," he said placatingly. "Pull yourself together and I'll get you a drink."

To his relief, she dabbed her eyes and heaved herself upright. Collapsing onto the sofa once more, she flashed him a resentful look. "You really are so uncool these days, Alan," she said sulkily. "Another couple of years and you'll be smoking a pipe and warming your slippers by the fire."

"A tempting prospect," he said drily. At least she wasn't making a scene any more, he thought. Perhaps if she had a last drink and cheered up a bit, they could part on good terms?

* * *

The doorbell rang for the second time that evening. Liz shot him a sharp glance. "Expecting someone?" she enquired acidly.

Alan groaned inwardly at the idea of a second unwanted visitor at this late hour. He heard a car door slam outside and moving towards the window, glimpsed the lights of a taxi pulling away from the kerb.

"Hadn't you better see who it is?" Liz prompted, getting to her feet and searching for her pack of cigarettes among the sofa cushions.

Alan heaved a sigh and went to open the front door. A girl stood there in the dark, wearing a beige trench coat and an orange silk scarf. She was carrying a very large brown leather suitcase. His heart lurched as he recognised Nathalie Lambert.

"Christ, what are you doing here?" he gasped in disbelief. She was the very last person he had expected to find on his doorstep, and she had arrived at the very worst time.

"*Bonsoir,*" she said pleasantly, ignoring his shocked expression. "Aren't you going to invite me in?"

Alan opened the door wider and picked up the suitcase, dumping it unceremoniously in the hallway. Nathalie took off her trench coat and hung it up as naturally as if she were a frequent visitor. She glanced at her reflection in the cracked hall mirror and ran her fingers through her dark hair in that now familiar gesture. She looked as effortlessly beautiful as she had in Paris.

"You're not very talkative this evening," she remarked with a smile. He tried to smile back, still in a state of shock and already dreading the inevitable confrontation ahead. He gestured awkwardly towards the front room.

Nathalie stopped in her tracks at the sight of Liz, who was now puffing on a cigarette and looking mutinous. There was a deafening silence as Alan racked his brains for something to say. He felt as if he were caught up in a French farce, cast in the role of distraught husband trying to avoid his wife and mistress coming face to face.

He cleared his throat. "Errr... Nathalie, this is Liz. Liz, this is Nathalie," he managed to say. He wished the earth would swallow him up and put an end to this nightmare. The two women nodded briefly and eyed each other. Nathalie took in Liz's sallow skin and lank hair, her cheesecloth blouse and shapeless gypsy skirt. Liz registered Nathalie's flawless face, her perfect figure, her crisp white shirt and Hermès scarf.

"Anyone like a glass of wine?" he offered desperately. The level of tension in the room was almost unbearable.

It was the first time in living memory that Liz turned down a drink. She shook her head and began to collect her belongings from the sofa. "No, I think it's time I split." She gave Alan a knowing look as she pulled on her frayed denim jacket. "So that's what you were up to in Paris," she mocked.

He gritted his teeth but did not respond. Heading for the front door, Liz couldn't resist a parting shot. "When I think how you used to take the piss about me and Simon," she sneered. "But who's the baby-snatcher now, eh? Better watch out, dearie, you're turning into a dirty old man!" She gave a humourless shriek of laughter and slammed the front door behind her as she left.

Alan turned to Nathalie, shrugging his shoulders helplessly and hoping he did not look as ridiculous as he felt. "Don't pay any attention to Liz, she was feeling a bit upset tonight," he mumbled.

Nathalie, hands on hips and glaring at him ferociously, was clearly uninterested in Liz's feelings. "Is that her?" she demanded. "Is that the woman you told me about in Paris? Alan, how could you live for fifteen years with someone like that? And her clothes, *mon Dieu...* she dresses like she's in some hippy time warp! *Qu'est-ce qu'elle est moche!"(1)*

"That's enough!" roared Alan. "Who the hell do you think you are anyway, coming here and passing judgement on people you don't even know? It's none of your bloody business!"

Nathalie met this onslaught unflinchingly, body rigid and fists clenched. Then he saw her shoulders slump and her expression soften. "You're right," she said in a small voice. "It's just that... I expected her to be beautiful. I imagined your standards would be... higher."

"Well, they aren't," Alan snapped. In a tiny corner of his mind, he registered the astounding fact that he had apparently occupied Nathalie's thoughts over the past three months. It was flattering to think that she looked up to him in some way. "You'd better sit down," he muttered. "And then you can explain exactly what you're doing in Notting Hill at this time of night."

Nathalie sat primly on the sofa just vacated by Liz. "I suppose I could have let you know I was coming," she conceded. "But I was afraid you wouldn't want to see me."

It was almost word for word what Liz had said earlier that evening, he thought in bemusement. What on earth was going on tonight? Two desperate females descending on him out of the blue, each with a private agenda that somehow involved him... Well, he would make it clear to them both that he wanted to keep his life uncomplicated right now. He had neither the time nor energy to take on either of these two women and their problems.

"Well, you're here now," he said grudgingly. "Can I get you a coffee or anything?"

Nathalie shook her head. "Let me get straight to the point," she began in her usual forthright manner. "The thing is, I told Papa I planned to move to London for the summer term and sign up for a course at LSE. He wasn't too keen at first, because he didn't want me to miss my end-of-year exams at Sciences-Po. But I managed to persuade him, and the good news is he's agreed to maintain my allowance until the end of June, plus a little extra for living expenses in London."

Alan looked at her dubiously. "Well, LSE does have various exchange programmes with Sciences-Po, but as far as I'm aware, they're always for a full university year. I've never heard of students being admitted at such short notice for just one term."

Nathalie cleared her throat. "You're not listening, Alan. I didn't say I *had* signed on at LSE for the summer term. I said I told Papa I had."

Alan groaned inwardly, not for the first time that evening. "So the bottom line is you lied to your father," he pointed out sternly. "Presumably, you have some other reason for moving to London that might not meet with his approval?"

"Evidemment," she retorted. "I'm considering starting up my own company here – skin care or cosmetics probably. I'm already working on a business plan, but I need to do some market research first."

Alan was not fooled. "Why does it have to be London? Why don't you start up a company in Paris?"

He listened distractedly as Nathalie launched into an unconvincing explanation about the relative merits of London and Paris. He strongly suspected there was an ulterior motive for her move and fervently hoped that, whatever it was, it didn't involve him. Admittedly, Nathalie was a beautiful girl but – as Liz had reminded him in no uncertain terms – she was far too young for him. Even putting her age aside, their tastes and lifestyle were worlds apart. It would be madness to embark on any kind of relationship with her.

"It all sounds very pie in the sky to me but frankly, it's none of my business what you do," he said dismissively. "You need to think about practicalities. Where are you going to live for a start?" Even as he uttered the words, he had a sinking feeling that he knew what the response would be.

"Well, of course I'm going to look for a place of my own," she said defiantly. "But I was wondering, obviously just for a couple of days or so, if you..." She let the question hang in the air, her huge dark eyes locking into his.

"So that's it!" he barked in exasperation. "You actually believe you can move in here with me! What the hell makes you think I'm responsible for you in any way? We barely know each other, for God's sake! Just because we had sex once—

322

" He stopped short as a horrifying thought occurred to him. "You're not pregnant, are you?"

Nathalie sprang to her feet, her eyes flashing with indignation. "*Mais non!* Of course I'm not pregnant!" she yelled at him. "How dare you speak to me this way? I haven't come here to beg and grovel, you know. I'm not some penniless hippy! I told you, I have an allowance – I can stay in a hotel if necessary. And you're under no obligation towards me at all." She was pacing up and down the room like a caged lion. "It's just that... you're the only person I know in London, and I thought you might actually want to help me. I didn't expect you to be so rude and bad-tempered. *Mon Dieu, quel sale type! (2)* Well, I won't bother you any more – I'm leaving!"

Alan strode across the room and grabbed her by the arm as she made for the front door. "All right, all right, calm down! If it's just for a couple of nights..." He was suddenly ashamed of his behaviour.

Nathalie was a young girl, alone and vulnerable in a big city. How could he simply throw her out into the night?

Still holding her arm, he led her to the tiny study where he had been working. Books and essay papers were still strewn on the desk, exactly as he had left them at the start of this momentous evening. "You can sleep here if you like." He indicated a dilapidated sofa in the corner. "This pulls out into a divan bed. I'll get you some sheets and a blanket."

Nathalie's eyes darted around the room disbelievingly. "But Alan," she burst out in bewilderment. "Where can I hang my clothes? There's nowhere to hang my clothes."

"That's right, there isn't," he said flatly, trying to repress a smile. "You're not in your penthouse flat now, you know. Look, do you want to stay here or not?"

"Oh yes, I do! Thank you, Alan. I promise I won't get in your way."

"It's a deal." She was standing tantalisingly close to him, so close that he could smell her perfume. His fingers tingled as he remembered how soft and smooth her skin had felt in Paris. Stick to your guns, he told himself. He swallowed hard and moved away from her. "It's just for tonight, Nathalie. No strings, no hassle..."

"No sex, you mean," she said. "It's a deal."

(1)   *She's so ugly!*
(2)   *My God, you're so gross!*

* * *

There was no sign of Nathalie next morning, and the door to the study was firmly shut. Alan showered, dressed and left a spare key on the kitchen table before leaving for LSE. All that day – in spite of a busy schedule of meetings, seminars and tutorials – his thoughts kept straying to the intriguing French girl in his home. In one-way he felt uneasy about her being there at all, as if he had fallen unwittingly into some kind of trap last night. On the other hand, the idea of her making breakfast in his kitchen, brushing her teeth in his bathroom, was strangely exhilarating. And what harm could there be after all in letting the poor girl stay over for a couple of days until she found somewhere to live? He decided it was the least he could do.

323

Alan returned to Notting Hill that evening with a sense of anticipation. He turned the key in the lock and hung up his coat in the hall as usual. He heard music playing from inside the house and pushed open the door to the living room.

He could hardly believe the transformation. His eyes popped in amazement as he surveyed his front room, now so spick and span as to be almost unrecognisable. The carpet had been hoovered to within an inch of its life, the furniture dusted, the cushions plumped and every book and magazine neatly stacked. Dirty coffee mugs and wine glasses accumulated over several days had been whisked away. He also noted that the contents of Nathalie's large suitcase were everywhere. Items of clothing were suspended on door handles, and an array of blouses and sweaters were draped over the back of the sofa.

"Hey, Nathalie," he called out but there was no reply. Still feeling stunned, he walked through to the kitchen and found her there with her back turned, washing dishes at the sink and listening to classical music on his transistor radio. There was an aroma of something delicious cooking on the stove, but what struck him first was the kitchen itself. Every surface from floor to ceiling had been cleaned and scoured. The shelves were now stocked with coffee, wine, pasta and a bewildering array of herbs and spices. He opened the gleaming fridge – depressingly empty that morning – to find it overflowing with terrines, smoked salmon, French cheese, mineral water and a veritable jungle of vegetables and salads. Nathalie had obviously discovered the local delicatessen, he thought in amusement.

She swung around and greeted him with a bright smile. "Alan, so you're back at last! Look how busy I've been... aren't you pleased?"

Alan was not sure whether he was pleased or not. He was both impressed by Nathalie's resourcefulness and slightly irritated by the disruption. "I liked the place the way it was," he said peevishly.

"*Mais c'est pas possible!*"*(1)* she burst out in exasperation. "Is that all you can find to say? When I got up this morning and saw your house in broad daylight, I couldn't believe you actually lived in such a mess. I've slaved away for hours to make it look nice, and now you have the nerve to tell me you liked it the way it was. *Mon Dieu,* your bathroom was disgusting! It looked as if it hadn't been cleaned for weeks."

This last remark was not far from the truth, Alan admitted to himself. He went to inspect the bathroom and found it as spotlessly clean as the rest of the house. Nathalie had even replaced the frayed old shower curtain and bought fluffy new towels. His few toiletries had been carefully moved to one side to make way for Nathalie's collection of perfumes, creams and cosmetics.

"It looks very nice," he conceded as he returned to the kitchen. "How much do I owe you for all this stuff?"

Nathalie waved her arms in protest. "I told you, I have an allowance from Papa," she said airily. "Don't let's talk about money. Come and see what I've made for dinner!" She lifted the lid of the casserole dish to reveal chunks of tender beef simmering in a red wine sauce. "*Boeuf bourguignon!* It's the only thing I know how to cook."

"Mmm..." said Alan appreciatively. He let out a low whistle as he spotted an expensive bottle of Bordeaux wine on the kitchen table.

"Now this is much more interesting than housework." Nathalie flashed him a triumphant smile and began to serve dinner.

They both relaxed over the delicious meal and chatted easily about the joys and tribulations of living in London. Nathalie proved to be insatiably curious about the British – their habits, their views, their politics. She absorbed his explanations like a sponge, and Alan sensed she was filing the information away in that sharp brain of hers.

"I take it you didn't have time for flat-hunting today," he remarked idly as they sipped cups of strong espresso coffee later that evening.

"Errr, no," she admitted. "But I haven't forgotten our arrangement, Alan. I'll start looking tomorrow."

Alan, feeling expansive after the best dinner he had eaten in a long time, was in no mood to argue. "Well, I suppose there's no rush. But tell me, Nathalie, how did you know where to find me in London? I'm pretty sure I didn't give you my address or phone number."

"No, you didn't." There was a hint of reproach in her dark eyes. "But it wasn't difficult. I just called Admin at LSE and asked."

"They're not allowed to divulge personal details," he pointed out.

"No, but they did for me. I put on a very strong French accent and said I was calling from Paris. I told them I was PA to the principal of Sciences-Po and that you had forgotten to complete the requisite forms with us."

Alan burst out laughing. He could not help feeling flattered that she had gone to so much trouble to see him again. "What a girl," he said admiringly.

She smiled at him enigmatically. "You'll see."

(1). *For heaven's sake!*

***

As the days lengthened and the spring sunshine inundated the streets of London, Nathalie's promise to find a place of her own gradually faded from Alan's mind. For the first week or so, she would tell him about the flats she had visited, but none of them ever seemed to be quite right. And Alan no longer pressed her to leave, for he had discovered that he enjoyed having Nathalie in his home. She was good company when he was feeling sociable and unobtrusive when he needed to work in peace and quiet. He looked forward to their evenings together, when they would talk or read or go out to a local restaurant. He was touched by the little ways she tried to please him, and appreciative of the tasty French food she seemed to conjure up so effortlessly.

Both of them went to great lengths to avoid any physical contact or sexual overtones in their discussions. For the time being, they were content to simply get to know each other – out of bed rather than in it. Neither of them ever referred to that afternoon in Paris when they had made love. Alan remembered uneasily how tense and inhibited Nathalie had been, how unfulfilled he had felt afterwards. Perhaps she was frigid? Perhaps they were sexually incompatible? Or perhaps Nathalie was not much interested in sex? So much the better, thought Alan. All such hypotheses served to reinforce his conviction that a serious relationship with Nathalie was out of the question.

She was distractingly beautiful of course, especially when she wandered about the house naked. Nathalie, who slept in the nude, could see no point in covering up first thing in the morning as she headed for the kitchen to make coffee. At other times, she would emerge naked from the bathroom, her perfect body still moist from the shower and her hair in a turban. She padded gracefully around his house *au naturel* and clearly saw nothing provocative in doing so.

At first, Alan felt a sharp shock of desire when a naked Nathalie glided past him at unexpected moments; her casual attitude was different from the other women he had known. He recalled that Liz, despite her stridently expressed views in favour of sexual liberation, had always kept nudity strictly to the bedroom. She had been as modest as a Victorian maiden about exposing her body publicly.

"Do you do this at home?" he asked her one Saturday morning as he walked into the kitchen to find her buttering toast at the counter. She was naked as usual, her dark hair tousled and her skin golden in the May sunshine.

"Do what?"

"Walk around with no clothes. I mean, in front of your family." He felt stupid as he said the words but curious nevertheless.

Nathalie gawped at him as if barely comprehending the question. "But of course," she said simply. "Don't you?"

Alan tried and failed to imagine himself with his parents, Geordie and Meggie Robertson, relaxing at home in Burnside in the nude. "Are you kidding?" he laughed. "It's too bloody cold up there."

"I didn't know it bothered you. I won't do it in future."

"No, no," he said hastily. "I'm used to it now."

Nathalie raised her eyebrows. *"Ah, les Anglais,"* (1) she mocked him gently and went back to buttering her toast.

(1). Ah, you English!

* * *

That spring, whenever Alan was invited to parties, pub gatherings or other social events, he took Nathalie with him. It seemed rude to leave her at home on her own, and in any case, he was secretly amused by the effect she had on his friends. The men swarmed around her like bees to a honeypot. They flattered her, flirted with her and generally behaved like gormless schoolboys in her presence. The general male consensus was that Alan was a 'lucky bugger'.

The women, initially wary and disparaging, gradually warmed to Nathalie. She took great pains to engage them in conversation, to take a genuine interest in their lives. And she rebuffed all male advances with a nonchalant laugh, making it clear to the women that she was not out to steal their men.

"Poor Nathalie," Alan joked one evening as they were coming home from a dinner party. "How do you manage to put up with us oldies? We must seem positively ancient to you."

"Don't be silly," she scoffed. "You're not ancient at all."

"Well, I'll be thirty-four next Saturday. I'd say that's pretty geriatric compared to you."

"Thirty-four isn't old," she protested. "A twelve year age difference is nothing." She suddenly squeezed his arm. "Oh Alan, I've just had a brilliant idea. Why don't we throw a party for your birthday?"

326

"Oh, no," he groaned. "Birthday parties are so embarrassing."

"We don't need to call it a birthday party if you don't want to," she persisted. "Let's just have a party anyway. Don't worry, I'll organise everything. You won't have to do a thing." Her dark eyes lit up with enthusiasm.

It must be two years, Alan reflected, since there had been a party in the house. He and Liz had thrown countless parties in the past, generally impromptu affairs. Their idea of party planning had been to empty packets of crisps into large bowls, turn the volume up full blast on the record player and let the festivities begin. The supply of alcohol was whatever the guests turned up with.

He was in an expansive mood that evening. "Okay," he said. "It might be fun."

Alan quickly realised that Nathalie's idea of a party was very different from his own. Ever the perfectionist, she threw herself into organising the event like an army general planning a military campaign. She issued invitations to a long list of guests and devised a theme for the evening: *Vive la difference!* Everyone, Alan discovered, had been asked to come disguised in typical British or French attire. The theme was echoed in the voluminous swathes of blue, white and red silk which she draped around the living room. Dozens of candles were also purchased and strategically placed to create atmospheric lighting.

On the day of the party, Alan found her hard at work in the kitchen, preparing large trays of exquisite *canapés* and intricate nibbles. "You're going to far too much trouble," he admonished her. "It's just a party, after all."

"Just a party?" Her voice rose disbelievingly. "This party is going to be fabulous. Absolutely fabulous!"

The evening, as Nathalie had promised, turned out to be a huge success. The living room and kitchen were soon packed full of guests, and the May weather was mild enough to encourage some of them to spill out onto the patio area at the back of the house. Alan noted with amusement that they had all taken Nathalie's dress code to heart and concocted extravagant costumes for the event. Punks in Union Jack t-shirts and bovver boots mingled with bewigged Versailles courtiers. English gentlemen in pin stripes and bowler hats chatted to French peasants in berets. Scotsmen in kilts and tam o'shanters drank wine with Parisian *gendarmes.*

Alan watched Nathalie admiringly as she moved easily among the guests, plying them with food and making sure glasses were constantly replenished. He had never seen her look so ravishing. She was dressed as a Moulin Rouge can-can dancer in red and black frilled satin. With her false eyelashes, rouged cheeks and scarlet lipstick, she exuded a blatant sex appeal totally at odds with her usual style of understated elegance. He saw Richard, one of his LSE cronies, slip his arm around her waist and whisper something in her ear that made her laugh. He was surprised how possessive he felt at that moment – an explosive combination of jealousy and desire.

As the evening wore on, the noise level rose to fever pitch. The guests, fuelled by good food and alcohol, were now in full swing. Most of them had started to dance to the rock music blasting from the loudspeakers. Richard, already drunk and perspiring heavily, was dancing with Nathalie, his hands on her hips and his body gyrating against hers.

Without thinking, Alan cut through the crowd and prised Nathalie away from Richard. "I need you to help me with something in the kitchen," he yelled over the din.

"Spoilsport," Richard grumbled and wandered off in search of more wine.

Nathalie looked both relieved and slightly bemused. "Thanks for coming to my rescue," she said drily. "What is it you need help with?"

Alan, unable to think of a suitable pretext, stared at her blankly. "Errr, I can't remember." He laughed awkwardly.

"Well, as it happens," said Nathalie, glancing at her watch. "I do need to get something from the kitchen." She left him standing there, rooted to the spot and feeling foolish.

Someone suddenly dimmed the lights, and Nathalie reappeared bearing a gigantic birthday cake, to cries of excitement and delight from the assembled guests. The cake, in the shape of an A, had been specially ordered for the party and was decorated with thirty-four lit candles. Alan, grinning from ear to ear, blew the candles out while everyone cheered and shouted, followed by a raucous rendering of 'Happy Birthday to You'.

Plates of cake were devoured and more bottles were opened. The guests were clearly in no hurry for the party to end, but at three in the morning Alan and Nathalie finally waved the last of them on their way. They collapsed in exhaustion on the sofa.

"The house looks like a bomb site," said Nathalie with a weary laugh. "I suppose we should really start clearing up."

"No way." He stretched his legs and yawned. Nathalie kicked off her high heels and curled up beside him. It was the first time they had both felt so utterly at ease with each other.

"Hilarious, isn't it?" he mused sardonically. "All the guys are green with envy, you know. They assume we're sleeping together. I'd love to see their faces if they found out we weren't."

He had expected her to say something amusing, but instead she snuggled closer. "What if we proved the guys right?" she said softly. She tilted her face to his and began to kiss him lightly. He felt her lips like butterfly wings on his eyelids, his nose, the corners of his mouth.

He vaguely recalled their pact; no sex, they had both agreed when she moved in. The very idea seemed ludicrous now. "Nathalie," he moaned, incapable of further resistance as her lithe body pressed urgently against his. He took her in his arms, caressing her velvety skin and breathing in her perfume. The red and black can-can dress slid away from her shoulders, revealing the swell of her small breasts.

"It'll be better this time," she whispered. "I know it will."

* * *

It had been better than better, thought Alan afterwards, it had been mind-blowingly fabulous. They had made love until dawn and lay in bed together now, their spent bodies entwined, listening to birds chirping on the back patio. He was overwhelmed by the transformation in Nathalie. The sensual, passionate woman in his arms was totally different from the tense, brittle girl he had encountered in Paris.

Perhaps they had simply needed to spend time together, to let their relationship evolve naturally. In Paris, he had been driven by sheer sexual desire and a certain form of opportunism; Nathalie had practically thrown herself at him after all. But tonight there had been raw emotion, a genuine connection between them.

As he gently stroked her soft skin, he was overwhelmed by a rush of tenderness. She turned her face to his, her brown eyes languorous. *"Mon amour...* was it better for you this time?"

"How can you ask?" he whispered. He saw that her eyes were closing as she drifted into sleep.

"It's just that..." Her voice was trailing away, barely audible. "It's just that I'm not used to men."

The words sounded strange and discordant to Alan, but he was too exhausted – physically and emotionally – to press her for more. He filed the words away in a corner of his brain and let himself fall asleep too.

* * *

The afternoon sun was high in the sky when they finally managed to crawl out of bed and face the post-party mayhem awaiting them. Neither of them was in the mood to start clearing up the mess. They sat at the kitchen table, surrounded by empty bottles and dirty glasses, nursing mugs of strong black coffee and feeling utterly content together.

Nathalie's words popped unbidden into his mind. "What did you mean last night?" he asked idly.

She looked at him blankly. "Don't you remember?" he continued. "You said you weren't used to men."

She stiffened slightly but did not attempt to elude the question. "I don't want there to be any secrets between us," she sighed eventually. "I suppose now is as good a time as any to tell you."

Alan had not expected such a serious reaction and was instantly alert.

There was an uneasy sense of dread in the pit of his stomach.

Nathalie raised her slender arms and ran both hands through her long dark hair, as if ordering her thoughts. She was wearing his shirt from the night before and looked disarmingly juvenile. "I'm twenty-two years old," she said finally. "And you'll probably be surprised to hear you're the first man I've ever slept with."

His first reaction was disbelief; young as she was, Nathalie was no innocent. "I don't understand, Nathalie. You're not a virgin, I know that much."

She nodded in agreement and looked him squarely in the eyes. "Before I met you, I had a very long affair," she said slowly. "With a woman."

"What?" shouted Alan, leaping to his feet and knocking over the kitchen chair in the process. Nathalie a lesbian? Nothing had prepared him for such a revelation. His heart was pounding from the shock.

She was on her feet too and caught his arm with a pleading look. "Please calm down, Alan, and let me explain. It's not exactly the way it sounds."

"What other way is there?" he burst out. Nevertheless, he felt it was only fair to hear her out. They both sat down again, and Nathalie poured more coffee into their mugs.

"Her name is Hélène," Nathalie began. "She's an interior decorator who did some work years ago on our second home in Deauville. That's how she and my mother became friends originally. They're about the same age, you see." Alan raised his brows but said nothing.

"I was fourteen when Hélène started to take an interest in me," Nathalie continued. Her voice was even, although he noticed her hands were trembling. "She kept offering to take me to museums, art exhibitions and so on at weekends. It was all very much above board, and Maman said Hélène would further my cultural education. So on Saturday afternoons, Hélène and I would go out and about in Paris together."

Alan stared at Nathalie with a mixture of horror and fascination. Every word she uttered was breaking new ground, leading him into unknown territory.

"I was instantly captivated by Hélène," she went on. "She was amusing and quirky and knowledgeable about so many things. I felt proud to be treated like a grown-up." She gave a short laugh. "Too much like a grown-up. I was so innocent that I didn't realise, you see. Everything happened so gradually, so naturally. At first when she hugged and kissed me, I thought she was just being affectionate. And then, instead of visiting museums we would end up spending more and more time at her flat, talking and kissing and—" She stopped short, her mouth working with emotion. "She seduced me, Alan, and afterwards it was too late."

"That's crazy, Nathalie," he protested. "Why didn't you tell your mother? This Hélène woman was supposed to be her friend, wasn't she?"

She shrugged dismissively. "Oh, Maman has never taken much interest in anyone but herself. She's never been there for me when I needed her… But you're missing the point, Alan. You don't know how clever Hélène is. She told me our love was too precious to be shared, like a secret garden no one else must enter. She charmed and manipulated me until in the end I was completely under her spell."

"But you were just a teenager," Alan interrupted. "Didn't you want to go out with boys, like other girls your age?"

Nathalie's dark eyes were intense as she tried to explain. "The thing is, I felt superior to the boys at school – cool and mature and experienced. I was caught up in Hélène's web and didn't realise that she was cutting me off from the normal experiences of growing up." She heaved a sigh, as if wishing she could turn the clock back.

"Even so, don't tell me the guys didn't come after you," Alan said disbelievingly. "A girl as good-looking as you—"

"I didn't let them anywhere near me. I made it clear I despised them all. You see, Hélène's a radical feminist and taught me to view all men as predators and oppressors. She thinks heterosexual romance is a myth, that social institutions like marriage are just tools invented by men to dominate women. She believes women should stand together to eliminate male supremacy from society. Being a lesbian is a political issue for Hélène, the ultimate form of resistance."

Alan let out a low whistle. He had met one or two women like Hélène in the intellectual, academic circles he frequented. But he hated the idea of Nathalie being methodically brainwashed to hate men before she was even old enough to formulate her own opinions. "And this… affair… went on for how long?"

"Seven years. As time went on, I realised how claustrophobic the relationship was becoming. I felt tied, body and soul, to Hélène. It was as if I couldn't see anyone or anything in life except through her eyes. But I couldn't seem to break away, I was afraid I couldn't cope without her. And the whole thing might have

330

gone on even longer if I hadn't found out…" Nathalie swallowed hard. "Last summer, I went around to her flat to return a book. She thought I was in Deauville for the weekend and wasn't expecting me. I had a key and let myself in." She gave a brittle laugh. "I found Hélène in bed with a girl as young as I had been when she first seduced me, fourteen or fifteen at most. I'm sure now there must have been others too, but I didn't stick around long enough to ask her. I felt such a fool, Alan, but at the same time, everything suddenly turned crystal clear. It wasn't men who were oppressing and exploiting me. The real predator in my life was her."

It was at that precise moment that Alan truly fell in love with Nathalie. He loved her all the more because she had not been afraid to bare her soul to him, expose her vulnerability. "Come here," he said, his voice thick with emotion, and stretched out his arms to her. She got up and went to sit on his lap, burying her face in his neck like a child.

"That was the last time I saw Hélène," she said after a while, willing herself to go on. "I shut myself away for weeks on end, going over and over it all, trying to get my head around those seven years. Eventually, I realised I had to pick up the pieces and make a fresh start. So when I went back to Sciences-Po in the autumn, I forced myself to go out on dates with a few of the guys. It was a fiasco! *Un désastre!*" She broke into peals of nervous laughter.

Seeing his questioning look, she continued more soberly. "None of them attracted me, that's all. They seemed so shallow and immature. I would pretend they were turning me on, but then I just couldn't go through with it. I soon got a reputation as an *allumeuse,* and after that most of them wanted nothing more to do with me."

In his mind's eye, Alan remembered Nathalie as she had been when he first saw her, in the amphitheatre at Sciences-Po. She had always sat by herself, apart from the other students. It was all starting to make sense now. "What's an *allumeuse?"* he asked curiously.

Nathalie grimaced. "It's a girl who deliberately lights a man's fire and then just lets him burn."

Alan grinned. "Ah! In English we have a less poetic term for such behaviour." He pulled her closer, and their lips met in a long, lingering kiss. "I think you're starting to light my particular fire again," he murmured. "But I still need to know one thing. Where do I fit into all this?"

Her face lit up. "Oh, that part is easy. I was drawn to you from the start, that day you gave your first lecture at Sciences-Po. You struck me like the proverbial thunderbolt. *Un vrai coup de foudre.* Love at first sight, as you English say."

"I can't think why," said Alan. "I'm not exactly the Prince Charming type."

Nathalie gave him a wry smile. "That much is true. Prince Charming doesn't usually come with a shaggy beard and atrocious clothes. But I knew instinctively you were the right man for me. And I must admit I found you rather sexy in a weird kind of way."

"Thanks," said Alan drily. "But if I was so irresistible, why did you never try to speak to me?"

"I was too nervous. And I suppose I was secretly hoping you'd speak to me."

"I tend to give female students a wide berth." Not for the first time, he suspected that Nathalie's sudden appearance in London was not entirely fortuitous. "Why did you really come here, Nathalie? Why did you tell that cock and bull story to your father about a summer course at LSE?"

She lowered her eyes in embarrassment. "You know the answer, Alan. I came here for you. I needed to be part of your life, and I knew you'd never come back to Paris for me."

He was relieved to hear the truth at last, and at the same time inexpressibly happy that she had loved him enough to go to such lengths. "So the story about starting a skin care company was cock and bull too?"

"Oh no," she rectified immediately. "That's a project that's been at the back of my mind for a while now. But it didn't have to be in London and it didn't have to be now."

In a way, he realised, he had been set up – by a woman who had wanted him so much that she had devised a very elaborate plan to ensnare him. It was a snare from which he no longer had any desire to disentangle himself. She was still sitting on his lap, her long legs barely covered by the shirt she had borrowed from him. His fingers stroked the flawless gold skin of her thighs.

"Still," he mused. "Fate played a hand in it too. If I hadn't run into you at the Rodin Museum, we'd never have met."

To his surprise, Nathalie averted her eyes and slid off his lap. She began collecting dirty glasses and stacking them furiously into the dishwasher. Alan stood up too and positioned himself squarely in front of her. He removed a couple of glasses, slowly and deliberately, from her hands. He put them back down on the counter and gently tilted her face towards his. "What is it, Nathalie? Don't tell me you…"

"Yes," she admitted ruefully. "I rigged that too. When you gave that last lecture in Paris, I couldn't bear the thought of never seeing you again. So I found out where you were staying, and the next morning I waited for you outside the hotel. It seemed like hours, I was frozen to death! When you finally emerged, I followed you to the museum. I kept at a safe distance until I finally plucked up the courage to speak to you."

Alan burst out laughing. The idea of Nathalie lurking outside the hotel, shadowing him like some modern Mata Hari, struck him as preposterous. It must be the first time in his life a woman had gone to such lengths to stage a meeting with him.

"Well, I have to say I admire your single-mindedness. Not to mention your good taste in men," he quipped. "Any other bombshells you want to drop on me today?"

"No, that's about it," Nathalie said. "Except… wait here a moment, will you?" She smiled enigmatically and padded barefoot out of the kitchen. Seconds later, she returned with a gift-wrapped package, which she handed to him diffidently. "I brought this with me from Paris, but I've been saving it for the right moment."

Mystified, Alan unwrapped the package and then caught his breath. The box inside contained a miniature replica of *Le Baiser*, the sculpture they had admired together on that first, not so accidental encounter at the Rodin Museum in Paris. His fingertips ran over the sensual lines of the naked couple, locked for eternity in their passionate embrace. He understood instantly that this was no ordinary gift; Nathalie had been thinking of him when she bought it. Rodin's lovers symbolised her aspirations and dreams for them both.

He set the sculpture down and took her in his arms. "I'm overwhelmed," he said. "It's as if you already knew we would—"

Nathalie stopped him with a soft kiss. "I didn't know," she whispered. "But I hoped."

* * *

Alan and Nathalie cleared up the aftermath of the party with dogged determination. The dishwasher went into overdrive, dozens of empty bottles were disposed of, decorations were taken down and every last crumb was hoovered into oblivion. Two hours later the little house in Notting Hill was deemed sufficiently spick and span to meet Nathalie's exacting standards. They collapsed in exhaustion on the sofa and spent the rest of the afternoon snuggled together, watching an old Hollywood movie on television. That evening, they lit candles, ate the leftovers and drank the last of the wine. They both felt blissfully, ridiculously happy.

They went to bed early and made love again, more languorously than the night before. Satiated and fulfilled, they kissed and said good night, still wrapped in each other's arms. Silence fell on the darkened room as they lay waiting for sleep to claim them. Alan listened to Nathalie's even breathing, although he sensed she was still awake.

"I love you," she said suddenly in a small voice. The words reverberated in the silence of the room and hung in the air expectantly.

"Oh Nathalie," he groaned, tightening his embrace. "You should know me enough by now. I'm no good at all that romantic stuff." Part of him wished he could give her the response she wanted, but he had never pronounced those three words in his life. There had certainly never been any talk of love with Liz; she would have scoffed at such bourgeois sentimentality.

"It's okay, I understand," Nathalie said gently. There was a short silence and then she stirred again, her face so close to his that their lips were almost touching. "You might find it easier to say in French."

Alan smiled to himself in the darkness. Nathalie, he was beginning to learn, was the kind of woman who stuck to her guns. "*Je t'aime,*" he whispered.

"*Moi non plus.*"(1) The words were light-hearted, but her sigh of contentment was unmistakeable. "*Bonne nuit, mon amour.*"(2)

(1).   *Me neither.*
(2).   *Good night, my love.*

Nick and Jenny (12)

It was a glorious summer's morning in late July, the kind of idyllic weather all too rare in Northumberland. The sun beat down from a bright cloudless sky as Nick and Jenny, struggling with a picnic hamper and various beach accessories, trudged across the pale golden sands of Embleton Bay. They found a sheltered spot in the lee of the high dunes and flopped down there, panting from the heat and exertion. After spreading out their beach towels and stripping down to their swimsuits, they looked around them, contemplating the huge expanse of the bay and the glinting blue swell of the North Sea at low tide. Although the beach itself was not completely deserted, the other holiday-makers were a long way off, reduced to insignificant specks on the long stretch of sand. At the far side of the bay, looming high above them on a headland, were the ancient ruins of Dunstanburgh Castle.

Nick lay back, propped on his elbows, taking deep breaths of the salty air. It was strange, he thought, how this rugged corner of Northumberland had come to fill him with a sense of belonging. This was where he had found his roots, where he and Jenny had fallen in love and where he felt at peace with the world. The windswept coastline, the picturesque villages, the country lanes and hillsides dotted with sheep were now a part of his very being.

And it was all thanks to Jenny, he reflected. Together they had journeyed into the past, stepped back in time to meet the Robertson ancestors who were now so familiar to him. And in doing so, the brash young television presenter of a few short months ago had morphed into a different person. He had a sense of his own identity now, a depth and substance he had lacked before. The Robertson family tree was now complete; he and Jenny had come to the end of that particular journey. Yet Nick hoped that a new journey awaited them, this time one of their own making.

They sunbathed in peaceful silence for a while, basking in the warmth. Eventually, they roused themselves sufficiently to lay out the contents of the picnic hamper – chicken salad, cheese and thick slices of crusty bread, fresh peaches and melon for dessert. Nick uncorked a bottle of rosé wine – still chilled from the cooler – and poured them both a glass.

"This is the life," he said contentedly. "I could stay here forever, just you and me."

Jenny grinned, her tawny hair blowing softly about her face. "Given the climate up here, we'd better make the most of it!" She sipped her wine reflectively. "I can hardly believe we'll be in America this time next week."

Their trip to Philadelphia was now imminent. They would be met at the airport by John Robertson, Chairman of the Robertson Realty Corporation, in person. They both hoped to learn more about John Robertson, the enigmatic young man in the portrait who had emigrated towards the end of the eighteenth century. Nick in particular was impressed that one of his ancestors – a poor, illiterate Northumbrian lad – had succeeded in founding a multi-million dollar business empire in America.

"It looks like we'll be getting red carpet treatment for the duration," he remarked. "John's laying on quite a show for our visit. It's amazing how kind and generous he's been."

"At least we'll be incognito in the States," sighed Jenny. "I can't take much more of this constant harassment from the paparazzi. It's so mortifying. How will I ever be able to face the kids at school after the holidays?"

"This kind of media buzz never lasts long," Nick reassured her. "They'll soon get tired of us and move on." The tabloid press and social media had finally picked up on their relationship, much to their dismay. For the last week or so, there had been much online gossip about their so-called budding romance – the star presenter of *In Those Days* and an unknown teacher from Newcastle. Various photos of Nick and Jenny, taken unawares, were currently circulating, accompanied by the usual innuendo and speculation. *Who's the hot new redhead in Nick Robertson's life? TV heartthrob finds love with Geordie schoolmistress...*

"What does your family say about it all?" she asked curiously.

"Oh, Charlotte's still away doing good works in darkest Africa. This kind of thing wouldn't even be a blip on her radar. And Maman is too busy negotiating the Inner Beauty acquisition deal to have picked up on it."

"What about Alan?" She had a feeling Nick's father would thoroughly disapprove of such sordid gossip.

"Dad? He's never read a tabloid in his life, and as for social media..." He raised his eyebrows in mock despair. "Dad's still getting to grips with the mysterious workings of the mobile phone."

Jenny laughed, and Nick patted her hand. "Don't worry, darling, it'll all blow over soon."

"I only hope you're right. I don't want to spend the rest of my life wearing dark glasses and avoiding flashlights." She giggled nervously.

Nick turned to her, looking suddenly much more serious. "And how *do* you want to spend the rest of your life?" he blurted out. He had not planned to broach the subject of their future today, but it seemed as good a time as any.

Jenny was completely taken aback. "Well, I... I... what do you mean?" she stammered.

Nick brushed her cheek gently with his hand. "Can't you guess, Jenny? Paparazzi or no paparazzi, I don't want you to go back to school after the holidays. I want you to come and live with me in London. I want you with me, darling, all day and every day."

"Oh, Nick," she breathed, her mind whirling as their lips met in a soft kiss. Until now, she had made a conscious effort not to jump to any conclusions about their relationship. Although she was sure of her feelings for Nick and equally secure in the knowledge that he loved her too, she had been determined not to make any assumptions about their future. They had after all only known each other for a few short months.

"Is that a yes?" His eyes were intensely blue.

"Yes, oh yes," she murmured. "I'm just stunned, that's all. There's so much to think about. Where would we live? What about your parents?"

Nick gave her a quizzical look. "My parents? I don't expect you to move into my den in South Ken, you know! It's high time I got a place of my own in any case, and I've already got an agent scouting for the perfect pad. Let's choose it together, Jenny! You can put your house in Jesmond on the market and move down to London by the end of the summer."

Jenny was still reeling from a heady cocktail of exhilaration and panic. Part of her longed to jump for joy or scream in delight. Wasn't this what she had secretly dreamed of all along? And yet the prospect of sharing Nick's life seemed unreal, almost too good to be true... so much so that she could think of nothing but mundane practicalities. "What about my job?"

Jenny had been let down by a man in the past, Nick reminded himself; she would not entrust him with her happiness lightly. "I know you love teaching, darling, but you can always apply for a position in London. Or for that matter, switch careers and do something completely different. You know I'll support you whatever you decide."

Something completely different... Jenny remembered yesterday's momentous phone call, the stupendous offer she had been mulling over ever since. Nick had a right to know, it was unfair to leave him in the dark any longer.

"Speaking of which," she began hesitantly. "There's something on my mind at the moment, and we need to talk about it." Seeing Nick's alarmed expression, she hastened to reassure him. "It's no big deal really, but I wasn't sure how you'd feel. I had a call from your boss, Mark Goodwin, yesterday. Apparently, One Better Productions wants me to present a new TV series."

It was the last thing Nick had expected. "Wow, that's amazing!" he managed to say. "Of course I knew Mark was very taken with you, he said as much when he sat in on the editing of *In Those Days*. But he didn't breathe a word to me about contacting you directly. Sneaky so and so!"

Jenny was distraught. "That's exactly how I was afraid you'd react. Oh Nick, I don't want anything to come between us, least of all Mark Goodwin and his crazy ideas. The whole thing has been preying on my mind for a while now, and I didn't know how to break it to you."

"For a while? But you said he only called yesterday." He knew he sounded peevish but couldn't help feeling annoyed with Mark for keeping him out of the loop. Mark must have suspected he was involved with Jenny, and yet he had deliberately gone behind his back.

Jenny took a deep breath. "Mark sent me a very complimentary e-mail last week. He's apparently convinced I've got what it takes to be a presenter in my own right. He asked me to come up with an original concept for a new series – a series I could put my own stamp on..."

"And?" Nick was listening attentively, although his expression was unreadable.

"Well, not surprisingly I started thinking about your family history, discovering the past and so on. And I remembered how difficult it was to find missing pieces in the mosaic, how long it took us to track down John Robertson in Philadelphia. Or the other John Robertson..."

"Is there another one?"

"Yes, have you forgotten? Your grandfather Geordie had an elder brother called John. He ran away from Burnside as a young lad, joined the Merchant Navy and eventually settled in Australia. As it happens, I've just managed to find his descendants. It turns out you have dozens of Robertson relatives in Brisbane!"

Nick could hardly wait to delve into this new chapter of the family history. Knowing Jenny, she was probably already planning their next holiday in Australia. But in this instance, he refused to be side-tracked. "So what does all this have to do with Mark Goodwin?"

Jenny's eyes flashed emerald in the sunlight. "There are so many of these stories, don't you see?" she cried passionately. "Think of all the thousands of families in the UK with long-lost relatives who emigrated – either voluntarily or forcibly – and were never heard of again. And at the same time, out there in America, Canada, Australia, South Africa and elsewhere there are thousands of other people desperately searching for their family roots in Britain. So I came up with an idea for a series that would bring these families together. I even have a working title for it – *Four Corners of the Empire.*"

Nick let out a low whistle. "Jenny, that's brilliant! And right up your street too... Have you discussed the idea with Mark?"

Jenny looked slightly shamefaced. "Yes, that was the reason for the phone call yesterday. I didn't believe for a moment he'd take me seriously. In fact, I didn't believe you'd take me seriously either, which is why I've kept it to myself until now. But amazingly, he loved the concept, Nick, he loved it! One Better Productions wants me on board, or so he kept saying. But I would hate you to think I'm trespassing on your territory, Nick, or that we're in some kind of competition. If you mind even the slightest, I'll tell Mark I'm not interested."

Nick caught the pleading tone in her voice. Did Jenny fear his male ego might be bruised, that he felt envious and resentful? She was even prepared to give up an exciting career opportunity for his sake. Surely this wasn't the kind of man he wanted to be? Loving Jenny didn't give him rights of ownership over her, like some male dinosaur from a bygone era. He must waste no time in impressing on her that he rejoiced in her success, and also that he was intensely proud of her.

He leaned towards her and clasped both her hands in his. "Mind? Jenny, of course I don't mind. This is wonderful news, I'm thrilled for you. And thrilled for me too."

"For you?" Jenny looked puzzled.

"Yes, because now you have absolutely no excuse to stay in Newcastle." He grinned triumphantly and reached for the wine to top up their glasses.

"Here's to *Four Corners of the Empire,*" he pronounced solemnly. "And here's to our new life together." They clinked glasses and sealed the toast with a kiss.

***

When they had cleared away the remains of the picnic lunch, they moved their beach towels into the shade and dozed for a while. There would be plenty of time to make plans and deal with the inevitable complications ahead. But for now, they were simply content to absorb the serenity of this perfect summer afternoon, to let the July sunshine permeate their bodies and souls.

"Come on, lazybones, time for a swim!" Jenny opened her eyes to find Nick towering above her, one arm encouragingly outstretched.

"Oh no, the water will be freezing!" Laughing and half-protesting, she allowed herself to be pulled to her feet. They strolled hand in hand towards the seashore.

It was then that they noticed a young man walking along the beach towards them, a large black dog bounding playfully at his side. The young man was tall and slim, dressed in a white t-shirt and jeans. Behind him, clearly delineated against the blue sky, the sombre ruins of Dunstanburgh Castle made a striking backdrop. Nick and Jenny stood rooted to the spot in the wet sand as the good-looking young man came closer, his fair hair ruffled by the summer breeze.

"Do you see what I see?" breathed Jenny, unable to take her eyes off the approaching figure.

Nick looked as if he had seen a ghost. "Incredible," he gasped. The young man striding towards them bore an uncanny resemblance to John Robertson, whose portrait they had studied so many times. His fair hair was cut in a modern style and a t-shirt had replaced the billowing white shirt of the painting, but the rest was identical... the set of the head on broad shoulders, the strong even features, the steady blue eyes, even the jagged silhouette of the castle in the background.

The young man looked somewhat mystified as he drew near, no doubt wondering why his appearance was causing such rapt attention. Nevertheless, he raised his hand in a friendly gesture. "Hi," he called out. "Lovely day, isn't it?" His dog had raced ahead and was splashing in the shallows.

If he didn't seize this opportunity, Nick thought, he would regret it for the rest of his life. He stepped forward, feeling foolish but his mind made up. "Hi," he managed to say. "Look, you probably think we're totally crazy staring at you like this, but..." His voice trailed away. How on earth could he tell a complete stranger that he was a dead ringer for an eighteenth-century portrait? The young man had stopped dead in his tracks and was gazing at him expectantly.

Nick tried again. "Let me introduce myself. My name's Nick Robertson, and this is my girlfriend Jenny." Taking her cue, Jenny smiled politely; at close quarters, she thought, the young man's likeness to John Robertson was even more startling.

"Nick Robertson? The name rings a bell." The young man's expression was puzzled for a moment. "Of course, I recognise you now! You're the guy on that TV show Mam always watches! The one about olden times..."

"That's right. *In Those Days.*" Nick was on more familiar ground now.

The young man's face broke into a broad grin. "Wow, that's incredible! Wait till I tell Mam I bumped into Nick Robertson on the beach."

"The thing is," Nick went on slowly. "My family originally came from this area, and I couldn't help noticing that you're the spitting image of a... relative of mine." He refrained from adding that the relative in question had been born over two hundred years ago. "I was wondering if by any chance, your name was Robertson too?"

The young man gaped open-mouthed at them both, his eyes travelling from Nick to Jenny in bewilderment. "Sorry to disappoint you, mate," he said with a nervous laugh. "But the name's Hunter. Dan Hunter."

Nick and Jenny felt as though a bucket of icy water had been thrown at them. Seeing their devastated expression, the young man attempted to make amends. "I'm a local lad, though. I'm from Eastfield Farm over in Dunstan, if you know where I mean."

338

"We know where you mean," Nick and Jenny chorused in unison, and they all burst out laughing.

"I'm home for the summer holidays at the moment. Still got another year to go at uni." The ice was broken now, and Dan Hunter sounded more relaxed.

He must be in his early twenties, Nick reckoned – roughly the same age as John Robertson when the portrait was painted. "What are you studying?" he enquired conversationally.

"Agriculture," said Dan. "I've got big plans for the farm once I've graduated. I want to take over the business side of things – go organic, open a shop selling local specialities, that kind of thing. We get a lot of tourist trade in summer, you know."

"Sounds really interesting – I'm sure you'll do well." Nick was genuinely taken with this bright, likeable young man.

"Hope so," Dan continued. "I'm looking forward to coming home for good. When I'm away at uni, I miss the farm, I miss the people, the countryside, the sea…" He made a sweeping gesture with his hands. "This is where I belong, if you know what I mean."

"We know what you mean," they chorused again, prompting more laughter all round.

The young man grinned good-naturedly. "Well, I suppose I'd better be off." He whistled to his dog and raised his hand again in farewell. "Nice meeting you."

Nick and Jenny watched Dan Hunter's retreating figure as he set off again along the beach. They stood hand in hand by the water's edge, tiny waves rippling over their feet.

It was ridiculous to feel so dashed, they knew. The striking similarity between Dan Hunter and the portrait of John Robertson had merely been wishful thinking on their part, a subconscious urge to connect this young man walking his dog to Nick's distant past. But there was no link between the two, except in their overwrought imaginations.

"Pity, isn't it?" sighed Jenny despondently. "It would all have fitted together so neatly. Still, we weren't too far off the mark. He is a local lad, after all."

Nick shrugged, resolving to put the episode behind him. He pulled her playfully into the water. "Come on, let's go for that swim!"

Jenny shrieked as they were enveloped to their waists in the cold swell of the North Sea; she could hardly stand upright in the strong current and crashing waves. "It's icy in here!" she gasped. "You can go for a swim if you like. I'll wait for you on the beach."

As she turned and began to wade into shallower water, she was startled to see Dan Hunter, the black dog still romping at his heels, purposefully walking back in their direction. He was waving to them energetically, obviously trying to catch their attention. Nick had spotted him too, and they both hauled themselves out of the sea to meet the young man at the shoreline. They stood squinting in the sunshine, salt water streaming down their bodies.

"Hey, I'm sorry to interrupt your swim," Dan began apologetically. "But I was thinking about what you said, and I suddenly remembered something. My grandmother was a Robertson before she married – Joyce Robertson, her name was. I thought you might like to know."

Nick and Jenny exchanged a quick, triumphant smile. So they hadn't been deluding themselves after all! John Robertson might have left Northumberland long ago, but the family genes had been passed on through the centuries, generation after generation, to reappear today with blinding clarity in this farmer's son from Dunstan.

"Oh my God, that's awesome!" breathed Nick. "You can't imagine how thrilled we are to hear you say those words. So there *is* a family connection after all, just as we thought when we first saw you."

"Looks that way, doesn't it? I can't wait to see Grandma's face when she finds out she's related to the famous Nick Robertson!" Dan looked almost as delighted as they were at the strange coincidence. "Look, I've just thought of something. Are you staying overnight in Embleton?"

"No, we have to get back to Newcastle tonight."

"Well even so, why don't you call in at the farm for a cup of tea on your way home? Mam and Dad would love to meet you both, and Grandma's over there visiting today. You can tell her about your relative – I'm sure she'll know who he is."

Jenny suppressed a smile. She very much doubted that Joyce Robertson's memory stretched as far as the eighteenth century. Nevertheless, she was already planning to trace the old lady's family tree back to where it met Nick's, if only to validate today's astounding revelation.

Nick was overjoyed. "We'd love to," he said, stretching out his dripping hand to clasp Dan's. They quickly arranged a time for the visit, and Dan gave them directions to Eastfield Farm.

Nick and Jenny watched the young man retreating for a second time, hugging each other for joy. "I feel as if I've just hit the jackpot!" he told her jubilantly.

"I know, it's like striking gold," Jenny agreed. Still soaking wet, she was starting to shiver. "Look, Nick, I'm definitely chickening out of this swim. The water's far too cold for my liking! I'm going to dry off and sunbathe instead."

"Coward!" he teased her. He ran back into the sea, plunging into the churning waves in a frenzy of celebration and then striking out into deeper water. Jenny observed his progress fondly before turning away. She found the dip in the dunes where they had left their belongings, towelled herself dry and flopped down on the sand, enjoying the sensation of the sun burning away the last drops of salty water from her skin. She reached for a bottle of water and drank thirstily, her eyes following Nick's bobbing head as his body thrashed through the deep blue water in a strong crawl.

Dan Hunter, Dan Hunter... There was something troubling her, although she couldn't quite put her finger on it. Where had she heard the name before? It was a common enough name, but there was something oddly familiar about it. She stretched out on the beach towel and closed her eyes, sifting through the possibilities.

Of course! Jenny sat bolt upright in sudden realisation. Almost four hundred years ago, Nick's distant ancestor, William Robertson, had married a Susannah Hunter! And Lancelot Hunter, Susannah's father, had been a shepherd on the Thorburn estate at Dunstan Manor. Jenny heaved a sigh of satisfaction. The knowledge that centuries later there were still Robertsons and Hunters in this remote corner of Northumberland, their lives still so closely entwined, gave new meaning to the journey through time she and Nick had made together. Dan Hunter, the farmer's lad from Dunstan with his Robertson grandmother, had been the missing link in their quest. She and Nick had come full circle today. She could hardly wait to tell him.

* * *

Jenny lay back again in blissful abandon and let her thoughts drift. In her mind's eye, she examined again the tiny fragments of the past which made up the mosaic of the Robertson family, certain pieces interlocking in marriage with her own family. She and Nick had enjoyed picking up the pieces of this particular mosaic and marvelling at the individual lives they encapsulated. The mosaic itself would always be incomplete of course, for with each generation new pieces were added. Nevertheless, its intricate pattern was now revealed at last.

But what did the pattern represent? What meaning did it hold? Maybe it would make more sense if she tried to see it in perspective? She took a mental step backwards, as she might do in a museum to view a large fresco. But in doing so, the Robertson family almost disappeared from view, a mere fragment in the gigantic mosaic of Northumbrian history. And if, with a supreme effort of the imagination, she took a further step backwards, the pattern of Northumberland itself was infinitesimal in the grander sweep of English history. The billions of minute pieces that made up the complex mosaic of a nation, from the dawn of time to the present day, defied comprehension.

She was afraid to step back too far, for the pattern that was England would then blur and recede into insignificance. England would become an ever-diminishing speck in the mosaic of Europe, the mosaic of the world, the mosaic of the cosmos. Jenny had always believed there was a pattern to the mosaic of time, but now she wondered whether she had simply been deluding herself. Perhaps the truth was less comforting? Perhaps there was no pattern at all?

Throughout history, she thought, great philosophers had puzzled over this conundrum. Eminent scholars and scientists had dedicated their lives to piercing the mystery, and there were still no definitive answers. She smiled inwardly. It was unlikely that she, Jenny Armstrong, would uncover the secret of the universe today. The warm breeze fluttered over her face, and the long grass in the dunes rustled softly. She fell asleep.

She was oblivious to Nick's approach, padding through the soft sand, until she felt the shock of ice-cold drops on her warm skin. Startled, she opened her eyes to see him standing over her, soaking wet from his swim and dripping salty water on her body.

"Go away!" she screeched in protest. But Nick, deaf to her pleas, had other plans in mind. He knelt down in the sand and ran his cold hands up her legs and thighs. She caught the familiar look of desire in his blue eyes and responding instinctively, pulled him down on top of her. She gasped with pleasure at the sensation of his cool skin and the salty tang of his mouth on hers. Deftly, he unfastened her bikini top to reveal creamy white breasts untouched by the sun. Her body arched as she felt his hands, gritty from sand and salt water, cupping their velvety softness. He held her tightly, exploring every inch of her body, turning her liquid with longing.

"What if somebody sees us?" she murmured feebly as he covered her face with kisses.

"Like who?" he whispered in her ear.

It was a pointless question, Jenny realised. They were safe from prying eyes in the lee of the dune, and in any case, the beach was deserted. Dan Hunter and his dog had long since disappeared from view. Wordlessly, she clung to Nick's taut body as he penetrated her, swiftly and urgently, on the sands of Embleton Bay. Turning her head in a moment of ecstasy, she caught a glimpse of Dunstanburgh Castle at the far side of the bay. Its sombre yet oddly benign presence filled her consciousness as she climaxed. The thought flashed through her mind that Nick was probably not the first Robertson to take a woman within view of the ancient castle.

They lay in each other's arms for a long time afterwards, their bodies loosely entwined and damp hair tangled together. Then Nick propped himself up on one elbow and looked deep into her eyes, translucent green after their lovemaking.

"I can't help thinking," he said tenderly. "Wouldn't it be lovely if we'd kick-started the next generation of Robertsons just now?"

Nick had never before alluded, directly or indirectly, to children as part of their future together. Caught off guard, Jenny felt a quick rush of soaring happiness which she instantly tried to quell. "I doubt we've kick-started anything," she murmured laconically. "You know I'm still on the pill."

"Don't be so prosaic," he laughed. "Let's look at it hypothetically."

She pretended to ponder the question. "Yes," she said finally. "It would be lovely." She felt his warm breath on her face as he gave a faint sigh of relief.

"Good," he pronounced firmly. "You've just ticked a box. The second one today."

She smiled up at him. "What was the first box?"

"Living together in London. You ticked that box this morning." He drew his face close to hers and ran his fingers delicately through her hair, brushing damp tawny strands away from her face.

"So I did. Things seem to be moving very fast at the moment." Their lips were almost touching, the words hovering between them like a butterfly's wings. "Are there any more boxes I need to tick?"

"Yes, one more." Nick paused briefly, searching for the right words. He had known for some time that this moment would come, although not when. He had planned to express his feelings in some fresh, original way; he had wanted to find sparkling new words that would imprint themselves forever in Jenny's heart. But there were no words, he realised now, which had not been uttered billions of times before, in every language known to man, by countless generations of lovers.

"My beautiful Jenny, the love of my life," he began, his voice breaking with emotion. "I love you and will always love you. Will you marry me, darling?"

Her heart was pounding as Nick's words coursed through her being, sweeping away hesitation and doubt. "Yes," was all she managed to say, but the kiss she gave him – deep and liquid, full of joy and hope – told him with absolute certainty all he needed to know.

Eventually, when the late afternoon sun dipped behind the dunes and their bodies began to chill, they pulled apart. They brushed the sand from their skin, pulled on their clothes and began to assemble their belongings.

"Oh dear, I've just thought of another box that needs ticking," said Nick casually, as if there had been no break in the conversation. There was a humorous glint in his eyes.

Jenny was busy folding their beach towels. "What other box can there possibly be?" she protested laughingly. "In the space of a few hours, I've agreed to move house, live with you, marry you and have your babies. That's a lot of ticks for one day, isn't it?"

"Oh, nothing out of the ordinary, I'd say," he remarked lightly. "After all, Robertson men often marry Armstrong women, don't they? Look at Tom and Annie, Bill and Hannah... So in a way, we're just following in their footsteps."

"That's true," she conceded with a mischievous smile. "You and I are treading very familiar ground. So what's this new box I need to tick? The suspense is killing me."

"Well, we need to think about the next line on the family tree. The crucial question being a name for our first son?"

Jenny's face clouded suddenly, afraid they were tempting fate by trying to see too far into the future. "Oh Nick darling, aren't you jumping the gun a bit? What if there are daughters but no sons? Or what if we can't have children at all?"

"We would still have a very long, very happy life together," he replied emphatically. "But let's look at it hypothetically. Let's assume we have a son." He drew her closer and circled her waist with his arms.

In spite of his bantering tone, Jenny sensed there was nothing frivolous about the question. Names, particularly family names, had special significance for them both. "I'd like to call our son William," she said slowly. "It was the name of your first Robertson ancestor, and it's a name that recurs in every generation of your family."

Nick nodded solemnly. "And I'd like to call our son George. It was George Armstrong, nearly two hundred years ago, who took young Tom Robertson under his wing and brought our families together. And you must admit Tom had good taste in women – he ended up marrying George's daughter."

"Little Annie Armstrong," she murmured fondly. "That's settled, then. Our son's name – hypothetically of course – will be William George. Box ticked." They exchanged a shy smile and kissed almost chastely, as if sealing a pact.

Nick and Jenny collected their belongings and began to retrace their steps across Embleton Bay. The soft sand was still warm underfoot, and the sea sparkled in the bright sunshine. Shading their eyes, they paused for a moment to look up at the oddly shaped ruins of Dunstanburgh Castle, looming high above them on the headland. In the castle's stark presence, they suddenly felt insignificant, two tiny transient figures on the beach below. Their joys and sorrows, they realised, were no different from the generations who had gone before them. Dunstanburgh itself had been battered by the elements over hundreds of years; its ancient stones had crumbled with the passing of time. Yet the castle had endured, unmoving and unmoved. It had watched over the destinies of countless Northumbrians who had played out their lives in its shadow. Nick and Jenny felt certain the castle would watch over their destinies too.

"William George," mused Nick after a while. "People will think we're copying the Royal Family."

Jenny giggled. "But we'll know differently, won't we?"